Gretel (Gretel Book One)

Christopher Coleman

This book is dedicated to my wife and children.

Subscribe to Christopher Coleman's Newsletter[1]

TO STAY IN TOUCH WITH Chris and receive exclusive cover reveals and sneak peeks, news about his latest releases, and other information, subscribe to his newsletter.

---

1. http://www.christophercolemanauthor.com/newsletter/

Description

Gretel

ALONE. FRIGHTENED. Captive. If you hear someone approaching, RUN. She is not there to help you.

There is an ancient evil in the Back Country, dormant for centuries but now hungry and lurking. When it sets its sights on an unsuspecting mother one routine morning along an isolated stretch of highway, a quiet farming family is suddenly thrust into a world of unspeakable terror, and a young girl must learn to be a hero.

CHAPTER ONE

SHE'D NEVER GOTTEN used to the taste. Even with the life and strength that teemed in every molecule, the russet fluid always went down heavy and crude. Like swallowing a fistful of thin mud that had been lifted from the bottom of a river.

There was a time in the early years of her life—this second life—when she was forced to mix the liquid with soup or tea, or to stir it into the batter of the sweet confections and pies that even today she took pleasure in baking. She had experimented relentlessly with temperatures and combinations—using ingredients she wouldn't have otherwise fed to a cockroach—hoping to create a formula that, if not tasty, was at least palatable enough to override the involuntary rejection by her mouth and throat.

But she'd had little success, and soon began believing the more she tampered with and diluted the delicate recipe, the more the regenerative effects were diminished. Her nails and hair didn't seem to grow quite as quickly, and her teeth, though they were restored, felt as if they had just a bit less length and severity.

Of course, it was plausible she was entirely wrong about the effects of the tampering, and she accepted the possibility that her observations were paranoid inventions of an overprotective mind. But she also wasn't taking any chances, and over time she had trained herself to drink the mixture straight. After all, it took mere seconds for the solution to make it over her taste buds and down to her belly. After that, it was ecstasy.

The mixture usually began its rolling boil within seconds of reaching the acid that lined her stomach, before shooting into her blood stream and picking up the platelets in perfect stride. From there the journey through the body took less than a minute, administering almost instant relief to pains both bitter and dormant alike. There was a sense of rejuvenation in the bones and ligaments that went beyond simply where they joined. It was cellular.

5

The feeling in those first few moments was literally indescribable. On the rare occasions she had tried to explain it aloud, she always found there was simply no adequate experience with which to compare it. The benchmark didn't exist. Sex—usually the standard by which all great feelings were measured—didn't come close. Though it had been decades since she'd had a man, and in her lifetime had little experience with them generally, she knew even with the greatest lover in history, sex was a laughable comparison. As was the feeling elicited by any other potion, and potions she knew. What she lacked in bedroom prowess, she made up for in a long resume of chemical experiences.

But the physical feeling, as glorious as it was, was inconsequential. A minor side effect of the greatest treasure the Old World had ever produced, and one that she had captured and preserved in the Northlands for centuries. Whether she alone was in possession of the knowledge she couldn't be sure; it certainly wasn't impossible that another had been given the precious gift to which she had clung so tightly for the last three hundred years. But if she did share it with another, she would likely never know; her isolation had become almost absolute. The Age of Transmission had transformed her existence from that of a private villager—having few social connections other than in passing and commercial exchanges—to one of complete withdrawal. There were no neighbors to speak of, and any mail or necessary supplies were delivered to the receiving station she had built for herself just over a half-mile from the cabin.

The woman picked up the large, stone container and swirled the liquid into a clockwise vortex, careful not to lose any of it over the top—though caution was mostly unnecessary, since what remained of the potable would have fit easily into a jigger.

This sip was different, however, and her careful attention was not without cause. This swig was the last of her batch. It was the final priceless ounce. She knew in her core it wasn't really enough for full revitalization; it would replenish for another year if she limited her energy, even two if she did nothing but sleep. After that she would decline quickly. And since the elixir didn't spare her from the necessary provisions of all human beings—food, heat, and so on—languidness and hibernation were no more a possibility for her than they were for the woman she was in her old life. In fact, she would need to exert more energy than most people, since she was not surrounded by the accommodations of a modern world. She would need to farm and gather, and even hunt if the harvest didn't last through winter, as well as keep an ample supply of kindling and wood. And she wasn't the youngest maiden in the court when she began the regimen—certainly past sixty years as she recalled—so though the potion sustained her and kept her strong, what was done was done: the contaminations of time did not reverse.

The woman raised the stone cup, which was little more than a small bowl, careful not to breathe the rancid aroma. As it reached her lips, the woman hesitated. This was it, she thought, this last drink would drain her supply, leaving her cabin empty of the fluid she'd come to worship over the many decades.

She willed a pragmatic moment into her addicted mind. Maybe she could hold out for a few months longer. Just a few, until she identified the source of her next supply. There really wasn't the urgency to drink today, she still felt strong and capable. Why, just this morning she had restocked the wood pile after several hours of brisk chopping. And besides, it had only been fourteen months since her last dose. Certainly she had gone without for much longer.

All of that was true. But the reality was that the effects had diminished over the years, and she needed larger doses now than in the past. As it was, her last drink had been meager, having been divided in half to leave today's swallow. No, she needed it today, all of it, and if it was enough to sustain her until the end of summer, she would be lucky. The woman figured by June she would need to be blending.

She pinched her nose and drank slowly, relaxing the pharyngeal nerve at the back of her throat to prevent gagging. The sickening warmth lingered on her soft palate, and then descended the length of her windpipe. The woman could feel the pulp of her victims organs catch and then release in her esophagus, and she lamented that, although she'd always spent days pestling, she had never been able to thin out the concoction completely. This part had always been the hardest—in the early days often inducing violent spasms of choking and expectoration. What she had coughed up over the years! The amount could have sustained her for another generation.

But those reactions had subsided long ago; aside from the taste, she had mostly gotten used to the process. Like the gypsy sword swallowers she had seen as a girl, so nonchalantly on the backs of their wagons immersing those giant blades, inconceivably, down into their bellies and back up again, before packing up and quietly moving on to the next village, she had learned to ingest the pungent broth with little effort.

But there was still the taste. She could never get used to the taste.

She placed the ceramic cup on the edge of the cast iron stove and gently walked to the lone wooden chair that occupied her kitchen. She sat wide-eyed and rigid on the edge of the seat, anticipating the impending experience of which she never tired. Then the slight hint of a bubble began in her abdomen, and a smile formed on the ancient woman's face.

WHEN SHE AWOKE IT WAS just before dawn, and she could hear the first whistling of the woodcocks as they began to pester the sun. Spring had arrived weeks ago, but the chill of the morning stung the back of her neck and prompted an exaggerated shiver. She reached instinctively for covering, and instead created finger tracks in the thick dust of the wooden floor. She grasped her hand again in a slight panic and was now quickly awake.

This wasn't the first time she had gone black—it had happened several times over the years—but those incidences had occurred mostly in the beginning, and never lasted this long, apparently, judging by the position of the sun, almost a full day. She was weaker than she thought, and the truth, which she had numbed her mind to, was that the mixture was old and diminished. Perhaps even toxic. She thought back to when the batch was originally concocted but couldn't recall. Forty years perhaps? Certainly well past the period for which she could reasonably expect it to remain fully viable. What if it had become inert and didn't deliver the effects this time? That seemed unlikely, since the immediate burn and thrill in her abdomen was just as magnificent as ever, but the unusual side effect of unconsciousness suggested a serious problem.

She tried to stand and was prostrated to the floor by a stab of lightning to her back. In disbelief, the old woman tried again, this time using the seat of the chair as a crutch. She was able to rise to her knees before the pain delivered another bolt. A scream attempted to escape her mouth but was immediately intercepted by phlegm and sickness. She laid her forehead on the chair and took deep, panicked breaths. It hadn't worked! This couldn't be happening! She lifted her head and glanced frantically around the room searching for the empty stone cup, hoping beyond reason that whatever trace amounts remained at the bottom of the urn would somehow be enough to release the magic. Maybe one last drop was all she needed.

She spotted the cup. It had rolled to the door of the cabin, the rim edging against the jamb as if waiting to be let out. She got down on all fours and crawled slowly toward the door, exaggerating every lift of her knees for fear of the returning agony to her back.

The woman reached the cup, took a deep, labored breath, and assumed a sitting position, leaning her back against the door for support. She sat that way for several moments until her breathing slowed and her thoughts leveled, and then closed her eyes in an extended blink. She then lifted the cup gently, cradling it from the bottom with both hands as if preparing to offer it in sacrifice, all the time feeling its cruel emptiness. She didn't bother to look inside, and instead placed the cup softly beside her before pushing herself forward and resting tall on her knees.

She closed her eyes again and bowed her head, thankful for the clarity that had presented itself. Her survival would not be dependent on whatever residue remained at the bottom. It would take faith and action. It was time again to accept what is and move on.

Of all the lessons she had learned in her long life, this one had come most grudgingly. But it *had* come, eventually, and once she embraced it, once she'd moved beyond just repeating the words to herself and had finally felt the power and truth of the phrase, it had been the greatest lesson of all. In the past, her reaction to this ruined batch of potion would likely have sent her into some uncontrolled rampage, screaming maniacally for hours, cursing the universe and destroying what few possessions she had. And then, once the fury subsided, she would conclude the episode by erupting into wild tears of self-pity, and then spending the rest of her precious day thinking of suicide and vengeful murder.

But that was in the past. Those futile thoughts of injustice and revenge were pollution to her mind and, for decades, had only weakened her. They were antithetical to what Life craved. She was still somewhat envious of those who had come to realize this fact in the span of a normal lifetime, but she was thankful it had eventually come to her. And thankful for her secret of immortality.

"I'll find it," she said softly.

She lifted her chin and stared out the window, as the sun's first rays provided just enough backlight to silhouette the multitude of lush trees that formed the spring forest. It was going to be a beautiful day. The sky would be clear, and the cool nip of the morning promised relief from the unseasonably warm days of the past week. It was perhaps a harbinger of a new start, she thought. The pain had vanished from her back, and her mind was as clear and unpolluted as ice. And silent. She reveled in the stillness, allowing every sensation of the surroundings to wash over her and soak into her skin. Yes, it was time to begin anew.

The old woman smiled widely, unleashing the large, jagged incisors and canines that crowded the front of her mouth. They were in need of replacement, but they were serviceable.

She stood from her kneeling position and walked to the makeshift wardrobe that anchored the rear wall of the small cottage. The wonder of faith now overwhelmed her, and she had no doubt that renewal loomed. It was only a matter of time—though time was leaking.

She removed the only piece of clothing that hung from one of a dozen wooden hooks that lined the back of the wardrobe's interior. The garment was a moth-ridden wool cloak, heavy and dark—a piece of clothing designed for frost and survival, from an era harsh and bygone. She placed the coat effortlessly over her torso and raised the oversized hood. She would undoubtedly be uncomfortable while the sun was up, since the day was likely to be warm and dry. But the cloak would protect her skin, which had become sensitive to direct sunlight—a thing she rarely received through the canopy of the forest—and if she were forced to camp overnight, the wool would keep her warm in the evening chill.

But such an adventure shouldn't be necessary, she thought. There was still time. Perhaps plenty of time. Going black was simply a sign that her moment had come to awaken and begin identifying the fresh source. To reconnoiter the landscape for the new point of supply. She had done it dozens of times since that first night so long ago, and, in fact, had become quite adept at tracking viable sources.

But identifying meant travel, a practice about which she had always been anxious and leery. Even as a young woman, before the Discovery, the unknown wilderness had always invoked feelings of dread and tragedy. By seven or eight years of age, her mother had so often explained the seemingly unlimited evils of men that she couldn't imagine any woman stepping off her property without being raped or beaten or enslaved. And she soon learned that the tales, though perhaps exaggerated, weren't simply cautionary. She had seen the truth of them first hand, and, indeed, had performed many of the cruel acts herself. Had those women she tortured been as cautious as she, they would have not been in that position, she often rationalized.

Yes, it was the quality of caution that had served her well and preserved her existence since The Enlightenment. But as always, caution was always overruled by necessity. It was time once again to hunt.

She stepped down gingerly onto the crude stone landing that served as a porch and settled for a moment without moving. She listened as a distant breeze pushed through the green of the forest, moving deliberately past each leaf and limb, before finally catching her in its wake. Yes, this would be a fine day. She lowered the cloak's hood, deciding she would begin the journey exposed to the wonders of the woods, figuring the sun would not be a factor for several miles, and the chances of encountering another person were remote.

She took another step on the porch and immediately recognized the adrenaline that had surged during her earlier moment of clarity was now waning. She could already feel the weakness of her joints and muscles returning. The sting of old age, a feeling she had forgotten, or perhaps never known, billowed down her spine and limbs, and the pain choked in a breath as she tried to exhale. Alarmed, she moved quickly toward the edge of the porch, convincing herself that by reaching the boardwalk at the bottom of the steps and beginning her journey on the overgrown pathway that led into the forest, she could somehow outpace the inevitable.

She reached the ledge of the stairs, barely, her legs giving out on the last stride, and narrowly avoided tumbling to the bottom. Only the stone wall that bordered the descent saved her from catastrophe. She held the barrier in a comic clutch, as if trying to keep a battleship from leaving port, and looked out at the seemingly endless timberland before her. She laughed aloud at the idea of venturing ten yards from home, let alone the ten miles or so it would require to reach the nearest source population. It was impossible. And rest was not the answer. Rest meant time and time meant decay. What the woman needed was help, and help—even more than companionship—had always been the greatest price of her isolation. The lack of companionship, or even the sound of another's voice, could certainly be brutal realities, but there were ways to deal with those. She had come to consider the trees and animals and insects important companions in her life and addressed them with respect and appreciation. And she had long since shed any embarrassment of speaking aloud or taking on different character roles. This, in fact—along with her baking—had become one of the few joys in her life, invoking the characteristics of women from her past that she had always envied or admired, playing the roles of huntress or princess or whore. Early on she had discovered that for even the most primal of human relationships there were always alternatives, as any thirteen-year-old boy could attest to.

But there was no substitute for the strength of men to remove an old iron stove, or fell a dying tree before it collapsed and demolish a house. Or for hands to help gather and hunt when the crops have failed and starvation is no further than a bad snowstorm away. She had paid for help in the past—and even kept slaves when the social climate allowed it—and though these servants had certainly alleviated many of the normal personal and practical burdens, the threat of loss had been too strong, and they never stayed on for long. Most of them she killed while they slept. Many were buried on this very property. Sadly, none of their innards were used for blending.

And now isolation would cost her immortality. The motif of so many legends and religions would evaporate with her last breath, as it may have done, for all she knew, with hundreds of other possessive hermits in the past.

She lowered herself down to a sitting position on the first step of the porch and rested her elbows on her knees. She coughed several times as if she had just finished a brisk winter walk and her lungs were struggling to adjust. She hung her head between her knees and watched as the wooden planks beneath her began to blur. She was about to go black again, perhaps permanently this time. Instinctively, she slid her buttocks to the next step down and continued this movement on to each lower tread until she reached the bottom. If she were going to die, she decided, it wouldn't be from a broken neck. There was one last impulse to get to her feet, but the message was never conveyed from her brain to her legs. Defeated, the old woman rolled onto her back and spread her arms wide, encouraging the world's embrace. She took in the bright blueness of the sky and wished that she could feel the wonder of rain one last time.

The blue canvas above her turned shadowy, not from the arrival of clouds, she assumed, but from her brain's lack of oxygen. She smelled the warm air rising from the ground, and tried to appreciate the last of life's sensory experiences. Surely this was death. She had escaped it for so long, but now here it was in front of her. The brew of life on which she had relied since the early times of the Northlands had finally failed her. Or she had failed it. It was true she trusted a source would come—her dreams had told her of its delivery—but it hadn't come, and she'd waited too long to move on. She'd trusted in her dreams and they had betrayed her, but it was *her* life, *her* responsibility. She had become careless and complacent. The supply was larger than ever these days, and she needed only to pull from it.

If only there was more time. A week. A day.

"I'm sorry," she whispered. "I'm sorry." She closed her eyes and slowed her breathing, as that relentless resistance to death which had dictated the bulk of her life now turned to acceptance. Without contention, she awaited sleep.

And then she heard the voice.

ANIKA MORGAN WAS COLD, and the mud that had gently cushioned the soles of her feet when she set out now enveloped her ankles and threatened to swallow her shins. Every step felt like someone was pressing down on the tops of her knees. She thought of quicksand. Was that a possibility? That this was quicksand? She knew—or at least had heard the stories as a child—about quicksand existing in the jungles of Africa and places like that, but not in the Northlands. Truthfully though, she couldn't be sure where it was found. Or if it was real at all. Was she really going to die such an improbable death as drowning in quicksand?

Anika cleared her head and focused. If she wanted to avoid death today, she figured it wasn't quicksand she had to worry about. Besides, quicksand was absurd, the forests of this territory were infamous for their swamps and mud; she had waded through much worse in her life. She had to stay on task.

"Just go," she scolded herself.

She wanted to scream the words, but her overworked lungs wouldn't allow it. Anika slowed her breathing and down-shifted her effort to an easy walk. The depth of the mud was making her progress comically slow, and trying to run through it was doing nothing but edging her closer to exhaustion. Adrenaline had its limits, and hers was almost reached. She would have to rest soon. In a few hours, the early morning chill would be giving way to the warmth of a typical spring day, and Anika could see the sun beginning its morning stretch upward. The sky was almost staggering in its clarity and blueness, and she was thankful at least to be dry; though had it been raining, she reasoned, she would never have attempted the forest to begin with, and probably would have been rescued by now.

But she *had* chosen the forest, and at the time had done so quite casually. But why?

Why would she have made such an unconventional decision? Such a bad decision? She was normally much more conservative in her approach to problems, and the woods in this country, even on a clear spring day, were risky to explore for the most well-conditioned of men, let alone a thirty-eight-year-old mother of two. So why hadn't she just walked the road? Or waited for help at the place where the car drifted off the shoulder? It was true she wasn't thinking clearly after the accident—everything had happened so quickly—but she hadn't suffered any trauma to her head. In fact, she was miraculously uninjured.

So the question remained: why?

It didn't matter now, she thought, the decision was made; all that mattered now was finding shelter and a telephone. Besides, with her car nestled at the bottom of what must have been a fifteen-foot embankment, with little hope of being seen from the road, it seemed somewhat reasonable that finding a place to call for help on her own was a safer play than standing alone on the side of a quiet road in the southern Northlands. Not that this part of the territory was particularly dangerous, but one could never be sure.

Anika spotted a log about forty yards in the distance and decided it would be a suitable place to rest. She wanted to keep going, but she knew forty yards was about all she had left in her. If she pushed beyond that, she might not come across another place to stop, and would end up having to rest in the mud she was desperately trying to escape.

And she was getting scared. And fear, she knew, would only make her judgment worse.

She needed to stop and think, try to orient herself with what little she knew of the land here, and get out of these woods and back to her family. She could only imagine the fears they would conjure if they didn't hear from her soon. She should have been home by now, and it wouldn't be long before they started to worry. Soon they would call to check on her and learn that she had left ahead of schedule and should have been home even earlier. And that would be bad. She loved Heinrich, but for all his pretensions of strength and masculinity, he was emotionally weak. And combined with his injuries, he would be in no condition to comfort and reassure the children.

She reached the large log and climbed atop to a sitting position, throwing one muddy leg to the far side to straddle it. She sat this way for a moment, legs dangling while she caught her breath, and finally lay down on her back, bringing her legs together and linking her hands behind her head for support. Under the circumstances, it felt strange to be assuming such a relaxed position, and she imagined that someone looking in might conclude that she was on some spiritual journey—albeit one that was oddly messy—and had come to the forest to contemplate the meaning of life or something.

If only.

It was still early and she'd only been up a few hours, but the grueling hike had tired Anika and she had to be mindful to stay awake. She had to keep her eyes wide and her mind active. She thought of her children and how they must miss her. She realized now it was the longest she had ever been away from them, only a little over a week, but it was eons compared to what they were used to, and, with Heinrich in his condition, it came at a time when she was needed at home most. They were both wonderful, mature children, exceptional for their ages, but they had no business carrying the responsibilities she had left them with this past week. Why hadn't she just waited by the road?

Anika sat straight on the log and took the last remaining bite of a stale candy bar. It had been in her car for days—weeks maybe—and she was thrilled now to have grabbed it before setting out. At least she'd made one good decision today.

She swallowed the chocolate and then laid back down to fully replenish her lungs and examine her options. She supposed she could try to retrace her steps and get back to the original point where she had entered the forest, and then wait on the shoulder of the road until someone passed by. The roads were certainly desolate on the stretch where she'd swerved off—in fact, she couldn't remember passing a car once in her short trip from Father's house—but surely someone would eventually motor by and help. Even if it took several hours. At this point, the fear of some lascivious stranger with devious motives paled to the fear she had of still being in these woods come nightfall.

But the truth was it was too late for the road, at least at the part where her car now lay abandoned and invisible. Whatever it was that had compelled her into the wilderness had now taken her beyond the point where she had the will to make it back. It would be a disheartening trek of over an hour through the now detestable mud, and at this point she wasn't sure she would even be able to find it. The turns she had made along the way to avoid the deeper swampy areas and larger thickets had disoriented Anika, and though she was fairly confident that she could head back in the general direction she had come, with fatigue and fear now a factor, there was no certainty she would reach the road at all.

Her other option—only option really—was to continue on. She realized she may only immerse herself deeper, but eventually she would reach a boundary. This was the Northlands, not the Amazon, after all. She had to keep going and cling to the fact that possibility rested in every new clearing.

She stood up on the log and slowly surveyed the forest in each direction, hoping by some wonder of the universe her eyes would focus past the camouflage and spot something other than trees. It wasn't a particularly dense woodland, so even with the lush spring leaves there was quite a bit of visibility. But she saw nothing. She jumped down off the log and searched the forest again, this time at ground level, figuring she may have more luck at a different angle. Nothing. She climbed the log again and this time stood tall, straightening her back, and cupped her mouth with her hands. She breathed deeply and screamed as loudly as possible.

"Help me! Can anybody hear me!"

The words seemed to float through the trees, echoing off the branches and carrying downwind. With the additional height of the log, her voice felt forceful, and the decision to yell now seemed less an act of desperation and more of an actual rescue strategy. She paused and listened, not expecting a response, and, of course, getting none. She screamed again, this time feeling a strained burn in her throat. She couldn't remember ever having yelled this loud as an adult. Still nothing, and the subsequent silence was stark, only reinforcing her desertion. She couldn't know that the sound waves of this particular bellow deflected at just the proper angle, avoiding perfectly the large oak trunks and dense clumps of leaves that should have absorbed them forever, traveling instead just far enough from their source to reach the auditory canal of an old woman who lay dying on a weathered terrace less than four miles away.

Anika moved down to a sitting position on the log, broke off a dying branch, and began clearing as much mud as possible from her shoes and pant cuffs. It was a futile exercise she knew—they'd be covered again in a matter of paces—but she needed whatever boost she could get. At least she hadn't worn a dress today, she thought. It could always be worse.

She placed her feet back down on the damp dirt floor and was startled by a rustle beneath the log. She stifled a gasp and watched as two chipmunks ran past her and headed up a nearby tree. Anika unconsciously cataloged the vermin as a potential food source; though if it came to that, how she would trap such small, fleeting creatures she had no idea. She watched the tiny animals disappear into the camouflage of the tree's top branches and then continued her upward gaze to the clear blue sky. It was indeed a marvelous day, she thought, and then she started walking.

THE OLD WOMAN OPENED her eyes and searched her surroundings with the vibrancy of an infant seeing the world for the first time. The voice was faint—perhaps the faintest sound she had ever heard—but that she had heard it there was no doubt. It may be the voice of Death, she thought, but if it was, he was incarnate. That sound had come in through her ears, not her imagination. She replayed the words in her mind. Over and over. The voice was feminine—beautiful and distressed. Strong. Alive. Not the voice of Death. The voice of Life. Delivering again.

CHAPTER TWO

"ANIKA!"

Gretel Morgan flinched violently at the sound of her father's voice, somehow managing not to drop the ceramic plate she had been drying over the sink. He was awake, and, as was usually the case lately, unhappy.

"It's me, Father, I'll be right there," she called, turning her head slightly toward the back bedroom, trying her best not to sound aggravated. She certainly sympathized with his condition but had grown tired of the demands it came with.

Gretel sighed and placed the dish on the sideboard. She had hoped to finish the cleaning before he woke since her tasks seemed to multiply when he was conscious. Cooking his meals alone was a day's work; add in laundering his clothes (including ironing) and general fetching, and the assignment was barbaric. Thankfully, Mother would be home today, at least to bear some of the constant attention, if not the heavy lifting.

Gretel walked the ten or so paces to her father's room and paused at the door, softly clearing her throat and assuming the statuesque, confident posture her mother always seemed to have when she entered a room. At fourteen, her shoulders and hips had begun to forge, and early indications suggested she would have her mother's shapely body. She had no delusions of striding in and conquering her father's petulance in the same effortless way her mother did, of course, but hopefully she could disarm him if only for a moment.

She formed what she believed was a serious, business-like look on her face and entered the room. She could see that her father was sitting up slightly in his bed, but avoided his eyes and walked briskly to the end table, feigning irritation at the crumbs and empty glasses that littered its surface.

"Where is your mother?" her father grumbled, his deep, accented speech at once both intimidating and divine. "She was to be home by now."

"She's probably not coming home," Gretel replied casually, letting the words drift just to the edge of uneasiness. "I wouldn't blame her. If I was her I would have changed my name and run away to a village in the south." She kept her eyes down, serious, staying excessively focused on her father's mess.

Her father frowned and stared coldly at his daughter. "Perhaps I'll send you to a village in the south."

Gretel stopped sponging the table in mid-motion, and stared up at her father with a look of both disbelief and anticipation. "Would you? Please! Promise me, Papa!" She held his gaze for as long as possible before losing control of the charade and erupting into a snorted laugh.

Her father shook his head slowly and grinned. Gretel could see the flicker of joy in his eyes, proud of how quick his daughter had become with her banter. Yet another gift inherited from her mother.

"How are you feeling, Papa?" Gretel said, now straight-faced, unable to conceal her weariness. She sat on the edge of the bed and examined her father's bandages.

"Better than I look."

"Well, you look terrible."

"So better than terrible then." He waved an absent hand and began shuffling to get on his feet, having reached the extent of how much he wanted to discuss himself or his maladies. "Get me up."

"You need to stay in bed, Papa. You're not ready."

"Then you had better be ready with the piss pot."

With that, Gretel stooped and leaned in toward her father, offering her shoulder as a crutch. She could see him size up her position, and with a soft, guttural grunt he threw an arm around his daughter's neck, embarrassment no longer the palpable element it had been six weeks ago. His white bedshirt was badly stained with some type of red sauce, and his ever-growing belly extended over the elastic of his tattered long underpants. It had amazed Gretel the short time it took for a man with such a long-standing trademark of pride and masculinity to concede to the often cruel circumstances of life; in the case of her father, those circumstances had come most recently in the form of three fractured ribs—not exactly the bubonic plague in the hierarchy of ailments, but painfully debilitating nevertheless. Particularly for a man nearing sixty.

Gretel boosted him from the bed and shuffled him slowly to the threshold of the washroom, grimacing throughout the process, and from there left him to his own maneuvers. The doctor had explained to her mother that the injury would likely cause a decrease in appetite, since even automatic bodily functions like swallowing and digesting could be painful, and limited activity would reduce his need for the same amount of nourishment he was getting before the accident. The opposite, however, was proving true; he ate constantly and, as a result, had become quite heavy. She couldn't be sure, but Gretel guessed that her father had gained at least forty pounds in little over a month.

"So where is your mother?" The voice from behind the bathroom door was less demanding now and contained the subtle hint of concern. Gretel had lingered outside since she would have to bring her father back when he was done.

"Delayed, I guess. But she must have left Deda's already or else she would have telephoned."

"Then why didn't she phone to say she would be delayed?" His pitch was now higher and layered with obstinance.

"Perhaps she was delayed on the road, I don't know Papa." She paused and asked, "Are you going to be in there much longer?" Gretel was now annoyed, both at her father for his current weakness and at her mother for being late. There were still dishes remaining in the kitchen, and she needed a break—if only for fifteen minutes—to sit and rest. Not working or helping or talking. Just to rest.

"Maybe you should bathe," she suggested, offering the words in the tone of a helpful reminder so as not to offend him. "You'll call Deda's when you're out." Her father mumbled something inaudible from behind the door, and then a grain of joy arose in Gretel at the abrupt sound of water being released from the tub's faucet.

She sighed with relief and walked back toward the kitchen, her desire to finish housework now dwarfed by the urge to rest. She averted her gaze from the sink as she passed it, and headed quickly for the back porch, where she collapsed forcefully in a white, weathered rocker. She tilted her face up toward the ceiling and closed her eyes, thankful for the chance to relax, but understanding that what she really needed was sleep. Sleep had now become the default thought in her mind throughout the day, and, in fact, had become of such value since her father's accident, that over the past three weeks Gretel had started her mornings by staring at herself in the small nightstand mirror by her bed and listing in her mind the things that she would be willing to give up for an undisturbed day of slumber. A full day. Not one chore. Not one knock. Not even a voice. Just complete serenity. Of course, she possessed virtually nothing of her own, so this exercise basically involved the sacrifices of treasures she would never see and powers she would never have, the latest offering being a horse that could fly. Later, in the throes of the day, she would scoff at how little value she would have gotten from her imagined trade-offs; but she was convinced that, at the time, she would have made the deal.

Gretel could feel herself drifting, and decided not to fight. The dishes remained, but her mother would be home soon, and though she would be in no mood to finish her daughter's chores after a long day of travel, Gretel concluded that as a parent she would recognize when her child was spent. If her father needed help back to his bed she would help, but aside from that, she was done for the day.

"SHE'S NOT HOME, GRETEL."

Gretel opened her eyes and was greeted by the orange glow of the twilight sky above her. She was momentarily disoriented, but smelled the oil from the lamps and remembered she was on the porch. Her late afternoon catnap had metastasized into solid sleep. By her estimation, she was out for at least four hours.

Her thoughts immediately went to her father, whom, for all she knew, was in the tub dead, a victim of immobility, hypothermia, and a neglectful daughter.

She got up quickly from the rocker and felt the effect of her sleeping position in the form of a dull stiffness at the back of her neck. No question she would be dealing with that misery for the rest of the night. Tentatively, Gretel turned back toward the house and screamed at the sight of her father sitting at the porch table, dressed and shaven, his elbows propped up and his head buried in his hands. He looked as if her were in a library reading—the way one might read a dictionary or an atlas—but there was nothing on the table below him.

Her initial thoughts were of relief, that her father was alive and that she was not a murderer. Then, registering his condition, her thoughts became more selfish, assuming his apparent improvement meant she would now get real relief. Physical relief. More sleep.

She stood staring at him, waiting for him to speak, but he sat in position, silent.

"Papa?" she said, "What's wrong?" Gretel spoke softly, but her tone had no sympathy and was one demanding an explanation. Her father didn't move and she became uneasy, then scared. "What's wrong!" she said again, this time louder, panicked and quivery, the film of sleep and the sureality of her father sitting upright in a chair on the porch, functional, now completely wiped away.

"She's not home, Gretel." Her father lifted his head from his hands and looked out through the trees at the small narrow lake that lined their property.

Gretel could see where the tears had been on his freshly-washed cheeks and she noted that this was as close to weeping as she'd ever seen from either of her parents.

"Something's happened," he said, "I know something's happened."

Her father's words caused Gretel's legs to wobble, and she sat back down slowly in the rocker. She couldn't speak, and looked off in the same direction as her father, as if they were both trying to spot the same object on the water. "Did you call Deda?" she asked finally, in a whisper, already knowing the answer.

"Of course I called him. She left even earlier than she had told me she would. She should have been home long before we expected her." There was no anger in her father's voice, only defeat.

"Perhaps there was traffic then. A very bad accident...and the road is closed."

"I've called The System. There is no report of any accident along the Interways."

Gretel could hear in her father's tone that the bases had been covered. Heinrich Morgan was a man of routine, as was his wife, and any break from that routine would immediately incite him to make it right again. To look at all the possibilities and rule them out, one by one, until the answer to the problem emerged. And if the remaining answers were out of his control, and he couldn't reset the routine to its proper function, he shut down. This was the point he had apparently reached.

The tears in Gretel's eyes seemed to be dripping to the floor before she even felt the sadness, and her face flushed with hate for her father's weakness. Nothing was wrong! Her mother was fine! He should be ashamed, a grown man crying in front of his teenage daughter because her mother is a few hours late. For a month he had contributed nothing to the house—NOTH-ING—other than dirty plates and whines of discomfort. Gretel and her mother had worked the fields for six weeks while he moaned over a few broken bones in his belly. If only that horse had kicked his head! And now, when strength was needed—when he was needed—he was a clammy dishrag, like a woman who's just watched her son leave for war.

Gretel erupted from the rocking chair and ran toward her room, ignoring the sharp pain that burned through her neck the whole way. She stumbled in and fell face down on the foot end of her bed, nearly crashing her head on the bench of the small white vanity that sat only inches away. Almost immediately, she stood back up and strode defiantly back to the open bedroom door, slamming it harder than she thought she was capable of. For that split moment she felt better than she could remember in weeks, as if the suppressed grievances of her fourteen-year-old body and mind were instantly alleviated.

She went back to her bed and took a more conventional position, curled fetal-like at the head with her cheek flat on the quilt cover.

The heavy sobs finally ended and Gretel lay still until her crying stopped completely. She rolled to her back and gazed vacuously at the brown wood that made up the cabin ceiling. Her thoughts became clear as she studied the evidence of the situation and soon became hopeful. This is all certainly an overreaction, she thought. Papa's condition has unsettled him and I've let it influence me. There's a good chance—better than good—that Mother is completely fine. In fact, there was a much higher likelihood that her mother was stranded on the road somewhere waiting for help to arrive, than lying dead on a river bank or in a landfill. True, she should have been home hours ago—if she left early, then at least six or seven hours to be more accurate—and she had taken the trip up North dozens of times over the past four or five years since Deda had become sick, so she wouldn't have become lost. But none of that evinced tragedy. Gretel reasoned that if something truly terrible had happened, someone would know by now and the family would have been contacted.

But her father's words bore the texture of truth; if not because of the sure somberness of his words—"Something's happened"—than for the possible explanations available. Even if Deda had suddenly been rushed away in an ambulance and died suddenly en route to a hospital (which, of course, hadn't happened since her father had spoken with him earlier), Mother would have called as soon as she reached the hospital. Mother always called. If she didn't call, there was a problem. In this case, Gretel proposed, that problem may simply be a blown tire or some mechanical malfunction in the car. But the Northlands were no more than two hours away on a clear spring day, so it was unlikely she wouldn't have found a telephone by now if it were something so benign. There was no logical reason she could think of that Mother wouldn't have called, other than reasons she didn't want to imagine.

She began to cry again softly, and her mind became overwhelmed with thoughts of never again seeing her mother. It was unimaginable, and physically nauseating. Her mother was everything to her. Everything. Gretel's image of herself as a good young girl—exceptional even—was due solely to the woman she had studied thoroughly and tried for as long as she could remember to emulate. Though Gretel rarely noticed it in the environment which they lived, her mother had a finesse and dignity about her that always astounded Gretel, and only became evident—almost embarrassingly so—when it was contrasted with the tactlessness of most women in the Back Country. She avoided the crude speech that most of the Back Country wives used in an effort somehow to endear themselves to their husbands' friends. Instead she maintained an easy poise that seemed almost regal and out of place. Consequently, of course, her mother stood out among her peers, earning the attention of the men and, Gretel supposed, the backstage scorn of her fellow ladies. She was far from what most people would describe as beautiful, but despite the physical advantages they may have had, other women always appeared intimidated by her mother's confidence.

Gretel got to her feet and walked to the vanity, where she sat on the bench and looked at her distraught face in the mirror as the day's last few rays of sunlight entered her window. It was almost dark and there was no sign of Mother. She turned on the lamp and examined the framed picture of her parents that sat on the vanity top. Her father had gotten very lucky, she thought, and Gretel became sad for him. He was twenty years older than his bride, and in his marriage had always been decided in his ways, insisting on the traditional roles of husband and wife: provider and caregiver, tough and understanding, et cetera.

But in that tradition he had never shown anything but respect and love for her mother. When choices of importance had to be made, concerning her and her brother, or otherwise, Heinrich Morgan always insisted on his wife's opinion. He knew between the two of them she was the smarter one, and he never pretended otherwise.

And though Gretel couldn't remember a time when her father was what she would describe as 'sweet' toward Mother, he certainly never gave her any reason to be docile or frightened around him. He never complained about a meal—whether overcooked or late or for any reason—and he always thanked her when it was over, even offering compliments if he found it exceptional. And if Mother needed to leave him for a day or a week—as in the current situation visiting her ill father—there was never a sense of trepidation when she told him, and the news was always delivered as a statement, with the full expectation that it would be received without protest, if not encouragement. "I'll need to leave for the North tomorrow," her mother would say. "Father's doing poorly. Gretel will handle the house while I'm gone." And father's replies would be nothing other than words of concern for his father-in-law.

The memory of these exchanges suddenly awakened Gretel to the fact that she was not ready to assume this position of authority. The surrogate role of housewife that Gretel had taken on for the last nine days, and that she had begrudgingly admitted to herself was, on some level, enjoyable, was beyond her capabilities. Well beyond. She couldn't do this for five or ten more days let alone years!

Gretel was startled by the muffled sound of the cabin door opening and then closing. She sat motionless, not breathing, and looked at nothing as she shifted her eyes in amazement around the room waiting for the next sound to decipher. Mother! It was definitely Mother. It had to be. Tired and with quite a story to tell, no doubt, but it had to be her. She waited for the booming sound of her father's voice, joyful and scolding, to ring through her room. She wanted to rush out and verify her belief, but she was paralyzed, fearing that somehow by moving she would lose the sound and her hopes would evaporate.

At the tepid knock on her bedroom door, Gretel smiled and lifted herself from the bench, banging her knee on the underside of the vanity and nearly knocking the lamp to the floor, catching it just before it fell. The door cracked and began to open. Gretel looked toward it, waiting for the miracle, holding her awkward lamp-in-hand pose.

It was her father.

"No!" she said, the word erupting from her mouth automatically, denoting both fear and authority, as if she were repelling a spirit that had ventured from hell to inhabit her room. Her father looked at her with sadness and acceptance. "Is she dead?" Gretel said, surprised at the bluntness of her question.

"I don't know, Gretel, we're going to look for her. Your brother is home."

<hr />

GRETEL LET OUT A RESTRAINED sigh as the family truck pulled in front of her grandfather's small brick house, amazed they had made it. The truck, she guessed, was at least thirty years old, and probably hadn't made a trip this far since before she was born. And each time her father had made one of his dozen or so stops along the way, exploring the considerable land surrounding every curve and potential hazard that the back roads offered, he turned the engine off to conserve fuel. She was sure with each failed effort to locate her mother, the key would click ominously in the ignition when her father tried to restart the engine, and they too would disappear along the road. But it had always started, and here they were.

She looked across the bench seat at her father and was disturbed by the look of indifference on his face. Her brother lay between them asleep.

Her father opened the door and said weakly, "Stay in the car."

"I'm seeing Deda," Gretel immediately responded, opening the door quickly and storming out of the truck, taking a more defiant tone than was indicative of how she actually felt. She had every intention of seeing her grandfather though. It had been months since she'd seen him, and even though she often felt awkward around him lately, more so now that he had worsened, she loved him enormously, and still considered him, next to her mother, the most comforting person in her world. If there was one person she needed right now, other than her mother, it was Deda.

She ran toward the house and as she reached the stoop she saw the tall, smiling figure of Deda standing in the doorway. She screamed at the sight of him. He looked so old, at least twenty years older than the seventy-five he actually was, and his smile was far from the thin-lipped consoling grin Gretel would have expected. Instead his mouth was wide and toothy, as if he had been laughing. He looked crazy, she thought.

"Hi, Deda," she said swallowing hard. "How are you feeling?"

At the sound of Gretel's voice, Deda's face lit up, morphing to normalcy and becoming consistent with that of a man seeing his beloved granddaughter for the first time in four months. "Gretel!" which he pronounced 'Greetel,' "my love, come in! Where is your brother?"

"He's in the car sleeping," she replied, and with that her brother came running into the house and into Deda's arms, which Deda had extended just in time to receive his grandson.

Deda held Hansel's shoulders and pushed him away to arms length. "Ahh, Hansel, you look so big!"

"You look really old, Deda," Hansel said, as respectfully as an eight-year-old could say such words.

Deda laughed, "I am so old, Hansel! I am so old!" He placed his palm on the back of the boy's neck and led him to the small sofa which was arranged just off the foyer. Deda sat down and lifted Hansel to his lap; Gretel followed and sat beside him on the cushion.

"Hello, Heinrich," Deda said, not taking his eyes from the children.

Gretel's father stood at the door, silently watching the interaction between his children and his wife's father. "Marcel."

"Why don't you sit?"

"We won't be staying."

Over the years Gretel had grown used to this style of conversation between her father and Deda, terse and factual, completely devoid of style. It wasn't that they disliked each other exactly, but more that they had failed to reach the level of trust normally achieved between two people at this stage in a relationship. Her parents had been married almost twenty years.

"Have you contacted The System?" Deda asked.

"Of course. They won't do anything for days," Gretel's father replied. And then, "Unless there's evidence of a crime."

Deda nodded in understanding. "Gretel," he said, "why don't you and your brother explore in the cellar for a while. I've some new books you would both like, just at the bottom of the stairs, on the first shelf there. You'll see them when you go down."

Deda stood and led the children to the cellar door, opening it and pulling the ribbed metal chain that hung just at the top of the stairs, unleashing a dull orange glow of light. The cellar was an obvious suggestion so that Deda could speak to her father alone, but Gretel didn't mind, and played along for her brother's sake. Besides, they were going to discuss her mother—and the possibilities of what might have happened—and she didn't have the emotional stamina to handle that right now.

As she and her brother reached the bottom of the cellar, Gretel saw that the books Deda referenced were the same ones he had had for at least two years now: Reptiles of the Northlands, Sea Life, and a few others containing topics Gretel had long since lost interest in.

"These books aren't new," Hansel complained. "I've read these a thousand times."

"Your Deda's old Han, he doesn't remember" Gretel replied, "And, anyway, you still like them."

"Fine."

Hansel opened the sea creature book absently and slumped heavily into a dusty club chair, once the centerpiece of Deda's living area but now in exile, having been replaced by a chair more conducive to Deda's frail condition. The dust from the chair puffed into the dim light and then dissipated. Normally Gretel found places like Deda's cellar repulsing—the dust was as thick as bread and seemed not to be spared from any section of furniture; and the scurrying sounds that clattered from the corners of the dark room conjured in her mind pictures of things much larger than mice. And she was sure that the spiders she had seen over the years had to be as large as any in the world.

But for all the impurities, Gretel had no memory of ever fearing the cellar. Lately, in fact, she felt drawn to it, mystified by the shrouded hodgepodge of books and tools and bric-a-brac that coated the surface of every shelf and table. There were candles and candle holders next to decorative plates and stemware; prehistoric preserve jars being used as paperweights for pictures of men and women Gretel had never seen in person; and dozens of other trinkets and curiosities that as a small girl she had considered junk—nuisances that cluttered up what might otherwise have been a play room for tea parties and dancing and such—but that she had recently come to admire.

The cellar, however, for all its antique charm, was also dark and difficult to explore. There was no window, and the one low-watt bulb that hung by the door illuminated only the area a few feet past the base of the steps; beyond that, a flashlight was required to make out any details of an object, if not just to walk. Gretel never asked Deda why he hadn't put a working lamp in the area, and now assumed it was to discourage her and Hansel from playing back there, though he had never explicitly forbade them from exploring that part of the house. Besides, as large as the cellar was, certainly large enough to convert into an apartment if Deda had ever decided to take in a boarder, most children didn't need to be warned about what may lurk in such a place.

But by eleven, and certainly now at fourteen, the illicitness of the "dark areas" only enhanced Gretel's curiosity, and, frankly, made the jaunts to Deda's bearable. What enjoyments she got at eight or nine were now almost completely nullified by her grandfather's health and her own adolescence. So the cellar had become her entertainment, and specifically the magazines.

Gretel found the flashlight that always sat on the seldom-used workbench and turned it on in Hansel's eyes.

"Stop, Gretel!"

Gretel chuckled. "I'm going to look for something in the back, I'll be right here, okay?" Gretel knew to be playful and delicate with her brother; he hadn't yet fully accepted that something bad might actually have happened to his mother, and if it occurred to him now, she thought, she was in no condition to help.

Hansel didn't respond, but looked up from the sea creatures book and followed Gretel with his eyes to the far end of the cellar, making sure the light was always visible.

Gretel felt her way to the antique bureau she was looking for and found the knob of the right-side drawer of the middle row. She could feel the weight of the magazines as she pulled, careful not to force the drawer and tear one of the covers. She pulled the top issue off the stack and thumbed through it, suddenly feeling nervous at the sight of the smiling, underclad women flipping past her. She leafed through to the end and put the first issue in the stack face down on the surface of the bureau so as to keep them in order when she put them all back, and took out the next issue, passively thumbing through it, staring at the women who were pretty much all the same. They weren't nude, but they were certainly there to provoke men and not to sell undergarments.

Gretel wasn't exactly sure why the women fascinated her. She didn't like girls in that way—at least she didn't think so—she certainly didn't get the same feelings looking at these women that she got when talking with certain boys at school. It was something else, something about their expressions. The way they smiled so easily for the camera when, Gretel had to assume, they felt ashamed and sad the whole time. She wanted to hug them, befriend them, let them know that she was fascinated by them, by their strength to do what she could never imagine. And that they were beautiful.

"Gretel, what are you doing?" Hansel called from the stairs.

Gretel flinched, nearly dropping the magazine, before fumbling it back to its proper place in the drawer and stacking the first one on top of it. "Nothing Han, looking at some old magazines. I'm coming."

She shut the bureau drawer and turned back for the stairs, and as the flashlight turned with her, the beam strayed wildly, just drifting over the thick black spine of a book. The book.

There it was.

The thick hardcover tome had presided from the top of Deda's tallest bookshelf for as long as Gretel had a memory of the house, which was from about age four. At that time, of course, the book was as mysterious and out of reach as space, and she hadn't the slightest clue as to what it might contain. But its sheer size and blackness had fascinated her even then.

The cover was absolute in its darkness, with no shine or reflection, as if it were overlaid with black wool. And there was no text or pattern on the spine—which was the only part Gretel would ever see for many years—and she imagined that someone looking up casually at the shelf could easily have mistaken the book for emptiness, a large gap in the middle of other books.

By age seven she got up the nerve to touch the book, which was no easy task given the height of the shelf and the book's position. It required delicate stacking of furniture and the tip-toe balance of a ballerina, but Gretel was determined, and soon became quite adept with her scaffolding.

During those years Gretel visited Deda's house regularly—at least once every other month—and with every visit she made a point to feel the book, to physically touch it, rubbing her fingertips on the exposed area. It was always cold—as were all of the books in the cellar—and its lack of any real texture, Gretel believed, gave an indication as to its age.

But she didn't touch the book because of any particular enchantment, or even because she thought it was magic, she did so more as a gauge, testing when she would be able to move forward on her stalled curiosity. As she grew taller, and as her level of comfort on the far ledges of stacked stools and empty milk crates increased, she began trying to flip the book out of its snug resting spot, placing her index finger at the top where the spine met the pages and then pulling backwards. At seven it never budged, as if cemented down, and the effort only enhanced Gretel's wonderment. It would be two years later when she would finally free the massive text and learn a word that would eventually come to hold a high place in her lexicon forever.

Gretel turned and faced the bookshelf and centered the beam of the flashlight on the book, which was no longer in its normal far left position on the top shelf, having moved to one center-right. In ten years it was the first time she had ever seen it out of place, other than when she was perusing it of course. Had it been in its current position when she was seven years old, she noted, it would have been a much easier endeavor to pull the book down, since this particular side of the shelf was far easier to access.

Now, at fourteen, the trick was to grab the book without attracting her brother's attention.

Gretel could see Hansel sifting through some boxes on the shelves near the stairs, and knew that his boredom would draw him to her soon; but the book was just out of her reach, and she didn't want to risk arousing his inquisitiveness by struggling and groaning on her tiptoes. Careful not to make any sudden motions, she pulled a large bucket from under the old wash basin and tossed aside a crusty towel that had dried crumpled and deformed inside, probably sometime in the last decade.

Gretel then placed the flashlight on the workbench, beacon down, reducing her visibility to a small halo of light on the table surface, and blindly flipped the bucket on its rim.

"Hey, what are you doing?" Hansel cried, his voice dripping with suspicion.

"Hansel, don't come over here, you'll trip on something," Gretel replied, trying to sound casual.

The sudden darkness had alerted her brother and Gretel silently cursed herself. She could hear him making tentative steps toward the bookshelf and Gretel quickly stepped up on the bucket, nearly missing the bottom brim and toppling to the floor. She began feeling for the black leather. She couldn't even make out the shadowy forms of the books without the flashlight, let alone any of the writing, but there was no doubt she would know her book by touch.

"Gretel?" Hansel again, edging closer.

"Han, I'm very serious, there are a million things that you could fall on and hurt yourself."

"I'll hold the light for you so you can see."

"I don't need the light, I've got it."

Gretel continued to feel for the book knowing she must be close. If it were in its proper spot she would have gotten it already and been done with it, now all this commotion would force her to make up some story about it. It didn't matter, he couldn't read the book anyway. She couldn't even read it. In fact, she couldn't even read the letters.

Gretel moved her hand over from a thin laminated book, and as instantly as the forefinger of her left hand brushed the cold, dead leather, she knew she had found it. By now Hansel had reached the shelf and was looking up at Gretel on the bucket.

"Han, shine the light up here," she barked in a loud whisper. "I don't want to knock anything off."

Hansel placed his hand on the flashlight, but before he could lift it to aid in his sister's search, a large beam of light shone in from the stairs, illuminating her face and the goal of her quest.

"Ah yes," her grandfather said, pointing the hanging bulb toward Gretel, "that book. It fascinates me, too."

CHAPTER T~~~

THE FIRST BITE OF CHILL came down just before the top of the red sun slipped behind the tallest cedars. Darkness was less than an hour away, and the waking moon was already visible, waiting to take its post in the night sky.

Anika Morgan hunkered in a small, weathered-out cavity that had formed in a hill bank and covered her face with her hands. She was lost and had not the faintest concept of where the treeline might be. The hope that had carried her through clearings and creeks, over countless bluffs and damp wastelands, was gone.

At least for today.

Her will had shut down and the prospect of death was now lodged tightly in her brain. What had she done? To her children? Her husband? Her life? In her unruliest imagination she wouldn't have seen herself like this! Dying in the woods of the Northlands. She lamented once again her decision to plunge unprepared into these strange woods, knowing full well that map reading and orienteering were a glaring weakness in her skill set.

But her instincts to survive—if not to navigate—seemed to be properly aligned. She knew she hadn't the skills to trap or make fire, but early on Anika recognized the unlikelihood of escaping the forest in the daylight, and had wasted no time seeking shelter. Hunger had come calling hours ago, and she had kept an eye out for anything that could pass for food. But the elements, she knew, were her biggest threat, even in the midst of a mild spring day.

And she had been fortunate to find the 'cave,' which was how she thought of it, though it was really nothing more than a deep indentation in the side of a hill she'd been following for the last several hours. It was barely deep enough to sit in, let alone lie down, but it was shelter, and it would protect her from

ight wind that was sure to come. The breezes she so welcomed dur-
heat of the day now terrified her.

shiver scurried the length of Anika's back, the night again teasing what
ahead, and Anika tucked her arms into the sleeves of her thin cotton
blouse, gripping the bottoms of her elbows, her forearms layered across her
abdomen below her bra. This was a bad sign, she thought: the sun had not
fully set and the early stages of hypothermia had already begun. If she made
it through the night, it wouldn't be without the help of God. Somewhere in
the back of her mind she considered that her faith would help, but she would
conserve her prayers for now, knowing the worst of the cold was still to come.
What she wouldn't give for a blanket.

Anika drifted to sleep but was awake within minutes, the result of another short, epileptic shiver. She was wide-eyed and focused for a minute, and
then drifted away again, repeating this cycle on and off for what may have
been an hour, with her shakes each time becoming increasingly violent, as her
muscles tried desperately to create warmth. She needed to move.

She crawled from the cave and stood outside in the open of the forest. It
was dark, but not as dark as she would have imagined this far from civiliza-
tion; the moon, thankfully, doing its part for her on this night.

She got to her feet and forced herself to run, at first in place, and then
occasionally in short bursts to about a ten-foot radius, making sure not to
lose sight of her shelter. She lifted her knees as high as possible, feeling the
blood in them resist, and then start to come alive. The short naps had been
frustrating and alarming—with death being the result of any deep sleep, she
feared—but they had momentarily revived her, and Anika suddenly felt she
could sustain the exercise long enough to get warm again. After that she
wasn't sure, and she knew running around wasn't the long-term solution to
her situation—after all, she was hungry, and her energy would fail soon. But
for now running felt good, and she went with it.

The crunch of her shoes on the leaf litter and dry twigs sounded abrupt
and panicky in the stillness of the forest, and the noise evoked in her some
long-forgotten sense of urgency, the primal need to continue even under
dire conditions and the harshest of circumstances. Though being lost in the
woods in early spring, Anika conceded, hardly qualified as the 'harshest of
circumstances.'

She felt suddenly energized, and desperately wished it were daytime so she could continue her lonely journey, ill-fated though it may be. She even considered, with the brightness of the moon, moving on at night; but her hunger, which was manageable now, wouldn't stay in the shadows for much longer, and if delirium was coming, she'd rather it arrive in the relative safety of her new burrow or in the light of day and not in the open of the forest darkness. Besides, if she did brave the forest tonight and was unable to find a cabin or some other artificial structure, it was unlikely she would again find natural accommodations like those she had now and would almost certainly freeze.

No, for now she would stay awake and keep her body moving as long as possible, conserving her water and resting when necessary. The night had a long way to go, but she felt she could make it.

Anika continued her pattern of light jogging, followed by short bursts of sprints, and then rest. As her legs began to tire, the jogging and sprint sessions became indistinguishable, and the rest periods became dozes. She resisted the urge to lie down, or huddle back in the cave, but sleep was inevitable.

<hr />

THE LOUD CRUNCH OF feet startled Anika, and with semi-cognizance she chuckled to herself, realizing she had fallen asleep while somehow walking in place. Wouldn't that be a great ability to have right now, she thought, and then realized she was doing it now, which inspired her in a groggy, abstract sort of way. Maybe she could figure out how to harness this newfound talent and sustain it.

The dreamlike concept turned to alert curiosity, and Anika opened her eyes to find herself lying in darkness on the ground in her "resting" spot. She wasn't sleepwalking, she was just sleeping. Mud and branches stuck to the side of her nose and lips, and something insectile quickly crawled its way up from the hairline at the back of her head toward the top of her scalp.

She scrambled to her feet and looked around, frantically ruffling her hair, trying in consternation both to rid herself of the parasite now nestled in her hair and to identify the potentially larger threat on the perimeter. Anika's slumbered eyes adjusted slowly to the night, and the once-bright moon had temporarily withdrawn behind a stray cloud cluster, making even the black forms of the trees virtually invisible. She was blind, and something was stalking her.

Her first thought was to climb, to locate the closest tree—fallen or otherwise—and get as high as possible. She was no great athlete, but she trusted her abilities given the situation. Besides, running was out of the question, since virtually any animal that she could think of would catch her easily before she took more than a few strides.

But if she were to get some height, Anika thought, maybe she could buy some time. Jab at whatever was after her with a stick or something and frustrate it until it gave up. Anika thought of wolves. Wolves couldn't climb trees could they? She'd heard somewhere that bears could, but were there really bears in these parts?

These initial plans and imaginings ran their course in a matter of seconds, and were quickly replaced with calmer, more reasonable thoughts. Anika now thought it much more likely that whatever was prowling her space was something more common and less deadly than a wolf or bear. A deer or fox perhaps. Maybe a moose. She stood her ground, motionless, now listening with conscious ears for the sound of steps to repeat.

She waited for what seemed like several minutes and then: Crunch. Crunch. Crunch.

The patient steps moved to Anika's left—perhaps ten yards away, maybe less—and then stopped.

Her guess of a deer now seemed most likely; the steps were heavy and deliberate—not the scurrying movements of a squirrel or rabbit—but not threatening either, secretive and apprehensive.

Anika breathed out for the first time in what must have been a full minute, and the passing thoughts of small game now made her stomach moan in hunger. She felt only slightly relieved, however, knowing the 'deer' could just as easily be one of a dozen other, less docile things, ready to pounce at any moment.

Anika slowly stooped down, blindly feeling for the largest stick in her immediate confines, which turned out to be a stray branch, two-feet long at most and no thicker than a billiard cue. She grabbed it and stood back up without moving her feet.

"Hello," she said softly, mildly aware that she was attempting to talk to what she had convinced herself was a deer.

The night answered back with only the distant chirping of crickets and the light rustle of the trees' topmost leaves. The moon had returned to the black sky, and Anika's eyes adjusted. She could now see the silvery reflection of the branches and rocks that crowded the area. If something large was still there, she would certainly see it when it moved.

Keeping as still as possible, Anika shifted her eyes from right to left, turning her head just slightly upon reaching the limits of her periphery.

Crunch! Crunch! Crunch!

This time the sound was plodding and aggressive with no pretense of stealth. Terrified, Anika turned toward the sound, and saw only a glimpse of something curved and dull smash down on her forehead, catching her brow above her left eye and splitting it like a grape.

CHAPTER FOUR

IT WAS ALMOST DAWN when the Morgan truck pulled back onto the gravel road that led to their cabin, and Gretel's doubts about seeing her mother again had grown stronger.

To this point she had been scared, and had concentrated this fear and directed it toward her father in a projection of overdue frustrations. But she hadn't really believed her mother was gone forever. Forever. She was too tired now to start adjusting to exactly what that meant to the rest of her life. And as much as her body pressured her to cry, there were simply no more tears.

The drive home from Deda's had been agony. Her father had stopped at every curve and intersection, every hill and possible hidden entrance, forcing her and Hansel out to wander the shoulders of the highways with him, branching off in opposite directions until he called them back with a barking "Let's go." They were the only words he spoke the entire drive.

And the searches were pathetic and hopeless in the vast darkness of the countryside, with only the narrow beam of the car's headlights to guide them. The only way they would have found their mother was if she happened to be sitting in the eight-foot wide stretch of light at the exact place where her father had pulled over. The ridiculousness of it made Gretel despondent and she cried nearly the whole time.

But as her father now pulled to a stop in front of their home, her sobs had been replaced with a more reserved depression and self-pity. If she had indeed lost her mother, then her loss, she knew, was greater than anyone's. Including her father. Whatever his weaknesses were as a man, he was an adult and was innately better built to deal with such losses. It was part of what separated adults from children, Gretel thought. She was sad for him, of course, but husbands lost their wives every day—or the other way around—it was an eventual fact of life. And with a home and a fair amount of land, he could marry again if that's what he wanted. Men with property rarely died alone in the Southlands.

There was Hansel, of course, who *was* a child, and Gretel did not discount the enormity of the loss her mother would be to him. Because of his age, he was more vulnerable than she was, and she knew there was no worse thing an eight-year-old boy could imagine than losing his mother. It would be devastating for her brother, of that she had no doubt. But she also knew that compared to virtually any girl born in the Southlands, a boy's life was charmed. And though his sadness would be deep and prolonged, his future would arrive unscathed. He would grow into a teenager and then a young man, and as he grew, so too would the respect of those in the community. Not that he would be any great pillar of society (it was the Back Country, after all)—or even a leader of men, she guessed—it's just the way it was here. Eventually Hansel would inherit the farm from their father, marry a girl, of which there would be several to choose from, and live as the Morgan men did for generations before him: long and average and in relative happiness. And it would go that way with or without his mother.

But it was different when a girl lost her mother. A girl truly *needed* her mother. It was true a girl's father protected her from physical harm, but her mother was her defender in the community, which, at fourteen, Gretel deemed far more important. And *her* mother was special, particularly suited for the task of raising a girl to womanhood. How brilliant she was! Having the ability not only to navigate the common pitfalls that consumed most of her friends' mothers, but also to float above all the ridiculous rules that most women accepted without protest. That role of an indentured servant, mothering unlimited offspring at her husband's command: that was never to be her mother's lot in life.

And until this moment, Gretel didn't think it was hers. She had anticipated and depended on her mother encouraging and reinforcing these values as she grew, molding her into something proud and independent. Not to lead armies into battle or found nations, but to become her own woman. And Gretel wasn't there yet. She wasn't ready to lose her mother.

She had, of course, considered another possibility: that her mother wasn't dead. That she had instead left them, fed up with domestic life on the farm.

Perhaps she even had the intention of retrieving her and Hansel once she was settled into whatever new life she'd found, one that had been blueprinted and dreamed of for years. It wasn't an impossible scenario; her father was no prince, and though he was by no measure evil or abusive, charming and inspiring he was not. It was no great stretch to imagine a woman like her mother trading up when the opportunity arose.

But this prospect, though obviously a better, happier one, didn't fit, and provided little comfort to Gretel. Somewhere within her, she knew the news was grim.

Her father turned off the truck's motor and left the keys in the ignition. He opened the door of the truck and walked to the front door of the cabin where he stood motionlessly, his head hung, staring at the ground in front of his feet.

"We'll go again tomorrow," he said, "when there is light." He then opened the door and walked inside quietly.

Gretel sat in the passenger seat of the truck and stared bleakly through the open car door at the spot where her father had stood just seconds before. The thought of another day combing the emptiness of the Interways was unbearable right now, and she pushed the thought aside. She could only pray that he would change his mind by tomorrow morning and let The System do its work.

But what her father said wasn't as dispiriting as how he was behaving. For starters, he had left Hansel sleeping in the back of the truck, having made no effort even to wake him, let alone carry him inside: something he had done without thinking dozens of times in his life. Her father was still ill, Gretel realized, and his injuries were far from healed and were probably flaring as badly as ever right now, but he hadn't even looked at his son. Hansel was certainly no toddler, of course, he was in fact rather tall and stout for his age, having always been a hearty eater and eager farmhand. But her father had always relished carrying his son to bed, whether from the truck after a long road trip or the large sofa in the den where Hansel liked to sit and read his magazines. It was something Gretel had observed in her father with great interest, even early in her brother's life, since the act was so out of place within her father's overall character.

But she was being too hard on him, perhaps. His wife was gone, and whether through force or by choice, the result for the rest of his life was essentially the same.

Gretel reached down and picked the book off the floor. In the context of the dirt road that made up the front yard of her cottage, the black tome now seemed somehow smaller and incomplete, losing some of its fascination to Gretel. But not all.

The blackness and sterility of it were still mesmerizing—appearing as shadowy in the dim light of the truck as it did on Deda's shelf—and the feel of it, that leathery coldness, remained.

Deda had allowed her to take the book home, and she had only asked to do so because she had seen the look in her grandfather's eyes when he saw her with it, struggling to reach it from the precarious edge of the work bench. His face had burst into the same smile she had seen when they first arrived, only this time his eyes were alert, craving. Instinctively, she had asked for it, feeling that doing so was a preemptive strike of sorts, though what exactly it was she was preempting she didn't know. She had always wanted to take it, of course, but knew on some level that it would be out of place with her outside the realm of the damp cellar. And that now seemed true.

Deda had told Gretel that the title of the book was *Orphism*, and according to him it was older than The Bible; how he knew that fact was unclear, since he claimed to have no idea what the word 'Orphism' even meant or what the book itself was about.

"But your grandmother treasured it," he had told her while they both sat in Deda's small kitchen, having exited the creepiness of the cellar. Deda's smile had been warm as he reflected on his deceased wife. "And it's one of the few possessions of hers that remains. So I have come to treasure it as well." It had seemed so strange to Gretel to be openly discussing the book that for so long had held such mystery, and she felt a bit silly that she had never asked her grandfather about it before. It was only a book after all.

"Why did she love it so much?" Gretel asked.

Deda paused and then said, "It was special to her." His smile waned slightly as he looked away from his granddaughter, appearing disappointed that she had posed such a question. He forced a cough and rose from the table, making his way to the stove and picking up the teapot that sat on the back burner.

The awkwardness of the silence that followed Deda's non-answer was striking, and Gretel had been relieved when her father entered the room. His face was stern and tired. And he had made no acknowledgment of Deda.

"Gretel, we're leaving," he said. "Your brother is in the truck." He turned and walked out, and the subsequent sound of the front door opening and closing had been deafening.

The ride back to the Southlands would be tortuous, Gretel knew, but she had been glad to be leaving.

She'd grabbed the book—*Orphism*—with both hands and stood up from the table. "Bye Deda," she said and turned to leave, not really expecting a reply. She had come to accept these periods of moodiness and depression in her grandfather over the years, and though her feelings were often hurt by them, she mostly felt sorry for him.

"Your grandmother was an amazing woman," Deda said, his voice crisp and loud, as if he was standing right behind her.

Gretel turned back toward the kitchen and saw Deda standing at the stove, casually firing up the teapot as he was before.

"You, Gretel, would have loved her. And she you."

"Okay, bye," Gretel had managed to stammer, and then quickly walked from the house and into the front seat of her father's truck, which her father had wasted no time shifting into park and driving away.

Deda's words had been eerie and out of place, Gretel now thought as she tried gently to stir her brother awake. But they were somehow comforting. She had never known her grandmother—she died when Gretel's mother was just a girl—but her mother had always spoken fondly of the woman, and that had always been important to Gretel.

Her mother. Gretel's eyes filled with tears once again. "Hansel."

"We'll never find her like this," he whined. "I want to go home!"

The fruitless searches had clearly traumatized her brother, and Gretel suspected there would be something akin to a revolution tomorrow morning when their father told him the plans for the day.

"We're home, Han. Let's go."

THE NEXT MORNING HANSEL woke first, followed by Gretel, and they both performed their daily tasks as minimally and quietly as possible, making every effort to ensure their father continued sleeping. And he had, almost until lunchtime, before he finally ventured out to the main area of the house, clumsily fixed a plate of eggs and toast, and retreated back to his room. No mention was made of a search effort, and neither child reminded him.

But Gretel was now torn. With a full night's sleep, in the clarity of the day, she thought her father had been right last night: they had to look for their mother. Who else if not them?

Gretel had been exhausted after the ride from Deda's, and it had made her selfish, but if her mother needed help, and if her father was right about The System not doing anything for days, then of course they had to go look for her! Were they to let her die in a ditch somewhere in the Northlands? No, they had to go.

But go where?

The truth was they had looked in the only place they knew—along the Interways—and though the daylight could certainly be the difference between spotting a footprint in the mud or a stray piece of fabric lingering on a branch, Gretel didn't suspect this would be the outcome. By now, if her mother had crashed the car along that stretch of road—not a major thoroughfare, to be sure, but not empty either—someone would have noticed. Certainly there would be some indication of an accident. She or her father would have seen it. On the way back from Deda's it had been dark and impossible, but driving *to* his house there had been plenty of light, and they had stopped everywhere it seemed. And had found nothing.

What Gretel also knew was there was little chance of getting help from anyone personally. Her father had already made all the calls to friends and family, including even the most fringe members of both sets, and according to him no one had heard anything or was in any position to help. Of course not.

Her mother's extended family consisted of Deda, who apparently offered nothing new during her father's conversation with him (though her father hadn't told Gretel any of the specifics), and the few members left of her father's family were either far away, feeble, or on less-than-stellar terms with her father. In some cases it was all three. The Morgan family—that is, her father's kin—as far as Gretel was concerned, did not extend beyond her family's cabin's walls.

And then there was The System of course, who Gretel, like most children in the Southlands, rarely, if ever, saw. Her father had told her they never patrolled the Back Country unless there was cause or summons, neither of which, if it could be at all helped, occurred here. The land policed itself for the most part, and this value of self-reliance was well-met by The System, who preferred to stay tight to the cities where their oversight was much more condensed and efficient. Whether they were respectful of Back Country rules or indifferent to the plight of its people, The System stayed away.

But they weren't completely foreign to Gretel. She had, in fact, seen their cars on two different occasions, and one of those times had been in the Back Country when the Stein farm had caught fire and Jonathan Stein's grandmother was killed. Gretel recalled the sight of the blood red car racing past her cottage, its siren blazing loudly as the black ghost of the exhaust lingered in the coupe's wake. Gretel had been struck most by the car's color and its stark contrast to the Back Country landscape, and the dark black tint of the windows. She had never actually seen a System officer, but had been told they were men of enormous size.

The reputation of The System was one that inspired fear in the general citizenry, but The System itself kept itself in the shadows as much as possible. They relied on local law enforcement—and in the case of the Back Country, the people—to deal with the lower crimes and complaints, focusing instead on the more serious, complicated situations. This enforcement formula had given The System a somewhat mythical quality for Gretel, as it did for most of the residents of the Southlands, particularly in the Back Country. And Gretel understood very well that this was kind of the point.

But as far as Gretel was concerned, The System was also corrupt and inadequate, and she knew of no incidences when they had actually helped anyone she knew. In fact, if there was one thing she believed about The System, it was that they did not exist to help her, her family, or anyone in her community, though she had come to realize years ago that most of her viewpoints about it were based on her father's beliefs and not her own experiences.

And there was one other thing she now believed about The System: that ultimately she was counting on them to bring her mother home.

So Gretel clung to hope in The System and their rules, which apparently required at least another full day for her mother to remain missing before they began a search. And when they finally did, Gretel guessed, they would do so under the assumption that their mother had left them for bluer skies and a new life, and not that she was in trouble or dead. Okay. That was fine. At least they would be looking. It was more than she and her family were doing now.

Gretel's hatred for her father flared with this thought and again she became disgusted with his lack of masculinity and fortitude. She knew her mother would be doing more for him if the situation were reversed, and even if he was hurting physically this morning—which no doubt he was after the chaos of last night—his wife was missing, and he should never give up.

As if on cue, Heinrich Morgan opened the door to his bedroom and walked out, passing through the kitchen to the porch where Gretel had first heard the news of her mother's absence only yesterday. Yesterday. It seemed like weeks, and Gretel's spirit was momentarily buoyed by the brief time span.

Heinrich put on his boots, still muddy and wet from last night's search, and walked toward the door.

"Where are you going, Papa?" Gretel's voice was calm, sympathetic.

"Check on your brother in a few minutes, Gretel. He's in the fields."

"Where are you going?" she repeated, this time with more urgency.

"You know where I'm going. Check on your brother." Her father opened the door and walked out toward the truck, Gretel right behind him.

"I'll come with you, Papa. Let me help. Last night it was too dark, but today—"

Gretel's words were interrupted by a voice Gretel hadn't heard come from her father's mouth in quite some time.

"You will stay and check on your brother as I've instructed! That is what you will do!" Heinrich frowned and opened his mouth as if to say more, then gingerly stepped up into his old pickup and drove off.

As Gretel watched him drive away, the tears came again in force, though this time in silence. She watched until the truck was out of view, confirming that her father was indeed heading north to the Interways, and then walked back to the house where she sat down on the porch again and began to thumb slowly through her dead grandmother's book.

It was a rather ridiculous waste of time, she thought, looking through the book, since she couldn't read a word of it. But it comforted her and made her feel more connected to her family somehow.

According to Deda, the symbols and letters that made up the text were similar to Ancient Greek, and the book itself contained the practices and mythologies of a religion hundreds of years older than Christianity. How he knew all this without being able to read it was still a bit unclear to Gretel, and her grandfather had deflected the question during their powwow in his kitchen. Clearly he had some familiarity with the language, or perhaps her grandmother did, and had explained it to him. Either way, as Gretel now reflected, he had been holding something back.

Gretel tried once again to decipher the sentences, recognizing that many of the letters in the book were the same as they were in English—the 'A's' and 'N's' and 'T's' and such—but it was all gibberish, and her light-hearted stab at amateur cryptography left her brain sore.

Still, the age of the words and the feel of the book kept her rapt, and she looked through the pages slowly, as if actually reading. The book kept her mind off her mother—and her father for that matter—and she suddenly felt very grateful that her grandfather had encouraged her to take it.

Orphism.

She would research the subject the next time she went to town and could stop in the library. Or maybe she would ask some of her teachers when she returned to school, though she doubted any of them would be familiar with such an exotic text.

If she and her family had still gone to church she would have asked one of the nuns, or perhaps the preacher after Sunday service; certainly they would have some knowledge of a book older than The Bible. But the routine of church-going had come to an abrupt end several years ago, with little forewarning or explanation, and though it was something that Gretel welcomed at first, she had grown to miss church, if only for the gathering of friends.

Gretel read for an hour or so and then closed the book and placed it on her lap. She sat meditatively for a few moments, staring out the window toward the elms in the back, before deciding she had better check on Hansel.

Her father had become far too overprotective of her brother lately, Gretel thought, but today she understood.

She took a deep breath and walked outside to the front stoop, leaving the book behind her on the chair. The air had quickly thickened with the emergence of the afternoon sun and the humidity stung her lungs instantly. Gretel looked off toward the fields and saw Hansel sitting in the dirt, playing with one of his many stick creatures that her father had made for him over the years. He was still such a young boy, she thought, and her eyes filled with tears.

Gretel cupped her hands around her mouth and lifted her chin, and as she inhaled to call her brother in from the fields, she noticed the cloud of dust that was rising from the end of the half-mile road that led past the fields to their cottage. It seemed to appear spontaneously, as if suddenly erupting from beneath the ground like a geyser of powder. The glare of the sun reflecting off the particles made it impossible for Gretel to see the source, but as the cloak of earth dissipated she saw the unmistakable red metal explode from the dust and go speeding insanely past Hansel toward the house. It looked as if the devil were coming, Gretel thought. But she knew better.

There was no mistaking it. It was The System.

CHAPTER FIVE

ANIKA FIDGETED AND grimaced, then rolled to her back and screamed. Reflexively, her left eye opened and the scream devolved into heavy breathing. She stared searchingly at the beams that ran along the ceiling above her, trying desperately to get her bearings. The daylight shone in from a small lunette window over her bed and illuminated the room, but nothing was familiar.

She touched her head where she had been struck and thought absently that it was probably a good sign of her condition that she even remembered the attack. The feel of her forehead made her dry heave. Her right eye was swollen shut and felt enormous; the entire area around it having the texture of a ripe plum, and probably looking about the same, she imagined. Anika pulled her fingers away from her head and looked at the white doughy substance that caked her fingertips. It had the consistency of batter, and she guessed it to be some type of moist medicinal powder.

Lying on her back, Anika surveyed the room and took note of the accommodations. They were far from charming, or even sterile, but they appeared fairly adequate—the wool blanket, sheeted bed, and apparent medicine on her wound even suggesting she was being nursed. It was a pleasant thought considering the attack she had received. Perhaps whoever assaulted her had done so mistakenly and was now atoning, believing perhaps that Anika was the wild creature she herself had imagined was lurking in the dark of the forest. Or maybe Anika had been unconscious for days and had already been rescued from her assailant.

Neither scenario seemed quite right to Anika, but whoever brought her to the comfort of the bed in which she now lay was certain to reveal himself soon. Her scream moments ago had been wild and echoing and, judging by the sounds of movement and clanging pots outside the door, there was definitely someone else in the house. And smells had begun to seep into the room, incredible smells that filled Anika's mouth with saliva and churned her stomach.

Despite the pain and fatigue gripping her head and muscles, she was eager to get up. Anticipating a rush of pain to her head, Anika lifted herself gently to a sitting position in the bed and pulled the wool blanket off of her lap. Surprisingly, there wasn't much protest from her body, though her head hurt badly, both inside and on the surface. But Anika was now confident she could get to her feet.

She swung her legs toward the floor and immediately felt the jolt of resistance on her right foot. Anika shrieked, immediately thinking someone had grabbed her from beneath the bed. But as she looked down to her feet she saw the black oval links running between the wall and the mattress before ending in a thick metal tube around her right ankle. She was chained.

She kicked her foot once, but there was little slack in the chain, and the effort was feeble. Now in a panic, she quickly cleared the blankets entirely from her legs and grabbed at the metal around her ankle. The clasp itself was fairly loose, but the metal was thick and appeared impenetrable to Anika.

She followed the chain from her ankle to the balled up quilt that had collected at the wall by her feet. She moved the quilt aside, looking down through the gap between the wall and the bed. There she could see a large metal plate with six thick bolts connecting the chain to the floor. She scooted down toward the foot of the bed, gripped the chain tightly with both hands and pulled up, again having no success as the length of the chain offered little leverage. The cold dark metal in her hand conjured thoughts of slavery and brutality, and only some primal sense of survival kept Anika from screaming again, though it was obviously no secret to her captor where she was being held.

A rush of pain shot through Anika's head, and she lay back down, supine, again feeling her wound and the mushy substance that coated it. It then occurred to her that she was indeed being nursed, but she was also a prisoner.

Suddenly the sounds outside the door—'kitchen sounds' is how Anika would come to know them—stopped, and Anika could hear the approaching rap of light footsteps followed by the creaking of her door as it opened slowly. The knob on the door rattled as it turned, and when the door finally opened,

Anika could see the flat edge of something black and heavy—cast iron perhaps—emerge through the portal, followed by the white deformed hands that gripped either side of the object.

With only one good eye, Anika first marked the object as some kind of blunt weapon, different than the one that had put her in her current state, but just as medieval and menacing. Her heart began to gallop, and she instinctively got to her knees, raising her arms to shoulder height and width in defense, fingers spread, as if prepared for a Roman wrestling match. And then she began to scream.

Anika's one working eye stayed fixed on the shape in the doorway and, as it began to focus, she realized the object being carried was not a weapon after all, but was, in fact, a tray. With food. A large plate of food.

It was a meal.

With some effort, Anika forced herself to look up from the tray to the face of the person carrying it, but his head was shrouded in a dark hood that was much too large for the figure underneath. He looked like a monk, she thought, and the slow, silent movements through the room only reinforced the image. Anika could only see the tip of the nose and lips—she couldn't identify a face—but as she studied the shape in full, there was no doubt about it: the figure in the robe was a woman.

Anika let out a sigh, if not of relief, at least of the pressure built up in the previous few seconds over the prospect of being raped and tortured. Something bad seemed certain to be looming of course, but at least a sexual assault and murder didn't seem to be in the cards. At least not for now. Instead, it appeared, she was about to be fed.

"Where am I?" Anika asked as sternly as possible, "Why am I chained?" She kept her eyes riveted to the cloaked figure and watched intently as the woman walked toward the corner of the room opposite the bed and set the tray on a thin black wrought iron table.

The woman paused for a moment at the tray, making sure everything was just so, and then stood erect, turning toward Anika and lowering her hood. "Which question would you like answered first?" she said pragmatically, without emotion.

Anika was surprised at the normalcy of the woman's features, expecting something closer to a stereotypical hag from the fairy tales, decrepit and grotesque, slightly green perhaps. In fact, Anika guessed the woman was maybe only twenty years older than she, though her skin appeared more weathered-looking and hardened than that. Anika supposed she would have described the woman as homely, and rather unremarkable in every way, though with a little effort she would have probably cleaned up decently. She did notice, however, her mouth seemed a bit large for her face.

A glint of recognition flashed in Anika's mind, but it was subtle, and Anika hadn't the luxury to pursue it at the moment. "Why am I chained?" she answered.

Without hesitation the woman responded, "You are chained because I don't know you. And though, admittedly, you don't look like much of a threat, I have been robbed by nicer-looking creatures than yourself. With no intended insult of course."

Anika detected an aged quality to the woman's voice, and perhaps an accent that had diminished over time. "So you keep an anchored chain in your bedroom—just in case you meet any strangers?"

The sarcasm wasn't lost on the woman and she smiled, picking up the plate of food and carrying it to Anika's bedside. "This room was at one time used as a slaughterhouse. Some of the instruments remain."

Anika was skeptical of this answer, but decided she would be well-advised not to challenge it; besides, the approaching plate of food quickly became the main subject of her focus. She had literally never been this hungry before, and tears filled her eyes at the prospect of eating.

The woman set the tray down at the foot of Anika's bed and then turned and walked toward the door as if to leave the room.

Anika's eyes were locked in on the three small pies that sat neatly on the tray, the smells arising from them suggesting a combination of both meat and fruit. Anika's throat convulsed in hunger, but as the door opened, she resisted her desires for a moment and said, "Why did you hit me?"

The woman stopped at the threshold of the door, as if surprised at Anika's restraint, and turned back toward the bed. This time the woman did not smile, but instead looked sympathetic, caring. "We all need to eat," she said, and then walked out.

Anika watched her leave, and then dug her fingers into the pie closest to her, shoving irregular pieces into her mouth, barely swallowing between bites. The tastes were delicious, and though Anika realized her hunger probably clouded her judgment, she could think of nothing else she had ever eaten that tasted quite this good. Moments later, before Anika had devoured the last pie, the cloaked woman entered the room again, this time carrying a large black pot.

"Your toilet," she said placing it beside the bed. "Summon me when it needs emptying." The woman turned to leave.

"Wait." Anika shoved the last piece of crust into her mouth. She swallowed the last morsel without chewing it, and then, "Thank you, these were delicious. You're quite talented." Anika was still unsure of the woman's motives, but she figured flattery couldn't hurt. And the pies *really were* amazing.

"You're welcome."

"I'm feeling much better. Food and rest: what better medicine is there?" Anika paused, waiting for some reciprocation to her attempt at rapport. The woman stayed silent. "Perhaps you could show me back to the road." Anika looked down at the chain around her ankle. "Clearly I'm no threat." She snorted a laugh at this last notion.

"You'll need more rest; and your wound will need another application." The woman's tone suggested there would be no further discussion, and she walked quickly to the door, opening it and then pausing. "And the road," she said, "you can see it from here."

THE NEXT MORNING ANIKA woke to the sound of wood being chopped just outside her window. There was a deliberate, grotesque nature to the sound that she had never noticed before, no doubt now occurring to her because of her current circumstances. Her first thoughts were of her children, and then her ankle, and she immediately thrust her leg away from the wall to reveal what she already knew: the chain remained.

The fresh smells from the kitchen continued to drift into her room, and once again her appetite was activated, the memory of last night's pies momentarily nudging its way into her mind. But Anika had eaten heartily only hours ago, and now that her hunger—along with the other necessities of warmth and sleep—had been appeased, the idea of escape strengthened and quickly positioned itself to its proper place at the helm of Anika's concerns. It was clear the woman intended to keep her; what her intentions were beyond that was still the question.

Geographically, Anika was close to the Interways, that much the woman had revealed. In which direction she could find the road she didn't know, but working on that mystery was putting the cart before the horse. As long as she remained chained to the cabin floor, she might as well have been on the moon.

She had already assessed the thick clasp of metal that was wrapped around her leg, and it looked on its face that the only way out of it—other than cutting off her foot—was with a key. Or else an extremely hearty tool, which she doubted would be conveniently resting somewhere nearby.

Instruments from a slaughter house.

Anika knew her share about slaughtering animals, she had been killing chickens since she was younger than Hansel and had never seen anything like the set up in this room. And it wasn't just because of the furniture. A slaughterhouse attached to the main living area? Who would ever design such a thing? What type of person would allow the gore and filth and violent noises that accompanied the killing of animals to be only paces from her kitchen and sleeping quarters? And there wasn't even an entrance to the room from the outside. Why would a woman want to herd filthy pigs and goats through her home when a door built into the wall was a much easier solution? Anika told herself it was possible that the room was originally intended as a bedroom and was later converted to a slaughterhouse, but on some level that theory was even more frightening.

Anika's mind leaped back to the current situation. She needed to get her bearings and plan out what to do next. Was it two days since her accident on the road? That seemed right, but she couldn't be entirely sure. She'd taken a blow to her head—a considerable one—and it was possible she'd been unconscious for longer than a day. Either way, Anika figured the longer she stayed locked in the room, the more her chances of escape diminished. She had to figure something out soon.

She suddenly realized her vision was improved and once again felt the area above her eye. She was astonished at how small it felt, shrunken and compressed and immediately reconsidered the length of time she had been out. She'd received her share of shiners after all—they were an accepted part of life on a farm, particularly as a child—but the injury she'd sustained in the forest was blunt trauma, a deliberate strike with a weapon. And this injury appeared to be healing in a fraction of the time of any normal black eye. She couldn't see her eye, of course, so there was probably still some discoloration, and judging by her fingers, the white paste was apparently still being applied while she slept, but the swelling was virtually gone.

There was no longer any question in Anika's mind that she was being nursed back to health, so perhaps the woman's intentions weren't sinister, just incredibly cautious. Why else would she be healing her? Maybe she really was harmless. Mad and harmless.

Either way, Anika thought, she was being held prisoner, and whether it was for the rest of her life or a few more hours, she had a right to know why. No more stalling or cryptic answers: the next time the woman came to her room, Anika was going to find out what was going on.

A surge of replenishment suddenly filled Anika, and she felt the need to get on her feet. The chain on her ankle was too short for her to dismount and stand beside the open side of the bed, but she thought if she were able to push the bed away from the wall and create a small gap there, she might be able to stand on the inside.

Anika could tell the bed was sturdy and well-made; there was very little wobble in it when she shifted, and it felt dense to the touch. But it also wasn't very big, and she figured with some effort she could scoot the legs just enough.

Anika wedged her right foot in between the wall and the frame of the bed, and with less force than she had expected, was able to leverage her body enough to pry the frame from the wood of the cabin wall, creating a small space between the wall and the thin mattress. She wiggled her foot down toward the floor, the metal clasp just clearing the gap, and moved her body upright.

She was now standing on one foot.

She nudged the bed further away with her right knee and dropped the other foot to the floor. She now stood erect against the wall, the chain snaking limply on the floor at her right foot.

Anika felt the ecstasy in her legs, as well as the weakness and atrophy, and a sudden sense of claustrophobia nipped at her nerves, as though she would lack the strength to regain her position on the bed when the time came. With all the strength in her unbound leg, Anika drove the foot of the bed away from her, pushing out with her left foot and sending it toward the middle of the room. She let out a long steady breath of relief and gave an internal prayer of thanks.

There was now enough space for her to squat and get some stretch in her muscles, so she did this several times, limbering her arms simultaneously with wide, rotating movements. The burn in her thighs and chest was both harsh and relieving, and Anna could sense the blood flowing throughout her body, giving her the alertness and energy she was chasing.

She stooped down again, and this time grabbed the iron hitch that connected the chain to the floor, wriggling it to test its permanence. The fastening was as she suspected, heavy and tight, sturdy in its feel and look, and the eye bolt that connected to the chain was as thick as her finger. She studied the wooden floorboard to which the hitch was connected, judging whether or not—over time of course—she would be able to pry it up, and with it the iron attachment. Anika figured if she could secure any type of tool—a spoon perhaps that the woman didn't notice missing from her empty meal tray—she could hopefully work up the plank. She would still have the problem of a chain around her ankle, but at least she would be mobile. She just needed to reach the road.

But the floorboards seemed solid as well, and even if she were able to get hold of some kind of instrument, with her ankle bound, she wouldn't have the range necessary to jimmy the boards at the proper angles. It was as if the contraption were built for just this purpose, she thought, and with that image Anika gripped the chain tightly with both hands, her knuckles bulging taut and white. In a controlled panic, she began to pull up on the chain, hoping to summon the extraordinary strength that she had always heard existed in everyone, but only erupted at just the right moment during times of crisis.

Her biceps strained as she desperately tried to hold her hands stable around the metal links and lift the chain from its anchor. Or at least bow the floor board slightly, just to give her hope. Her effort, though, was feeble, as her palms, sweaty and slick from both exertion and fear, kept sliding up the metal cable. She needed leverage.

Anika sat down on the floor and faced the wall, her back straight, straddling the square bracket. She wedged her ankles at the juncture where the floor and wall met, the soles of her feet flat against the wall and her toes pointing to the ceiling. She wrapped the chain once around her right wrist and grabbed it with both hands near the anchor. It was a bit awkward with her ankle bound, but she now had the strength of her thighs. Anika pushed her body out with the last of the stamina that remained in her for now.

Nothing. She felt not the slightest movement from the anchor or wood boards.

Defeated, she leaned her head back gently to the bed which was now behind her and closed her eyes, fighting back the tears. The woman would be in soon, would see the bed in the center of the room and the exposed eye bolt, and she would know Anika was trying to escape. Perhaps she already assumed that, but this would be the proof. Maybe the woman would kill Anika right there on the floor, or maybe she would explain everything first, and then kill her. Or let her leave. Either way Anika would know her fate soon.

As if her thoughts had been screamed aloud, Anika heard the chopping sounds outside her window suddenly stop. She waited in fear, breathless, hoping for the sickening thump of metal on wood to resume, having not calculated exactly what the next step in her plan would be.

Other than to survive.

She wasn't ready to die. She thought of her children again, this time less abstractly, conjuring their faces in her mind. Hansel was only a baby, he wouldn't understand. And Gretel. All of the obligations that were Anika's, formed by decisions that she had made willingly since she had left home at seventeen, and that had ultimately shaped her life to this point, would fall to Gretel. It wouldn't just be unfair, it would be an atrocity. Her daughter's future promised value, significance; it wasn't to serve her elderly grandfather in the Back Country, or to spend the remainder of her youth as a surrogate mother to her brother and servant to her father.

This old woman seemed reasonable and lucid, Anika thought, though she was obviously a little askew. If she could maybe evoke some more information from her, possibly find some common ground with the woman to build on, she could buy a little time and figure an escape. Maybe convince the woman to let her go. Anika again thought of the accent. There was something familiar in it, the way the woman cut off the 'Rs', rolling them slightly. It wasn't a sound heard often in this country, but Anika was sure she recognized it, from her childhood perhaps. The memory, however, was faint and seemed to dissolve before she could approach it.

The cabin door thundered closed and the sound rang through Anika's room like a gunshot. She needed to arrange the room back to normal. She wasn't ready to die. Not yet. If she hurried she could pull the bed back to the wall and the woman would never know she was up, scheming.

The usual sounds of clanging pots and plates that seemed never to stop for long rattled outside Anika's door. The woman was cooking again, probably Anika's breakfast. There was still time. From her knees, Anika stretched her left arm toward the right rear post of the bed, and was able to grab it, wrapping her fingers around the adorning iron bulb. The chain on her ankle limited her reach, but Anika was able to use it for leverage to pull the bed back in. The bed was heavy on its return, but she was able to slide it slowly on the wooden floor, being careful not to make too much noise.

The sounds in the kitchen stopped, and the ensuing silence unnerved Anika, as if someone was waiting, listening. She had five or so more planks to navigate before the bed would be back to its original place, though even if she had all day she wouldn't have the leverage to get it flush against the wall again. She would have to leave a gap to get out and back on the mattress, and she certainly couldn't push the bed while on top of it. That was fine, it would be close enough.

The lull from the kitchen suddenly erupted into one last *Clang!*, as if a dozen dishes were dumped in a heap into a basin, and then the now familiar footsteps began to click quickly down the hall. Anika didn't have the bed repositioned yet, it was still slightly diagonal, and there were more planks to go; if the woman walked in now, the crookedness would be obvious to her.

Ignoring the noise it would make, and with her full effort, Anika yanked the top of the post, pulling the bed toward her like a rower on a Viking ship. It slid with less resistance than Anika had anticipated, leaving her off balance, and making it impossible for her to offset the effect of the clawed foot at the bottom of the right post catching on a slightly raised floor plank.

The bed almost turned entirely over on top of Anika, but instead rocked back to its side, forming a trench-like barrier in front of her, as if she had taken cover in preparation for a bomb blast.

Anika felt a fearful laughter well up inside of her, but resisted it, pushing the bed back on all fours, and missing by only inches the woman who now stood in front of her.

Anika screamed and recoiled, her back slamming forcefully against the solid wall.

The woman stood staring at Anika for a moment, expressionless, as if watching fish in an aquarium. There was no detectable sense of anger in her face, and Anika stared back at her, keeping eye contact and trying to gauge her next move.

The woman smiled slightly at Anika, and then made a peek over the bed, making sure Anika was still bound and hadn't somehow escaped the shackles. The look was warm and playful, and Anika felt a compulsion to smile back, but resisted. Instead she said, "I have to go. My children are—"

"What are their ages?" she interrupted. "Your children, what are their ages?"

Anika paused, weighing the consequences of revealing this seemingly benign fact. "Fourteen and eight," she replied. "My daughter is fourteen and my son is eight."

"Only two?" The woman looked away as if annoyed at this answer, and then rhetorically asked, "When did women stop having children?"

Anika was well past feeling insulted, and instead experienced a twinge of encouragement from the common ground they seemed to have found. "How many do you have?" she asked.

The woman's eyes seemed to flicker at the question, and Anika noticed the slightest downturn at the edges of her mouth.

"Certainly you have children?" Anika was almost challenging in her tone and knew it was a gamble; but the woman showed interest in *her* children, and whatever wound Anika may have opened on the matter she figured she could sew up on the back end. She wanted to keep the woman talking.

"I don't," the woman responded, clearly not interested in telling her own story.

"Really? When did women stop having children?" Anika forced a laugh, hoping to convey a sense of camaraderie and not insolence.

The woman turned back toward Anika, her eyes wide and focused, a slight smile forming at the edges of her mouth as if amused at Anika's boldness. "At one time I had six," she said. "They've all been dead many years."

Anika felt the blood rush to her face, a reaction indicative of both fear and embarrassment. Her stomach convulsed and she felt like vomiting."I'm sorry," she whispered. "I didn't mean..." Wide-eyed, Anika watched the woman's face, hoping she would say something—anything—to fill the empty space where Anika's words should have been, thereby letting her off the mat.

But there was only silence, and the woman continued her cold stare, forcing Anika to drop her gaze to the floor.

Finally Anika looked up and said, "Are you going to kill me?"

The woman considered the question for a moment, seeming to give it sincere thought, and then said, "Why are you here?"

Somewhat relieved, Anika digested the question, took a deep breath, and replied, "I was attacked...you attacked me and..."

"No!" the woman yelled.

The word was shrill and reflexive, causing Anika to flinch, and for the first time since she had been here, Anika saw in the woman the first real evidence of derangement. She'd assumed from the beginning it was there, of course, waiting restlessly underneath all the properness and hospitality, waiting for any imbalance to release it. And now here it was surfacing, from little more than a wrong answer.

"Why am I here?" Anika asked.

"No! No! I asked you, 'Why are you here?' Answer the question!" The woman was screaming now, enraged, her lips curling back from her teeth with every word, revealing the huge, dirty gray and brown triangles that clustered in her gums.

Anika coughed nervously and began to cry softly. She could feel the nausea again rising in her throat. What were those teeth? she thought. Oh my God, they were inhuman!

She felt hysteria coming on and realized she had to get control. Panic would just feed into the woman's outrage and that might just wrap things up for good. Anika thought again of her children. What answer was the woman looking for?

Anika took another deep breath and closed her eyes for a moment, and then opened them and said, "I was in a car accident."

She said the words stoically, looking directly into the woman's eyes, as if she had known all along this was the answer the woman wanted. She felt empowered on some level, though she couldn't have said why.

"My car went off the road," she continued, "and I went for help. I got lost in the forest."

Anika measured each word, each syllable, as if writing a sonnet, careful not to get the meter wrong. It was working. The woman was riveted, as if she were a child listening to a knight's tale. But there wasn't much more to tell without getting into the details, and somehow Anika didn't think the woman was interested in her muddy shoes.

What else? Just give the facts, she thought, and then said, "So I screamed for help."

The woman's eyebrows perked up at this last bit of the story, and a broad smile curved up her cheeks. Anika again shuddered and stopped talking. She felt lucky to have said this much without upsetting her captor. She didn't want to push it.

The woman's eyes softened on Anika, and she tilted her chin down slightly, cocking her head to the side, as if sympathizing with a petulant child who needed only to sleep to be right again. "You need more rest..." she began and then paused, "Angela?"

"Anika. How...how did you know my name?"

"Evidently I didn't."

"Yes, but...you were very close. How did you know?"

"I'll be in shortly with your breakfast. If you displace your furniture again, I will cut off your hands."

Anika felt a chill from the threat, but realized she had little to lose now. "You never answered my question. Are you going to kill me?"

"The proper word is 'Slaughter,' Anika," the woman replied. "One does not 'kill' an animal, one slaughters it."

CHAPTER SIX

GRETEL FINALLY EXHALED, and then began to hyperventilate. She knew instinctively the car was not headed toward any fire this time: that car was headed for her.

"Oh my God," Gretel managed to whisper, and her eyes shifted desperately from the approaching red machine to her brother. "Oh my God! Hansel!" she screamed, "Hansel come in now!"

Hansel jerked up quickly, and Gretel could tell by his posture that he recognized immediately the panic in her voice. She regretted frightening him, but if she had been casual in her summons, she would have surely wasted time arguing with her brother about staying out for just a few more minutes.

Gretel wasn't quite sure why she was so afraid for her brother—after all, it was the police that were heading toward them, not a herd of buffalo—or why she wanted him to come home to begin with; if the approaching System officer was a real threat, Hansel would have been safer staying in the fields. But Gretel wanted her brother with her, instinctively, as a mother would her child.

Hansel watched in awe as the speeding blaze of metal passed him, barely slowing as it turned toward the house. He heard his sister's voice again and the spell was broken; he was now running with frenzy toward Gretel, leaving the homemade toys behind him in the field.

Gretel watched as the car pulled to a stop about twenty yards from the front of the house where it sat idling for several minutes. She realized she had never seen a System car from the front before, or from such a close distance, and she was mesmerized by it. It seemed massive to her. Not in its length or height, necessarily, but in its bulk, the way a cow doesn't look very large from the road—it's only when one stands next to it that its size is appreciated. And the headlights were like nothing she had ever seen, they were huge and ellip-tical, with the organic quality of staring eyes that Gretel guessed must have been the intention of the engineer. The grill was cased in solid black with sil-ver plates running vertically along the front where, again, the resemblance to teeth on a living face was undeniable. The car reminded Gretel of a squinting dragon.

She stood motionless on the porch staring wide-eyed at the hulking red machine, only raising her arm slightly to take in her brother as he finally lum-bered up beside her. The size of the car and the deep rumbling of the idling engine made Gretel think of a bull sizing up a bullfighter, only instead of the confidence of a matador, Gretel was frozen with fear. The System was there to help—to find her mother—that was their job; but it all felt wrong, and Gre-tel couldn't help feeling terrified.

"Who is that, Gretel?" Hansel asked, not taking his eyes off the car.

Her brother was fairly composed, Gretel thought, given the menacing mass of metal that loomed in his front yard.

"Is it The System?"

Gretel cleared her throat. "Yes," she replied with a feeble attempt at con-fidence.

"We should get Father. Is he awake?"

"He's gone. He went to look for Mother."

Hansel glanced toward his sister, who intercepted his look before he could draw some horrible conclusion.

"He'll be back soon. He just wanted to search again in the daylight. You saw how impossible it was last night."

This seemed to assuage whatever worry was brewing in Hansel, and he fo-cused again on the current circumstances. After a moment he said, "Maybe they know something about Mother."

Gretel knew The System had come there about her mother, obviously, but she assumed it was to get information. A photograph, a description of what her mother was wearing, who her friends were, things like that. Information to help them in their search. Admittedly, Gretel even had a thought while she stood gawking at the car that they had come to question Father about his role in her mother's disappearance, though his alibi was indisputable. What she hadn't considered, however, was that they had come with news. "Yes. Maybe."

The prospect of answers turned Gretel's fear into tempered anticipation, though she realized that if the car was indeed bringing news, it almost certainly wasn't good. Otherwise, she figured, they would have called. Or brought her mother home. Wasn't that how it was done? She had seen bad news delivered that way in movies after a soldier had been killed in battle or a child had gone missing.

The eagerness for closure was now strong, and Gretel considered approaching the car. It was parked on her property, after all, and she would have been in her perfect right walking up to the cloudy black driver's side window and knocking delicately on the glass.

But that didn't feel right. It seemed rather dangerous in fact, and Gretel now imagined her face pressed down in the dirt driveway with the barrel of a pistol digging into the back of her skull. No, she would stay put for now. Even her father, Gretel suspected, wouldn't have been so bold as to approach a System car without being ordered to do so. If The System sent a car this far out to the Back Country, they obviously did so for a reason, and it wasn't for the purpose of parking outside her house to do nothing. Whatever they had to bring—whether it was questions or news—they would bring it eventually.

"Let's go inside."

Gretel put her arm around her brother's neck and led him back into the house, glancing over her shoulder at the snoring metal beast as she did so. Hansel clucked softly in protest but followed his sister, and once inside immediately dashed to the front window to continue his surveillance.

"Hansel! Get away from there," Gretel scolded.

Ignoring his sister, Hansel pressed his face against the glass and cupped his hands around his eyes. "Why are they not coming out of the car? What are they waiting for?"

"They're probably gathering papers and things," Gretel replied, "and reviewing our case. So they know what questions to ask."

Hansel pulled his face from the window, as if detecting a tone of insincerity in his sister's voice, and stared at Gretel. "Is she dead, Gret?"

Gretel could see the welling of tears in Hansel's eyes and the large lump that formed and then disappeared in his throat, and she knew this was the first time her brother had accepted the possibility that his mother was not coming home. She felt remorse at having triggered this truth in him, wishing her acting had been a bit better. But ultimately she knew this acceptance would help to soften the slamming news if it was indeed coming.

She reached out to her brother, beckoning him and took him into her arms, holding him as the muffled sobs erupted into her belly. "No, Han," she said, "I don't think she is."

Gretel closed her eyes and rested her cheek on top of her brother's head, rocking him gently as his tears poured into her shirt. She shushed him half-heartedly, but only to convey her compassion, not in any way to stifle his crying. She wanted him to cry as long as he needed.

The siblings stood embraced by the window for several minutes, and Gretel temporarily forgot about the mysterious officer watching their home. She considered instead the answer she had given Hansel: that her mother wasn't dead. Did she really believe that? Was her mother alive somewhere, unharmed? She had no reason to believe that, but in the pit of her heart, she knew it was true. No scenario had emerged in her mind over the past twenty-four hours to logically support that belief, but she believed it anyway. And if she was wrong—and the longer her mother stayed missing, the likelihood that she was wrong grew—then she'd be wrong. But until then, she'd go with her instincts and keep hope close.

Gretel opened her eyes and gasped at the figure walking toward her house. He was coming. Finally. She released Hansel from her clutches and placed her hands on his shoulders as he turned toward the focus of his sister's stare.

Gretel and Hansel inched closer to the window for a clear view and watched as the man approached slowly, almost leisurely, seeming to take inventory of the surroundings of the house. He was a law officer, of course, an investigator, so his interest in the house wasn't by itself unusual, but the insouciance of his mannerisms were so unlike anything resembling 'official' that if Gretel had seen this man walking on the street somewhere, or in a park, she would have guessed him drunk.

The two children watched the man disappear from view as he neared the front door and then waited in silence, listening to his footsteps on the porch stairs. The two loud raps on the door that followed, though expected, were startling, and Hansel couldn't suppress a yelp.

"Stay here," Gretel said, as she walked to the door, turning back to her brother before opening it. "Remember, he's here to help us."

Hansel nodded meekly to his sister, and then Gretel lifted her head, threw back her shoulders, and opened the door slowly. For the first time in her life, she stood face to face with The System.

The officer stood with precise posture in the doorway, respectfully distant from the entrance. He wasn't particularly large in stature, certainly not to the degree that the myths perpetuated System officers—Gretel guessed he was probably shorter than her father. And neither was there anything in his dress that inspired fear; in contrast to the car he drove, his clothes were rather customary. In fact, his overall appearance had a rather retroactive quality that was comforting.

"Good afternoon," he said smiling. "My name is Officer Stenson."

The words came out quietly, but unmistakably clear, as if he were disclosing very important information in the stacks of a library. He presented a small metal shield—which might just as well have been a dead fish as far as Gretel was willing to question his authority.

"I'm looking for Heinrich Morgan," the man continued. "Does he live here?"

"Yes," Gretel squeaked, somewhat pleased with herself that she was able to manage even a word.

"May I speak with him?"

Officer Stenson stood casually now, leaning slightly forward with his hands clasped behind his back. He was clearly making an attempt at coming across friendly, and Gretel thought he was doing an excellent job.

"No," Gretel replied. She stared unblinkingly at the man, on some level expecting him to eventually morph into the robotic giant that she had envisioned since her earliest memories.

The System officer held his smile and raised his eyebrows slightly, as if humored by the precociousness of the adolescent girl in front of him. "No?"

"I mean, he's not home. He left."

Officer Stenson frowned and stared to his right, as if thinking about what to do with such a perplexing answer. He turned back to Gretel and said, "May I ask your name, young lady?"

Gretel paused, and then with a bit of a defiant stare said, "Yes."

The officer stood waiting, and then realizing she had answered his question, threw back his head in laughter.

There was a glowing sincerity to the officer's face and movements, and Gretel couldn't help but smile herself. Something about this man she liked instinctively, but there was something deeper she remained cautious of. Perhaps, she considered, it was just his position as a System officer.

Officer Stenson composed himself, exhaling the last few chuckles from his chest, and then, nodding approvingly, said, "You're a smart girl. I should think you'll have all the boys under your command very shortly."

Gretel blushed.

"In fact, my son is about your age, perhaps I should drag him out of the car so you can help get *him* under control. I certainly can't seem to do it."

He laughed again at the answer the girl had given, and Gretel peeked behind him, amazed at the fact that there was both a boy her age in that devil-car in her front yard, and that this man in front of her was old enough to have such a child. He looked half her father's age.

The officer took note of Gretel's stare. "Ah yes, my son. That's why I was so long outside. He's had some trials lately."

Gretel detected a flare in the officer's eyes, but it evaporated as quickly as it rose.

"Now, more directly this time, young lady, what is your name?"

"Gretel," she replied with a smile of satisfaction. "Gretel Morgan."

"Gretel. Morgan." The officer wrote each name down with great concentration, maintaining a very formal demeanor, and this made Gretel laugh out loud. "Well, Gretel Morgan, do you know when..." Officer Stenson caught himself this time. "When will your father be back?"

"I don't know." Gretel frowned. "He went to look for my mother." Gretel looked away from the officer, suddenly flooded with the reminder of why he was here.

Gretel looked back toward the man, who had now assumed a slightly crouched position, bringing himself to her eye level. "Gretel," he said solemnly, "may I come in?"

Whatever fear Gretel had for the officer was now all but gone, and she figured that if he had come to hurt her, he could have done so at any time. She opened the door wide and stepped aside, and Officer Stenson entered, immediately catching sight of the anxious boy standing statue-like in the kitchen.

Gretel walked quickly toward her brother, framing her arms around him. "This is my brother Hansel."

Officer Stenson gave a delicate nod toward the boy, looking him squarely in the eye. The man reminded Gretel of someone who has encountered an unfamiliar dog and is trying to gauge its temperament based on the slight signals of posture and expression. There was an inferred tension in the silence, and Gretel could feel the distrust in her brother's body.

"It's all right, Han. This is Officer Stenson."

Hansel looked at his sister, and then back to the man. "Why is Officer Stenson all right?" he replied, maintaining the stare of a gunfighter, if not the confidence.

"Because he's here to help us," she replied, but immediately realized that the officer had not yet actually stated his reason for being there, and she was ready to get to the matter. "Isn't that right, Officer Stenson? You're here about our mother?"

The officer looked toward Gretel and then back to the boy. "I am," he said. "Is there somewhere we can sit down?"

◦◦◦

PERCHED PATERNALLY on a weathered leather ottoman, Officer Stenson sat opposite the two children, who waited anxiously side by side on the sofa in the living room. Gretel recalled how she and her brother had sat this way countless times over the years, listening to their father's stories—or, occasionally, his scoldings—and Gretel felt a sort of comfort in this reverie. This man in front of her wasn't her father, but he was a protector by trade, and that was important right now.

The officer clasped his hands together and frowned, and then looked down at the floor, gathering his thoughts before beginning. "Normally I would wait for your father, but you both seem to understand the situation at hand, and I'll need to leave soon." Officer Stenson paused. "First of all, we haven't found your mother."

He stared intently at the children's faces, waiting, and Gretel could see the uncertainty in his eyes, realizing the news could be taken either way. Gretel instinctively reached over and grabbed her brother's hand, giving it a reassuring squeeze.

"We're searching the portion of the Interways that lead to your..." the officer lingered on the 'r' and pulled a small notebook from his breast pocket, flipping it open to the proper spot, "...grandfather's house. If something happened along that stretch, we'll know."

"You mean an accident?" Gretel said.

"Yes, an accident." And then, "Or if the car was abandoned."

"You mean like if the car broke down and she left it there? Why would she do that?"

"I don't know Gretel, she probably didn't. It's just a possibility that we need to think about."

"Do people do that a lot?" Gretel hadn't really thought about this as an explanation, but now that the officer had mentioned it the hope she'd kept ablaze flickered higher.

"No," Officer Stenson said without hesitation, "not a lot. But on that stretch of road there is very little traffic and there have been instances of people leaving to look for fuel or a phone to call for help."

The hope fire rose higher.

"But honestly, Gretel, we're not hopeful of that being the case with your mother. We've driven the route—I drove a large portion of it myself—we would have found the car."

Gretel closed her eyes and frowned. The scenario of her mother leaving for help wasn't completely unthinkable to Gretel. Her mother wasn't exactly what Gretel would describe as hearty, but she was a survivor, and if walking the countryside for help was the practical solution to a situation—like being stranded on the road—she would have pursued it. On the other hand, the officer had a point: if she had left the road for help, where was the car?

"Maybe the car was towed away?"

"The car would only be towed from the Interways under System direction, and no request was put in. Look, Gretel, we know what to look for and we're looking for it."

Gretel detected a hint of agitation in Officer Stenson's voice, and she blushed, embarrassed now that she had presumed to know more than the man in front of her.

Officer Stenson grabbed Gretel's hand. "You're obviously a very smart girl, Gretel, and I do need your help to find your mother. So perhaps I can ask you the questions and you can give me the answers?"

Gretel smiled weakly at the compliment and nodded.

"And Hansel, I'll need your help too." The officer took a masculine tone with the boy, curt and direct. "Will you help me?"

Hansel nodded bravely, seriously, eager to play a role in solving the puzzle.

Before the officer uttered the first syllable of his question, a voice boomed through the house, thunderously, as if God Himself had spoken. "Hansel, go to your room."

The voice was calm, even-toned, but the energy in the words nearly knocked the wind from Gretel's chest. It had come invisibly from somewhere behind the walls of the kitchen.

Father.

He appeared slowly in the entryway, locking his eyes on the stranger holding court with his children. He stood tall and still, his eyes narrowed. There wasn't quite rage in her father's face, Gretel thought, it was something closer to disgust. The way one might look at a person who has once again violated a recently regained trust. She was thankful that his hands were unclenched and visible at his sides; if there had been a gun in one of them, it wouldn't have surprised her.

Officer Stenson smoothed the creases in his pants and stood, and Hansel scuttled off to his room. Gretel shifted her eyes between the two men and began to follow her brother toward the back of the house.

"Gretel," her father barked, "stay here."

Heinrich Morgan stuffed his hands in his pockets and walked toward Officer Stenson, a passive-aggressive casualness in his demeanor, stopping only inches from The System officer. Gretel's jaw hung loosely at her father's boldness, both by his irreverence toward The System and the contrasting display of masculinity as compared to the withering he'd shown the day before. He had perhaps gone over the edge, Gretel thought, and this frightened her. She sat back down on the couch, a spectator to whatever would unfold.

"Mr. Morgan," the officer began, "my name is Officer Stenson. I'm with the fourth division of the Southlands System. I'm here about your wife, Anika."

Officer Stenson's voice was deep and clear, unaffected by the intrusion. The leisurely softness he had shown toward the children was now a sterile recitation of business. He stared directly into the eyes of the man before him, never blinking, and his mouth showed not the hint of a smile. This, Gretel thought, was The System of which her father had spoken.

"Really?" Gretel's father replied sarcastically. "You're here about my wife?" He laughed. "No doubt it was the first case on the docket this morning."

"Mr. Morgan..."

"Why are you here?" Gretel's father growled.

"You called us, Mr. Morgan."

Gretel recognized her father's smile at this response as one of sincere amusement.

"I was born in the Back Country, Officer Stenson, have lived here my whole life, and I've seen The System here maybe four times in those years. System officers don't show up to a person's home lightly—anywhere in the Southlands—never mind in the Back Country. I called you only yesterday because my wife went missing—not from here but from along the Interways—and yet here you are at my house speaking to my children? So I'll ask you again, why are you here?"

Gretel sat riveted as she watched Officer Stenson hold her father's stare and then look away, frowning. Clearly, there was more to tell.

The officer smiled sympathetically. "I understand how upset you must be Mr. Morgan, so perhaps this isn't the best time. And anyway, I haven't the time tonight to do a proper interview. I'll be in contact with you in a day or so—by phone. I'll show myself out."

He walked toward the door and then stopped with his hand on the knob, turning back toward the living room. "And Mr. Morgan, I may have some questions for you concerning the nature of your relationship with Mrs. Morgan. Domestic problems. Things like that."

"Leave my house, Officer Stenson."

Officer Stenson opened the door, looking past his newly-acquired enemy to the flabbergasted girl sitting on the couch. "Goodbye Gretel," he said. "You're a very charming young lady. I hope to talk with you again soon. Maybe you'll meet my son one day."

He left and closed the door behind him, the uncomfortable silence that lingered finally broken by the sound of Heinrich Morgan walking slowly toward his room, holding his side as he went.

The burping eruption of the engine starting outside made Gretel lurch: Officer Stenson awakening the sleeping dragon. Gretel examined again the mismatch between the demon car that approached her like a deranged Visigoth and the rather even-mannered man that controlled it. The opposition was almost comical. The officer had spoken to Hansel and her with such consideration and ease, without even the hint of an angle or condescension, while at the same time maintaining an authority that was without question. But Gretel had also glimpsed the nettles beneath the placidness, and intuitively knew to remain skeptical of anyone who could change his demeanor with such little effort.

She sat motionless on the sofa, waiting anxiously for the diminishing sounds of gravel crackling beneath rolling tires indicating the car's departure. But the idling rumble of exhaust endured for several minutes; evidently more business with the delinquent son. Or perhaps a transmission was being sent requesting backup for the arrest of one Heinrich Morgan. Gretel hoped it wasn't the latter for the obvious reasons, but also because she knew her father wasn't well, and jail was the last place he needed to spend the night.

The soft knock on the window above the sink made Gretel shriek, and she covered her mouth with her hands. Her nerves were threadbare, and she momentarily doubted the prism of a face in the window over the sink. She stood and walked cautiously to the window, where the face of a dark-haired boy, frowning, came into focus. He lifted his hand to the window and pointed to the door.

Gretel walked toward the door and she could see outside that the boy was following her lead. She was more curious than apprehensive, and so opened the door, instantly meeting the eyes of, unquestionably, the most exquisite looking person she had ever seen in the flesh.

It wasn't just his face, which as far as Gretel could tell was flawless, it was that the boy seemed to be a perfect amalgamation of all the qualities one calculates in defining a person's attractiveness. His cheekbones and shoulders were high and broad, and the shape of his mouth and nose seemed to be transposed from a Roman statue. Even the way he stood was just right, with his feet shoulder width apart and hands behind his back, his head tilted slightly forward in cool humility. Even his clothes fit him perfectly. Only in magazines had she seen people of such beauty.

The boy gave a shy grin and rolled his eyes, embarrassed. "Sorry, hi," he said, "my, uh, Dad sent me to get his binder. He says he left it on the floor next to the ottoman."

"His binder?" Gretel remained locked on the boy, and her words came out robotic like she had been bewitched by an evil master and was repeating a benign test phrase to make sure the spell had taken.

The boy was her age, maybe a year older, and the exotic combination of dark curls and cold blue eyes were the stuff of key-locked diaries, so atypical in this land of straight blond hair and pink cheeks. She was transfixed.

"Yeah, you know, like his notebook thing." The boy mimed his hands in the shape of the object.

"Oh. Okay." Gretel opened the door. "Come in."

The boy shifted his eyes and looked back at the waiting car, and then stepped through the door; clearly he had expected the girl to just bring him the binder. Gretel noticed the action and blushed, but it was too late to rescind the invitation.

He took a tentative step inside the house and, spotting the ottoman in the next room, walked quickly toward it, recovering the binder and tucking it under his arm. He lingered a moment in the living room and looked at Gretel. "It obviously isn't any of my business or anything, but was he able to help you?"

"I'm sorry?" Gretel responded automatically. It was more a delay tactic than a misunderstanding of the question.

"My father. Did he help you with whatever he came here for?"

Gretel considered the question a moment. "He helped me feel a bit better, I suppose, but my mother's gone missing, and there's been no sign of her since early yesterday." Gretel glanced toward the back bedrooms and lowered her voice, "And my father told him to leave."

The boy nodded thoughtfully, and Gretel could see him mentally catalog her case. As the son of a System officer, Gretel supposed stories like hers were as common as the sunrise.

"I'm sorry," he said.

The words were unexpected, and they hit Gretel like an iron pan. They were the first true words of sympathy she'd heard since her family's recent implosion, and it took every bit of composure not to run to the boy, throw her arms around him, and pour her tears onto his shoulder.

"Thank you," she murmured instead, clearing her throat much louder than she'd intended. And then, changing the subject to thwart any oncoming wave of emotions said, "Do you ride with your father often?"

The question was a perfect change of pace, and a proud surge of butterflies danced in Gretel when the boy smiled. It was an adult comment, something her mother would have said.

"Almost never. And certainly not if I can help it." He paused, and his smile flattened. "I've had some trouble with schools lately...always really, and my parents are sending me off in the fall. Boarding school. Outside the city."

The boy shifted his eyes around the house, as if indicating its simplicity and rusticness.

"Not quite this far off, I guess, but near the edges of the Back Country. There's an academy for boys there—The Hengst Academy?"

Gretel shook her head and shrugged. Never heard of it.

"Well, anyway, I'll be starting there in the fall, I suppose. If my interview today was acceptable."

He stopped for a moment and looked at nothing, seeming to consider his life after the summer.

"So anyway, my father said he'd gotten a new case that was out this way and he needed to stop here before we went home. Though, truthfully, your house is quite out of the way."

That was the second jab the boy had tossed at Gretel about where she lived. The first she ignored, but now she was suddenly insulted and angry at the implications. That this land was somehow outside the borders of consideration. And how could anyone possibly survive in such territory? It was an attitude that was by no means new to Gretel—condescension toward Back Country folk, if not outright discrimination, was routine behavior from Urbanists. But she was in her own house and she'd be damned if she would take it here and—especially—now.

"What is your name?" Gretel's voice was steel, though her face showed no sign of bitterness.

"Petr," the boy replied, "Petr Stenson." He flashed his perfect smile at Gretel, pleased she had asked.

Gretel countered with a sarcastic half-smile of her own and said, "Well now that you've gotten your father's things Petr Stenson, please leave my home."

Petr's face twisted into an expression of confusion and humor, not quite sure if the girl was serious. "Did I say something..?"

"You don't know better, none of you do," Gretel clipped. "Goodbye."

Petr stepped past Gretel out the door, and Gretel followed him onto the porch, standing defiantly with her arms crossed as she watched the boy descend the porch, a look of bemused bewilderment on his face. He took a few steps toward the waiting car and stopped, looking back at Gretel.

"Just so you know, Gretel," he said in a way that Gretel could only describe as sad, "and I'm not sure why I'm telling you this." Petr paused, "but I don't think he's here to help you. I know he probably seemed that way. He does that very well."

Without hesitation, Gretel snapped back, "Well what is he here for then?"

Petr scanned Gretel's body, starting from her feet and working his way up. He then moved his head in a slow arc from left to right, up and down, studying the house and its surroundings, letting his eyes drift over each wooden beam and crooked branch and lowly piece of gravel, suspicious of everything, as if the answer to her question might be found in any one of the millions of insignificant objects that composed the Morgan property.

"I don't know," he said finally, shaking his head slowly, pausing for just a moment in the event the answer appeared at that last moment of surrender. "I don't know."

Gretel opened her mouth to speak but couldn't invoke a word, and she stood that way as she watched Petr Stenson walk back to the car and the red metal rocket speed down her driveway toward the Interways.

CHAPTER SEVEN

"YOU'RE LOOKING MUCH better Heinrich, but now it's time for rest."

The young nurse walked from Heinrich Morgan's room and gently shut the door, the smile on her face evaporating instantly. Gretel had witnessed this transformation in the woman's look almost daily since her arrival almost two months ago, and it made Gretel wince every time. It wasn't a cruel gesture—the frown—Lord knew that if anyone could sympathize with the woman's duties it was Gretel—but there seemed to be something beyond fatigue and frustration in her face, something measured. Maybe it was hate. But if it was, Gretel couldn't even say she didn't understand that.

Odalinde Merth had come to the Morgan house as a part-time nurse and had stayed well beyond the time Gretel originally imagined. She was certain her father would have improved to normal health by now, since that day Gretel had found him sprawled on the kitchen floor clutching his belly, blood streaming from his mouth. And though Gretel obviously appreciated the care Odalinde was giving her father, it struck her as unusual that the nurse remained with them. Not only had her work proven ineffective in recuperating her patient—a sign that it's probably time to move on—as far as Gretel could tell, she also wasn't receiving any pay for her work. As it was, the money wasn't enough for food to sustain the three of them, let alone pay for the services of a private nurse. Since their mother had vanished, Gretel and her brother usually went without at least one meal a day, and occasionally two. Perhaps a deferment arrangement had been made and Odalinde would collect payment for her nursing activities when times improved, but it was simply impossible that she was being paid now.

Heinrich Morgan's previously damaged spleen had flared and lacerated the first day Gretel and Hansel had returned to school after their mother's disappearance. Gretel had arrived home that day to find her father collapsed in a half-naked ball of flesh at the threshold between the kitchen and porch, and on first glance, seeing only the back of him, Gretel would have sworn he was dead. His motionless body was contracted, fetal-like, his arms clutched around his torso as if trying to stay warm. Gretel had stood staring at the lifeless heap on the floor, and almost instantly began preparing for her new life as an orphan, which she supposed would play out in the Northlands with Deda. It would be a hard adjustment, and Gretel knew that though he would take them in, Deda would be reluctant to assume the burden of children so late in life. But they would survive, and Gretel would take on the duties of raising her brother. There were worse lots in life to be sure, particularly for orphans in the Back Country, and Gretel swelled with an unlikely feeling of gratitude. She would take care of Hansel and Deda, and that would be the way it was.

The moan from the floor had frightened Gretel back to reality, and she quickly re-focused. Her father wasn't dead. She ran to him, stepping over his body and kneeling down to examine his face, which was bloated with pressure and contorted in pain. He was struggling to breathe, not because of any blockage in his windpipe, but because of the agony that breathing induced. Gretel could see the dried blood on his lips and chin, and when a weak coughing breath finally escaped his lungs, she could see the blood was coming from somewhere inside her father's body.

Gretel's next thought was that Hansel would be home soon, and she would have to mitigate the trauma caused by seeing his father in this condition, so vulnerable, sprawled unnaturally on the floor. Looking back on it now, she remembered that her instincts had been sharp that day, clear and unhesitating, and she was proud of the perfect steps she had taken: dialing the doctor's number from memory, repositioning her father and covering him with blankets, encouraging him to breathe. Hansel was certainly scared when he finally saw his father that day, but Gretel was all smiles and stoicism, and easily calmed him with the promise that everything would be fine.

And it *had* turned out fine, with Gretel the hero. The doctor later credited Gretel with saving her father's life through a combination of quick action and shock reduction. But, truthfully, she hadn't really surprised herself at all: the world had unleashed upon Gretel the most lethal of blows—taking her mother—and Gretel had endured. She had thrived, in fact, and the scar tissue of the wound now insulated her from both terror and hysteria. It was her role now, she realized, to be nurturer and parent, and what she had been consciously unprepared to do a few short months ago when her mother first vanished, nature had activated within her.

And that had been the difference: the newly-nested concept that something else in the universe was in control of such important matters.

Odalinde glanced up at Gretel and then looked away immediately. "Gretel," she said, the smile on her face unable to cloak the disdain in her voice.

"Hello, Odalinde," Gretel replied in a similar tone, keeping her eyes on the woman as if challenging her to a conversation. The exchanges between the women had devolved to become strictly perfunctory, and if the nurse remained much longer, Gretel knew they would cease entirely.

But Gretel had considered that end unacceptable—Odalinde had become far too friendly with Father in such a short time, and there were too many unanswered questions. "How's he doing?"

Odalinde looked up to meet Gretel's stare, a look of defensiveness in her eyes. She blinked slowly a few times and nodded, resetting her demeanor, and with a smile said, "Much, much better."

"Really? So not just *much* better today, but much, *much* better?"

Odalinde's smile straightened and Gretel felt her own stomach tighten. The words had escaped Gretel's mouth immediately, automatically, but it certainly wasn't an unusual thing for her to say. There was a new combativeness to Gretel that had started that day with The System officer's son, the day after her mother had gone missing. Gretel had become unrestrained with her challenges and often looked for a confrontation where none existed. And she needed—*needed*—to have the last word in any debate, no matter how explicitly her point may have been tested and discredited. This new quality had already resulted in more than one afternoon home from school, and kids who had previously spoken to her in class or on the walk home started avoiding her entirely. If she was honest, there wasn't one person—other than Hansel—whom she could truly call a friend.

At first she blamed it on a perceived awkwardness from others about her mother and Gretel's needing space to cope, and to some extent she thought that to be true; but those same kids spoke with Hansel quite easily, and even when they did speak with her, it wasn't with sympathy or deference, but rather with an abruptness that indicated a certain disapproval and hostility.

But that was a price Gretel had been willing to pay. She owed it to her mother to become the woman she was meant to be, that her mother had always envisioned. Strong and confident, controlling the situation when it was necessary and appropriate. Gretel knew that she still had a lot of refining to do, and that her mother certainly wouldn't have approved of her occasional rudeness or insubordination in school and otherwise. But if she had used her mother as an excuse to pity herself, to disappear into a tent of silence and demureness, that would have been altogether dishonorable.

There had been no official recognition of Anika Morgan's death. The System had instead 'Suspended' the case three weeks into the investigation. But according to the opinions of most, suspensions were rarely taken up again without the emergence of obvious evidence.

Similarly, Heinrich Morgan's dedication to his wife's disappearance lost momentum. He had driven the Interways for the few days following her disappearance, but his poor health, as well as an increasing build up of hopelessness, had left him spending most of the ensuing days in bed. Thankfully, he had been self-sufficient in the basic necessities, and Gretel had mostly avoided him. It wasn't until the day she found him on the floor that she realized how bad his state was, and Odalinde had shown up at the house only days later.

Gretel held Odalinde's look without blinking. If Gretel had been able to retract her last words, to erase the last few seconds of this scene, she would have. But it was said, and she would let the words play out. And besides, that feeling of instant regret had become typical to Gretel, and on some level it was comforting.

"Do you have schoolwork, Gretel?" It was a common play of Odalinde's to take the role of the mother. "Your father isn't been pleased with how it's been slipping of late."

And there the line was crossed. For the most part Gretel had not resisted Odalinde periodically slipping into the character of the maternal head of the house. She was the adult, after all, and performed most of the duties that role required—less one, Gretel hoped and assumed. But Odalinde had increasingly used her own intimacy with Heinrich as a weapon against Gretel, becoming the filter through which any expression of her father ran. "Your father is ready for you" or "Your father wants you to know that he loves you." And so on.

And indeed, even the disciplining and disappointments were now being contracted out. Of course, Gretel knew that Odalinde had to be lying in some of the cases, but Gretel had confirmed too many of the reports with her father to dismiss them out of hand.

Gretel clenched her teeth and glared at Odalinde, holding the look for a long moment before walking away, muttering as she left, "My mother would have hated you."

She spoke loudly enough that Odalinde certainly could hear her voice, though Gretel couldn't be sure she could understand the words. If she did, she didn't reply.

What Gretel was certain of, however, was that the words were true.

Gretel hurried into her room and closed the door, and immediately snatched the book from the top shelf in her closet, holding it to her chest as she lay down on her bed. She hadn't learned any of what the bizarre symbols meant since the day she brought the book home from Deda's, and she hadn't been able to find anyone who could translate it. Gretel had hoped that Deda would be able to tell her more about it, but she had seen him only once since that night, and on that occasion he had been distant and cold. The other candidates whom she had hoped would at least have knowledge of the book didn't, and, in fact, had never even heard of the term 'Orphism.'

But the book had become a security blanket for Gretel, and even though she didn't know what it was about, she always felt better with it in her hands.

Gretel lay still with her eyes closed and took deep breaths, imagining what she usually did during the quiet periods: her mother walking through the door, weary from her unbelievable ordeal, a wry smile of relief on her face. Occasionally, the image made her hopeful, but mostly it made her cry.

The creak of the bedroom door shattered Gretel's vision, and she turned to see Hansel slump in, his mouth slightly open and eyes half-closed. Gretel frowned at him and turned her body toward the wall. "What do you want Hansel?"

"I'm hungry," he whined.

"Odalinde is finished with Father; ask her to make you something."

"I did. She said there's no food."

Gretel turned back toward her brother, slightly alarmed. "No food? Is she sure?"

Hansel shrugged. "I haven't eaten today, Gretel."

Gretel's heart began to race, and she soon realized she hadn't eaten either. She, however, had gotten used to not eating much, and to share her portions with Hansel when she could stand it. But never had she not eaten all day. And Hansel! Hansel needed his food. He was a growing boy!

Gretel put the book aside and lifted herself from the bed, suddenly aware of her empty stomach. She left Hansel standing by the door as she exited her room and crossed the hall, opening her father's door without knocking. She heard him groan in his sleep as he shifted in his bed.

"Father," she whispered loudly. He moved again but didn't turn to her. Gretel registered the bowl on the side table, half-filled with soup. "Father," she repeated, her voice booming this time, commanding attention as if in preparation to scold him.

Heinrich Morgan raised his head with a grunt and turned wide-eyed toward his daughter. "Gretel? What is it?" His voice was raspy and slow, his eyes cloudy and disoriented.

Gretel got right to the point. "There's no food, Father. Hansel hasn't eaten today. Nothing." She paused, debating whether to say her next line. "But I see you have." She stared at the bowl on the table. Heinrich followed her stare and studied the bowl, confused.

"No food?" The words came out clumsily, as if Heinrich were repeating a nonsense phrase, mimicking what he'd heard to make sure he'd gotten it right. Heinrich looked back toward his daughter and over her shoulder to the door. "Odalinde?"

Gretel turned to see the nurse standing behind her at the threshold, a smiling look of mock sympathy on her face, the way a mother might observe a crying toddler who has fallen after trying to take his first steps.

"I've only to go to the market, Heinrich. There's been so much to do around here, what with the children and your condition, that I'm afraid I've gotten behind on the shopping. There's not much money left, but enough."

"And the crops? Has anything come in?"

Odalinde looked away from her patient and down to the floor, embarrassed for him. There would be no harvest of any kind this year, and even she didn't have the stomach to say otherwise.

Why would father think a harvest was coming? Gretel thought. There had been no one to work the fields since his injury and mother's subsequent disappearance, and he couldn't possibly think Odalinde was tending them. As it was, their crops had been in decline for years, and without severe attention and care, it would have been impossible to keep them bountiful.

"Not yet," she said, and a more serious look enveloped her face. "But Gretel has no reason to worry." Odalinde placed a hand on Gretel's shoulder. "I'll head off now for some rice and bread, perhaps some sweets. I'll be back shortly." She flickered a glance at Gretel as she began to walk out, and then turned back toward Heinrich. "Oh, and I'll take Hansel along."

The back of Gretel's neck tingled at the nurse's words, and for the first time she suspected Odalinde was more than simply unpleasant and coarse. Perhaps, Gretel thought, she was malevolent.

"I could go, Father. I can drive the truck—"

"Don't be ridiculous, Gretel," Odalinde interrupted. "It's part of my duties. And you've yet to do your schoolwork. Now let your father rest." She grabbed the knob of the door and shut it, corralling Gretel out to the hall in the process.

Gretel would have put up more resistance, but she saw that her father had laid back down and was again drifting toward unconsciousness. She would be surprised if later he even remembered the conversation. Something wasn't right with him lately, and it was more than his spleen.

"Hansel's staying here!" Gretel snapped after they were out in the hall, and she immediately walked over to her brother who had migrated to the living room. She stood slightly in front of him, protectively.

Odalinde raised her eyebrows, "Really? Perhaps we should let him decide."

Hansel locked eyes with his sister; there was defiance in his stare. "I'm going with Odalinde, Gretel. She's going to buy me a sweet bun with jam." A meager smile drew across Hansel's face as he looked timidly toward the nurse. "Right Odalinde?"

"That's right, Hansel. Or whatever you want." Odalinde turned to Gretel, "I'd ask you to come along too, Gretel, but what with your father's condition and your schoolwork and all."

Gretel looked away from Odalinde to her brother. She could see the fear on his face, but it acted only as a backdrop to his hunger, and she was suddenly glad he was going to town. Gretel knew Odalinde wouldn't hurt him—in fact, she was pretty certain that the nurse would buy him the treat that was promised. And if not, at the very least he would be offered a sample of fresh breads or pastries from one of the stalls at the markets.

But there was an obvious motive underneath Odalinde's gesture; whether it was simply to win Hansel's favor and divide the siblings or something more nefarious, Gretel couldn't be sure. As far as today was concerned, however, Gretel knew her brother was safe.

Gretel watched as Odalinde unlocked the cabinet beneath the sink and fetched her bag, squatting insect-like in the opening as she sifted through the satchel, inventorying the contents. The cabinet, tall and narrow in design, had previously been used as storage for household cleaning items and canned goods; but Odalinde had requested her own private depository when she arrived—'one that was secure from children'—and Heinrich had obliged her and cleared out the cabinet, customizing it with a lock. The reorganization had made for a messy kitchen at first, but as the canned goods and supplies dwindled, counter space was no longer an issue.

Gretel had kept a close watch on Odalinde's trips to this private space, and in particular to the time she spent huddled by the opening. As far as Gretel could tell, the bag was the only thing in the cabinet, or at least the only thing she tended to. And Odalinde always squatted, never sat, so as to always keep her bag completely covered and hidden while she shuffled and rechecked the contents. When she did finally take the bag out, it was always double-zipped and clasped, and clutched tightly to her breast or rib. And it was never left unattended—never—which for Odalinde's sake was a good thing. Because Gretel was waiting.

Odalinde shepherded Hansel out the door and down the porch stairs to the truck. Gretel followed them to the bottom of the stairs, leaving her brother with a look that said 'stay aware,' and then watched as the truck crept slowly away, disappearing over the hill toward town.

Gretel could feel the time until her family completely fell apart was short. They were starving and sick, their mother was missing and presumed dead, and now a stranger had come from nowhere and taken control of the household. Things were dire indeed. In the past, these realities would have overwhelmed Gretel and brought her to tears, but she now looked at them with pragmatism, prioritizing them as problems needing to be solved.

The first of these problems was, of course, her mother. Though she had promised herself never to give up on the possibility that her mother was still alive, there were few actions Gretel could think of taking to help find her. The System officer had never again come calling on her for help—help for which he had told Gretel in no uncertain terms he would need from her. Perhaps her father's invasion that night had dissuaded the officer. Or perhaps he'd never intended on returning, and had only told her that to make her feel useful.

And then there was the problem of her father, who apparently was not as far along as Gretel had believed. Or else his recovery had slipped. She knew nothing of medicine, but the doctor had prognosticated her father's recovery weeks ago, and indeed, based on the immediate signs, seemed to be accurate in his assessment. But there had been a slide in his recuperation—not in terms of his actual internal injuries, but in his overall energy and clarity. Even his intellect, Gretel thought. She didn't know what to do about the problem of her father, other than to wait it out.

As for Odalinde, this problem was becoming increasingly formidable, particularly after today's exchange. At the very least she was not to be trusted; at worst, she was a danger. Her threats were only passive at this point, however, and there was nothing specific Gretel could say or do to fix this problem right now. She would have to let that play out a bit more as well. And if the opportunity arose, she would get into that cabinet and see what mysteries lurked there.

That left the problem of food. It was the most pressing problem and the one that Gretel felt she had the most control over. Gretel didn't know where Odalinde's money had come from to buy the food for which she was now on her way to purchase, but it obviously couldn't be counted on to feed Hansel and her. With two children in the house, the nurse had let the supplies dwindle to nothing, having not fed either of them all day. But yet there had been a bowl of soup for Father. Had that bowl been from today? Or even last night?

Gretel admitted to herself that she couldn't be sure, though she was fairly confident that if there had been enough for only one person, Hansel and Gretel would have been the last two names on the meal list. For the time being, and perhaps from now on, it would be up to Gretel to figure out where the meals would come from for her and her brother.

She mentally ran through the names of friends and neighbors in the Back Country, some of whom had helped out in one way or another since her mother's disappearance. Since most were poorer than Gretel's family, the help had come mainly in the form of labor and childcare. But since the arrival of Odalinde, it had mostly stopped, with the occasional visit of obligation to "see if there was anything they could do." There was certainly nothing in the form of financial help, the perception being, Gretel assumed, that anyone affording a private nurse could certainly afford food. Gretel could never quite follow this line of thinking though; after all, they were a farming family, their income depended on selling crops, and if no crops were being harvested and sold, how could they be taking in any money?

But Gretel didn't judge them too harshly. She supposed people had their own problems and usually looked only as deeply as necessary to satisfy their consciences. There may have been life insurance, after all, or a family grant to see the Morgans through. It wasn't the burden of neighbors to ask *how* they were making it with no crops or occupation to speak of—questions like those might easily be construed as nosy and intrusive. Apparently they were making it and that's all that mattered.

Besides, Gretel had always been taught it was the job of family to help navigate the straits of life, and Gretel's family was nothing short of conspicuous in their absence. Her father's side of the family had never been close to begin with, and they had drifted even further when Anika disappeared. And Deda, whom Gretel had barely seen since her mother vanished, had become, according to her father, 'a bona fide hermit,' and now refused to take calls or visits from anyone, including his own grandchildren.

Gretel walked around to the back of the house and continued into the small clump of trees that divided the rear of the house from the small lake that formed the back of the Morgan property. She walked to water's edge, absently picking up a small stone and tossing it in. Across the lake, Gretel could see the trees of the Klahr orchard approaching full bloom, the apple and pear trees perhaps a week away from perfect ripeness. In a few days the extended Klahr relatives and a dozen or so other workers would descend on the trees like caterpillars, furiously climbing and picking until the last of the fruit was sifted through and basketed, ready to be sold at market, or further processed into jam, bread, and wine.

The Klahrs were what passed for wealth in the Back Country, having a small stable of horses, a tractor, and two trucks, as well as, by all accounts, a profitable business. They were an older couple—Gretel imagined they were on the other side of sixty by now—and as far as Gretel knew they had no children of their own. At least none Gretel had ever seen. Presumably if they did have heirs, they were now grown men and women—men and women who had perhaps decided to see their land only as a future inheritance, pursuing instead a career more sophisticated than farmer. But Gretel didn't think this was the case. The Klahrs had lived across the lake from her family since before Gretel was born, and she had never heard of any Klahr children.

There was nothing at all ostentatious about the couple, but by all measures they were deeply proud of their farming operation, and ran it with great organization and efficiency. They kept to themselves for the most part—Gretel couldn't remember her mother or father ever engaging them in conversation—with her only interaction coming in the form of the occasional wave from across the lake. They seemed friendly enough, dealing with merchants in town or whatever, but work was always the order of the day, the exception being Sunday, of course.

So Gretel had no illusions that what she was planning was acceptable, and she justified it only on the most practical of levels: Her family needed to eat, and there was food in her sights.

Her decision made, Gretel walked back through the trees to the house. She wasted no time on preemptive regret or future plans of atonement, figuring those would only distract from what was required. If her family was to eat, focus and will were all that mattered.

There would be no school tomorrow. Tomorrow Gretel would become a thief.

GRETEL AWOKE JUST AFTER two o'clock in the morning, feeling well-rested and sparked with adrenaline. She had gone to her room just before Hansel and Odalinde returned from the market and had stayed there, forgoing whatever dinner had been brought home for her. More than food she had wanted to sleep, knowing she would need to be fully rested to take on the task ahead. And since Hansel hadn't come to her, Gretel assumed he had been fed, and that was her main concern.

As she had done dozens of times in her life, Gretel quietly slid open her bedroom window and slipped out, easing herself down the four-foot drop to the ground below. The sound of her feet in the overgrown garden bed was amplified in the serenity of the night, but Gretel didn't anticipate anyone investigating it. In a place where nocturnal animals were as common as weeds, rustling sounds outside your house rarely caused alarm in the Back Country.

She ran slowly on her toes until she was through the tree clump to the lake edge, and then stopped to get her bearings. It was darker than she'd expected; the light she had hoped to get from the moon was swallowed up by clouds. But her eyes would adjust, and she had the lantern.

After she'd made her decision yesterday, Gretel spent the rest of her time alone preparing for the early morning raid. She had fetched the lantern from the shed, checking the battery twice to make sure it worked. And the canoe, once a fixture along this sliver of beach, Gretel had untarped in the yard and dragged down to the shoreline. The skeleton of a mouse had welcomed her when she first pulled the covering from the small boat, and the accompanying oars had long been broken and discarded, but otherwise the craft seemed in decent condition. As long as it didn't sink, Gretel thought, that's all that mattered. If she had had to paddle with her hands she would have—the distance across was short enough that she could have swum it—but Gretel had been able to find a hollowed-out guitar among the ever-increasing junk in the yard, a fossil from merrier Morgan days when things like music were a part of their lives. It would do fine as a replacement for an oar.

Gretel now stood on the shore beside the boat and slowly scanned the water. She felt inside the hull of the canoe and found the lantern, lifting it out and lighting it. It was so bright! She was aware there wasn't a way to adjust the intensity of the lantern, unlike the oil lantern they'd owned when Gretel was younger, but in the daylight that hadn't seemed to be an issue. In fact, if she had any concern it was that the light wouldn't be enough. But now, in the cape of Back Country blackness, it seemed the light must have been visible for miles, as if a star had been born from the union of water and trees.

Gretel breathed deeply, trying to relax. The truth was there was no one out to see the light at this hour. These were farming folk, early risers; the only potential witnesses were likely to be either philandering or drunk—or most likely both. No one to worry about, Gretel thought. And in any case, witnesses or not, she was crossing the lake. Crossing the lake now. Life would decide her fate from there.

She moved the light over the canoe and checked again that both the guitar and buckets were intact. Gretel had decided on four buckets, figuring that four would hold enough fruit to last her and Hansel—and her father if necessary—for at least a week, more if she could keep it cool. She hadn't considered exactly how to store and preserve the fruit yet, or how to explain their origin if her father—or God help her, Odalinde—were to ask, but there were more immediate concerns at the moment.

With everything in order, Gretel placed the lantern in the front of the boat and shoved the canoe easily into the water, dexterously avoiding wetting her shoes as she grabbed either side of the stern end, and bounced in, landing in perfect sitting position at the stern seat. She moved the lantern to the bow, picked up the guitar and gently began to row across the lake toward the Klahr orchard.

In the daylight, the lake looked like hardly more than a large pond, but now, under the shroud of night, it seemed larger, frightening. There was a quietness to it that implied undisclosed secrets and demanded trepidation. Gretel thought she would have preferred raging rapids under sunny skies to the lake at this moment.

She distracted herself by trying to remember when she'd last been on the boat, but she couldn't recall, imagining it must have been when Hansel was just a toddler, and their father would row them past the entire Klahr orchard, down to the Stein mill where the lake ended. Gretel remembered being mostly bored by the trips, other than seeing the joy it brought to her brother and father. She would have given just about anything to have such stability and leisure in her life right now.

The canoe nudged into the silty bottom of the lake just a few feet off the shore of the Klahr side of the lake. Gretel was already across! She let out a breathy laugh at how quick the ride had been; she'd barely paddled the guitar more than a few times it seemed.

So far the plan was working as well as she could have hoped.

Gretel pulled the lantern and buckets from the canoe, and was now grateful for the lantern's brightness; she was completely unfamiliar with the landscape on this side of the lake, and began to imagine bottomless pits and angry dogs waiting for her just outside the circumference of the light's rays. She walked slowly up the slight slope of the muddy beach, focusing on the two or three feet that were illuminated just in front of her steps. Soon she crossed a threshold into a patch of wild grass and then saw the first of the trees planted closely together in the perfectly manicured row of dirt that formed the back of the Klahr orchard. She was there.

Gretel exhaled and then breathed in deeply, taking the clean, candied air into her lungs and holding it there, savoring it, before releasing it to the breeze. Her stomach reacted instantly, awakening from its slumber.

She lifted the lantern branch-high and her eyes were overwhelmed with pears. There were pears everywhere on the tree, bulbous and perfectly shaped, nestled in clusters, clinging to the leaves like giant green raindrops. There were dozens, maybe hundreds on the one tree, and Gretel's mind conjured a picture of the entire orchard, which ran as long and deep as human eyes could see, even from across the lake in the clear of day. She began to extrapolate out how many pears and apples there must be in the entire orchard and realized it was inconceivable. Millions, she thought.

Gretel's impulses stirred and she scrambled for a bucket. The trees were taller than she'd imagined, and Gretel would certainly have needed a ladder to pick one clean, but she only had four buckets to fill, and the low-hanging fruit would be just fine. Besides, there were hundreds—maybe thousands—of trees to choose from.

The buckets were filled quickly, and as Gretel began the first trip back to the canoe—one hand holding the lantern, the other lugging a bucket of pears—she lamented not bringing more than four. She could imagine sitting with Hansel and devouring all the pears in a single morning, and the Klahrs would miss four buckets of pears no more than the beach would miss four buckets of sand. But four was all she had, and she needed to stay on task. Besides, she could always come back for more.

With three buckets secure in the canoe, Gretel made her last trip back to the orchard for the remaining bucket when she heard a dull metallic click. She knew instantly it was the unmistakable sound of a round of ammunition being loaded into the chamber of a shotgun.

"Place the bucket on the ground," a voice commanded. The man's voice was neither loud nor aggressive. In fact, Gretel thought, there was a soothing, instructive quality to it.

Gretel did as she was told and now stood frozen, suddenly realizing the vulnerable position she was in. She had been caught trespassing and stealing—no small offenses, particularly in the Back Country—and was now being held alone by a man with a gun, a man who, Gretel assumed, was either going to kill or rape her. Or both. Property crimes in the Back Country were not turned over to The System—and they never went unpunished. She had never associated the Klahr family with anything other than piety and work, but the truth was she didn't know them at all. For all she knew they could have spent the bulk of their days offering sacrifices to Satan himself.

"Hold the lantern up to your face." The steady voice was coming from in front of Gretel, maybe ten or fifteen feet away.

Gretel obeyed, closing her eyes to avoid the glare of the light.

"Gretel Morgan."

Gretel opened her eyes in surprise, narrowing them, trying to force her vision through the darkness. She listened with both fear and anticipation as the heavy footsteps approached.

Finally, the figure came into view, but the light only illuminated his torso. The man was tall, and Gretel lifted the light over her head to try to see his face.

"It's all right, Gretel, let me have the lamp," the voice said, wrapping his long fingers around the handle. Gretel released her grip and dropped her hands to her sides, assuming a tall, penitent posture, as if waiting for a scolding.

The stranger lifted the lantern to his face and stooped to Gretel's height, revealing his face. It was Georg Klahr. "Let's go," he said.

AMANDA KLAHR PLACED the soup gently in front of Gretel, who instinctively grabbed the sides of the bowl and raised it just slightly off the table. She caught herself in time, but Mrs. Klahr had seen her, and Gretel immediately imagined how appalled her mother would have been.

"Here Gretel," Mrs. Klahr said, placing a spoon beside the bowl. The woman hovered for a moment, frowning down at Gretel. "I know the face of hunger child, and it's been many years since I've seen it as I do on your face right now. Eat the soup as you like; your bread will be ready soon."

Gretel's eyes filled with tears as she picked up the spoon and began ladling the soup into her mouth. "Thank you, Ma'am," she choked out between swallows, but the warm broth and the smell of the bread from the kitchen overwhelmed her, and the gratitude she felt yielded to eating.

The front door opened and closed, and Gretel looked up sheepishly from her bowl as Mr. Klahr walked into the kitchen.

"Anyone there, Georg?" Mrs. Klahr inquired, setting a steaming plate of bread beside the soup bowl.

"No," he replied, "seems not." Mr. Klahr placed his hat on the table and sat down across from Gretel, watching her as she dipped her bread in the soup and shoved it in her mouth.

Gretel kept her eyes on her bowl, afraid that lifting them and making contact with Mr. Klahr would somehow end the magic that was happening in front of her.

"You've a brother," Mr. Klahr stated. "Greener than you as I recall."

Gretel met Georg Klahr's eyes and hesitated. "Yes, sir."

"Did he eat yesterday?"

Gretel looked at Mrs. Klahr and then back to the man across the table, suddenly feeling guilty at her newfound bounty. "My father's nurse took him to town. She told him she would buy him something to eat there. I was in bed before they returned, but I guess she did."

The uncertainty in Gretel's voice was obvious, and she did nothing to disguise it. There was no point pretending things were just dandy at home when you've been caught stealing apples at four o'clock in the morning. The tone was not lost on George Klahr, and he glanced sideways at his wife.

"Mrs. Klahr will pack some food for you to take to your brother. Make sure it gets to him." Georg Klahr frowned and looked away, clearly disgusted at the abject position of the poor girl in his kitchen. Still looking away he said, "Is your father going to marry that woman?"

"No, sir!" Gretel snapped her head up from her plate and stared wide-eyed at the side of Mr. Klahr's face. Her voice was louder than she'd intended, and she repeated the words, this time more softly. "No, sir. She's his nurse, that's all."

Gretel hadn't known the Klahrs were even aware of Odalinde, never mind that she'd been with them long enough to ask such a question. But that's how it was in the Back Country: news about the arrival of strangers traveled with the speed of electricity, and often with greater detail than one would expect.

The thought of her father marrying Odalinde had frankly never occurred to Gretel, though now that the question had been posed it seemed like a legitimate possibility. Likely even. Gretel's stomach turned slightly and she put her hands to her mouth to suppress the nausea.

Mercifully, Mrs. Klahr quickly changed the subject. "How *is* your father?" She shot her husband a dirty look and Mr. Klahr looked away unruffled. "I know he was very ill for a while there. A mule kick, was it? To the gut?"

Still wallowing in the dreadful idea of her new stepmother, Gretel looked at Mrs. Klahr as if she had asked this question in Latin. "Ill? Uh...yes ma'am," she replied finally, "except it was a horse."

"Ah yes, a horse. But he's doing better?"

Gretel considered the question for a moment. "I don't really know. It seems sometimes that he is. Like he's fully recovered, though perhaps a bit sore still, and then later he's in bed for days. And sometimes when I talk to him it's as if he hardly knows me."

At this revelation, an awkward noiselessness enveloped the kitchen, and Gretel blushed at having disclosed so much in her answer to what was, more or less, a rhetorical question.

Mrs. Klahr had cleared her bowl and Gretel now sat with her hands hanging by her sides, suddenly feeling like a prisoner undergoing a soft interrogation who has just been coerced into willingly revealing everything about herself, without so much as a harsh word from her captors. These were her neighbors, yes, but as she reminded herself again, she didn't really know them at all.

She picked up her spoon again and began to scrape the bottom of the bowl.

"So what should we do about the apples you've stolen?" Mr. Klahr asked flatly.

Gretel glanced up at the man across the table from her, a look of regret in her eyes, though secretly she was thankful to be done with the personal questions and back on the topic of why she was sitting in the Klahr kitchen to begin with.

"I don't know, sir," she replied, and then thought a moment, her eyes glancing toward the ceiling. "I have no money to pay for them. I suppose my father will have to make amends." Gretel paused, perhaps dramatically she would later consider, "Unless you're to call The System."

The words blurted from Gretel's mouth with the tone of a hopeful alternative, and Gretel blushed immediately. It was true she was no longer afraid of The System, and in the context of the situation, she would have much preferred discussing this matter of the apples with Officer Stenson than with George Klahr.

But it was ludicrous to think The System would handle such a relatively petty crime as the one at hand. So why would she have made the suggestion? It wasn't to do with her mother's disappearance, Gretel thought. If The System did take the time to respond to this apple complaint, they would focus on the crime at hand—not on giving information about another case to the accused!

And Gretel knew in her bones that there was nothing about her mother for them to offer anyway. At least nothing they were willing to share.

So what then?

But Gretel knew the answer, of course. There was only one reason The System would have popped into her mind, and it was a reason Gretel had thought about on and off for weeks. It was The System officer's son. Petr.

George Klahr formed a quizzical smile at Gretel's suggestion of The System and sat studying her for a moment, as if he'd missed something in the story. "I think that might be a bit excessive. Don't you?"

Gretel shrugged shyly.

"And I'd also prefer not to involve your father...or that woman. What is her name?"

"Odalinde. Odalinde Merth."

"Or Odalinde Merth."

George Klahr rose from his chair and walked to the cupboard, taking out a ceramic mug and pouring himself a cup of coffee, mumbling to himself something about not going back to sleep.

Gretel frowned at the hint of blame.

"Instead Gretel," George Klahr continued, "I'd like you to repay me another way."

Gretel's eyes widened, and she eagerly followed Mr. Klahr as he paced back toward the window and looked out past the orchard to the first glint of morning sunlight. His words scared her slightly—Gretel wasn't naive to the deviant wishes of some (maybe all) men. But she also didn't sense evil in Mr. Klahr, neither in his tone or his character generally. And the fact that his wife stood not eight feet away comforted Gretel further (though she was not naive to the perversions of certain women either).

Gretel waited for the proposition silently, steeling herself not to speak, afraid that she might blurt out an offer beyond what was to be pitched—though what she would have volunteered she couldn't have said.

"As you obviously know," Mr. Klahr started, smiling and nodding toward the bucket of apples beside the table, "the orchard is just about ready for harvest. Starting Thursday in fact, I have men coming from across the Back Country, some even from the Northlands, to pick the fruit. They'll be here for the next several weeks."

Gretel sat riveted, still not quite sure what was coming.

"These men will need to be fed, and their clothes and linen will need to be cleaned. They're a quiet, respectful bunch generally, not very fussy, but there is still a lot to be done in regards to their care. It isn't easy work."

Mr. Klahr paused.

"Mrs. Klahr has been insisting on help with these duties for, what is it now dear, twenty years?" George Klahr looked at his wife and gave the same quizzical smile Gretel had received only minutes before.

"I lost count somewhere around year ten," Mrs. Klahr replied without looking up.

Mr. Klahr continued. "So...I'd like to offer you a job, Gretel, assisting Mrs. Klahr with these duties." He paused to let the offer penetrate. "You can work after school and on Saturday, even before school if you like. I'll pay you by the hour, the same wage as the pickers, and you can work as much or as little as you like, though if you say you will be here on a particular day I'll expect you to be. And you're not to miss school."

Tears began to form behind Gretel's eyes before Mr. Klahr had finished speaking. Her stomach knotted nervously and she couldn't contain the smile that fought through her pursed lips and spread as wide as her face. She couldn't quite believe what she was hearing, and said nothing in response, waiting for a 'catch' to the offer.

"So?" Mr. Klahr said, "Will I see you Thursday?"

Gretel cleared her throat and sat up straight in her chair. "Yes sir, you will," she said professionally, "Thursday. I'll be here before and after school. As early as I can."

Mrs. Klahr spoke up, "As long as it isn't as early as you showed up today."

Gretel blushed again, but her excitement instantly transformed it into a glow of joy. "Yes, ma'am."

With the deal in place, the Klahr's began hustling Gretel back home before the sun rose completely, so as not to raise the eyebrows of Odalinde. Generally, Odalinde didn't give much thought to Gretel's comings and goings, which would make her newly-gained employment not much of an issue, but there was no point inciting unnecessary suspicion. To be safe, Gretel and the Klahrs developed a believable story for how Gretel acquired her job, just in case anyone should ever ask. Though, truthfully, the only person Gretel could imagine caring much at all about the story was Hansel, and he would believe whatever his sister told him.

Gretel confessed to the Klahr's about the three buckets already in the canoe, and Mr. Klahr told her to keep them, along with the one by her side. "We've more apples and pears than we could ever sell or process in a season," Mrs. Klahr said, "Better you eat them than the pigs. And I want you to give that bread to your brother as soon as he's awake."

"Yes, ma'am." Gretel raised the wrapped hunk of bread to show she'd remember, and then thanked the Klahr's for what must have been the thousandth time as she stood in the doorway, the bucket of apples in the other hand. She soon realized this was the best night she'd had since her mother vanished, and she wanted to linger in it.

Finally, she turned from the house to leave when Mr. Klahr's voice struck her like an iron bar. "I'm sorry about your mother, Gretel," he said.

Gretel stopped but didn't turn back.

"We wanted to come so many times but…" his voice drifted off to a whimper, "…well, I'm sorry. We both are."

Gretel closed her eyes and sighed. "I'll see you Thursday," she said, and then walked away.

CHAPTER EIGHT

FOR WEEKS FOLLOWING that night in the Klahr kitchen, Gretel was as busy as she'd ever been in her life, and that included those weeks her mother had gone to care for Deda.

Each day, except for Sunday, began at five o'clock in the morning and ended close to eight o'clock at night. Ten o'clock if you included homework. And Gretel loved it. All of it.

She was learning new things every day from Mrs. Klahr, mostly about cooking, but other, less tangible things as well. And, most importantly, Gretel was making money. Mr. Klahr paid her in cash every morning for the previous day's work, and she was provided a meal for each shift worked, which basically meant breakfast and dinner every day, and lunch on Saturdays. Admittedly, Sundays were a blessing, and Gretel more or less stayed in her room and slept all day, but she was as enthusiastic and eager as a shrew come Monday morning, and often arrived at the Klahr house before Mr. and Mrs. Klahr had even dressed for the day. On these mornings, Gretel gave her sincere, albeit pride-laced apologies, but the Klahrs always dismissed them, rebuking themselves instead for their sluggishness.

Gretel's only apprehension about her new job was how it would play out at home and the effect it would have on her brother. Naturally, Hansel had become both dependent on and protective of his sister since their mother's disappearance and Gretel feared he would take her new schedule badly. He didn't have many friends to begin with, and the last thing Gretel wanted was for her brother to experience any additional feelings of loneliness on top of those which already gripped him. But he had been surprisingly calm about the news—nonchalant even—the buckets of ripe pears and apples no doubt contributing to his casualness.

And her father hadn't uttered a word of protest either. He was in fact relieved, both that his daughter was exerting her independence through the healthy outlet of work, and that desperately needed money would now be coming into the household. He hadn't asked about her salary, and Gretel hadn't offered to tell him, but the shine in his daughter's eyes had revealed to him that their worries could subside for a few weeks. In this exchange, which Gretel was determined to keep fresh in her mind for as long as possible, Gretel saw a glimpse of the man her father was before their mother went missing, before his injury even, and she laughed boisterously in his arms as he hugged her and told her how proud he was.

Gretel didn't know what would happen when the harvest eventually ended, or how they would continue to survive, but she wasn't ready to submerge herself into that concern just yet. She had done as she set out to do that night in the canoe: feed herself and her brother. Certainly, her goal hadn't been realized quite the way she'd intended, but that's how it usually went. Knowing what you wanted and then doing something—anything—about it was a big part of the battle.

And in this case, it turned out a hundred times better than she'd ever dreamed. She was now able to feed her entire family, keep some of her family's creditors at bay, and, since most of her meals were provided by the Klahrs, which meant less money was needed for food, she could even buy a few 'luxuries' like new dinner plates for the house and shoes for Hansel. To Gretel, it was all a miracle; two weeks ago such a scenario seemed far beyond impossible.

Even Gretel's school work had improved. Her grades, which had been dropping steadily, quickly began to trend upwards, and the combative behavior which had shortened so many of her school days over the past couple of months suddenly became agreeable and helpful. Gretel even became somewhat amicable with her classmates, and though her schedule allowed little time for outside socializing, she had made one or two friends.

Of course, she recognized many of these changes were due to her fear that any news of mischief in school might find its way back to the Klahrs, but it was also more than that: for the first time in months, Gretel felt happy. And it wasn't that fleeting kind of happiness which arrives seemingly from nowhere and then evaporates with the same lack of reason. It was a consistent happiness—that underlying peace that seems always to flow beneath the surface of certain people, subliminally repeating to them throughout the day that everything is okay. That no matter what happens, everything is okay. Those people who have never been without the feeling might label it 'contentment,' but Gretel was new to the feeling, and it was one she was now dedicated to for life.

"Gretel, the pies!" Amanda Klahr barked her raspy command at Gretel as she carried the oversized platter of biscuits out the front door to the waiting table of hungry pickers.

The men were mostly quiet and undemanding, particularly when it came to Mrs. Klahr, but she was as adamant as any city restaurant manager about having their meals to them hot and on time. Gretel surmised this came from a combination of pride and motivation, figuring the men would work hard for her if she worked hard for them. Plus, as far as Gretel could tell, the picking months were the only time of the year the Klahrs had company, and Mrs. Klahr enjoyed the entertaining part of the whole thing.

The Klahrs had long ago moved the daily meals of the workers outside where cleanup would be easier and space wouldn't be an issue. Georg Klahr had constructed a large wooden table for the purpose, with permanent benches on either side and a flat patio area made of clay brick. The giant table ran the entire length of the patio and was quite a marvel of construction. She had never measured it, but Gretel figured the table must have been twenty feet long. It was the length of a table that kings might dine at, Gretel thought, though its impurities and unfinished design made it suitable only for the environment in which it now stood. The whole area was actually quite beautiful, though Gretel couldn't imagine that the space was used much at any other time of the year. But it served its purpose well, and the scene of men seated around the table resembled something closer to a family reunion than a migrant worker lunch hour.

"I've got them, Ma'am! I'm right behind you." Gretel slipped on the oven mitts and took two pies from the oven, setting them on the stove top and grabbing the remaining two from the back of the rack. She placed the four pies on a large serving board and followed Mrs. Klahr through the door which, mercifully, she had left open.

Saturday: Gretel's favorite day of the week. And her busiest. She'd been at work for five hours now and it was only eleven a.m.

Gretel set the first pie at one end of the huge table and continued down toward the other end, spacing the remaining pies evenly so as to make them accessible to everyone. Gretel could feel the eyes of the men—not on her, but on the food. With great restraint the men sat sturdy, watching, waiting for the women to finish their roles and signal for them to begin. And when the signal came, the men wasted no time moving in.

They were courteous, of course, taking one biscuit at a time, or one spoon of potatoes or chili, and then passing the dish on. But when they began, they ate everything. Soup pots were bone dry when the hour was up. The boards of roast beef or game hens or whatever main course was served that day were cleaned by the workers as if they had come from the wash bin. The tea pitchers, the greens, and the seemingly never-ending bowls of apples and pears were drained without pause.

And then there were the pies.

Amanda Klahr's pies were staggering and had become so popular among the men that Gretel had suggested to Mrs. Klahr they be served first. Mrs. Klahr put up a mild protest at first but came around after testing the idea and receiving applause from the men when she placed them on the table at the beginning of the meal. From that point on, pies had been the appetizer at each lunch and dinner, whether they were made with fruit, meat or potatoes.

Gretel placed the last pie on the table and stepped back, placing her hands properly in front of her, waiting as a servant in a mansion might for any further requests. Gretel loved to watch the men as they began the feast. She reveled in it. There was such joy in that first moment, and the moments just after the first bites, from men who spent most of the day looking stoic and grim. The ear-touching smirks and agreeable nods that sprang up around the table when Mrs. Klahr finally said 'enjoy' in her ironic, understated manner made Gretel glow inside. She wanted to clap for the men, encourage them to 'take more, there's plenty!'

Of course, she said nothing and waited for Mrs. Klahr to flap her back to the kitchen for the next task.

"They're not children," Mrs. Klahr scolded amusingly. "You shouldn't watch them like that."

Gretel smiled, nodding toward the table. "I don't think they mind. In fact, I don't think they would notice if I was standing here naked."

Mrs. Klahr laughed and put her arm around Gretel, leading her back to the house where, once inside, Gretel went right for the kitchen and began cleaning the floors and range top. She worked fast, knowing that the dishes that awaited her after the men finished would take up most of her time until dinner, which she would need to help Mrs. Klahr prepare.

"Pace yourself child! My goodness! You'll be an old woman before you become a young woman!"

Gretel smiled conspiratorially and continued scrubbing. "With all the food I eat now, I'll get fat if I don't move this fast."

"Well I can't afford you getting sick, so don't overdo it."

And this was a truth Gretel had come to accept.

For the Klahrs, Gretel had evolved from a charity case to a necessity in only a few short weeks. She didn't know how they ever got through a harvest without her, though Gretel assumed they must have hired some kind of temporary helper, perhaps the wife or daughter of one of the pickers. The fact was: this day was a typical day for Gretel, and Mrs. Klahr's cautions to take it easy were simply courtesies. The work Gretel had been given was hard and heavy, and the pace at which she moved was what was required for it to get done. And Gretel was naturally suited for it.

At first, of course, the hours and work seemed impossible, particularly during those first two or three days; but Gretel's body adjusted quickly, not just in terms of her stamina, but also in her physique. The carrying of pots and baskets, as well as her newly-discovered love for rowing (the Klahr's had gifted Gretel a set of old oars), had quickly transformed her biceps and shoulders and thighs into those of an athlete. Gretel was accustomed to hard work on her land and household, but those duties had mostly been limited to feeding livestock, cleaning stalls, and mopping floors. The work she was doing now had made her lean and wiry, and she even seemed to have grown an inch or two.

She was becoming the woman her mother had always envisioned.

"Hi Gretel."

Gretel paused at the sink, trying to place the voice before turning around. It was young, male, and definitely one she had heard before. Not one of the workers—they rarely spoke to Gretel except to say 'please' or 'thank you.' Certainly never to engage in idle kitchen talk

Gretel flipped the dishtowel across her shoulder and spun toward the voice. A smile reflexively spread across her face at the sight of the boy in front of her. It was Officer Stenson's son.

For the moment, Gretel couldn't recall his name, which was odd considering she had replayed her encounter with the boy virtually every night for almost a month following their whirlwind meeting.

But so much had changed since then. She'd quickly began to rebuild her life—thanks almost entirely to the Klahrs—and had spent as little time as possible on the 'what ifs?' of the past few months. What if The System had found her mother? or What if Petr was her boyfriend? There was no room for fantasy in Gretel's life right now. Her actual life was working, and she wasn't going to waste it wishing she were somewhere or someone else.

Even with her mother, whom she still thought about several times a day, Gretel refused to descend the path of 'if only Deda hadn't gotten sick and mother hadn't gone to take care of him and...' She had learned at fourteen what most people never did: regrets were a waste of time.

But now, months later, here was the mysterious son of The System officer. Petr Stenson. That angelic face from the window was now appearing to Gretel in the center of the Klahrs' kitchen, as if in a dream, looking as beautiful as she'd remembered him.

Gretel forced down her smile and shook her head quickly, blinking in confusion. "Hi," was all she could manage.

"It's Petr," he said, recognizing that perhaps his name had escaped her.

"Right, Petr. Are you...here with your father? Is there news about my mother or something?" There was only the hint of hope in Gretel's voice, mostly the tone was bewilderment.

"No, no, nothing like that. I'm sorry, I didn't mean to...I'm actually working here during the final weeks of the harvest. The academy agreed to accept me for the fall, with the condition I enroll immediately. They wanted to see if I'm suitable, I suppose. Anyway, the spring session has ended and the summer session doesn't start for a few weeks, and my father wanted me to work during my time off instead of staying home. I guess he thinks it will keep me out of trouble."

"So your father knows the Klahrs?" Gretel asked.

"I don't think so. But my roommate this spring at Hengst worked for them last season, and he told me they always need workers to finish up the season."

None of this sounded plausible to Gretel, but she continued with the conversation. "This isn't too far out for you?" she asked.

Petr laughed, "Of course it's too far, but what am I to do? I don't make the decisions." He bounced his gaze around the kitchen before his eyes landed back on Gretel. "Besides, I kind of like it out here."

Gretel blushed and looked away, swallowing hard, the sting of the boys piercing blue eyes lingering on hers. She composed herself and met the boy's look again, quickly running through the circumstances of this meeting, none of which added up, of course. That she had met Petr at all that first day was unlikely—he'd happened to be with his dad, and his dad had happened to leave his notebook behind in her living room?

And now she was expected to believe that this same kid had been referred to the Klahr orchard by a schoolmate at some snooty academy? Most of the workers in the orchard had never made it past grade school, let alone been to private secondary schools.

With these calculations, Gretel's defenses rocketed to the surface, with anger leading the way. She had little patience for lies—especially from teenage boys—and even less patience for those who looked to take advantage of the people she loved.

"What is his name?" Gretel asked.

Petr's smile dipped slightly and his eyes widened for an instant. "Who's that?"

"Who's that?" she repeated, mimicking the look on Petr's face and tone of his voice. "You know damn well who I mean! What is the name of your roommate? He worked here last summer, did he? Don't you think that's an easy enough thing for me to check?"

Gretel was close to yelling now, and had taken a step forward. She was now only a foot or two from Petr's face.

"What is his name?" she asked again, enunciating each word in staccato jabs.

"Gretel!" a voice barked.

Shaken from her hypnotic attack, Gretel turned to see Mr. Klahr standing tall in the foyer, his chiseled face expressionless and his eyes locked on hers. He had called her name the way a parent might to a disorderly child in a public place, whispery, with jaws clenched.

"Yes, sir," she whispered. She was breathing heavily now, her eyes blurred with a mixture of fear and anger.

"What has gotten to you, Gretel?" Mr. Klahr's voice contained more concern than anger. "This is how you speak to our workers now?"

"No, Mr. Klahr, but—"

"That's enough then."

Mr. Klahr walked slowly to Gretel, his eyes softening as he extended his arms and placed his hands on her shoulders.

"That's quite enough, Gretel. I want you to go home now. You've worked far too much lately, and with all of your schoolwork, I fear you're exhausted."

Gretel had plenty of words to come back with—how this outburst had nothing to do with work or school, and that Petr was suspicious, and that she needed the money—but she knew speaking them would be a waste. When Mr. Klahr made his decision, it was made.

Besides, she *was* tired, and a day of rest wasn't the worst thing she'd ever been told to do. She silently slid the dishtowel from her shoulder and placed it over the basin and then walked toward the door, glaring once more at Petr Stenson before turning the knob.

"His name was Francis," said Mr. Klahr.

Gretel looked over her shoulder at her employer.

"Petr's roommate, his name was Francis."

PETR'S FIRST WEEK HAD come and gone with him saying little more than 'Hello' to Gretel, and she now regretted her tirade. It was more than just the scolding she'd received from Mr. Klahr, she'd completely overreacted, showing no grace in her behavior.

She still believed Petr's employment at the Klahr orchard to be an unbelievable coincidence, but apparently coincidences did happen, as was confirmed by Mr. Klahr himself. And now the result was that she'd alienated a potential friend. And maybe something more.

But what did it matter really? The harvest was ending soon and Petr would return to school. And Gretel had far more pressing thoughts to consider, the most important of which being her plans for after the harvest. Her family had come to depend on the money she was earning—for food, for medicine, for everything—and though the end had always been in sight, there was nothing in place for the future. But why was this her concern anyway? Gretel was just fourteen after all, and yet the primary adult in her life, her father, had become reliant on his daughter's temporary, part-time job. It was despicable to Gretel, and she had all but shed any remaining sympathy for his sickness. His recovery had plateaued, apparently, and though Gretel had been able to pay a doctor to reexamine him, he hadn't found any real reason for her father's lack of progress. 'Some people just recover more slowly,' the doctor told them, 'there's not much that can be done.' But he was bed-bound twenty hours a day, and Gretel began to regard him, fairly or not, as just plain lazy.

And frankly, Hansel was Gretel's only real concern now, though she saw very little of him lately; he certainly must have missed his sister just as she did him. But that was a consequence of necessity, and they would all be better off for it. In fact, her being gone was probably good for the boy's development, not having his sister around all the time to impart feminine softness into his personality. He needed to become strong, male, and, with an invalid as a father, Hansel would need to learn this from the world. And, indeed, Hansel was slowly making friendships with other boys in the community—not all of them Gretel's first choices, but safe enough. There certainly hadn't been adequate dedication and follow-through on his schoolwork—Gretel could only do so much—but Hansel had always been a solid student, and as long as he stayed away from trouble, she figured that part would work out fine. And so far, as much as Gretel could tell, her brother was keeping his nose clean.

It was Odalinde Gretel most worried about. She'd kept out of Gretel's hair for the most part, as it concerned her work and other things, but the longer she stayed on, working for free, the more Gretel distrusted her. The Morgan farm was no great land treasure—in fact it was slowly becoming ruinous—but it was property, and if Odalinde had her sights on it, who knew what intentions she had ultimately.

Gretel had been saving though, putting some cash away after each day's wages, leaving only enough for Odalinde to pay the creditors and feed herself and her father. Gretel had splurged some in the beginning, but she'd been frugal otherwise, and had saved up a decent stipend. When the Klahr gig was up, she would offer it all to Odalinde, with the condition that she leave quietly. She wasn't sure what she'd tell her father, or how she would care for him, but she needed that woman out of her house. Of course, Gretel had no illusions the payoff would work—she was old enough to understand that if Odalinde was the evil figure Gretel imagined her to be, the woman could have robbed them long ago—but maybe a lump payment was just what she was waiting for, and Gretel had to try.

Gretel finished her dinner duties and after the dishes were cleared and cleaned—and she herself had finally eaten—Gretel said her goodbyes to the Klahrs and rowed back across the lake, deciding to forego her normal routine of canoeing down to the Stein mill before going home.

She walked inside and instinctively put on a pot of coffee before checking on a sleeping Hansel, and then unpacked her schoolbooks and walked out to the porch, where she piled the considerable stack on the table. Among a few other assignments, she had her final biology test tomorrow. It would be a late night.

She dove right in, opening to a chapter on Mendel and his discoveries in genetics. She read the first page and then thought better of it, figuring such dry reading should wait until the effects of the caffeine had been fully realized. Instead she just sat quietly, reflecting on her day in the orchard and Mrs. Klahr's kitchen, feeding and cleaning and bantering with the Klahrs and the pickers. And Petr Stenson, with whom she guessed she should try to make amends.

The thoughts started well and then began to careen again into the darkness of her future once the harvest ended. Gretel had visited the outskirts of this topic in her mind for weeks, but always backed away, not ready to face it. Everything had happened so quickly! The Klahr's, the job, the sudden abundance of food—it was all so wonderful that she hadn't really made any plans beyond. But it would come to an end when the last pickers left the orchard, and Gretel didn't know what she would do then.

The pot on the stove began to percolate, and Gretel walked to the kitchen and poured a cup of coffee. She immediately drank half of it—black—and then refilled the mug, flavoring it now with milk and sugar. Before her work at the Klahr orchard, Gretel had occasionally drunk coffee in the morning, usually on a lazy Sunday or holiday, but now she drank it habitually at night, and thanked God that He had blessed the Earth with such a miracle. She'd have never lasted the first week on the job without it.

The caffeine hit Gretel almost immediately, and the energy made her feel a notch better about the future. She was determined to maintain this life she'd made over the past few weeks, and if she had to knock on the door of every farmer in the Back Country to find work, she'd do it. She had experience now, and an apparent talent, and the Klahrs would certainly give a good reference to any potential employer. It wouldn't be easy, but that she would find work she had little doubt. She would make herself irreplaceable to the family that took her on.

Gretel now surged with inspiration and decided a row on the lake was exactly what was needed. She would study the biology chapter later; right now there was too much inside her to focus on the inherited traits of pea plants. Her canoe excursions were peaceful and cleansing and helped to untangle the thoughts that had silently built up during the day but which Gretel had not been able to tackle fully. She seldom missed a night on the lake, as she had done tonight, and now, with her mind overrun with thoughts of the future, she knew why.

When Gretel first started at the orchard, Mr. Klahr had offered to pick her up in the mornings and take her home at night—offers which Gretel had politely refused. At first she had done so because she didn't want to burden her employer or be bound by their schedules—she wanted to arrive as early as possible and leave when it was time to go. But eventually the rowing had become the reason. She cherished it. Every part of it. The smell of the wood and the water, the air on her face and neck as it drafted past her, and, of course, the results of her efforts, both on her mind and muscles. The short canoe ride home had become such a pleasure to Gretel that by the third day she had expanded her commute, rowing down to the Stein mill or up toward the abandoned cannery. Some nights the paddling was leisurely and calm, other nights it was as fierce as a slave galley. Tonight would be the latter. Gretel felt the need to be strong.

Gretel poured the last swallow of coffee into the sink and washed the cup out, turning it face down to dry on the towel next to the basin, and then walked to the front door.

"Gretel," a voice said from somewhere in the house.

It was her father, and though the words were calm and measured, they bit into the back of Gretel's neck as if they had been screamed.

Gretel stepped away from the door and walked back through the kitchen to get a view of the family room where it sounded like her father had spoken. And there he was, sitting on the couch smiling, Odalinde next to him with a similar look on her face.

"What's going on, Papa?"

"Sit down," her father said, pointing at one of the chairs that sat opposite the sofa.

Gretel walked slowly to the chair, never taking her stare off the couple sitting across from her. Her father looked misplaced on the couch, artificial, like a mannequin strategically positioned to showcase the couch in some bizarre showroom. Tears welled in Gretel's eyes though she couldn't have said why at the time.

"Gretel," her father said, "Odalinde and I have some news."

Gretel said nothing, waiting.

"We're getting married, Gretel."

There was a feeling in Gretel's body of collision and nausea, and she stifled a gag as her hand reached reflexively for her stomach. She had the sudden urge to release her bowels. Her face flooded with blood and adrenaline; somehow—incredibly—she kept her tears at bay.

Gretel immediately thought of Mr. Klahr's question that first night, and the look on his face at the time. He knew this was coming and had felt sorry for her. How naive she was! Of course they were getting married! It was obvious even to Mr. Klahr, a stranger at the time, a man who saw her family only occasionally from across a lake. And yet Gretel hadn't seen it coming!

Instinctively, protectively, her thoughts went to the lake. She wished more than anything that she was drifting on it now, listening to the groan of the bullfrogs and the light *plop, plop* of jumping fish. Why hadn't she rowed tonight instead of coming straight home? Ultimately it wouldn't have made a difference, the revelation she'd just heard would have been told eventually, but maybe it would have been put off for the night.

"Married?" Gretel finally said, not able to manage even a trace of joy in her tone or expression.

"I proposed this morning and Odalinde accepted." Heinrich Morgan managed a dull smile and looked to his fiancé. "The wedding will be in the winter. Just after Christmas perhaps."

Her father's words seemed to be coming from somewhere in Gretel's imagination, as if she were playing a game in her mind, conjuring the most horrible scenes that could possibly occur in her life, just so that she may better appreciate what her life actually was. Her stomach tightened further and Gretel prepared to run for the bathroom, but the wave subsided.

"I'd like you to be in my wedding, Gretel," Odalinde said flatly, though with a mock formality that was appropriate for the occasion.

Gretel ignored her and said to her father, "Is she pregnant?"

"Gretel!" her father snapped.

Gretel finally looked at Odalinde, stunned, realizing the hurtfulness of her question. But the inquiry wasn't meant to be mean-spirited; it was the only genuine reason Gretel could come up with for the engagement.

"I'm sorry," she said, and with those words the tears finally came.

Gretel ran from the family room and out the front door down to the lake. Tonight she would row as she'd never rowed before.

THOUGH SULLEN AND SPIRITLESS, Gretel rose the next morning and, as usual, arrived early for work. She tried to keep things to herself, but the morning chaos had hardly begun before Mrs. Klahr uncovered the source of her young apprentice's mood.

"Surely you must have suspected this could happen, Gretel?" Mrs. Klahr said. She spoke softly, in a tone intended to diminish the impact of her recent upset, not to point out Gretel's naiveté.

"Yes ma'am, I suppose I did," Gretel replied. "That first night, in this very kitchen, Mr. Klahr asked me if those were my father's intentions, so I must have had some idea. I tried not to think of it, I guess. I just wanted to go home one day and have her be gone." Gretel looked at the ceiling as she spoke, as if the feelings inside of her were suddenly organizing themselves in a way that made sense. "She doesn't love my father."

Mrs. Klahr let Gretel's words resonate, being in no position to confirm or deny the statement.

The two women sat without speaking for several moments before the sound of Mr. Klahr's boots striding thunderously in from the orchard fractured the silence. He sensed the mood instantly, and Mrs. Klahr filled him in on the relevant facts. He nodded thoughtfully, his discomfort palpable. "I'm sorry," he said, "I...I know how you feel about her."

Gretel mouthed an inaudible 'thank you', and sat frowning with her elbows splayed on the kitchen table and her fists screwed into her cheeks.

Mr. Klahr shot his wife a glance. "Gretel, we need to talk to you about something else," he said.

Gretel felt her stomach tighten and her eyes flicked up wide to meet Mr. Klahr's. "Yes? What is it?" She guessed maybe it was to do more with her behavior toward Petr and braced for admonishment.

"As you know, the harvest is ending. By the end of next week, we'll be done." Mr. Klahr paused for a moment and stared at Gretel intensely. "When we took you on, it was temporary, with the understanding that when the season is over, your work would be done here."

"I know," Gretel said. Her voice wobbled, pitching upwards on the word 'know.'

She sat up straight and closed her eyes, focusing whatever restraint remained inside her on not shedding tears. She'd done far too much of that lately. She felt a tear creeping over her bottom lashes and quickly caught it with her thumb. She squeezed her eyes tight and shivered once to clear any remaining sobs, then smiled weakly at Mr. Klahr, embarrassed at her fragility.

"Gretel, you don't understand." Mr. Klahr grabbed Gretel's hands. "We want you to stay on with us."

The words hung in the air, drifting around the kitchen like ghosts.

Gretel's smile fell straight. "What?"

It was Mr. Klahr's turn to smile now. "In case you hadn't noticed Gretel, we're old."

"You're the strongest people I know," Gretel said absently, irrelevantly.

"We do fine, Gretel, and we don't complain much. But we ache as much as the next people, and we aren't beyond needing help." He squeezed her hands tighter. "We'd have never made it through this harvest without you."

Gretel sat staring, stupidly she imagined, and as the reality of the offer set in, she couldn't restrain herself anymore, and the sobs came out in huge coughing waves. Her mother would have been mortified, but Gretel didn't care.

Then, as if possessed, she launched herself toward Mr. Klahr and threw her arms around him, his eyes widening in reflexive fear. He caught her and briefly held her at a distance, before bringing her into a full embrace. "It's true! You've been a godsend!"

Gretel pulled away and looked at Mr. Klahr quizzically, wiping her nose with her sleeve the way a five-year-old might. "But what will I do?" she said, almost panicking, "when the harvest is done?"

Amanda Klahr laughed. "Oh, my dear, there are plenty of things in your life to worry on, having enough work to do around here is not one of those things."

Gretel laughed at this and then stopped abruptly, suddenly awestruck by the strong, plump woman that sat before her. Gretel walked around the table to Mrs. Klahr and gently wrapped her arms around the old woman's neck, making a silent vow to take care of her for the rest of her life. "Thank you," was all she could manage.

"You're very welcome, love," Mrs. Klahr said, "but you don't seem to understand that this is not charity. We really do need you."

"Thank you anyway, both of you."

"And this also doesn't solve the problem of your father."

This fact sobered Gretel only slightly. "No, it doesn't. But one thing at a time. Right now I'm too happy to care. Besides, I haven't even started on breakfast and I hear the men mulling around outside already."

"Oh please," Mrs. Klahr said, "they're glad to wait. It only means they get to start working later. They get the same wage either way. But I imagine you are right, we should get going."

Mr. Klahr stood to leave. "Welcome to the family, Gretel. For good." And with that he walked out.

The rest of that day Gretel worked with an energy she'd never felt before. She took no break at lunch, instead grabbing a roll on the fly and a slice of pie while she waited for the dishes to come in. At dinner, she playfully teased the pickers as she placed their food on the table, and after, when the final plate was cleared, she alone wiped down the huge table and swept the patio clean (a chore that usually waited until morning). And when Saturday evening arrived, and her week was down to its final hour, the fierceness of her work endured, as she scrubbed the cabinets to a shine.

"I want you to take next week off," Amanda Klahr stated flatly, continuing to dry a bowl and not looking at Gretel.

Gretel giggled, wiping the pantry door down. "Yes ma'am, thank you. Perhaps I'll fly off to the tropics and catch up on my sun."

"I'm not joking, Gretel, I want you to rest. I've spoken with Mr. Klahr and he agrees."

Mrs. Klahr caught Gretel's stare, hardening her face to demonstrate the seriousness of her words.

"There's not enough work in the field for all the pickers anyway, so I'll put some of them to work in the house. Most of the meals have already been prepared so the cooking will be easy. It's just a matter of heating the food." She softened her tone. "Listen, if you're going to work here, you'll need to establish some balance in your life, and we're both concerned that you aren't focusing enough on being a young girl. I don't think I've ever even heard you mention friends."

This wasn't what Gretel had in mind with her new duties, and was speechless. And scared at the prospect of a week without pay.

As if reading Gretel's mind, Amanda Klahr said, "We'll pay you of course. It's our decision, not yours, so of course we'll pay you."

"I couldn't..." Gretel said weakly, still dazed by the order.

"You can and you will. I don't want to see you anywhere near this property until next Monday. We will give your regrets to the workers since most of them will be gone by then."

"Most?"

"Petr will stay for a few weeks longer, as a favor to his father."

Gretel tried to think of more reasons to protest her hiatus—some necessity the Klahrs hadn't considered perhaps—but she came up with nothing, and as the reality of a vacation slowly took hold in her imagination, she quickly warmed to the idea. Not only for the much-needed rest, but school was coming to an end, and with her final tests looming at the end of the week, time off would be an invaluable gift.

But perhaps the best part was she could finally reconnect with Hansel—at least enough to find out if there were any major problems that needed tackling. From afar things seemed fine with the boy, but a closer look wouldn't hurt.

And she could spend extra time rowing as well, perhaps take the canoe past the cannery one day and picnic in Rifle Field. Because of her schedule at the orchard, her leisure rowing was always done at night, in complete darkness or the gloom; and all her plans for Sunday jaunts to explore the lake always disintegrated into more sleep. Not this week. This week she'd row in the light of the sun every day.

Of course, time off from work also meant more chances to clutch horns with Odalinde. The two women had spoken very little since Gretel started working, and though to an outsider that might have appeared to strain them further, in Gretel's mind this was a mutual benefit. The edges of their relationship had sharpened severely in the days just prior to Gretel starting at the orchard, and time apart was needed medicine.

But if storm clouds did start forming this week, Gretel figured she had enough outlets to keep away from the nurse.

She also made the promise that this was the week she'd get into her future stepmother's cabinet beneath the sink.

CHAPTER NINE

AS SHE DID MOST SUNDAYS, Gretel spent the bulk of her day in her room sleeping and reading. But by Monday afternoon, with the school day over and her body rested, she was eager to begin her vacation.

She was still struggling with the idea of so much free time, and all that was still to be done for the final week of harvest, but the order had been given to take the time, and she was determined not to waste it.

An appreciable relief had filled the room when Gretel relayed the news to her family—including Odalinde—regarding her newly-gained permanent employment, and she was proud to have provided that relief. Her father had wept at the news, as did Hansel (no doubt because his father had), and her soon-to-be stepmother gave a wide, quizzical smile that Gretel found unusual, almost as if she were reassessing Gretel, that she had perhaps underestimated her.

The other part of the deal—that Gretel would spend the upcoming week free from her duties (and would be paid for it)—Gretel decided to keep to herself, figuring it was no one's business but hers and would only result in requests for her time. She had a lot to do this week and she couldn't be bothered with other people's concerns.

Gretel's first order of business was figuring a way inside Odalinde's cabinet beneath the sink. This was, she reasoned, her house, and now that she was providing for the house, including paying for the food that filled the cabinets, she had every right to know what else was inside them. Even that one.

And if it turned out not to be the repository of danger and mystery that Gretel suspected it was, the nagging curiosity of the whole thing would at least be settled.

Odalinde's only routine outing each week occurred on Thursdays, when she left precisely at four in the afternoon and returned sometime around eight; this according to Hansel, who hadn't a clue where she went. Gretel mentally added the uncovering of that mystery to the list of things she would attempt to tackle this week.

But that was a problem for later. Gretel's concern now was to discover the contents of the cabinet, and how, if at all, they affected her family. If, in the end, it turned out Odalinde was only storing photos of her dead grandmother, or some ancient love letters from a teenage sweetheart, then so be it. But Gretel knew instinctively it was more than that.

The current lock on the cabinet was formidable, and, in fact, was a replacement for the one Gretel's father had put in originally when Odalinde first arrived—Odalinde declaring *that* lock to be 'perfectly unsuitable.' She had made some reference to 'Back Country burglars,' but Gretel had never heard of such a thing and concluded 'Back Country burglars' was just code for 'Hansel and Gretel.'

Gretel's first idea to access the cabinet was to go in through the side of one of the adjoining cabinets, removing it, or even cutting a small hole that could be glued back once the contents were known. But the walls of the cupboard were solid wood, oak probably, and to go through them would have required more destruction than she'd be able to cause and repair in one short evening.

Her other idea was to go in from the top, through the sink above the cabinet; but, similar to the walls, the basin was heavy, and would have been far too difficult for her to remove, especially with all the attached plumbing. And she hadn't the time to find someone with the skills to deal with all that. No, the only way in, she decided, was through the door. And that meant she needed the key.

This conclusion sat well with Gretel, and she was filled with hope. Getting the key would surely prove difficult, but not impossible, and she'd have to plan the thing carefully. But that it could be done, she was more than hopeful.

Gretel ruminated on the framework of a plan for a while before dropping the subject entirely and spending the remainder of Monday rowing on the lake, clearing her mind of any plans or plots or fantasies of the future. She'd only recently learned the sacredness of quiet, and the cleansing properties of it, and considered this new exercise in nothingness—she thought of it as having a 'white mind'—to be no less valuable than engaging her brain in the throes of work. The natural marvel of trees and water and untarnished air that had surrounded Gretel since birth were suddenly awakened to her, and she now basked in their stillness whenever possible. There was a time for designing and scheming, obviously, and she took pride in her industrious and conspiratorial inclinations, but she also had no doubt that peril awaited the unrested mind. And, in fact, it was often in the times of total clarity and peace that the ideas she needed most came to her.

And here it had come again, just as she began to turn the small boat that had become her sanctuary back toward home: the keys to Odalinde's cabinet were always kept in her bag, and her bag was never left unattended. If Gretel could pull her away from the bag, distract her for just a minute, she could grab them.

She had an idea, and she would need Hansel's help. It was by no means an infallible plan, but it was something.

THE NEXT DAY GRETEL decided to walk with Hansel from school, which was something she hadn't done since she started working at the orchard. She needed to discuss the newly-devised plan with him, and this, she figured, would be the safest time. Other than her erratic shopping jaunts, and the Thursday night outing, Odalinde always seemed to be around, and had a knack for appearing from the shadows of a tree or the back of a dimly-lit room during a conversation, or entering a room just when the gist of a thought was being spoken. She was sneaky—it was always the first word that came to Gretel's mind when she thought of her future stepmother—and she, Gretel, was taking no chances of being overheard.

But Gretel also regretted the pretense of 'catching up' with her brother as the reason she was walking with him today, and despite her eagerness to construct the plan, and the reasonable explanation that she was off work for the week, she aborted the discussion for the time being. She realized the time together *should* be used to catch up with him, to rediscover Hansel's life; the plot against Odalinde could wait a few hours, even a day if necessary.

"Are you going to try for any teams next year? Soccer maybe? You like soccer, right?"

"I'm not good at soccer," Hansel replied flatly, "I'm not fast enough."

"What? That's silly! You're plenty fast for soccer! And besides, you don't need to be fast for all the positions." Gretel was giving it a go, but it felt forced. Clearly she was rusty at engaging her brother. And she really did want to encourage him to go out for a team!

"I don't like it anyway," Hansel said, and that was the end of that. The boy was going to play or he wasn't, and what she said wasn't going to change anything.

The siblings walked the road in silence for several minutes.

"Do you like her, Hansel?" Gretel finally said, "Odalinde, I mean."

Hansel looked over at his sister, trying to gauge the answer she wanted. But Gretel kept her face as casual and neutral as the tone of her voice.

"I don't know. Sometimes, I guess," Hansel answered.

Gretel nodded, maintaining her breezy air.

"I know you hate her though."

Gretel stopped walking and Hansel followed suit, sheepishly avoiding his sister's eyes in the process. She scrunched her forehead and smiled weakly at Hansel. "What? No. I...I don't...I don't really *hate* her." She glanced at the sky. "No, that's not the right word. I just...I guess I just don't trust her. And that's only because I don't know anything about her." Her voice became shrill. "And now, all of a sudden, she's marrying Father, moving into our house for good, and we don't really know anything about her."

Gretel stopped, and then dropped her voice to its normal pitch and slowed her tempo.

"I know that Odalinde and I have had our conflicts, but we're both women, Hansel, and sometimes...I don't know, sometimes women take a little longer to get along. It doesn't really make sense, but it's true."

Gretel felt she was losing control of the conversation, and in doing so making Hansel feel more insecure, which was the opposite of her intention. If she wasn't going use this time to pitch her brother on being an accomplice to some future cabinet raid, she wanted at least to restore some stability to his psyche. Maybe even make him laugh a time or two. What she didn't want was to get him thinking that his future stepmother was out to steal their home and Father, and that she couldn't be trusted. And that seemed to be right where the conversation was headed.

They both started again toward home and Gretel stayed quiet the rest of the way, disappointed at her clumsiness. She decided she may not ask for Hansel's help at all. It meant she would have to come up with another idea since her original plan called for his diversion, but so be it. If he wasn't ready, then it wasn't fair to involve him. But either way, Hansel or not, Gretel still had every intention of finding out what was in that cabinet.

The children reached the long, dusty driveway that led to the Morgan house when Hansel finally spoke. "I know something about her," he said.

From the tone of her brother's voice, Gretel could instantly tell this 'something' was not insignificant, and she stopped quickly, grabbing Hansel's arm lightly and turning him toward her. She studied his eyes and could see that he had struggled with this knowledge for a while now, and probably had more than one internal debate about whether to share it. Gretel felt a bit angry at first—that he hadn't trusted her with this information—but the feeling fell away as quickly as it developed. The truth was if he had known this thing two months ago—this secret—there was no doubt he'd have confided in his sister. But Gretel's work at the orchard had abruptly snatched her out of his life, and with the new figure of Odalinde now tending to Hansel's daily needs, as cold and neglectful as that figure may have seemed to Gretel, Hansel's loyalties had become less defined.

"Is it something you want to tell me?" she replied.

Hansel nodded.

Gretel was careful to take it slow. "I understand if you're scared, Han, and if you don't want to tell me, whatever it is you know, or you want to tell me some other time, that's okay." She placed her finger under her brother's chin and lifted it to meet his eyes with hers. It was a move her mother had perfected with both her children. "But no matter what," she said, "I'll never let anything happen to you. Okay?"

Hansel nodded again, this time more contemplatively. "What about you though? I don't want anything to happen to you." He looked away, embarrassed.

Gretel gave a sad smile and sighed, a glaze of tears suddenly blurring her vision. She pulled her brother close and hugged him, resting her cheek on his dirty blond hair. Finally she said, "Do you still think about Mom?"

Hansel paused for a moment, thoughtful, and then said, "I used to think about her every day, "but now sometimes I don't."

"That happens to me too. That's okay. But then I remember to think about her and I get happy. So it's important that we don't forget her, okay? She loved us very much. So very much." And then, "And she wanted us to be happy."

Hansel let this sink in. "But what if thinking about her makes me sad?"

Gretel squeezed her eyes tight and the tears began to drop on Hansel's head. "Just don't forget her, Han," she said, and used all her will to stifle the sobs forming inside her.

The children stood silently embraced for a moment in the openness of the faded gravel driveway, like two figures holding on for their lives in the eye of a raging storm.

Hansel finally pulled away from his sister and stared coldly into her eyes. "I want to tell you what happened, Gretel. But I don't want to tell you here."

RIFLE FIELD RESTED just past the Weinhiemmer Cannery and derived its name from the late afternoon sounds of factory workers, ostensibly drunk, finishing their shifts and then honing their marksmanship skills on those containers deemed unsuitable for market. The cannery itself, once a Back Country pillar of capitalism, had long been abandoned as a result of short-sighted management and a debilitating class-action lawsuit brought about by the families of dozens of botulism victims, several of whom had apparently died.

These days, in addition to being a blot on the landscape, the cannery, with its surrounding fence and sprawling rusted paneling, acted as a barrier to Rifle Field. And with the winding lake that swept past the opposite side of the large swath of land, the field could really only be reached by water.

When Gretel was younger, the Morgan family often picnicked in the field, and occasionally had even kept the name relevant by taking target practice at the side of the cannery. At one point, Heinrich Morgan had even taken steps to maintain the landscape of Rifle Field, hauling the mower out on the canoe to level the grass as well as by planting shrubs and flowers. The constant demands of the farm, however, saw this practice die quickly.

And now, after remaining deserted for so long, Rifle Field had been resurrected as an asylum for Gretel, her own private hideaway from the demands of family and employer. She had, in fact, only taken to land there twice since she began her rowing excursions (she usually couldn't spare the time and preferred to be on the water anyway), but she considered the field 'hers' now, and by all accounts, she was the only person to step foot on it in years. Until today, when her brother disembarked from the canoe and helped lay down the tarp on which they both now sat.

"It was a couple of Saturdays ago." Hansel began. "Not that long after you started working at the orchard." He paused. "I think it was Saturday...I know it wasn't Sunday because you weren't home."

Gretel smiled, struggling not to pressure Hansel to the point. He was only eight, after all, and she didn't want to hurt his feelings or embarrass him by pointing out irrelevancies. They were in no hurry, and if it took all day, Gretel had every intention of letting her brother meander his way to the crux.

"Anyway, Odalinde was getting into her cabinet like she does; you know how she gets into that creepy stoop in front of it?"

Gretel smiled and nodded. Oh, she knew all right.

"I was on the porch watching her, and she knew I was there but she didn't know I was watching. But she was still covering everything up and staying really close to the door. And then when she was done looking at her stuff or whatever she does, and she was about to lock the door, right at that second Dad called out to her, loud, like he was hurt or scared or something. Right when she was about to lock it."

He stopped for a moment and his eyes widened. "It was like it was supposed to happen. It was weird."

Gretel was rapt with attention, not at all surprised at the timing of her father's call. "And then what?" she said gently.

"And then Odalinde jumped, and almost fell off her heels onto her back. But she caught herself, and then got up and ran to Dad's room."

Hansel stopped and looked at Gretel, waiting for the revelation to sink in.

Gretel stared back and finally said, "So?"

"I didn't think she locked it, Gretel. I could tell, just the way it happened and how she got so surprised. After Dad's scream, she took the key out of the lock, but I could tell she didn't turn it to lock the door. I could just tell. And then when she came out of Daddy's room, she rushed out the front door and drove off in the truck."

Gretel felt a pang for her brother whenever he regressed to 'Daddy,' but she kept silent and her expression fixed.

"I don't know if she went to get medicine or food or what," Hansel continued, "but she didn't say anything. Or even look at me."

Gretel could see where the story was going, and she hoped more than gold it arrived there.

"So I looked inside, Gretel. I opened it and looked inside."

Gretel couldn't believe what she was hearing. Was this true? A grin the length of the lake formed on her face. She was so excited she wanted to grab her brother and squeeze him until he popped. All the elaborate thoughts of taking apart the cabinetry, and her plan of using Hansel as a decoy to pull Odalinde away from her bag so that Gretel could somehow steal the key and...and do what? She didn't really know, and it didn't matter! Hansel. Beautiful Hansel!

But Gretel had to be realistic and temper her enthusiasm; what Hansel found only mattered to the extent that he could relay it to her. "What did you find, Han?"

Hansel focused his stare in concentration, trying to get it all right. "I thought there was going to be all kinds of junk inside," he said, "like loose papers and stuff. But when I opened the door, all I saw was that huge brown bag. You know the one?"

Gretel nodded slowly, hanging on every word.

"So I undid the clasp and started to open it, but then I saw the bag wasn't all that was inside the cupboard. Behind it, all the way against the back, there was a book. A black book."

Gretel stared at her brother in astonishment.

"It was your book, Gretel," he said flatly, "except it wasn't yours. I checked, yours was still where you always keep it."

Gretel's throat tightened and a true fear took hold of her senses. She was terrified, speechless, trying at once both to understand how what Hansel was telling her could be, and what was to be done about it. Finally she managed, "Are you sure?"

"I checked Gretel, your book was there. I know I'm not supposed to know where you keep it, but I..."

Gretel cut him off, "I mean are you sure that it's the same book? Maybe it just looked the same. Maybe it was just another big black book. About something else."

"*Orphism,* Gretel, I read it on the cover. And all those crazy letters inside. It was the same book." He stopped for a moment, remembering. "But there was something different about hers."

"What do you mean? Different how?" Gretel was losing her poise now and the shrillness in her voice was returning. She caught herself. "What was different, Han?"

"There was lots of writing in her book—like handwriting, with pencil and ink. It was all over the pages, on every page, in between the sentences and at the tops and bottoms. Everywhere."

"Writing? Could you read it? Was it English?"

"I could read most of it. It was definitely English, but a lot of it was sloppy and I didn't really pay that much attention to what it was about. I just flipped through some of the pages—a lot of the pages—and the writing was everywhere."

It took a moment—longer than she would later admit—to occur to Gretel what it all meant, but when it finally did sink in, she gave a throaty giggle and then started laughing. It could only be one thing. A translation! The words had to be a translation!

She quickly stood up on the tarp and walked off it into the tall grass where she began pacing in short laps, staring at the sky in wonder. Virtually every day for months she'd been looking at this book, trying to decipher a word here and there, hoping to get some idea what it was about. And had been utterly dreadful in doing so. And it turned out, apparently, that she'd been walking past the knowledge every time she entered or left the kitchen. Unbelievable!

Gretel's head was spinning with the fact that her father's nurse—whom she trusted no further than she could toss her—was somehow in possession of the same book her grandfather had given her, and which had fascinated her for years. But even that mystery was superseded by the idea of finally knowing what the book was about, and Gretel quickly paced back toward the tarp.

"Did you see at all what it said, Han, anything at all that might have told you what the book was about?"

"I told you, I just flipped through it. I was scared and I...I'm sorry, I..."

"It's okay, Han," she interrupted, sensing his fear that she was disappointed in him, "you did great." Gretel stepped toward her brother and stooped down to his level, taking his head in her hands. She smiled at him and repeated, "You did great."

Gretel stood up again and walked back onto the grass, this time continuing through the field toward the cannery. She needed a minute to consider everything. The plan was back on: she would still need to get into the cabinet—now more than ever. Whether Odalinde found out that she'd been snooping was less of a concern now that Gretel had probable cause; but at the same time, it was perhaps even more important to be discreet, and she revisited her plan, mentally tweaking the details. Hansel. A diversion.

After a few more moments, Gretel walked back to the tarp where her brother sat cross-legged, his face scrunched in his palms and his elbows propped on his knees. She stared at him a moment and detected a sadness in the boy that she hadn't noticed before. "Are you okay, Han?"

The boy looked up at his sister and sighed, catching her eyes for just a moment before looking away.

"What's the matter? Are you upset about the book? This is good, Han. I'm just excited to know what it's about, that's all. It doesn't mean that Odalinde is bad. I mean, it *is* strange that she has the same book that Deda had, but that doesn't necessarily mean anything. It could just be a coincidence."

"There's more, Gretel."

Gretel's face twisted into confusion. "More what? You said you didn't know what the book said."

"I'm not talking about the book." With that Hansel met his sister's stare and held it. "I'm talking about the bag."

The bag. Odalinde's bag! It was the main reason Gretel wanted to get into the cupboard in the first place, and now she had completely forgotten about it. She'd gotten so excited—elated—about the book she'd forgotten there was anything else in the cabinet and assumed the book was all Hansel would have cared about as well.

Gretel sat down next to her brother slowly, mimicking his Indian-style posture, and scooted close to him, resting her hands in her lap. She saw the seriousness about him and wanted to offset it by assuming a relaxed manner.

"What did you find in the bag, Hansel?"

Hansel looked down into his own lap and then looked over at his sister. "I found another book, a smaller one, with names and stuff on it. Like a phone book, but one you write your own numbers and names in."

Some type of organizer, Gretel got it. "And did you see a name in there that you knew?" she asked.

Hansel nodded.

Gretel waited for it, deciding to let her brother reveal the name without any further questions.

"There were lots of names on the pages in the book, and I didn't know any of them at first. Why would I, right?"

"Right."

"But then I was closing it, to put it back in the bag and be done with it, and I saw a name written on the inside cover, down at the bottom."

Hansel stared warily at Gretel, preparing her for the name.

"Officer Stenson, Gretel, that officer from The System who came out here."

"What?" Gretel's reply was a reflexive whisper, her mouth lingering wide, her eyes alert. Clearly not a name she was expecting.

Hansel nodded in confirmation. "I saw it written there, Gretel, with no first name either, just Officer Stenson. And there was a phone number next to it."

Hansel paused as his sister digested this latest morsel.

"I guess it could be another Officer Stenson, but I don't think it is."

Gretel didn't think so either. It wasn't impossible, of course, but neither was a spaceship landing on the roof of their house.

She conjured the image of Officer Stenson now in her mind—not the breezy, affable man she'd first met at the door, but the cold-mannered lawman that walked out of it, so completely unaffected by her father's demeanor and subtle threats. Amused by them almost.

And she also recalled Petr's words that day as she stood on the porch watching the boy walk away admonished: *I don't think he's here to help you.*

"Why do you think Odalinde has Officer Stenson's name in her book, Gretel?"

Snapped from her reverie, Gretel stood quickly, giving the indication that it was time to leave. "I don't know, Hansel, I haven't one clue," she said absently.

"Are you going to ask her?"

"No!" Gretel replied sharply, "and neither are you!" For the moment, Gretel was done with any fragile emotions still brewing in her brother. "Let's go."

Hansel helped Gretel fold up the tarp and they carried it back to the canoe before pushing the boat back into the water and paddling away from Rifle Field. It was the last time Hansel would ever set foot on that particular piece of land.

Gretel was quiet until they reached the shoreline of their property. "Hansel," she said finally, "I'm going to need your help."

GRETEL STOOD WITH HER hands stuffed in her pockets, the key on the tips of her fingers, and watched casually as Odalinde scurried about the kitchen, double-checking that she had all her things in order before her mysterious Thursday excursion. It was just as Hansel said: she was leaving for the evening, and the urgency of the woman's movements led Gretel to believe that the outing was not unimportant. She was shallow-breathed and fidgety, all the time having a whispered dialogue with herself as she glanced at the clock about every thirty seconds.

It was strange to see her in such a fuss, her default demeanor being one of such weariness and indifference, and Gretel played mentally with the possibilities. A lover was certainly not unreasonable—perhaps she had a standing tryst with some young ram from town, a weekly roll in the field to satisfy nature's insistence. Maybe it was even Officer Stenson who was on the receiving end.

But if that were the routine, Gretel would have expected Odalinde to be a bit more adorned than she was at the moment. She wasn't an ugly woman by any stretch—in fact Gretel thought she had the natural makings to be rather pretty—but there was a vacant, weathered look to her, and she always wore her hair and face with such plainness. And since her arrival, her wardrobe had gradually descended into outright sloppiness, with tonight being no exception. There was little to distinguish her appearance from any regular day around the house, her clothes wrinkled and large on her frame and her hair and face in need of washing.

The other possibility Gretel played with was that Odalinde was off to meet her lawyer or accountant, or perhaps some business-minded partner who would aid her in snatching the Morgan farm out from under the shoes of its familial heirs—namely Gretel and Hansel. It certainly fit with the impression Gretel had of Odalinde as cold and ruthless.

But that fantasy didn't quite make sense either. Odalinde and her father were engaged after all, and once they were married, the farm would essentially be Odalinde's anyway. And after father died, which he most certainly would before Odalinde, she would have full authority and ownership of the property. Why would she risk all the fighting and legal tanglings for something that would more or less belong to her in a matter of months?

But then again, patience didn't appear to be Odalinde's most renowned characteristic, and the more Gretel considered conspiracy as the back story behind her rendezvous, the more it felt like the truth.

The whole business of staging a diversion to steal the key from the satchel was far easier than Gretel had imagined, and all the planning she and Hansel had done for that purpose now seemed laughable. Odalinde had been so anxious and intent on leaving for the evening, that Hansel's scream from the bathroom, and the subsequent appearance of a two-foot garter snake in the tub, was more than enough to engage her long enough for Gretel to raid the bag and secure the key.

The only real issue had been the timing: Hansel had to be sure that Odalinde had already taken the bag from the cabinet before sounding his alarm, and Gretel had to be out of the room when it happened, since it was unlikely the woman would have left her alone with it.

But in the end it had all been synchronized perfectly, and by the time Hansel and Odalinde finally wrangled the reptile and secured it in an old hat box, Gretel had the key at the bottom of her pocket and was back outside watering the flowers.

"Will you be gone long?" Gretel asked.

Odalinde gave a measured look toward Gretel and held her eyes, all the time continuing with the details of her departure.

"I only ask because I'm usually not here at this time and I wanted to know if there is anything I need to do for Father while you're away. Medications and such."

"He's fine," Odalinde replied flatly, dropping her gaze and focusing it on Hansel, "and your brother knows what to do if he has any pain."

Gretel noted that Odalinde hadn't answered her original question and decided not to arouse further suspicion by pushing it. She'd really only asked because she thought it might appear suspicious if she took *no* interest in Odalinde's outing, being that Gretel had yet to see the woman ever leave the house for any reason other than to shop. Besides, Hansel said she was usually gone for several hours, and Gretel figured that if the answers she sought were to be found in the cabinet, she'd need less than a half hour or so to discover the real story of why the nurse had invaded her family.

"Have you and father set a date yet?" Gretel asked, silently cursing herself immediately after for continuing to engage Odalinde. It was in her own best interest to let the woman get on with her evening, but Gretel couldn't help herself. Her displeasure and suspicions about the marriage had been on full display over the past week, and she rarely missed an opportunity to highlight them with a snide remark or probing question. In this case, the question was innocent enough, but the suggestion of accusation was unmistakable.

"We've got a few in mind," Odalinde replied tersely, "I'll be sure to let you know the moment we decide."

The quick smile on Odalinde's lips was contrasted by the uneasiness in her eyes, and Gretel grinned, proud at the jab she'd landed.

Gretel stood tall in the kitchen and watched her stepmother-to-be glance at the clock one last time and then shoot a reflexive peek at her before leaving without another word. Just to be sure, Gretel loped to the bedroom window and watched the truck drive off. She was taking no chances.

Once the old Morgan truck was out of sight, Gretel immediately raced to the kitchen and found Hansel waiting eagerly next to the cabinet.

She had some concern that her brother's feet would get cold about what they were doing, that he would feel he was somehow betraying Odalinde and would then be saddled with this secret throughout his childhood. But his posture and expression indicated only that he was ready to get on with it.

Gretel fished the key from her pocket and kneeled in front of the forbidden cabinet. She slid the key gently into the lock and turned it clockwise. The click of the latch sounded refreshing in her ears, and she looked up at Hansel and flicked her eyebrows conspiratorially.

The light from the kitchen flooded the inside of the cabinet and Gretel saw instantly that it did not contain anything resembling the bulky tome that was *Orphism*. In fact, the cabinet was empty except for a small address book, presumably the one described by her brother.

Hansel stood behind Gretel, his head nearly resting on her shoulder, and he became immediately defensive by the book's absence. "It's not there!" he cried. "It's not there! But it was! I swear!"

"Of course it was," Gretel replied, "I believe you. She obviously moved it." Gretel couldn't hide her disappointment, and even though it obviously wasn't Hansel's fault the book was gone, she was annoyed at him.

"It was there."

Gretel had to bite her lip to keep from snapping at her brother to forget it and was glad when he didn't add on further to his deflated words. Besides, all was not lost. There was still the address book. It wouldn't be the Rosetta Stone to *Orphism* she was hoping for, but it might answer some questions about Odalinde and her business there.

Gretel's first observation about the book was that, though apparently well-traveled, it was rather new, certainly newer than she had imagined. Gretel had envisioned something more exotic—a homemade piece with a leather jacket and filled with parchment paper perhaps—something more closely resembling her *Orphism* book. But this book was ordinary, cheap, the type found in any dime store.

She flipped through the thin pages and found nearly every line filled with names, with only a few blank pages scattered throughout. She stopped randomly on several of the pages and scanned them, looking for any name that she recognized, but found none. There were, of course, several familiar names, but they were common surnames and no matches with first names that she could see.

Gretel finally dropped the wad of pages to the back cover and stared at the name "Stenson" on the inside of the front cover, just as Hansel had said. But it wasn't *exactly* as Hansel had said. There was the name 'Stenson,' and there was also a phone number, but instead of the word *Officer*, only an 'O' was written. It was understandable her brother would have made that connection, but it was possible there were other possibilities.

"Hansel, get me a piece of paper."

"For what?"

"Just do it! Hurry!"

Hansel fetched a small leaf of notepaper from the porch and handed it to Gretel, who checked twice the phone number of *O. Stenson* and then transcribed it to the sheet. She flipped through the organizer one last time and then placed it back in its exact location in the cabinet, checking one last time to see if, perhaps, *Orphism* had magically appeared in the meantime, which, of course, it hadn't. She then locked the cabinet and stuffed the key back in her pocket where it would rest until later in the evening when it would reappear for the presumably more difficult trick of being returned to Odalinde's bag.

But this first task was done. Easy enough. Gretel wasn't completely satisfied, of course since she still couldn't decipher her book, but something about seeing the inside of the cabinet and the seeming innocuousness of it made her feel better.

"Gretel?"

Gretel let out a yelp and snapped her head toward the deep rasp that blasted through the kitchen. It was Father, standing hunched in disbelief at the threshold.

"What in God's name are you doing?"

Gretel was silent and looked to her brother, as if he alone held the answer to their father's question. But Hansel only looked to the floor.

"Answer me, Gretel. What are you doing?"

Gretel closed the cabinet door and locked it, and then rose to her feet, locking eyes with her father, trying to gauge his anger and lucidity; but his face implied only a jumble of emotions which resulted in something closest to confusion.

He wasn't right—still—after all these weeks of convalescence from a common spleen injury—a serious injury to be sure, but certainly not one which normally resulted in such lethargy and feebleness. He looked as old and disoriented as the days following his collapse, as if he were healing from a stroke or some other brain trauma. Something was perverse about her father's recovery, and the lingering doubts that Gretel had about Odalinde's culpability in the matter were now erased.

"Nothing father," Gretel replied, "Odalinde let me borrow her book and I'm just returning it to her. Go back to bed."

"How did you get into that cabinet? You shouldn't be in there. I prepared that space for Odalinde, and you and your brother were never to go in there."

Her father's voice was low and weary, but far from calm, and Gretel saw that patronization wasn't going to work with him.

"I'm suspicious of her, father, and you should be too. Aren't you at all curious as to why you aren't getting better? You should be back working by now. Or at least not spending your entire day in bed. What's wrong with you?"

"I'm getting better," Heinrich Morgan replied, and then looked at the floor, unconvinced of his own words.

"You're not! And every time I mention it to Odalinde she says, 'All he needs is more rest.' Well, rest isn't making you better, and I've got money now. I'll take you into the city. Tomorrow. We'll have real doctors examine you. Good doctors that can run tests and..."

"No!" her father interrupted, "No more doctors, Gretel. Heinrich Morgan closed his eyes and took a deep breath, and then reached for the wall to crutch his stance. When he finally spoke again, his voice was barely more than a whisper. "You can't go into her cabinet, Gretel," he said. "You just can't." He paused again, as if he'd momentarily fallen asleep, and then said, "And that goes for you too." He nodded toward Hansel, his eyes still closed, and then turned and staggered back to his bedroom.

Gretel's anger at her father's weakness and her amplified hatred for Odalinde combined to brew the beginning stages of tears and fury, but she contained her emotions. It was a skill she hadn't yet mastered, but one she'd been working on daily.

In truth, she wanted nothing more than to run down to her boat and shove off into the lake and row for hours, sweating off the frustrations of her home while building her muscles in preparation for some impending showdown. Perhaps she would even dock at Rifle Field and spend the rest of the evening on her back staring at the stars, developing her strategy for making her life right again.

But none of that would be possible tonight. There was still the matter of returning the key, an operation that would require two people, and one that, even if it could be done alone, was too serious to delegate to someone as young and vulnerable as Hansel. Besides, Gretel would need to talk to her brother about what had just occurred with their father, assure him that although he was still sick, he would get better at some point, soon probably, and that he still loved them. And that he would keep to himself what he saw in the kitchen. Gretel couldn't really be sure that any of these things were true, of course, but reassurances like these were required of her now, and she accepted this responsibility with less reluctance as each day passed.

It was after ten o'clock when Odalinde finally returned, and though Gretel would normally have been sleeping at such an hour, especially on a school night, she was instead sitting at the kitchen table when the nurse walked in. Odalinde gave Gretel a curious look and grumbled her name in weary acknowledgment. Gretel saw this as a good sign that she was none the wiser about the key missing from her bag.

Now for the tricky part.

"Odalinde," Gretel said, rising from the chair, her eyes fixed on the woman, "I have something to show you. I realize it may upset you, and if it does, I would just like to say that I'm sorry in advance."

Now Odalinde's attention was rapt on Gretel, and she followed the girl's hands as she brought the figurine from behind her back into the light of the kitchen.

"I'm not quite sure how it happened, but..."

As if the script had been rehearsed for weeks, Odalinde placed her bag on the floor and took the porcelain swan from Gretel, cradling it delicately and holding it up to the light.

"What is it?" she asked rhetorically, without any of the alarm in her voice Gretel had expected.

Odalinde turned the fragile piece over gently with her fingers, squinting desperately to find the flaw, and as she examined the piece, Hansel appeared silently behind her, stooped with assassin-like grace, and nestled the cabinet's key down into the bottom of her canvas bag.

Gretel shifted her eyes to Hansel's squirrel-like movements, gave a slight grin, and then focused back on Odalinde and the figurine. It had, in fact, been Hansel's idea to use the swan as a diversion, and only to pretend that it had been broken, as opposed to actually breaking it, which had been Gretel's suggestion. Frankly, Gretel had barely noticed the figurine's appearance on the mantel, though apparently it had been there since the day Odalinde arrived; that the piece was important to Odalinde, Gretel hadn't the slightest idea. Whether it had any real value Gretel wasn't sure either, but Hansel insisted she cherished it, and had witnessed her take special care in cleaning it, even speaking to it on occasion when she was in one of her more airy, carefree moods.

"I knocked it to its side while dusting this evening," Gretel lied. "I'm sorry, but I think I've cracked it. Just there." Gretel pointed to the base of the swan's neck, placing her fingernail in a thin crevice at the point where the wing joined with the gray collar of the bird.

"There?" Odalinde squinted her eyes tighter.

"Yes. There, at the neck."

"That's no crack, silly girl! Those are its feathers, separated on the wing!"

Gretel took a deep breath and smiled, feigning relief, though in fact the smile reflected pride in her performance.

"Thank goodness!" she said, "I've never seen the figure close up before. I really thought I'd cracked it."

"Perhaps you should leave the dusting to me from now on." Odalinde sighed and walked the figurine back to the mantel and placed it in its proper spot, noting the dirty mantel. "Been dusting have you?"

"Yes, well..." Gretel snorted a laugh, "as you say, I should probably leave that to you."

With tragedy averted, Odalinde's fatigue returned, and she slinked back to the kitchen and grabbed her bag from the floor, fishing the key from the bottom. Gretel watched anxiously as the woman opened the cabinet door and went through her routine of restocking the space. But instead of simply shoving the bag in and locking the door as Gretel had seen her do dozens of times, Odalinde paused, suddenly, as if noticing something slightly off. It was only for an instant, the pause, and there was no suspicious glance back toward the kitchen, but that she paused was without doubt. Did she know? How could she know? Gretel had put the book back exactly as it had been. And there was nothing else in the cabinet to be moved.

At last, Odalinde closed the door and locked it, keeping the key in her clenched fist, and she walked slowly back to her bedroom. She opened the door, and just before she entered she turned to Gretel. "Gretel," she said stoically, "if you have any interest in my things, please don't be afraid to ask."

CHAPTER TEN

THE CONCOCTION WAS coming along, but slower than the woman would have liked. The extractions proved painstaking—much more difficult than she'd remembered—and required every bit of the training she'd received in the Old Country. She had the book of course, which gave every detail of the procedures, but she still had to be precise with every slice and suture. No amount of instruction could correct for a shaky hand or poor intuition. Acquiring fluids from such delicate organs without killing was difficult, and the woman, to say the least, was rusty.

But she remained focused and disciplined, methodical with every incision and took only what was absolutely safe to keep the Source alive. The Source would die in the end, of course; once the liver was removed and the bile taken there was no chance of survival, but all the acids had to be just so, and that meant she would have to eat the pies for another week or so. If the Source was slaughtered too early, everything would be lost. It was always better to wait too long.

The woman re-read the instruction from the book that rested on the tray, and added the precise number of drops to the mixture, stirring slowly as she did so, folding the red liquid into the mash with a thin piece of flat steel she called a 'Fin', a tool she'd designed long ago for just this purpose. She was careful not to over-mix, and used a wooden spatula to gently scrape the excess potion from the Fin, sliding the utensils back and forth against each other until all the mixture was off. None of it could be spared.

Once properly combined, the woman placed a glass covering over the bowl and then draped a white cloth on top of the glass. It didn't need to be kept airtight, but the mixture couldn't afford the additions of dust or large insects either. Or, God forbid, mice. The white cloth prevented her from having to look at the vile broth all day.

A dull scream bellowed from the back room, signaling to the woman it was time for the evening feeding. She'd been expecting it would come soon. She'd learned by now to differentiate between the screams of sleep and those of confusion and fear, but either way they affected the woman's nerves little more than a clock striking on the hour.

The 'real' screams did mean, however, that the drug was beginning to wear off, and it was important the Source was kept as tranquil and unruffled as possible. The woman was convinced that adrenaline and hormones affected the potency of the mixture, more so even than the drug itself.

She filled a small cup with water and dropped in a pinch of the powder from the saucer next to the stove. She placed the cup on the feeding tray, which she'd already loaded with two small pies, and then walked with them back toward the bedroom where her victim lay chained. She opened the door quickly and entered, and was immediately hit with the smell of fresh urine. Again. An irritating side effect of the drug. She could only hope the Source had found the pot this time, as she was getting tired of cleaning and replacing the sheets. But that was just another part of it: she also couldn't risk the Source being defiled from lying around in her own piss all day.

"Breakfast," the woman said coldly, not looking up.

The Source groaned and attempted to talk, instead only managing garbled nonsense. The drug made intelligible speech virtually impossible, since one of its functions was to boggle the part of the brain controlling syntax and tenses. It was amusing at first, the blathering, but now it just frustrated and annoyed the old woman, and she had wasted too much time already trying to elicit meaning from the subconscious ramblings. 'Hansel' and 'Gretel' came up a lot—no doubt the names of the Source's children—but the other words and names always stopped short of significance. Except for one.

It was tempting for the witch, living in such isolation, to ease up on the drug and allow some sort of dialogue with the girl, but the old woman knew nothing good would come of it. It wasn't that she feared feeling sympathy for the girl—she'd long since shed the ability for that emotion—but she was old, and she wasn't foolish enough to think she was incapable of being tricked by a mind more nimble than her own. She didn't know if this creature had such a mind—in fact, she doubted it—but there was no point in taking chances.

It had been months since the young gift lying before her had appeared, miraculously, as if fused from air and earth, a flower planted in the wood waiting to be plucked and drained of its nectar. Life had responded to her on that horrifying morning, almost instantly. Now it was her task to complete the work.

And that task would need to be completed soon. That morning on the stoop, when 'death' had been so close, had turned out to be nothing more than a bout of withdrawal, and it was only the hope and anticipation of a continued long life—and a new focus—that had seen her through it. But hope alone wasn't enough, and death would eventually come. She was tiring again, and she would need to drink soon.

The old woman rolled her eyes at the girl's garbled words and placed the tray on the end table, harder than she'd intended, almost spilling some of the powdered water.

The Source had figured out almost immediately after her capture that it was the water which was tainted, and at first had refused to drink it. But the slightest singe of a hot nail just below her left eye, along with the promise that the next time she refused it the nail would go an inch higher, had quickly reversed her resistance. There had been no 'next time.' The stress wasn't good for the hormones, of course, but a necessary evil to establish the rules.

"You're to drink first, then you eat."

The woman grabbed the chamber pot—which was full—and opened the door to leave.

"Tonight I'll take more," she said and slammed the door behind her.

ANIKA WATCHED THE WOMAN leave through a cloud, and then registered the slam of both the bedroom and front doors. Two doors closing, she was positive.

The drug or poison or whatever it was, was wearing off, but it still lingered, and she had to be definitive in her thought process. The woman had left her room and then the house. That made sense. That had been her usual routine just after bringing the meals.

Anika figured out months ago that it was almost always the water that was drugged, but she also suspected it may sometimes have been the food as well, and as she lay staring at the knots of wood in the beams above her, she decided there would be no drinking tonight. She would have to eat—there was no real way to hide the food—but water was something else. She was banking it was in the water this time, and she needed to sober up.

In the beginning, the woman had sat like a barn owl from the vanity bench, ensuring Anika drank every drop of water and ate every crumb of pie. But it had been weeks since she'd last waited in the room for Anika to finish a meal, and after the tattoo had been branded on Anika's face, she hadn't needed to. The scar beneath her left eye and the memory of the pain kept Anika obedient to the regiment.

But Anika could sense the time left was short. Any day—any moment—could be her last. Something had to change. Soon.

As she recalled, her shackles were last removed only days ago after she'd wet the bed, but Anika was barely conscious at the time and had only a foggy memory of it now. She had a drowsy recollection of sitting against the wall naked, rubbing her legs with a wet cloth as the old witch changed the bed covers. But she couldn't remember changing into the clothes she now wore, and probably wouldn't have remembered the episode at all if it hadn't been for the hag's screaming. She assumed the scolding was directed toward her, but it didn't register that way at the time. In fact, Anika vaguely remembered laughing, which meant she was at the apex of the drug's effects.

But Anika swore the next time the shackles came off the scene would be very different.

Anika glanced over at the tray beside her and the waft of plum hit her immediately. The smell disgusted her. All the pies disgusted her now. She wasn't sure if it was a reaction to the drugs or what the food now represented—or perhaps the recipe for the pies she found so delicious in the beginning had changed—but her stomach now immediately lurched even at the sight of them. The ones with meat were the worst. She ate them, she had no choice, but Anika promised herself if she was still alive at the end of this ordeal, she would never again eat another piece of pie.

She scooted to the end of the bed, threw the chain over the post, and pushed herself over the foot and onto the floor. Her legs wobbled a bit, but she steadied them quickly. They were getting stronger, at least compared to a month ago.

Anika stood still for a moment, feeling her muscles adjust to standing and focused her mind again. She took a deep breath and bowed her back, forcing her legs and spine to stretch as far as they would go. The cracking of joints and tendons reverberated through the room, adding to the exhilaration of the maneuver.

Following that first day on the floor, when the old woman had caught Anika testing the room for weaknesses—and told Anika about her morbid intentions—Anika was reluctant to leave the bed; and, in fact, she had not gotten out of it for several weeks. But her body's craving for motion had eventually won out over her fear, and she now got up at least three times a week. Sometimes for only a minute of two, but usually closer to an hour.

The movements were a blessing and seemed to be making her stronger, though with the shackle on her ankle she was mostly limited to stretching and isometrics. And, of course, Anika did this only when she was certain the woman was gone, though truthfully she began to doubt the necessity of that. On the one other occasion, the woman had caught her up and about she had only given Anika a mild scolding. Anika reasoned the woman needed her to stay healthy, and healthy did not include atrophied muscles and bed sores. But still, she didn't want to push it.

The other thing Anika figured was that the woman meant to eat her.

She had never told her this explicitly, but the fact that she considered Anika an animal to be slaughtered was as obvious a clue as one could expect to gather. As was the constant supply of pies. Too much food was better than starving, Anika supposed, and she couldn't have cared less about her appearance, but Anika could feel herself getting fat, particularly in her legs and feet, though she probably singled out those extremities because those were the parts of her anatomy she was forced to stare at most of the day. She wasn't anywhere near obese, but she was significantly heavier than the day she arrived. She labeled this fact as bad, since she needed to maintain some level of fitness on the off chance a window of escape opened. At this point, knee bends and back stretches weren't keeping her weight down, and she felt a lot like a turkey the week before Thanksgiving. And unless she did something soon, she'd end up like one.

Anika laced her fingers together and raised her arms over her head, pressing her palms toward the ceiling. She raised herself up on her toes and lowered her head with her eyes closed, holding that position for as long as she could.

When she opened her eyes, she saw a red patch of gauze attached to her gut and blood pouring down her side. Another incision. By her count, that made a total of five that she could see, and she was almost certain there were at least three on her back, near her spine between her shoulder blades. This one was fresh though—from when she couldn't say for sure—but it was probably from early this morning. The drugs had hit her hard this time and now she knew why: they'd been dosed up to serve the purpose of both anesthetic and pacifier. Anika recognized the feeling from the other times.

The patch of gauze was about the size of a cracker and was taped to the side of her abdomen just below her ribcage. It was bright red, but not entirely soaked through, which meant the sutures had probably just opened during her stretches. Quickly Anika climbed back on the bed and, on her back, gently pushed her way back toward the head next to the night table. She had to stop the bleeding before the woman returned. If there was one thing Anika had learned about the woman since her capture, it was that she disliked instability. On the occasions that she had lost her temper, either with Anika or otherwise, it stemmed from things not working out just as she'd planned. Anika ruminated that this was probably the source of most anger in the world, but a deranged person's anger was a bit more to deal with.

Anika picked up the napkin from the tray—the old witch usually forgot to include it, but not today—and dipped it in the water. Looking at the glass, Anika now realized if she didn't drink the water the unnoticed cut on her belly would be all too noticeable to her in a few hours when the anesthesia wore off. Hopefully, she thought, the stuff works as a local anesthetic as well.

She reclined slightly and then placed the wet napkin on the incision, wiping away the excess blood. The cut was relatively small, about three inches she guessed, and the stitchwork looked precise. She'd need to be more careful with her stretching.

Anika sat up and reached to dip the napkin again, but this time froze, her eyes locking in on the large black book lying next to the pies. She'd completely missed it before. Even now, as she focused on the form, it looked more like the shadow of a book than an actual book, and she considered the drugs may still be working their charms.

To be sure what she was seeing was real, she reached over and touched the tome, feeling the dull, cold leather. Certainly real.

She turned the tray toward her, hoping to get a better look at the cover, but whatever words or symbols may have been etched during the original printing had long since faded. She had to restrain herself from instantly picking up the book and opening it. The woman may be back any minute, and who knew what the punishment would be for snooping. And there remained the more urgent matter of her cut.

Still, this seemed like some form of an opportunity, if not for an escape, then at least to gather information which could help her.

Anika moved the pies from the tray to the night table and as she did, spotted a thin piece of straw sticking from the top of the book. A bookmark. She wedged a finger between the pages on either side of the straw and pulled the book open, gravity thumping the weight of the first three-quarters of the book down to the tray, nearly spilling the glass of water. Anika clenched her teeth and whispered a curse.

She stared wide-eyed at the pages and instantly saw that the writing was foreign to her—Greek perhaps—and that the surrounding margins were littered with handwritten notes. In fact, she noted, all of the white space was taken up with pencil and pen marks, including above and below the type. The space between the lines was wide, so the letters were perfectly legible, and as Anika studied the text further, she saw this writing was in English. Cursive, sloppy, and grammatically atrocious, but definitely English. In some instances there were just single words, often capitalized and underlined or with exclamation points. But most of the words seemed to be a translation of the text and not the aimless writings of a lunatic. And as Anika continued to read, she now realized one thing was certain: there wasn't much time left.

CHAPTER ELEVEN

GRETEL'S FIRST WEEK back at the orchard was bittersweet; she was happy to be with the Klahrs again, working and feeling productive, but there was an anxiety that nagged, lingering in her belly, reminding her that things at home were tenuous and unresolved. That her father may be dying. Perhaps being murdered slowly.

She thought of Hansel almost constantly, imagining the unbearable guilt she would forever live with if anything happened to him. There hadn't been any further mention from Odalinde concerning the swan figurine, and apparently father had kept the cabinet breach a secret, but Gretel perceived a difference in Odalinde since that night in the kitchen, a new sort of quietness that implied restraint and plotting.

Still though, it was nice to be back at work, and compared to the madness of the weeks during the harvest, Gretel had it easy. All of the workers were gone, having migrated to further corners of the region where various other crops were about to be born, so Gretel's work mainly consisted of cleaning the Klahr house to the point of sterilization, dividing the newly picked fruit for their various uses, and helping prepare the meals for Mr. and Mrs. Klahr.

Petr was staying on for a few weeks more, but apparently would only be making appearances on Fridays, as well as the weekends. So in addition to not being particularly busy, Gretel's first week back was also quite lonely.

But she worked hard and tried to stay occupied, and Mrs. Klahr, bless her heart, seemed to make the point regularly to Gretel that her presence was critical to keeping the Klahrs out of the graveyard and the house from crumbling to splinters. Still, she wasn't used to the downtime and boredom that filled much of her day, so when Friday finally came and Gretel saw Petr standing on the bank of the orchard as she eased her canoe to the shore, she couldn't help but smile and wave. She was instantly embarrassed by the act, of course, and was still blushing when she walked up to the boy, who himself wore the look of giddy unease.

She'd barely spoken to Petr since that day in the Klahr kitchen—she'd been so focused on her work and the harvest—but she had always been keenly aware of his presence at the house and felt a nervous comfort whenever he smiled at her or offered to help with a chore, only to be told "No, thank you" in a way that implied everything was exceedingly simple to Gretel and in her complete control.

Now, though, having spent a mostly restful week away from the orchard and returning to find the feverish regimen of the place substituted with an almost placid routine of thorough maintenance, Gretel regarded Petr as an old friend, a domestic soldier like herself, who'd fought beside her in some recent battle and now waited for her in the clearing dust.

"You're here early," Gretel said, arching her eyebrows to show she was mildly impressed.

"I got in last night. Something came up and it was the only time my father could drop me off."

Gretel nodded, still smiling, and stared at Petr, measuring him, until finally he looked away, embarrassed.

It was strange. As beautiful as Petr was physically, Gretel was not at all intimidated by him. Of course, she didn't really know him well, so there was still a certain self-consciousness she felt around him; but whenever they met, within a minute or two she always felt like she had the upper-hand. Even on that first night in her kitchen, when she first collided with those sky blue eyes and dark curls, she had been more stunned by his looks than threatened by them. Not that she normally came unhinged in front of boys anyway, but she would have thought a boy like Petr would have made her far more uncomfortable than he did.

"It's good to see you, Gretel."

Gretel's smile widened with this brave revelation, as if she was proud of Petr for his boldness, and she let out a good-natured laugh. "It's good to see you too, Petr. Are the Klahrs awake?"

Gretel and Petr split the chores evenly that day, with Petr taking on most of the outdoor duties and Gretel minding the interior of the house. But by Saturday, the two children decided the work could be done in the same amount of time if they tackled the tasks together, and they would enjoy the added pleasure of companionship. Mrs. Klahr met this suggestion with a thin smile, and then an exaggerated nod signifying the resourcefulness of the idea. Petr and Gretel both knew what she was thinking—that love was blooming or some such thing—but they initiated no corrections to this assumption, as they were both just happy to have a friend to work with and conversation to fill the day.

And if love blossomed, that was fine too.

"What do you do on your days off?" Petr lifted a full bucket of pears onto the flatbed of the Klahrs' truck, wiping the sweat from his forehead.

It was an unseasonably hot day for the Southlands, even for early summer, and though he'd only worked two full days that week, Gretel could see the boy was tired and looking forward to Sunday. Unlike Gretel, Petr technically had to work on Sundays, but the work was laughably light, and even he understood his pay for that day was mostly charity.

"I sleep mostly. And row. That's the bulk of it. The two things that keep me away from my...my father's nurse."

Petr stared at Gretel for a moment and then heaved another full bucket to the unhinged tailgate. "Is she cruel?" he asked bluntly. "Your father's nurse, that is."

Gretel glanced sideways at Petr, not really wanting to get into her home affairs. She liked Petr, and they seemed to have enough in common to become real friends, if not more, but her instincts told her it was too early to fully trust him. Especially with his father's name (maybe?) etched in Odalinde's address book.

"Maybe," she offered, "I'm not sure yet."

Petr nodded as if understanding not to push it further, and then changed the subject. "Well, I was thinking...if you...if you are going to be around tomorrow...I only work until noon, and my father won't pick me up until around four." The boy looked away and swallowed hard. "So I was wondering if you wanted to have lunch tomorrow. With me. A picnic maybe."

The corners of Gretel's mouth turned up slightly, reflexively, and she cocked her head in a move indicating both flattery and delight. "I...sure...I would love to."

"Okay! That's great! Do you want to meet somewhere here in the orchard?"

Gretel thought for a moment and then said, "Do you know Rifle Field?"

Petr shook his head.

Gretel was suddenly embarrassed for Petr, and realized she had just hijacked his plans by inserting Rifle Field into the date. "I'm sorry," she said, "it doesn't matter. The orchard is fine."

"No, it's okay. I'm not sold on the orchard. What's Rifle Field? It sounds great."

Gretel smiled and recognized a new sweetness in Petr. She saw a mature quality, one that just wanted happiness for the ones he cared about and didn't need to control the feeling or be credited for bringing it about.

"It's just on the other side of the cannery. From here you can only get there by boat. If you want I could pick you up and we could go there."

After the suggestion had left her mouth Gretel realized how forward she must have sounded, but she felt comfortable in the offer. "Or, again, the orchard's fine too. Wherever."

"No! No, it's fine. Rifle Field sounds perfect. I'd really like to see it."

"Okay then, I'll pick you up at noon."

CHAPTER TWELVE

ANIKA'S MIND SPUN AS she read the gruesome recipe in front of her, the matter-of-fact tone in which the steps and measurements were explained only adding to the horror.

She frantically began to investigate her incisions and scars more closely, desperately craning her neck over her shoulders, trying to figure out what had been taken already. And what surgeries were still to be performed. Surely she wouldn't survive these procedures much longer! Specifically the removal of her liver, which, apparently, judging by the bookmark and what she could decipher of the markings, could occur any day. Maybe this day. The woman had said she'd 'take more tonight,' and though Anika didn't get the sense that the 'more' she was referring to would be the death blow necessarily, she simply couldn't risk waiting any longer. Even if the woman 'only' tapped her spine for a few driblets of fluid, she could easily sever a nerve or crack a vertebra. And what good would survival be at that point? She had to get out of there today.

As Anika read further, she saw that the book also contained ingredients for the pies she'd been eating.

As she suspected, those pastries indeed seemed critical in making the final product (which is how Anika now thought of herself) and contained a bizarre assortment of things. Some of the ingredients hadn't been translated, and others Anika had never heard of, but even the sounds of them had a sinister quality. Goose Proventriculus. Aged Lynx Bladder. Baneberry. Not exactly the stuff of Christmas desserts, she thought. And where this crazy old woman even found such things or knew where to look for them, baffled Anika.

But really, what was the difference? The ingredients could have been candy canes and jellybeans for all it mattered. The planned conclusion was for

Anika to die, painfully, and if she wanted to thwart those plans, she had to move soon.

Anika closed the huge black book, poured the glass of water into the bedpan, and began on the pie.

As she ate, her thoughts surged with the idea that this was the last pie she would ever eat in her life, whether that life ended today or fifty years from now.

The taste of the thing was horrible, of course, but she took down every shard of crust and sludgy finger scoop of black saucy meat, using all her will to suppress her constant gags. As she finished and wiped her mouth and hands on the bed sheets in long streaks, Anika mentally finalized her plan.

The inside of the bowl was still slick and hard to hold, but she resisted cleaning it—when it dried it would become sticky and create the perfect grip. She placed the heavy ceramic bowl by her hip beneath the sheet and waited. The woman would be home by nightfall, Anika presumed. There was nothing left to do but wait.

THE OLD WOMAN HAD WAITED for just such a morning to make the journey. A cool day at the end of a long dry spell. It had been eleven days since the last rainfall, so the floor of the forest was well-parched and navigable. With her strength as it was, long morasses or wide creek beds would have been impassable. But on a day such as this, she felt confident about the trek. As long as she could find what she sought quickly.

Most of the signs that her Source traveled these parts only recently had long since eroded or been covered by leaves. But one clue had endured, miraculously, to quite literally light the way. A food wrapper, small and rectangular, used for enclosing something store-bought and processed. The casing was silver, highly reflective, and like a beacon it flashed just a glint as it caught a renegade ray of sun that had maneuvered past the canopy. It winked at the woman, beckoning. The woman considered it afterward and determined there must have been two hundred feet between her and the small discarded foil, but it had pointed the direction exactly, and without backtracking a step, the haggard woman found the abandoned car.

Life again delivering.

There were no signs that the car had been discovered by anything other than Northland fauna, but the old woman opened the passenger door warily anyway, as if suspecting a trap had been set. But if indeed they were responsible for sending her Source, certainly there'd be no point in trapping her. It was she who made the potion. Not them!

And there was no trap. Instead the door creaked lazily open, and the leaves which had perched between the door and the roof frame fell harmlessly to the ground. The woman stood back from the car and stared inside, searching.

There wasn't much, other than an empty mug and the balled remains of what appeared to be an old newspaper. Cars had certainly changed quite a bit since her last experience, but the compartment below the dash—the glove box they called it, for storing a driver's gloves in case the day was cold—remained.

She pulled the lever and dropped open the door of the small box, and was instantly greeted with a stack of papers, along with a set of miniature tools and a near-empty container of what appeared to be some type of lotion. The woman fished out the papers and shuffled through them, tossing those she found useless to the floor until she found what she was looking for: Anika Morgan's identification card.

Anika Aulwurm Morgan.

The Source had given her first and last name on that first day in the slaughter room, when she still held a small level of trust—and even gratitude—for the old woman. It was a common enough name, Morgan, and not one she could attach to him in any way.

But another name had emerged, six nights ago, in the fever of poison, during the woman's routine room inspection. The young Source had let slip the name *Aulwurm*. She'd said the name twice, groggily yet distinctly, but had attached it to no other name. The old woman had frozen at the sound of the word, and the tingle in her eardrums had cascaded down her back.

Aulwurm.

It was a name the old woman knew well: a surname that formed branches not far from her own on her family's tree.

And beyond just her recognition of the name, Aulwurm was unusually distinct. It was the maiden name of her grandmother and, as the old woman recalled, her Aulwurm uncles and aunts had taken great pride in the rarity of their name, claiming that it was born and existed in only a very segregated section of the Old World.

She'd heard the name only once since she'd been in the New Country—during that one night over a year ago when the men had come. Other than that time, over the centuries now that she'd been alive, the old woman couldn't remember ever hearing the name outside of her family. And certainly never in the New Country.

But just as the woman suspected, upon hearing the name ring from the lips of her Source only nights ago, Aulwurm was the middle part of Anika Morgan's full name—as it had been the middle name of her mother, no doubt—having been passed on through generations to all girls born to the family, by parents who wished to keep Old Country traditions and birthrights alive not only in their male offspring, but in the females as well. Certainly young Gretel's middle name was no different.

The moment she'd heard the name the woman wanted to wake her Source immediately, and use all her means to coerce the girl into revealing her family's full history. But since learning of her fate, the Source talked very little now and was explicitly silent on the issues of her personal life. She asked and answered only those questions that dealt with her most basic needs, and there was little doubt in the old woman's mind that her Source would die before exposing her children any further. She had considered torture again, another branding to the face perhaps, but she was too close now and didn't want to risk an infection so close to the end.

And besides, she wanted to explore for herself the truth of what happened. If indeed this was the Source of her dreams. If the memory was real. If the men had indeed come to her—in the flesh—and not in the dementia of her mind. She wanted to know if they *had* sent the girl—as her imagination dictated. She wanted to know if it was time for her to pay.

She recalled it all again: it was evening, cold, and the old man had sat relaxed in her kitchen, with the younger one beside him, anxious. The old one had explained how it would happen: there would be an accident, and a woman would be delivered to her. She would need to trust in the powers, allow them to guide her, but the Source would come to her, and she needed only take in the prey.

And then prepare it. Perform the blending which she had mastered.

How they had known of her cabin—or even her own existence—was a mystery to the woman, and she uttered not a word that night, feigning feebleness and madness, as well as a language barrier. It was the first men she had seen in ages, and she was terrified by the intrusion and aggressiveness, particularly of the older one, as well as the overall surprise of their arrival.

But the older one had been undeterred by the woman's condition, and he had simply laid out his plans—as well as his expectations—as she stood quivering, panicked, hunched by the window which overlooked the cabin porch.

And as quickly as they arrived they were gone; the sound of the departing car engine had roared in her head for days.

But then the weeks passed and the encounter faded, until soon the woman believed it hadn't happened at all, but was instead a dream, or one of her many fantasies she played out in the absence of intimacy. It was a strange fantasy to be sure, but so were many of them.

But then Aulwurm brought it back to reality.

This strange, surreal meeting *had* taken place, and now, as the old woman stood beneath the huge Northland trees breathing in the warm autumn air, the entire one-sided conversation flooded back to her, and she knew her time was even shorter than she thought.

CHAPTER THIRTEEN

GRETEL WAS ON THE LAKE by eight o'clock the next morning, which was two hours earlier than she'd been awake on a Sunday in as long as she could remember. Her lunch with Petr wasn't for several hours, and though she'd get some rowing in on her way to Rifle Field, the type of rowing she'd use for that excursion wasn't the effort Gretel was accustomed to on her day off. Sunday was her day of rigor on the lake, the day she sweated out those frustrations and grievances that couldn't be expressed through words or work. On some days the brutality of her catharsis was so severe that Gretel imagined any onlooker would think she was in the midst of some desperate escape, fleeing the bonds of slavery or the eager jaws of a crocodile, perhaps.

But to Gretel the feeling was nothing short of wonderful, and once she finally reached exhaustion, usually somewhere just beyond the last scattered stretch of the Klahr orchard, a substitute feeling of peacefulness slipped into her body, as if filling the gap left by her concerns. Gretel would drench herself in the feeling, at once studying and devouring it, always knowing on some level that she was experiencing the sensation of normalcy: the natural state of being where God had intended humans to dwell.

She dipped the blades of the oars into the water and gave a long exaggerated pull, propelling the boat forward down the middle of the narrow lake, closing her eyes to experience the full pleasure of the draft on the back of her neck. She repeated these long, slow strokes, gradually building up speed while stretching the muscles of her chest, shoulders and back. She focused on the strain of each tendon, visualizing as they stretched and contracted, slowly unloading the buildup of anxieties from the previous week.

And then the fury began.

Gretel thrust the shafts of the oars from bow to stern, pivoting them at breakneck speed on their fulcrums, the blades slashing the surface of the water in hypnotic ferocity. She puffed her cheeks with each exhalation, and focused the air back into her lungs with every breath, watching absently as the banks of her property diminished. She was two hundred yards or so when the film of sweat began to form on her cheeks and forehead, and the world of confusion and problems began to drift steadily away. How laughably easy it was, Gretel thought, to simply leave a situation, to simply turn away and run, or row, as the case was here. When she was home, chest-deep in the chaos and responsibility of what her life had become, constantly being forced to decide on this and argue her points on that, she seemed utterly trapped, hopelessly surrounded by walls so tall and thick they could never be scaled or penetrated. But from the distance of only a hundred yards or so, surrounded by the vastness of earth and water, the truth was uncovered. The walls were a mirage. Escaping her world was no more difficult than thrusting a rowboat down a lake and leaving, and then watching with cold detachment as her house and property faded around a bend. She could never *actually* leave it of course, there was too much at home that she loved and needed to see through, but if she really wanted to, if she could ever summon the boldness and courage, she was free to just keep going.

The other part of rowing that Gretel had grown to love was the utter blindness of it—that feeling of never being sure, not entirely, what lie in wait. Of course, after all these weeks, she now knew this lake as well as anyone on earth probably, but there was always that possibility that some unknown log or critter had surfaced just up ahead, or even that another boat, heading just as blindly in the opposite direction, was on course to collide with Gretel and plunge her unconscious into the water. And when those fears didn't satisfy her adventure, Gretel would create other fantasies: imagining hazarding some exotic river perhaps, all the time being watched by cannibals; or unknowingly bounding toward the shelf of some plunging waterfall.

She watched as the trees in the orchard began to diffuse, signaling the end of the Klahr property, and she summoned what remained of her reserves, ferociously clenching her jaws while ignoring the burn in her triceps and thighs. When her muscles had nothing left to serve, Gretel stopped abruptly and unleashed a scream that started deep in her belly and ended in a fit of hoarse, violent coughing. The burn in her chest was cold and harsh, but it lasted only a second or two, and her breathing steadied quickly.

Gretel flexed her biceps and stared down at them, rubbing them with her open palms, the sweat and oil accentuating their definition. She loved the thin, wiriness of her body now, and she figured she was at least as strong as any boy she knew her age, including Petr. She thought of her mother and how she would be in awe of Gretel if she could see her now. Gretel stared at the sky and thought of what that encounter might look like. Her mother would first hug her desperately, of course, but then she would push her to arms length and examine her, laughing incredulously at the transformation that had taken place in her daughter. Gretel looked at herself in a mirror everyday and couldn't believe the change; imagine what her mother would see!

Gretel turned the boat around and headed back for home, this time taking the long easy strokes one would normally expect to see from a Sunday morning oarsman. As she reached the plush, perfect lines of the orchard, she heard the sounds of light work from somewhere beyond the treeline. Petr, no doubt, passing the morning with busy-work.

Gretel was tempted to pull to the bank and visit, but it would only be a few hours before their lunch date, and even though she imagined Petr would be more than happy to see her beforehand, she didn't want to seem pushy. She liked the boy, he was friendly and funny, and certainly he was handsome enough, but she wasn't ready for the complexities she imagined would accompany having a boyfriend. And she wasn't even sure she liked him in that way. She had always remained fairly demure in his company, but she never felt that nervous, chest-gripping sensation that she'd had around a handful of boys in the past. Maybe she'd been hardened by the loss of her mother and the unnatural burden of taking care of her family, but Gretel felt instinctively it was more than that. It was him. It was Petr. She couldn't pinpoint the component exactly, but some chemical or current that naturally combined to form that swell of passion wasn't being properly received by her or transmitted by him. Maybe it was that ever-elusive component of trust, she thought, and figured this might be her lot with men for the rest of her life.

Gretel drifted into the bank behind her home and hopped out of the rowboat, pulling it up far enough onto the shore to keep it from floating away. She then turned and sprinted toward the house, burning off the last of the energy that remained in her from the morning.

As she reached the porch stairs leading to the front door, Gretel dropped her head in concentration, placing her feet on each step just right, so as not to tumble during her ascension. And as she reached the top of the steps, Gretel plowed the top of her head into the center of Odalinde's chest, barreling her over as a bull might do to an overconfident matador.

Gretel's first thought was that she had just run over Hansel, the force of the impact was so solid and the body had put up such little resistance, but when Gretel looked to see Odalinde on the ground at her feet, staring back at her with such astonishment and fear, Gretel couldn't hold back the grin on her face.

"What...Gretel watch where you're going!" There wasn't anger in Odalinde's voice; her tone was more instructive, as a mother teaching manners to her child.

Gretel's grin flattened, though it was hardly replaced with the look of concern. "I'm sorry. I didn't see you there."

"Well, I should hope you didn't see me! You could have killed me!"

"I think that's a bit of an exaggeration. Are you all right?" Gretel didn't wait for the reply as she stepped over the fallen woman and past the threshold into the house.

"It's not an exaggeration! What if I had been knocked down the stairs?" Odalinde asked rhetorically. There was a shrillness now to her voice that teetered on yelling, but it remained motherly, as if combating the petulance of a child. "You need to pay attention when..."

"I said I'm sorry!"

Gretel now stood back on the porch at the woman's feet, staring down at her as a fighter would to his fallen opponent. It was a posture of intimidation and warning.

Gretel waited for a response from the nurse and, receiving none, walked back into the house. She wiped the sweat from her face with a towel and poured herself a drink of water, and then began making the lunches for the picnic. She listened attentively for the opening of the truck door, signaling Odalinde was leaving, or else the sounds of her coming back into the house. Several minutes passed with no movement from the porch. Finally the front door creaked open and Gretel heard Odalinde walk slowly into the kitchen. Gretel didn't look up.

"Gretel?" Odalinde said softly, as if waking her from a nap.

Gretel looked up.

"I'm leaving for the market. I'll be home in an hour or so." Odalinde paused for a moment and looked down at the floor before raising her head again and making eye contact with Gretel.

"I'm sorry for my tone on the porch. It was an accident, I know that, and my screaming at you was uncalled for." She paused again. "While I was outside I was thinking, perhaps we could talk later. There are some important things—very important things—I've been wanting to tell you. You and Hansel. And I think now is the time."

Gretel looked at Odalinde suspiciously and then returned her attention to the picnic lunch. "I suppose that will be okay," she said casually, "but I'll be having lunch with a friend today, so I won't be home until this afternoon."

"A friend?

Gretel glanced at the nurse and dropped her eyes quickly, as she wrapped a loaf of bread in a damp towel. "Yes," she said, "a friend. You know, someone whose company you enjoy and they enjoy yours."

Odalinde didn't respond to the jab. "Is it that boy from the orchard?" she said flatly.

Gretel ignored the question. "As I said, Odalinde, I'll be back this afternoon."

Gretel placed the remaining items for the picnic into a shallow woven basket and left it on the counter by the door, and then walked toward her room to begin changing for lunch.

"If Hansel is around later, I'll be happy to participate in that wildly important talk."

"He's The System man's son, correct?"

Gretel stopped frozen in stride.

"That officer that was looking for your mother, right?"

"How do you know him?" Gretel whispered. "The System officer, how do you know him?"

Gretel had mentioned to her father that a new boy had come to work at the orchard and, as she now tried to recall, had perhaps even told Odalinde.

But she had never mentioned his name, and certainly had never told them that he was Officer Stenson's son. In fact, Gretel had never told either of them about that first night when Petr had come to the door for his father's binder. She had even kept it a secret from Hansel. She couldn't have said why exactly, but Petr's cryptic statement on the porch that night, as well her general instincts, impressed upon her to keep Petr in the shadows. After all, if she had remarked to her father that next morning that Officer Stenson's son had stopped by just after he'd gone to his room, and oh, by the way, implied that his father, whom Gretel's own father had bounced only minutes before, was less than genuine about his intentions to find their mother, that may have pushed her father over the edge. He may have even tried to find Officer Stenson, or filed a complaint to The System itself, which certainly wouldn't have improved the chances of finding her mother.

"I don't know him," Odalinde replied, "not really. But I did meet him. He stopped by one day when you were at school, not long after you began working at the orchard."

Gretel was floored by this revelation. "What did he want?" Her breathing was now frantic and labored. "Was there something found?"

"No, no, nothing like that. It was more of a courtesy visit, I suppose. He said his son worked at the orchard, just like you, and since he was in the area he wanted to see how all of you were getting on. He asked for you."

Gretel said nothing as she digested this news.

"He left his number with me and wanted you to call him if you felt up to it. I wrote it down. Stenson, I believe his name was. I wanted to tell you, I had every intention in fact, but your father forbade it."

"Did father talk to him?" Gretel asked.

"Your father was in a very bad state at that time. He had no idea the officer was even here."

"Well, what did he say? Was there any news at all on my mother? He had to have said something?"

Odalinde frowned and her look softened. "I'm sorry, Gretel, he didn't. He just wanted to know how you were getting on."

Gretel searched the room with her eyes, trying to place the meaning of this revelation.

Odalinde watched Gretel silently, until finally she said, "I should have told you sooner."

"Yes," Gretel replied, "you should have."

CHAPTER FOURTEEN

THE RUSTLING OF LEAVES snapped Anika to attention; despite focusing all of her will to stay awake, she'd drifted off to sleep.

But early on in her captivity the sounds of the forest nestled in her subconscious, and now, after...months (?)...she could detect the nuances distinguishing the crackle of the witch breaching the treeline and the sounds of a deer trepidatiously grazing outside her room.

The old whore was back. Finally.

The crunching steps quickly turned to clicks as the ancient monster reached the boardwalk and made her way toward the porch steps and front door. Anika's mind suddenly flooded with doubt. The woman would sense her plotting. Smell it maybe, or taste it on her tongue like a snake. If nothing else she would notice the bowl missing from the tray, or even see the bulge beneath the sheets. And then what?

Anika reached beneath the blanket for the bowl she'd stored next to her hip, but felt only linen. She felt lower, down to her thigh and past her knee, but still nothing. She spread her fingers wide and pressed the mattress around her frantically with both hands on either side of her legs. Where was it! She arched her back and felt under her torso. The sugars from the pie had cemented on her fingers and palms, and the sheets stuck to them as she hunted the bowl, making the search more difficult. The bowl was nowhere!

She sat up in fear and lifted the sheets over her head, hoping that the ceramic container had just rolled to a blind spot in her grasps, but she saw nothing.

She was now overcome with panic and her vision began to blur with tears. How could she have let it go? After having it in her grasp for so many hours! Waiting. Preparing.

Anika steadied her mind and made the rational assumption that the bowl had to be close. Perhaps it had rolled to her feet. Or off the bed. She slowly leaned her head over the side of the mattress, closing her eyes as she did so, sensing the importance of what she might see when she opened them: the bowl shattered on the floor would mean it was all over. It would mean she was to die in this room at the hands of a madwoman—this woman who intended to harvest Anika's body for some demented concoction. It would mean she had botched her last chance.

It meant she would never see her children again.

Anika opened her eyes and exhaled, seeing nothing other than the bedpan full of poisoned water. There was still a chance. For another day at least. For another plan to be formed. She couldn't give up now.

The door of the cabin closed with a gruesome thump, and the hurried steps of the witch marching toward the bedroom were immediate. There was no more time to look for the bowl.

Anika twisted her body into a sleeping posture, her back to the door, making one last fruitless search beneath her pillow in the process. She closed her eyes and prayed silently.

The bedroom door creaked open and Anika could sense the witch hesitate before slowly walking in. She listened carefully to the woman's steps, trying to gauge her location as she stalked the room surveying the scene. The woman had been gone for longer than she'd ever been before, and Anika could sense her uneasiness at what may have transpired in her leave. But other than the missing bowl, Anika was pretty sure she'd kept things as they were.

"Get up!"

The scream was deafening, and Anika's eyes shot open in panicked surprise.

"Get up now you filthy pig! This will not do! This will not do at all! Filthy, filthy pig!

Anika's mind erupted in terror, and tears filled her eyes as she braced herself for the weapon—perhaps the same one used to hunt her in the forest—to plow down upon her. The woman's rage certainly meant the end this time. She must have seen the bowl (and the book! Anika had forgotten about the book!) and was finally going to kill her.

"I leave you alone for only a few hours, a few hours longer than usual, and you...you scat yourself! Filthy pig! Get up. Get up now and get off the bed. I will not have you lying around in your own filth!"

At first Anika had no idea what the woman was screaming about, but as she turned to the woman and obediently started off the bed, she looked down at the sheets and saw the long brown streaks. The pie stains where she'd wiped her hands. The woman thought Anika had foregone the bed pan and defecated on the bed.

"Get up!" the woman shouted once again, this time hunching toward the bed in short quick steps, her eyebrows sloped at a cartoonishly angry angle.

Anika slowly but deftly scooted to the front of the bed and pushed herself off, almost catching her chain on the bedpost in the process. She should have still been groggy from the poison, incapable of such a move, but the woman made no sign of noticing, focusing instead on the mess of linen before her.

"There can be no impurities for the last step," the woman murmured to herself, carefully removing the pillows from the bed as she assessed exactly what she had in front of her. "It's almost ready. Almost ready and look at this filth!"

Anika stood statue-like, removed from the scene, watching the old hag lament as she began to strip the sheets. The words "almost ready" didn't sound promising.

The woman shuffled the wool blanket to the dusty floor and then snatched the top sheet from under the bed corners, gathering it into a ball and walking it back to the door.

And Anika saw it immediately, resting in the crease between the mattress and the wall.

The bowl.

With the woman's back still turned, and without thinking, Anika grabbed the ceramic hollow off the bed and shoved it beneath her gown, holding on to it through the fabric, trying to appear as casual as possible.

Did the woman notice the move? Or hear it? If she did, she didn't care, and without looking at Anika, the witch walked back to the bed, still grumbling about the mess. There was still the bottom sheet to contend with, and that contained the lion's share of the clean-up challenge.

Starting at the foot of the bed, not twelve inches from where Anika stood frozen in uncertainty and anticipation, the woman began to remove the fitted corners of the bottom sheet. It was a struggle at first, the sheet perhaps a bit small for the bed, but eventually she released it and moved toward the head of the mattress to unbind the other end.

And then, at the midpoint of the bed, she stopped.

She didn't look back at Anika, but instead looked down at the brown streaks that marked the white sheets. With barely a turn of her head, the witch peeked back toward the tray with which she now stood parallel, and then back to the mattress again. Casually she placed two fingers from her left hand on the edge of the brown stain and then brought them to her nose, smelling the mistake she had made.

The witch never saw the girl fumble frantically beneath her gown, nor did she hear the whispered word 'Die' as the clay bowl smashed onto her left cheekbone. She did, however, feel the collapse of her eye socket and the ensuing rattle of splintered bone in her sinus cavity, as well as the stiff, mercilessness of the wooden floorboards on the back of her skull.

She had felt it all before she blacked out.

THE OLD WOMAN WOKE in a panic, coughing and gasping for air. Her windpipe was blocked with what had to be a shattered piece of her own skull.

She tried to stand, but her legs had been bound at the ankles and thighs, and her arms at the wrists and behind her back. She fell back to the floor face down, her eyes bulging, wheezing in terror. She tried again to stand, using the leverage of the bed, and this time made it to her knees, desperately trying to take air into her lungs. The lack of oxygen began to fog her head and blur her vision. She was dying.

Behind her she felt the bed frame brush her back, and she reached for it with her elbow, trying to gauge its exact position. With a last act of will and survival, the old woman leaned her torso forward, almost touching her head to the floor, and then rocked back violently, slamming her upper back against the steel of the bed.

There was a simultaneous flash of pain and light as the bone shot from the witch's throat like a prehistoric bullet. She closed her functioning eye and collapsed back to the floor, now lying on her side, replenishing her cells with precious gasps of air.

She lay in that position for several minutes until her breathing steadied and then focused on her body as the pain set in. Her face was destroyed. The left side felt as if someone had removed her cheekbone. She had no sight in her left eye and had to assume she would never regain it. That was okay; it was her weaker eye anyway.

The throbbing ache that now filled the space between her shoulder blades where she'd smashed her back to the bed added slightly to her misery, but it was the mildest of her physical problems at the moment. It was the sickening looseness in her head that concerned her most, and she feared that without the attention of a skilled surgeon her brain would begin to leak from its cavity. She could deal with the pain—that would go away in time—but she needed to know that her body was stable and that she wasn't going to hemorrhage slowly over the next few days.

The potion. If she could complete the last stages of the mixture, she reasoned, adding the liver parts, specifically, she could mend enough of her body to carry on. It wasn't quite perfect yet, the mixture, there was perhaps another week of aging and feeding that needed to be done to get it exact, but it was close enough. She'd never tempted it before, always fearing the worst if it wasn't precise, but certainly the recipe allowed for slight degrees of error.

As for her permanent injuries, she could always find a doctor later to fix her face—if not her sight—and continue living for a hundred more years. Longer.

But first she needed the Source.

That the young girl left her alive didn't surprise the witch. She'd met very few people in her long life that could kill mercilessly unless it was in direct defense of themselves or their children. It was no small feat to slice the throat of an old lady lying unconscious on the floor, or even to chain her and leave her to starve, even if it that old lady's intentions were to harvest your organs.

Undoubtedly the Source hoped the blow she'd struck would kill her captor, but if it didn't, she hadn't the will to make sure. And for that she would pay.

The woman wiggled her way back up to a sitting position and leaned gingerly against the bed. She tested the strength of the rope on her wrists and could tell the girl had done a competent job with the knotting. The witch pushed her back hard against the bed now and screamed, extending her knees out and sliding her shoulders onto the mattress. She took three heavy breaths, accepting the pain in her back, and then slithered the rest of her torso onto the bed. She was now able to stand.

There was enough slack at her ankles that she could shuffle to the kitchen, and once there she began looking for something to slice through the cords at her wrists.

There was nothing accessible that she could see immediately, but if she could open the front door, there were plenty of items in the yard that would serve the purpose. With the height of the doorknob, however, that would be a challenge all its own.

As the witch's mind began to construct a way to wedge a butcher's knife between a drawer and the counter, her eye caught sight of a brown shard of pottery at her feet. Her heart raced, and as she stumbled too quickly past the kitchen counter, nearly collapsing from her bound ankles, she instantly saw the rest of the pot along with the soupy mixture splattered across the floor.

The potion.

It was destroyed.

✧

THE ROAD WAS INDEED close to the cabin and Anika found it quickly. Thankfully the witch hadn't been lying about that. Anika was coughing and wheezing as she reached it and collapsed hard on her buttocks, her back finding a tall, roadside evergreen to lean against.

She'd not stopped running since leaving the cabin, and despite the relatively short distance, her lungs—and legs—were exhausted. Anika was frustrated by her fitness level and wanted to continue farther down the road, but will alone wasn't going to overcome months of muscle atrophy. She would only rest a minute though, and then would start walking; she wasn't going to risk being missed by a passing car. If she had to, she thought, she would strip naked and run to the middle of the road.

She rubbed her lower leg just above her ankle where the chain had been clasped. The gesture was part massage and part reassurance that the shackle was really gone. The sensation that it remained was still strong and Anika imagined she'd be feeling it for some time. Maybe for the rest of her life.

She replayed the events of the last hour in her head, wondering if she'd killed the witch (she doubted it) and thought of all that could have gone wrong. What if Anika hadn't seen the pie bowl in time? What if the blow hadn't knocked the woman unconscious? What if the woman didn't have the keys with her? This last thought was most frightening, since Anika would have been forced to kill the old woman—if she hadn't been killed already—and then solve the puzzle of escaping the chains before starving to death alone in the slaughter room. Perhaps she would have gnawed off her foot, though what good that would have done she didn't know since she was still in the middle of the forest and she doubted there was a phone in that cabin.

But none of these thoughts occurred to her at the time—at the time it had all been instinct. Even her decision to slide that bowl of unspeakable broth to the floor was impulsive, though one she was now glad she'd made. Had the cauldron not been sitting out in the open, so easily accessible, Anika wouldn't have risked the time to find it.

She stood gently, unsure of her thighs' ability to make such a movement, and was encouraged by the result. They seemed to relish the motion, aching for long steady movements. Well, they would certainly get them, Anika thought, maybe for the next several hours, though she hoped it wouldn't be quite so long.

She began to walk the Interways toward the Southlands. With any luck, she'd reach the Back Country by nightfall.

ONCE THE ROPES ON HER wrists were free the woman dropped to her knees, leaned forward on her elbows, and began lapping the liquid from the floor like a cat. The ropes, it turned out, were old and brittle, and escape had been fairly easy. Four or five strokes against an exposed wall beam and she was free. The adrenaline induced by the sight of the wasting concoction drying at her feet didn't hurt either, and her sawing motions had been frantic and fearless.

Much of the soupy mixture had congealed, forming a protective, awful, skin-like film. But the hag didn't have the luxury to care, and she scooped the broth up indiscriminately, splashing it into her mouth like a wanderer in the desert who's just stumbled upon a lone puddle of water.

The taste was far from good, but nothing like it had tasted in the past. Perhaps it was the bile that gave the potion its putridity, she thought, or maybe the direness of her situation was muffling her taste buds.

It didn't matter; as it was, there was no guarantee that drinking it would render any benefit at all. In fact, it was more likely to sicken her, she thought, since all of the ingredients weren't included.

But she had nothing to lose. She could feel herself slipping. It was a feeling similar to the one she had that morning, just a few months ago, before Life had brought her back.

The woman stopped drinking only to breathe, the burgundy mess slogging down from her chin in thick webs. She leaned in to drink again, and as she pooled her hands together to scoop she felt the first tingle. It was like the sprinkle of water from a distant splash, tickling the left side of her skull where her former prisoner had shattered the empty pie bowl. It was slight at first, the tingle, and then quickly crescendoed into something nearing an electrical surge. Initially, there was *only* the feeling, and then the old woman recognized an ease and slowness to her breathing. It was as if her nasal passages had suddenly doubled in size. She gluttoned for the air, taking giant, vacuumed breaths through her nose and exhaling through her mouth, the huge swallows of oxygen as refreshing as any drink she could ever remember tasting.

She took another deep breath and then stopped in a gasp when she spied the open door to her left. The front door to the cabin. Wide open. Had it been open this whole time? Or was her Source back to finish the job, deciding she had the will to kill after all, and was now hiding somewhere in the room, armed and cocking some organic weapon?

Confused, the old woman turned suspiciously toward the door and jumped as the kitchen and back hall suddenly appeared in her periphery. And it was then she understood what was happening.

The door had indeed been open all along—open at least since her Source had escaped—it was just the woman hadn't been able to see it. Until now. Until the potion. She could see. From both eyes.

She was being healed.

The old woman untied the knots at her feet and moved slowly, delicately, to the lone chair in her cabin, afraid any jarring movements might impact the potion's effects. She sat upright in the chair, stiff, anticipating what was to come, just as she had done only months ago in the same spot. This time, however, she knew instinctively there would be no blacking out or painful contractions; this combination was fresh, beautiful (perhaps with the bile it would be perfect!), and it was going to make her whole again.

The electric tingle moved from her skull to the space between her shoulder blades, tightening the muscles there and then loosening them to just the right tension. From there it moved swiftly past her legs to her feet—drained from so much hiking through the restrictive forest—and lavished them with warmth and health and nutriment.

The old woman sat for what must have only been an instant, basking as the potion stormed everything from her complexion to her toenails, inundating her body with minerals and magic, cleansing each cell of decades of decay and pollutants, to regenerate a physique many generations past its intended time and purpose.

Nausea entered her stomach briefly but was quickly invaded and tamed, the potion not allowing any form of discomfort or disease to sustain itself. From her gut the magic formula flowed downward, stimulating her between her legs, moistening her crotch and evoking a smile and shiver. It rushed the length of her body to her teeth, at once filling cavities and filing incisors. The feeling swarmed upward through her newly-repaired skull and rippled over her scalp, vaccinating each follicle and patch of dander. Reflexively, the witch finger-combed through her hair and closed her eyes in ecstasy at the ease in which her hands glided through. Her tangled locks had existed for so many years she'd forgotten what healthy strands felt like.

This feeling was different. All of it was different. She'd taken the potion for close to two hundred years, she guessed, and had never experienced anything like what was happening today. It was as if decades of mixture had been concentrated into one pot, accelerating and magnifying all of the potion's wondrous effects.

She'd heard of this before—this exceptional regeneration—eons ago in another world and language, when knowledge of the potion itself—if not the ingredients—had been known by many, and witchcraft and magic weren't the metaphors and caricatures they were today. And though few ever had the will and stomach to explore it then, there were plenty of stories from The Ancients that implied its truth.

Even the book, of which she was told several still existed in the world, did not mention this rumored secret, for reasons even the old hag could understand on some level. It was said, she recalled, that the fluids of a kinsman could produce what she was now experiencing. That the closer the relation of whose blood and fluid was being extracted, the more magnificent the effects would be to the one ingesting it. It was obvious now; she understood it all. Life never failed its end of the deal.

Aulwarm.

Anika Morgan was her blood.

CHAPTER FIFTEEN

GRETEL WAS LATE MEETING Petr at the orchard and had considered not showing up at all. Odalinde's news about the visit from Officer Stenson—Petr's father—had left her melancholy, and though she didn't necessarily feel required to act bubbly for Petr's sake—they were just a pair of friendly co-workers meeting for lunch after all—she also didn't want to be a downer.

But by the time noon rolled around the walls of the bedroom started closing in on Gretel, and she decided a picnic was just the thing she needed. Besides, it was about time to push the elephant out of the room and talk about that night on the porch—and Petr's declaration that his father was not really there to help. Maybe there was nothing substantial to Petr's ominous words, but she felt she knew him well enough now that he owed her an explanation.

"You're late," Petr said, holding the boat steady as he stepped apprehensively onto the wooden bottom. Gretel thought he looked like an old lady as gingerly as he was stepping.

"You're not afraid of the water are you?" Gretel said playfully.

"No. Not really. Not as long as I'm on top of it and not in it. I can't really swim that well. And when I say 'not that well' I mean not at all."

"Can't swim?" Gretel was floored by the revelation. "Whoever heard of a boy in the Back Country who can't swim?'

"I may be *in* the Back Country, but I'm not *from* the Back Country. Just in case you forgot. And there aren't many lakes and rivers in the Urban lands."

Petr maneuvered his way to the center of the boat and reached blindly for a seat.

"You'd better hope the Klahrs keep you in the orchard and never ask you to fish for them," Gretel teased, gripping a single oar with both hands and launching the boat from the bank.

Petr, who now sat only a few feet away on the bow seat facing Gretel, grimaced at her and she smiled back.

Gretel liked her current position of power, helming the vessel, responsible for the life of her passenger as she gently glided them both toward the cannery. If there was ever a time to ask Petr about that first night they met, she figured now was it. "So how is your father?"

Petr held tightly to the sides of the boat and kept his stare fixed on the water, clearly uncomfortable with his current location so far from shore. "Uh, he's fine, I guess. Do we need to go this far out?"

"There are some shallow dunes that form close to the bank," Gretel lied. "We need to stay out far enough to avoid them." Realistically, they could have stayed twenty feet from the bank and been just fine, but Gretel wanted to keep Petr vulnerable for as long as possible, and hopefully get some answers.

"He came by one day to check on me," Gretel continued, "a while ago. I wasn't there. Did you know about that?"

Petr didn't hesitate. "Yeah, I think I remember him saying something like that." And then, "Is it much further?"

Gretel ignored the question. "Speaking of your father, do you remember that first day at my house, when your father sent you back for his binder?"

Petr looked up at Gretel and nodded. "Yes, of course."

"Do you remember what you said when you were leaving?"

"You mean before you kicked me out?"

"Okay, fine, before I kicked you out," Gretel repeated coldly. Now that the subject was afoot she was in no mood for bantering, and her words were curt and focused. She kept her gaze on the boy in front of her and steered the rowboat around the bend in the lake, intuitively heading for Rifle Field.

"I don't remember exactly," Petr replied, this time more serious in his tone. "I think I asked you why my father was there. Why he came out to your house in the first place." Petr's eyes were now back on the murky water and he was shifting slightly back and forth on the seat, trying to find the true middle.

"Wrong!" Gretel barked, snapping Petr's head to attention. She locked on his eyes and held them steady. "You actually said, 'I don't think he's here to help you,' those were your exact words." Gretel lowered her voice and then continued. "You already knew why he was there because I had told you in the house. And then when I asked why he *was* there if not to help us, you said, 'I don't know,' and, by the way, you looked very suspicious while saying it."

"I...I guess I don't..."

"We're here," Gretel interrupted, slipping off her sandals and hopping into the shallow water bordering Rifle Field. "Help me pull it in."

She'd, of course, pulled the boat on the bank dozens of times by herself, but she felt barking orders would keep Petr off his guard and manageable. Gretel slung the blanket over her shoulder and grabbed the loaded basket and walked off alone while Petr finished docking the boat. He sprinted to catch up with her, and the two children silently acknowledged a spot in the field and spread the blanket.

Gretel sat on her knees and unloaded the basket, arranging the bread and fruit on the blanket in her own private categories.

"So, do you remember now?" she said finally, after several minutes of speechlessness.

"I remember," Petr replied.

Gretel broke off a large piece of bread from the loaf and handed it to Petr. And waited.

"Okay," Petr said, absently crumbling the bread piece as he searched for the words to his confession. "The truth is my father sent me to the door and told me to talk to you. I think he left his binder on purpose."

"But why? What did he want you to talk to me about?"

"I really don't know. He didn't say anything specific. I think he just wanted me to meet you. When he came back to the car that night he described you to me and told me that you made a good impression on him. He said you were very sophisticated or something, and asked me why I couldn't be as mature and polite as you."

Gretel felt a flush in her cheeks. "So why did you say he wouldn't help me?"

"I was just mad at him for insulting me, I guess, wishing I was more like some stranger he'd just met for only a few minutes." Petr dropped his eyes and smiled. "And a girl to boot."

Gretel couldn't hold back a smile and she shook her head in playful irritation.

"Plus," the boy continued, "I was already unhappy about the meeting at the boarding school. It was just a long day. And by the time he sent me to your door—and then you threw me out—I ...I was trying to scare you, I guess. I'm sorry."

Petr gave an epiphanic sideways glance and then nodded. "My father was right, I'm not as mature and polite as you are. Your mother had just disappeared. I should have been more understanding."

Gretel's look was hard as she stared at Petr's shamed face, but she wasn't mad at him. She put herself in his position, and though she wouldn't have behaved exactly as he did if the roles were reversed, she certainly would have acted out in some way. Not to mention that, as she recalled, he had remained incredibly cordial and sophisticated throughout the encounter.

"And I want to be honest with you about something else," Petr said.

Gretel stared in anticipation, swarming with relief that she had finally reached this point with Petr.

"My father knew that you were starting at the orchard, and that's why he asked the Klahrs to take me on."

On some level Gretel knew this fact, but she was stunned to hear it admitted. "So Mr. Klahr was lying about your friend from school?"

"No! Of course not! Mr. Klahr would never lie to cover me. He'd choose you over me any day."

This fact was so self-evident Gretel didn't even bother disputing it.

"My roommate really did work there last summer. That was just a coincidence, and a good excuse to use for finding the work in the first place."

Gretel stayed quiet for several moments, and then started giggling softly.

"What's funny?"

"Your father sure thinks highly of me!"

Petr laughed. "I guess."

"I mean, I only met him for ten minutes!" Gretel was in full-blown laughter now. "Maybe he wants you to marry me someday!"

Petr's laughter had crescendoed to match Gretel's.

"Maybe," he replied "but I don't think your father would approve!'

This last quip sent Gretel into hysterics, and the laughter and joking continued throughout the better part of lunch, at one point causing Gretel to spit out the apple she'd been chewing, nearly causing her mortal embarrassment. It was the most fun she'd had in months, and maybe longer.

Finally, when the chortling subsided, Gretel said, "I'm sorry too."

"For what?"

"Mainly for being mean to you that day at my house—and most of the days during the harvest—but also for your dad getting you involved that day. That wasn't fair of him." Gretel watched the boy closely to see if he became defensive about his father, which he didn't seem to, and she pressed him. "Why do you think he would have done that? Really?"

Petr shook his head and shrugged.

Gretel decided to let the gesture suffice, and then asked, "Do you get along with him?"

"As much as most kids get along with their fathers, I guess," Petr answered. "I don't see him that much anymore since the academy, and now with work and everything. Plus he's not home much."

Since Petr seemed open to conversation, Gretel plowed on, asking about his home and the rest of his family, what it was like to live in the Urbanlands, and the benefits and drawbacks of having a System officer for a father, of which there seemed to be plenty on both accounts. Petr was vague on the subject of his mother, who had died when he was six, but was otherwise candid about his life, and by the end of the conversation, when Gretel had formed her image of what he'd told her, it all seemed fairly ordinary. Not quite boring, but certainly nothing like she'd have guessed only months ago.

She watched his expressions throughout the lunch, recognizing the shine of pride in his eyes as he recounted the pistoleer award he'd won when he was ten; and, alternately, the devastation at the loss of his grandmother—the woman who had raised him—only the year before. Gretel was rapt by his voice, so lush and sincere, and when the discussion lagged, it seemed the most natural action in the world for her to lean over and kiss him. He kissed her back, awkwardly yet gently, and when Gretel pulled away Petr remained puckered and shut-eyed for just a moment too long, and this made Gretel giggle and Petr blush.

After the kiss, neither child said a word until time dictated they begin the process of leaving. Gretel would have stayed until nightfall if she could have, and she knew Petr felt the same.

In blissful silence the two teenagers walked back to the rowboat, occasionally stealing glances and smiling, though Petr's smiles possessed something more than Gretel's. Gretel had enjoyed the kiss—later, what she would always consider her first—but it was being with Petr that she enjoyed more. It was friendship that she wanted most from him right now, and though their relationship had certainly crossed into something more since this morning, Gretel wasn't in love. At least not yet. Not in the holding hands, having babies kind of way.

The silence continued for the entire ride back to the orchard, with Petr in his same position on the bow seat and Gretel at the helm. When they finally reached the bank, Petr lingered for a moment, staring at Gretel and smiling. She thought he was going to kiss her again, which would have been perfectly appropriate, she thought, but he didn't, and that was okay too.

"Thank you," he said finally, "for the picnic. I had a great time. I wish I could stay longer."

"Me too," Gretel replied softly, smiling. And then, as if needing something to segue from the mushiness, said, "And good luck on the ride home with your father."

"Thanks."

Petr disembarked with a hop, displaying a confident acumen not seen during boarding, and Gretel watched with a sympathetic smile as he jogged up the bank into the first cut of grass lining the orchard.

At the tree line he turned back toward the water and called with a wave, "And good luck with your stepmother. Everything's going to be fine."

Gretel waved back and watched the boy as he ran on air toward the Klahr house. When he was out of sight, she shoved off toward home, pressing the oars back and forth with steady deliberation. She had considered an afternoon rowing session, but decided to pass. It wasn't that she was tired—in fact she had more energy than she'd had that morning—but her talk with Petr had created a longing for her family—Hansel mainly, but father as well—and she decided to go directly home to see them.

She was halfway across the lake when the knot formed low in her belly, and by the time she'd reached the bank of the Morgan property something akin to panic had set in. She stepped from the boat and stood statue-like on the rocky shore, her eyes wide and searching, her breath shallow as she rummaged through her memory, replaying each of the encounters she'd had with Petr over the last few weeks: today at the picnic, that day in the Klahr kitchen when he'd reappeared like a vivid memory, the past few days in the fields and in Klahr house working as partners and forming a real friendship. She even thought about each of the dozen or so perfunctory conversations they'd had during the harvest.

And she was sure.

Gretel knew the answer to her internal question: she'd never referred to Odalinde as anything other than her father's nurse.

She'd never mentioned to Petr that Odalinde was going to be her stepmother.

CHAPTER SIXTEEN

THE CAR PRESENTED ITSELF to Anika first in a dream, as a low sustained thunder somewhere miles off on the horizon, a benevolent warning to an inevitable storm.

The dream itself was almost an exact replica of Anika's current situation: she had escaped from an isolated cabin in the woods and was now desperately looking for help along the Interways. Only in her dream she was not alone, Hansel and Gretel were with her, and Anika's desperation to find safety for her children was a burning sickness in her abdomen. And in her dream, unlike in reality (thank God), rain was apparently on the way.

On any other day the rumbling thunder would have been inaudible to Anika, or unperceived, a white noise drifting above the trees until simply vanishing into the atmosphere. But Anika's senses were heightened, and even in her sleep her mind indexed the sound, cross-referencing it with latent experiences of the past. Her mind told her the sound was an impending storm, but the rumble was continuous and growing, unlike the crescendo and decrescendo of thunder. And, as she recalled, the sky had been clear before she'd fallen asleep.

Anika opened her eyes and glanced around, instinctively keeping the rest of her body still, afraid that moving would somehow expose a secret hiding spot in which she'd been hunkering. But she hadn't been hiding. In fact, her position was rather exposed and precarious, less than four feet from the pavement of the Interways. She quickly got to her feet and breathed deeply, rubbing the confusion from her eyes while giving silent thanks that her children, though she missed them terribly, weren't actually with her.

Anika realized now that her energy levels were lower than she originally thought when she first started her journey home—she'd only walked a few miles by her estimate, and already was asleep. Exposed.

She peeked toward the horizon for storm clouds and saw nothing but dusky blue clarity. She was mostly pleased with this sight, though thirst was beginning to factor in, and the thought of rain triggered a lumpy swallow in her throat.

Then, as if keen to Anika's inquisitiveness, the wind brought forth the low rumble of thunder from her dream. But the sound, she now realized, wasn't thunder, it was the mechanical growl of an engine—a large engine by the sound of it—and it was getting louder. A car was coming. Finally.

Anika stood and began to walk down the middle of the road toward the oncoming sound, and then broke into a slow lope, her arms hanging at her sides. She hadn't the strength to run properly, but she needed to get to that noise and confirm her miracle. Her mind was shrouded by hope to the actual danger of running toward oncoming traffic, but she absently figured that at the long stretch of road she'd started down, any car headed toward her would see her well before reaching her.

Anika squinted in desperation, trying to adjust the lenses of her eyes to the dimming afternoon light, hoping to catch the first flicker of metal heading toward her. She knew she'd been right about the sound. There was no question it was the sound of a car motor, or perhaps a motorcycle, and it was growing louder every second. In less than a minute she could be rescued, on her way home to Heinrich and her children, beginning her life again. She started to cry and began running faster. 'Thank you! Thank you, God!' she sobbed.

She ran another thirty yards before the sound that began as a subtle reverie finally materialized into reality. Anika stopped running and leaned slightly forward, hands on her thighs, measuring the distance and the validity of what her eyes were seeing. It was true. A car was headed straight for her.

She started laughing hysterically and waving her hands in front of her face in a frantic, scissor-like motion. The headlights grew larger as the car neared, and Anika could hear the downshifting gears as the car began its deceleration. Exhausted, she dropped to her knees and put her palms flat on the street, her head hanging as she simultaneously laughed and coughed and spat. It was implausible that she had made it to this place, free and unbound, seemingly in good health with her sanity still intact, though this last part she knew was yet to be fully determined. At no point had she ever completely given up hope, but, if she were honest with herself, at her core, she assumed she was going to die in that cabin.

Anika tried to will the muscles in her neck to raise her head to the approaching stranger, but it was useless; her exhaustion was almost absolute. A whispered 'thank you' was all she could manage before collapsing face down on the street, her arms no longer able to support her torso. She listened as the footsteps quickened and she elicited the trace of a smile when she felt the blanket fall across her shoulders and back.

But the cover didn't warm the chill that flashed in her neck and spine when her rescuer spoke.

"Anika Morgan," the voice said confidently, "so you're not dead after all."

ANIKA SAT QUIETLY IN the front seat of The System officer's car and held the woolen blanket tightly over her shoulders, sweeping it across the front of her neck and chest. The constant speed and steady hum of the tires on the road caused her to drift in and out of sleep, and with each brief awakening she brought the meticulously clean blanket under her nose to inhale the scent. She'd forgotten the smell of cleanliness, so accustomed had she become to the slaughter room's gradual descent into filth and disgrace; and now, as she held the blanket to her face, the fresh fragrance of laundered fabric made her think of summertime as a small girl.

Anika felt the car slow dramatically and then turn sharply to the left, and she woke instinctively to brace herself from toppling toward the driver. She opened her eyes and glanced at the window where a wall of daylight confronted her.

Out of the front windshield Anika could see a narrow dirt road which had been divided down the middle by an overgrowth of grass and weeds. With some reluctance, she shifted her attention to the figure on the seat beside her, expecting either to be met by a face familiar to her, or else one not quite human, signaling she was in the midst of a dream. Instead, the smiling face she saw in the driver's seat was as normal and unintimidating as any she'd see on a busy Saturday in the local market, though she supposed a bit more handsome. And not one she recognized.

Anika sat straight on her portion of the bench seat and rubbed her palms down her face to clear the grogginess from her head.

"You're the man who helped me I suppose," she said, her voice sounding raspy and timid. She cleared her throat. "I can never thank you enough."

"You're welcome," the man replied, not taking his eyes from the road in front of him.

Anika vaguely remembered that the man had spoken her name as she had lain in the street, just before her last memory of the blanket being draped across her shoulders. "Do I know you?"

The man smiled quizzically and finally looked at Anika. "I don't think so," he said, "do I look familiar to you?"

"No, it's just that...back on the street...I think you said my name. At least I think I remember that."

The man's smile straightened and a serious look emerged on his face, an expression which hovered between interest and concern. He looked back to the road. "Yes, Anika, I know your name. Every System officer in this area knows your name."

Anika flinched at the man's words, and an icy tremble trickled the length of her nape and dispersed across her blanketed shoulders.

With her eyes now adjusted, Anika slowly surveyed the car's interior and immediately noticed the bulbous metal switches and steep buttons, as well as the standard two-way radio, which indicated she was indeed among a man of The System. This wasn't the first time she'd been in a System vehicle, and she was deluged with thoughts of her childhood when, as a girl of twelve, Anika rode quietly in the back of a cruiser as she was shuttled behind an ambulance carrying her father to the hospital following a rather severe traffic accident. At the time that short trip had seemed like a dream—Anika's mind protecting her from considering all the possible fates of her father, she supposed—and she'd been unusually distracted by the car's interior. She'd seen nothing like it in her world before, the stark leather of the seats and door panels, the chrome lines outlining every hard feature, and the various multi-colored blinking lights that spanned the dashboard. There was an alien feel to the car that made Anika feel both helpless and safe, and now, as she sat rigid and wary in the passenger seat of this more modern, yet still familiar cruiser, that same feeling possessed her again.

"The System." Anika was suddenly flooded with hope as she recognized her good fortune, and her mouth exploded into a huge grin. "You're from The System! But how did you know it was me? On the street?"

The officer chuckled. "I know everything about you Mrs. Morgan: your age, your hair and eye color, even how you were dressed the day you disappeared." He glanced at her again. "Which doesn't seem to fit with what you're wearing now by the way."

Anika started to respond, but held back, deciding that an explanation regarding the difference in her attire wasn't the proper place to begin her story.

"Besides, Mrs. Morgan, how many possible women do you think one would expect to find in the middle of the road, especially in this part of the country?"

Anika processed this reasoning as sound, though slightly off, but explored that notion for only a moment before the reins on her instincts snapped. "My family! You must have spoken with my family then? How are my children?"

"We have spoken with your family, Anika, on several occasions, and everyone is fine. Though your husband was quite ill for a while after your disappearance."

"Ill? In what way? Who's been looking after the children?"

Anika realized the rather one-sidedness of her concern, inquiring about her husband's condition only to gauge the impact it had on Gretel and Hansel, but at the moment her children were all she could think of.

The officer stopped in front of what appeared to be a small warehouse and shifted the car into park. "As I said, your family is fine, including your children. In fact—and I don't tell you this to upset you in any way—but your daughter seems to have thrived since you went missing. Shall we?"

Anika hadn't noticed the warehouse or even that they'd stopped, and she stared baffled at the officer for a few moments before finally understanding his suggestion to enter the building standing before them.

"What? What is *this* place?"

"It's a place for gathering information. Yours was a very complicated case, Mrs. Morgan, and there's a lot we need to investigate concerning what happened. You'll just need to stay here for a while, and I promise to get you home as soon as possible."

"A while? How long is a while?"

The officer sighed impatiently. "I don't know exactly, Mrs. Morgan. I suppose until we have the information we need."

Anika glanced toward the stark building and then back to the officer. "Does my family know that I've been found? Has anyone contacted them?"

"Yes, certainly. Of course. We had an officer visit them as soon as I was able to verify your identity. They've been contacted."

Anika noticed at a fairly young age that most men of power were poor liars, she imagined it was for the simple reason that they usually reached their ends through force or intimidation, and lying wasn't a skill necessary to master. And she recognized this lie at once. The shift of the officer's body, the loss of eye connection, the change in pitch and excessive affirmation: all obvious signs of deceit.

She could now feel the rise inside her toward hysterics, but fought the emotion, catching it in her chest and driving it back to her belly. Her nerves had been shredded in the slaughterhouse, and her psyche going forward in life would be as fragile as butterfly eggs; but the ordeal had also assured Anika that within her was an involuntary prowess of survival, a fundamental determination to keep her heart beating and blood flowing, at least until that final moment when it was no longer hers to decide. She'd always believed everyone possessed this strength to some degree, and over the last several months it had been revealed that hers was exceptional.

"I'll take all the time you want to answer questions," she said calmly, "of course, every detail. I would just like to see my family first."

The officer stared at Anika for a moment, as if considering her request, and then said flatly, "Let's go."

"No!" she screamed, and then as if speaking an echo, "No." Anika sat hugging the blanket around her torso, staring forward, looking as petulant as a four-year-old who's been told to eat her vegetables. She could sense the officer considering whether the time had come to use force, but then, with a sigh, he continued the act.

"Listen, Mrs. Morgan," he said, "the longer we wait to get the information from you, the better chance whoever did this to you will go free. Is that what you want?"

"What makes you think someone did anything to me?" she replied, her eyes wide and crazed. "I never told you anything about another person. Maybe I was just lost."

The officer frowned. "If you had just become lost in the woods, Mrs. Morgan, you would have died weeks ago. Only the most skilled survivalist would have been able to find food in those forests. And I assume you didn't sew a new set of clothes for yourself while wandering through the wilderness."

Anika looked away, slightly embarrassed at her 'Aha!' attempt.

"Besides, some of the injuries I've seen on you don't come from tree branches or a slip on a wet rock. Or even a wild animal. A person caused those wounds."

"Then if I can't see my family yet at least let me see a doctor. I definitely do need a doctor." Anika softened her tone, sensing she had struck a chord of sympathy within the man.

"Your medical needs will be taken care of promptly. Once we're inside."

It was obvious The System officer's intentions were deeply anchored, and that going anywhere other than inside the building was not a possibility for Anika. And though her will was steel, she simply hadn't the physical strength to fight or run; that would have been tantamount to suicide. Her only choice was to obey.

The absurdity of the scenario nearly caused her to erupt in laughter. It was nearly impossible to imagine: not a full day had gone by since she escaped the most atrocious nightmare she could have conceived—being slowly harvested by a monstrous hermit for some obscene recipe—and now here she was again, being held without choice, and this time by a public servant under oath to protect her!

Anika tossed the blanket to the backseat and exited the car without another word, and then walked ahead of the officer to the front of the structure. The building wasn't much bigger than a large house, but the design and lack of windows suggested it was used for something other than living, and its modern, utilitarian appearance was in complete opposition to the rustic road they'd just traveled. The officer followed Anika to the metal door which stood at ground level and then fished a single key from his pocket, inserting it into the deadbolt above the knob. Anika had one last thought to flee, but the bleakness of the perimeter was daunting and hopeless.

With a push, the door opened to a large, brightly lit room with high ceilings, though several rows of overhanging fluorescent lights made them feel much lower. Stacks of empty metal shelves lined the side walls, which were made of unfinished concrete. The floor was wood and dusty to the point of slick, and the holes between the planks were so gaping that Anika could see through to the natural ground on which the warehouse stood. And perfectly centered in the room, a couch and two brown, leather chairs had been placed on top of an area rug, and a small table and lamp set was positioned beside the couch.

"Have a seat, Mrs. Morgan," the officer ordered.

Anika walked to one of the chairs and sat down, the dust exploding into the air and clouding her face. At this stage she'd resigned herself to do as she was told, at least until the request became unreasonable. When that time came she hoped to still have the resolve to put up some iteration of a fight, whether verbal or otherwise. She still left room for hope that the officer's intentions weren't sinister, that he really did just want to ask her questions and get some answers about her disappearance. Maybe he didn't trust her, she thought. Maybe her case had caused him to snap, and now his fanaticism was leading him to inappropriate, or even illegal, procedures. That certainly made him a bad System officer, but it didn't necessarily make him dangerous.

But that didn't change the fact he was being less than truthful about something. About that she had no doubt.

The officer locked the door behind them, walked toward Anika, and stood behind the couch, facing her. "Mrs. Morgan," he said, his tone now very official, "my name is Officer Oliver Stenson. I was assigned to your case soon after you were reported missing by your family."

Anika leaned back in the chair and placed both arms on the rests, assuming a look of comfort that contradicted the feelings inside her.

"After your father told us you'd gone missing along the Interways, a team of several officers was dispatched that day to find evidence. What we found instead was..."

"My father?"

Officer Stenson stared at Anika for a moment, confused. "Yes, Mrs. Morgan. Your father, Marcel Gruen."

"Yes, I know my father's name, I was curious that my father called you and not my husband. Or my daughter. My father wouldn't have known that anything was wrong once I left him. How would he have known to call The System?"

Officer Stenson glanced away, searching, as if the explanation lay somewhere on the warehouse floor. He looked back at Anika and then smiled. It was a full, toothy smile, one Anika hadn't seen before.

"Perhaps your husband called your father and then he called us," Office Stenson said, "I suppose I can't be certain of the telecommunication pattern exactly. Are you suggesting that I'm lying?"

Anika locked the officer's gaze, resisting any displays of the fear she felt. "I didn't mean that at all. It's just that it's odd to me. My father reporting me missing, that is."

Officer Stenson dropped his stare and started walking toward a door at the back of the warehouse. It seemed to Anika to be an interior door that led to some unseen backroom of the building. The door appeared solid metal on the bottom with a framed mirrored window on top. A one-way mirror she supposed, of the kind she'd seen in police movies.

"I'll return in a moment for questioning," he said flatly, "please wait for me here. The door to the outside is locked securely. In case you were wondering."

"When do I see a doctor? You said I would see a doctor. And I need to eat something. And can I at least have water?"

"Of course. I'll bring you something now. The doctor should be arriving shortly."

With that Officer Stenson walked into the back room of the warehouse and closed the door behind him. Within a few seconds Anika could hear talking behind the door. Though she couldn't make out the words being spoken, the conversation seemed somewhat confrontational. There was a moment of quiet, and then the door opened slowly and a taller, much older man emerged from the back room. It was the last man she'd seen before she was seized and tortured.

It was her father.

GRETEL LAY MOTIONLESS in her bed, the sheets to her chin, searching the ceiling above her as she considered the picnic and what Petr had said to her on the bank. Her mind was exhausted of explanations, and Gretel was now virtually certain she'd never mentioned the engagement to Petr. Which left only one explanation: someone else told him.

Gretel quickly eliminated the Klahrs as the source, since they had never offered any personal information about Petr to Gretel, and she couldn't imagine them acting any differently when it came to her private affairs. On the one or two occasions when Gretel had asked something about Petr, they either didn't know or told her to ask him. That's how they were: very respectful of a person's personal business.

So who? And why?

Gretel was startled by a knock on her bedroom door. "Who is it?"

"It's me." Odalinde. "You've been in there quite a while Gretel. I figured you would be on the lake by now. Are you feeling okay?"

"Yes, I'm fine." Gretel tried to keep the irritation out of her voice but fell short. "I just didn't sleep well last night, that's all. I'll be out in a minute."

This was the price of routine and dedication, Gretel thought: once you falter even slightly, everyone's eyebrows shoot to the ceiling.

She willed her feet to the floor and within ten minutes was twisting the knob of the front door. She made no eye contact with Odalinde, but could feel the woman shifting glances toward her.

"Do you think you'll be on the lake long today?" Odalinde asked for the first time ever.

Gretel paused at the threshold and then turned toward Odalinde, squinting, confused by the question. "What?" she asked.

"I was just asking if you planned on spending a lot of time rowing today, or if you would be home a little earlier." Odalinde's voice was eager, nervous.

"Why would you want to know that?" Again, there was no bite in Gretel's reply, only confusion.

Odalinde frowned and her eyes softened. "Remember earlier when I said there were some things I needed to tell you and your brother?"

Gretel nodded.

"Well those things can't wait much longer, Gretel." Odalinde walked to the kitchen table, pulled out a chair, and sat. "And if you're ready," she said, "I'd like to tell you now."

"HELLO, ANIKA."

"Father?" Anika whispered.

Anika had never been one to believe in ghosts and magic, but seeing the form of her father, now, at this moment and in this setting, could only be the result of a force supernatural. Or perhaps she was hallucinating—the workings of her brain stressed to its limit.

"I suppose I'm the last person you expected to see come through that door, eh?" Marcel forced a sad smile and nodded slightly, answering silently for his stunned daughter.

"Father...What...Why are you here? Are you being held here? I think I'm being imprisoned! Again! I don't know what's happening. Who is that man?"

"It's okay, Anika, it's okay. He is who he says he is. He is a System officer."

Anika's father turned back toward the door and yelled for Officer Stenson, calling for him as simply "Stenson," before erupting into a rasping cough. The episode subsided for a moment, and then continued again, this time more violently, forcing the old man to double over, hands to his knees. He stumbled around the sofa, using the back as a crutch, and then dropped to the cushion, bouncing comically and nearly toppling to one side. As if prompted by the act, Officer Stenson walked back through the door carrying a plate and a ceramic cup of water. He kept his eyes to the floor, brooding.

Anika stayed focused on her father, watching him with a mixture of concern and terror, both at his condition and his apparent knowledge of the situation. In fact, she observed, he seemed not just knowledgeable, but in control.

"This was not the plan, Marcel," Stenson said through tightly clenched teeth, "what are you doing?"

Anika's father tried to speak but was still in the throes of sickness, and waved a dismissive hand instead.

"What is happening?!" Anika screamed, rising like a piston from the chair. She walked to the couch and sat next to her father. "Give me the water! Now!" she barked at Stenson, reaching her hand behind the couch but keeping her eyes to her father.

Officer Stenson handed the water to Anika and she put it to her father's mouth, gently tipping a steady sip over his lips as she'd done dozens of times over the past year.

He swallowed the water and then pushed the glass away, gulping down several frantic breaths, trying to fill his lungs as fully as possible before the coughing resumed.

"I'm dying, Anika," he said, "and...I don't want..." was all he had managed before the hacks started again.

"You're okay, Papa, don't talk," she whispered, stroking the back of his head. She glared back toward the officer who was standing alone, away from the oasis of furniture, awkwardly watching the domestic scene play out as if he'd stumbled upon it accidentally.

"My father is not well. He should not be here!"

"Your father is here of his own will, Mrs. Morgan," Stenson replied. "In fact, it is your father who..."

"No!" It was Marcel. He stood, precariously and with some effort, but much quicker than Anika would have thought possible given his condition, his chest bowing forward, his shoulders high and receded. "No. If she is to hear it she will hear it from me."

"I don't *want* her to hear it, Marcel. There is no purpose served by it. That was never the plan and it shouldn't be the plan now."

"I want her to hear it, Oliver," Marcel said, his words soft now, a plea for understanding.

The officer shook his head disapprovingly, but remained quiet.

Anika's father closed his eyes for what must have been twenty seconds, and then breathed deeply, exhaling comfortably, the coughing fits mercifully over for the moment. "I know what has happened to you, Anika," he said finally. "I know where you've been."

Anika shook her head in a combination of confusion and denial. "What?" The word was barely audible, and the tears in Anika's eyes felt poisonous.

"I know all that you've been through. At that cabin."

"You have no idea what I've been through! How could you know! What is happening here? Papa, what did he mean that you want to be here? What does that mean?"

Anika looked back and forth between the two men, hoping the pieces would suddenly come together and the answers to her questions made apparent. She watched as Officer Stenson walked toward her and set the plate on the table beside the couch. The dish contained an assortment of cheeses and surprisingly fresh-looking bread, but Anika's appetite was lost.

Officer Stenson said nothing more as he strode to the back of the warehouse and disappeared through the interior door.

"I'm trying to tell you, Anika," her father continued, "I'm dying. Soon. I can feel it in my chest and hear it in my cough. You know it as well as anyone. You can hear it too. And you've seen how I've rotted over the years."

Anika cringed at the word choice.

"You know I'm dying. You do. But the problem is my girl, I am a selfish man, and I don't want to die." He paused, and his eyes widened just slightly before saying, "And I don't intend to."

Marcel sat down again on the couch, this time easily and controlled.

"I had always hoped, Anika, and at times even prayed, that as the years piled on me and my body began failing that I would accept death as everyone does, as people have done for thousands of generations: ideally, with grace, but if not grace, then at least concession." He paused, calculating the words. "But once I learned of it, of the miracle, and the truth of what it meant, I..."

He stopped suddenly, recognizing the frenzied crescendo of his voice. The volume and tenor reminded Anika of a carnival barker.

"I could never unlearn it, Anika," he continued slowly, "I could never not try." He paused again, and this time stared intently at his daughter. "That is where you come in."

The words drifted in the room, each molecule of air now saturated with the solution to the riddle of why Anika's father was sitting before her in a warehouse at the end of the world. Anika shook her head in disbelief, the tears now streaking steadily.

"I don't understand," she lied, "what are you saying?"

Marcel's look was rigid, but his voice had the tone of kindness, "You know what I'm saying, Anika."

"But why? Why me? And how could you have...It was just an accident. I wandered into the woods. What you're saying doesn't make sense!"

"Sit down, Anika, the story is a long one."

"I don't want to sit down!" Anika screamed, now teetering on hysterics, but her father's look was fierce, and one Anika had known since her earliest memories. It was a look that, even under the circumstances, she'd been conditioned to obey.

She moved backward to the chair and sat, waiting for her father to begin the story of why her life had been shattered.

CHAPTER SEVENTEEN

GRETEL STARED AT ODALINDE, who was now seated in the kitchen, her shoulders and chin high, her back stiff against the chair. Gretel's hand was still firmly wrapped around the door knob, her expression mixed with fear and confusion.

"I don't mean to be rude, Odalinde, but I really had plans to row today. I..."

"Sit down, Gretel. Please."

Odalinde's stare was hypnotic, and Gretel could see in the woman's eyes that whatever she had to say was not insignificant.

"It's about your mother."

Gretel relaxed her hand and let it slide from the knob, the feeling of urgency now replaced with one of anxiety. "What is it? What's happened?"

Gretel walked to the kitchen table and sat down next to Odalinde.

"And I want your brother to hear this too."

Gretel quickly called for Hansel, who emerged from his room moments later. Seeing his sister and guardian seated together instantly made him curious, and he too sat down, facing his sister from across the table.

Hansel and Gretel stared unwaveringly at Odalinde, waiting for her revelation. Gretel could sense the woman's nervousness as she looked to the floor, studying her thoughts and trying to figure where to begin.

"I've wanted to talk to you both for quite some time now. And it's taken me much longer than it should have. And before I begin, I just want to say I'm sorry—for many things really, but most of all I'm sorry for that. For waiting so long."

Neither child said a word in response to this preamble, and Odalinde continued.

"I'm going to tell you why I'm here, why I came here at all, to your home." She paused a moment, waiting for any interruptions that may come, and hearing none said, "and to tell you what I believe happened to your mother."

"Mother?" Hansel said, the word coming off his tongue as if only generally familiar to him.

"That's right, Hansel, your mother."

"What do you mean 'why you came here?'" Gretel backtracked, "you're a nurse, our father was...is ill."

Odalinde's mouth turned down in a guilty frown, and she sighed deeply through her nose. "Yes Gretel, but there's more. Much more. Now I want you both to listen to me carefully."

She stopped and looked back and forth between the siblings, making sure she had their attention.

"What I'm going to tell you must not be discussed with anyone. Not with your friends, not with your teachers, or even the Klahrs. No one. You'd be wise even to keep it from your future husband or wife. Do you understand me?"

Hansel nodded, rapt with intrigue.

"Okay," Gretel said, "but why are *you* about to discuss it with *us*?"

Odalinde smiled. "Because Gretel, you're at the center of this story. You were always to know."

"Know what?" Hansel asked.

Odalinde began.

"YOUR MOTHER WAS BORN during a time of enormous upheaval and discontent in the Old Country. The kings and emperors of the assorted lands—men who had known the greatest power ever held over humankind—were abruptly and successfully being challenged by their people. The uprisings were fleet and merciless, and within a decade each had watched helplessly as his power receded to the past like broken waves. In their place chaos and strife emerged."

Marcel was settled back on the couch now, motionless, his eyes barely slits, his mouth effortlessly and eloquently unleashing the story to the ether.

"Most in the nobility and clergy were killed during this time, or banished to the wilderness to die a much lonelier death, one filled with cold and hunger. Those of the tradesmen and peasant classes fared only slightly better though, since once their rulers fell, they were essentially leaderless and naturally distrustful of anyone who tried to assume a position of authority. And this distrust fractured not only regions and villages, but neighbor and family as well. The ultimate result was a continent of borderless nations and mob rule."

Anika hung on every word, both fascinated by her father's fecundity and frightened by the delusions that had apparently infected him. He'd obviously been sick for a long time—and *very* sick lately—she'd never been in denial about the truth of that, but it was a sickness that until now had seemed not to affect his mind. Where did this depiction of her mother's childhood come from? Old kings and emperors? Peasant classes? He was describing a world hundreds of years before her mother was born.

"But there were other peoples in these lands," he continued, "groups that existed outside of the classes—villages whose families could trace their ancestors as accurately and distantly as the pharaohs of Egypt. They lived beyond the kings' reaches mostly, in the hills and forests or other grueling geographies abhorred by soldiers and uncharted on most maps of the time. These were places thought to be strategically and culturally irrelevant, and so were largely ignored by leaders and forgotten by historians. Even tax collection was considered folly in such lands, since the cost to reach them was often far more expensive than what could be seized. Those clans that made their homes in these regions were considered at the time to be primitive, tribal, unlearned in the modernity of things like architecture, weaponry and fashion; and indeed, by the standards of the ruling classes and those beneath them, they were comparatively uncivilized in those subjects.

"But in many areas they were genius, intensely curious of the world, scientifically sophisticated and meticulous in their calculations. And perhaps more importantly, they were literate, and therefore able to pass on their discoveries not only through speech and pictures, but through the invention of hundreds of unique written languages, each containing uncommon alphabets and symbols, languages that were frequently known only to the tiny society in which they were formed, where members often lived and died having never spoken a word to a person outside the territory. It was in a place like this that your mother entered the world."

"That's enough!" Anika screamed, rising to her feet once again. "You've gone mad, Papa! I won't listen anymore!" She stifled the sob boiling in her chest and breathed deeply. "I don't understand, Papa, your mind was well when I left you, your memory as nimble as ever. What's happened to you?"

Marcel gave a patient look to his daughter and offered a subtle gesture for her to sit, a command she obeyed with a sigh of aggravation.

"I won't argue that I'm not insane, Anika, to you the evidence must seem quite staggering at the moment. But what I've told you, and everything I'm going to tell you, is true."

"You're speaking of Mother as if she were born in medieval times! What...what are you saying?"

"I'm telling you now, Anika. If I may continue?"

Anika gave a permissive nod and listened.

CHAPTER EIGHTEEN

"I'M NOT HERE TO NURSE your father," Odalinde began, "not primarily anyway."

Gretel studied the woman's face, which seemed now to have become softer, more innocent. But Gretel's wariness remained, and she even left open the possibility that this conference was a trick, though intuitively she knew it wasn't. "I don't think I ever believed that," she replied, "I don't think I've believed most of what you've said since you came here."

She could feel Hansel's eyes on her, wide and disbelieving, but Gretel's eyes stayed fixed on Odalinde.

"I've tried not to lie to you, Gretel, to either of you. I've been brusque at times, I realize that, but..."

"Why *are* you here then?" Gretel interrupted, not interested in rationalizations or anything resembling an apology.

"To put it concisely, I'm here to protect you."

"Protect us?" Gretel snorted, her eyes wide with astonishment. "*Protect* us?" She repeated the phrase, as if offering Odalinde a chance to rethink her word choice.

"I know that seems odd to you right now, but..."

"No, Odalinde, it doesn't *seem odd right now*, it actually seems insulting and deranged right now! Protect us. How have you protected us? By starving us? By threatening us?"

"I've never..."

"You've done nothing to protect us! Hansel and I have been protecting ourselves since the day father got sick. And every day after. And you coming here has made it all worse!"

Gretel stopped abruptly and stared at Odalinde, waiting for her to fire back with shouts of her own, or perhaps with one of her moderately concealed threats. Instead the woman stayed silent, her hands folded in front of her as if encouraging Gretel to finish.

"Why is my father still sick?"

Odalinde nodded, as if understanding this question was inevitable. "Your father is a good man," she said, "and I've grown very fond of him."

"*Very fond of him*? Have you grown fond of him? You're marrying him! I should hope you're fond of him!"

Odalinde looked away. "Yes, well, we'll need to discuss that as well." She looked back to Gretel and waited for another barrage, but Gretel had, for the moment, said her peace. Odalinde then leaned forward conspiratorially. "But to answer your question, I'm keeping your father sick to protect you from him."

Gretel's face again twisted in anger and disbelief at the woman's brazenness, and all the blood in her body seemed to hurtle toward her head, flooding her brain with the energy it would need to defend her father from this villainous slanderer.

"As I said, Gretel," Odalinde added, holding up an open hand in anticipation of Gretel's eruption, "your father is a good man. A good father and husband. I know that. And so do you. And what you also must know is, that above all else, he loves you both. Very much."

Hansel was now crying, the combination of fear and love and anger too much for him to contain all at once. Gretel put her arm around his shoulders and offered a reassuring shush.

"Then why..." Gretel could no longer arrange her thoughts into a rational sentence.

"But your father is also weak. Weak emotionally, temperamentally, and, increasingly so, physically. He would never withstand the temptation once offered. There are few men who could, and your father is not one of those men."

"Temptation? What temptation?" Hansel asked, "I don't understand what you're talking about."

"It's a very long story, Hansel—centuries old—and most of it doesn't concern either of you. Or me for that matter. But some of it does. Some of this story involves you both quite directly. So I suppose the place to start is at the beginning. Or at least at the beginning of when it matters to you."

"And when is that?" Gretel asked.

"It's the day I met your grandmother," Odalinde said.

She paused a beat and tilted her head slightly forward, narrowing her eyes, making sure the children understood that what she was about to say was true, and that she, Odalinde, recognized the preposterousness of how it sounded.

"Long before your mother was born."

"BY THE TIME YOUR MOTHER was born the elixir was already discovered and, as your mother recounted to me many years ago, it was spoken of throughout her early childhood, though apparently none in her particular village knew the precise recipe at that time. Or even if the stories were true."

Marcel seemed adrift in his chronicle of an era to which he'd never belonged; Anika thought he looked almost melancholy, sad that his experience of the time would never be more than vicarious and obscure.

"It was a bit of legend at first I suppose, the elixir, but most believed in it, believed at least that there was some truth to it, though the full extent of the power was surely doubted."

Anika's skepticism was unshaken, but she listened carefully, resigning herself to hearing the tale. Besides, she'd never known much about her mother's youth, her schooling and adolescence and such, and even considering the setting in which she now found herself—imprisoned for the second time in as many days—there was comfort in the idea that even a portion of what her father was telling her might be true.

"It was not until your mother reached sixteen or so that the magic was revealed to her explicitly." Marcel paused and stared intensely at his daughter, as if considering whether to continue with the revelation.

Anika could see in her father's eyes that he believed every word he was saying. And that his madness was rampant.

"The magic came in the form of a book, written in a language spoken by so few people that the number could have been measured in dozens. And among those who spoke it there were even fewer who could read it. Your mother was one who could."

The excitement had returned to Marcel's voice, signaling the impending climax to his tale.

"It was true magic, Anika. Of the kind you've always read about in stories. It was, in fact, the unearthing of the most quested possession since the birth of humankind. Truly! And not one whose value was found only in the sentiment of religion or culture, like the Holy Grail or some Pharaoh's sarcophagus," Marcel grimaced at the insignificance of such things, "but one of true power. Life unending, Anika. Immortality."

Anika sat stone-faced, disinterested, a complete opposite reflection of her father's face across from her, which was alert and grinning maniacally, his eyes carefully searching his daughter's face for the look that conveyed, due to the marvel of his story, that she now understood his motives and forgave him his actions.

"Anika. Did you hear me? There exists the formula to let me live forever."

"So for you to live forever requires me to die?" Anika retorted. Her voice was low and clear, her expression never changing.

"Yes, well, it is..." Shame returned to Marcel's face and he looked away from his daughter quickly. He rubbed his hands together in a nervous gesture and then covered his face with them. He sat motionless for a few seconds, and then removed his hands and soberly answered his daughter's question. "Unfortunately, the answer is yes," and then almost as an afterthought, "you or one of your children."

Anika was now at full attention, but she stayed balanced and icy. "And what is it about me...and *your grandchildren*...that makes us so perfect for this priceless recipe of immortality? Surely the pollution that *your* blood contributes can't be it."

Marcel attempted no defense. "There is nothing about you or Gretel or Hansel that is particularly unique, for the formula that is, except that you *are* my blood, and therefore a necessary match for what I need."

Anika glared hatefully now. "I don't understand."

"According to your mother, virtually any human under the age of sixty or so can be used to create the mixture. The measurements must be exact and the timing perfect, but those parts contained within the natural anatomy of any normal human being are all that is required. Only those with the rarest of deformities or genetic conditions are exempt. In other words, any transient on the street can be harvested for the miracle."

Anika closed her eyes and turned away in disgust at her father's morbid detachment, then breathed deeply and resumed her confident stare.

"If I had decided earlier in my life to participate in this evil, I, of course, would have used the degenerates of society—the criminals, the molesters—all of the monsters that feed on the weak and drag humankind toward the sewer. Of course I would have done that!' Marcel stifled a cough and then softly said, "It is what your mother did for all those years."

Anika wanted to interrupt, pursue this off-handed charge by her father that his wife—her mother—was in fact some kind of serial killer, albeit one utilitarian to society. Instead she stayed silent, not wanting to veer the story away from the substance.

"But I resisted, Anika. Steadfastly! I kept a vigil for my soul. I knew that even immortality wouldn't last forever. And when that final day came, even if millennia in the future, I would face the judgment awaiting all of us and would have to answer for my actions. It is this belief that kept me unaddicted. And when your mother finally died, my sobriety was only reinforced."

Marcel sighed, and his mouthed turned down in sadness.

"But the truth is this, Anika: when death is upon you, when the horizon is no longer an abstraction, when morbidity is no longer a passive thought but rather a place you can feel in your belly and taste in your mouth, your decisions waver. The concept of death and the reality of it are two very different things. And death is upon me now, and I plan to fight it. I..."

"You haven't explained where I come in," Anika interrupted finally. Her words were curt and emotionless, intended to be in harsh contrast to her father's dramatic explanation and tacit plea for sympathy.

"The concoction is not a potion of youth; it does not undo disfigurement or trauma or disease. A man with one leg could not drink the mixture and suddenly grow a new one. Nor will a cripple walk or a dwarf grow. The potion simply feeds those healthy cells that exist, and, more importantly, arrests their natural march toward degeneration."

Anika could tell it was the first time her father had ever explained the details of the potion, as he knew them to be, and now that he'd begun the words spilled from him with ease.

"Oh, there have always been stories of course, according to your mother there were certain additives that would strengthen bones and taper teeth, perhaps even make them grow larger. And of course there are always the vanity claims of clearing complexions and strengthening hair. But even if those rumors are true, Anika, by the measure of rumors, they're rather benign. It is a well-accepted, centuries-old truth that the restorative powers of the potion are limited. It is not a cure for death. It is a prevention."

He paused then, signaling the import and relevance of the words that were to follow.

"Unless the subject is close kin. In that case, there may be the exception. There the possibilities may become more variable."

Anika nodded slowly in disappointed understanding. Then she smiled softly and shook her head. "So this is why I've gone through all of this? This is why my family was destroyed? My children made to suffer? My husband left to raise them alone?"

"Anika, Heinrich is..."

"Shut your mouth! Don't you dare speak aloud the name of anyone in my family!"

Anika gave her father the chance to challenge her command, and when he didn't, she continued.

"Not even the promise of youth? You'll have me tortured—and my children if necessary—to live a few more decades—a century maybe—as a deranged old man?"

"Not Gretel and Hansel! I did not..." Marcel broke into a desperate bout of coughing. He stood awkwardly, attempting to get leverage on it.

"And what is it about life that you so cherish, father? Tell me. Is it the loneliness of it? Or perhaps it's your lack of contribution to the world? And lifelong lack of ambition. Yes, that must all be it. Who would want to forfeit such a meaningful life as that?"

"I was good to you, Anika." Marcel extended his arm and formed his crooked hand into an accusatory point. His other hand he kept pressed to his mouth in anticipation of another coughing bout.

"Yes, father, you were. But what now? Your children are raised. Your wife is gone. And even if you can be cured by my death, you're old and frail. What will you do with your immortality other than hoard and treasure it for its own sake?" The edge had left Anika's voice now, as if she were offering her father one last chance to recognize how horribly wrong all of this was.

"My new life will be different." Marcel's eyes shifted in doubt. "I will make it into something valuable."

"Your life *was* valuable father. To me. To Mother. And to Gretel and Hansel. But it's become rotted. Nothing good will come in the future. Death is necessary, father, for everyone."

Marcel sat back on the sofa and stared into his daughter's eyes. "No, Anika," he said, "today only your death is necessary."

CHAPTER NINETEEN

"BUT MY MOTHER IS...was older than you."

"No Gretel, she's not," Odalinde replied. "Not by quite a bit."

The woman hesitated a moment and then strode the few steps to her secret cabinet behind her, simultaneously fishing something from her pouch. Without seeing it, Gretel knew at once it was the key she and Hansel had 'borrowed' only days ago. She plugged the key into the lock casually, with no concern of the potent little spies that ostensibly surrounded her. It was so unlike the times Gretel had seen her in the past, hunched and secretive, a compact wall of back and shoulders.

Both children sat mesmerized as they watched Odalinde reach into the cabinet, fumbling only briefly before pulling out the large black book that Gretel now recognized, without an ounce of doubt, as *Orphism*.

"I told you!" Hansel whispered.

Odalinde frowned and gave Hansel a narrow sideways stare, which the boy received and dropped instantly. "I suspected it was you, young man," she said.

"I'm sorry. I didn't..." Hansel's tone was more pleading than whimpering, but he was teetering on tears.

"It's okay, Hansel. It really is." Seeming to sense Hansel's descent toward a breakdown, Odalinde walked slowly to the boy and kneeled by him, resting her upper arm across the back of his chair, keeping her forearm raised to gently pet the back of his head with her hand. "It was never either of you I was worried about."

It was the first act of real warmth Gretel had seen from Odalinde since her arrival, and the gesture comforted Gretel in a way she hadn't felt since she'd lost her mother. But the scent of the ongoing mystery was strong, and she had no intention of losing it.

"How is it that you can be old enough to remember my mother being born?" Gretel asked. "That's not possible."

Odalinde looked squarely at Gretel and then stood straight, gripping the book with both hands so that the front cover faced forward. She framed it against her chest and said, "As I said, the story is long, but the short answer to your question is this book. This book is how it's possible."

"*Orphism*?"

Odalinde's eyes sparkled at the sound of the word, and a sad smile drifted across her lips and then receded. "Yes, Gretel, *Orphism*."

Gretel shook her head slowly in disbelief, blinking several times. She realized now that she hadn't truly believed Hansel's story about his discovery in Odalinde's cabinet. Particularly after searching it herself and finding it empty. If pressed for the truth, she would have said she even considered that Hansel had made the whole thing up to get her attention, and that she was willing to entertain him, thankful for the fact that he was talking to her at all, thankful that he had weathered the loss of his mother with such courage. It was true she had hoped the book would be there, but wasn't so surprised when it wasn't. It couldn't have been her same book.

"Is that...is it the same as the one I have?"

Odalinde nodded. "It is."

"I told you," Hansel said again, this time to no one in particular.

"How many copies are there?"

Odalinde smiled again, this time fully and warm. "It's an excellent question, Gretel. An excellent question. There are a handful maybe. I know of at least two others. But the truth is I don't really know for sure."

Odalinde straightened her smile now. "Your book, it was given to you by your grandfather? Is that right?"

Gretel nodded.

"When was that?"

"The night my mother disappeared. When we drove to his house trying to find out what happened to her."

"Before that day, the day he gave it to you, did your grandfather ever talk about the book? Or mention anything about it that you might remember?"

Gretel didn't need to think about the answer. "No. Nothing. I don't think he knew that I'd ever even seen it until that day. I used to look at it all the time though. Up on the shelf in the basement. And when I got older and could reach it I used to read it—well, look at the words anyway. But I never let him know that I'd found it. It always seemed like a thing to keep secret."

At this last remark Odalinde nodded again. "Yes, it does seem like that type of thing."

"But when he saw me with it," Gretel continued, "that night in the basement, he just gave it to me. Like he wanted me to have it and was waiting for me to ask. So maybe he did know that I'd found it. I guess I can't be sure."

"Did he tell you anything about it after he gave it to you?"

"Why? What does it say?" Hansel chimed in. "What's the book about?"

"In a moment, Hansel, okay? I'll tell both of you. I promise." Odalinde's voice was calm and reassuring, and she stroked the boy's head as she stepped toward Gretel and kneeled in front of her, waiting for the answer to her question. "What did he tell you, Gretel?"

"He just said that it was very old. That not many people could read it. And that my grandmother liked it. 'Treasured it,' I think he said."

Odalinde nodded politely and then asked slowly, "Could *he* read it, Gretel? Did he say whether *he* could read it?"

Gretel immediately shook her head. "No. He couldn't read it. At least that's what he told me."

Odalinde let out a sigh and stood up again.

"But..." Gretel stopped.

Odalinde froze, her eyes encouraging.

"I think he was hoping that *I* would be able to read it. Or that I could learn to read it. I don't know exactly. He wanted me to have it, that's for sure, but he was strange about it. Sad or something."

Gretel thought back to the scene in Deda's house and then shook her head quickly.

"But he's sick—dying I think. He was probably just having a spell. That's what my mother always called it when Deda acted strange."

Odalinde nodded and let this last piece of information sink in.

"This book is bad, isn't it?"

Odalinde's eyes searched the room for an answer to the question, a signal to Gretel that the woman had never thought about the book in these terms. "Yes Gretel," she said finally, "it is bad."

"And it's bad because..." Gretel's eyes darted furiously as she was suddenly flooded with the rain of discovery. "...it's some kind of black magic book, right? A book that tells how to live forever. That's how you knew my grand-mother. And how you were there when my mother was born. That's right isn't it?"

Odalinde gave a tired grin. "You have amazing intuition, Gretel, as I knew you would."

Gretel said nothing, her look never wavering as she dismissed the compliment and waited for actual confirmation. She couldn't have said exactly how she figured everything out so quickly, but she suspected Odalinde was right, she did have exceptional instincts.

"Perhaps not forever," Odalinde admitted softly, "but yes, in essence, that is what the book does."

"How old are you then?" Gretel asked, and saw instantly in Odalinde's face that this question was one that tortured her, one that she fought every day to keep her mind from exploring.

"I don't know exactly, but very old. Much older than I should ever have allowed myself to become."

Hansel smiled, almost laughing at this exchange. He looked to Gretel for the whimsical reveal of a teasing punchline, a wink or a punch to the shoulder perhaps; but he saw only cold seriousness in his sister's eyes.

Reflexively, he reached for his face, forming a dome over his nose and mouth as if ready to sneeze. Gretel at first took the gesture for one of shock, the stifling of a gasp, but her brother then lurched forward from his chair, his hands fixed in place as he dashed toward the front door, fumbling with the knob until finally turning it just in time to direct his cascade of vomit away from the kitchen floor and onto the porch. He stumbled a few more steps until he was fully out of the cabin and in the sanctuary of cool Back Country air. He descended the stairs until he reached the gravel driveway where he could freely release whatever sickness remained. Gretel listened to her brother wretch once again and then heard his breathing steady as he let out some hybrid of a wretch and a scream.

Odalinde retraced Hansel's path across the kitchen floor, following it to the threshold of the open front door. She paused, submitted a brief check of the situation in the driveway, and then closed the door until it was open just a crack.

"He'll be fine," she said, "everyone is frightened the first time they hear about the book. It's not an easy thing to digest." Odalinde rolled her eyes and smiled weakly at her unintended pun.

"Is it really true though?" Gretel asked, now fully realizing the significance of what was being revealed here. She wasn't worried about Hansel; it wasn't the first time nerves had caused the reaction she'd just witnessed. "Is it true anyone that can read this book could live forever?"

"Well, it's not quite that simple."

Odalinde walked back to the table and sat across from Gretel.

"Even if you know the language, or it's been translated for you, there are delicate skills you'd need to master—medical skills among them—and there are several quite obscure ingredients you'd need to be able to recognize and find." Odalinde paused and then nodded. "But, yes, eventually you could figure it out. More practically though, you could find someone who already had all of these skills."

Gretel was curious about the "medical skills," but she put it aside for the moment.

"So then I don't understand," she said, "why is the book a bad thing? I mean, I know people have to die to make room for new people, but...I don't know...life is good, right?" Gretel lingered on the last word, not sure exactly what she was trying to say.

"This is not about life, Gretel, this is about death: what happens to your physical body after it's been born into this world and then deteriorates from time or is ravaged by trauma or disease. We are meant to die. All of us. Avoiding death is unnatural. It's the opposite of nature, in fact."

Odalinde spoke quickly, never taking her eyes from Gretel. She stopped and searched the girl's face, looking for a sign of understanding that the truth she'd just heard should never be doubted. Odalinde took a slow breath and then continued, this time with less frenzy.

"Life, however, is something else. Life is always with you. Even after your body dies. Life is energy, and energy can't be destroyed. Life is your spirit or soul or a dozen other names that have been given to that thing—that force inside of you—which lets you know you're alive. It's the force that comforts you and motivates you, makes you love and sympathize. You, Gretel, have a strong awareness of Life. Stronger than most. That is part of your heritage and it will never go away."

"My heritage? What does that mean? I don't understand."

"The energy of the universe is available to all of us, Gretel. It flows through everyone and makes us who we are. And, if we wish, often with much trial and persistence, we can manipulate this energy to make things happen for us. To direct things toward us. For some, like you—and me, I suppose—that ability comes much easier."

"So is it some kind of magic?"

"I suppose that's a way to look at it, except that magic implies something otherworldly and exclusive. This isn't witchcraft. The energy of Life is the most common force in the universe. So common, in fact, that most of us ignore it. The way we ignore sunlight or oxygen."

"So this book, *Orphism*, explains this power? How to use it?"

"In a way that's what it does, yes. But the truth is the power of Life can't fully be explained in a book. It must be felt, experienced, individually harnessed for whatever purpose a person wishes to use it. Most people, even if they could read the language in the book, wouldn't have the discipline or insight to understand—on the deepest level—exactly what the book explicates. But the people who wrote the book, Gretel, they understood these things quite well. They were a group very strongly aware of the world and the offerings available to them."

"But you said the book was bad. So people can use this power to do bad things?"

Odalinde gave a tired sigh and rubbed the heels of her palms against her temples. "I don't believe the intention of the book was bad. Not originally. It was just the result of natural curiosity and exploration. And to answer your question: Oh yes, Gretel, people can use Life to provoke a great number of bad things. Unbounded really. You see, Life doesn't distinguish between good and bad—those are human adjectives that we assign to things based on an accepted set of social values. If a man were to inherit a family, for example, and then kill the children so that he may bear and raise only his own, we would consider that man bad, and our system of justice would likely deem it so bad he would be killed as a result. But when a lion does the very same thing—kills the offspring of other lions so that only his genes move on—we distance ourselves from judgment, accepting that the world of the lion operates by different rules. Well, in a way, Life sees the world the way we see the lion: objectively, without prejudice. If a person is knowledgeable of this Life power, he can use it however he sees fit. Even in a way that we would describe as bad."

Odalinde stood and walked back to the door, opening it just wide enough to check on Hansel again, before walking back and sitting at the table.

"I know this is a lot to hear right now, Gretel, and much of it you probably don't believe. That's okay. Where this power comes from and how it's used is not important right now. All of that is something you'll need to explore and come to believe on your own."

Odalinde stretched her arms across the table, her palms facing up, beckoning for Gretel's hands. Gretel offered them freely, and the touch of the woman's hands again awakened some hibernating memory of her mother.

"But the power of this book is real. And I have the feeling it has to do with your mother's disappearance."

Gretel's breathing shortened, and she could feel the muscles in her shoulders tighten. She squeezed Odalinde's hands tightly. "You think she's alive, don't you?"

"Honestly, Gretel, I don't know, she may *not* be. But I think if *you* believe she's alive—truly believe it—that's a very good sign. Do you believe she is?"

Gretel could only nod.

"Okay then," Odalinde said, "Okay."

"But how? Where would she be?"

"The whole process of creating the formula is complicated; it takes time. The source needs to be healthy and strong to start, and then it needs to be fed correctly. And the extractions can often take months depending..." Odalinde's eyes had grown wide, and the first two fingers of her right hand instinctively went to her lips as if giving an emphasized signal to a child to stay quiet.

Hansel now stood in the doorway, frozen, listening to this impossible conversation. His mouth hung wide and Gretel thought he looked a bit like a nutcracker.

"What are you talking about?" Gretel asked, nearly whispering. "Extractions? Fed?"

"I'm so sorry..." Odalinde began.

"What are you talking about!" Gretel violently recoiled her hand from Odalinde's.

Odalinde closed her eyes and exhaled. "The book—*Orphism*—is about a lot of things, much of it to do with what we discussed earlier, controlling the powers of Life and all that."

"But it's also about living forever," Gretel added, her impatience brimming.

Odalinde opened her eyes. "Yes. It's about that too. The first part—the part about Life and spirit and the ways of the universe—is not only powerful, it's also quite beautiful. The people who wrote it were unusually synchronized with the world. These were an ancient people, untraceable to any known descendants. Perhaps as old as those of Asia and Mesopotamia."

She paused, signaling a transition.

"But there is the other part of the book. The part on solving death." Odalinde gave a deep, nervous swallow. "This part was written by your people, Gretel. And yours, Hansel."

Odalinde waved for Hansel to come back and sit, which he did, reluctantly.

"This part is not beautiful. In fact, it's quite horrifying."

"Hansel, maybe you should go," Gretel snapped, her tone signaling she would have no tolerance for any more weak-stomach distractions.

"I'm fine," he replied, unconvincingly.

Gretel glared at her brother with a "you'll be sorry if you're wrong" look, and then immediately shot her attention back to Odalinde.

"It's a recipe, essentially, for a potion that stops the dying process. The brew is ingested, in small amounts at first, and then gradually, over decades, the doses need to increase for the formula to continue working. I don't think anyone knows exactly how it works, and it isn't like it's ever been studied properly in a laboratory."

Odalinde stopped for a moment to arrange her words, and Gretel tried to appreciate her aim to be delicate.

"Many of the ingredients—not all, but many—are derived from the human body."

Hansel brought a fist to his mouth but quickly composed himself. "That's disgusting," he said.

"Yes, it is, Hansel. It's despicable. But what is even more despicable, and what you would correctly assume, is that people don't usually give of their body parts willingly." Odalinde dropped her eyes ruefully. "There are victims."

"So they're killed?" Hansel asked, each word coming out with a beat in between.

"The final part is always fatal. Some die sooner than others. Those are..." Odalinde stopped and shook her head as if to strike the beginning of the sentence.

"Those are what? What is it?" It was Gretel this time.

"Those are the fortunate ones." Odalinde frowned and bounced a sad stare between the two children. "The true horror is the torture. The mutilation. It's abominable."

Gretel narrowed her eyes and sneered. "But you've done this," she challenged, unable to pitch down the shrillness in her voice. "You *are* one of the people who has tortured. You *are* someone who has eaten people. You must be, right?! You've lived for what? Centuries!"

"I have killed and tortured people, Gretel. Yes, I have done those things. More times than I could ever count or wish to remember. And the shame that I feel now—not just for those deaths, but also for the lack of feeling that I had for them at the time—I will feel that shame until I am buried."

Odalinde stood again and walked away from the table, her back to the children.

"And that time will come. I haven't blended for several years now. And I won't do it again."

"So you've decided to die then," Gretel stated flatly, with satisfaction. "Why?"

Odalinde turned back toward Gretel.

"For all the reasons I've explained. This discovery is a mistake. It's monstrous. I understand that. I've always understood it but...I couldn't stop. I just couldn't. If Hell exists I will burn there for what I've done. But it has been done. And I can't undo it. All I can do is try to help you and Hansel. And your mother."

The fury in Gretel was rising, and she clenched her teeth, struggling not to leap at the murderer standing in her kitchen.

"So if you made this decision, why did you wait so long? Why did you not help us right away! My mother could have been saved!"

"I didn't know your mother's disappearance had to do with any of this. At least...I wasn't sure. I truly wasn't. My reason for coming here wasn't to protect you from your father, it was just to take care of you because of a promise I made to your grandmother. A promise that I would take care of your mother—or her unborn children—if they were ever in need."

"But you're not making sense. You said you were here to protect us from our father," Gretel said, quick with her challenge.

"Protecting you from your father was not the reason I came here, it was the reason I stayed."

Gretel closed her eyes and spread her hands across her face, and then quivered her head back and forth in a short, vibratory twitch, trying to shake the mountain of puzzle pieces in her head into something flat and orderly. "None of this makes sense," she said, "what does my father have to do with this?"

"I didn't think anything at first. But then..." Odalinde paused and looked away.

"What?"

"On your bed, soon after I got here, I saw the book, the copy of *Orphism* your grandfather gave you. I didn't know if your father could read it—I still don't actually—but if he could, he was a danger to both of you. A sick man, in the last quarter of his life, that is the most dangerous man of all to know this secret. So I've kept him as he is, just sick enough to...make him weak."

"Why didn't you tell me about any of this? You knew I had this magic book the whole time and you never told me? Didn't you think everything was connected? My mother's disappearance? All of it?"

"No, I didn't. Not necessarily. Your grandmother had a copy of the book, I knew that, so it wasn't impossible to think your grandfather had simply handed down her copy to you or your mother as a keepsake."

Gretel was quiet, considering the possibility there may be logic in this reasoning.

"And I don't know if any of this *is* connected, Gretel, it may not be."

"It is," Gretel replied without hesitation, "I know it is."

Odalinde frowned and nodded, offering no challenge to the teenager's intuition.

"I handled all of this badly. I'm sorry to both of you. I didn't know what I was doing. I haven't raised a child or nursed a man in...I don't know how long. A very long time."

"You're not good at it." The words had left Gretel's mouth before she had a chance to consider them.

Odalinde smiled. "I know I was hard on you, Gretel, and neglectful to both of you, but I didn't want either of you to grow fond of me. When I left, I wanted you to be glad for my riddance. Plus it was how I was raised, and how I was taught to raise children, building them for survival. If your father were to..." She stopped suddenly, rethinking her words. "If he were not able to care for you, if he didn't get better, you would have to grow up quickly, on your own."

A lump grew in Hansel's throat, and the first tear bubbled in the bottom of his eye. "So you're not staying?" he asked. "You weren't going to stay?"

"No Hansel, I can't stay."

"So you never planned to marry him?" Gretel asked, the sadness in her voice conveying sympathy for her father and not sorrow at the news that she was losing a stepmother.

"No, Gretel. I have another life, other commitments. People I care for. That is where I would go in the evenings on..."

"Thursdays," Gretel finished for her.

Odalinde smiled again. "Yes, on Thursdays. But when your father asked me to marry him it was a very awkward situation. If I had said 'no' I would have had to leave immediately. It would have been too uncomfortable. And even though I never really knew if your father had to do with this, I believed something was wrong. And I was right, something *is* wrong."

Gretel sat quietly for a moment, and then she rose slowly, locking eyes with Odalinde, her chest burning at the question she was about to ask. "And how do you know Officer Stenson? How do you *really* know him?"

The confusion on Odalinde's face was instant, and Gretel trusted it.

"Who is..? You mean that System officer that came to check on you? I *don't* know him, Gretel. As I said the other day, he came by to check on you and you weren't here."

Gretel stared coldly into the woman's face, searching for the tell, the flicker or swallow or shift of the eyes. "Hansel saw his name in your book," she said finally. "And I saw it too."

Odalinde glanced toward Hansel and frowned and then looked back to Gretel.

"I told you, he gave me his name and number and told me to give it to you. I wrote it in my book where I keep all of my other numbers. I didn't give it to you because I didn't trust him. There was something insincere about him. I still believe that to be true."

"You told me father wouldn't allow it. You said that was why you didn't tell me."

"That was a lie. Your father never knew he was here."

"So you never told Officer Stenson about your engagement to Father?"

"Of course not! Why would you think that?"

Gretel dismissed the question with a quick head shake.

"He was here only a few minutes, we barely spoke at all, let alone that I would disclose anything like that. Particularly that topic. I just wanted him gone."

Odalinde's answers were coming to Gretel quickly, logically, in a way that only the truth could. She sat back down and took a deep breath, and the buzz of nature filled the otherwise silent kitchen.

"So do you think he knows where my mother is?" she said finally, wearily. "If she is alive, do you think he knows where she is?"

Odalinde opened her mouth as if to answer, but instead took a deep breath and then pressed her lips into a thin, sad smile. "Honestly? Yes, I think he knows something about what's happened. But if Officer Stenson is part of this, he's only one part."

"So who else then," Hansel asked before Odalinde could get to it.

"You're not going to like my answer. Neither of you."

Hansel's eyes widened and his mouth dropped in a short gasp. "Father?" he said.

"No Hansel," Gretel said, her voice deep and controlled, "she means Deda."

CHAPTER TWENTY

OLIVER STENSON'S RED System cruiser turned sharply down the hidden path leading to the old woman's cabin and then abruptly stopped, its tires skidding across the dirt driveway, leaving a haze of dust that hovered effervescently for a moment, and then deflated to the ground. It had been months since he'd come here, as a skeptical neophyte on the subjects of witchcraft and magic potions, terms for which he was always chided by Marcel for using. This wasn't wizardry or spell-casting he was told, this elixir was natural, accessible to everyone.

In the beginning, of course, at the very center of his beliefs, he doubted nearly all of what he'd been told about the bizarre brew; and the fulfillment of the promises that were made to him for his part in the scheme he accepted with equal doubt. But if it *was* true, even in part, even if it was something akin to a vitamin that allowed him twenty years beyond his natural life—or fifteen—his investment in the plan seemed worth it, especially if those years proved strong and healthy. After all, his role would be minimal: to monitor the case of a missing Back Country woman who would vanish along the Interways one spring morning; and then to make sure any leads in the case were steered in a direction away from certain sections of the Interways and this cabin. It sounded simple. It was simple. With his System experience and knowledge of the area, his part required little more than rigging a few clues here and there, and maybe leaving off a few more off the reports. Simple.

And in fact, as it turned out, it had been rather simple. Stenson wasn't even needed for the actual crime. Marcel had told him exactly how it all would happen: that Anika Morgan's car would drift off the road, and she, in a foolish search for help, would stumble directly into the clutches of the old woman. And it had happened just that way!

214

The poor woman, Anika, had somehow—impossibly—disappeared from the Interways and ended up in this time-forgotten, wooden shack in the bleakest part of the Northlands. Untraced. Unwitnessed. And he, Stenson, hadn't needed to do a thing! Even the car was virtually invisible, almost perfectly camouflaged at the bottom of that embankment. Only the most basic of additional cover had been necessary to keep it from being seen by anyone walking along at more than eight or ten feet away. And when the day came that it was finally discovered—if that day ever came—the obvious assumption would be that Anika Morgan had simply wandered into the woods after an accident looking for help and then died, her body overcome by the elements before being ravaged by some hungry animal (and in a way, Stenson thought, that is what happened), her clothes rotted and buried forever beneath countless layers of mud and leaf litter. Yes, finding that car now would do no good; it was far too late to find the connection between Anika Morgan and this cabin.

But there was a problem now: Anika Morgan was still alive. Recaptured, thank God, but still alive.

Marcel had known immediately that she'd escaped—*had felt it*—and within hours Stenson was rumbling his cruiser up to a defeated Anika Morgan lying prostrate in the middle of the road. It *was* magic. It was the only explanation. If anyone else had found her, the whole plan would have collapsed. She would have been taken to a hospital or barracks, or perhaps even home, and the whole story of her nightmare would have been unfurled. And by this time, instead of standing quietly outside the door of his cruiser, debating whether to walk to the front of the cabin door ahead of him and knock, or to investigate around back to keep the element of surprise intact, he and the rest of the Northlands unit would be ransacking the old shack for clues, of which there would be plenty. Perhaps even enough to connect him to the case.

But it hadn't happened that way. *He* had found Anika Morgan, just one more of an increasing number of fortuitous events that fell in his favor, and another example of why Oliver Stenson had steadily grown to become a believer in the potion. Devout. He'd yet to see any actual proof of the elixir's life-giving effects, but still, all of what Marcel had told him would happen had, from the accident, to the capture, to the hiring of the woman's daughter at the orchard. He hadn't predicted the escape, of course, but even magic contained some degree of variability, Stenson supposed. Yes, Stenson was a true believer now, and over the past few months he had become vigilant in his role of protecting the secret.

But he was also ready for the payoff. He was ready for that feeling that had been described to him by Marcel as described to him by his wife. And he was ready to bring Petr home from that school and, more importantly, to get him out of that orchard for good. 'We need to watch her,' Marcel had told him, referring to his own granddaughter. 'Gretel knows more than she knows.' Stenson had no idea what Marcel was talking about at the time, and after his visit with the girl he understood even less. Gretel seemed like a typical teenage girl to him—mature certainly, but typical—naturally distrustful of authority, and devastated that her mother had gone missing. But ultimately Stenson had deferred and agreed to position Petr at the Klahr orchard to act as their unknowing spy.

But it was time for all of this to be over. It was time to become untangled from all of this villainy.

Stenson exited his cruiser and stood tall, surveying the surroundings, squinting for any sign of the old woman. "Hello," he called out. He wanted to follow with the woman's name but realized he didn't know it. He wondered if even she knew it at this point. "Hello," he called again and closed the cruiser door, deciding to take the direct route to the front of the cabin.

Stenson imagined a flurry of scenarios as he approached the front door—an exercise that, as a System officer, was automatic to him. He didn't conjure any images that were particularly dangerous, especially since the escaped prisoner had already been caught, but the quietness made him wary. The most likely scene, he thought, was that the woman was dead, or else severely wounded. The prisoner had escaped after all, and Stenson could only believe that she'd done so using force. Perhaps the story was even known by now, revealed to Marcel by his daughter in some gleeful rage. He suddenly wished there was a way to contact the warehouse.

But what did it really matter? Stenson's only real concern—besides keeping his own freedom—was the potion. The beautiful potion. He realized now that he was addicted to it without ever tasting a drop! Ha! That was madness, of course, but it was true. It was the first and last thing he thought about each day. Every day. He'd risked his career, farmed out his son, and been an accomplice to kidnapping, torture and attempted murder. What more evidence was needed to show he was a slave to it? And the more he thought of it, the worse the addiction grew.

And now, with months of images of the brew stirring slowly in the middle of his mind, he almost couldn't stand it. His respect for Marcel on this matter was immense; how had he had resisted it all those years? But this respect was somewhat offset by Stenson's hatred about the fact that the old man never learned the recipe himself, that he had never taken the path of his wife. Of course, Stenson never considered that if Marcel had known the recipe, Stenson's role in the whole plan would have been unnecessary and he would have been left out. But that was addiction.

He forced his mind back to the top concern on the docket: The potion, and the fact that it wasn't completed. The Source was still alive, which according to Marcel meant, at the very least, the final ingredients had not been included. Stenson was pretty sure he'd been told that piece involved the heart, but it could also have been the liver. Whichever. It was close to finished. Very close. It had to be!

He knuckled five aggressive raps on the cabin door, the thick, solid design of the structure muffling the sound into something dull and impotent, like knocking on a tree trunk. He waited a moment and then walked a few steps to the porch-level window, bending over at the waist and cupping his hands around his eyes as he put his forehead to the glass to peer in. But he could see only vague outlines and darkness, the result of decades of built-up grime and dust.

The System officer walked back to the door and this time turned the knob slowly. It twisted easily, ironically almost, considering the daunting mass of the door itself. He pushed the door open about three feet and was immediately assaulted by the unmistakable stench of flesh. Old and rotten. Dead. He turned back to the air of the porch and breathed deeply, instinctively lifting his uniform shirt to cover his nose and mouth while blinking out the film of water that had formed protectively over his eyes.

"Oh my God," he whispered.

His mind instinctively formed a few additional, more precarious, scenarios for what might be in the cabin, and after processing them almost simultaneously, the officer pushed the door firmly with both hands so that it opened as wide as possible, offering the awful odor an undisturbed route of escape. The width of the doorway allowed Stenson to see most of the inside of the cottage from the porch, the only exceptions being the two bedrooms off to the side. And with this expansive vantage point, his conditioned brain went through the progressions. A disturbance had occurred. Violent. In the kitchen area. The escape had been through the back door (it was open). And there was something else. Something much worse.

Stenson's breathing became rapid and his throat tightened at the sight. Something had been shattered, something ceramic—a bowl or plate—and the dark mixture that it had contained was now splattered grotesquely across the floor.

"Oh God, no!" The words came out in something resembling a whine, and Stenson raced into the cabin, now completely unaware of the foulness in the air. He reached the scene on the floor and knew instantly—not with magic or witchcraft (screw you, Marcel!), but with the knowing instincts of a seasoned detective—that his chance at immortality was finished.

Oliver Stenson stood with his legs slightly apart and his head hung, his eyes closed as if saying a prayer in front of a gravesite. He opened his eyes and stared absently at the dried black puddle, making sure to keep his boots clear, just in case...just in case it was still...viable.

With his index finger extended, he began to kneel toward the floor. He needed to touch the black sludge, to feel for himself whether there was truly power there. The tip of his finger was only inches away when a sound from the back of the cabin broke the stillness. It was rustling and quick, and Stenson's hand instinctively repositioned itself away from the puddle to his sidearm. He knew it was unlikely to be anything too concerning, probably just an animal, lured by the sickening promise of decaying flesh. But he was cautious anyway, as he'd been trained to be in even the most seemingly benign situations, and he unholstered his weapon as he walked toward the open kitchen door.

More noises came from the back, this time heavier and more methodical, though still quick. Stenson reconsidered his original assessment and now thought the sounds were footsteps. Human footsteps. He stood in the doorway and faced the outside, his toes just across the threshold. He gripped the gun tightly and laid it close to his chest.

"Who's there?" Stenson called, deepening his voice an octave. He waited a few beats for an answer, sensing attentive ears just outside the door. "My name is Officer Oliver Stenson. I'm a System officer. If there is anyone there show yourself or respond to me now."

"What can I do for you, Officer?"

The words imploded the silence almost before Stenson had finished barking his commands. The voice was clear and robust, young and feminine, and for a moment Stenson felt like a child, seven or eight maybe, whose mother has just caught him sneaking sweets before dinner. It was almost comforting. But not quite. There was something else in the voice, in the tenor perhaps, something vibratory in the pitch that was ancient and unfriendly. And the words had come not from the backyard but from inside the cabin, near the front door in fact, on the opposite side of the house from where he'd heard the footsteps.

Stenson spun toward the voice and raised his weapon. His eyes were wide and locked, not with fear exactly, but something close to it, uneasiness perhaps. Enhanced uneasiness.

"And what is your answer to my question, officer." The words were slightly playful and challenging. "Again, in case you weren't ready for it the first time, the question was 'What can I do for you?'"

Officer Stenson lowered his sidearm and stared at the figure which stood rigid and motionless; the dusky gray robe it wore gave it the appearance of a shadow, faded and strayed from its source. The eyes and cheekbones were blanketed by a large hood which draped forward several inches past the figure's face; the only features Stenson could see with any clarity were the nose and lips. It was the old woman, he was sure of that, the general outline matched, and she had worn the same robe on the other occasion they had met. And besides, who else would it be?

But she was different now, transformed in some way. And it wasn't just her voice, which had lost all trace of the off-key, aged hoarseness he remembered from the few words she'd spoken that day. She was...taller, sturdier. Imposing even. Or maybe it was just that her posture was better—perfect in fact—that she appeared taller. And from what he could see of her face she was younger, judging by the smoothness of the skin on her nose and color of her lips, by at least a decade. Maybe more.

"Were you outside?" he stammered finally. "Did you hear me call you? How did you get in here so fast?"

"I *was* outside and I *did* hear you call," the woman challenged in a tone conveying the question 'and what are you going to do about it?'

The woman stood waiting for a reply to her implied question, but Stenson stayed silent.

"And I'm fast, Officer Stenson," she continued, "that's how I got in here so fast." At this remark her eyes flickered. "Now, one more time: What can I do for you?" The old woman's words had lost their airy edge and were now sardonic and impatient.

"What can you do for me? *Do* for me?" Stenson's voice rose considerably on the second sentence, and he opened his eyes wide, presenting that slightly crazed look signifying that a punch in the nose for asking such a question wouldn't be unreasonable. "Perhaps you hadn't noticed..." Stenson again wanted to address the woman by name but remembered, once again, that he didn't know it. "The young woman who was sent to you, that was arranged for you to...blend...or whatever it is you call it, is no longer here! So maybe the first thing you can *do for me* is tell me *why* she isn't here anymore and, instead, is sitting alive in a System holding house. And she's there, by the way, only because *I* found her lying in the middle of the Interways! That's what you can do for me!"

The old woman stood motionless for a moment, staring at him, and though he couldn't see her eyes, Stenson knew it was a look of hate. She then formed her lips into a pleasant smile, while at the same time raising her hands and gripping the flopping edges of the oversized hood. Stenson noted again the smooth unblemished skin, this time on her hands and wrists, as she pulled the hood back slowly, revealing the truth about what the officer had thought may have been just a trick of the shadows and sunlight. She *was* younger. By twenty, even thirty years, he guessed. For a moment he thought he may have been wrong about his initial certainty that this was the same person; but no, it was definitely her, the woman he'd conspired with to murder a young mother in order to use her innards for his own youthful quests. But how? The woman in front of him now looked barely older than a young mother herself.

If he was being honest, he would have described her as attractive. Beautiful maybe. Her skin was taut and unblemished, and the dullness of her eyes was replaced by the alert glitter of a schoolgirl's. And her hair. Her hair erupted from the hood of the cape in a mane of auburn silk, pouring down her shoulders and chest like diluted honey.

Stenson opened his mouth to speak but stopped, not knowing exactly what to say. Then, suddenly, he made the obvious connection. It was the potion. And it was better than what he'd been promised. Younger. It could make him younger!

The woman again stood still, as if showcasing herself for the man. But Stenson stared for only a moment. He knew the woman was studying him, and he'd seen her lips, barely splitting apart, revealing the stark whiteness of her newly polished enamel. The twitch of her mouth was slight, unnoticeable by the average citizen, but to Stenson it was a common tell, and it snatched him back to the moment. He took a breath and gripped his fingers tightly around his firearm, anticipating action. He was in that stage of an encounter—he'd been there dozens of times, he figured—when a perpetrator is weighing the options of whether to flee or attack, and by what means he'll carry out the decision. In almost every other case, Officer Stenson would have guessed correctly as to which move this perp was going to make. Given the two choices, a child would have guessed the same. First of all this was a *woman* in front of him, and an older woman at that (though not as old as she used to be). And, ostensibly, she was unarmed, as well as uniquely familiar with the environment having lived there for what, a hundred years? This suspect was no threat to him. This suspect was a runner ('and I'm fast, Officer Stenson, that's how I got here so fast'). It was System Work 101.

These calculations were processed in the mind of Officer Stenson automatically, only seconds before the witch glided across the room, as if carried from behind by a blast of sudden wind, and slammed against the torso of The System officer.

She's flying! he thought, *like a real witch*. It was the last conscious thought of Officer Stenson's life, just before the enormous fingernails of the woman entered his gut below the ribcage, piercing his stomach and severing his large intestine. With her other hand she gripped the back of his head and pulled it close, like a lover overcome by passion. But instead of a kiss, the woman exposed her fangs, newly filed and razor sharp, and tore out the left side of her victim's neck with the ease of an African lion. She clung tightly to the man, her mouth open in anticipation of a struggle, but the attack had left the officer instantly paralyzed.

She was stronger now, much stronger, and it would take some time to learn the appropriate effort needed to kill her prey in the future. But she had time now. So much time.

She spat the hunk of flesh toward the sink and discarded the body of Officer Oliver Stenson to the floor with the care of sock tossed to a hamper. His skull popped against the countertop on the way down before joining the rest of his body in a puddle of bodily fluids—a mixture that included both his and those of the woman he'd helped capture. His chest lurched in its last few attempts to get oxygen to his lungs, but his mouth hung agape, frozen, unable to suck any air past the shroud of blood and saliva that had built up on his tongue and in his cheeks. And with his windpipe shredded, the air would have never made it anyway.

"You're rather lucky," the old woman said absently, "in another life I would have kept you to die much slower."

WITH BLOOD DRIPPING from her chin, the woman walked outside through the back door and looked to the place where she'd been digging. Interruptions! She'd been expecting the officer of course, especially since the girl's escape, but she had work to do; there was no time for distractions. She needed to recapture her prisoner, somehow keep her alive and remake the potion. It would take time, certainly, and there was no guarantee the prey would survive the ordeal again. But if she didn't, all was not lost. There were others. Others who were nearby with perfection in their blood. Other Aulwurms.

The cabin, however, was no longer safe. If only she'd sampled the mixture earlier! She'd have her prisoner without this hassle! But she knew that wasn't completely true either. Even if she still controlled the girl, the old woman knew the extorting thieves would be coming. The mixture was overdue: she could recall the schedule perfectly now in her revived brain. And it was 'Marcel.' Yes, that was his name. That was the man who had sent the lovely Source to her, and she reveled in the purity of this truth. But it was she alone who could make the brew. It was she alone with the knowledge of the recipe. Not them!

And things took time. There was no patience in this modern world; everyone needed things now. And this System officer, Stenson, he seemed particularly hasty. She could see in the way he leaped for the spilled potion that he'd grown addicted to the idea of it. To the idea of immortality. It was a pattern she'd seen dozens of times in her past. No temperament to handle the wait. And as she'd also witnessed, the pursuit of the broth had caused his early expiration, an irony never lost on her.

But Stenson's death was unimportant. Nothing more than a mess to clean. Her aims were different now. She'd found the true serum. The one she'd heard whispered of in the Old Lands by her ancestors. The myth sought by all. She could stay young. Forever. She was strong again, of mind and body. And Life. She would reconnect with It. Control It as she once had when she was young and zealous.

She walked back to the kitchen and stood over the twisted body of Officer Stenson, which now lay still, dead. The witch's feet were planted irreverently in the remaining mixture on the floor, and she almost chuckled at the locked expression of fear and pain on the officer's face. She kicked the left side of his body and heard the sound she was listening for—the jingle of keys—in his right pocket. She reached over and pulled the ring of keys free, and then dangled them in front of her face, smiling at the confidence she felt inside of her. It was almost impossible to believe what she was considering—no, not considering, what she was *going* to do. The world now seemed a platter to her, a buffet of opportunity and treasure. Every second in this cabin now seemed a waste of the eternal time she now possessed. If even yesterday she'd been granted this opportunity, the opportunity to drive off in this machine, she would have certainly hidden from it, afraid of the technology she'd shunned for so long. She'd driven a car in the past, in the days before secrecy and privacy had taken over her life, but it had been years, and she'd certainly never controlled anything like the monster parked outside. Yes, her old self would have spent days, weeks maybe, figuring out some method to dispose of the car without ever starting the engine or even getting inside. But now the machine excited her and the thought of driving released a burst of saliva across her tongue. The energy under her. The power and speed at her control. And, most importantly, the utility of the thing. There were more sources to find before this day ended, and the car would help her find them.

It was time to hunt.

CHAPTER TWENTY-ONE

"SO IT WAS YOU WHO ARRANGED for the Klahrs to hire me."

Gretel's statement came out sad and robotic, not quite a question. She kept her head still and her eyes forward, watching the pavement pass beneath the truck. They were on their way to Deda's, and the sickening memory of the trip she and Hansel made with their father on the day her mother disappeared regurgitated in her stomach.

Everything Odalinde had told her in the kitchen was too much to process: that her mother may be alive and that it was likely Deda who stole her away to begin with. That it was Deda who was the villain in this mystery. This possibility was devastating, and Gretel wasn't ready to explore her true beliefs about the tale just yet. Instead, she circled the issue, attempting to talk her way in from the edges until she reached a point in the middle where everything came together to make sense.

"No, Gretel, that was you," Odalinde said, "you alone." Odalinde took her eyes from the road and stared hard at Gretel, searching for a signal of belief that what she'd just said was true. She looked back to the road and frowned. "But I was also wrong. I was wrong to have forced you to that point—the point where you were scared and stealing food. I was just...I just wanted to instill in your heart that you were strong. Stronger than you believed. And that if you were pressed to survive—forced to save yourself and your brother—you would find a way."

She turned to look at Gretel again, this time giving a look that was softer, sympathetic.

"And you did, Gretel. You found a way. I knew you would. I could tell that resolve was in you the second I met you." Odalinde paused and then said, "It was like I'd met your grandmother all over again."

225

Gretel felt the swell in her throat and she turned quickly toward the window. It wasn't that she cared about crying in front of Odalinde necessarily, but crying at the mention of her grandmother seemed to negate the strength for which she'd just been commended. Besides, she didn't want to trust Odalinde completely, and crying at this point would make her vulnerable. And, of course, there was Hansel. She had to stay strong for him.

"I'm sorry, Gretel. For everything."

Gretel stayed quiet, with her forehead and nose pressed against the side window. She gave a hard blink to wring out the last threat of tears, and when she opened her eyes, she could see in her periphery that Hansel had fallen asleep in the back. She sat straight again, now feeling encouraged to continue questioning Odalinde more directly.

"Petr referred to you as my stepmother." Gretel paused, setting up the blow. "But I never told him about you and Father getting married. Why would he have said that? How would he have known?"

Odalinde furrowed her brow and smiled, nearly snickering. "I don't know, Gretel. I told you, I never said anything about marrying your father to anyone. And certainly not to Petr or his father."

"So how then?"

"Maybe he just made a mistake. Or..." Odalinde paused, "is it possible you *did* tell Petr and just forgot?"

Her tone was delicate, one intended to encourage Gretel to explore this explanation more deeply. But Gretel *had* explored it exhaustively and was positive she'd never mentioned the engagement. The whole affair had weighed on her far too heavily to have one day tossed it out casually and forgotten about it.

"No, it isn't possible."

"So you never told anyone then? Not even at school?"

"No," Gretel hesitated, "except...Well, I told the Klahrs. But no one else."

Odalinde's eyebrows flickered up and she cocked her head slightly, her eyes staying focused forward. It was a gesture that said, 'Perhaps there's your answer.'

"They wouldn't have told Petr," Gretel protested.

"No? And why is that?"

Gretel started in on her defense of the Klahrs, but decided too much time had been wasted already on the ill-fated marriage of Heinrich and Odalinde, and she instead changed the subject entirely. "That figurine-thing, the swan on the mantle, that was my grandmother's wasn't it?"

Odalinde smiled and nodded, again fascinated by Gretel's instincts. "She gave it to me when your mother was born. It's an old custom for a mother to give a gift to the godparents upon the birth of a child. I've treasured it for a long time. And when I came here it seemed proper to bring it along." She paused. "I'm going to leave it for you, Gretel. It's yours now."

Gretel was touched by the gift, and wanted to ask a thousand more questions about how Odalinde came to the responsibility she now owned. And about her grandmother. And how she died.

But the subjects felt out of place to explore at the moment, as if they were stories from a different book to be read later. So instead Gretel asked, "What will we do if my grandfather is there?"

The sympathy returned to Odalinde's face, and she reached out and stroked Gretel's hair. "I've thought about that. Obviously we can't simply walk into his house and accuse him of kidnapping your mother. I do believe he's involved in this, but I don't have proof. So, we'll say we're there to visit, that's all."

"What about Hansel? I don't know if he'll be able to stay quiet."

"I won't say anything," Hansel chimed from the back, "I promise."

And for the rest of the trip to Deda's, no one said a word.

ANIKA AWOKE IN THE chair and saw her father sitting on the couch in the same position he was when he told her of her impending death. It hadn't been a dream. Anika hadn't suspected as much, but the soulless man next to her now left no doubt.

She tried to gauge how long she'd been asleep, but without windows, she had no idea. Clearly her body was still recovering from its ordeal, and she was thankful for the rest.

"Who is the woman?" Anika asked coldly, "The woman whose face I smashed?"

Marcel was sober now, no longer convulsively trying to sell the merits of his diabolical decisions. It seemed to Anika that he'd recognized his daughter was right—he was deranged—and that continuing to advocate for what he was prepared to do only amplified that assessment.

"She's your kin, Anika," he answered, "distantly related, but your blood."

Anika nodded at this, the truth of her father's words obvious to her now that they'd been spoken.

"She, however, didn't know of the relation. At least your mother didn't believe so."

This too made sense to Anika—she'd never gotten the sense the woman viewed her as anything other than a common animal. If she *had* known, based on what her father believed about the potion, Anika suspected the woman's ferocity and precision would have been even greater.

"Your mother had known the woman was in this country the day she arrived, so many years ago. She was young then, the woman, and alone." Marcel looked to the floor. "And not yet inoculated with the potion."

"Was she looking for Mother? Why did she come here to begin with, to the Northlands?"

"The Northlands have always been a common refuge for Old Country folk, surely you know that. Just think of all the like surnames in these parts. The reasons for coming are always changing—when the woman came it was probably for opportunity and adventure, a drive far less coercive than the persecution from which your mother fled. But in any case, it has never been unusual for ancestors to settle in common areas."

Anika had never been close with her relatives, but it was true there were many around. "So Mother welcomed this woman when she arrived? They bonded?"

"No, Anika, that's not how it was. I don't think they ever met. Your mother had been here long before the woman arrived. Long before she was ever born."

"So how did she know this woman was coming at all? If people arrived regularly, and she had no real connection to her, why was her coming here of any note to Mother? I don't understand."

"It was the book, Anika. It was, of course, the book. Your mother knew she had the book."

"That doesn't help me to understand."

"The copies were tracked carefully back then. There were only a few dozen or so in existence, most of which were kept by members of your mother's family. When a copy traveled, so did word of its movement. Your mother learned of the book's voyage to the Northlands and she took it as her duty to make sure the secrets it contained stayed safe."

"But how did she know the book was coming? Who relayed that message?"

Marcel rubbed his brow with the tips of his fingers and closed his eyes. He inhaled slowly, careful not to trigger another fit of coughing. His exhaustion was palpable to Anika.

"I don't know every detail, Anika. Your mother told me this story long ago. I just know your mother was afraid—terrified—that the secret would become known, known here in a land that lacked the context and history to respect it. It's why she never taught it to me."

Anika was relentless with her questioning, leaving no room for her father to change the subject. "But the woman knew the secret. How would it stay safe if that woman knew?"

"You mother knew she had the book, but it was possible she didn't know of the black secrets it contained. She thought it quite unlikely actually. And that was the primary reason your mother stayed away from her. She was afraid if she befriended the woman, and made their common ancestry known, that eventually the secret would be revealed. So instead your mother kept her distance, watching for signs from afar, listening for news of unusual deaths...murders."

"May not have known the secret? Why would Mother have assumed she didn't know?"

"Many of the inheritors of the books, even in those days, revered the document only for what it symbolized, the beauty of life and the powers of nature. Things like that. But they never *truly* believed or attempted to practice all that was inside. Not most of them. They didn't believe in the practical nature of the book. Much the same way millions of people own Bibles but don't live their lives by the letter of The Word. Some do, but most don't. These books eventually became keepsakes, family heirlooms, an inheritance with a medieval backstory that few believed."

"But there is..." Anika paused suddenly and closed her eyes. She exhaled slowly and continued. "There's the recipe. I don't recall in the Bible a menu for cannibals." Anika could see her father draining further, and knew he had no energy for banter or argument.

"Once the books became two or three generations removed from their original scribes, there were few people in the world anymore who could read them. There were a handful of families who kept the language sacred and passed it on, but most didn't. The world was moving on, on to the one we live in today, a world of enlightenment and science—things like *Orphism* were suddenly viewed with fear and contempt—and ultimately mythology. It was why your mother left her home."

"So Mother didn't know if the woman could read the book? Is that what you're saying?"

"She doubted it but had no way of knowing for sure. But even if she could, your mother thought it unlikely the woman would ever attempt to practice it. Not the blending part."

"But Mother was wrong."

Marcel leaned back in his chair and frowned. "It so happens that, yes, she was wrong. In many ways I wish she hadn't been but...well, there it is."

Anika stared at her father and said nothing, and then stood suddenly with her cup of water and walked to the main door of the building, twisting the handle for good measure, but showing no surprise when it didn't turn.

"You didn't think it would be that easy did you?" Marcel's tone was mild, as if trying to soften the natural sinisterness of the phrase.

"I suppose not," Anika said as she began to stroll the interior perimeter of the warehouse. "But what now, Father? Your plan failed. I'm here, alive, and as far as you know I've killed the woman, leaving you with no one to complete the recipe. You're a dead man after all."

"The woman isn't dead, Anika. I know she isn't."

"How can you be sure of that?" Anika's tone was challenging, almost cocky, and she continued sauntering the warehouse floor, clutching her mug nervously in both hands, passing the empty metal shelving until she reached the back wall and the interior door where Officer Stenson had ducked out.

"Your mother never taught me the secret to immortality, but the book contains more than that. Much more. There are things inside—lessons—powerful and wonderful things which your mother did teach me. Ways to connect with the life force inside of everything, and to feel that force, intuit it, guide it when necessary. It took years to learn and control it, but I have done it. And I feel Life in the old woman. I feel it as strongly as ever."

"So is that where your slave has gone? That System officer? To bring her here? To kill me?" Anika tried the knob of the interior door but it too was locked, and though she hadn't expected anything different, she let out a disappointed sigh.

"They'll be here soon, Anika." Marcel paused and then said, "I know it means nothing at this point, but I truly am very sorry."

Anika let out a sound that was a mixture of laughter and scream. She stood bewildered at the back of the warehouse, staring wide-eyed at the tall ceiling, resetting all that had happened since she'd been found on the road this morning. It didn't seem possible.

"So why did you never teach me any of these great lessons, Papa?" Even now, Anika knew the sarcastic lilt she attached to 'Papa' would sting her father.

"I tried, Anika, when you were very young. But you didn't grasp it. It didn't come naturally to you. I always intended—when you were older—to resume the lessons, but your mother died and, well, I just didn't. I'll admit I was disappointed you weren't naturally able to feel it, feel it the way Gre..." Marcel stopped, as if speaking his granddaughter's name was forbidden.

"Gretel? The way Gretel does?"

Marcel nodded slowly. "Yes, Anika, the way Gretel does."

GRETEL WASN'T SURPRISED to find Deda's house empty when they arrived, nor was she surprised that an aimless search for clues as to Deda's whereabouts rendered nothing.

Odalinde and Hansel took the main floor while Gretel searched the basement. At once the musty smell of the cellar transported her back to the last time she'd been down there, the night her mother disappeared, the night she and Hansel waited anxiously as their father and grandfather discussed what could have happened to the only woman in the world that loved all of them.

Gretel rummaged again through the drawers of the old desk—including the one that held the dirty magazines—and was momentarily amazed that she and the girl who had mischievously perused those pictures only months ago were the same person. It seemed almost impossible, and she nearly giggled at the embarrassment she felt at the time. Such innocence.

She scanned the dusty bookshelves where Orphism had sat for so many years, that empty slot now as vacant and black as the book itself. A montage of all the times she'd constructed makeshift scaffolds and had secretly leafed through the book's pages instantly flashed through her mind. It was all so distant now. How she wished that book was still there. How she wished everything was still here.

As for clues, the basement contained nothing tangible, a fact Gretel knew to be true before she touched the first step down. But there *was* something—an inkling—a memory to pursue maybe, something peculiar about that night that went unnoticed. At the time it didn't stick—there was far too much to process about that night— but there was something. Gretel couldn't quite find it, however, and if it was still in her brain, whatever that "it" was floated mockingly out of reach, and Gretel didn't feel she was very close to it. Deda was involved, however, about that she was convinced, and her impatience to find him—and her mother—was festering.

"Let's go," she said to no one in particular as she reached the top of the cellar stairway, "we're wasting our time here."

"Okay, but where?" Odalinde asked.

Gretel knew the woman's question wasn't rhetorical. Her ex-stepmother-to-be believed in Gretel's intuition, and she, Gretel, now felt the pressure of that belief. "I don't know! I just know there is nothing here and we have to hurry!"

"Stop yelling, Gret!" Hansel snapped, the boy once again precariously close to tears.

"Gretel, it's okay," Odalinde said, her voice soft and measured. "I think you're right. I don't think we're going to find anything here."

"Then why did we come here at all?"

"Your grandfather is involved, Gretel. I was being delicate about that before, but you know he's involved."

"Yes, I do know that. But he isn't here. I knew he wouldn't be here."

"Where is he then Gretel!" Hansel's voice was as loud as Gretel had ever heard. "I need to find Mother!" The boy slapped his hands to his face, covering his cheeks and eyes, while deep, guttural sobs exploded from him. He dropped down to the floor like a sack of flour and cried, his back and head convulsing with each bawl.

Gretel frowned at her brother and walked to the front door. "Let's go," she said coldly, as she turned the knob on the door.

GRETEL SAT RIGID IN the front seat of the truck while Odalinde, ostensibly, consoled Hansel. She brushed aside any feelings of guilt about her treatment of her brother, and instead used the time instructively, focusing her intuition. She closed her eyes, squinting them in concentration, and placed her hands flat on the top of her head. She was missing something.

She sat this way for several minutes, still, waiting for the answer to arrive from the ether, when, finally, the front door to Deda's opened and Odalinde stepped out holding Hansel's hand.

"I'm sorry, Gretel," Hansel said as he climbed into the back of the truck, "I didn't mean to yell at you. I just miss her."

Gretel sighed and had to fight the reflexive eye roll that surfaced. "I miss her too, Hansel. And don't be sorry. You didn't do anything."

Hansel was quiet for a moment, and then said, "I guess I just never believed it, you know? I always thought she was coming back. Especially on that first day, the day she didn't come home. I was scared just like you and Papa, but I also thought you were both wrong. I thought when we came here that night that...that Deda would know. I thought Deda would tell us everything was fine, that Mother had just been delayed or...I don't know. Something."

Gretel's eyes welled at the sincerity and eloquence of her brother's words, and she turned toward him, awkwardly pulling him close and hugging him. "It's okay, I know."

With Odalinde sitting unobtrusively beside them, the siblings remained embraced momentarily when Gretel's eyes flashed open.

"Wait a minute," she whispered, pushing her brother away. She turned her eyes to the roof of the truck, exploring her memory.

"What is it, Gretel?" Odalinde asked.

"That night—that night Hansel and I came here, when Mother went missing—Deda had nothing to tell us that could help. He never told us anything."

"We already know it's Deda, Gretel," Hansel said, "We know he's involved in this."

"But that's just it," Gretel shook her head as if fanning away her brother's obviousness, "Deda didn't tell *us* anything. Remember Han? We were shooed to the basement. Deda and Papa wanted to talk in private. Why in private?"

"So we wouldn't hear if something bad had happened. They didn't want us to get more upset. Deda wanted to protect us."

"But protect us from what? If Deda didn't know anything, what could he have said that would have upset us any more than we already were? And yet, he wanted to talk to Father alone."

"What are you saying, Gretel?" Odalinde's voice was low and clear.

"I don't know exactly," she replied, "we need to talk to Father. And we need to go now."

CHAPTER TWENTY-TWO

THE OLD WOMAN SAT MOTIONLESS in The System cruiser, her eyes closed, a long, thin smile drawn across her face. Her breathing was slow and rhythmic and her mind was clear. The smells accompanying her meditation were foreign and wonderful, and the feel of the leather on her palms, so lithe and cool, calmed her even further. And the sound. Those sounds which had surrounded her, which had imprisoned her for generations, were now virtually extinguished by the insulation of this perfectly built machine.

Resting on the seat beside her, contained securely in a bowl no larger than the one she'd been assaulted with, were the remnants of the broth, salvaged with great effort from the floor of her kitchen. There was no need to bury it now, she wouldn't be coming back.

Almost instantly after turning the ignition, the old woman heard a voice. "Hello officer," the female voice said, "where would you like to go?"

The old woman instinctively spun her body toward the back seat, teeth bared, looking for the intruder. But the back of the cruiser was empty, and the old witch quickly realized it was not a woman, but rather the car, that was speaking. A robot. To assist her.

The old woman glanced fervently about the cab of the cruiser, looking for some clue, a note perhaps, containing the magic words that would unlock her destination. Did the words have to be perfect? Would there be some alert if she spoke errantly? Or worse, would she trigger some self-destruction mechanism?

No.

This was her new life. Her Orphic life. A life without paranoia, only perfection. A life where only the powers of the universe worked for her, constantly thrusting her forward toward her ever-evolving completeness.

"Anika Morgan," she said. "Take me to Anika Morgan."

The robot was silent for several beats, every one of which pulsed through the old woman's blood as she sat wide-eyed, anticipating.

"There is no match for Anika Morgan," it said finally. And then, "Do you mean Gretel Morgan?"

"Yes," the old woman said, almost laughing, her face as cheerful and alive as a child's on a playground, "take me to Gretel Morgan."

CHAPTER TWENTY-THREE

BEFORE THE TRUCK WAS at a full stop, Gretel had opened the passenger-side door, hopped out to the driveway, and was racing toward her house and the boy sitting on her porch steps.

It was Petr.

She had no idea why he was there, and why his father hadn't come to pick him up, but she didn't care; a fury had overtaken her, and now that he *was* here, it was time he filled in his part of the mystery.

The boy stood quickly, a weary smile on his face; it was a look that showed both surprise and pleasure at Gretel's apparent excitement to see him. "Hey Gretel," he called, "since I guess my..."

"Who told you?" she demanded, braking the last steps of her run just before slamming into Petr. She was gasping heavily and had to bend at the waist to allow the air in. "Who told you?" She wanted to say more, berate the boy really, but she had to catch her breath, and the three words were all she could manage.

"What? Who told me what? Gretel, what's wrong? Where were you?"

"Who told you!" Gretel was now only inches from Petr's face, eye to eye with him, screaming. Over the boy's shoulder, she could see what appeared to be the outline of a car. It was covered by an old faded tarp, and for a moment Gretel's mind flashed to her canoe and thoughts of rowing.

"Gretel I don't know—"

Gretel snapped back to attention. "About my father and Odalinde getting married! You know Goddamn well what I'm talking about!" Gretel took a deep breath and lowered her voice. "I never told you about them getting married, Petr. So who told you? Was it the Klahrs?"

"No!" Petr chirped, quickly, a clue to Gretel that Petr hated even the suggestion that the Klahrs were somehow involved in any of this. But it also signaled that Petr was hiding something, and it was time to come clean.

Odalinde parked the pickup truck and had now arrived with Hansel to stand beside Gretel. Petr Stenson had an audience now, and they were rapt with attention.

"It wasn't the Klahrs," he began, and then quickly veered into an apology. "I'm sorry, Gretel, I..."

"I don't care, Petr. Later I might, but not now." Gretel's eyes shifted again to the tarp. What *was* that?

Peter nodded and continued. "My father told me, Gretel."

"Your father?" she whispered, and then glared at Odalinde. "You said you never told him."

Odalinde frowned. "I didn't Gretel." Her voice was low and weary, disappointed at Gretel's continued skepticism about her. She turned back to Petr. "Who told your father, Petr? Do you know?"

Petr looked to the ground and kicked a stray pebble. "I can't be sure, but I..." he paused for a moment, considering his speculation, and then blurted, "I don't know. I don't know who told him. I'm sorry. And what does it matter anyway?"

"Dammit, Petr!" Gretel barked, her patience exhausted, "It *does* matter, and you *do* know! Now who told your father!?"

"I told him."

The voice of Gretel's father boomed down to the huddle below, startling it to attention like a herd of deer stumbled upon by hikers. Heinrich Morgan stood tall at the top of the porch stairs, his posture healthy and majestic, as if addressing peasants from his chamber balcony.

Gretel stared disbelieving at the man, her face now flush and her throat and mouth as dry as the ground she stood on. "Father?" She couldn't remember the last time she'd even seen him outside. It had to be months she guessed.

"Papa!" Hansel whimpered.

Gretel turned to the boy in fear as he began walking toward his father. She couldn't speak, and then almost vomited as she watched her brother nearly bare his teeth when Odalinde grabbed his shoulders to restrain him.

"No, Hansel," Odalinde said calmly

Hansel's wild stare lingered on Odalinde for a moment, and his breathing was panicked and wheezing. Gretel knew what he was imagining. Their father was back. Finally. And now they had to go to him and reunite. After all, what was the point of all these months of suffering and neglect if they were only going to shun him upon his recovery? What were they doing all of this for?

But Gretel now realized what her brother did not. Things had changed. Her father, it seemed, was the enemy.

"I don't understand, Father," Gretel said. "Why...how..." Her thoughts were coming too quickly and they jumbled into incoherence.

Heinrich took his first step down when Odalinde froze him in stride. "We'll hear your story, Heinrich—from the porch."

Gretel's father smiled at what he clearly inferred as brazenness, but he obeyed, and Gretel took this as a good sign. Perhaps he knew of Odalinde's secret and feared the powers that it implied.

"I think on some level you do understand Gretel, just as you always have. Since you could talk, you always understood things very quickly."

There was nothing menacing in her father's tone, but his words now left little doubt in Gretel's mind that he had participated in her mother's disappearance. Petr had now turned toward Heinrich, and the group of four stood in anticipation. Gretel's instinct was to get back in the truck—with Petr and Hansel—and drive away, but she stood hypnotized.

"I didn't plan any of this, Gretel, not initially. When your mother disappeared that day, I was as grief-stricken and devastated as you were. More perhaps. I loved her very deeply."

Gretel glanced over at her brother and felt a sense of pride in his attempt to control his emotions. Tears had begun to stream, but he was silent, listening to every word. She looked back to her father. "Then why?"

"This explanation, Gretel, you would not understand. You wouldn't believe any of it. I don't suppose I believed it, not truly. Not until today."

Gretel's eyes were locked on her father. "What happened today?" she asked, her words slow and suspicious.

"Magic, Gretel. True magic."

A smile formed on Heinrich Morgan's face, and as his lips parted, Gretel screamed at the teeth that emerged through the opening. They were larger than before, inhumanly angled.

Petr began backing away, instinctively pulling Gretel's hand, which she snatched away. "What in...your tee..?"

"Odalinde what is that!?" It was Hansel, his voice resonating with a sound of terror Gretel had never heard from her brother.

"It's okay. Hansel, it's often part of it. Your father has the potion. I don't think it's much but...Oh my God, he has the potion." Odalinde was speaking as if to herself, trying to understand how any of this could be happening. "I don't know..."

"I thought he couldn't read the language!" Gretel cried. "You told me he couldn't!"

At this Heinrich boomed out his voice again. "So perhaps you *would* understand what has happened." He stood for a moment, silent, studying his daughter curiously, a bemused smile on his face.

"You murdered your wife—our mother—for this?"

Heinrich turned his head quickly to the side, as if slapped, and then returned his focus to his daughter. "I had nothing to do with it," he said flatly. "It was only after that I...participated."

"Who did then? Who killed her?" Gretel waited, and then, receiving no answer asked, "Was it Deda?" Gretel could sense the tension in her father, restraining his reflex to look away once again. She was like a boxer offering quick, stinging jabs. "Or maybe you're lying; maybe you did kill her."

At this last suggestion, Heinrich became very still, almost frozen, and then, almost impossibly for a man of his age and condition, set off down the steps in a rage, like a rodeo bull ungated. He reached the landing area at the bottom of the porch and turned in the direction of his daughter. Instinctively, Odalinde and Petr both stepped forward, flanking Gretel, preparing to meet the deranged attacker head on. That encounter, however, was averted by the woman now occupying Heinrich's position at the top of the porch.

"Heinrich!" the woman shouted.

Heinrich Morgan's feet stopped instantly, as if programmed, but the momentum of his body did not, and he fell forward, putting his hands in front of him to brace his fall and breaking his left wrist as a result. His screech of pain was ignored by everyone. The group instead stood gazing, incredulously, at the stunning woman in the cloak above them. Her heavy robe and clear, white skin gave her an apparition-like appearance, and it would have surprised no one if she simply vanished into the forest—a memory to be doubted later in life. But the figure remained, unmoving, a serene image at the top of the porch, seemingly incapable of the command she'd just barked at Heinrich.

"You'll not move again, Mr. Morgan until you are instructed." The woman's eyes lingered on Gretel's father for a moment, ensuring he'd understood his orders, and then she looked back to the woman and the three children on the driveway beneath her. "Gretel and Hansel," she said, "I've heard about you."

Gretel strode forward, pushing past Odalinde and Petr. "Heard about us from whom?"

"Why from your mother, of course. Your lovely, delicious mother."

"Murderer!" Hansel screamed, and Odalinde again had to snatch the boy back by his collar.

At this accusation, the woman raised her eyebrows and frowned. "I am that, yes, many times over. It's a title which your guardian, no doubt, assumes as well. Am I wrong on that count?" The witch cocked her head toward Odalinde.

Odalinde stayed silent and looked away, one hand still firmly on the back of Hansel's shirt and the other ready to restrain Gretel if necessary.

"Yes, well, perhaps that discussion is for another time. As far as your mother is concerned, however, I cannot quite claim her as my victim. At least not yet."

"She's alive?" Gretel knew the answer to the question before she'd asked it, and her joy quickly turned to fear when she realized why the woman had come. She took a step back and glanced again at the tarp-covered car beside the house.

The old woman caught the glance and grinned. "My new toy," she said, "perhaps you'd like a ride?"

"No thanks," Gretel replied quickly, "unless you want to take me to my mother."

With this statement, the old woman threw back her head and laughed. The sound was awful to Gretel, much closer to the cackle of the witches of myth than of the relatively attractive woman at the top of the porch.

"If I knew where your mother was, I wouldn't be here with you." The witch pondered a moment and then said, "Well, again, at least not yet."

"What do you want then?" It was Odalinde who spoke now. "We don't know where she is."

"Oh, I know you don't." She paused. "But," the woman continued, now pointing at Petr, "I was hoping that perhaps he does."

Gretel looked back at Petr, and could see by his expression that he didn't know what the woman was talking about—or at least he didn't *know* he knew. "Petr?" she said.

"I never met Gretel's mother. I don't know her and I don't know where she is."

Petr's voice was bordering on panic, and Gretel knew he was still shaken by the crazed look on her father's face only moments ago. And the teeth.

"Oh, but you may, Petr. Certainly your father showed you things. Took you places. Yes?"

"What places? How do you know my father?" Petr's words were now spoken with nothing less than terror.

The old woman descended the porch stairs slowly, gracefully, and when she reached the bottom, she turned sharply and headed toward the side of the house where the car was parked. Without breaking stride, she clutched the tarp where it covered the hood of the car and walked it back toward the trunk until the full view of the machine was revealed. As Gretel suspected—or perhaps knew—it was The System cruiser.

Petr's mouth fell open slightly, just parting his lips, and he shook his head in a short rhythmic spasm of disbelief. "That's my father's car," he said, his voice vibrational from fear, as well as the shaking of his head.

"Why yes it is, Petr, and he keeps a lovely picture of the two of you right there on the ...hmm...I'm not sure what it's called! But it's wonderful at shielding the sun!"

"Where's my father?" Petr asked, nearly in tears.

The old woman walked back to the front of the car and stood centered in front of the grill. She narrowed her eyes and steeled them on Petr. "Your father is dead. He's been dead for several hours now." The tone was aggressive and menacing—nothing less than a dare to the five sets of ears in the range of her voice. "And unless you want to join him—along with your girlfriend and her brother—I suggest you tell me where I can find Anika Morgan."

"Don't you dare threaten them!" Odalinde snarled.

As fast as Gretel's thoughts could process what was happening, the old woman's feet had left the ground, effortlessly, and she had flown—literally flown—from the front of the cruiser to the spot where Odalinde had stood only a second before. The cape of her cloak was flattened by the wind as she flew, giving her the appearance of some evil super villain from the pages of any number of comic books. The old woman's hands were raised above her as she flew, with her fingers pointing to the ground, sharp, spearlike nails protruding from the tips. She looked like a wizard attempting to cast a midair spell on some poor peasant or toad perhaps. As she landed, Gretel could see the woman's teeth bared to the top of the gumline, wolf-like; except instead of the wide canines and blunt incisors of a dog, the teeth were severe and jagged, like those of a shark.

The event happened in an instant—Gretel hadn't time even to scream. Instead she stood silently, paralyzed, her mind reflexively beginning to cope with the loss of Odalinde.

But Odalinde was fast too. She'd moved off her spot, two feet or so, just far enough to avoid the slashing fingers and fangs of the flying demon. The old woman's momentum carried her forward on her landing, and as she stumbled forward, Odalinde clutched both of her hands together and hammered the back of the witch's head, sending her face-first onto the gravel. "Run! Odalinde commanded. "All of you run!"

"Odalinde, I can..." Gretel began to protest.

"Go Gretel. Now. Take your brother and your friend and go." It was Gretel's father this time. He stood tall, clutching his wrist to his chest, a look of sadness and disgust on his face. "Go to the Klahrs. Tell them what's happened."

The old woman had returned to her feet, her serene, ghost-like appearance now diminished by dirt and rage. "Heinrich!" she shouted and took several steps backward, trying to keep her enemies in her periphery. She regained her poise. "I'll find them, Heinrich, no matter what. The only difference is now you'll be dead too." The old woman then turned to Odalinde. "But first, you."

Heinrich Morgan looked at his daughter one last time, the sadness in his eyes was a look Gretel would remember for the rest of her life. "Now," he repeated.

Gretel grabbed her brother's hand and barked at Petr to follow, and listened in agony as Hansel screamed, "Father!" while the three children made their way down to the lake.

CHAPTER TWENTY-FOUR

THE OLD WOMAN HADN'T expected a challenge, not really, not on a physical level anyway. She had arrived cautious of Gretel, of her ostensible intuition and fortitude—particularly being that she was the daughter of the woman who had nearly killed her. But she hadn't counted on this mystery woman who apparently had her own reservoir of courage. This woman who reminded her of herself in many ways.

"So you're an Orphist," she said, as a statement, not a question. "I sensed that in you the moment I looked at you. I could see it in your eyes. It stops the aging, but it does little for the weariness."

"I will die now, quietly, at your hand if you prefer," Odalinde replied.

Apparently the woman's fellow Orphist had no interest in camaraderie.

"I've done this life as far as I wish," Odalinde continued. Then, perhaps overplaying her hand said, "You can use me for blending. Just leave them alone. All of them. Heinrich included."

Ignoring her compromise, the old woman said, "How long have you lived—'Odalinde' is it? How long have you lived Odalinde?"

Odalinde stayed quiet, the old woman recognizing her reticence to reveal anything capable of weakening her position.

"It doesn't matter," the old woman said, "I'm sure it's been long enough. Far too long in fact. Certainly you know your body will do me little good at this point. And besides, I've found it. I've found the treasure. The Prize of Prizes if you will. And I'll never let it slip away."

Had it been only a few days earlier, the old woman would have been killed by the stone in Heinrich Morgan's hand. It would have landed solidly on the back of her skull and sent shards of bone into her brain. At the very least she

245

would have been rendered unconscious, with no chance of a second clemency, as there certainly would have been additional blows that followed.

But her senses were heightened now, and she could "see" the rock at its apex just before beginning its descent. Like a dervish, the old woman took a step to the side and then back, and then spun three hundred and sixty degrees, easily avoiding her assailant while assuming the position of strength. She was now behind Heinrich Morgan, restraining his arms to his sides, her breasts flat against his back and her mouth just inches from the man's neck.

The woman knew instantly after arriving that it would end this way for the Morgan father. He'd been part of Marcel's plan after all, a fact she'd uncovered so easily with just a taste of the broth; but as a result of his ongoing poisoning—no doubt being administered by the Orphist woman—he had temporarily forgotten his commitment.

And so it had been a dangerous play for her to strengthen him, allowing him that tiny, delicate taste; the woman knew it the moment she'd touched it to his lips. But it was only done as a temporary measure, an aid to learn what she could from the feeble man. Certainly he'd have some clue as to his wife and daughter's whereabouts. Besides, whatever strength he regained was meaningless; the amount of brew was trivial and the effects wouldn't last the day. It was nothing at all compared to what she'd lapped up. And, of course, Mr. Morgan wasn't a blood relative of his wife. That was the main difference.

The old woman turned her right hand so that her palm faced outward, away from her body, and then she plunged her nails into the side of Heinrich Morgan's neck, letting them glide naturally through the flesh. She flushed in excitement again at her newfound strength, admiring the ease at which her fingers penetrated the skin and muscle. She let her hand rest for a beat, relishing the sounds of asphyxiation and screams ("NO!" from Odalinde), before flinging her hand violently forward and tearing out the man's throat. With her other hand, the old woman held up the corpse of Gretel's father for a few seconds, showing off her strength to her next opponent, and then tossed the body to the dirt. "Are you ready to die?"

CHAPTER TWENTY-FIVE

"HOW ARE THEY, PAPA? Do you even know how your grandchildren have been doing?"

"They're fine, Anika, but it's best we not speak about them now. It will only upset you further. Please." Marcel nodded with a smile and waved a hand toward himself, beckoning his daughter to come and sit.

Anika kept her distance, remaining instead at the back door of the warehouse. Ready. For what, she wasn't sure. Perhaps when the officer returned—if he returned through the same door from which he left—she could make a run for it. Or maybe ambush him. He and that horrible witch. It was no plan at all really, a wild grasp at survival, but whatever happened, she wasn't going to surrender again. And she was done obeying her father.

"And how do you know they're fine?" she asked. "Have you seen them? Or spoken with them?"

"Oliver..." he paused, "Officer Stenson, the man who found you, he has seen them. He tells me they are well."

Anika bit her upper lip to restrain a scream. The thought of that hideous officer looking at or being anywhere near her children sickened her.

"In fact, if I'm not mistaken, he spoke with Heinrich just a week or so ago. Everything with your children is fine."

"Spoke with Heinrich? Why?"

Marcel peered at his daughter across the room, squinting her into focus, pausing long enough to give her time to come to the answer to her question.

"No," she whispered.

"I'm sorry, Anika."

"No!" Anika screamed. "No!" And with that final scream, a foreign rage erupted in Anika, a rage she hadn't felt even at the moment she'd crushed the skull of the hag. In one fluid motion, Anika gripped the mug of water tightly by the handle, spilling its contents to the warehouse floor, and then, torquing her body violently for leverage, smashed the bottom of the cup against the door's mirror.

At first the sound was electrical in nature, sharp and piercing, and then it turned heavy and liberating as the shards of silver glass rained to the floor. Instinctively, Anika shielded her eyes from the exploding shrapnel, and then, realizing there was nothing else to do now but keep going, she floated her arm slowly through the new opening in search of the knob on the opposite side. The cup had left a sizable hole where the mirror had been, but jagged shards from every direction of the perimeter still threatened. She would obviously have to hurry, but she needed to avoid shredding her arm if it could be helped.

As she groped for the doorknob, Anika could also see through the opening to a small room which contained an exit door leading to the outside, the unmistakable neon beacon shining red on the wall above.

Her hand found the opposing doorknob and then felt its cruel resistance as she twisted it. That should come as no surprise, she thought, the door *is* locked. She continued her blind search, fine-tuning it, using now the tips of her fingers to locate the locking mechanism. Within seconds, she'd found the dial and unlocked the door, and then pulled her arm back through the opening. She was free.

Having not wasted any precious time worrying about what her father was doing during her escape, Anika turned back now to gauge him. Perhaps he was letting her leave.

As she considered this possibility, she felt the palms of her father's hands plunge into the middle of her chest, knocking the air from her lungs, the sound like a baseball bat on an old pillow. Her body spun slightly to the right before crashing against the cold metal scaffold behind her. The metal shelving held her upright for a moment, and then she slumped to the floor, dropping slowly before coming to rest on one knee. With her head bowed in a look of prayer, Anika blinked several times at the floor, reflexively taking inventory of her condition. She wasn't seriously hurt. Luckily, her right arm (which would have a nasty bruise later but wasn't broken) had taken most of the impact;

had her spine taken the brunt, she thought, she may have been finished. Just survive, she thought. Just keep surviving.

"I can't risk you anymore, Anika," her father spoke, this time making no pretensions at niceness. "When they arrive, she'll have to use you as you are."

Anika turned her eyes to her father, glaring. Any trace of love or sorrow for him was gone. There was only hatred, a searing contempt for the man who'd raised her.

And as this transmutation took place—from sympathy to loathing—everything in front of Anika crystallized. The shard of mirror. The side of her father's neck. The resolve. She'd felt this before, at the witch's cabin: a focused rage—a rage unlike the wild fury she'd released on the mirror minutes before.

<hr />

ANIKA HAD KNOWN EVERY move before it happened. It almost wasn't fair, she thought. And as she was walking through the door, pebbles of glass crunching beneath her shoes, she fixed back on the body lying frozen on the floor. As she stared at the corpse, the shard of mirror that protruded neatly from her father's neck, just below his right ear, caught the light and seemed to wink at Anika. Anika winked back and walked out.

<hr />

GRETEL HAULED THE CANOE toward her, backpedaling up the bank, making certain to keep the boat from drifting, and then raced behind Petr and Hansel through the orchard to the Klahr's house. Every gram of her body wanted to go back and fight, to help save Odalinde and her father—but she couldn't risk Hansel and Petr following her. And she wanted to see her mother again.

"What is it, Petr? Gretel?" Mrs. Klahr was on the porch, welcoming the children as she untied her apron at the back and then crumpled it into a ball. It was Amanda Klahr's version of preparing to fight, Gretel thought absently.

Gretel spoke rapidly, breathing heavily and stuttering. "Mrs. Klahr, it's my father, and...and Odalinde...and my mother...and a woman...she's a monster...or..."

"Gretel, slow down." Mrs. Klahr twisted back toward the house. "Georg!" she called. "Come out here, George! It's the children!" She turned back to the kids, this time addressing Petr. "Petr, what's going on?" Mrs. Klahr's tone sounded almost amused as if suspecting a prank.

"It's true, Mrs. Klahr. There's a woman...she...I think my father..." Petr stumbled, not sure how to relay anything that could make sense in only one or two sentences.

"Okay, settle down Petr. My goodness!" Mr. Klahr had arrived on the porch next to his wife. "George," she said to him, "scamper over to the Morgan house and see what all's happening there. These children are quite hysterical."

"No! Mr. Klahr, no!" Gretel's face twisted in terror. "Don't go over there! She's dangerous!"

"But Gretel," Hansel cried, "someone needs to help them!"

Hansel was right, of course: it was likely her father and Odalinde needed help (the woman had flown!). But the thought of losing Mr. Klahr was too much for her to imagine. Gretel knew her father was gone—dead or alive she couldn't know—but that he was a man who had passed the post of redemption, about this she was sure. And Odalinde. Odalinde had come here for them, exclusively, almost as a sacrifice—or salvation even—for the horrors she'd brought upon the world. Gretel felt she was meant to die protecting Hansel and her. Perhaps she's dying right now, she thought.

But the Klahrs played a different role in this story. They weren't part of this twisted history that her grandmother brought here so long ago. They were of *this* world. Back Country folk. Righteous and charitable. They had saved Gretel when her mother went missing (not dead, Gretel remembered again, her mother wasn't dead). Even when Odalinde suggested the Klahrs had betrayed Gretel, in the car on the way to Deda's, Gretel knew she was wrong. She knew they were as pure a people as she could ever expect to know, and Gretel would never bear losing them. Even if she found her mother—when she found her—Gretel would always need the Klahrs.

"It's okay, Gretel, I'll be extra careful. Got my companion, you know." Mr. Klahr unhinged the twin barrels of his shotgun and loaded the chamber. "I'll be just fine."

Gretel's fear hadn't shaken Mr. Klahr, but Mrs. Klahr's face was now serious and concerned. "Be careful, Georg. If something's happening you can't handle, you come back here."

Mrs. Klahr's tone left no space for discussion, and Mr. Klahr simply nodded, then walked briskly to his truck and drove off.

ANIKA OPENED THE EXIT door and could see instantly that night would be arriving soon. She had freed herself from captivity, but her struggle to get home remained, and darkness would present a formidable obstacle. She had no idea where she was, and The System officer would surely be back soon, likely with that savage witch in tow. Wandering these foreign parts in the dark seemed all but suicidal.

But as Anika stepped on the ground outside the bleak building, a flood of recognition overtook her. The smells and landscape, and even the siding and structure of the building itself, all became familiar. She knew this place. Perhaps not the exact earth she stood on, but for certain, she knew this ground. Or at least the area surrounding it. She looked to the sky and inhaled deeply, attempting to coax a memory from her senses. It was there, this memory, bulging at the surface of her mind; and from what she intuited, it wasn't some stray thought from a single moment in her distant past—this memory was close, with a feeling of security and routine. It was a memory of Home.

As Anika stood recollecting, she absently took note of the land extending before her at the back of the property, and how it proceeded quite differently from that in the front. When she'd arrived at the warehouse, she recalled the road leading to the front of the building had been long and flat, innocuous and rural and had ended rather lazily at the front door. But the back sloped steadily away from the house until, at a distance of perhaps thirty yards or so, the land dropped off dramatically, sloping at such an angle that she couldn't see the ground below. The building, it seemed, was atop a large hill.

Anika walked toward the edge of the slope, not knowing exactly what to expect, and at about halfway to the drop-off could see another building enter into view. It was just the roof at first, and then, as she proceeded closer to the edge, the whole of the large industrial complex below came into view. And the memory was complete. Anika knew exactly where she was.

She jogged zombie-like the rest of the way to the edge of the hill and looked down, breathing spastically in disbelief, consciously slowing her inhalations to keep from hyperventilating.

It was the cannery.

There was no mistaking it. The rusted out factory shell and overly secure barbed wire fencing that strangled the grounds were as recognizable to Anika as her own reflection. She'd seen it a thousand times. It had been years, but her family—and at times, before the children, just she and Heinrich—had spent countless hours at Rifle Field picnicking and playing games, or, in their somewhat wilder and more adventurous days, shooting their guns through the fence at the broadside of the building. She was staring down on the Weinheimmer Cannery. It was impossible, Anika thought. Her house was right across the lake! She'd no way to get to it from this spot, of course—even if she were to get over the fence she'd need a boat to get across the water—but if not for the trees and cannery, she would be able to see her house from where she stood! She wouldn't speculate as to why her father would have held her so close to her home until much later; her thoughts now were soaked of her children.

During the times she'd spent at Rifle Field she'd barely even noticed the hill upon which she now stood, and she'd certainly never dreamed there had been a warehouse at the top. It made sense now of course, this warehouse—maintenance workers and others would have needed a place to store supplies and tools or whatever—but it just wasn't something you thought of, particularly since the cannery had been closed now for so many years. And with the dense foliage of the Backwoods and its location so far from the main road, the warehouse simply wasn't visible from any place she'd ever been. She supposed that had the imposing fence that surrounded the cannery not existed they may have explored Rifle Field further, but the fence *had* always been there, and they'd never even considered what was beyond it.

Anika's initial instinct was to scream for help. Their neighbors with the orchard, the Klahrs, lived on this side of the lake, had for decades, so it was possible—probable even—that *they* were aware of this place, and would have heard her voice if the sound carried right. Perhaps she'd even be heard at her own house. But Anika was disoriented and felt wildly insecure about her judgment of the distance. She'd never been great with directions and ranges to begin with, and after all she'd been through, she felt even less certain of her internal gauges. Besides, even if someone were to hear her, the noise would be faint and directionless, likely to be dismissed as far off children at play, or perhaps a bird. And, more importantly, for all Anika knew, the officer and the witch were rolling to a stop in front of the warehouse at this very moment, and the yelling would be as good as wrapping a chain around her neck and locking it to one of the warehouse shelves. Never again, she thought, I'll die before ever being a prisoner again.

But could she make it over the fence? As fences went, it wasn't particularly tall, and the portion of it that formed the barrier was standard chain link; she assessed it would be easy enough for her to scale to the top. But it was at the top where things got problematic. Four or five rows of gruesome barbs formed a wide V-shape that ran the entire length of the fence, making it as difficult to get on top of it as across it. From where she stood now, the jagged steel canopy appeared as some giant metal crocodile, waiting for her entry into its agape jaws, perhaps promising to take her across the lake—a painful retelling of the fable about the mischievous gingerbread boy, Anika thought, only this time she would star in the ill-fated title role.

But Anika knew a choice had to be made, and there were really only two options: head back down the long, dirt road on which she'd arrived, risking imminent darkness and the openness that seemed certain to expose her to The System officer; or, scale the fence in front of her and take her chances with the barbs and the awaiting lake beyond. She hadn't swam in years, she suddenly realized, but she was comfortable enough in the water, and she trusted that instincts and desperation would take her the distance she needed.

It was the fence that would be the challenge though, and if that was to be her choice—the fence—she would need to move quickly.

Anika descended the hill and walked up to the fence, pushing the weight of her body against it and gripping her fingers through the links like a prisoner of war. It felt strong, stronger than she would have suspected after so many years. She could see through to Rifle Field the exact spots where she and her family used to lay out their blanket and set the picnic platters, Heinrich always meticulous in his combing of the patches to avoid settling on an ant hill. The grass was wildly overgrown now though it appeared certain areas had been recently trampled and used.

This scenario, her precise position standing at the fence, reminded her of something from a nightmare: pursuing some elusive goal—in this case, her freedom—yet ultimately able only to observe it in silent frustration as the monsters steadily moved in.

But this wasn't a dream; here she was able to make choices, and Anika's mind instantly sharpened as she assessed the fence and the possible ways over. The barbs atop were even more imposing at this close angle, and a panic started in Anika's chest at the sight of the rusty aluminum thorns. She could bear the pain, she thought, but if she got caught—stuck—it would almost certainly spell the end.

She walked the length of the fence to the front wall of the cannery which stood only a few feet from the barrier. Rifle Field stared at her, mocking her with its closeness. Anika surveyed everything, not sure exactly what she was looking for, but loosely hoping that, perhaps, time had created a gap at the base of the fence, some opening wide enough for her to squeeze through. She wasn't as thin as she'd ever been, that was certain, but even if she were as thin as Gretel it wouldn't have mattered, the spaces between the bottom of the fence post and ground were sound, and not big enough for her even to put an arm through.

She dropped to her knees and raked her hand into the grass, clawing it like a badger. The earth was surprisingly loose, and Anika came away with a mound of wet dirt that left an ample hole just to the side of the fence post. With the cannery situated so close to the lake, the ground below the fence was essentially mud, and could be removed without much effort. But who knew how deep the fence went, and even with the ground being damp, her fingers would be numb in no time. If she had a day to dig, or even several hours, and if she were rested and nourished with the morning sun above her, and if virtually every single thing about how she felt right now was different, she was sure she could tunnel under using her hands alone. But Anika figured she didn't have that time, and her strength was dwindling.

Once again Anika stared up at the evil barbs above her. It was impossible, she thought—over or under—she simply didn't have the energy.

Anika slowly dropped her head to her chest and, for the first time in months, after all she'd seen and been subjected to, after all of the betrayal and cruelty that had become her daily life, she began to cry. Her weeping was almost silent as she stood and turned to face the cannery. Her eyes remained closed while she tilted her face to the darkening sky. The bout of tears lasted only a few seconds—Anika would later consider this burst of sorrow was somehow necessary, physiologically, as a means of cleansing her mind, ultimately allowing to enter the thought that would free her.

With her head still angled up toward the roof of the cannery, Anika opened her eyes. And she saw it. A window.

At first Anika rejected what she was seeing as an illusion, a mirage, a cruel trick of her desperate mind. But her memory instantly reacted, assuring Anika the window was real. She'd seen it before, of course, during any number of the Rifle Field visits, but each time it had gone unregistered: an unnoticed speck on the landscape.

Anika bolted toward the foot of the hill to the cannery entrance on the opposite side of the building, nearly losing her footing on the grass as she navigated the corner and then braked, almost instantly, in order to avoid passing the thick metal door. She stood tall and looked indifferently at the threshold, and then let out a disbelieving chuckle at the unlatched door before her. The rusted metal ring that normally, presumably, would have been looped through with the steel shackle of a thick padlock, was empty. Anika unfolded the latch, which barely resisted despite its worn, corroded look, and opened the cannery door.

The interior of the cannery was mostly empty, except for the large canning tables and various-sized tubes of copper piping—some as large as tree trunks—which ran in maze-like fashion from floor to ceiling along the walls. There was little else, however, to indicate that this building had ever been a cannery. There was no heavy machinery or shelving, no stacks of cans or old Weinheimmer signs, and Anika assumed everything had either been gutted by the failed owners or repossessed by the State.

But there were tools strewn about the facility, everything from hammers to pickaxes, which, Anika presumed, had been used to extract sealers and conveyors and whatever else of value existed from their moorings. She figured she wouldn't need much to get through the window, and she scooped a thick, wrought iron claw hammer from the dusty floor. There was also a wide barn shovel leaning against the far wall, and Anika briefly reconsidered the tunneling-under plan. She decided to stay the course and head to the window, but she grabbed the shovel anyway. You never knew.

From there everything moved like a storm. She scaled the steps leading to the second floor of the cannery and then stopped in front of the window—the window she'd taken notice of, remarkably, for the first time only minutes ago. The glass panes were missing almost entirely, probably broken out decades ago, but the frame of the window remained. It was weak-looking and well rusted, but the grid which once divided the panes was intact and would need to be broken out. But Anika was sure in her plan, she had seen everything play out the moment she spotted her escape route from the ground below, and knew the frame would pose little difficulty. She gripped the iron hammer and banged once on the cross grill of the window and then again. Anika suspected the window would be frail, but when it virtually disintegrated on the second gavel-like blow, she was incredulous.

She placed her first foot on the sill, and then her second; her body was still plenty thin enough to fit between the jambs, though she did have to crouch slightly to avoid the head of the window. She looked just beyond the fence to her landing spot, and then back to the floor of the cannery.

The shovel.

Without really knowing why, Anika stepped down from the sill, grabbed the spade, and tossed it out of the window and over the fence to Rifle Field. She then climbed back up and re-squatted, and with both of her hands gripped to the sill on either side of her feet, Anika took one last breath, and jumped.

CHAPTER TWENTY-SIX

"YOU CAN'T LIVE FOREVER." Odalinde's words were weary, a desperate attempt at reason with the mad woman who now stood above her, measuring the setting, timing the moment for her final, fatal attack. She was so strong, Odalinde thought. Hopelessly strong.

"In theory, that seems not to be true." The witch's reply was quizzical as if lightly considering the concept for the first time. "Though practically I'm sure you're right. But, my fellow Orphist, these types of philosophical dialectics have never been of interest to me, in any area of study really, but particularly in the subject of..."

She paused, and Odalinde noted the trepidation in the witch's voice in the words that followed.

"...the subject you've presented," she continued. "My role is only to take the opportunities as they are presented to me. And as I've promised to those Universals who are greater than the sum of us all, I shall never reject one again."

With a squint, Odalinde locked eyes with the remade woman, and then, never losing the gaze, shook her head slowly in disgust. "You're no Orphist. You believe yourself one, talk as one, but you are not. Just as I was not. But what I know now is that you are much worse than I am, or ever was. You care nothing for life—you're not even human."

Odalinde had given up on survival, and this type of banter would all but guarantee her death. But there was no discomfort in that thought—her time had arrived to forfeit what she should never have possessed. And as this judgment became realized, a feeling of warmth drifted over her. She'd done what she could for Gretel and Hansel, and her only goal now was to draw out this moment, to stall—for as long as her heart forced blood through her veins—the infandous demon above her.

"You're a common being. Like a tree." Odalinde laughed at her somewhat childish analogy. "Destined to live on for centuries, alone and soulless—loveless—with nothing to offer the world." Odalinde looked away in confusion, a visible display of her rethinking the comparison. "So, to be accurate then, you're much lower than a tree. A tree is an object which lavishes on the world fruit and habitation, air to breath and shelter from heat and rain. You give nothing. You're a parasite. An immortal parasite. What worse thing could ever exist on this earth?"

The witch's expression stayed frozen. The confident smile, which emerged instantly after sending Odalinde to the ground with the force of a stallion's kick, remained. But Odalinde could now detect the effort behind the smile, and the rage bubbling beneath it. Would she kill her now? Odalinde prayed not, not for her own life, but to give the children just a bit more time.

"I was like you. For years. I know the addiction as well as anyone who's ever been in its grips." Odalinde's tone was softer, now trying slowly to unreel the witch, just enough to keep her on the line while still maintaining the attention she'd won. "But I returned to Orphism—true Orphism—not the horrid recipe that has become its legacy. I rediscovered—or perhaps found for the first time, it had been so long I couldn't remember—the remarkable book of The Ancients. The beauty and truth of a spectacular people, who informed of a message that, had it been widely read, was potent enough to catapult humanity centuries forward. Perhaps further. I felt the pride in that, the responsibility." Odalinde smiled flatly. "And I changed. It took some time, but I changed."

Odalinde paused, hoping the witch would give her some measure of reply, some morsel of conversation which Odalinde could latch onto and steer into a dialogue. But she stood frozen above her, her teeth bared in that insidious smile, fingernails protruding down to the ground.

"You've enough now to live for as long you'd ever want to," Odalinde continued. "Look at you! You're...quite stunning really. I imagine you were rather old once—old!—and now you've replenished. You've found that elusive fountain of myth!" Odalinde lowered her voice, sensing an impact of her words on the witch. "Look at you. You don't need more. These aren't animals of the forest, these are your kin."

Odalinde knew any word she uttered could topple the delicate interest she'd acquired, and she measured each carefully.

"You don't want to be a destroyer forever. You've already taken this gift—despite what you've done to get it—it's yours now, and there's nothing that can be done to return it. So take it, live a long life, and then, centuries from now, let your spirit return to the universe, the way Life has intended it always to be. For all of us."

Odalinde reveled in her eloquence, not out of pride, but because she recognized that her filibustering words and the truth of what she was saying were one and the same. Yes, if it was time to die, she was ready; she had never been as certain of anything in her long, damaged life. She would welcome it now, the moment she believed the children were safe, she wanted not another second in this world.

But she would never know if her words would have been enough to change the witch, or if another few minutes could have made any difference at all for the children. The scene was broken, interrupted, as the sound of popping gravel cascaded from beneath the truck of Georg Klahr.

CHAPTER TWENTY-SEVEN

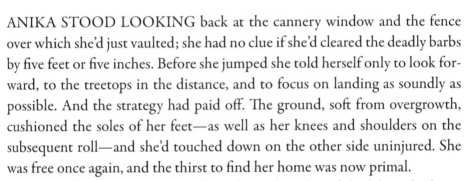

ANIKA STOOD LOOKING back at the cannery window and the fence over which she'd just vaulted; she had no clue if she'd cleared the deadly barbs by five feet or five inches. Before she jumped she told herself only to look forward, to the treetops in the distance, and to focus on landing as soundly as possible. And the strategy had paid off. The ground, soft from overgrowth, cushioned the soles of her feet—as well as her knees and shoulders on the subsequent roll—and she'd touched down on the other side uninjured. She was free once again, and the thirst to find her home was now primal.

She walked slowly across Rifle Field to the edge of the lake—the latest hurdle in Anika's seemingly endless maze of obstacles—took off her shoes and rolled her pants to her knees, and then waded to the middle of her shins, gauging the depth of the water and the amount of swimming that would be required. Once she left the grounds of Rifle Field and started up the lake, she knew there would be no bank on which to rest, not until she reached the Klahr orchard—or her own property on the opposite side. Was that a quarter mile? A half? Surely it wasn't a mile! Really she hadn't any idea. She could wade much of the way she supposed, and at no point would she be required to swim at breakneck speeds or fight currents; but once she was out there, beyond plodding distance, there was no going back.

And darkness had arrived.

The night was clear and the moon, not yet high, was a solid gibbous that in little over an hour she estimated, would offer a beacon to follow. It wasn't visibility that worried Anika, it was her stamina. Even the numerous nocturnal critters, some of which were potentially harmful, never even entered Anika's thoughts; had she found herself in this situation a year ago, having never endured the ordeal that would now shape her life forever, thoughts of snakes and eels would have paralyzed her. But she trusted herself now, trusted her instincts and decision-making. And there was little choice besides.

She stepped back to the shore and disrobed to her underwear, figuring the weight of her clothes would only add to her burden, and then waded back into the lake, this time pushing forward, feeling the cold murkiness of the lake seep over her crotch and hips before settling at her midriff. She looked back to the shore, briefly regarding her shoes and clothes, considering whether the smart move was to toss them into the water, erasing evidence that she'd been there at all. She quickly decided against it—if she were to drown, she figured, those may be the only clues to finding her body and eventually punishing the guilty. The System would certainly crack the case! she thought, smiling in spite of the dreadful truth of her cynicism.

Anika began sidestepping slowly down the bank toward her destination, careful to have one foot planted firmly before lifting the other, and thankful for every inch she made closer without being forced to swim. At the onset, the going was steady, and the ground at her feet was sturdy. Maybe she could walk most of the way, she thought. It wasn't likely, but not impossible. Per-haps the water levels affected the bed beneath and deposited dirt and gravel at the borders, making this trip achievable by foot alone! She was getting carried away, she knew, particularly since she knew as much about lakes and tides and submarine sediment as she did about the mating habits of the striped pole-cat. Nothing. But her mind was occupied, and though the waterline had risen since her departure—closing in on her breasts—the rise was gradual, and she was confident in her progress.

Her foot set down on something hard, Anika assumed a rock until it moved slowly away, and then she assumed a turtle. If the only thing she en-countered in this lake tonight were turtles, she thought, she'd label herself happy. She'd been lucky to this point, not just in the lake but since she'd left the warehouse.

Since she'd killed her father. (This was not the time to explore that part, she thought. Later she'd be happy to run through the emotions associated with that act, but not now.)

Of all the scenarios, things had fallen into place for her. Finally. She'd es-caped the warehouse before the officer returned, had found her escape route through the cannery window before nightfall, and, miraculously, found herself no more than a short boat ride from home, though this last part, she supposed, would have been luckier with the provision of an actual boat. But, all in all, things could have gone much worse.

And when the report of the shotgun exploded over the lake, she assumed they were about to.

GRETEL SCREAMED AT the sound of the blast, turning sharply toward the window that looked out on the orchard and the lake beyond.

Reflexively, Petr draped his arm across Gretel's shoulders, pulling her close to him. She moved into his clutch, but her eyes were wide with shock and focused on Mrs. Klahr, whose look was akin to Gretel's.

The four of them—Gretel, Hansel, Petr, and Mrs. Klahr—stood frozen, breathless, waiting for the next shotgun blast to erupt. Did Gretel want a second shot or not? She couldn't decide. Did one shot mean Mr. Klahr had killed the witch? Or did it mean the witch had descended on Mr. Klahr, flown across the lot as she'd done to Odalinde, and the one blast was just an aimless discharge? She was suddenly praying for the second report, but it never came. Gretel's eyes darted crazily from the window to Mrs. Klahr to Hansel and back to the window again.

"It will be all right, Gretel," Mrs. Klahr stated flatly, without conviction.

Gretel pulled away from Petr and walked briskly over to Hansel. She kissed him gently on the forehead and then pulled him close. She held him that way for just a moment and then turned and walked to the door, opening it wide.

"Gretel, no!" It was Petr

"I have to go, Petr. I should have never left them." And then, "And he needs me."

"He tried to kill you, Gretel," Mrs. Klahr said sharply, without apology. "And may have helped murder your mother."

Gretel stood still, hesitating, her back to Mrs. Klahr and the others. "I love you, Mrs. Klahr. Until my last day on this earth, as long as my mind is sound and my body able, I will do anything for you. And when I said, "he needs me," I meant Mr. Klahr."

Gretel could hear the sounds of Mrs. Klahr crying as she walked down the steps of the porch toward the lake and the waiting canoe.

CHAPTER TWENTY-EIGHT

NO! ODALINDE THOUGHT, as she turned to see the headlights of the weathered pickup. It was Mr. Klahr, the man who had saved Gretel, the man who, along with his wife, had given the girl a job and a purpose, and thus a new hope about what her life could be. She was relieved at first, knowing that the children had obviously made it to the Klahrs and reported on the madness presently unfolding, but then panic set in. She'll kill him, of course, Odalinde knew, but worse, she'll torture him, use his pain as a path to the children.

"Go away!" Odalinde screamed the instant the truck door opened.

The man inside ignored the command, and instead stepped to the driveway, a twin-barreled shotgun steadied upon his shoulder before his second foot touched the ground.

"I'll go away when you're in the truck 'side me, ma'am," replied Georg Klahr, his voice slow and gentle. "Not before then, however. You there, locksy lady with the chompers, I'll need you to step away from the children's guardian. Now!" Mr. Klahr slid the fore-end of the shotgun back and then forward, stripping the shell from the magazine and loading the chamber.

The witch did nothing at first, standing completely motionless, and her pause seemed aggressive to Odalinde, calculating. And then, as if finally comfortable with the plan she'd formulated, the witch obeyed, and stepped away from Odalinde, slightly forward, toward the threat before her, her eyes remaining fixed on the man.

"You know the children? Those two in her charge?" the witch asked. Her words sounded intrigued and pleased.

"Be quiet!" Odalinde shouted from behind the woman, "You don't know me, or anything about my children. You're just that old fool from across the lake! Get out of here! This is none of your concern!" Odalinde tried to sound demented and fierce; she'd never met the Klahrs, but from what Gretel had no doubt told them about her over the last several months, the man was likely to be convinced of her madness.

The witch moved quickly back toward Odalinde, like a large spider scurrying to a cricket, and, using a single hand, reached down and snatched Odalinde by the hair, standing her straight and positioning her to act as a shield.

The moment for Georg Klahr to shoot was then, Odalinde knew, there wouldn't be another opportunity. But the witch's movements were lightning fast, and with the natural stress of the situation, combined with the incredulousness of the overall scene—including the dead body of his neighbor Mr. Morgan, bloody and shredded on the driveway—it was no doubt Mr. Klahr couldn't squeeze the trigger. It was likely he would have missed, of course, or even shot the wrong target, Odalinde thought, but it was a chance, and though the woman was still at bay, in that few seconds the advantages had turned dramatically.

"What do you know of the children who were here?" the witch said calmly.

"I know I can see the older boy's father's cruiser parked there behind you," Mr. Klahr replied in a similarly calm tone. "And I know if you make another move without being told, you'll wish you hadn't. Now tell me now about where I'd find that boy's father."

"Why, I'd be happy to do more than that! I'll take you right to him! I know just where he is!" The woman paused, and Odalinde could imagine the hate emitting from her eyes as she glared at Georg Klahr, a wide, mocking smile lifting her cheeks. "But I believe I asked you for some information first. You see, after I'm done slaughtering this one," the witch glanced at Odalinde, who was stagnant, doll-like in the grip of the woman, "I'll need to find those children. The siblings especially. I just have some questions, of course." The woman's voice then dropped an octave, becoming serious and threatening, as if she'd tired of the pretense. "And as she's just reminded you, this has nothing to do with you."

"Well seeing as the children you're so eager to talk with's father's corpse is growing cold behind you there, I'm thinking I won't tell you where they've gone. No, instead, I'm going to leave it up to you to decide whether to release your claws from that woman right now, and then rest quietly until The System gets here, or to have this conversation end with your face full of buckshot and your brains scattered about this property for the scavengers to feed on. I don't mean to rush you, ma'am, but I'll need a decision soon." Mr. Klahr's tone was steely and the squint of his eye through the sight steady and focused. The next time the witch moved any faster than a tree sloth, the trigger would feel the squeeze. Odalinde knew it, and no doubt the witch did too.

Odalinde could feel the woman's breath and heartbeat quicken, and the grip on Odalinde's neck tightened. The witch was ready to attack.

Almost before the thought had formed in her mind, Odalinde felt herself lifted from behind as if a large condor had swooped down and snatched her in its talons. "Shoot!" was all she could manage to scream—though she couldn't be sure it was audible—as she catapulted through the night, the woman attached to her from the back. They were barely two feet off the ground she guessed as they hurled directly toward Mr. Klahr. She could see the surprise in his stillness as they approached him, a frozen disbelief at what he was witnessing. Odalinde tried to scream again, but upon opening her mouth felt a pinch just above her collarbone. The last thing she heard before collapsing in the witch's grasp, unconscious, was the sound of the shotgun.

CHAPTER TWENTY-NINE

THE NARROW LEDGE THAT ran along the bank at the bottom of the lake had run out, and Anika was now forced to swim. She'd been fortunate to this point, and was now trying desperately to stay calm, positive, knowing her energy would deplete much more quickly if she let her thoughts descend into panic. But the gunshot had been close, and judging by the direction of the report, it had come from the other side of the lake. Anika didn't want to admit it to herself, but if she'd had to guess, it had come from her house.

The swimming had come naturally to this point and she'd felt remarkably capable in the water—she'd kept her strokes long and smooth, keeping her head above the surface and stopping every minute or so to tread water and rest. She'd make it, she now believed—based on her assessment of her strength and pace thus far, she'd make it. At least to the orchard. But once there—at the orchard—she'd have to stop and rest before heading home. Home—where a gun had been fired only minutes ago. Why was there a gunshot? Certainly no one was hunting in the dark, she could be sure of that, and knowing what she did now about her husband's role in all of this, Anika's mind invoked it's most awful scenarios.

She tried desperately to banish the thoughts and focus on the progress she was making, watching the stripe of moonbeam on the lake approach. But thoughts of tragedy became pervasive and soon merged with a weariness Anika never thought possible. Anika was now crying and coughing in fear. She stopped again to rest, to rein in her hysteria, but she was struggling now just to remain afloat, her arms were weakened by fear and exhaustion and her breathing was spastic.

"Don't panic!" she scolded herself, aloud. "You've come too far to die here!"

She pushed off again, trying to breast-stroke her way forward, but was forced to stop almost immediately. Her energy was crippled now, and evidently Anika was much weaker than she'd believed herself to be. Adrenaline could fuel someone for only so long, she knew—at some point a person needed real strength and actual energy. And hers was spent.

She stretched one leg as far down toward the bottom of the lake as possible, reaching with her foot and toes, hoping to feel the cold slime of the mud floor, indicating she'd be reaching the bank soon. But she felt nothing, and though she wanted to stretch farther, dipping her head under until she felt exactly how deep the water was, she decided against it, fearing she might never resurface.

Anika's eyes filled with tears, not at her impending death, but at her failure to complete her journey to find her children. To save them. Were they dead already? Every cell in her body told her no. So why couldn't she summon the strength!

She was now paddling laboriously at the surface, and her feet beneath were kicking down frantically, running and stepping furiously just to keep her nose above the water line. She stared out at the ribbon of placid moonbeam, coughing out the lake water that was now lapping over her lips and into her mouth. A beautiful night, she thought absently, the water in the distance as still as pavement.

Anika's nostrils filled with water, forcing another reflexive, gasping effort from her to stay alive. She pushed herself back above the water line, squeezing her eyes shut and snorting the water from her nose. And as she opened her eyes, Anika saw the beam on the lake waver, rippling only slightly at first, and then a bit more. A gust of wind, Anika thought though she'd not felt it herself. And then she saw the real source of the disturbance. It wasn't a mirage—she wouldn't allow herself to consider that possibility—it was real. There was only the tip of the vessel at first, and then a silhouette of oars, slapping machine-like at the water, blended into view.

Anika filled her lungs with air in one last stab at survival, and then screamed, "Help me!" at the canoe cutting through the moonlight.

CHAPTER THIRTY

THE OLD WOMAN COULD feel the warmth of blood on her neck and face and instantly knew she was hurt—perhaps badly. It had been a dangerous strategy using the woman as a shield the way she had, but in truth, she hadn't thought about it at all; the strategy had chosen her more than she it. It was pure instinct.

But now, with the armed man in front of her preparing to reload his weapon, she needed to make a decision: attack again, unprotected and weakened—her new gliding ability was wonderful, but afterward left her temporarily exhausted—or retreat.

Without looking back, the witch rose to her feet, stumbling badly at first but somehow maintaining her balance and began running to the back of the house and down the slope toward the lake. She kept her body crouched all the while, like a soldier avoiding sniper fire, and her eyes focused on the porch steps which would provide some measure of cover.

The witch ran past the porch and grabbed one of the wooden steps, the momentum swinging her body left and underneath the open staircase. She paused for a moment, listening, and then continued down the gravel slope of the Morgan property toward the lake. If the man decided to pursue her, which she'd no doubt he would, she'd be trapped at the water's edge. She had no aversion to swimming (in fact, she imagined, it was likely she'd now be quite adept at the activity), but even if she were as quick as a porpoise she'd be an easy target for a shooter on the bank.

The woman stepped down onto the mud of the lake bank, noting the footprints of the children who had fled the property earlier—as well as the drag marks of the boat they'd set off in. In an attempt to limit visibility, she ducked low behind a clump of small trees that were skirted in a patch of ivy.

And listened. But it wasn't steps she heard, it was the sound of an old truck engine starting and the dusty growl of spinning tires. He was leaving, and seconds later, he was gone. Out of fear for himself or to return to protect the children he'd spoken of, the witch didn't much care, she knew only that she was safe for the moment. And moments she could not waste.

Her first thought was of the Orphist, Odalinde. She assumed she was dead. That the shotgun blast had ripped her apart; after all, *she'd* been hit—and hurt—how was it possible her human shield survived? But there had been no time to check to make certain.

Reluctantly the woman raised her hand to her ear and neck, and, finding the source of her gruesome injury, winced with nausea. Her right ear was gone and her neck was missing a chunk, though apparently one not vital to her immediate survival since she wasn't feeling the encroaching blackness of death's approach that she'd felt in the past. She had the potion, of course, which would certainly heal her. The thought kept her calm for the moment, but she'd need to attend to her wounds soon.

But first the woman. It was time for the woman—Odalinde—to die.

The witch stepped from behind the tree cover and looked out across the lake at the orchard—the orchard owned by the man who had just attempted to murder her, she assumed—and mentally listed it as her next stop. It would be more difficult now—with the home fortified and the element of surprise now gone—but guns or not, she'd need to get to Gretel and Hansel. Perhaps there was a gun in the cruiser, she thought, certainly the officers kept weapons in the trunk. She wasn't so confident as to count on it, but she hadn't checked before, and securing her own arms was a possibility that was strong. If only she'd thought to take the officer's weapon before leaving her cabin! But she hadn't, and there was no point ruing the decision. And in her own defense, she'd never envisioned these difficulties. She had never counted on a struggle.

She turned back to the house and took two steps up the slope toward Odalinde when she heard the scream.

It was a scream she'd heard a dozen times before.

CHAPTER THIRTY-ONE

GRETEL SCREAMED IN reply, reflexively, and slammed the oars to the water, adroitly rotating the canoe toward the sound. At first she didn't believe what she'd heard—the 'voice'— and decided it was nothing more than a combination of night sounds and her imagination.

"Help me!"

This time the voice was clear and belting, but also desperate, struggling. Drowning, Gretel thought.

"Wait...wait for me. I'm coming!"

Gretel dunked the oars and gave one long thrust. There was nothing but darkness in this direction, and she could easily row right over the floundering soul if she wasn't careful. But her stroke was perfect, and Gretel saw immediately the shape bobbing just above the surface.

"I'm here," Gretel said nervously. "Give me your hand."

Without looking up, the drowning woman lifted a feeble hand from the water. Gretel grabbed it with one hand and with the other reached down past the thin woman's elbow to her triceps, gripping it firmly. The woman reached up with her free hand and grabbed the side of the canoe, and with a manic tug from Gretel, pulled herself into the boat. She lifted her head and met the eyes of her savior, and there was nothing left in her to restrain her emotions.

"How did you get so strong?" The question blurted from Anika's mouth in a fit of laughter and crying. It was a benign question, an act of maternal instinct aimed at calming her daughter.

Gretel was hysterical in her joy, and couldn't lift her sobbing head off her mother's shoulder. Anika wasn't much better in her composure, but knew the proper reunion would have to wait.

"Where is your brother, Gretel?" Anika stroked the back of her daughter's head, coaxing her to lift it and speak to her.

Gretel had a look of bewilderment and terror on her face as she lifted her head. "I think Father's dead. I don't know for sure, but..." she kept herself stiff and upright, but unleashed another fit of tears at the sound of her own words.

Anika turned away and closed her eyes, squeezing them tightly in an effort to keep stable.

"But Hansel is fine," Gretel continued. "He's at the Klahr's. He's safe."

"Oh, thank God," Anika sighed and pulled Gretel close, relishing the warmth of her daughter's body.

Gretel sniffled like the child she was. "Where were you, Mother? How did you...? What happened...?"

"It's too much for now, Gretel," Anika said. "Far too much for now." Then she paused and looking in the direction of her home said, "What was that gun shot?"

Gretel's eyes flashed wide, suddenly reminded of why she was out on the lake to begin with.

"What is it, Gretel?"

"Mr. Klahr. And Odalinde."

"Who?"

"There's no time, Mother, we have to go!"

CHAPTER THIRTY-TWO

THE OLD WOMAN COULD hear the voices—female voices—on the lake, but the whispers were faint and she couldn't make out the words. But she'd heard those first two words that had snared her attention and recognized them instantly. Those familiar words contained in the scream. The first time she'd heard them was all those months ago, when she lay dying at the base of her porch, debilitated, anticipating the approaching clutch of death's grasp. And they had rung through the forest like the song of an angel, to save her—quite literally—and to draw to the surface a reserve of power she'd never dreamed existed inside her.

Help me!

The witch gave one last glance to the front of the Morgan house, mildly considering the option to continue up the path to the front of the house to ensure the children's guardian was indeed dead in the driveway. But this detail suddenly seemed far less important than pursuing the voices on the lake. The Orphist woman wasn't going anywhere, the witch decided, and she crept warily back toward the water line.

A mixture of laughter and crying was all she could interpret from the sounds, and the witch quickly deduced that the invisible scene adrift on the water was a reunion of mother and daughter.

She made it home.

The smile and twitch of pride in the witch came not from an admiration of her Source's individual effort, but from the blood that flowed in her veins, the blood that had fueled the remarkable accomplishment. Her own blood, the witch thought.

She waded slowly into the water until it reached her shins, careful to stay clear of the moon's glow. She now had another decision to make: should she swim to them? It seemed an absurd idea at first, considering all the advantages she now possessed—particularly that of knowing their current location, as well as where they lived—but time was against her. No doubt The System was en route already—the marksman neighbor having certainly made that call—and though the one officer, Officer Stenson, had been a puppet in Marcel's plan, as far as she knew, there was no influence on them otherwise.

The ability to swim the distance to the boat wouldn't pose the problem; it was the ability to do it quietly, she reckoned. The lake was deathly still, and even with the occasional jumping frog or fish periodically rippling the surface, she didn't see how she wouldn't be noticed before getting even halfway to them. The witch considered her choices again, and as she stood on the lake bank, she heard the voices become clearer. The tones were hushed and deep, but they were steadily approaching. She wouldn't need to swim to them, they were coming to her!

The witch ducked back in the thicket of trees where she had taken cover from the never-approaching neighbor. She narrowed her eyes and covered her head as far as possible with her cloak. Without a light source, she knew she was invisible from the bank.

The woman saw first the arrowhead shape of the canoe's bow, followed instantly by the silhouetted shapes of her prey. She held her breath, exhaling only slightly during the rattle of the boat as the two women parked it on the gravel shore. She extended her fingers, brushing the back of her saber-like nails against the trunk of one of the small trees in the clump. It was the preparatory move of an animal, instinctive and lethal. She stood slowly from her crouch and opened her mouth wide, touching the tip of her tongue to one of her incisors, relishing the bite of the blade-like point.

The two Morgan women—mother and daughter—started up the slope to the house, apprehensive and focused in their movements. The witch stayed still as stone as they passed her, no small restraint given she could have touched Gretel—killed her, easily—without even having to extend her arm fully. But that wasn't the perfect moment. She couldn't risk letting the older one get away. Not again.

The witch ducked a branch and stepped out from the thicket, assassin-like, placing her first foot firmly on the path before bringing the second foot out beside it. She stood pleased for just a moment, smiling at the seemingly endless talents the potion now endowed her with, watching the women obliviously make their way up the path. They never sensed her as she appeared behind them, closing in with claws extended.

She'd made the decision to kill the older one—Anika—and to keep the girl for further blending. She was strong now, but there was simply too much to risk trying to capture and hold two prisoners, particularly since she didn't yet know where she'd be living past today. So, yes, she'd kill the mother, and once she'd found a new location—a new lair—and had blended the new potion, she'd come back for the boy. She couldn't let that much power go free.

Her clarity about the future was suddenly staggering, with thoughts and strategies now flooding her mind, giving her confidence and energy. Her mind felt *organized*, without disease or ambiguity.

The witch drew her arm back as if to throw a punch, but instead of forming her hand into a fist, she kept it open with her palm down and fingers stretched, the tips of her nails pointed directly at the base of Anika's skull. The women had walked about ten yards from the witch when she began her advancement. She took two long strides at first and then skipped into some form of a human gallop.

Five yards away. Two. Her grin was wide with teeth shining.

And then the madness in her face changed at the sound of screams.

They had come from the women—both of them—and their shrieks had been bloodcurdling, as if the witch had suddenly materialized in front of them. But she hadn't, and they hadn't turned to see her; they had, in fact, made no sudden turns or suspicious pauses at all. Why the sudden terror?

And then she saw it—the figure—emerging from between the two Morgan women, crashing toward her like a giant warped arrow. Stunned, the witch opened her mouth to scream but the figure slammed into the bottom of her chin before a sound could escape. There was a sickening sound of cracking bone from the back of the witch's jaw, and the bottom row of her teeth exploded in every direction, including down her throat.

The Orphist!

CHAPTER THIRTY-THREE

"GRETEL GO!"

In the moonlight, Gretel could see Odalinde at the edge of the lake, her face coated in what appeared to be a mixture of blood and mud. Her eyes were open, but they were weary and fading.

"Odalinde? Odalinde! What's happening?"

"Go!" Odalinde repeated, this time with a wet cough culminating the statement.

"Let's go, Gretel," Anika said, beckoning her daughter up the hill.

"No!" Odalinde shouted, pulling herself to her knees. "Not that way. You'll be trapped." She caught her breath. "The canoe. Take it and go back to the Klahrs. Your father's dead."

"What about Mr. Klahr?" Gretel asked.

"He's gone."

"What?" Gretel cried.

"No, I mean...I mean he left. He's okay. There's no time Gretel. Go back!"

Gretel and her mother stood paralyzed, not sure whether to disobey the woman's instructions—who, after all, may have just sustained a violent head injury—or to trust her and go.

"She's still here, Gretel. She'll have you trapped up there. Go back. You have to get back to the Klahrs!" Odalinde looked to the ground, composing herself, and then continued in an even tone. "Go back, call The System, and get ready with every gun the Klahrs have."

Gretel suddenly considered the witch—whom she'd forgotten temporarily—scanning the area immediately in front of her and down by the lake. But darkness blanketed most of the area and she saw no one.

And then it came to her: the witch had been behind them. Hunting them. Ready to kill them both. And Odalinde had saved them.

Gretel grabbed her mother's hand and they descended the path together, back toward the lake from where they'd just come, to the spot where Odalinde lay.

"Fine," Anika said, kneeling beside Odalinde, "but you're coming with us."

"I can't," Odalinde said.

Her exhaustion was palpable, and Gretel could see by the wounds on the side of her head that she was badly injured.

"You can and you will," Anika replied, "My daughter came back for you, risked her life for you, so you're coming."

"Anika," Odalinde whispered, the faint trace of a smile forming on her face.

Anika grabbed the woman under her armpit and lifted. "It's nice to meet you. It looks like you've been through a lot. But still, I think you'll find my story trumps yours. And I'll never live with myself if I don't discover whether or not you agree."

Gretel had always marveled at this ability of her mother's. She'd seen her do this trick with her father a thousand times, expressing things in such a way as to create the impression that any option other than the one she proposed was nothing short of absurd.

Odalinde was wobbly as she stood, and her eyes looked like they were fading into unconsciousness; but somehow she made it to her feet, and Anika held her steady as they shuffled toward the canoe where Gretel waited alertly, oar in hand and ready to push off.

"She's coming," Odalinde whispered, her words coming out dreamy and delirious.

"It's okay," Anika replied, "It's going to be..."

But Anika Morgan never had the chance to finish her underscore of assurance. Before her muscles could react, before she could offer any semblance of protection, the witch had ripped Odalinde from her, yanking her by the hair. She held her still for just a beat, elevated, resting against her torso, before inserting her top row of fangs into the side of Odalinde's neck. The image was nauseating, something from a nightmare, and made all the more grotesque by the witch's twisted jaw and missing row of bottom teeth.

The witch tossed Odalinde's corpse to the ground and stood glaring at Anika and Gretel, who were now screaming in horror by the canoe. There was no hesitation from the witch this time, and she lurched furiously toward Anika, focused only on the final slaughter of her once-captive Source.

The opportunity flashed in a blink, but Gretel saw it, clearly, and speared it like a fish. The witch's single-mindedness toward her mother had given Gretel a moment of advantage, and, almost automatic in her motion, she swung the oar forward, rotating her hips and torso, creating drag with the weapon, and clipped the hag's head just above the temple. Two inches lower and the witch would have been dead, Gretel lamented, but she'd stunned her badly, and the witch collapsed to the ground like a satchel of wet clay.

Wasting not another second, Gretel pounced into the canoe and anchored the oars in place. "Mother, let's go!" she shouted, and before her mother's second foot was off the muddy bank, Gretel was launched and rowing.

Positioned facing the bank as the canoe pulled away, Gretel stared in disbelief at the wreckage in front of her, assessing the danger which—unbelievably—was already recovering from the blow. Gretel's breathing had been heavy and rasping from exhaustion and trauma, but was now escalating to panic at what she was witnessing. The witch was on her feet—already!—standing tall over Odalinde's body with her arms high above her head. She was pulling and struggling, reaching for the sky, and Gretel quickly calculated the woman was disrobing, a suspicion that was confirmed when the witch's ample cloak fluttered through the moonbeam into the clump of trees. But she didn't appear to be stopping with the cloak, and continued to strip down to her underclothing, and possibly beyond. She was coming after them.

Gretel had launched the canoe in the direction of the Klahrs and had no plans to deviate from the course, frantic now to get across to the orchard and up to the house where she could warn the others and help fortify the grounds.

"She's coming, Gretel. She's coming after us." Her mother had been watching the scene on the bank as well, and now turned her head back toward the front of the boat and Gretel, aware of the direction they were headed. "We can't lead her to the Klahrs, Gret. Not to Hansel. Not to those people."

"What?" Gretel continued in her current direction, not properly inferring her mother's words.

"Rifle Field, Gretel, head down the lake to Rifle Field." Anika's words were restrained but tense, carefully intoned to elicit obedience. "She'll follow us, Gretel, away from your brother. I need you to do this."

"But Rifle Field! We'll be trapped!"

"It's the only place close enough. And if you can get us there—get us there fast—I have a plan."

Gretel recognized the insistence in her mother's voice, and, with a grunt of reluctance, deftly turned the canoe south toward Rifle Field and began carving the oars into the water with the possessed repetition of a galley slave, guiding them and turning them over as hard and fast as she'd ever done before. The canoe glided easily, rapidly, as though it were motor-powered or thrust by a blast of wind. Her mother was right—she was strong. And she was going to get them to their new destination.

Her mother had again turned away, looking to the bank where the witch had been standing only seconds before. "I can't see her anymore, Gretel. I think she's in."

Gretel thought so too. In the dark, however, the bank had drifted too far away to see much, so she couldn't be sure the witch had taken to the water. But Gretel, and apparently her mother, had sensed it. Surely they couldn't be caught with the boat travelling at this speed, though, Gretel thought—particularly by a woman who was severely wounded. But...the woman had flown. Flown!

Gretel could see the first signs of the clearing to Rifle Field, and effortlessly decelerated the canoe and steered it toward the bank, guiding it slowly toward shore.

"I can't believe I'm back here again," Anika said flatly as she hopped from the stern seat into the shallow water at the shoreline, rushing to where she'd left her clothes.

"I never stopped believing you'd be back," Gretel replied. She was winded, and the words came out rushed and emotionless, but as she looked over to see her mother dressing, she realized what she meant. "Wait. You mean here? At Rifle Field? You were here? Why?"

"Let's go, Gretel, I promise you'll know everything later. Right now, we have to dig."

CHAPTER THIRTY-FOUR

ANIKA THREADED HER arms through the sleeves of her shirt and pushed her head through the neck hole; how thankful she was now that she had left her clothes and shoes behind, dry on the bank. She looked over at her daughter, who seemed to have already created a gap beneath the fence large enough for both of them to squeeze through and was continuing to dig with abandon.

Anika would never be able to explain what had inspired her to toss the shovel from the cannery window, only that it seemed the prudent thing to do at the time. Perhaps it had to do with the instincts that apparently ran in her family, a result of her mother's unique gift—a gift that had been revealed to Anika only hours ago—that had been genetically passed on to Anika, ever-ready to manifest itself in certain life-threatening situations to pull her to safety. She suspected this was the reason for her decision, but couldn't honestly commit to it. Maybe her instincts had just sharpened over the last several months and were much more dependable now. Or maybe she was just lucky. Sometimes your decisions were spot on, she thought, and other times (trudging through the woods after a car accident, for example) they weren't.

"Are we good, Gret?" Anika asked.

"I think so," Gretel replied. "I know *I* can fit."

Anika gave her daughter a cold stare. "Well, thanks a lot for that!"

Gretel let out a quiet burst of laughter. "I hardly mean it like that," she said. And then, "Do you think she's still coming?"

"I don't know, honey, but let's leave the canoe on the bank. I want her to know we're here."

Gretel walked back to her mother at the shoreline and, as the two women stepped toward the boat, they were halted by the twisted face of the tortuous witch rising from the lake.

Her face was gruesome, bloodied from head to chin, her mouth deformed and vacant, with a demented grinning overbite. In the dark of night, with her hair and body dripping with water, she looked like a corpse that had crawled from a tomb buried long ago at the bottom of the lake.

Anika stood palsied by the emerging face, stunned at the transformation it had undergone. Everything back on the bank had happened so quickly—the attack and Gretel's heroics—that nothing had registered in Anika's mind. But it was obvious now what was happening—even with all that destruction to the woman's face—Anika understood clearly what she was seeing. The torture. The blood. All of the extractions and the rank pies, all of the forced, unnatural rest and nursing, it had all been for this. This metamorphosis. This conversion of the hideous beast from the woods of the Northlands into a younger, more maniacal version of itself. A stronger version of itself.

"Now Gretel! Follow me now!"

Anika broke from her paralysis and sprinted to the fence and the awaiting burrow beneath it, with Gretel following obediently, barely a step back from her heels. She ushered her daughter through first, and Gretel slithered under the fence as nimbly as a human could. Anika was on the ground following before her daughter's feet had cleared the hole, sneaking peeks behind her, expecting the monster to grab her at any moment.

But the woman didn't pursue them, and Anika and Gretel made it through, quickly heading to the front side of the cannery. Anika opened the door and shuffled Gretel through, narrowly squeezing in herself before slamming the door behind them. Anika briefly considered that perhaps the warehouse would have been the better option, but the hill leading up to it was steep, and she didn't trust her legs at this point. And there were tools in the cannery. Weapons.

When Anika had been inside the cannery earlier—escaping the very grounds on which she now sought sanctuary—there had still been a hint of daylight by which to navigate. But it was nearly pitch black inside the building now, with only the radiance of the moon through the second-level window to see by.

Ideally, Anika would have blocked the door with a table or piece of large machinery, but she recalled the emptiness of the cannery floor and decided there was nothing accessible to serve that purpose, and there was no time to explore. Besides, Anika thought, the door swung out—not in—and any blockade would be easily conquered.

Anika grabbed her daughter's hand and, extending her other arm, felt the space immediately in front of her for any looming obstacles. The path to the stairs had been clear previously, she was relatively confident on that count, but she could little afford to be hobbled by a stray iron post or corroded hole in the floor. She and Gretel had to get to the second level.

"Where is she? Why isn't she following us?" Gretel asked, her tone hopeful, suggesting that perhaps the woman hadn't seen the hole they'd created, or perhaps hadn't been able to fit.

Or maybe she decided the effort was too taxing after all. Or, with God's Grace, had finally succumbed to her injuries. That was the one they needed. But Anika knew better; she'd seen the glee and determination on the woman's face. She was wounded, but she'd never stop chasing them. Any of them.

"She is, Gretel. But maybe she suspects a trap."

Anika stepped forward and felt the toe of her shoe against the side of the bottom step. "We're going upstairs, Gretel. There's no railing, so be careful."

With the moonlight shining through to the landing at the top of the stairs, the ascent got progressively easier as they reached the top, and Anika quickly looked around for the hammer she'd used earlier to clear out the window.

"Is there one?" Gretel asked.

"One what?" Anika replied, focusing on the floor, squinting her eyes in adjustment to the shadows on the floor.

"A trap? You said, 'Maybe she suspects a trap.' Is there a trap?"

"No. Not really. Not one that I've planned anyway. But if she suspects one, that's good. It will give us time to think of one." Anika realized this logic was somewhat specious, but the alternative—having the witch bounding up the stairs to maul them—was certainly worse.

Anika was on her knees now, feeling the dusty wood of the floor in search of the hammer. It had been here! She'd dropped it right here!

"Gretel," she whispered, "there's a hammer up here. On the floor some-where. It should be here by the window. Help me find it."

A crackling sound on the ground below froze Anika, and she could hear Gretel's breathing stop midway through her exhalation. It could have been just an animal—a raccoon likely—Anika thought, and on any other night it would have been. She considered for a moment that maybe Gretel had been right: maybe the blow from the oar had been more severe than realized, and it was only the witch's adrenaline that had seen her through the lake. Maybe she'd staggered out of the water toward them in a last desperate attempt at murder until her body simply refused to go any further.

Maybe, Anika thought, but she was alive. And as long as she was alive, she'd be coming.

Every atom in Anika's body wanted to crawl to the window and peek out, just to get a glimpse of the ground below, to see if the woman was there, waiting for them, starving them out perhaps. But she knew if the witch was there—recovered and virile—that to give away their position at this point was suicidal; the witch knew they were inside the cannery, but not where in-side. Anika and Gretel had to hold that advantage, no matter how slight.

"She's down there, Mother," Anika said, her voice so tempered that 'mother' came out as "other."

"I know."

"What are we going to do?"

"We'll hide here for now." Anika hadn't prepared for this recess. She'd fig-ured that after they ran for the cannery the witch would have been a step be-hind them and that all of it—one way or the other—would be over by now. But that hadn't happened, and now she needed a real plan. "We'll move away from the window for now, out of the light, against the wall."

"And then what?" Gretel asked.

"I don't know, Gretel!" Anika immediately regretted her whispered bark, but let the effect of it stand. "Just move to the wall."

Anika scooted to the side wall of the cannery and frowned at Gretel, who had decided to move away from her to the opposite wall. Not really a good time for brooding, Anika thought, but she's just a child. And God only knew what she'd been through. A tear formed in Anika's eyes and her mind raced to red over the struggle that wouldn't be rewarded. The reward she deserved! Her life! Her children!

Anika quickly erased the tear, flicking it away in a redirection of anger. No. No. No. She wouldn't let her mind straggle off in a countenance of the inequities of life. Not now, and not ever again. There was simply no gain in it. There were gains from love—and sometimes from fight—but never from blame. Never from self-pity. Those were the things that bred regret. Those were the things that dissolved power.

"Mother." It was Gretel from the opposite wall, whispering only as loud as necessary to be heard.

"I love you, Gretel," Anika replied.

"I love you too, Mother. I can't wait until Hansel sees you."

This time Anika let the tear fall, and she wanted to run to Gretel, to spend her last seconds on earth—if that what was meant to be—in the arms of her daughter.

"And Mother," Gretel continued.

"Yes, angel?"

"I found the hammer."

CHAPTER THIRTY-FIVE

THE WITCH STAGGERED to the dry ground of the clearing and collapsed, gasping for air. She was thankful the women had run off—had they stood and fought, she may not have had the strength to defeat them both. She was desperately tired, and her injuries were not insignificant.

But this challenge was a mere formality, a honing of her abilities, a further test of her dedication to Life. Rest was all she needed to continue. Rest and more potion.

The old woman lay flat on her back now, breathing heavily through her damaged jaws. She could feel the effects of the magic broth trying to restore her once again, as it had earlier in the cabin after she'd been brutally attacked and left to die. But already she sensed the potency diminishing. In her bones and muscles she still felt young and strong, but she wasn't healing the same.

She needed more. She needed everything blended properly this time. And her earlier plans to kill the older one, her original Source, had to be recalibrated. She would need all of them. All of the Aulwurms. The girl and the woman she would get now, and later, when she'd regained control of the situation, the boy.

She watched her prey squeeze beneath the wire barrier, scattering like so many vermin she'd hunted in her day. Her rest would be short-lived it seemed, and the witch felt a pang of panic as she watched the women disappear into the darkness on the opposite side of the fence. She was confident she could scale the fence, or even fit beneath it, but such efforts would take their toll, and leave her vulnerable in whatever conflict eventually awaited her.

Still, she had to move.

She climbed back to her feet and stepped slowly to the fence, peering through into the blackness. She took a step back and scanned the metal barrier top to bottom, calculating what efforts would be needed to lift herself over the barbed wire. Certainly burrowing under would be far easier, but there would be several seconds of defenselessness, and it wasn't impossible that the women were waiting with a raised axe just on the other side.

But the witch was anemic, and even the idea of taking flight exhausted her. She couldn't wait to recover, and she couldn't risk a failed attempt that would leave her caught in the barbs. The hole at the bottom of the fence seemed like the only decision.

She kneeled back to the soft ground, preparing to follow the path the women had taken only minutes before, and froze at soft muffled sounds coming from the huge rusted building in front of her. There was silence for a few beats, and then the sounds again, coming from within. At first the woman assumed it was rats or bats, but then, magically, the faint hiss of whispers drifted down from the window above. The witch's smile grew wide with joy, and she had to cover her half-mouth like a schoolgirl to keep from chuckling.

She lay back down, this time at the foot of the fence just in front of the tunnel, and closed her eyes, listening to the sweet sounds above her, waiting for her power to return.

CHAPTER THIRTY-SIX

"HOW LONG ARE WE GOING to stay here?" Gretel asked.

It was the first words either woman had spoken in at least ten minutes, both Gretel and Anika seeming to understand that silence was safer. But Gretel was growing restless, and with every minute that passed, more wary of the situation. This plan of her mother's to hide and fortify seemed as good as any before, but now it felt wrong, like it was working against them. Like they were trapped.

"It hasn't been that long, Gretel. It just feels that way," Anika replied.

Gretel could hear the doubt in her mother's voice and capitalized on it.

"We can't just sit here, Mother. Maybe she's gone by now. She doesn't know we came in here, right? How could she? Maybe she went off into the woods somewhere looking for us, and now's the time we should be leaving."

This didn't feel right to Gretel either—she suspected the witch was still near—but she wanted to move, be proactive. Sitting and waiting, as a rule, always seemed to Gretel like the wrong course of action.

"And if she's down there, waiting for us, what then?"

Gretel paused a moment and said, "Then we'll fight her...and kill her."

Gretel's words lingered for several beats, and then she saw the figure of her mother creep into view and head toward the window. She had her head bowed well below the height of the sill, like a bank robber dodging pistol fire with the local sheriff in some old movie.

"I'm going to take a look," Anika whispered, "but just understand, if she sees me, you'll get your wish. There will be a fight. So keep the hammer ready."

Gretel held the hammer up, and then, not sure whether she or the hammer was visible to her mother from where she sat, replied, "I've got it."

Gretel watched the back of her mother's head rise slowly up to the opening of the window, turning first in the direction of Rifle Field, and then rotating back in the direction of their property down the lake. She then stood up further to get a view of the ground directly below, and instantly collapsed back to the floor and turned toward Gretel, wide-eyed and stunned.

Assuming her mother had seen the witch walking below, Gretel stayed quiet, and simply turned her palms up and matched her mother's expression.

"She's down there. Outside the fence near the hole." Anika was barely auditory, doing little more than mouthing the words. "I think she might be dead."

Gretel looked toward the window. "Let me see."

Anika nodded, indicating she wanted Gretel's assessment about whether she also believed the witch dead.

Gretel walked on her knees over to the window and looked out, scanning the ground below, waiting for her eyes to adjust to the dark. The night was still clear and the moon offered plenty of light past the fence. But Gretel didn't see anyone. She scanned the grounds for a few seconds more and then turned back to her mother. "I don't see her. You said by the fence, right?"

"Yes, right next to the hole. Let me see."

Gretel backed off and allowed her mother to move in again.

Anika peered once again out the window. "I don't understand. She was..."

A hoarse, high-pitched cry shattered the quiet of the night and rang through the cannery like the bellow of a bull elephant. Anika, screaming in disbelief, lurched in terror away from the window—so far, in fact, that had she backed up even another foot, Gretel could see she would have gone tumbling down the open stairway.

A dark, amorphous blotch now filled the space of the window, blocking the full light of the moon, allowing only small strands of silver rays around its perimeter. It was the witch, and she was perched like a giant spider in the window, gripping the top corners of the frame with her long fingers. Her feet were wedged in the bottom corners. Gretel thought she looked like an enormous, disfigured bat.

"That's impossible!" Anika screamed. "How?"

"You, my sweet Source," the witch replied, "You are 'How.'" Her words were breathy and, with her mouth and neck mangled, nearly unintelligible.

Gretel watched the woman in the window silently, unable to look away from her destroyed face.

The witch stepped down from the sill and stood tall, dropping the hood of her cloak, never taking her eyes off Anika. Gretel noticed instantly the woman had not even glanced in her direction, and had instead stayed locked on her mother during the entire exchange. As Gretel had suspected earlier with her mother, it was possible the witch couldn't see her in the shadows.

"You've given me so much trouble, Anika Morgan, more trouble than I ever would have believed you capable of. But you've also given me so much life. And you will continue giving. You and your family." Blood and mucous dropped from the woman's lips, occasionally bringing with it a stray tooth or shards of bone.

Gretel's hatred was searing as she knelt, frozen in self-preservation, listening to the mutilated woman threaten her mother. This horrible, deranged creature—miscreation—who'd fragmented her life, first by stealing her mother, and then by killing her father. And Odalinde, whom Gretel had hated for so long, yet in less than a day had grown to care deeply for. Perhaps one day she'd understand Odalinde's tough love approach—and in some ways she supposed she did already—but there was no doubt now in Gretel's mind that she was there to protect them. To save them.

And now here this freak of life was again, threatening more torture and destruction, wielding the genius of Gretel's own descendants, shamelessly, to destroy everyone she loved, as if everyone's life belonged to the old witch and was lived for her pleasure alone. Gretel's own life. And Hansel's. And what of the Klahrs? And Petr? Certainly she wouldn't stop until they were dead too.

"I'll kill myself first," Anika shot back, "or, even better, I'll kill you."

The witch chuckled. "That opportunity has passed young pigeon, and it shall not come again." The witch took a step forward. "And though it is often thought so, killing one's self is not as easy as one might think. Besides, I know of your will, and the love you hold for your progeny. You, I know, would use any breath of hope—however vaingloriously—to keep me from them.'

Gretel placed her fingertips on the floor and began to gently push herself up to a standing position. She held her breath as she rose, thankful for the silence in her young bones and muscles. But the floorboards of the cannery were not so young, and as Gretel stood, the old wood detonated in a barrage of creaks and pops. The witch pivoted in the direction of the sound, but as she stopped to stare, her gaze was askew, off to the right slightly, in the direction of the window, hoping perhaps the light would drift over the source of the noise. Gretel knew, with certainty now, she was all but invisible.

"Ah, there you are. Gretel, yes? The very special Gretel. Your grandfather—and your father more recently—have told me of your talents, talents which they tell me you have not even begun to explore yourself. You are young now, with no one to show you. But I will. I will show you. I will bring these talents from within you. Why don't you come where I can see you better."

"I'll go with you," Anika blurted. "I'll go with you now." She hurried to her feet, nearly tripping over them and down the stairwell, and then lingered at the top of the opening, as if ready to follow the witch to whatever fate she had in store. "If you leave her alone, I'll go with you. I'll go with you and you can do what you will to me."

The witch looked over her shoulder at Anika and chuckled again, this time with more confidence. "You *will* go with me," she said, and spun her head back in the direction of Gretel, this time lining her gaze up almost correctly, but not quite. "And so will she." The words were bitter and hostile this time, her patience with coaxing and civility clearly at an end. "And once you're both secure—confined—I'll be back for the boy. Hansel, yes? I believe your brother's name is Hansel."

Hearing the monster speak her brother's name—threatening him—was the last evil Gretel could endure, and before she could consider the consequences of failure—consequences not only for herself, but for everyone still alive that she loved—she gripped the hammer, claw-end forward, and erupted from the shadows on the second floor of the cannery.

The sound of fear in the witch's scream, and the look of surprise and defeat in her eyes, fueled Gretel to the point of possession, and were the final sparks of power Gretel needed to bring the wide metal spikes of the hammer down and into the middle of the witch's forehead.

"No...no!" the witch begged uselessly, the words sounding gurgled and infantile, her hands flailing in the direction of the hammer, grasping at the iron lodged above her eyebrow but not quite able to touch it.

Gretel held the handle of the hammer tightly and pulled the woman close to her, staring at her coldly as she extracted the claw from the woman's head, causing a bloodfall across the witch's eyes and cheeks. And then, with more leverage and fury than before, Gretel brought the hammer down once again, this time to the top of the old woman's head.

The witch's eyes and mouth grew grotesquely wide, mummified in a silent scream, the blood and damage to her face now leaving her all but unrecognizable as human. Her body was still for a beat, and then began to convulse, wobbling ninety degrees at a time until the dying woman was facing forward and staggering drunkenly toward the stairs, the hammer jutting from her head like a deformed horn.

Anika took one step to the side as the old woman stumbled past her. The witch paused a moment, looking blankly at the women, and then, involuntarily, her foot drifted to the empty space of the stairwell. She collapsed like a stone to the ground floor of the cannery, hitting only the bottom step as she fell, her body ending face down in a crumpled mass, the hammer still jutting from her scalp.

Anika would later recall that the sound of the woman hitting the floor reminded her of a pie hitting a concrete wall.

CHAPTER THIRTY-SEVEN

PETR AND GRETEL DESCENDED the porch steps jointly carrying the last piece of major luggage: a large, antique trunk—the piratey kind, enveloped by bulleted leather banding and secured with brass lockplates. Gretel always imagined her mother had seen it fall from an old circus train one day and had decided to keep it for herself, perhaps to use one day when she, herself, ran off to join the circus. It was one of the first items Gretel had looked for the day after her mother went missing and was disappointed to find it.

The teenagers heaved the trunk onto the tailgate of the truck and pushed it cozy with the rest of the things. Anika stood in the bed of the pickup, arranging space for the small items that still remained.

"Is there anything else, Mrs. Morgan?" Petr asked. His voice was timid and whispery.

"No Petr," Anika replied without looking up, her tone with the boy curt and dry. "Perhaps Gretel has something."

Gretel had witnessed—without interfering—similar interactions between her mother and Petr over the last three weeks, and felt sympathy for both of them. But mostly she felt for Petr, who craved her mother's acceptance and seemed to be adjusting pretty well to his new life with the Klahrs.

He was certainly adjusting better to his new life than her mother was to her old one.

With Hansel, her mother had recalibrated fine, and had returned to being as sweet as she ever was to the boy. Perhaps she crossed the threshold into overbearing on occasion, but Gretel assumed such behavior was perfectly normal. With Gretel, she was also still loving, except that Gretel now detected more of a demureness from her mother, a newfound reverence toward her daughter that contained a dusting of dread. Awe was the word, Gretel guessed. Her mother was in awe of her.

But with everybody else her mother had been cold. Even to the Klahrs, whom she'd lathered with thanks and blessings for days afterward, there was an uncomfortable distance—a mistrust that only the saintly Klahrs could and did understand. And with Petr the feelings seemed to be especially true, though for Gretel the reasons why were no great mystery. So, as difficult as it was to witness, Gretel didn't intervene during these implied slights or moments of aloofness, and instead allowed her mother the room to recover. There was trauma to be worked through, and who could blame her for not being chipper and friendly after only a few weeks?

Petr lingered by the truck looking down at his shoes, which surprised Gretel since normally he took any opportunity her mother gave him to scurry out of the kill zone of awkwardness. But today he stood pat.

"I'm sorry," Petr said, his voice solid, though tears had begun to plop down to the gravel below. "I know you're angry at me. For what my father did to you. I never knew anything." He paused, "And that's not who I am."

The sentences came out quickly and evenly, as if he'd rehearsed them a hundred times; but there was emotion in every word, and on the last sentence Petr's voice cracked, and he turned from the truck and broke into a trot toward the house.

"Petr!"

Anika's voice stunned the boy, who was nearly past the porch and on the path down to the lake. He stopped immediately and stood tall, though he didn't turn to look at her.

Gretel moved aside as her mother stepped over the trunk to the tailgate and down to the driveway before running to where Petr stood, turning him toward her and pulling him in close.

The boy collapsed in Anika's arms, sobbing like an infant. And for the first time in Gretel's life, she heard her mother cry.

An hour later the truck was loaded with everything that would be travelling with the Morgan family—whatever remained now would simply remain. Gretel's mother mildly alluded to 'coming for it another day,' but Gretel doubted that day would ever arrive.

Gretel said her goodbyes to Petr—whom she imagined would live in her story as her first love, though love wasn't quite what it was. But it was something. Something to grow and learn from. And she would see him again. About that she was as certain as the sunset.

"We have to stop at the Klahrs, Mother," Gretel reminded, "don't forget."

"I want you to give them this." Gretel's mother handed her daughter a note. "It has all the information about where we're going. Once they have it, Gretel, they'll be the only ones—other than the three of us—who know where we are. I want you to tell them that."

"Where *are* we going?" Hansel asked, a pitch of pleasure and adventure in his voice. If his mother had said to the other side of the moon, Gretel knew Hansel would have been okay with that answer. She was home. They were together. That's all he cared about. He had it right.

"Pretty far, sweetheart," his mother replied, "pretty far."

Gretel had asked the question the night before and, essentially, had gotten the same answer, with the additional provocation of 'We're going to get some answers.'

But Gretel had already begun getting answers.

She opened Odalinde's copy of *Orphism* at the bookmarked page and began reading. Not much had made sense when she started a few days ago, even with the translation, and she had gotten only ten or twelve pages in.

But it was beginning to come together.

DEAR READER,

Thank you for reading GRETEL. I hope you enjoyed it.

The story continues with Marlene's Revenge[1], which has a jaw-dropping, chilling twist that will leave you wanting more.

In Marlene's Revenge, the witch has returned and no one is safe.

Almost a year has passed since Anika and Gretel's horrifying night in an abandoned cannery in the Back Country, and the subsequent beginning of their quest to the Old Country for answers to the mysteries of Orphism. But

---

1.   https://www.amazon.com/Marlenes-Revenge-Gretel-Book-psychological-ebook/dp/
B01LX8R3LD/

rumors are reaching the far shore that the evil Witch of the North, presumed dead since that night of terror, is alive and strong. And hunting again. But this time no one is safe. Everyone Gretel loves is in danger, and she must summon a new level of power and conviction to end her family's nightmare forever.

Start reading Marlene's Revenge today.[2]

---

2.   https://www.amazon.com/Marlenes-Revenge-Gretel-Book-psychological-ebook/dp/
B01LX8R3LD/

More from Christopher Coleman

Marlene's Revenge (Gretel Book Two)[1]
Hansel (Gretel Book Three)[2]
Anika Rising (Gretel Book Four)[3]
They Came with the Snow[4]
The Sighting[5]

---

1. https://www.amazon.com/Marlenes-Revenge-Gretel-Book-Two-ebook/dp/ B01LX8R3LD/

2. https://www.amazon.com/Hansel-Gretel-Book-Three-Suspenseful-ebook/dp/ B072L8C5SN/

3. https://www.amazon.com/Anika-Rising-Gretel-Book-Four-ebook/dp/B0784MXFHD/

4. https://www.amazon.com/They-Came-Snow-Christopher-Coleman-ebook/dp/ B06XPL2Q4L/

5. https://www.amazon.com/Sighting-Suspenseful-Mystery-Horror-Thriller-ebook/dp/ B076MJ5GVC/

Leave a review for Gretel[1]

https://www.amazon.com/Gretel-Book-One-spine-chilling-thrilling-ebook/dp/B01605OOL4/

IT DOESN'T HAVE TO be long, just a sentence or two is all that is needed. Thank you so much.

---

1. https://www.amazon.com/Gretel-Book-One-spine-chilling-thrilling-ebook/dp/B01605OOL4/

What inspired Christopher Coleman to write Gretel?

I HAVE BEEN ASKED BY readers what inspired me to write GRETEL.

I always found Hansel and Gretel to be one of the scariest of the classic fairy tales for two reasons: one, because of the lost-in-the-woods setting (a personal phobia), and two, because the central characters were children. Who could be more vulnerable? Throw a witch into the mix, and you've got real terror.

Gretel incorporates all of these components, but it goes a bit further.

I wanted to explore the dread of capture, as well as the pain caused by the separation of children and their parents.

And then, ultimately, demonstrate the fight and strength necessary to overcome hopelessness. It's not the Grimm tale, but all the elements of the original tale are there.

I hope you enjoyed reading Gretel.

To learn more about me, visit my website: http://www.christophercolemanauthor.com

Sample from Marlene's Revenge (Gretel Book Two)
Prologue

AS ALWAYS, TIME WAS the enemy. Not bad luck or people or ambition—the scapegoats she often turned to in crisis—but time. Time was always flowing relentlessly, unaware of its destruction, like a herd of buffalo striding across a plain of anthills.

The men would be coming soon, and if they found her here alive, there wasn't even the sliver of a chance of her survival. She would be the one to make sure of that.

Her mind went to the Source and her mouth watered instantly. Even in her current state, with death looming above her like a buzzard, ready to descend upon her at any moment, she couldn't keep her mind away from it. It was the smell, she now realized, that triggered the thought. . That candied aroma of her former prisoner still lingered in the damp air of the cannery, wafting down from the top floor in subtle waves. It wasn't that exact smell though, the one she had grown to lavish over all those weeks while the young woman lay trapped and shackled in the back room of her cabin; this smell was mixed with the even sweeter fragrance of another. Her daughter. Gretel.

Gretel.

The silent sound of the word in her mind elicited a tingle in her shoulders and groin.

The witch lay mangled on the stone floor, the fall from the loft leaving her body a twisted heap, with arms and legs pointed at unnatural angles. The top half of her body felt like it was on fire; the bottom half she felt not at all. At the crest of her head, she could feel the pressure of the weapon used to strike her only hours earlier, the weight of it unstable and sickening. There was no pain at the entry point, but the damage was certainly unimaginable. My head and face have been through a lot over the past few days, she thought, belching out a deep, hoarse cough, a sound representing both laughter and disgust.

You must go. Now. They're coming. The voices registered as whispers in her brain, urgent and quick, not unlike the manner she imagined deranged women in institutions had heard just before they sunk their children, one by one, below the waterline in the bathtub.

The witch tried to open her eyes, but they felt sewn shut. She tried again but felt only the stretch of her closed eyelids. She wiggled one finger on her right hand, then two, tapping them on the floor, the tips splashing in the shallow pools beneath them—her blood, no doubt, and judging by the depth, not an insignificant amount. She made a fist, barely bringing her hand together at first but then progressively working up to a tight clench. She relaxed her grip and stretched her fingers wide before slowly bringing them to her face, using her thumb and index finger to crush the crust of caked blood from her eyelids. She could now see the handle of the weapon staring at her, taunting her from an inch away, the business end of the thing still clinging tightly to her skull. She resisted the urge to pull it away, fearing the hemorrhaging that would ensue.

Moving only her eyeballs, the woman surveyed her surroundings, glancing wildly from wall to stairs to ceiling to floor. This last area—the floor—was a horror show, and the newly risen sun hid none of the massacre. The fallow, brown ground where she lay was now a dark purple lake of viscous blood, the color matching perfectly that of her palms and sleeves.

The woman maneuvered her hand under her cloak and then reached down toward the top of her thigh, touching herself lightly at first, and then, feeling nothing, grabbing her leg with the force of panic. Her leg muscles tightened reflexively with the clench, bringing a sigh of hope and relief to the woman. She had feeling in her legs. She was not paralyzed.

They're almost here, the voices warned again. You'll die here. Die here.

The last two words drifted away, but she followed them until they disappeared from her thoughts.

"I will not," the woman spoke aloud, her warm breath bouncing back at her off the base of the hammer. "I'll never die."

The woman inhaled to her lungs' capacity, and on the exhale rolled herself flat against the floor, chest down, before pushing herself to her knees. She stretched her back straight and stared up through the opening of the loft, listening for life. They had long since gone, of course, the women, but she would never again assume anything.

The ditch. Get to the ditch.

She thought of her cabin and the holes she had dug following her Source's escape, just after resurrecting her life with the most brilliant taste she would ever know. The instinct to dig had been odd, but she'd followed it, using her newfound strength to move quickly through the sod and dirt. She'd buried some of the potion there, and now she needed to find her way home to drink it.

The witch finally stood, the effort of it immense considering the trauma her body had suffered. But the potion seemed to have staved off any truly debilitating injuries. And as long as she was mobile, she had a chance.

She walked to the door of the cannery and opened it slowly, half-expecting one of the Morgan women—or perhaps a System officer—to be standing outside, waiting with pickax in hand to finish the job they had come so close to completing. But there was only the clean, cool air of the Back Country, as it entered the cannery. The feel of the breeze on her wounds was exhilarating. She walked outside the boundaries of the dilapidated structure to the openness of the cannery grounds and listened again for anything that may indicate her odds of escape—sirens, voices, gunshots—but she heard only the sounds of the morning.

She strolled to the chain link fence and stared through to the lake, reliving last night's hunt. She had lost control. Lost sight of her goals. Lost her chance at Gretel.

She retraced her steps back past the cannery and began to ascend the hill at the rear of the grounds. With the industrial hammer still projecting from the top of her head, she imagined she must have looked like some type of mythical woodland beast, the kind hundreds of people claim to have seen but which is widely dismissed as legend by the rest of the world.

She had not a clue what the top of the hill held for her, but at this point, it was her only chance of escape. If it was more fencing, like that which ran along the front of the cannery, she would be in serious trouble. In her condition, she couldn't conceive lifting herself six inches off the ground, let alone the eight or ten feet that was necessary to clear a fence. She'd fly again one day, but not today.

Halfway up the hill, she saw the shape of a roof come into view, and soon after, the warehouse. There was no fence barring her from the structure, and this, she acknowledged, was a small sign of hope. And when she slowly pushed open the back door of the warehouse and saw the corpse of the man who had started her on this latest path of addiction and murder, she knew Life had returned for her.

CHAPTER ONE

"THERE IT IS. I TOLD you it was here."

The woman's eyes sprung open and she caught her breath at the apex of an inhale. Voices. Voices and footsteps. Her mind deciphered the sounds even before she was fully awake. There were three of them. She knew it instantly. Three intruders. Pre-adolescent. She could detect the pitch of their voices and their vibrations through the ground.

"It really is here," another boy replied. "I can't believe it. I didn't think it was true."

The woman turned her head toward the sound of the words and was greeted by one of the earthen walls of her bunker. She could feel the rays of the sun beaming through the grass canopy that had so effectively camouflaged her for what must have been, at this point, months. Maybe even a year. These young travelers on the perimeter of her yard were the first to come since those days immediately following the horrific night in the cannery. The first she had detected anyway. It was likely others had come and gone during her deepest of slumber, and now the thought of laughing gawkers defacing and stealing her property made her gag. She thought back to the first days of hiding, the days when the men had come for her, scouring her property and desecrating her cabin. But they had come to do more. They had come to take her as their prisoner. To rob her of her potion. And, no doubt, to kill her.

The potion.

She felt beside her and touched the small jar that still contained several viable ounces of the elixir—the extraordinary brew that had allowed her to rest and heal. The grave had been her shelter and concealment, but the potion had allowed her to go without food and water, to get perfect—almost—once again. Perhaps these plodding boys had awoken her a few weeks earlier than the optimum recovery time, but her mind was clear and her body lithe. She felt fresh. Reborn.

The woman stood in the ditch and peered over the ledge, pushing the twigged canopy up with the top of her head, stooping slightly to keep her eyes at a level barely above the dirt wall that surrounded her. Through the foliage in the distance, she could only see the shoes of the intruders, but she could tell by their voices they weren't much older than twelve. She held her breath for several beats and then exhaled slowly, never blinking the eye that remained. Her left eye had been beyond repair; the combination of the ceramic bowl and hammer claw had proven too costly. She had feared the damage would be permanent, agonizing over the dire possibilities during her grueling trek from the Back Country, and she now accepted the obvious truth of it. But it was only an eye. The rest of her seemed to have healed quite well. She blinked her eye fully now, feeling the bulge of the orb beneath her lid, savoring it setting in its socket. There will be a price to pay for the other one, the woman thought. Revenge. A smile followed this last thought as the literal manifestation of the biblical metaphor took hold in her mind.

"Wait," one of the voices uttered. It was the third boy this time, younger and more frightened than the others. "What if she's there? What if she's waiting for us?"

The woman listened closely to the reply, ready to strike if the answer was inadequate, ready to erupt from the ground like a tarantula if the boys suddenly became spooked and began the first movements and utterances of flight. Instead, she smiled wildly at the sound of the other boys as their crackling voices spilled into mocking laughter.

The first boy coughed out a few more chortling breaths and then said with defiance, "She's dead, you pillock. Her skeleton is at the bottom of a lake somewhere in the Back Country."

"So everyone says, but how do you know that's true? If they never found her body, how can you know?"

"Because the girl killed her. And her mom was there and saw the whole thing. They saw her dead body splayed across the ground as they left. That's how I know. Are you the only person from the Southlands who hasn't heard the story?"

"I've heard the story, but back to my same question then: where is the body? Why is there no body?"

"How many laps do you want to take around this 'body' track? Hmm? I don't know where the body is exactly. It was probably dragged off and eaten by dogs. Or something. The System doesn't seem too concerned about it, so why are you?"

"I'm not concerned about it, I just..."

"Or maybe," the first boy interrupted, "maybe they did find the body and the System is covering that whole night up. Did you think about that?"

"No." The boy paused, indicating he was considering the explanation. "But why would they do that?"

"Because that's the kind of crap they do! I don't know. It doesn't matter." The first boy's tone was curt now, irritated, and any more talk about the body's location was likely to propel him into raw anger.

The woman groaned in ecstasy.

"And anyway, she's not here. How could she be here? She was killed in the Back Country, not here at her cabin. Think about things before you spit up your stupid theories. Besides that, the System has probably been through this place a million times by now. The cabin is empty. There's no one here waiting for us."

The boy paused, and the woman could almost see his eyes widen and his chin jut out slightly, taunting another challenge.

"But...I guess if you're scared, you should stay back here. I honestly don't give a crap. I knew I shouldn't have brought you along."

The woman listened intently, in some ways hoping the boy would call the bully's bluff and keep away from the property. So soon after her hibernation, she was somewhat concerned she would only have strength for one of the boys right now—maybe even two if she was quick with the first. But three would be a definite challenge, so if one of them had to escape, she'd rather it be the sensible one. Not that she was more concerned about him than the others, she just figured the more prudent boy would be too frightened to tell his tale to anyone who mattered. At least not for a few days anyway. And by then she would be gone. By then she will have started hunting again.

"I'll go with you," the boy relented. "I was only saying."

The witch watched as the three boys came into full view, clearing the last of the branches and crossing the threshold of the tree line. They stood motionless, standing in the clearing that bordered the side of her home. The woman could now see them clearly. They were average in height and build, gangly and unsure in their movements, typical mannerisms of boys that age. She could no longer see them below their knees, their shoes and lower legs now completely enveloped by the ryegrass and thistle that had overtaken the property. They look like apparitions gliding over the weeds, she thought.

"Let's go," said the first boy, the leader, the one who, moments before, had mocked his frightened friend—or possibly brother, which, if that were true, would give her less time if he escaped. His voice was quick and full of energy and adventure, and the witch knew that if they headed toward the back of the house, he would be her first victim. It was always the eager ones who made the most mistakes. Bless their hearts.

The thought of new prey now elicited ecstasy. She licked her tongue across the bottom of her top row of front teeth, groaning as she did so. The sound was low and guttural, starting deep in her chest and rattling up through her throat. The noise came out in a loud rumble, louder than she had intended, and she saw the boys stop and pivot, now facing toward the back-yard and the ditch where she was lurking. She ducked below the brim of the narrow channel, the canopy closing the small gap, and waited, listening for the scatter of terrified footsteps. If they did run, she stood poised to attack. This was a gift she wouldn't deny herself.

"What was that?" a voice asked, his tone playfully suspicious. It was the second brave boy in the group, the other teaser, and his question was clearly directed toward the coward with the intention of pushing the boy into panic.

"Oh that was definitely her," the leader declared. "I mean, what other ex-planation could there be? The Old Witch of the North lives!"

The second boy laughed at this and said, "You're crazy, Tomas." But the fear behind his brave veneer was now detectable to the woman. She could al-most smell it.

"Okay, well what was it then?" It was the coward this time, he making no pretensions at bravery. "We should leave. There's probably bums back here anyway. Or wild animals."

"Or..." the leader replied, "wild bums! Terrifying wild bums!"

The first two boys burst into laughter, loud enough now to veil the woman if she chose this moment to attack. But she restrained herself, not quite confident that her legs were charged and ready for a guerilla attack at this distance. Soon, but not yet. Instead, she waited and listened, trying to anticipate the boys' next moves.

"Well something is back there. You heard it. And I'm not going to find out what it is. Have fun being brave; I'll have fun being alive."

"Leave then. Bye. Don't forget your bottle, baby."

The witch couldn't tell which one of the bullies supplied this last taunt, but there was a malignancy in the tone that was unmistakable. It was the sound of the rotten men she'd known all her life.

Suddenly the bullies began laughing like rabid jackals, and the woman could hear the coward's footsteps trotting off and diminishing into the distance, a slow gallop at first, and then, just before breaking into the trod of a full sprint.

"Do you still want to check it out?" said the second in command.

"Of course. Why wouldn't I? Wait a minute. Don't tell me you're scared too."

"Shut up, Tomas. I was just asking." There was a pause. "You're such a whaling prick."

"Stop pouting and come on then. Of course, we're going to check it out. Let's see if this crazy bitch has something cool in her attic or something."

"Wait. You want to go inside? I don't know about that. I mean, maybe we—"

"You are scared! Ha! I knew it."

The woman could imagine the look of gleeful satisfaction on the face of the leader, his dominance once again established by the apprehension of his companion.

"Go off with Billy then! You can probably catch up! Ha! I don't care. I'll go alone. Faggot."

"Shut up, Tomas!" the second boy screamed, the fury in his voice real.

The witch's eyes opened wide, and the trace of a smile returned to her face.

"Or what?" Tomas replied. The words were threatening, daring.

"You don't want to find out."

"Really? You won't do crap. Pussy."

And with that, the scuffle was on. The jocular conversation of the adolescents was replaced with grunts and screams and slaps of skin.

With the delicacy of a new mother rousing her infant, the woman pushed up on the canopy and slid it aside, just far enough so she could clear her head fully from the ditch. Fascinated, she watched the boys as they grappled themselves into a human knot of head and leg locks, pinning each other helplessly into a stalemate of limbs. She rotated the canopy further, with less care this time, and then nestled her foot on an earthen step that had formed naturally on the side of the trench. Effortlessly, she propelled herself to the ledge of the ditch and then pulled herself easily from the grave.

Now on level ground, the woman strode steadily toward the boys, focused and menacing; her dark cloak and the cake of mud on her hair and face made her appear like an encroaching black blot against the sun-filled landscape. The boys, still caught up in the scrap and whines of their own meaningless struggle, took no notice of the evil that was now less than twenty yards from them.

It wasn't until the old woman's blade-like thumbnail pierced the back of the leader's head, just at the neckline, that the second boy knew what was happening. His scream lasted only a second or two, but it was loud enough to be heard by a third boy who was now sprinting in terror through the woods of the Back Country.

◦◦∽◦◦

THE BOARDWALK THAT led to the defaced cottage was warped and mildewed, and the witch recalled the day—a day that to her seemed like decades ago but was probably only a year or two past—when she lay dying, lamenting the universe as the energy of Life seeped from her bones and organs, bringing blackness to her mind. It had seemed so final that day, death so absolute in its certainty. Until the moment when the gift of Anika Morgan was presented to her in the form of a desperate scream from miles deep in the Northlands forest. It was the moment of her rebirth.

She recalled how expertly she had stalked her prey that night, seeing all the moves clearly in her mind hours before executing them. And when she'd captured her Source and finally learned the secret of Anika's family and the power of Life in the cells and blood of all of them, her mission became clear:

to take all of them—Anika, Gretel, and Hansel—and become truly immortal.

She'd done well at first, killing the father and disposing of the nurse. The latter killing, that of the Orphist, had not come without a struggle. The woman had been fierce and heroic in her efforts before finally succumbing to a strength and brutality the witch thought impossible for her ever to possess.

And then she was there. So close. So near to her destiny, only a movement or decision away from seizing the women, both of them, and finalizing the greatest power ever conceived. They had been trapped, positioned there just for her, hopelessly sealed in that cannery by the lake; the old woman needed only to use the cunning and patience she had imparted that first night in the forest.

But it had ended in disaster. The Morgan women escaped, and she had been critically wounded in the process.

In the end, it was her great failure, and now, as she stood on the porch of her decrepit shack of a home, she knew that if she didn't find the family again, her failure would be fatal.

The woman opened the large wooden door that led to her cottage and stepped inside, proceeding directly to the kitchen. It was evident—mainly due to the presence of the many sets of large, dusty footprints—that more men had walked through her house in the past six months than had ever walked through in the home's existence. She'd been right that she'd missed some of the invaders who'd come during her slumber, but things inside weren't quite as different as she expected. A few remnants of the round black crock remained on the floor by the counter, and the witch's eyes widened for just a moment. Was it possible that some of the potion...?

No. Of course not. She reined in the idea. What she hadn't collected the day of the escape had long since dried away or been eaten by vermin. It was never going to be that easy.

The woman again fantasized about the power of the brew at its full potency after the bile of Gretel Morgan was added to the already powerful mélange.

She had work to do, and it started with finding them. The Morgans. All of them. Finding out where they had gone. She had no idea where they might be just now, but she knew there was someone who would.

CHAPTER TWO

GEORG KLAHR LIFTED the dusty rag from his back pocket and snapped it once, watching the dust scatter to the wind before methodically wiping his face. The sweat began collecting on his brow almost from the moment he stepped off the porch this morning, and he was forced to stop every minute or so to clear it. It was the hottest day of the year, no question about it. He only had about another half hour in him, and by that time, the sun would have peaked. He knew he was stronger than most men half his age, but he didn't want to push his limits. Amanda had been through enough; nursing her husband back from a stroke was more than even she could handle.

The thought of his incapacitation invoked a vague image of Heinrich Morgan, and then a clearer one of Gretel. It had been nearly a year since the day she and her family left for the Old Country, and the Klahrs hadn't heard a word from them since, a fact about which Georg had grown slightly angry. Anika had written them the mysterious letter before they left, detailing where they were headed, and emphasizing that they were not to be contacted unless absolutely necessary. He'd not had a chance to question this clause—the letter had been given to him just before the Morgans departed on their quest—and as difficult as it had been these last eleven months, neither Georg nor Amanda ever felt there was proper cause to disobey it. Amanda had cried on and off for several days after Gretel left, and as the months ticked by, her worry had only ripened.

The girl couldn't call? Or send a letter?

Georg stuffed the damp rag back into his pocket and stared across the lake at the Morgan property. He closed his eyes and thought of that day of death and carnage. Of the spectacle he had witnessed. Of the woman—witch—who had attacked him. And of the things he hadn't done to save the nurse. He had failed her, and he now lived with that thought every day, just as he would until the day he died. He squeezed his eyes tightly and shook the memory clear. Not now. It was too early in the day to descend into this thinking.

"I'm leaving, Georg."

Georg spun to see his wife stalking the back porch, studying her lavender and jasmine, sniffing them gently before moving on to tease up her hydrangeas.

"What's that, dear?"

"I'm leaving for a bit. Got some things to buy for the garden. Don't want you out here too much longer. Hottest I've felt it in a long while." Amanda Klahr stopped and stared defiantly at her husband, imparting the seriousness of her statement.

"Would you like me to go instead? To the store?"

"I would not. If you do my hobbies for me, they're no longer my hobbies."

Georg smiled. "All right then. Be safe, will ya?"

"Course hon. Always am."

Amanda paused and stared at her husband, as if waiting for the answer to her question before she asked it. Finally, she said, "Have you seen Petr today?"

Georg forced a smile. "Not yet. He'll be around soon."

Amanda nodded, gave one last pluck to a rose bush, and then faded from the porch into the cottage.

Georg stared his wife back into the house, wincing at the sucking sound of the sliding glass door sealing behind her. He closed his eyes and sighed. Petr.

Petr Stenson had worked at the orchard for almost a year and a half, and after the death of his father at the hands of the faithless she-devil, there had never been a question as to where the boy would live. The Klahrs had never given a second thought to taking the boy in. He was an orphan now, his mother having died years earlier, and both Georg and Amanda had grown to love him like a grandson.

But the new arrangement had been difficult, and the truth was they hadn't expected such a dramatic shift in Petr's behavior, at least not so immediately after becoming their responsibility. Georg realized this was probably a naïve way of thinking, given the boy's age and the trauma he'd been exposed to, but the adoption itself was only a formality—Petr had essentially been living with them anyway—so they both thought the transition would be less rocky.

But Petr now stayed out late most nights—sometimes even all night, as in the case of this previous evening—and his friends were not of the type the fathers of the Back Country hoped their daughters would marry. Neither he nor Amanda suspected Petr was getting into any dire trouble, but his pattern of disappearing was becoming a concern.

But Georg knew it wasn't the recent living arrangements or even the death of his father that was the most trying on Petr. It was losing Gretel.

Georg opened his eyes and turned back to his work, lifting the hoe high above his head before slamming it into the brittle earth. He loved the power and ferocity of this move—whether with the pick, the axe, or the hoe—and from that first day when spring quietly snuck a day in in March, he had come to the orchard every day, building his strength this way for hours at a time. Georg Klahr's days of working the harvest had been effectively done years ago, so during the season, as he continued his violent work of chopping an empty field, the workers simply watched with odd fascination while they did their business of picking the blossoming apples and pears.

Georg raised the hoe again and slammed it to the earth, unconcerned what the migrant workers may have thought. Or what anyone thought. He was training. Getting strong. Building the muscles of his shoulders and biceps and thighs. Working his lungs until they burned and tormented him. And if he ever got the chance again, he would kill without consideration the person who threatened him or his.

"Georg."

He registered his name and the voice that spoke it, but the sound didn't quite file as real, as if it were uttered from a dream.

"Georg!"

Georg barked out a scream this time, lurching toward the sound of his name and raising the hoe high above his head, directing it toward the intruder. He stopped before swinging it, blinking wildly at the boy standing before him.

"Petr?" Georg was frozen, his eyes now dilated in madness, the garden tool still poised to strike. "Petr, I'm sorry. I was deep in thought...work."

Petr grinned slightly and nodded. "I know those thoughts, Georg. Trust me, I do."

Petr had recently gone from using the moniker "Mr. Klahr" to "Georg," and Georg was still not quite comfortable with it. It was fine, of course—"Mr. Klahr" seemed too formal for their relationship, and "Dad" or "Grandad" wasn't right either—but Petr's use of the title somehow put him on a level of adulthood that Georg wasn't ready for. Thankfully, Petr hadn't yet made the transition to "Amanda," and Georg quietly hoped he never would.

"Where were you last night? Mrs. Klahr was worried." Georg now held the hoe down by his waist, gripping it in front of him casually with both hands.

Petr frowned and looked away. "I needed to be away last night."

Georg waited for more, and when he got nothing, he said, "Searching?"

Petr looked back at Georg, whose eyes were set in marble. "She's alive."

Georg frowned at the statement, but this time he resisted the urge to diminish the boy's beliefs further with a shake of the head or a snicker as he'd done dozens of times since Petr first declared his theory.

"I know you don't believe that, and that's your choice, but she's alive...or at least...she didn't die that night in the cannery. Not the way they said she did."

"Gretel was there, Petr. And Mrs. Morgan. Gretel was the one who ki—" Georg stopped, not wanting to attach Gretel to the violence that had occurred that night.

"They didn't see her die, Georg," Petr replied. He was delicate with his words, detached from the emotion of the events. "They saw her fall. They saw her lying on the ground. But they never saw her die. They jumped from the cannery window and never saw..."

"Where is she then, Petr?"

"It's a big world out there, Georg."

The theory, which Petr had recited to Georg within the first month of moving in, was that the witch was alive, and she would be coming once again for Gretel. Likely Anika and Hansel too, but Gretel for sure. This discussion, which they now had once or twice a month, never reached the point where Petr told him exactly how it was that the woman was still alive or where she had been living. Or why the System had her officially listed as dead. When

Georg had asked Petr about this last part, Petr had simply laughed at him and replied something sarcastic like, "Yeah, you're right Georg. the System would never do anything like that. No way."

Georg supposed he had a point there.

And here they were again, back in the throes of the subject, speeding down the bumpy road to nowhere. Georg decided to veer off. "Where were you searching last night?"

Petr was clearly caught off guard by this indirect validation of his belief, but he answered calmly. "It's better you don't know."

Georg nodded and let the tension of the words set in. Finally, he said, "You know that you aren't the only one who misses her, right? You know we love her too. And that Mrs. Klahr still cries at night. Not every night, but often, out of the blue, because she misses her and has no idea whether or not she's okay."

"But you know where she went! That's what I don't get. Why don't you just find out if she's okay?"

Georg felt the sting of the boy's words, accusatory and hurt.

A tear rolled down Petr's cheek. "Why can't you just tell me? Why don't you trust me? Still?"

Georg grabbed Petr by the back of the neck and pulled him to his chest, holding him there for a few beats. "We do trust you Petr. With our lives. But this secret is not ours to give to anyone. Including you. Mrs. Morgan was explicit about that."

Petr pulled away and looked hard into his guardian's eyes. "But what happens when something happens to you? How do I tell Gretel? How will I get in touch with her?"

"What do you mean, 'when something happens to us?' Nothing will happen to us. Not any time soon anyway. And we will hear from her soon. I believe that. Gretel is fine. She's fine. She's doing what you're doing, that's all. She's searching." He smiled. "And if something does happen to me, then Aman—Mrs. Klahr will know how to get in touch with her. And she will, I promise. We just have to wait for her a little longer, Petr. We swore we would, so that's our only real choice right now."

Petr gave a reluctant nod, never releasing Mr. Klahr's gaze. "Just stay careful, Georg. Please stay careful."

Georg flashed a wide smile at this warning, holding the hoe up to his chest, gripping it tightly with both hands. "You sound like Mrs. Klahr." His smile softened, and then, "I promise I will be careful. Too old to push myself too hard."

"Not that Georg. Keep doing that. Keep getting stronger. You need to stay careful because this isn't over. She is alive. I know she is. And we're going to have to be ready."

End of sample. Did you enjoy this preview of Marlene's Revenge? Download your copy today.[1]

To stay in touch with Chris, and be among the first to be notified of upcoming releases, giveaways, cover reveals, exclusive excerpts and other goodies, subscribe to his newsletter.

http://www.christophercolemanauthor.com/newsletter/

---

1.   https://www.amazon.com/Marlenes-Revenge-Gretel-Book-psychological-ebook/dp/
B01LX8R3LD/

Made in the USA
Middletown, DE
18 November 2018

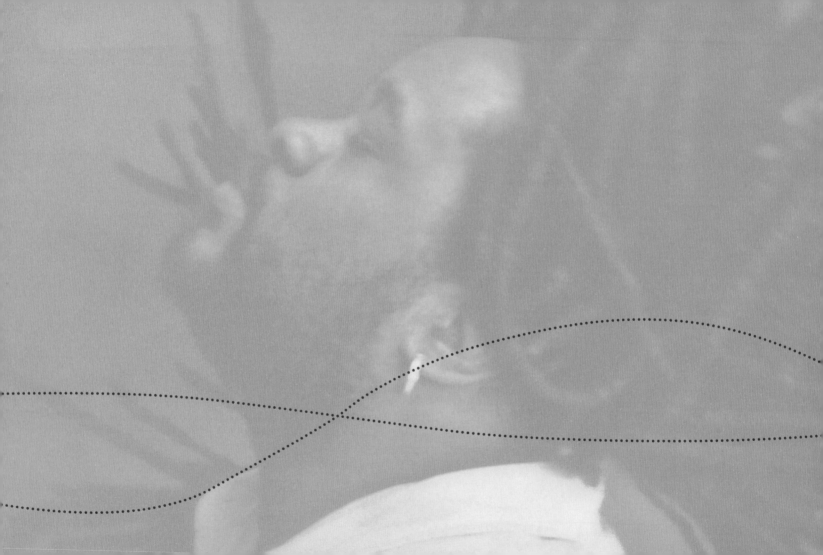

SOUL INFINITY
NEW TESTAMENT

New Living Translation

SECOND EDITION

TYNDALE HOUSE PUBLISHERS, INC.

CAROL STREAM, ILLINOIS

Visit Tyndale's exciting Web site at www.tyndale.com

O-wrap and interior photograph of break-dancers copyright © by Dream Pictures/Getty Images. All rights reserved.

O-wrap and interior photographs of people in car, man jumping, woman in hat, and man in sweater copyright © iStockphoto. All rights reserved.

O-wrap and interior photographs of man with locks and man with headphones by Dan Farrell.

O-wrap back photograph of man with headphones by Dan Farrell.

Soul Infinity copyright © 2009 by Tyndale House Publishers, Inc. All rights reserved.

Content developed in partnership with Urban Spirit!

This New Testament is an edition of the *Holy Bible,* New Living Translation.

Holy Bible, New Living Translation, copyright © 1996, 2004, 2007 by Tyndale House Foundation. All rights reserved.

ISBN-13: 978-1-4143-1444-0   ISBN-10: 1-4143-1444-2   Softcover

Printed in China

16   15   14   13   12   11   10   09
 9   8   7   6   5   4   3   2   1

Tyndale House Publishers and Wycliffe Bible Translators share the vision for an understandable, accurate translation of the Bible for every person in the world. Each sale of the *Holy Bible,* New Living Translation, benefits Wycliffe Bible Translators. Wycliffe is working with partners around the world to accomplish Vision 2025—an initiative to start a Bible translation program in every language group that needs it by the year 2025.

CONTENTS

THE NEW TESTAMENT

ALPHABETICAL LISTING OF BIBLE BOOKS

SOUL INFINITY USER'S GUIDE

Substance . . . swagger . . . style . . . strength. Could we be talking about you—or about the emerging hip-hop generation? *Soul Infinity* will help you discover how you can have all these traits by building your life on a strong foundation—a foundation that rests securely on faith in Jesus Christ. Whether you use this book in your personal study or in your youth group, you will discover how God's Word can change your life!

In *Soul Infinity*, you will gain a better understanding of the Word and find tools to help apply it to the situations you face. You'll soon see a new swagger and confidence in your daily walk, and your style will be noticed and emulated. When faced with tough decisions, you'll have a resource to help you act and speak with substance, and your search for the ultimate source of strength will be over.

If you've already read the Bible, now read it again—in words you can really understand. Check out each feature. You'll find they're written in your own language. It will be like talking to your closest friend. (This isn't your mama's Bible!) But even so, if you take what you read to heart, even your pastor will be impressed with your understanding. This New Testament is designed to communicate to you and your friends, where you're at right now!

By putting you in contact with God's truth, *Soul Infinity* is sure to strengthen your walk with the Lord. It's also a great tool to reach out to your friends with God's hope and guidance. God's Word is the best place to start the renewal and recovery of anyone's soul! Check out *Soul Infinity*—a little bit every day—and put yourself in position to experience God's life-changing power.

FEATURES OF SOUL INFINITY
Book Introductions
Each New Testament book opens with an introduction and event list that highlight key themes and events found in the book, offering helpful perspective to enhance its reading and study.

The Point
This feature is located close to a passage where an important point comes to light. These look at really important ideas that you've just got to understand, like the fact that Jesus reaches out to people who've got issues (not just people who have it all together) or that Jesus was a totally unique individual—both God and man. This feature often takes a theme mentioned in the book introduction and then digs deeper.

Power Choices
Here's a feature that looks at some of the tough choices you have to make and helps you think through how to do things God's way. The New Testament is full of wisdom to help us make better choices and live better lives. This feature ends

with a statement that recommends a course of action in the right direction.

Keeping Your Swagger Strong

This feature highlights biblical principles for success and leadership. Nobody wants to go through life as a failure. God's Word has practical wisdom to help us succeed in the real world, and this "Swagger" feature helps you discover God's truth to keep you headed in the right direction.

Prayer

As we wrestle with the truth we find in God's Word, we begin to realize we need help to live it out. You'll find prayers near other key features, leading you to ask for God's help in living out the truth.

Flow

The New Testament is full of wisdom for living well, building healthy relationships, and keeping in touch with God. The Flow feature calls out a great verse from the Bible text and then restates the truth in a fresh way to help you remember and think about it. These show up sprinkled throughout the text.

A NOTE TO READERS

The *Holy Bible,* New Living Translation, was first published in 1996. It quickly became one of the most popular Bible translations in the English-speaking world. While the NLT's influence was rapidly growing, the Bible Translation Committee determined that an additional investment in scholarly review and text refinement could make it even better. So shortly after its initial publication, the committee began an eight-year process with the purpose of increasing the level of the NLT's precision without sacrificing its easy-to-understand quality. This second-generation text was completed in 2004 and is reflected in this edition of the New Living Translation. An additional update with minor changes was subsequently introduced in 2007.

The goal of any Bible translation is to convey the meaning and content of the ancient Hebrew, Aramaic, and Greek texts as accurately as possible to contemporary readers. The challenge for our translators was to create a text that would communicate as clearly and powerfully to today's readers as the original texts did to readers and listeners in the ancient biblical world. The resulting translation is easy to read and understand, while also accurately communicating the meaning and content of the original biblical texts. The NLT is a general-purpose text especially good for study, devotional reading, and reading aloud in worship services.

We believe that the New Living Translation—which combines the latest biblical scholarship with a clear, dynamic writing style—will communicate God's word powerfully to all who read it. We publish it with the prayer that God will use it to speak his timeless truth to the church and the world in a fresh, new way.

The Publishers
October 2007

TRANSLATION PHILOSOPHY AND METHODOLOGY

English Bible translations tend to be governed by one of two general translation theories. The first theory has been called "formal-equivalence," "literal," or "word-for-word" translation. According to this theory, the translator attempts to render each word of the original language into English and seeks to preserve the original syntax and sentence structure as much as possible in translation. The second theory has been called "dynamic-equivalence," "functional-equivalence," or "thought-for-thought" translation. The goal of this translation theory is to produce in English the closest natural equivalent of the message expressed by the original-language text, both in meaning and in style.

Both of these translation theories have their strengths. A formal-equivalence translation preserves aspects of the original text—including ancient idioms, term consistency, and original-language syntax—that are valuable for scholars and professional study. It allows a reader to trace formal elements of the original-language text through the English translation. A dynamic-equivalence translation, on the other hand, focuses on translating the message of the original-language text. It ensures that the meaning of the text is readily apparent to the contemporary reader. This allows the message to come through with immediacy, without requiring the reader to struggle with foreign idioms and awkward syntax. It also facilitates serious study of the text's message and clarity in both devotional and public reading.

The pure application of either of these translation philosophies would create translations at opposite ends of the translation spectrum. But in reality, all translations contain a mixture of these two philosophies. A purely formal-equivalence translation would be unintelligible in English, and a purely dynamic-equivalence translation would risk being unfaithful to the original. That is why translations shaped by dynamic-equivalence theory are usually quite literal when the original text is relatively clear, and the translations shaped by formal-equivalence theory are sometimes quite dynamic when the original text is obscure.

The translators of the New Living Translation set out to render the message of the original texts of Scripture into clear, contemporary English. As they did so, they kept the concerns of both formal-equivalence and dynamic-equivalence in mind. On the one hand, they translated as simply and literally as possible when that approach yielded an accurate, clear, and natural English text. Many words and phrases were rendered literally and consistently into English, preserving essential literary and rhetorical devices, ancient metaphors, and word choices that give structure to the text and provide echoes of meaning from one passage to the next.

On the other hand, the translators rendered the message

more dynamically when the literal rendering was hard to understand, was misleading, or yielded archaic or foreign wording. They clarified difficult metaphors and terms to aid in the reader's understanding. The translators first struggled with the meaning of the words and phrases in the ancient context; then they rendered the message into clear, natural English. Their goal was to be both faithful to the ancient texts and eminently readable. The result is a translation that is both exegetically accurate and idiomatically powerful.

TRANSLATION PROCESS AND TEAM

To produce an accurate translation of the Bible into contemporary English, the translation team needed the skills necessary to enter into the thought patterns of the ancient authors and then to render their ideas, connotations, and effects into clear, contemporary English. To begin this process, qualified biblical scholars were needed to interpret the meaning of the original text and to check it against our base English translation. In order to guard against personal and theological biases, the scholars needed to represent a diverse group of evangelicals who would employ the best exegetical tools. Then to work alongside the scholars, skilled English stylists were needed to shape the text into clear, contemporary English.

With these concerns in mind, the Bible Translation Committee recruited teams of scholars that represented a broad spectrum of denominations, theological perspectives, and backgrounds within the worldwide evangelical community. (These scholars are listed at the end of this introduction.) Each book of the Bible was assigned to three different scholars with proven expertise in the book or group of books to be reviewed. Each of these scholars made a thorough review of a base translation and submitted suggested revisions to the appropriate Senior Translator. The Senior Translator then reviewed and summarized these suggestions and proposed a first-draft revision of the base text. This draft served as the basis for several additional phases of exegetical and stylistic committee review. Then the Bible Translation Committee jointly reviewed and approved every verse of the final translation.

Throughout the translation and editing process, the Senior Translators and their scholar teams were given a chance to review the editing done by the team of stylists. This ensured that exegetical errors would not be introduced late in the process and that the entire Bible Translation Committee was happy with the final result. By choosing a team of qualified scholars and skilled stylists and by setting up a process that allowed their interaction throughout the process, the New Living Translation has been refined to preserve the essential formal elements of the original biblical texts, while also creating a clear, understandable English text.

The New Living Translation was first published in 1996. Shortly after its initial publication, the Bible Translation Committee began a process of further committee review and translation refinement. The purpose of this continued revision was to increase the level of precision without sacrificing the text's easy-to-understand quality. This second-edition text was completed in 2004, and an additional update with minor changes was subsequently introduced in 2007. This printing of the New Living Translation reflects the updated 2007 text.

WRITTEN TO BE READ ALOUD

It is evident in Scripture that the biblical documents were written to be read aloud, often in public worship (see Nehemiah 8; Luke 4:16-20; 1 Timothy 4:13; Revelation 1:3).

It is still the case today that more people will hear the Bible read aloud in church than are likely to read it for themselves. Therefore, a new translation must communicate with clarity and power when it is read publicly. Clarity was a primary goal for the NLT translators, not only to facilitate private reading and understanding, but also to ensure that it would be excellent for public reading and make an immediate and powerful impact on any listener.

THE TEXTS BEHIND THE NEW LIVING TRANSLATION

The Old Testament translators used the Masoretic Text of the Hebrew Bible as represented in *Biblia Hebraica Stuttgartensia* (1977), with its extensive system of textual notes; this is an update of Rudolf Kittel's *Biblia Hebraica* (Stuttgart, 1937). The translators also further compared the Dead Sea Scrolls, the Septuagint and other Greek manuscripts, the Samaritan Pentateuch, the Syriac Peshitta, the Latin Vulgate, and any other versions or manuscripts that shed light on the meaning of difficult passages.

The New Testament translators used the two standard editions of the Greek New Testament: the *Greek New Testament*, published by the United Bible Societies (UBS, fourth revised edition, 1993), and *Novum Testamentum Graece*, edited by Nestle and Aland (NA, twenty-seventh edition, 1993). These two editions, which have the same text but differ in punctuation and textual notes, represent, for the most part, the best in modern textual scholarship. However, in cases where strong textual or other scholarly evidence supported the decision, the translators sometimes chose to differ from the UBS and NA Greek texts and followed variant readings found in other ancient witnesses. Significant textual variants of this sort are always noted in the textual notes of the New Living Translation.

TRANSLATION ISSUES

The translators have made a conscious effort to provide a text that can be easily understood by the typical reader of modern English. To this end, we sought to use only vocabulary and language structures in common use today. We avoided using language likely to become quickly dated or that reflects only a narrow subdialect of English, with the goal of making the New Living Translation as broadly useful and timeless as possible.

But our concern for readability goes beyond the concerns of vocabulary and sentence structure. We are also concerned about historical and cultural barriers to understanding the Bible, and we have sought to translate terms shrouded in history and culture in ways that can be immediately understood. To this end:

- We have converted ancient weights and measures (for example, "ephah" [a unit of dry volume] or "cubit" [a unit of length]) to modern English (American) equivalents, since the ancient measures are not generally meaningful to today's readers. Then in the textual footnotes we offer the literal Hebrew, Aramaic, or Greek measures, along with modern metric equivalents.

- Instead of translating ancient currency values literally, we have expressed them in common terms that communicate the message. For example, in the Old Testament, "ten shekels of silver" becomes "ten pieces of silver" to convey the intended message. In the New Testament, we have often translated the "denarius" as "the normal daily wage" to facilitate understanding. Then a footnote offers: "Greek a denarius, the payment for a full day's wage." In general, we give a clear English rendering and then state the literal Hebrew, Aramaic, or Greek in a textual footnote.

- Since the names of Hebrew months are unknown to most contemporary readers, and since the Hebrew lunar calendar fluctuates from year to year in relation to the solar calendar used today, we have looked for clear ways to communicate the time of year the Hebrew months (such as Abib) refer to. When an expanded or interpretive rendering is given in the text, a textual note gives the literal rendering. Where it is possible to define a specific ancient date in terms of our modern calendar, we use modern dates in the text. A textual footnote then gives the literal Hebrew date and states the rationale for our rendering. For example, Ezra 6:15 pinpoints the date when the postexilic Temple was completed in Jerusalem: "the third day of the month Adar." This was during the sixth year of King Darius's reign (that is, 515 B.C.). We have translated that date as March 12, with a footnote giving the Hebrew and identifying the year as 515 B.C.

- Since ancient references to the time of day differ from our modern methods of denoting time, we have used renderings that are instantly understandable to the modern reader. Accordingly, we have rendered specific times of day by using approximate equivalents in terms of our common "o'clock" system. On occasion, translations such as "at dawn the next morning" or "as the sun was setting" have been used when the biblical reference is more general.

- When the meaning of a proper name (or a wordplay inherent in a proper name) is relevant to the message of the text, its meaning is often illuminated with a textual footnote. For example, in Exodus 2:10 the text reads: "The princess named him Moses, for she explained, 'I lifted him out of the water.'" The accompanying footnote reads: "Moses sounds like a Hebrew term that means 'to lift out.'"

Sometimes, when the actual meaning of a name is clear, that meaning is included in parentheses within the text itself. For example, the text at Genesis 16:11 reads: "You are to name him Ishmael *(which means 'God hears')*, for the LORD has heard your cry of distress." Since the original hearers and readers would have instantly understood the meaning of the name "Ishmael," we have provided modern readers with the same information so they can experience the text in a similar way.

- Many words and phrases carry a great deal of cultural meaning that was obvious to the original readers but needs explanation in our own culture. For example, the phrase "they beat their breasts" (Luke 23:48) in ancient times meant that people were very upset, often in mourning. In our translation we chose to translate this phrase dynamically for clarity: "They went home in deep sorrow." Then we included a footnote with the literal Greek, which reads: "Greek went home beating their breasts." In other similar cases, however, we have sometimes chosen to illuminate the existing literal expression to make it immediately understandable. For example, here we might have expanded the literal Greek phrase to read: "They went home beating their breasts in sorrow." If we had done this, we would not have included a textual footnote, since the literal Greek clearly appears in translation.

- Metaphorical language is sometimes difficult for contemporary readers to understand, so at times we have chosen to translate or illuminate the meaning of a metaphor. For example, the ancient poet writes, "Your neck is *like* the tower of David" (Song of Songs 4:4). We have rendered it "Your neck is *as beautiful as* the tower of David" to clarify the intended positive meaning of the simile. Another example comes in Ecclesiastes 12:3, which can be literally rendered: "Remember him . . . when the grinding women cease because they are few, and the women who look through the windows see dimly." We have rendered it: "Remember him before your teeth—your few remaining servants—stop grinding; and before your eyes—the women looking through the windows—see dimly." We clarified such metaphors only when we believed a typical reader might be confused by the literal text.

- When the content of the original language text is poetic in character, we have rendered it in English poetic form. We sought to break lines in ways that clarify and highlight the relationships between phrases of the text. Hebrew poetry often uses parallelism, a literary form where a second phrase (or in some instances a third or fourth) echoes the initial phrase in some way. In Hebrew parallelism, the subsequent parallel phrases continue, while also furthering and sharpening, the thought expressed in the initial line or phrase. Whenever possible, we sought to represent these parallel phrases in natural poetic English.

- The Greek term *hoi Ioudaioi* is literally translated "the Jews" in many English translations. In the Gospel of John, however, this term doesn't always refer to the Jewish people generally. In some contexts, it refers more particularly to the Jewish religious leaders. We have attempted to capture the meaning in these different contexts by using terms such as "the people" (with a footnote: Greek *the Jewish people*) or "the religious leaders," where appropriate.

- One challenge we faced was how to translate accurately the ancient biblical text that was originally written in a context where male-oriented terms were used to refer to humanity generally. We needed to respect the nature of the ancient context while also trying to make the translation clear to a modern audience that tends to read male-oriented language as applying only to males. Often the original text, though using masculine nouns and pronouns, clearly intends that the message be applied to both men and women. A typical example is found in the New Testament letters, where the believers are called "brothers" (*adelphoi*). Yet it is clear from the content of these letters that they were addressed to all the believers—male and female. Thus, we have usually translated this Greek word as "brothers and sisters" in order to represent the historical situation more accurately.

  We have also been sensitive to passages where the text applies generally to human beings or to the human condition. In some instances we have used plural pronouns (they, them) in place of the masculine singular (he, him). For example, a traditional rendering of Proverbs 22:6 is: "Train up a child in the way he should go, and when he is old he will not turn from it." We have rendered it: "Direct your children onto the right path, and when they are older, they will not leave it." At times, we have also replaced third person pronouns with the second person to ensure clarity. A traditional rendering of Proverbs 26:27 is: "He who digs a pit will fall into it, and he who rolls a stone, it will come back on him." We have rendered it: "If you set a trap for others, you will get caught in it yourself. If you roll a boulder down on others, it will crush you instead."

We should emphasize, however, that all masculine nouns and pronouns used to represent God (for example, "Father") have been maintained without exception. All decisions of this kind have been driven by the concern to reflect accurately the intended meaning of the original texts of Scripture.

LEXICAL CONSISTENCY IN TERMINOLOGY

For the sake of clarity, we have translated certain original-language terms consistently, especially within synoptic passages and for commonly repeated rhetorical phrases, and within certain word categories such as divine names and non-theological technical terminology (e.g., liturgical, legal, cultural, zoological, and botanical terms). For theological terms, we have allowed a greater semantic range of acceptable English words or phrases for a single Hebrew or Greek word. We have avoided some theological terms that are not readily understood by many modern readers. For example, we avoided using words such as "justification" and "sanctification," which are carryovers from Latin translations. In place of these words, we have provided renderings such as "made right with God" and "made holy."

THE SPELLING OF PROPER NAMES

Many individuals in the Bible, especially the Old Testament, are known by more than one name (e.g., Uzziah/Azariah).

For the sake of clarity, we have tried to use a single spelling for any one individual, footnoting the literal spelling whenever we differ from it. This is especially helpful in delineating the kings of Israel and Judah. King Joash/Jehoash of Israel has been consistently called Jehoash, while King Joash/Jehoash of Judah is called Joash. A similar distinction has been used to distinguish between Joram/Jehoram of Israel and Joram/Jehoram of Judah. All such decisions were made with the goal of clarifying the text for the reader. When the ancient biblical writers clearly had a theological purpose in their choice of a variant name (e.g., Esh-baal/Ishbosheth), the different names have been maintained with an explanatory footnote.

For the names Jacob and Israel, which are used interchangeably for both the individual patriarch and the nation, we generally render it "Israel" when it refers to the nation and "Jacob" when it refers to the individual. When our rendering of the name differs from the underlying Hebrew text, we provide a textual footnote, which includes this explanation: "The names 'Jacob' and 'Israel' are often interchanged throughout the Old Testament, referring sometimes to the individual patriarch and sometimes to the nation."

THE RENDERING OF DIVINE NAMES

All appearances of 'el, 'elohim, or 'eloah have been translated "God," except where the context demands the translation "god(s)." We have generally rendered the tetragrammaton (YHWH) consistently as "the LORD," utilizing a form with small capitals that is common among English translations. This will distinguish it from the name 'adonai, which we render "Lord." When 'adonai and YHWH appear together, we have rendered it "Sovereign LORD." This also distinguishes 'adonai YHWH from cases where YHWH appears with *'elohim*, which is rendered "Lord God." When *YH* (the short form of *YHWH*) and *YHWH* appear together, we have rendered it "Lord God." When *YHWH* appears with the term *tseba'oth*, we have rendered it "Lord of Heaven's Armies" to translate the meaning of the name. In a few cases, we have utilized the transliteration, *Yahweh*, when the personal character of the name is being invoked in contrast to another divine name or the name of some other god (for example, see Exodus 3:15; 6:2-3).

In the New Testament, the Greek word *christos* has been translated as "Messiah" when the context assumes a Jewish audience. When a Gentile audience can be assumed, *christos* has been translated as "Christ." The Greek word *kurios* is consistently translated "Lord," except that it is translated "Lord" wherever the New Testament text explicitly quotes from the Old Testament, and the text there has it in small capitals.

TEXTUAL FOOTNOTES

The New Living Translation provides several kinds of textual footnotes, all designated in the text with an asterisk:

- When for the sake of clarity the NLT renders a difficult or potentially confusing phrase dynamically, we generally give the literal rendering in a textual footnote. This allows the reader to see the literal source of our dynamic rendering and how our translation relates to other more literal translations. These notes are prefaced with "Hebrew," "Aramaic," or "Greek," identifying the language of the underlying source text. For example, in Acts 2:42 we translated the literal "breaking of bread" (from the Greek) as "the Lord's Supper" to clarify that this verse refers to the ceremonial practice of the church rather than just an ordinary meal. Then we attached a footnote to "the Lord's Supper," which reads: "Greek *the breaking of bread*."

- Textual footnotes are also used to show alternative renderings, prefaced with the word "Or." These normally occur for passages where an aspect of the meaning is debated. On occasion, we also provide notes on words or phrases that represent a departure from long-standing tradition. These notes are prefaced with "Traditionally rendered." For example, the footnote to the translation "serious skin disease" at Leviticus 13:2 says: "Traditionally rendered *leprosy*. The Hebrew word used throughout this passage is used to describe various skin diseases."

- When our translators follow a textual variant that differs significantly from our standard Hebrew or Greek texts (listed earlier), we document that difference with a footnote. We also footnote cases when the NLT excludes a passage that is included in the Greek text known as the *Textus Receptus* (and familiar to readers through its translation in the King James Version). In such cases, we offer a translation of the excluded text in a footnote, even though it is generally recognized as a later addition to the Greek text and not part of the original Greek New Testament.

- All Old Testament passages that are quoted in the New Testament are identified by a textual footnote at the New Testament location. When the New Testament clearly quotes from the Greek translation of the Old Testament, and when it differs significantly in wording from the Hebrew text, we also place a textual footnote at the Old Testament location. This note includes a rendering of the

Greek version, along with a cross-reference to the New Testament passage(s) where it is cited (for example, see notes on Proverbs 3:12; Psalms 8:2; 53:3).

- Some textual footnotes provide cultural and historical information on places, things, and people in the Bible that are probably obscure to modern readers. Such notes should aid the reader in understanding the message of the text. For example, in Acts 12:1, "King Herod" is named in this translation as "King Herod Agrippa" and is identified in a footnote as being "the nephew of Herod Antipas and a grandson of Herod the Great."

- When the meaning of a proper name (or a wordplay inherent in a proper name) is relevant to the meaning of the text, it is either illuminated with a textual footnote or included within parentheses in the text itself. For example, the footnote concerning the name "Eve" at Genesis 3:20 reads: "*Eve* sounds like a Hebrew term that means 'to give life.'" This wordplay in the Hebrew illuminates the meaning of the text, which goes on to say that Eve "would be the mother of all who live."

As WE SUBMIT this translation for publication, we recognize that any translation of the Scriptures is subject to limitations and imperfections. Anyone who has attempted to communicate the richness of God's Word into another language will realize it is impossible to make a perfect translation. Recognizing these limitations, we sought God's guidance and wisdom throughout this project. Now we pray that he will accept our efforts and use this translation for the benefit of the church and of all people.

We pray that the New Living Translation will overcome some of the barriers of history, culture, and language that have kept people from reading and understanding God's Word. We hope that readers unfamiliar with the Bible will find the words clear and easy to understand and that readers well versed in the Scriptures will gain a fresh perspective. We pray that readers will gain insight and wisdom for living, but most of all that they will meet the God of the Bible and be forever changed by knowing him.

The Bible Translation Committee
October 2007

BIBLE TRANSLATION TEAM

HOLY BIBLE, *NEW LIVING TRANSLATION*

PENTATEUCH

Daniel I. Block, Senior Translator
Wheaton College

GENESIS

Allen Ross, *Beeson Divinity School, Samford University*
Gordon Wenham, *Trinity Theological College, Bristol*

EXODUS

Robert Bergen, *Hannibal-LaGrange College*
Daniel I. Block, *Wheaton College*
Eugene Carpenter, *Bethel College, Mishawaka, Indiana*

LEVITICUS

David Baker, *Ashland Theological Seminary*
Victor Hamilton, *Asbury College*
Kenneth Mathews, *Beeson Divinity School, Samford University*

NUMBERS

Dale A. Brueggemann, *Assemblies of God Division of Foreign Missions*
R. K. Harrison (deceased), *Wycliffe College*
Paul R. House, *Wheaton College*
Gerald L. Mattingly, *Johnson Bible College*

DEUTERONOMY

J. Gordon McConville, *University of Gloucester*
Eugene H. Merrill, *Dallas Theological Seminary*
John A. Thompson (deceased), *University of Melbourne*

HISTORICAL BOOKS

Barry J. Beitzel, Senior Translator
Trinity Evangelical Divinity School

JOSHUA, JUDGES

Carl E. Armerding, *Schloss Mittersill Study Centre*
Barry J. Beitzel, *Trinity Evangelical Divinity School*
Lawson Stone, *Asbury Theological Seminary*

1 & 2 SAMUEL

Robert Gordon, *Cambridge University*
V. Philips Long, *Regent College*
J. Robert Vannoy, *Biblical Theological Seminary*

1 & 2 KINGS

Bill T. Arnold, *Asbury Theological Seminary*
William H. Barnes, *North Central University*
Frederic W. Bush, *Fuller Theological Seminary*

1 & 2 CHRONICLES

Raymond B. Dillard (deceased), *Westminster Theological Seminary*
David A. Dorsey, *Evangelical School of Theology*
Terry Eves, *Erskine College*

RUTH, EZRA—ESTHER

William C. Williams, *Vanguard University*
H. G. M. Williamson, *Oxford University*

WISDOM BOOKS

Tremper Longman III, Senior Translator
Westmont College

JOB

August Konkel, *Providence Theological Seminary*
Tremper Longman III, *Westmont College*
Al Wolters, *Redeemer College*

PSALMS 1–75

Mark D. Futato, *Reformed Theological Seminary*
Douglas Green, *Westminster Theological Seminary*
Richard Pratt, *Reformed Theological Seminary*

PSALMS 76–150

David M. Howard Jr., *Bethel Theological Seminary*
Raymond C. Ortlund Jr., *Trinity Evangelical Divinity School*
Willem VanGemeren, *Trinity Evangelical Divinity School*

PROVERBS

Ted Hildebrandt, *Gordon College*
Richard Schultz, *Wheaton College*
Raymond C. Van Leeuwen, *Eastern College*

ECCLESIASTES, SONG OF SONGS

Daniel C. Fredericks, *Belhaven College*
David Hubbard (deceased), *Fuller Theological Seminary*
Tremper Longman III, *Westmont College*

PROPHETS

John N. Oswalt, Senior Translator
Wesley Biblical Seminary

ISAIAH

John N. Oswalt, *Wesley Biblical Seminary*
Gary Smith, *Midwestern Baptist Theological Seminary*
John Walton, *Wheaton College*

JEREMIAH, LAMENTATIONS

G. Herbert Livingston, *Asbury Theological Seminary*
Elmer A. Martens, *Mennonite Brethren Biblical Seminary*

EZEKIEL

Daniel I. Block, *Wheaton College*

David H. Engelhard, *Calvin Theological Seminary*
David Thompson, *Asbury Theological Seminary*

DANIEL, HAGGAI—MALACHI

Joyce Baldwin Caine (deceased), *Trinity Theological College, Bristol*
Douglas Gropp, *Catholic University of America*
Roy Hayden, *Oral Roberts School of Theology*
Andrew Hill, *Wheaton College*
Tremper Longman III, *Westmont College*

HOSEA—ZEPHANIAH

Joseph Coleson, *Nazarene Theological Seminary*
Roy Hayden, *Oral Roberts School of Theology*
Andrew Hill, *Wheaton College*
Richard Patterson, *Liberty University*

GOSPELS AND ACTS

Grant R. Osborne, Senior Translator
Trinity Evangelical Divinity School

MATTHEW

Craig Blomberg, *Denver Seminary*
Donald A. Hagner, *Fuller Theological Seminary*
David Turner, *Grand Rapids Baptist Seminary*

MARK

Robert Guelich (deceased), *Fuller Theological Seminary*
George Guthrie, *Union University*
Grant R. Osborne, *Trinity Evangelical Divinity School*

LUKE

Darrell Bock, *Dallas Theological Seminary*
Scot McKnight, *North Park University*
Robert Stein, *The Southern Baptist Theological Seminary*

JOHN

Gary M. Burge, *Wheaton College*
Philip W. Comfort, *Coastal Carolina University*
Marianne Meye Thompson, *Fuller Theological Seminary*

ACTS

D. A. Carson, *Trinity Evangelical Divinity School*
William J. Larkin, *Columbia International University*
Roger Mohrlang, *Whitworth University*

LETTERS AND REVELATION

Norman R. Ericson, Senior Translator
Wheaton College

ROMANS, GALATIANS

Gerald Borchert, *Northern Baptist Theological Seminary*
Douglas J. Moo, *Wheaton College*
Thomas R. Schreiner, *The Southern Baptist Theological Seminary*

1 & 2 CORINTHIANS

Joseph Alexanian, *Trinity International University*
Linda Belleville, *Bethel College, Mishawaka, Indiana*
Douglas A. Oss, *Central Bible College*
Robert Sloan, *Baylor University*

EPHESIANS—PHILEMON

Harold W. Hoehner, *Dallas Theological Seminary*
Moises Silva, *Gordon-Conwell Theological Seminary*
Klyne Snodgrass, *North Park Theological Seminary*

HEBREWS, JAMES, 1 & 2 PETER, JUDE

Peter Davids, *Schloss Mittersill Study Centre*
Norman R. Ericson, *Wheaton College*
William Lane (deceased), *Seattle Pacific University*
J. Ramsey Michaels, *S. W. Missouri State University*

1–3 JOHN, REVELATION

Greg Beale, *Wheaton College*
Robert Mounce, *Whitworth University*
M. Robert Mulholland Jr., *Asbury Theological Seminary*

SPECIAL REVIEWERS

F. F. Bruce (deceased), *University of Manchester*
Kenneth N. Taylor (deceased), *Translator, The Living Bible*

COORDINATING TEAM

Mark D. Taylor, *Director and Chief Stylist*
Ronald A. Beers, *Executive Director and Stylist*
Mark R. Norton, *Managing Editor and O.T. Coordinating Editor*
Philip W. Comfort, *N.T. Coordinating Editor*
Daniel W. Taylor, *Bethel University, Senior Stylist*

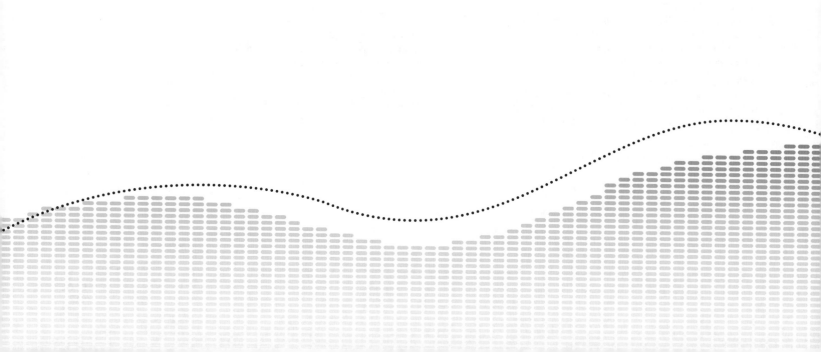

THE BOOK OF MATTHEW was written by a cat named Levi. After he started chillin' with Jesus, his life would never be the same. Remember back in the day, there was always someone on the block you ducked and dodged whenever you saw him coming, kinda like Omar on *The Wire?* Well that's what used to happen to Matthew. People would see him comin' and run because they knew he was about to gank them for their ends. You see, before Matthew became boys with Jesus, he was a tax collector—a gangsta tax collector. Even though it was his job, Matthew was collectin' for the enemy—the Romans. And he was takin' from his own people—the Jews—and likely skimmin' some off the top. But when Jesus called him out, his whole life changed!

Matthew's Gospel tells the story of Jesus from beginning to end. Matthew was all about his paper, and he was pretty organized. So when he wrote the book, it was pretty much in the order it happened, starting from Jesus' birth until his burial and resurrection. Matthew, more than any of the other Gospel writers, used prophecies from the Old Testament to back up that Jesus was the promised Messiah—the One who came to save us all.

MATTHEW

CHAPTER **1**

The Ancestors of Jesus the Messiah

This is a record of the ancestors of Jesus the Messiah, a descendant of David* and of Abraham:

2 Abraham was the father of Isaac.
Isaac was the father of Jacob.
Jacob was the father of Judah and his brothers.
3 Judah was the father of Perez and Zerah (whose mother was Tamar).
Perez was the father of Hezron.
Hezron was the father of Ram.*
4 Ram was the father of Amminadab.
Amminadab was the father of Nahshon.
Nahshon was the father of Salmon.
5 Salmon was the father of Boaz (whose mother was Rahab).
Boaz was the father of Obed (whose mother was Ruth).
Obed was the father of Jesse.
6 Jesse was the father of King David.
David was the father of Solomon (whose mother was Bathsheba, the widow of Uriah).
7 Solomon was the father of Rehoboam.
Rehoboam was the father of Abijah.
Abijah was the father of Asa.*
8 Asa was the father of Jehoshaphat.
Jehoshaphat was the father of Jehoram.*
Jehoram was the father* of Uzziah.

9 Uzziah was the father of Jotham.
Jotham was the father of Ahaz.
Ahaz was the father of Hezekiah.
10 Hezekiah was the father of Manasseh.
Manasseh was the father of Amon.*
Amon was the father of Josiah.
11 Josiah was the father of Jehoiachin* and his brothers (born at the time of the exile to Babylon).
12 After the Babylonian exile:
Jehoiachin was the father of Shealtiel.
Shealtiel was the father of Zerubbabel.
13 Zerubbabel was the father of Abiud.
Abiud was the father of Eliakim.
Eliakim was the father of Azor.
14 Azor was the father of Zadok.
Zadok was the father of Akim.
Akim was the father of Eliud.
15 Eliud was the father of Eleazar.
Eleazar was the father of Matthan.
Matthan was the father of Jacob.
16 Jacob was the father of Joseph, the husband of Mary.
Mary gave birth to Jesus, who is called the Messiah.

17All those listed above include fourteen generations from Abraham to David, fourteen from David to the Babylonian exile, and fourteen from the Babylonian exile to the Messiah.

1:1 Greek *Jesus the Messiah, son of David.*   **1:3** Greek *Aram*, a variant spelling of Ram; also in 1:4. See 1 Chr 2:9-10.   **1:7** Greek *Asaph*, a variant spelling of Asa; also in 1:8. See 1 Chr 3:10.   **1:8a** Greek *Joram*, a variant spelling of Jehoram; also in 1:8b. See 1 Kgs 22:50 and note at 1 Chr 3:11.   **1:8b** Or *ancestor*; also in 1:11.   **1:10** Greek *Amos*, a variant spelling of Amon; also in 1:10b. See 1 Chr 3:14.   **1:11** Greek *Jeconiah*, a variant spelling of Jehoiachin; also in 1:12. See 2 Kgs 24:6 and note at 1 Chr 3:16.

The Birth of Jesus the Messiah

¹⁸This is how Jesus the Messiah was born. His mother, Mary, was engaged to be married to Joseph. But before the marriage took place, while she was still a virgin, she became pregnant through the power of the Holy Spirit. ¹⁹Joseph, her fiancé, was a good man and did not want to disgrace her publicly, so he decided to break the engagement* quietly.

²⁰As he considered this, an angel of the Lord appeared to him in a dream. "Joseph, son of David," the angel said, "do not be afraid to take Mary as your wife. For the child within her was conceived by the Holy Spirit. ²¹And she will have a son, and you are to name him Jesus,* for he will save his people from their sins."

²²All of this occurred to fulfill the Lord's message through his prophet:

²³ "Look! The virgin will conceive a child!
   She will give birth to a son,
and they will call him Immanuel,*
   which means 'God is with us.'"

²⁴When Joseph woke up, he did as the angel of the Lord commanded and took Mary as his wife. ²⁵But he did not have sexual relations with her until her son was born. And Joseph named him Jesus.

CHAPTER 2

Visitors from the East

Jesus was born in Bethlehem in Judea, during the reign of King Herod. About that time some wise men* from eastern lands arrived in Jerusalem, asking, ²"Where is the newborn king of the Jews? We saw his star as it rose,* and we have come to worship him."

³King Herod was deeply disturbed when he heard this, as was everyone in Jerusalem. ⁴He called a meeting of the leading priests and teachers of religious law and asked, "Where is the Messiah supposed to be born?"

⁵"In Bethlehem in Judea," they said, "for this is what the prophet wrote:

⁶ 'And you, O Bethlehem in the land of Judah,
   are not least among the ruling cities* of Judah,
for a ruler will come from you
   who will be the shepherd for my people
     Israel.'*"

⁷Then Herod called for a private meeting with the wise men, and he learned from them the time when the star first appeared. ⁸Then he told them, "Go to Bethlehem and search carefully for the child. And when you find him, come back and tell me so that I can go and worship him, too!"

⁹After this interview the wise men went their way. And the star they had seen in the east guided them to Bethlehem. It went ahead of them and stopped over the place where the child was. ¹⁰When they saw the star, they were filled with joy! ¹¹They entered the house and saw the child with his mother, Mary, and they bowed down and worshiped him. Then they opened their treasure chests and gave him gifts of gold, frankincense, and myrrh.

¹²When it was time to leave, they returned to their own country by another route, for God had warned them in a dream not to return to Herod.

The Escape to Egypt

¹³After the wise men were gone, an angel of the Lord appeared to Joseph in a dream. "Get up! Flee to Egypt with the child and his mother," the angel said. "Stay there until I tell you to return, because Herod is going to search for the child to kill him."

¹⁴That night Joseph left for Egypt with the child and Mary,

1:19 Greek *to divorce her.*   **1:21** *Jesus* means "The LORD saves."   **1:23** Isa 7:14; 8:8, 10 (Greek version).   **2:1** Or *royal astrologers;* Greek reads *magi;* also in 2:7, 16.   **2:2** Or *star in the east.*   **2:6a** Greek *the rulers.*   **2:6b** Mic 5:2; 2 Sam 5:2.

his mother, [15]and they stayed there until Herod's death. This fulfilled what the Lord had spoken through the prophet: "I called my Son out of Egypt."*

[16]Herod was furious when he realized that the wise men had outwitted him. He sent soldiers to kill all the boys in and around Bethlehem who were two years old and under, based on the wise men's report of the star's first appearance. [17]Herod's brutal action fulfilled what God had spoken through the prophet Jeremiah:

[18] "A cry was heard in Ramah—
    weeping and great mourning.
Rachel weeps for her children,
    refusing to be comforted,
    for they are dead."*

The Return to Nazareth

[19]When Herod died, an angel of the Lord appeared in a dream to Joseph in Egypt. [20]"Get up!" the angel said. "Take the child and his mother back to the land of Israel, because those who were trying to kill the child are dead."

[21]So Joseph got up and returned to the land of Israel with Jesus and his mother. [22]But when he learned that the new ruler of Judea was Herod's son Archelaus, he was afraid to go there. Then, after being warned in a dream, he left for the region of Galilee. [23]So the family went and lived in a town called Nazareth. This fulfilled what the prophets had said: "He will be called a Nazarene."

CHAPTER 3

John the Baptist Prepares the Way

In those days John the Baptist came to the Judean wilderness and began preaching. His message was, [2]"Repent of your sins and turn to God, for the Kingdom of Heaven is near.*" [3]The prophet Isaiah was speaking about John when he said,

"He is a voice shouting in the wilderness,
'Prepare the way for the LORD's coming!
    Clear the road for him!'"*

[4]John's clothes were woven from coarse camel hair, and he wore a leather belt around his waist. For food he ate locusts and wild honey. [5]People from Jerusalem and from all of Judea and all over the Jordan Valley went out to see and hear John. [6]And when they confessed their sins, he baptized them in the Jordan River.

[7]But when he saw many Pharisees and Sadducees coming to watch him baptize,* he denounced them. "You brood of snakes!" he exclaimed. "Who warned you to flee God's coming wrath? [8]Prove by the way you live that you have repented of your sins and turned to God. [9]Don't just say to each other, 'We're safe, for we are descendants of Abraham.' That means nothing, for I tell you, God can create children of Abraham from these very stones. [10]Even now the ax of God's judgment is poised, ready to sever the roots of the trees. Yes, every tree that does not produce good fruit will be chopped down and thrown into the fire.

[11]"I baptize with* water those who repent of their sins and turn to God. But someone is coming soon who is greater than I am—so much greater that I'm not worthy even to be his slave and carry his sandals. He will baptize you with the Holy Spirit and with fire.* [12]He is ready to separate the chaff from the wheat with his winnowing fork. Then he will clean up the threshing area, gathering the wheat into his barn but burning the chaff with never-ending fire."

The Baptism of Jesus

[13]Then Jesus went from Galilee to the Jordan River to be baptized by John. [14]But John tried to talk him out of it. "I am the one who needs to be baptized by you," he said, "so why are you coming to me?"

2:15 Hos 11:1.   2:18 Jer 31:15.   3:2 Or has come, or is coming soon.   3:3 Isa 40:3 (Greek version).   3:7 Or coming to be baptized.   3:11a Or in.   3:11b Or in the Holy Spirit and in fire.

¹⁵But Jesus said, "It should be done, for we must carry out all that God requires.*" So John agreed to baptize him.

¹⁶After his baptism, as Jesus came up out of the water, the heavens were opened* and he saw the Spirit of God descending like a dove and settling on him. ¹⁷And a voice from heaven said, "This is my dearly loved Son, who brings me great joy."

CHAPTER 4
The Temptation of Jesus
Then Jesus was led by the Spirit into the wilderness to be tempted there by the devil. ²For forty days and forty nights he fasted and became very hungry. ³During that time the devil* came and said to him, "If you are the Son of God, tell these stones to become loaves of bread."

⁴But Jesus told him, "No! The Scriptures say,

'People do not live by bread alone,
but by every word that comes from the mouth of God.'*"

⁵Then the devil took him to the holy city, Jerusalem, to the highest point of the Temple, ⁶and said, "If you are the Son of God, jump off! For the Scriptures say,

'He will order his angels to protect you.
And they will hold you up with their hands
so you won't even hurt your foot on a stone.'*"

⁷Jesus responded, "The Scriptures also say, 'You must not test the LORD your God.'*"

⁸Next the devil took him to the peak of a very high mountain and showed him all the kingdoms of the world and their glory. ⁹"I will give it all to you," he said, "if you will kneel down and worship me."

¹⁰"Get out of here, Satan," Jesus told him. "For the Scriptures say,

'You must worship the LORD your God
and serve only him.'*"

¹¹Then the devil went away, and angels came and took care of Jesus.

The Ministry of Jesus Begins
¹²When Jesus heard that John had been arrested, he left Judea and returned to Galilee. ¹³He went first to Nazareth, then left there and moved to Capernaum, beside the Sea of Galilee, in the region of Zebulun and Naphtali. ¹⁴This fulfilled what God said through the prophet Isaiah:

¹⁵ "In the land of Zebulun and of Naphtali,
beside the sea, beyond the Jordan River,
in Galilee where so many Gentiles live,
¹⁶ the people who sat in darkness
have seen a great light.
And for those who lived in the land where death casts its shadow,
a light has shined."*

¹⁷From then on Jesus began to preach, "Repent of your sins and turn to God, for the Kingdom of Heaven is near.*"

The First Disciples
¹⁸One day as Jesus was walking along the shore of the Sea of Galilee, he saw two brothers—Simon, also called Peter, and Andrew—throwing a net into the water, for they fished for a living. ¹⁹Jesus called out to them, "Come, follow me, and I will show you how to fish for people!" ²⁰And they left their nets at once and followed him.

²¹A little farther up the shore he saw two other brothers, James and John, sitting in a boat with their father, Zebedee, repairing their nets. And he called them to come, too. ²²They immediately followed him, leaving the boat and their father behind.

"The people who sat in darkness have seen a great light. And for those who lived in the land where death casts its shadow, a light has shined" (Matthew 4:16).

There is light where there was once darkness. The people who lived in the shadow of death have seen the light.

3:15 Or *for we must fulfill all righteousness.* 3:16 Some manuscripts read *opened to him.* 4:3 Greek *the tempter.* 4:4 Deut 8:3. 4:6 Ps 91:11-12. 4:7 Deut 6:16. 4:10 Deut 6:13.
4:15-16 Isa 9:1-2 (Greek version). 4:17 Or *has come,* or *is coming soon.*

Crowds Follow Jesus

²³Jesus traveled throughout the region of Galilee, teaching in the synagogues and announcing the Good News about the Kingdom. And he healed every kind of disease and illness. ²⁴News about him spread as far as Syria, and people soon began bringing to him all who were sick. And whatever their sickness or disease, or if they were demon possessed or epileptic or paralyzed—he healed them all. ²⁵Large crowds followed him wherever he went—people from Galilee, the Ten Towns,* Jerusalem, from all over Judea, and from east of the Jordan River.

CHAPTER 5

The Sermon on the Mount

One day as he saw the crowds gathering, Jesus went up on the mountainside and sat down. His disciples gathered around him, ²and he began to teach them.

The Beatitudes

³ "God blesses those who are poor and realize their
   need for him,*
   for the Kingdom of Heaven is theirs.
⁴ God blesses those who mourn,
   for they will be comforted.
⁵ God blesses those who are humble,
   for they will inherit the whole earth.
⁶ God blesses those who hunger and thirst for justice,*
   for they will be satisfied.
⁷ God blesses those who are merciful,
   for they will be shown mercy.
⁸ God blesses those whose hearts are pure,
   for they will see God.
⁹ God blesses those who work for peace,
   for they will be called the children of God.
¹⁰ God blesses those who are persecuted for doing right,
   for the Kingdom of Heaven is theirs.

¹¹"God blesses you when people mock you and persecute you and lie about you* and say all sorts of evil things against you because you are my followers. ¹²Be happy about it! Be very glad! For a great reward awaits you in heaven. And remember, the ancient prophets were persecuted in the same way.

Teaching about Salt and Light

¹³"You are the salt of the earth. But what good is salt if it has lost its flavor? Can you make it salty again? It will be thrown out and trampled underfoot as worthless.

¹⁴"You are the light of the world—like a city on a hilltop that cannot be hidden. ¹⁵No one lights a lamp and then puts it under a basket. Instead, a lamp is placed on a stand, where it gives light to everyone in the house. ¹⁶In the same way, let your good deeds shine out for all to see, so that everyone will praise your heavenly Father.

Teaching about the Law

¹⁷"Don't misunderstand why I have come. I did not come to abolish the law of Moses or the writings of the prophets. No, I came to accomplish their purpose. ¹⁸I tell you the truth, until heaven and earth disappear, not even the smallest detail of God's law will disappear until its purpose is achieved. ¹⁹So if you ignore the least commandment and teach others to do the same, you will be called the least in the Kingdom of Heaven. But anyone who obeys God's laws and teaches them will be called great in the Kingdom of Heaven.

²⁰"But I warn you—unless your righteousness is better than the righteousness of the teachers of religious law and the Pharisees, you will never enter the Kingdom of Heaven!

Teaching about Anger

²¹"You have heard that our ancestors were told, 'You must not murder. If you commit murder, you are subject to judg-

"God blesses those who are poor and realize their need for him, for the Kingdom of Heaven is theirs" (Matthew 5:3).

say what?

The Kingdom of Heaven belongs to people who know they need God's help.

4:25 Greek *Decapolis.*   5:3 Greek *poor in spirit.*   5:6 Or *for righteousness.*   5:11 Some manuscripts do not include *and lie about you.*

ment.'* ²²But I say, if you are even angry with someone,* you are subject to judgment! If you call someone an idiot,* you are in danger of being brought before the court. And if you curse someone,* you are in danger of the fires of hell.*

²³"So if you are presenting a sacrifice* at the altar in the Temple and you suddenly remember that someone has something against you, ²⁴leave your sacrifice there at the altar. Go and be reconciled to that person. Then come and offer your sacrifice to God.

²⁵"When you are on the way to court with your adversary, settle your differences quickly. Otherwise, your accuser may hand you over to the judge, who will hand you over to an officer, and you will be thrown into prison. ²⁶And if that happens, you surely won't be free again until you have paid the last penny.*

Teaching about Adultery

²⁷"You have heard the commandment that says, 'You must not commit adultery.'* ²⁸But I say, anyone who even looks at a woman with lust has already committed adultery with her in his heart. ²⁹So if your eye—even your good eye*—causes you to lust, gouge it out and throw it away. It is better for you to lose one part of your body than for your whole body to be thrown into hell. ³⁰And if your hand—even your stronger hand*—causes you to sin, cut it off and throw it away. It is better for you to lose one part of your body than for your whole body to be thrown into hell.

Teaching about Divorce

³¹"You have heard the law that says, 'A man can divorce his wife by merely giving her a written notice of divorce.'* ³²But I say that a man who divorces his wife, unless she has been unfaithful, causes her to commit adultery. And anyone who marries a divorced woman also commits adultery.

Teaching about Vows

³³"You have also heard that our ancestors were told, 'You must not break your vows; you must carry out the vows you make to the LORD.'* ³⁴But I say, do not make any vows! Do not say, 'By heaven!' because heaven is God's throne. ³⁵And do not say, 'By the earth!' because the earth is his footstool. And do not say, 'By Jerusalem!' for Jerusalem is the city of the great King. ³⁶Do not even say, 'By my head!' for you can't turn one hair white or black. ³⁷Just say a simple, 'Yes, I will,' or 'No, I won't.' Anything beyond this is from the evil one.

Teaching about Revenge

³⁸"You have heard the law that says the punishment must match the injury: 'An eye for an eye, and a tooth for a tooth.'* ³⁹But I say, do not resist an evil person! If someone slaps you on the right cheek, offer the other cheek also. ⁴⁰If you are sued in court and your shirt is taken from you, give your coat, too. ⁴¹If a soldier demands that you carry his gear for a mile,* carry it two miles. ⁴²Give to those who ask, and don't turn away from those who want to borrow.

Teaching about Love for Enemies

⁴³"You have heard the law that says, 'Love your neighbor'* and hate your enemy. ⁴⁴But I say, love your enemies!* Pray for those who persecute you! ⁴⁵In that way, you will be acting as true children of your Father in heaven. For he gives his sunlight to both the evil and the good, and he sends rain on the just and the unjust alike. ⁴⁶If you love only those who love you, what reward is there for that? Even corrupt tax collectors do that much. ⁴⁷If you are kind only to your friends,* how are you different from anyone else? Even pagans do that. ⁴⁸But you are to be perfect, even as your Father in heaven is perfect.

5:21 Exod 20:13; Deut 5:17. **5:22a** Some manuscripts add *without cause.* **5:22b** Greek uses an Aramaic term of contempt: *If you say to your brother, 'Raca.'* **5:22c** Greek *if you say, 'You fool.'* **5:22d** Greek *Gehenna;* also in 5:29, 30. **5:23** Greek *gift;* also in 5:24. **5:26** Greek *the last kodrantes* [i.e., quadrans]. **5:27** Exod 20:14; Deut 5:18. **5:29** Greek *your right eye.* **5:30** Greek *your right hand.* **5:31** Deut 24:1. **5:33** Num 30:2. **5:38** Greek *the law that says: 'An eye for an eye and a tooth for a tooth.'* Exod 21:24; Lev 24:20; Deut 19:21. **5:41** Greek *milion* [4,854 feet or 1,478 meters]. **5:43** Lev 19:18. **5:44** Some manuscripts add *Bless those who curse you. Do good to those who hate you.* Compare Luke 6:27-28. **5:47** Greek *your brothers.*

Teaching about Giving to the Needy

"Watch out! Don't do your good deeds publicly, to be admired by others, for you will lose the reward from your Father in heaven. [2]When you give to someone in need, don't do as the hypocrites do—blowing trumpets in the synagogues and streets to call attention to their acts of charity! I tell you the truth, they have received all the reward they will ever get. [3]But when you give to someone in need, don't let your left hand know what your right hand is doing. [4]Give your gifts in private, and your Father, who sees everything, will reward you.

Teaching about Prayer and Fasting

[5]"When you pray, don't be like the hypocrites who love to pray publicly on street corners and in the synagogues where everyone can see them. I tell you the truth, that is all the reward they will ever get. [6]But when you pray, go away by yourself, shut the door behind you, and pray to your Father in private. Then your Father, who sees everything, will reward you.

[7]"When you pray, don't babble on and on as people of other religions do. They think their prayers are answered merely by repeating their words again and again. [8]Don't be like them, for your Father knows exactly what you need even before you ask him! [9]Pray like this:

Our Father in heaven,
    may your name be kept holy.
[10] May your Kingdom come soon.
    May your will be done on earth,
        as it is in heaven.
[11] Give us today the food we need,*
[12] and forgive us our sins,
        as we have forgiven those who sin against us.
[13] And don't let us yield to temptation,*
        but rescue us from the evil one.*

[14]"If you forgive those who sin against you, your heavenly Father will forgive you. [15]But if you refuse to forgive others, your Father will not forgive your sins.

[16]"And when you fast, don't make it obvious, as the hypocrites do, for they try to look miserable and disheveled so people will admire them for their fasting. I tell you the truth, that is the only reward they will ever get. [17]But when you fast, comb your hair and wash your face. [18]Then no one will notice that you are fasting, except your Father, who knows what you do in private. And your Father, who sees everything, will reward you.

Teaching about Money and Possessions

[19]"Don't store up treasures here on earth, where moths eat them and rust destroys them, and where thieves break in and steal. [20]Store your treasures in heaven, where moths and rust cannot destroy, and thieves do not break in and steal. [21]Wherever your treasure is, there the desires of your heart will also be.

[22]"Your eye is a lamp that provides light for your body. When your eye is good, your whole body is filled with light. [23]But when your eye is bad, your whole body is filled with darkness. And if the light you think you have is actually darkness, how deep that darkness is!

[24]"No one can serve two masters. For you will hate one and love the other; you will be devoted to one and despise the other. You cannot serve both God and money.

[25]"That is why I tell you not to worry about everyday life—whether you have enough food and drink, or enough clothes to wear. Isn't life more than food, and your body more than clothing? [26]Look at the birds. They don't plant or harvest or store food in barns, for your heavenly Father feeds them. And aren't you far more valuable to him than they are? [27]Can all your worries add a single moment to your life?

6:11 Or *Give us today our food for the day;* or *Give us today our food for tomorrow.* **6:13a** Or *And keep us from being tested.* **6:13b** Or *from evil.* Some manuscripts add *For yours is the kingdom and the power and the glory forever. Amen.*

²⁸"And why worry about your clothing? Look at the lilies of the field and how they grow. They don't work or make their clothing, ²⁹yet Solomon in all his glory was not dressed as beautifully as they are. ³⁰And if God cares so wonderfully for wildflowers that are here today and thrown into the fire tomorrow, he will certainly care for you. Why do you have so little faith?

³¹"So don't worry about these things, saying, 'What will we eat? What will we drink? What will we wear?' ³²These things dominate the thoughts of unbelievers, but your heavenly Father already knows all your needs. ³³Seek the Kingdom of God* above all else, and live righteously, and he will give you everything you need.

³⁴"So don't worry about tomorrow, for tomorrow will bring its own worries. Today's trouble is enough for today.

CHAPTER 7

Do Not Judge Others

"Do not judge others, and you will not be judged. ²For you will be treated as you treat others.* The standard you use in judging is the standard by which you will be judged.*

³"And why worry about a speck in your friend's eye* when you have a log in your own? ⁴How can you think of saying to your friend,* 'Let me help you get rid of that speck in your eye,' when you can't see past the log in your own eye? ⁵Hypocrite! First get rid of the log in your own eye; then you will see well enough to deal with the speck in your friend's eye.

⁶"Don't waste what is holy on people who are unholy.* Don't throw your pearls to pigs! They will trample the pearls, then turn and attack you.

Effective Prayer

⁷"Keep on asking, and you will receive what you ask for. Keep on seeking, and you will find. Keep on knocking, and the door will be opened to you. ⁸For everyone who asks, receives. Everyone who seeks, finds. And to everyone who knocks, the door will be opened.

⁹"You parents—if your children ask for a loaf of bread, do you give them a stone instead? ¹⁰Or if they ask for a fish, do you give them a snake? Of course not! ¹¹So if you sinful people know how to give good gifts to your children, how much more will your heavenly Father give good gifts to those who ask him.

The Golden Rule

¹²"Do to others whatever you would like them to do to you. This is the essence of all that is taught in the law and the prophets.

The Narrow Gate

¹³"You can enter God's Kingdom only through the narrow gate. The highway to hell* is broad, and its gate is wide for the many who choose that way. ¹⁴But the gateway to life is very narrow and the road is difficult, and only a few ever find it.

The Tree and Its Fruit

¹⁵"Beware of false prophets who come disguised as harmless sheep but are really vicious wolves. ¹⁶You can identify them by their fruit, that is, by the way they act. Can you pick grapes from thornbushes, or figs from thistles? ¹⁷A good tree produces good fruit, and a bad tree produces bad fruit. ¹⁸A good tree can't produce bad fruit, and a bad tree can't produce good fruit. ¹⁹So every tree that does not produce good fruit is chopped down and thrown into the fire. ²⁰Yes, just as you can identify a tree by its fruit, so you can identify people by their actions.

True Disciples

²¹"Not everyone who calls out to me, 'Lord! Lord!' will enter the Kingdom of Heaven. Only those who actually do the will of my Father in heaven will enter. ²²On judgment day many

---

6:33 Some manuscripts do not include *of God*.   **7:2a** Or *For God will judge you as you judge others*.   **7:2b** Or *The measure you give will be the measure you get back*.   **7:3** Greek *your brother's eye*; also in 7:5.   **7:4** Greek *your brother*.   **7:6** Greek *Don't give the sacred to dogs*.   **7:13** Greek *The road that leads to destruction*.

will say to me, 'Lord! Lord! We prophesied in your name and cast out demons in your name and performed many miracles in your name.' 23But I will reply, 'I never knew you. Get away from me, you who break God's laws.'

Building on a Solid Foundation

24"Anyone who listens to my teaching and follows it is wise, like a person who builds a house on solid rock. 25Though the rain comes in torrents and the floodwaters rise and the winds beat against that house, it won't collapse because it is built on bedrock. 26But anyone who hears my teaching and doesn't obey it is foolish, like a person who builds a house on sand. 27When the rains and floods come and the winds beat against that house, it will collapse with a mighty crash."

28When Jesus had finished saying these things, the crowds were amazed at his teaching, 29for he taught with real authority—quite unlike their teachers of religious law.

CHAPTER 8

Jesus Heals a Man with Leprosy

Large crowds followed Jesus as he came down the mountainside. 2Suddenly, a man with leprosy approached him and knelt before him. "Lord," the man said, "if you are willing, you can heal me and make me clean."

3Jesus reached out and touched him. "I am willing," he said. "Be healed!" And instantly the leprosy disappeared. 4Then Jesus said to him, "Don't tell anyone about this. Instead, go to the priest and let him examine you. Take along the offering required in the law of Moses for those who have been healed of leprosy.* This will be a public testimony that you have been cleansed."

The Faith of a Roman Officer

5When Jesus returned to Capernaum, a Roman officer* came and pleaded with him, 6"Lord, my young servant* lies in bed, paralyzed and in terrible pain."

7Jesus said, "I will come and heal him."

8But the officer said, "Lord, I am not worthy to have you come into my home. Just say the word from where you are, and my servant will be healed. 9I know this because I am under the authority of my superior officers, and I have authority over my soldiers. I only need to say, 'Go,' and they go, or 'Come,' and they come. And if I say to my slaves, 'Do this,' they do it."

10When Jesus heard this, he was amazed. Turning to those who were following him, he said, "I tell you the truth, I haven't seen faith like this in all Israel! 11And I tell you this, that many Gentiles will come from all over the world—from east and west—and sit down with Abraham, Isaac, and Jacob at the feast in the Kingdom of Heaven. 12But many Israelites—those for whom the Kingdom was prepared—will be thrown into outer darkness, where there will be weeping and gnashing of teeth."

13Then Jesus said to the Roman officer, "Go back home. Because you believed, it has happened." And the young servant was healed that same hour.

Jesus Heals Many People

14When Jesus arrived at Peter's house, Peter's mother-in-law was sick in bed with a high fever. 15But when Jesus touched her hand, the fever left her. Then she got up and prepared a meal for him.

16That evening many demon-possessed people were brought to Jesus. He cast out the evil spirits with a simple command, and he healed all the sick. 17This fulfilled the word of the Lord through the prophet Isaiah, who said,

> "He took our sicknesses
> and removed our diseases."*

The Cost of Following Jesus

18When Jesus saw the crowd around him, he instructed his disciples to cross to the other side of the lake.

8:4 See Lev 14:2-32.   8:5 Greek *a centurion;* similarly in 8:8, 13.   8:6 Or *child;* also in 8:13.   8:17 Isa 53:4.

POWERCHOICES

WHO DO YOU ROLL WITH? NOW THAT YOU'RE SAVED AND ALL UP IN CHURCH, DO YOU JUST HANG WITH CHURCH FOLK? OR ARE YOU SOMEONE WHO HASN'T YET SEEN THE LIGHT—AND WON'T GIVE GOD-FREAKS THE TIME OF DAY? HOW DO YOU CHOOSE TO RESPOND TO WHAT OTHERS SAY ABOUT YOUR CREW? BEFORE COMIN' TO FAITH, MATTHEW WASN'T RAGGIN' ON JESUS OR CALLIN' HIM AND HIS BOYS GOD-FREAKS. HE INVITED THEM TO DINNER. HE WANTED TO SEE WHAT THESE BROTHAS WERE ABOUT. ONCE HE FOUND OUT THEY WERE THE REAL DEAL, MATTHEW WENT TO GREAT LENGTHS TO SHOW PEOPLE WHO HATED HIM THAT GETTING TO KNOW JESUS HAD MADE A BIG CHANGE IN HIS LIFE. ¶ THE GOSPEL OF MATTHEW IS FULL OF OLD TESTAMENT PROPHECIES, WHICH PROVES MATTHEW HAD DONE HIS HOMEWORK. HE WASN'T JUST FOLLOWIN' JESUS ALL WILLY-NILLY; MATTHEW KNEW THE WORD FOR HIMSELF. HE DIALOGUED WITH THE MASTER FACE TO FACE—AND THE WORD BECAME FLESH. (WE'LL DEAL WITH THIS A LITTLE LATER IN THE GOSPEL OF JOHN.) MATTHEW CHECKED OUT WHAT THE PROPHETS HAD TO SAY, AND THEN HE WROTE IT DOWN AND MADE IT PLAIN FOR OTHERS TO READ. ¶ *LIKE MATTHEW, CAN YOU TELL JESUS' STORY? CAN YOU SPEAK TO WHAT JESUS HAS DELIVERED YOU FROM AND GET CRUNK FOR CHRIST?*

---

¹⁹Then one of the teachers of religious law said to him, "Teacher, I will follow you wherever you go."

²⁰But Jesus replied, "Foxes have dens to live in, and birds have nests, but the Son of Man* has no place even to lay his head."

²¹Another of his disciples said, "Lord, first let me return home and bury my father."

²²But Jesus told him, "Follow me now. Let the spiritually dead bury their own dead.*"

Jesus Calms the Storm

²³Then Jesus got into the boat and started across the lake with his disciples. ²⁴Suddenly, a fierce storm struck the lake, with waves breaking into the boat. But Jesus was sleeping. ²⁵The disciples went and woke him up, shouting, "Lord, save us! We're going to drown!"

²⁶Jesus responded, "Why are you afraid? You have so little faith!" Then he got up and rebuked the wind and waves, and suddenly there was a great calm.

²⁷The disciples were amazed. "Who is this man?" they asked. "Even the winds and waves obey him!"

Jesus Heals Two Demon-Possessed Men

²⁸When Jesus arrived on the other side of the lake, in the region of the Gadarenes,* two men who were possessed by demons met him. They lived in a cemetery and were so violent that no one could go through that area.

²⁹They began screaming at him, "Why are you interfering with us, Son of God? Have you come here to torture us before God's appointed time?"

³⁰There happened to be a large herd of pigs feeding in the distance. ³¹So the demons begged, "If you cast us out, send us into that herd of pigs."

³²"All right, go!" Jesus commanded them. So the demons came out of the men and entered the pigs, and the whole herd plunged down the steep hillside into the lake and drowned in the water.

³³The herdsmen fled to the nearby town, telling everyone what happened to the demon-possessed men. ³⁴Then the entire town came out to meet Jesus, but they begged him to go away and leave them alone.

CHAPTER 9

Jesus Heals a Paralyzed Man

Jesus climbed into a boat and went back across the lake to his own town. ²Some people brought to him a paralyzed

---

8:20 "Son of Man" is a title Jesus used for himself.   **8:22** Greek *Let the dead bury their own dead.*   **8:28** Other manuscripts read *Gerasenes;* still others read *Gergesenes.* Compare Mark 5:1; Luke 8:26.

man on a mat. Seeing their faith, Jesus said to the paralyzed man, "Be encouraged, my child! Your sins are forgiven."

³But some of the teachers of religious law said to themselves, "That's blasphemy! Does he think he's God?"

⁴Jesus knew* what they were thinking, so he asked them, "Why do you have such evil thoughts in your hearts? ⁵Is it easier to say 'Your sins are forgiven,' or 'Stand up and walk'? ⁶So I will prove to you that the Son of Man* has the authority on earth to forgive sins." Then Jesus turned to the paralyzed man and said, "Stand up, pick up your mat, and go home!"

⁷And the man jumped up and went home! ⁸Fear swept through the crowd as they saw this happen. And they praised God for sending a man with such great authority.*

Jesus Calls Matthew

⁹As Jesus was walking along, he saw a man named Matthew sitting at his tax collector's booth. "Follow me and be my disciple," Jesus said to him. So Matthew got up and followed him.

¹⁰Later, Matthew invited Jesus and his disciples to his home as dinner guests, along with many tax collectors and other disreputable sinners. ¹¹But when the Pharisees saw this, they asked his disciples, "Why does your teacher eat with such scum?*"

¹²When Jesus heard this, he said, "Healthy people don't need a doctor—sick people do." ¹³Then he added, "Now go and learn the meaning of this Scripture: 'I want you to show mercy, not offer sacrifices.'* For I have come to call not those who think they are righteous, but those who know they are sinners."

A Discussion about Fasting

¹⁴One day the disciples of John the Baptist came to Jesus and asked him, "Why don't your disciples fast* like we do and the Pharisees do?"

¹⁵Jesus replied, "Do wedding guests mourn while celebrating with the groom? Of course not. But someday the groom will be taken away from them, and then they will fast.

¹⁶"Besides, who would patch old clothing with new cloth? For the new patch would shrink and rip away from the old cloth, leaving an even bigger tear than before.

¹⁷"And no one puts new wine into old wineskins. For the

9:4 Some manuscripts read *saw.*   9:6 "Son of Man" is a title Jesus used for himself.   9:8 Greek *for giving such authority to human beings.*   9:11 Greek *with tax collectors and sinners?*
9:13 Hos 6:6 (Greek version).   9:14 Some manuscripts read *fast often.*

THE POINT

Jesus chooses folks with issues. Matthew probably had a hard time makin' folks see that Jesus was the promised One—the Messiah. Matthew was the brotha standin' on the corner waitin' to catch peeps and take their cash—why should anyone trust what he said? The point was, Jesus knew Matthew's issues and still chose him.

As Jesus was walkin' along, he saw a man named Matthew sittin' at his tax collector's booth. "'Follow me and be my disciple,' Jesus said to him. So Matthew got up and followed him" (Matthew 9:9).

Later Matthew invited Jesus and the disciples over to his crib for some grub. When the religious folks saw this, they had a fit. They asked the disciples, "Why does your teacher eat with such scum?" (9:11). Jesus peeped their question and snapped on them right then:

"Healthy people don't need a doctor—sick people do . . . Now go and learn the meaning of this Scripture: 'I want you to show mercy, not offer sacrifices.' For I have come to call not those who think they are righteous, but those who know they are sinners." (Matthew 9:12-13)

Jesus was serious about this. He was truly about savin' souls. He knew Matthew was out there in the streets jackin' people. But he also knew Matthew was a brotha out there every day gettin' his hustle on. And even though people didn't particularly like Matthew, they gave him his props. He was just the type of person Jesus could use to spread the Good News of the Kingdom in the hood. Jesus knew that if people saw ole boy Matt on the straight and narrow, they would know somethin' was righteous about this Kingdom stuff.

keeping your swagger strong

BIBLICAL PRINCIPLES FOR SUCCESS AND LEADERSHIP

Success and faith are linked. If you want to succeed, you have to do like Matthew: get up and follow Jesus when he calls. Matthew was a true baller; nothing about him was fake. He was about gettin' paid, and there was no shame in his game. He was probably skimmin' money; we know he was harassin' folks—he did it all. Still, he became the spokesperson that connected, for the Jewish people, the old with the new. The entire book of Matthew is a testimony to his life's work. He was the first one who presented evidence that Jesus was the promised Messiah.

How's your witness? How many folks do you know that would benefit from hearing your story? From hearing Jesus' story? Sometimes the best evidence of God's goodness is to tell someone what happened after Jesus asked you to get up and follow him—and you did. Can you tell the story?

old skins would burst from the pressure, spilling the wine and ruining the skins. New wine is stored in new wineskins so that both are preserved."

Jesus Heals in Response to Faith

[18]As Jesus was saying this, the leader of a synagogue came and knelt before him. "My daughter has just died," he said, "but you can bring her back to life again if you just come and lay your hand on her."

[19]So Jesus and his disciples got up and went with him. [20]Just then a woman who had suffered for twelve years with constant bleeding came up behind him. She touched the fringe of his robe, [21]for she thought, "If I can just touch his robe, I will be healed."

[22]Jesus turned around, and when he saw her he said, "Daughter, be encouraged! Your faith has made you well." And the woman was healed at that moment.

[23]When Jesus arrived at the official's home, he saw the noisy crowd and heard the funeral music. [24]"Get out!" he told them. "The girl isn't dead; she's only asleep." But the crowd laughed at him. [25]After the crowd was put outside, however, Jesus went in and took the girl by the hand, and she stood up! [26]The report of this miracle swept through the entire countryside.

Jesus Heals the Blind

[27]After Jesus left the girl's home, two blind men followed along behind him, shouting, "Son of David, have mercy on us!"

[28]They went right into the house where he was staying, and Jesus asked them, "Do you believe I can make you see?"

"Yes, Lord," they told him, "we do."

[29]Then he touched their eyes and said, "Because of your faith, it will happen." [30]Then their eyes were opened, and they could see! Jesus sternly warned them, "Don't tell anyone about this." [31]But instead, they went out and spread his fame all over the region.

[32]When they left, a demon-possessed man who couldn't speak was brought to Jesus. [33]So Jesus cast out the demon, and then the man began to speak. The crowds were amazed. "Nothing like this has ever happened in Israel!" they exclaimed.

[34]But the Pharisees said, "He can cast out demons because he is empowered by the prince of demons."

The Need for Workers

[35]Jesus traveled through all the towns and villages of that area, teaching in the synagogues and announcing the Good News about the Kingdom. And he healed every kind of disease and illness. [36]When he saw the crowds, he had compassion on them because they were confused and helpless,

like sheep without a shepherd. ³⁷He said to his disciples, "The harvest is great, but the workers are few. ³⁸So pray to the Lord who is in charge of the harvest; ask him to send more workers into his fields."

CHAPTER 10

Jesus Sends Out the Twelve Apostles

Jesus called his twelve disciples together and gave them authority to cast out evil* spirits and to heal every kind of disease and illness. ²Here are the names of the twelve apostles:

first, Simon (also called Peter),
then Andrew (Peter's brother),
James (son of Zebedee),
John (James's brother),
³ Philip,
Bartholomew,
Thomas,
Matthew (the tax collector),
James (son of Alphaeus),
Thaddaeus,*
⁴ Simon (the zealot*),
Judas Iscariot (who later betrayed him).

⁵Jesus sent out the twelve apostles with these instructions: "Don't go to the Gentiles or the Samaritans, ⁶but only to the people of Israel—God's lost sheep. ⁷Go and announce to them that the Kingdom of Heaven is near.* ⁸Heal the sick, raise the dead, cure those with leprosy, and cast out demons. Give as freely as you have received!

⁹"Don't take any money in your money belts—no gold, silver, or even copper coins. ¹⁰Don't carry a traveler's bag with a change of clothes and sandals or even a walking stick. Don't hesitate to accept hospitality, because those who work deserve to be fed.

¹¹"Whenever you enter a city or village, search for a worthy person and stay in his home until you leave town. ¹²When you enter the home, give it your blessing. ¹³If it turns out to be a worthy home, let your blessing stand; if it is not, take back the blessing. ¹⁴If any household or town refuses to welcome you or listen to your message, shake its dust from your feet as you leave. ¹⁵I tell you the truth, the wicked cities of Sodom and Gomorrah will be better off than such a town on the judgment day.

¹⁶"Look, I am sending you out as sheep among wolves. So be as shrewd as snakes and harmless as doves. ¹⁷But beware! For you will be handed over to the courts and will be flogged with whips in the synagogues. ¹⁸You will stand trial before governors and kings because you are my followers. But this will be your opportunity to tell the rulers and other unbelievers about me.* ¹⁹When you are arrested, don't worry about how to respond or what to say. God will give you the right words at the right time. ²⁰For it is not you who will be speaking—it will be the Spirit of your Father speaking through you.

²¹"A brother will betray his brother to death, a father will betray his own child, and children will rebel against their parents and cause them to be killed. ²²And all nations will hate you because you are my followers.* But everyone who endures to the end will be saved. ²³When you are persecuted in one town, flee to the next. I tell you the truth, the Son of Man* will return before you have reached all the towns of Israel.

²⁴"Students* are not greater than their teacher, and slaves are not greater than their master. ²⁵Students are to be like their teacher, and slaves are to be like their master. And since I, the master of the household, have been called the prince of demons,* the members of my household will be called by even worse names!

10:1 Greek *unclean*.   **10:3** Other manuscripts read *Lebbaeus;* still others read *Lebbaeus who is called Thaddaeus.*   **10:4** Greek *the Cananean,* an Aramaic term for Jewish nationalists.   **10:7** Or *has come,* or *is coming soon.*   **10:18** Or *But this will be your testimony against the rulers and other unbelievers.*   **10:22** Greek *on account of my name.*   **10:23** "Son of Man" is a title Jesus used for himself.   **10:24** Or *Disciples.*   **10:25** Greek *Beelzeboul;* other manuscripts read *Beezeboul;* Latin version reads *Beelzebub.*

26"But don't be afraid of those who threaten you. For the time is coming when everything that is covered will be revealed, and all that is secret will be made known to all. 27What I tell you now in the darkness, shout abroad when daybreak comes. What I whisper in your ear, shout from the housetops for all to hear!

28"Don't be afraid of those who want to kill your body; they cannot touch your soul. Fear only God, who can destroy both soul and body in hell.* 29What is the price of two sparrows—one copper coin*? But not a single sparrow can fall to the ground without your Father knowing it. 30And the very hairs on your head are all numbered. 31So don't be afraid; you are more valuable to God than a whole flock of sparrows.

32"Everyone who acknowledges me publicly here on earth, I will also acknowledge before my Father in heaven. 33But everyone who denies me here on earth, I will also deny before my Father in heaven.

34"Don't imagine that I came to bring peace to the earth! I came not to bring peace, but a sword.

35 'I have come to set a man against his father,
    a daughter against her mother,
and a daughter-in-law against her mother-in-law.
36   Your enemies will be right in your own household!'*

37"If you love your father or mother more than you love me, you are not worthy of being mine; or if you love your son or daughter more than me, you are not worthy of being mine. 38If you refuse to take up your cross and follow me, you are not worthy of being mine. 39If you cling to your life, you will lose it; but if you give up your life for me, you will find it.

40"Anyone who receives you receives me, and anyone who receives me receives the Father who sent me. 41If you receive a prophet as one who speaks for God,* you will be given the same reward as a prophet. And if you receive righteous people because of their righteousness, you will be given a reward like theirs. 42And if you give even a cup of cold water to one of the least of my followers, you will surely be rewarded."

CHAPTER 11

Jesus and John the Baptist

When Jesus had finished giving these instructions to his twelve disciples, he went out to teach and preach in towns throughout the region.

2John the Baptist, who was in prison, heard about all the things the Messiah was doing. So he sent his disciples to ask Jesus, 3"Are you the Messiah we've been expecting,* or should we keep looking for someone else?"

4Jesus told them, "Go back to John and tell him what you have heard and seen—5the blind see, the lame walk, the lepers are cured, the deaf hear, the dead are raised to life, and the Good News is being preached to the poor. 6And tell him, 'God blesses those who do not turn away because of me.*'"

7As John's disciples were leaving, Jesus began talking about him to the crowds. "What kind of man did you go into the wilderness to see? Was he a weak reed, swayed by every breath of wind? 8Or were you expecting to see a man dressed in expensive clothes? No, people with expensive clothes live in palaces. 9Were you looking for a prophet? Yes, and he is more than a prophet. 10John is the man to whom the Scriptures refer when they say,

'Look, I am sending my messenger ahead of you,
    and he will prepare your way before you.'*

11"I tell you the truth, of all who have ever lived, none is greater than John the Baptist. Yet even the least person in the Kingdom of Heaven is greater than he is! 12And from the time John the Baptist began preaching until now, the

10:28 Greek Gehenna. 10:29 Greek one assarion [i.e., one "as," a Roman coin equal to 1/16 of a denarius]. 10:35-36 Mic 7:6. 10:41 Greek receive a prophet in the name of a prophet. 11:3 Greek Are you the one who is coming? 11:6 Or who are not offended by me. 11:10 Mal 3:1.

Kingdom of Heaven has been forcefully advancing,* and violent people are attacking it. 13For before John came, all the prophets and the law of Moses looked forward to this present time. 14And if you are willing to accept what I say, he is Elijah, the one the prophets said would come.* 15Anyone with ears to hear should listen and understand!

16"To what can I compare this generation? It is like children playing a game in the public square. They complain to their friends,

17 'We played wedding songs,
    and you didn't dance,
  so we played funeral songs,
    and you didn't mourn.'

18For John didn't spend his time eating and drinking, and you say, 'He's possessed by a demon.' 19The Son of Man,* on the other hand, feasts and drinks, and you say, 'He's a glutton and a drunkard, and a friend of tax collectors and other sinners!' But wisdom is shown to be right by its results."

Judgment for the Unbelievers

20Then Jesus began to denounce the towns where he had done so many of his miracles, because they hadn't repented of their sins and turned to God. 21"What sorrow awaits you, Korazin and Bethsaida! For if the miracles I did in you had been done in wicked Tyre and Sidon, their people would have repented of their sins long ago, clothing themselves in burlap and throwing ashes on their heads to show their remorse. 22I tell you, Tyre and Sidon will be better off on judgment day than you.

23"And you people of Capernaum, will you be honored in heaven? No, you will go down to the place of the dead.* For if the miracles I did for you had been done in wicked Sodom, it would still be here today. 24I tell you, even Sodom will be better off on judgment day than you."

Jesus' Prayer of Thanksgiving

25At that time Jesus prayed this prayer: O Father, Lord of heaven and earth, thank you for hiding these things from those who think themselves wise and clever, and for revealing them to the childlike. 26Yes, Father, it pleased you to do it this way!

27"My Father has entrusted everything to me. No one truly knows the Son except the Father, and no one truly knows the Father except the Son and those to whom the Son chooses to reveal him.

28Then Jesus said, "Come to me, all of you who are weary and carry heavy burdens, and I will give you rest. 29Take my yoke upon you. Let me teach you, because I am humble and gentle at heart, and you will find rest for your souls. 30For my yoke is easy to bear, and the burden I give you is light."

CHAPTER 12

A Discussion about the Sabbath

At about that time Jesus was walking through some grainfields on the Sabbath. His disciples were hungry, so they began breaking off some heads of grain and eating them. 2But some Pharisees saw them do it and protested, "Look, your disciples are breaking the law by harvesting grain on the Sabbath."

3Jesus said to them, "Haven't you read in the Scriptures what David did when he and his companions were hungry? 4He went into the house of God, and he and his companions broke the law by eating the sacred loaves of bread that only the priests are allowed to eat. 5And haven't you read in the law of Moses that the priests on duty in the Temple may work on the Sabbath? 6I tell you, there is one here who is even greater than the Temple! 7But you would not have condemned my innocent disciples if you knew the meaning of this Scripture: 'I want you to show mercy, not offer sacrifices.'* 8For the Son of Man* is Lord, even over the Sabbath!"

"Come to me, all of you who are weary and carry heavy burdens, and I will give you rest. Take my yoke upon you. Let me teach you, because I am humble and gentle at heart, and you will find rest for your souls" (Matthew 11:28-29).

say what?

If you are faced with hardship, trade your troubles for God's troubles because his load is lighter. You'll learn that his heart is gentle, and your soul will be able to rest.

11:12 Or the Kingdom of Heaven has suffered from violence.   11:14 See Mal 4:5.   11:19 "Son of Man" is a title Jesus used for himself.   11:23 Greek to Hades.   12:7 Hos 6:6 (Greek version).
12:8 "Son of Man" is a title Jesus used for himself.

Jesus Heals on the Sabbath

[9]Then Jesus went over to their synagogue, [10]where he noticed a man with a deformed hand. The Pharisees asked Jesus, "Does the law permit a person to work by healing on the Sabbath?" (They were hoping he would say yes, so they could bring charges against him.)

[11]And he answered, "If you had a sheep that fell into a well on the Sabbath, wouldn't you work to pull it out? Of course you would. [12]And how much more valuable is a person than a sheep! Yes, the law permits a person to do good on the Sabbath."

[13]Then he said to the man, "Hold out your hand." So the man held out his hand, and it was restored, just like the other one! [14]Then the Pharisees called a meeting to plot how to kill Jesus.

Jesus, God's Chosen Servant

[15]But Jesus knew what they were planning. So he left that area, and many people followed him. He healed all the sick among them, [16]but he warned them not to reveal who he was. [17]This fulfilled the prophecy of Isaiah concerning him:

[18] "Look at my Servant, whom I have chosen.
   He is my Beloved, who pleases me.
 I will put my Spirit upon him,
   and he will proclaim justice to the nations.
[19] He will not fight or shout
   or raise his voice in public.
[20] He will not crush the weakest reed
   or put out a flickering candle.
   Finally he will cause justice to be victorious.
[21] And his name will be the hope
   of all the world."*

Jesus and the Prince of Demons

[22]Then a demon-possessed man, who was blind and couldn't speak, was brought to Jesus. He healed the man so that he could both speak and see. [23]The crowd was amazed and asked, "Could it be that Jesus is the Son of David, the Messiah?"

[24]But when the Pharisees heard about the miracle, they said, "No wonder he can cast out demons. He gets his power from Satan,* the prince of demons."

[25]Jesus knew their thoughts and replied, "Any kingdom divided by civil war is doomed. A town or family splintered by feuding will fall apart. [26]And if Satan is casting out Satan, he is divided and fighting against himself. His own kingdom will not survive. [27]And if I am empowered by Satan, what about your own exorcists? They cast out demons, too, so they will condemn you for what you have said. [28]But if I am casting out demons by the Spirit of God, then the Kingdom of God has arrived among you. [29]For who is powerful enough to enter the house of a strong man like Satan and plunder his goods? Only someone even stronger—someone who could tie him up and then plunder his house.

[30]"Anyone who isn't with me opposes me, and anyone who isn't working with me is actually working against me.

[31]"So I tell you, every sin and blasphemy can be forgiven—except blasphemy against the Holy Spirit, which will never be forgiven. [32]Anyone who speaks against the Son of Man can be forgiven, but anyone who speaks against the Holy Spirit will never be forgiven, either in this world or in the world to come.

[33]"A tree is identified by its fruit. If a tree is good, its fruit will be good. If a tree is bad, its fruit will be bad. [34]You brood of snakes! How could evil men like you speak what is good and right? For whatever is in your heart determines what you say. [35]A good person produces good things from the treasury of a good heart, and an evil person produces evil things from the treasury of an evil heart. [36]And I tell you this, you must give an account on judgment day for every idle word you speak. [37]The words you say will either acquit you or condemn you."

"And I tell you this, you must give an account on judgment day for every idle word you speak" (Matthew 12:36).

say what?

On the day of judgment, you will have to fess up to anything you said that was meaningless.

12:18-21 Isa 42:1-4 (Greek version for 42:4).   12:24 Greek *Beelzeboul;* also in 12:27. Other manuscripts read *Beezeboul;* Latin version reads *Beelzebub.*

The Sign of Jonah

[38] One day some teachers of religious law and Pharisees came to Jesus and said, "Teacher, we want you to show us a miraculous sign to prove your authority."

[39] But Jesus replied, "Only an evil, adulterous generation would demand a miraculous sign; but the only sign I will give them is the sign of the prophet Jonah. [40] For as Jonah was in the belly of the great fish for three days and three nights, so will the Son of Man be in the heart of the earth for three days and three nights.

[41] "The people of Nineveh will stand up against this generation on judgment day and condemn it, for they repented of their sins at the preaching of Jonah. Now someone greater than Jonah is here—but you refuse to repent. [42] The queen of Sheba* will also stand up against this generation on judgment day and condemn it, for she came from a distant land to hear the wisdom of Solomon. Now someone greater than Solomon is here—but you refuse to listen.

[43] "When an evil* spirit leaves a person, it goes into the desert, seeking rest but finding none. [44] Then it says, 'I will return to the person I came from.' So it returns and finds its former home empty, swept, and in order. [45] Then the spirit finds seven other spirits more evil than itself, and they all enter the person and live there. And so that person is worse off than before. That will be the experience of this evil generation."

The True Family of Jesus

[46] As Jesus was speaking to the crowd, his mother and brothers stood outside, asking to speak to him. [47] Someone told Jesus, "Your mother and your brothers are outside, and they want to speak to you."*

[48] Jesus asked, "Who is my mother? Who are my brothers?" [49] Then he pointed to his disciples and said, "Look, these are my mother and brothers. [50] Anyone who does the will of my Father in heaven is my brother and sister and mother!"

CHAPTER 13

Parable of the Farmer Scattering Seed

Later that same day Jesus left the house and sat beside the lake. [2] A large crowd soon gathered around him, so he got into a boat. Then he sat there and taught as the people stood on the shore. [3] He told many stories in the form of parables, such as this one:

"Listen! A farmer went out to plant some seeds. [4] As he scattered them across his field, some seeds fell on a footpath, and the birds came and ate them. [5] Other seeds fell on shallow soil with underlying rock. The seeds sprouted quickly because the soil was shallow. [6] But the plants soon wilted under the hot sun, and since they didn't have deep roots, they died. [7] Other seeds fell among thorns that grew up and choked out the tender plants. [8] Still other seeds fell on fertile soil, and they produced a crop that was thirty, sixty, and even a hundred times as much as had been planted! [9] Anyone with ears to hear should listen and understand."

[10] His disciples came and asked him, "Why do you use parables when you talk to the people?"

[11] He replied, "You are permitted to understand the secrets* of the Kingdom of Heaven, but others are not. [12] To those who listen to my teaching, more understanding will be given, and they will have an abundance of knowledge. But for those who are not listening, even what little understanding they have will be taken away from them. [13] That is why I use these parables,

For they look, but they don't really see.
They hear, but they don't really listen or understand.

[14] This fulfills the prophecy of Isaiah that says,

'When you hear what I say,
   you will not understand.
When you see what I do,
   you will not comprehend.

12:42 Greek *The queen of the south.*   12:43 Greek *unclean.*   12:47 Some manuscripts do not include verse 47. Compare Mark 3:32 and Luke 8:20.   13:11 Greek *the mysteries.*

15 For the hearts of these people are hardened,
 and their ears cannot hear,
and they have closed their eyes—
 so their eyes cannot see,
and their ears cannot hear,
 and their hearts cannot understand,
and they cannot turn to me
 and let me heal them.'*

16"But blessed are your eyes, because they see; and your ears, because they hear. 17I tell you the truth, many prophets and righteous people longed to see what you see, but they didn't see it. And they longed to hear what you hear, but they didn't hear it.

18"Now listen to the explanation of the parable about the farmer planting seeds: 19The seed that fell on the footpath represents those who hear the message about the Kingdom and don't understand it. Then the evil one comes and snatches away the seed that was planted in their hearts. 20The seed on the rocky soil represents those who hear the message and immediately receive it with joy. 21But since they don't have deep roots, they don't last long. They fall away as soon as they have problems or are persecuted for believing God's word. 22The seed that fell among the thorns represents those who hear God's word, but all too quickly the message is crowded out by the worries of this life and the lure of wealth, so no fruit is produced. 23The seed that fell on good soil represents those who truly hear and understand God's word and produce a harvest of thirty, sixty, or even a hundred times as much as had been planted!"

Parable of the Wheat and Weeds
24Here is another story Jesus told: "The Kingdom of Heaven is like a farmer who planted good seed in his field. 25But that night as the workers slept, his enemy came and planted weeds among the wheat, then slipped away.

26When the crop began to grow and produce grain, the weeds also grew.

27"The farmer's workers went to him and said, 'Sir, the field where you planted that good seed is full of weeds! Where did they come from?'

28"'An enemy has done this!' the farmer exclaimed.

"'Should we pull out the weeds?' they asked.

29"'No,' he replied, 'you'll uproot the wheat if you do. 30Let both grow together until the harvest. Then I will tell the harvesters to sort out the weeds, tie them into bundles, and burn them, and to put the wheat in the barn.'"

Parable of the Mustard Seed
31Here is another illustration Jesus used: "The Kingdom of Heaven is like a mustard seed planted in a field. 32It is the smallest of all seeds, but it becomes the largest of garden plants; it grows into a tree, and birds come and make nests in its branches."

Parable of the Yeast
33Jesus also used this illustration: "The Kingdom of Heaven is like the yeast a woman used in making bread. Even though she put only a little yeast in three measures of flour, it permeated every part of the dough."

34Jesus always used stories and illustrations like these when speaking to the crowds. In fact, he never spoke to them without using such parables. 35This fulfilled what God had spoken through the prophet:

"I will speak to you in parables.
 I will explain things hidden since the creation of the world.*"

Parable of the Wheat and Weeds Explained
36Then, leaving the crowds outside, Jesus went into the house. His disciples said, "Please explain to us the story of the weeds in the field."

13:14-15 Isa 6:9-10 (Greek version). 13:35 Some manuscripts do not include *of the world*. Ps 78:2.

37Jesus replied, "The Son of Man* is the farmer who plants the good seed. 38The field is the world, and the good seed represents the people of the Kingdom. The weeds are the people who belong to the evil one. 39The enemy who planted the weeds among the wheat is the devil. The harvest is the end of the world,* and the harvesters are the angels.

40"Just as the weeds are sorted out and burned in the fire, so it will be at the end of the world. 41The Son of Man will send his angels, and they will remove from his Kingdom everything that causes sin and all who do evil. 42And the angels will throw them into the fiery furnace, where there will be weeping and gnashing of teeth. 43Then the righteous will shine like the sun in their Father's Kingdom. Anyone with ears to hear should listen and understand!

Parables of the Hidden Treasure and the Pearl

44"The Kingdom of Heaven is like a treasure that a man discovered hidden in a field. In his excitement, he hid it again and sold everything he owned to get enough money to buy the field.

45"Again, the Kingdom of Heaven is like a merchant on the lookout for choice pearls. 46When he discovered a pearl of great value, he sold everything he owned and bought it!

Parable of the Fishing Net

47"Again, the Kingdom of Heaven is like a fishing net that was thrown into the water and caught fish of every kind. 48When the net was full, they dragged it up onto the shore, sat down, and sorted the good fish into crates, but threw the bad ones away. 49That is the way it will be at the end of the world. The angels will come and separate the wicked people from the righteous, 50throwing the wicked into the fiery furnace, where there will be weeping and gnashing of teeth. 51Do you understand all these things?"

"Yes," they said, "we do."

52Then he added, "Every teacher of religious law who becomes a disciple in the Kingdom of Heaven is like a homeowner who brings from his storeroom new gems of truth as well as old."

Jesus Rejected at Nazareth

53When Jesus had finished telling these stories and illustrations, he left that part of the country. 54He returned to Nazareth, his hometown. When he taught there in the synagogue, everyone was amazed and said, "Where does he get this wisdom and the power to do miracles?" 55Then they scoffed, "He's just the carpenter's son, and we know Mary, his mother, and his brothers—James, Joseph,* Simon, and Judas. 56All his sisters live right here among us. Where did he learn all these things?" 57And they were deeply offended and refused to believe in him.

Then Jesus told them, "A prophet is honored everywhere except in his own hometown and among his own family." 58And so he did only a few miracles there because of their unbelief.

CHAPTER 14

The Death of John the Baptist

When Herod Antipas, the ruler of Galilee,* heard about Jesus, 2he said to his advisers, "This must be John the Baptist raised from the dead! That is why he can do such miracles."

3For Herod had arrested and imprisoned John as a favor to his wife Herodias (the former wife of Herod's brother Philip). 4John had been telling Herod, "It is against God's law for you to marry her." 5Herod wanted to kill John, but he was afraid of a riot, because all the people believed John was a prophet.

6But at a birthday party for Herod, Herodias's daughter performed a dance that greatly pleased him, 7so he prom-

13:37 "Son of Man" is a title Jesus used for himself.   **13:39** Or *the age;* also in 13:40, 49.   **13:55** Other manuscripts read *Joses;* still others read *John.*   **14:1** Greek *Herod the tetrarch.* Herod Antipas was a son of King Herod and was ruler over Galilee.

ised with a vow to give her anything she wanted. ⁸At her mother's urging, the girl said, "I want the head of John the Baptist on a tray!" ⁹Then the king regretted what he had said; but because of the vow he had made in front of his guests, he issued the necessary orders. ¹⁰So John was beheaded in the prison, ¹¹and his head was brought on a tray and given to the girl, who took it to her mother. ¹²Later, John's disciples came for his body and buried it. Then they went and told Jesus what had happened.

Jesus Feeds Five Thousand

¹³As soon as Jesus heard the news, he left in a boat to a remote area to be alone. But the crowds heard where he was headed and followed on foot from many towns. ¹⁴Jesus saw the huge crowd as he stepped from the boat, and he had compassion on them and healed their sick.

¹⁵That evening the disciples came to him and said, "This is a remote place, and it's already getting late. Send the crowds away so they can go to the villages and buy food for themselves."

¹⁶But Jesus said, "That isn't necessary—you feed them."

¹⁷"But we have only five loaves of bread and two fish!" they answered.

¹⁸"Bring them here," he said. ¹⁹Then he told the people to sit down on the grass. Jesus took the five loaves and two fish, looked up toward heaven, and blessed them. Then, breaking the loaves into pieces, he gave the bread to the disciples, who distributed it to the people. ²⁰They all ate as much as they wanted, and afterward, the disciples picked up twelve baskets of leftovers. ²¹About 5,000 men were fed that day, in addition to all the women and children!

Jesus Walks on Water

²²Immediately after this, Jesus insisted that his disciples get back into the boat and cross to the other side of the lake, while he sent the people home. ²³After sending them home, he went up into the hills by himself to pray. Night fell while he was there alone.

²⁴Meanwhile, the disciples were in trouble far away from land, for a strong wind had risen, and they were fighting heavy waves. ²⁵About three o'clock in the morning* Jesus came toward them, walking on the water. ²⁶When the disciples saw him walking on the water, they were terrified. In their fear, they cried out, "It's a ghost!"

²⁷But Jesus spoke to them at once. "Don't be afraid," he said. "Take courage. I am here!*"

²⁸Then Peter called to him, "Lord, if it's really you, tell me to come to you, walking on the water."

²⁹"Yes, come," Jesus said.

So Peter went over the side of the boat and walked on the water toward Jesus. ³⁰But when he saw the strong* wind and the waves, he was terrified and began to sink. "Save me, Lord!" he shouted.

³¹Jesus immediately reached out and grabbed him. "You have so little faith," Jesus said. "Why did you doubt me?"

³²When they climbed back into the boat, the wind stopped. ³³Then the disciples worshiped him. "You really are the Son of God!" they exclaimed.

³⁴After they had crossed the lake, they landed at Gennesaret. ³⁵When the people recognized Jesus, the news of his arrival spread quickly throughout the whole area, and soon people were bringing all their sick to be healed. ³⁶They begged him to let the sick touch at least the fringe of his robe, and all who touched him were healed.

CHAPTER 15

Jesus Teaches about Inner Purity

Some Pharisees and teachers of religious law now arrived from Jerusalem to see Jesus. They asked him, ²"Why do your disciples disobey our age-old tradition? For they ignore our tradition of ceremonial hand washing before they eat."

"Then Peter called to him, 'Lord, if it's really you, tell me to come to you, walking on the water.' 'Yes, come,' Jesus said" (Matthew 14:28-29).

Then Peter said to Jesus, "Lord, if you are real, tell me to walk to you on the water." Jesus told him, "Come on!"

14:25 Greek *In the fourth watch of the night.*   **14:27** Or *The 'I AM' is here;* Greek reads *I am.* See Exod 3:14.   **14:30** Some manuscripts do not include *strong.*

³Jesus replied, "And why do you, by your traditions, violate the direct commandments of God? ⁴For instance, God says, 'Honor your father and mother,'* and 'Anyone who speaks disrespectfully of father or mother must be put to death.'* ⁵But you say it is all right for people to say to their parents, 'Sorry, I can't help you. For I have vowed to give to God what I would have given to you.' ⁶In this way, you say they don't need to honor their parents.* And so you cancel the word of God for the sake of your own tradition. ⁷You hypocrites! Isaiah was right when he prophesied about you, for he wrote,

⁸ 'These people honor me with their lips,
    but their hearts are far from me.
⁹ Their worship is a farce,
    for they teach man-made ideas as commands from
        God.'*"

¹⁰Then Jesus called to the crowd to come and hear. "Listen," he said, "and try to understand. ¹¹It's not what goes into your mouth that defiles you; you are defiled by the words that come out of your mouth."

¹²Then the disciples came to him and asked, "Do you realize you offended the Pharisees by what you just said?"

¹³Jesus replied, "Every plant not planted by my heavenly Father will be uprooted, ¹⁴so ignore them. They are blind guides leading the blind, and if one blind person guides another, they will both fall into a ditch."

¹⁵Then Peter said to Jesus, "Explain to us the parable that says people aren't defiled by what they eat."

¹⁶"Don't you understand yet?" Jesus asked. ¹⁷"Anything you eat passes through the stomach and then goes into the sewer. ¹⁸But the words you speak come from the heart—that's what defiles you. ¹⁹For from the heart come evil thoughts, murder, adultery, all sexual immorality, theft, lying, and slander. ²⁰These are what defile you. Eating with unwashed hands will never defile you."

The Faith of a Gentile Woman

²¹Then Jesus left Galilee and went north to the region of Tyre and Sidon. ²²A Gentile* woman who lived there came to him, pleading, "Have mercy on me, O Lord, Son of David! For my daughter is possessed by a demon that torments her severely."

²³But Jesus gave her no reply, not even a word. Then his disciples urged him to send her away. "Tell her to go away," they said. "She is bothering us with all her begging."

²⁴Then Jesus said to the woman, "I was sent only to help God's lost sheep—the people of Israel."

²⁵But she came and worshiped him, pleading again, "Lord, help me!"

²⁶Jesus responded, "It isn't right to take food from the children and throw it to the dogs."

²⁷She replied, "That's true, Lord, but even dogs are allowed to eat the scraps that fall beneath their masters' table."

²⁸"Dear woman," Jesus said to her, "your faith is great. Your request is granted." And her daughter was instantly healed.

Jesus Heals Many People

²⁹Jesus returned to the Sea of Galilee and climbed a hill and sat down. ³⁰A vast crowd brought to him people who were lame, blind, crippled, those who couldn't speak, and many others. They laid them before Jesus, and he healed them all. ³¹The crowd was amazed! Those who hadn't been able to speak were talking, the crippled were made well, the lame were walking, and the blind could see again! And they praised the God of Israel.

Jesus Feeds Four Thousand

³²Then Jesus called his disciples and told them, "I feel sorry for these people. They have been here with me for three days, and they have nothing left to eat. I don't want to send them away hungry, or they will faint along the way."

15:4a Exod 20:12; Deut 5:16.   **15:4b** Exod 21:17 (Greek version); Lev 20:9 (Greek version).   **15:6** Greek *their father;* other manuscripts read *their father or their mother.*   **15:8-9** Isa 29:13 (Greek version).   **15:22** Greek *Canaanite.*

³³The disciples replied, "Where would we get enough food here in the wilderness for such a huge crowd?"

³⁴Jesus asked, "How much bread do you have?"

They replied, "Seven loaves, and a few small fish."

³⁵So Jesus told all the people to sit down on the ground. ³⁶Then he took the seven loaves and the fish, thanked God for them, and broke them into pieces. He gave them to the disciples, who distributed the food to the crowd.

³⁷They all ate as much as they wanted. Afterward, the disciples picked up seven large baskets of leftover food. ³⁸There were 4,000 men who were fed that day, in addition to all the women and children. ³⁹Then Jesus sent the people home, and he got into a boat and crossed over to the region of Magadan.

CHAPTER 16
Leaders Demand a Miraculous Sign

One day the Pharisees and Sadducees came to test Jesus, demanding that he show them a miraculous sign from heaven to prove his authority.

²He replied, "You know the saying, 'Red sky at night means fair weather tomorrow; ³red sky in the morning means foul weather all day.' You know how to interpret the weather signs in the sky, but you don't know how to interpret the signs of the times!* ⁴Only an evil, adulterous generation would demand a miraculous sign, but the only sign I will give them is the sign of the prophet Jonah.*" Then Jesus left them and went away.

Yeast of the Pharisees and Sadducees

⁵Later, after they crossed to the other side of the lake, the disciples discovered they had forgotten to bring any bread. ⁶"Watch out!" Jesus warned them. "Beware of the yeast of the Pharisees and Sadducees."

⁷At this they began to argue with each other because they hadn't brought any bread. ⁸Jesus knew what they were saying, so he said, "You have so little faith! Why are you arguing with each other about having no bread? ⁹Don't you understand even yet? Don't you remember the 5,000 I fed with five loaves, and the baskets of leftovers you picked up? ¹⁰Or the 4,000 I fed with seven loaves, and the large baskets of leftovers you picked up? ¹¹Why can't you understand that I'm not talking about bread? So again I say, 'Beware of the yeast of the Pharisees and Sadducees.'"

¹²Then at last they understood that he wasn't speaking about the yeast in bread, but about the deceptive teaching of the Pharisees and Sadducees.

Peter's Declaration about Jesus

¹³When Jesus came to the region of Caesarea Philippi, he asked his disciples, "Who do people say that the Son of Man is?"*

¹⁴"Well," they replied, "some say John the Baptist, some say Elijah, and others say Jeremiah or one of the other prophets."

¹⁵Then he asked them, "But who do you say I am?"

¹⁶Simon Peter answered, "You are the Messiah,* the Son of the living God."

¹⁷Jesus replied, "You are blessed, Simon son of John,* because my Father in heaven has revealed this to you. You did not learn this from any human being. ¹⁸Now I say to you that you are Peter (which means 'rock'),* and upon this rock I will build my church, and all the powers of hell* will not conquer it. ¹⁹And I will give you the keys of the Kingdom of Heaven. Whatever you forbid* on earth will be forbidden in heaven, and whatever you permit* on earth will be permitted in heaven."

²⁰Then he sternly warned the disciples not to tell anyone that he was the Messiah.

16:2-3 Several manuscripts do not include any of the words in 16:2-3 after *He replied.*   16:4 Greek *the sign of Jonah.*   16:13 "Son of Man" is a title Jesus used for himself.   16:16 Or *the Christ. Messiah* (a Hebrew term) and *Christ* (a Greek term) both mean "the anointed one."   16:17 Greek *Simon bar-Jonah;* see John 1:42; 21:15-17.   16:18a Greek *that you are Peter.*   16:18b Greek *and the gates of Hades.*   16:19a Or *bind,* or *lock.*   16:19b Or *loose,* or *open.*

Jesus Predicts His Death

²¹From then on Jesus* began to tell his disciples plainly that it was necessary for him to go to Jerusalem, and that he would suffer many terrible things at the hands of the elders, the leading priests, and the teachers of religious law. He would be killed, but on the third day he would be raised from the dead.

²²But Peter took him aside and began to reprimand him* for saying such things. "Heaven forbid, Lord," he said. "This will never happen to you!"

²³Jesus turned to Peter and said, "Get away from me, Satan! You are a dangerous trap to me. You are seeing things merely from a human point of view, not from God's."

²⁴Then Jesus said to his disciples, "If any of you wants to be my follower, you must turn from your selfish ways, take up your cross, and follow me. ²⁵If you try to hang on to your life, you will lose it. But if you give up your life for my sake, you will save it. ²⁶And what do you benefit if you gain the whole world but lose your own soul?* Is anything worth more than your soul? ²⁷For the Son of Man will come with his angels in the glory of his Father and will judge all people according to their deeds. ²⁸And I tell you the truth, some standing here right now will not die before they see the Son of Man coming in his Kingdom."

CHAPTER 17

The Transfiguration

Six days later Jesus took Peter and the two brothers, James and John, and led them up a high mountain to be alone. ²As the men watched, Jesus' appearance was transformed so that his face shone like the sun, and his clothes became as white as light. ³Suddenly, Moses and Elijah appeared and began talking with Jesus.

⁴Peter exclaimed, "Lord, it's wonderful for us to be here! If you want, I'll make three shelters as memorials*—one for you, one for Moses, and one for Elijah."

⁵But even as he spoke, a bright cloud overshadowed them, and a voice from the cloud said, "This is my dearly loved Son, who brings me great joy. Listen to him." ⁶The disciples were terrified and fell face down on the ground.

⁷Then Jesus came over and touched them. "Get up," he said. "Don't be afraid." ⁸And when they looked up, Moses and Elijah were gone, and they saw only Jesus.

⁹As they went back down the mountain, Jesus commanded them, "Don't tell anyone what you have seen until the Son of Man* has been raised from the dead."

¹⁰Then his disciples asked him, "Why do the teachers of religious law insist that Elijah must return before the Messiah comes?*"

¹¹Jesus replied, "Elijah is indeed coming first to get everything ready. ¹²But I tell you, Elijah has already come, but he wasn't recognized, and they chose to abuse him. And in the same way they will also make the Son of Man suffer." ¹³Then the disciples realized he was talking about John the Baptist.

Jesus Heals a Demon-Possessed Boy

¹⁴At the foot of the mountain, a large crowd was waiting for them. A man came and knelt before Jesus and said, ¹⁵"Lord, have mercy on my son. He has seizures and suffers terribly. He often falls into the fire or into the water. ¹⁶So I brought him to your disciples, but they couldn't heal him."

¹⁷Jesus said, "You faithless and corrupt people! How long must I be with you? How long must I put up with you? Bring the boy here to me." ¹⁸Then Jesus rebuked the demon in the boy, and it left him. From that moment the boy was well.

¹⁹Afterward the disciples asked Jesus privately, "Why couldn't we cast out that demon?"

²⁰"You don't have enough faith," Jesus told them. "I tell you the truth, if you had faith even as small as a mustard

16:21 Some manuscripts read *Jesus the Messiah.*   16:22 Or *began to correct him.*   16:26 Or *your self?* also in 16:26b.   17:4 Greek *three tabernacles.*   17:9 "Son of Man" is a title Jesus used for himself.   17:10 Greek *that Elijah must come first?*

seed, you could say to this mountain, 'Move from here to there,' and it would move. Nothing would be impossible.*"

Jesus Again Predicts His Death

²²After they gathered again in Galilee, Jesus told them, "The Son of Man is going to be betrayed into the hands of his enemies. ²³He will be killed, but on the third day he will be raised from the dead." And the disciples were filled with grief.

Payment of the Temple Tax

²⁴On their arrival in Capernaum, the collectors of the Temple tax* came to Peter and asked him, "Doesn't your teacher pay the Temple tax?"

²⁵"Yes, he does," Peter replied. Then he went into the house.

But before he had a chance to speak, Jesus asked him, "What do you think, Peter?* Do kings tax their own people or the people they have conquered?*"

²⁶"They tax the people they have conquered," Peter replied.

"Well, then," Jesus said, "the citizens are free! ²⁷However, we don't want to offend them, so go down to the lake and throw in a line. Open the mouth of the first fish you catch, and you will find a large silver coin.* Take it and pay the tax for both of us."

CHAPTER 18

The Greatest in the Kingdom

About that time the disciples came to Jesus and asked, "Who is greatest in the Kingdom of Heaven?"

²Jesus called a little child to him and put the child among them. ³Then he said, "I tell you the truth, unless you turn from your sins and become like little children, you will never get into the Kingdom of Heaven. ⁴So anyone who becomes as humble as this little child is the greatest in the Kingdom of Heaven.

⁵"And anyone who welcomes a little child like this on my behalf* is welcoming me. ⁶But if you cause one of these little ones who trusts in me to fall into sin, it would be better for you to have a large millstone tied around your neck and be drowned in the depths of the sea.

⁷"What sorrow awaits the world, because it tempts people to sin. Temptations are inevitable, but what sorrow awaits the person who does the tempting. ⁸So if your hand or foot causes you to sin, cut it off and throw it away. It's better to enter eternal life with only one hand or one foot than to be thrown into eternal fire with both of your hands and feet. ⁹And if your eye causes you to sin, gouge it out and throw it away. It's better to enter eternal life with only one eye than to have two eyes and be thrown into the fire of hell.*

¹⁰"Beware that you don't look down on any of these little ones. For I tell you that in heaven their angels are always in the presence of my heavenly Father.*

Parable of the Lost Sheep

¹²"If a man has a hundred sheep and one of them wanders away, what will he do? Won't he leave the ninety-nine others on the hills and go out to search for the one that is lost? ¹³And if he finds it, I tell you the truth, he will rejoice over it more than over the ninety-nine that didn't wander away! ¹⁴In the same way, it is not my heavenly Father's will that even one of these little ones should perish.

Correcting Another Believer

¹⁵"If another believer* sins against you,* go privately and point out the offense. If the other person listens and confesses it, you have won that person back. ¹⁶But if you are

17:20 Some manuscripts add verse 21, *But this kind of demon won't leave except by prayer and fasting.* Compare Mark 9:29.   17:24 Greek *the two-drachma [tax];* also in 17:24b. See Exod 30:13-16; Neh 10:32-33.   17:25a Greek *Simon?*   17:25b Greek *their sons or others?*   17:27 Greek *a stater* [a Greek coin equivalent to four drachmas].   18:5 Greek *in my name.*   18:9 Greek *the Gehenna of fire.*   18:10 Some manuscripts add verse 11, *And the Son of Man came to save those who are lost.* Compare Luke 19:10.   18:15a Greek *If your brother.*   18:15b Some manuscripts do not include *against you.*

unsuccessful, take one or two others with you and go back again, so that everything you say may be confirmed by two or three witnesses. [17]If the person still refuses to listen, take your case to the church. Then if he or she won't accept the church's decision, treat that person as a pagan or a corrupt tax collector.

[18]"I tell you the truth, whatever you forbid* on earth will be forbidden in heaven, and whatever you permit* on earth will be permitted in heaven.

[19]"I also tell you this: If two of you agree here on earth concerning anything you ask, my Father in heaven will do it for you. [20]For where two or three gather together as my followers,* I am there among them."

Parable of the Unforgiving Debtor

[21]Then Peter came to him and asked, "Lord, how often should I forgive someone* who sins against me? Seven times?"

[22]"No, not seven times," Jesus replied, "but seventy times seven!*

[23]"Therefore, the Kingdom of Heaven can be compared to a king who decided to bring his accounts up to date with servants who had borrowed money from him. [24]In the process, one of his debtors was brought in who owed him millions of dollars.* [25]He couldn't pay, so his master ordered that he be sold—along with his wife, his children, and everything he owned—to pay the debt.

[26]"But the man fell down before his master and begged him, 'Please, be patient with me, and I will pay it all.' [27]Then his master was filled with pity for him, and he released him and forgave his debt.

[28]"But when the man left the king, he went to a fellow servant who owed him a few thousand dollars.* He grabbed him by the throat and demanded instant payment.

[29]"His fellow servant fell down before him and begged for a little more time. 'Be patient with me, and I will pay it,' he pleaded. [30]But his creditor wouldn't wait. He had the man arrested and put in prison until the debt could be paid in full.

[31]"When some of the other servants saw this, they were very upset. They went to the king and told him everything that had happened. [32]Then the king called in the man he had forgiven and said, 'You evil servant! I forgave you that tremendous debt because you pleaded with me. [33]Shouldn't you have mercy on your fellow servant, just as I had mercy on you?' [34]Then the angry king sent the man to prison to be tortured until he had paid his entire debt.

[35]"That's what my heavenly Father will do to you if you refuse to forgive your brothers and sisters* from your heart."

CHAPTER **19**

Discussion about Divorce and Marriage

When Jesus had finished saying these things, he left Galilee and went down to the region of Judea east of the Jordan River. [2]Large crowds followed him there, and he healed their sick.

[3]Some Pharisees came and tried to trap him with this question: "Should a man be allowed to divorce his wife for just any reason?"

[4]"Haven't you read the Scriptures?" Jesus replied. "They record that from the beginning 'God made them male and female.'* [5]And he said, 'This explains why a man leaves his father and mother and is joined to his wife, and the two are united into one.'* [6]Since they are no longer two but one, let no one split apart what God has joined together."

[7]"Then why did Moses say in the law that a man could give his wife a written notice of divorce and send her away?"* they asked.

[8]Jesus replied, "Moses permitted divorce only as a concession to your hard hearts, but it was not what God had

18:18a Or *bind,* or *lock.*   **18:18b** Or *loose,* or *open.*   **18:20** Greek *gather together in my name.*   **18:21** Greek *my brother.*   **18:22** Or *seventy-seven times.*   **18:24** Greek *10,000 talents* [375 tons or 340 metric tons of silver].   **18:28** Greek *100 denarii.* A denarius was equivalent to a laborer's full day's wage.   **18:35** Greek *your brother.*   **19:4** Gen 1:27; 5:2.   **19:5** Gen 2:24. **19:7** See Deut 24:1.

originally intended. ⁹And I tell you this, whoever divorces his wife and marries someone else commits adultery—unless his wife has been unfaithful.*"

¹⁰Jesus' disciples then said to him, "If this is the case, it is better not to marry!"

¹¹"Not everyone can accept this statement," Jesus said. "Only those whom God helps. ¹²Some are born as eunuchs, some have been made eunuchs by others, and some choose not to marry* for the sake of the Kingdom of Heaven. Let anyone accept this who can."

Jesus Blesses the Children

¹³One day some parents brought their children to Jesus so he could lay his hands on them and pray for them. But the disciples scolded the parents for bothering him.

¹⁴But Jesus said, "Let the children come to me. Don't stop them! For the Kingdom of Heaven belongs to those who are like these children." ¹⁵And he placed his hands on their heads and blessed them before he left.

The Rich Man

¹⁶Someone came to Jesus with this question: "Teacher,* what good deed must I do to have eternal life?"

¹⁷"Why ask me about what is good?" Jesus replied. "There is only One who is good. But to answer your question—if you want to receive eternal life, keep* the commandments."

¹⁸"Which ones?" the man asked.

And Jesus replied: "'You must not murder. You must not commit adultery. You must not steal. You must not testify falsely. ¹⁹Honor your father and mother. Love your neighbor as yourself.'*"

²⁰"I've obeyed all these commandments," the young man replied. "What else must I do?"

²¹Jesus told him, "If you want to be perfect, go and sell all your possessions and give the money to the poor, and you will have treasure in heaven. Then come, follow me."

²²But when the young man heard this, he went away sad, for he had many possessions.

²³Then Jesus said to his disciples, "I tell you the truth, it is very hard for a rich person to enter the Kingdom of Heaven. ²⁴I'll say it again—it is easier for a camel to go through the eye of a needle than for a rich person to enter the Kingdom of God!"

²⁵The disciples were astounded. "Then who in the world can be saved?" they asked.

²⁶Jesus looked at them intently and said, "Humanly speaking, it is impossible. But with God everything is possible."

²⁷Then Peter said to him, "We've given up everything to follow you. What will we get?"

²⁸Jesus replied, "I assure you that when the world is made new* and the Son of Man* sits upon his glorious throne, you who have been my followers will also sit on twelve thrones, judging the twelve tribes of Israel. ²⁹And everyone who has given up houses or brothers or sisters or father or mother or children or property, for my sake, will receive a hundred times as much in return and will inherit eternal life. ³⁰But many who are the greatest now will be least important then, and those who seem least important now will be the greatest then.*

CHAPTER 20

Parable of the Vineyard Workers

"For the Kingdom of Heaven is like the landowner who went out early one morning to hire workers for his vineyard. ²He agreed to pay the normal daily wage* and sent them out to work.

³"At nine o'clock in the morning he was passing through the marketplace and saw some people standing around doing nothing. ⁴So he hired them, telling them he would

19:9 Some manuscripts add *And anyone who marries a divorced woman commits adultery.* Compare Matt 5:32.   19:12 Greek *and some make themselves eunuchs.*   19:16 Some manuscripts read *Good Teacher.*   19:17 Some manuscripts read *continue to keep.*   19:18-19 Exod 20:12-16; Deut 5:16-20; Lev 19:18.   19:28a Or *in the regeneration.*   19:28b "Son of Man" is a title Jesus used for himself.   19:30 Greek *But many who are first will be last; and the last, first.*   20:2 Greek *a denarius,* the payment for a full day's labor; similarly in 20:9, 10, 13.

pay them whatever was right at the end of the day. ⁵So they went to work in the vineyard. At noon and again at three o'clock he did the same thing.

⁶"At five o'clock that afternoon he was in town again and saw some more people standing around. He asked them, 'Why haven't you been working today?'

⁷"They replied, 'Because no one hired us.'

"The landowner told them, 'Then go out and join the others in my vineyard.'

⁸"That evening he told the foreman to call the workers in and pay them, beginning with the last workers first. ⁹When those hired at five o'clock were paid, each received a full day's wage. ¹⁰When those hired first came to get their pay, they assumed they would receive more. But they, too, were paid a day's wage. ¹¹When they received their pay, they protested to the owner, ¹²'Those people worked only one hour, and yet you've paid them just as much as you paid us who worked all day in the scorching heat.'

¹³"He answered one of them, 'Friend, I haven't been unfair! Didn't you agree to work all day for the usual wage? ¹⁴Take your money and go. I wanted to pay this last worker the same as you. ¹⁵Is it against the law for me to do what I want with my money? Should you be jealous because I am kind to others?'

¹⁶"So those who are last now will be first then, and those who are first will be last."

Jesus Again Predicts His Death

¹⁷As Jesus was going up to Jerusalem, he took the twelve disciples aside privately and told them what was going to happen to him. ¹⁸"Listen," he said, "we're going up to Jerusalem, where the Son of Man* will be betrayed to the leading priests and the teachers of religious law. They will sentence him to die. ¹⁹Then they will hand him over to the Romans* to be mocked, flogged with a whip, and crucified. But on the third day he will be raised from the dead."

Jesus Teaches about Serving Others

²⁰Then the mother of James and John, the sons of Zebedee, came to Jesus with her sons. She knelt respectfully to ask a favor. ²¹"What is your request?" he asked.

She replied, "In your Kingdom, please let my two sons sit in places of honor next to you, one on your right and the other on your left."

²²But Jesus answered by saying to them, "You don't know what you are asking! Are you able to drink from the bitter cup of suffering I am about to drink?"

"Oh yes," they replied, "we are able!"

²³Jesus told them, "You will indeed drink from my bitter cup. But I have no right to say who will sit on my right or my left. My Father has prepared those places for the ones he has chosen."

²⁴When the ten other disciples heard what James and John had asked, they were indignant. ²⁵But Jesus called them together and said, "You know that the rulers in this world lord it over their people, and officials flaunt their authority over those under them. ²⁶But among you it will be different. Whoever wants to be a leader among you must be your servant, ²⁷and whoever wants to be first among you must become your slave. ²⁸For even the Son of Man came not to be served but to serve others and to give his life as a ransom for many."

Jesus Heals Two Blind Men

²⁹As Jesus and the disciples left the town of Jericho, a large crowd followed behind. ³⁰Two blind men were sitting beside the road. When they heard that Jesus was coming that way, they began shouting, "Lord, Son of David, have mercy on us!"

³¹"Be quiet!" the crowd yelled at them.

But they only shouted louder, "Lord, Son of David, have mercy on us!"

³²When Jesus heard them, he stopped and called, "What do you want me to do for you?"

20:18 "Son of Man" is a title Jesus used for himself.   20:19 Greek *the Gentiles*.

³³"Lord," they said, "we want to see!" ³⁴Jesus felt sorry for them and touched their eyes. Instantly they could see! Then they followed him.

CHAPTER 21
Jesus' Triumphant Entry
As Jesus and the disciples approached Jerusalem, they came to the town of Bethphage on the Mount of Olives. Jesus sent two of them on ahead. ²"Go into the village over there," he said. "As soon as you enter it, you will see a donkey tied there, with its colt beside it. Untie them and bring them to me. ³If anyone asks what you are doing, just say, 'The Lord needs them,' and he will immediately let you take them."

⁴This took place to fulfill the prophecy that said,

⁵ "Tell the people of Jerusalem,*
  'Look, your King is coming to you.
He is humble, riding on a donkey—
  riding on a donkey's colt.'"*

⁶The two disciples did as Jesus commanded. ⁷They brought the donkey and the colt to him and threw their garments over the colt, and he sat on it.*

⁸Most of the crowd spread their garments on the road ahead of him, and others cut branches from the trees and spread them on the road. ⁹Jesus was in the center of the procession, and the people all around him were shouting,

"Praise God* for the Son of David!
  Blessings on the one who comes in the name of the
  LORD!
  Praise God in highest heaven!"*

¹⁰The entire city of Jerusalem was in an uproar as he entered. "Who is this?" they asked.
¹¹And the crowds replied, "It's Jesus, the prophet from Nazareth in Galilee."

Jesus Clears the Temple
¹²Jesus entered the Temple and began to drive out all the people buying and selling animals for sacrifice. He knocked over the tables of the money changers and the chairs of those selling doves. ¹³He said to them, "The Scriptures declare, 'My Temple will be called a house of prayer,' but you have turned it into a den of thieves!"*

¹⁴The blind and the lame came to him in the Temple, and he healed them. ¹⁵The leading priests and the teachers of religious law saw these wonderful miracles and heard even the children in the Temple shouting, "Praise God for the Son of David."

But the leaders were indignant. ¹⁶They asked Jesus, "Do you hear what these children are saying?"

"Yes," Jesus replied. "Haven't you ever read the Scriptures? For they say, 'You have taught children and infants to give you praise.'*" ¹⁷Then he returned to Bethany, where he stayed overnight.

Jesus Curses the Fig Tree
¹⁸In the morning, as Jesus was returning to Jerusalem, he was hungry, ¹⁹and he noticed a fig tree beside the road. He went over to see if there were any figs, but there were only leaves. Then he said to it, "May you never bear fruit again!" And immediately the fig tree withered up.

²⁰The disciples were amazed when they saw this and asked, "How did the fig tree wither so quickly?"

²¹Then Jesus told them, "I tell you the truth, if you have faith and don't doubt, you can do things like this and much more. You can even say to this mountain, 'May you be lifted up and thrown into the sea,' and it will happen. ²²You can pray for anything, and if you have faith, you will receive it."

The Authority of Jesus Challenged
²³When Jesus returned to the Temple and began teaching, the leading priests and elders came up to him. They demanded,

21:5a Greek Tell the daughter of Zion. Isa 62:11.   21:5b Zech 9:9.   21:7 Greek over them, and he sat on them.   21:9a Greek Hosanna, an exclamation of praise that literally means "save now"; also in 21:9b, 15.   21:9b Pss 118:25-26; 148:1.   21:13 Isa 56:7; Jer 7:11.   21:16 Ps 8:2.

"By what authority are you doing all these things? Who gave you the right?"

²⁴"I'll tell you by what authority I do these things if you answer one question," Jesus replied. ²⁵"Did John's authority to baptize come from heaven, or was it merely human?"

They talked it over among themselves. "If we say it was from heaven, he will ask us why we didn't believe John. ²⁶But if we say it was merely human, we'll be mobbed because the people believe John was a prophet." ²⁷So they finally replied, "We don't know."

And Jesus responded, "Then I won't tell you by what authority I do these things.

Parable of the Two Sons

²⁸"But what do you think about this? A man with two sons told the older boy, 'Son, go out and work in the vineyard today.' ²⁹The son answered, 'No, I won't go,' but later he changed his mind and went anyway. ³⁰Then the father told the other son, 'You go,' and he said, 'Yes, sir, I will.' But he didn't go.

³¹"Which of the two obeyed his father?"

They replied, "The first."*

Then Jesus explained his meaning: "I tell you the truth, corrupt tax collectors and prostitutes will get into the Kingdom of God before you do. ³²For John the Baptist came and showed you the right way to live, but you didn't believe him, while tax collectors and prostitutes did. And even when you saw this happening, you refused to believe him and repent of your sins.

Parable of the Evil Farmers

³³"Now listen to another story. A certain landowner planted a vineyard, built a wall around it, dug a pit for pressing out the grape juice, and built a lookout tower. Then he leased the vineyard to tenant farmers and moved to another country. ³⁴At the time of the grape harvest, he sent his servants to collect his share of the crop. ³⁵But the farmers grabbed his servants, beat one, killed one, and stoned another. ³⁶So the landowner sent a larger group of his servants to collect for him, but the results were the same.

³⁷"Finally, the owner sent his son, thinking, 'Surely they will respect my son.'

³⁸"But when the tenant farmers saw his son coming, they said to one another, 'Here comes the heir to this estate. Come on, let's kill him and get the estate for ourselves!' ³⁹So they grabbed him, dragged him out of the vineyard, and murdered him.

⁴⁰"When the owner of the vineyard returns," Jesus asked, "what do you think he will do to those farmers?"

⁴¹The religious leaders replied, "He will put the wicked men to a horrible death and lease the vineyard to others who will give him his share of the crop after each harvest."

⁴²Then Jesus asked them, "Didn't you ever read this in the Scriptures?

'The stone that the builders rejected
    has now become the cornerstone.
This is the LORD's doing,
    and it is wonderful to see.'*

⁴³I tell you, the Kingdom of God will be taken away from you and given to a nation that will produce the proper fruit. ⁴⁴Anyone who stumbles over that stone will be broken to pieces, and it will crush anyone it falls on.*

⁴⁵When the leading priests and Pharisees heard this parable, they realized he was telling the story against them—they were the wicked farmers. ⁴⁶They wanted to arrest him, but they were afraid of the crowds, who considered Jesus to be a prophet.

21:29-31 Other manuscripts read *"The second."* In still other manuscripts the first son says "Yes" but does nothing, the second son says "No" but then repents and goes, and the answer to Jesus' question is that the second son obeyed his father.   21:42 Ps 118:22-23.   21:44 This verse is not included in some early manuscripts. Compare Luke 20:18.

CHAPTER 22

Parable of the Great Feast

Jesus also told them other parables. He said, [2]"The Kingdom of Heaven can be illustrated by the story of a king who prepared a great wedding feast for his son. [3]When the banquet was ready, he sent his servants to notify those who were invited. But they all refused to come!

[4]"So he sent other servants to tell them, 'The feast has been prepared. The bulls and fattened cattle have been killed, and everything is ready. Come to the banquet!' [5]But the guests he had invited ignored them and went their own way, one to his farm, another to his business. [6]Others seized his messengers and insulted them and killed them.

[7]"The king was furious, and he sent out his army to destroy the murderers and burn their town. [8]And he said to his servants, 'The wedding feast is ready, and the guests I invited aren't worthy of the honor. [9]Now go out to the street corners and invite everyone you see.' [10]So the servants brought in everyone they could find, good and bad alike, and the banquet hall was filled with guests.

[11]"But when the king came in to meet the guests, he noticed a man who wasn't wearing the proper clothes for a wedding. [12]'Friend,' he asked, 'how is it that you are here without wedding clothes?' But the man had no reply. [13]Then the king said to his aides, 'Bind his hands and feet and throw him into the outer darkness, where there will be weeping and gnashing of teeth.'

[14]"For many are called, but few are chosen."

Taxes for Caesar

[15]Then the Pharisees met together to plot how to trap Jesus into saying something for which he could be arrested. [16]They sent some of their disciples, along with the supporters of Herod, to meet with him. "Teacher," they said, "we know how honest you are. You teach the way of God truthfully. You are impartial and don't play favorites. [17]Now tell us what you think about this: Is it right to pay taxes to Caesar or not?"

[18]But Jesus knew their evil motives. "You hypocrites!" he said. "Why are you trying to trap me? [19]Here, show me the coin used for the tax." When they handed him a Roman coin,* [20]he asked, "Whose picture and title are stamped on it?"

[21]"Caesar's," they replied.

"Well, then," he said, "give to Caesar what belongs to Caesar, and give to God what belongs to God."

[22]His reply amazed them, and they went away.

Discussion about Resurrection

[23]That same day Jesus was approached by some Sadducees—religious leaders who say there is no resurrection from the dead. They posed this question: [24]"Teacher, Moses said, 'If a man dies without children, his brother should marry the widow and have a child who will carry on the brother's name.'* [25]Well, suppose there were seven brothers. The oldest one married and then died without children, so his brother married the widow. [26]But the second brother also died, and the third brother married her. This continued with all seven of them. [27]Last of all, the woman also died. [28]So tell us, whose wife will she be in the resurrection? For all seven were married to her."

[29]Jesus replied, "Your mistake is that you don't know the Scriptures, and you don't know the power of God. [30]For when the dead rise, they will neither marry nor be given in marriage. In this respect they will be like the angels in heaven.

[31]"But now, as to whether there will be a resurrection of the dead—haven't you ever read about this in the Scriptures? Long after Abraham, Isaac, and Jacob had died, God said,* [32]'I am the God of Abraham, the God of Isaac, and the God of Jacob.'* So he is the God of the living, not the dead."

[33]When the crowds heard him, they were astounded at his teaching.

22:19 Greek *a denarius.*   22:24 Deut 25:5-6.   22:31 Greek *read about this? God said.*   22:32 Exod 3:6.

The Most Important Commandment

[34] But when the Pharisees heard that he had silenced the Sadducees with his reply, they met together to question him again. [35] One of them, an expert in religious law, tried to trap him with this question: [36] "Teacher, which is the most important commandment in the law of Moses?"

[37] Jesus replied, "'You must love the LORD your God with all your heart, all your soul, and all your mind.'* [38] This is the first and greatest commandment. [39] A second is equally important: 'Love your neighbor as yourself.'* [40] The entire law and all the demands of the prophets are based on these two commandments."

Whose Son Is the Messiah?

[41] Then, surrounded by the Pharisees, Jesus asked them a question: [42] "What do you think about the Messiah? Whose son is he?"

They replied, "He is the son of David."

[43] Jesus responded, "Then why does David, speaking under the inspiration of the Spirit, call the Messiah 'my Lord'? For David said,

[44] 'The LORD said to my Lord,
Sit in the place of honor at my right hand
until I humble your enemies beneath your feet.'*

[45] Since David called the Messiah 'my Lord,' how can the Messiah be his son?"

[46] No one could answer him. And after that, no one dared to ask him any more questions.

CHAPTER 23

Jesus Criticizes the Religious Leaders

Then Jesus said to the crowds and to his disciples, [2] "The teachers of religious law and the Pharisees are the official interpreters of the law of Moses.* [3] So practice and obey whatever they tell you, but don't follow their example. For they don't practice what they teach. [4] They crush people with unbearable religious demands and never lift a finger to ease the burden.

[5] "Everything they do is for show. On their arms they wear extra wide prayer boxes with Scripture verses inside, and they wear robes with extra long tassels.* [6] And they love to sit at the head table at banquets and in the seats of honor in the synagogues. [7] They love to receive respectful greetings as they walk in the marketplaces, and to be called 'Rabbi.'*

[8] "Don't let anyone call you 'Rabbi,' for you have only one teacher, and all of you are equal as brothers and sisters.* [9] And don't address anyone here on earth as 'Father,' for only God in heaven is your spiritual Father. [10] And don't let anyone call you 'Teacher,' for you have only one teacher, the Messiah. [11] The greatest among you must be a servant. [12] But those who exalt themselves will be humbled, and those who humble themselves will be exalted.

[13] "What sorrow awaits you teachers of religious law and you Pharisees. Hypocrites! For you shut the door of the Kingdom of Heaven in people's faces. You won't go in yourselves, and you don't let others enter either.*

[15] "What sorrow awaits you teachers of religious law and you Pharisees. Hypocrites! For you cross land and sea to make one convert, and then you turn that person into twice the child of hell* you yourselves are!

[16] "Blind guides! What sorrow awaits you! For you say that it means nothing to swear 'by God's Temple,' but that it is binding to swear 'by the gold in the Temple.' [17] Blind fools! Which is more important—the gold or the Temple that makes the gold sacred? [18] And you say that to swear 'by the altar' is not binding, but to swear 'by the gifts on the altar' is binding. [19] How blind! For which is more important—the gift

"'You must love the LORD your God with all your heart, all your soul, and all your mind.' This is the first and greatest commandment" (Matthew 22:37-38).

There are many commandments, but the most important is to love God with all your heart, mind, and soul.

22:37 Deut 6:5.   **22:39** Lev 19:18.   **22:44** Ps 110:1.   **23:2** Greek *and the Pharisees sit in the seat of Moses.*   **23:5** Greek *They enlarge their phylacteries and lengthen their tassels.* **23:7** *Rabbi*, from Aramaic, means "master" or "teacher."   **23:8** Greek *brothers.*   **23:13** Some manuscripts add verse 14, *What sorrow awaits you teachers of religious law and you Pharisees. Hypocrites! You shamelessly cheat widows out of their property and then pretend to be pious by making long prayers in public. Because of this, you will be severely punished.* Compare Mark 12:40 and Luke 20:47.   **23:15** Greek *of Gehenna; also in 23:33.*

on the altar or the altar that makes the gift sacred? ²⁰When you swear 'by the altar,' you are swearing by it and by everything on it. ²¹And when you swear 'by the Temple,' you are swearing by it and by God, who lives in it. ²²And when you swear 'by heaven,' you are swearing by the throne of God and by God, who sits on the throne.

²³"What sorrow awaits you teachers of religious law and you Pharisees. Hypocrites! For you are careful to tithe even the tiniest income from your herb gardens,* but you ignore the more important aspects of the law—justice, mercy, and faith. You should tithe, yes, but do not neglect the more important things. ²⁴Blind guides! You strain your water so you won't accidentally swallow a gnat, but you swallow a camel!*

²⁵"What sorrow awaits you teachers of religious law and you Pharisees. Hypocrites! For you are so careful to clean the outside of the cup and the dish, but inside you are filthy—full of greed and self-indulgence! ²⁶You blind Pharisee! First wash the inside of the cup and the dish,* and then the outside will become clean, too.

²⁷"What sorrow awaits you teachers of religious law and you Pharisees. Hypocrites! For you are like whitewashed tombs—beautiful on the outside but filled on the inside with dead people's bones and all sorts of impurity. ²⁸Outwardly you look like righteous people, but inwardly your hearts are filled with hypocrisy and lawlessness.

²⁹"What sorrow awaits you teachers of religious law and you Pharisees. Hypocrites! For you build tombs for the prophets your ancestors killed, and you decorate the monuments of the godly people your ancestors destroyed. ³⁰Then you say, 'If we had lived in the days of our ancestors, we would never have joined them in killing the prophets.'

³¹"But in saying that, you testify against yourselves that you are indeed the descendants of those who murdered the prophets. ³²Go ahead and finish what your ancestors started. ³³Snakes! Sons of vipers! How will you escape the judgment of hell?

³⁴"Therefore, I am sending you prophets and wise men and teachers of religious law. But you will kill some by crucifixion, and you will flog others with whips in your synagogues, chasing them from city to city. ³⁵As a result, you will be held responsible for the murder of all godly people of all time—from the murder of righteous Abel to the murder of Zechariah son of Barachiah, whom you killed in the Temple between the sanctuary and the altar. ³⁶I tell you the truth, this judgment will fall on this very generation.

Jesus Grieves over Jerusalem

³⁷O Jerusalem, Jerusalem, the city that kills the prophets and stones God's messengers! How often I have wanted to gather your children together as a hen protects her chicks beneath her wings, but you wouldn't let me. ³⁸And now, look, your house is abandoned and desolate.* ³⁹For I tell you this, you will never see me again until you say, 'Blessings on the one who comes in the name of the LORD!'*"

CHAPTER 24
Jesus Foretells the Future

As Jesus was leaving the Temple grounds, his disciples pointed out to him the various Temple buildings. ²But he responded, "Do you see all these buildings? I tell you the truth, they will be completely demolished. Not one stone will be left on top of another!"

³Later, Jesus sat on the Mount of Olives. His disciples came to him privately and said, "Tell us, when will all this happen? What sign will signal your return and the end of the world?*"

⁴Jesus told them, "Don't let anyone mislead you, ⁵for many will come in my name, claiming, 'I am the Messiah.' They will deceive many. ⁶And you will hear of wars and

---

23:23 Greek *tithe the mint, the dill, and the cumin.* **23:24** See Lev 11:4, 23, where gnats and camels are both forbidden as food. **23:26** Some manuscripts do not include *and the dish.* **23:38** Some manuscripts do not include *and desolate.* **23:39** Ps 118:26. **24:3** Or *the age?*

threats of wars, but don't panic. Yes, these things must take place, but the end won't follow immediately. ⁷Nation will go to war against nation, and kingdom against kingdom. There will be famines and earthquakes in many parts of the world. ⁸But all this is only the first of the birth pains, with more to come.

⁹"Then you will be arrested, persecuted, and killed. You will be hated all over the world because you are my followers.* ¹⁰And many will turn away from me and betray and hate each other. ¹¹And many false prophets will appear and will deceive many people. ¹²Sin will be rampant everywhere, and the love of many will grow cold. ¹³But the one who endures to the end will be saved. ¹⁴And the Good News about the Kingdom will be preached throughout the whole world, so that all nations* will hear it; and then the end will come.

¹⁵"The day is coming when you will see what Daniel the prophet spoke about—the sacrilegious object that causes desecration* standing in the Holy Place." (Reader, pay attention!) ¹⁶"Then those in Judea must flee to the hills. ¹⁷A person out on the deck of a roof must not go down into the house to pack. ¹⁸A person out in the field must not return even to get a coat. ¹⁹How terrible it will be for pregnant women and for nursing mothers in those days. ²⁰And pray that your flight will not be in winter or on the Sabbath. ²¹For there will be greater anguish than at any time since the world began. And it will never be so great again. ²²In fact, unless that time of calamity is shortened, not a single person will survive. But it will be shortened for the sake of God's chosen ones.

²³"Then if anyone tells you, 'Look, here is the Messiah,' or 'There he is,' don't believe it. ²⁴For false messiahs and false prophets will rise up and perform great signs and wonders so as to deceive, if possible, even God's chosen ones. ²⁵See, I have warned you about this ahead of time.

²⁶"So if someone tells you, 'Look, the Messiah is out in the desert,' don't bother to go and look. Or, 'Look, he is hiding here,' don't believe it! ²⁷For as the lightning flashes in the east and shines to the west, so it will be when the Son of Man* comes. ²⁸Just as the gathering of vultures shows there is a carcass nearby, so these signs indicate that the end is near.*

²⁹"Immediately after the anguish of those days,

the sun will be darkened,
    the moon will give no light,
the stars will fall from the sky,
    and the powers in the heavens will be shaken.*

³⁰And then at last, the sign that the Son of Man is coming will appear in the heavens, and there will be deep mourning among all the peoples of the earth. And they will see the Son of Man coming on the clouds of heaven with power and great glory.* ³¹And he will send out his angels with the mighty blast of a trumpet, and they will gather his chosen ones from all over the world*—from the farthest ends of the earth and heaven.

³²"Now learn a lesson from the fig tree. When its branches bud and its leaves begin to sprout, you know that summer is near. ³³In the same way, when you see all these things, you can know his return is very near, right at the door. ³⁴I tell you the truth, this generation* will not pass from the scene until all these things take place. ³⁵Heaven and earth will disappear, but my words will never disappear.

³⁶"However, no one knows the day or hour when these things will happen, not even the angels in heaven or the Son himself.* Only the Father knows.

³⁷"When the Son of Man returns, it will be like it was in Noah's day. ³⁸In those days before the flood, the people were enjoying banquets and parties and weddings right up to the time Noah entered his boat. ³⁹People didn't realize what was

24:9 Greek *on account of my name.*   24:14 Or *all peoples.*   24:15 Greek *the abomination of desolation.* See Dan 9:27; 11:31; 12:11.   24:27 "Son of Man" is a title Jesus used for himself.
24:28 Greek *Wherever the carcass is, the vultures gather.*   24:29 See Isa 13:10; 34:4; Joel 2:10.   24:30 See Dan 7:13.   24:31 Greek *from the four winds.*   24:34 Or *this age,* or *this nation.*
24:36 Some manuscripts do not include *or the Son himself.*

going to happen until the flood came and swept them all away. That is the way it will be when the Son of Man comes.

⁴⁰"Two men will be working together in the field; one will be taken, the other left. ⁴¹Two women will be grinding flour at the mill; one will be taken, the other left.

⁴²"So you, too, must keep watch! For you don't know what day your Lord is coming. ⁴³Understand this: If a home-owner knew exactly when a burglar was coming, he would keep watch and not permit his house to be broken into. ⁴⁴You also must be ready all the time, for the Son of Man will come when least expected.

⁴⁵"A faithful, sensible servant is one to whom the master can give the responsibility of managing his other household servants and feeding them. ⁴⁶If the master returns and finds that the servant has done a good job, there will be a reward. ⁴⁷I tell you the truth, the master will put that servant in charge of all he owns. ⁴⁸But what if the servant is evil and thinks, 'My master won't be back for a while,' ⁴⁹and he begins beating the other servants, partying, and getting drunk? ⁵⁰The master will return unannounced and unexpected, ⁵¹and he will cut the servant to pieces and assign him a place with the hypocrites. In that place there will be weeping and gnashing of teeth.

CHAPTER 25

Parable of the Ten Bridesmaids

"Then the Kingdom of Heaven will be like ten brides-maids* who took their lamps and went to meet the bride-groom. ²Five of them were foolish, and five were wise. ³The five who were foolish didn't take enough olive oil for their lamps, ⁴but the other five were wise enough to take along extra oil. ⁵When the bridegroom was delayed, they all be-came drowsy and fell asleep.

⁶"At midnight they were roused by the shout, 'Look, the bridegroom is coming! Come out and meet him!'

⁷"All the bridesmaids got up and prepared their lamps.

⁸Then the five foolish ones asked the others, 'Please give us some of your oil because our lamps are going out.'

⁹"But the others replied, 'We don't have enough for all of us. Go to a shop and buy some for yourselves.'

¹⁰"But while they were gone to buy oil, the bridegroom came. Then those who were ready went in with him to the marriage feast, and the door was locked. ¹¹Later, when the other five bridesmaids returned, they stood outside, call-ing, 'Lord! Lord! Open the door for us!'

¹²"But he called back, 'Believe me, I don't know you!'

¹³"So you, too, must keep watch! For you do not know the day or hour of my return.

Parable of the Three Servants

¹⁴"Again, the Kingdom of Heaven can be illustrated by the story of a man going on a long trip. He called together his servants and entrusted his money to them while he was gone. ¹⁵He gave five bags of silver* to one, two bags of silver to another, and one bag of silver to the last—dividing it in proportion to their abilities. He then left on his trip.

¹⁶"The servant who received the five bags of silver began to invest the money and earned five more. ¹⁷The servant with two bags of silver also went to work and earned two more. ¹⁸But the servant who received the one bag of silver dug a hole in the ground and hid the master's money.

¹⁹"After a long time their master returned from his trip and called them to give an account of how they had used his money. ²⁰The servant to whom he had entrusted the five bags of silver came forward with five more and said, 'Master, you gave me five bags of silver to invest, and I have earned five more.'

²¹"The master was full of praise. 'Well done, my good and faithful servant. You have been faithful in handling this small amount, so now I will give you many more responsi-bilities. Let's celebrate together!*'

25:1 Or *virgins*; also in 25:7, 11.   25:15 Greek *talents*; also throughout the story. A talent is equal to 75 pounds or 34 kilograms.   25:21 Greek *Enter into the joy of your master* (or *your Lord*); also in 25:23.

²²"The servant who had received the two bags of silver came forward and said, 'Master, you gave me two bags of silver to invest, and I have earned two more.'

²³"The master said, 'Well done, my good and faithful servant. You have been faithful in handling this small amount, so now I will give you many more responsibilities. Let's celebrate together!'

²⁴"Then the servant with the one bag of silver came and said, 'Master, I knew you were a harsh man, harvesting crops you didn't plant and gathering crops you didn't cultivate. ²⁵I was afraid I would lose your money, so I hid it in the earth. Look, here is your money back.'

²⁶"But the master replied, 'You wicked and lazy servant! If you knew I harvested crops I didn't plant and gathered crops I didn't cultivate, ²⁷why didn't you deposit my money in the bank? At least I could have gotten some interest on it.'

²⁸"Then he ordered, 'Take the money from this servant, and give it to the one with the ten bags of silver. ²⁹To those who use well what they are given, even more will be given, and they will have an abundance. But from those who do nothing, even what little they have will be taken away. ³⁰Now throw this useless servant into outer darkness, where there will be weeping and gnashing of teeth.'

The Final Judgment

³¹"But when the Son of Man* comes in his glory, and all the angels with him, then he will sit upon his glorious throne. ³²All the nations* will be gathered in his presence, and he will separate the people as a shepherd separates the sheep from the goats. ³³He will place the sheep at his right hand and the goats at his left.

³⁴"Then the King will say to those on his right, 'Come, you who are blessed by my Father, inherit the Kingdom prepared for you from the creation of the world. ³⁵For I was hungry, and you fed me. I was thirsty, and you gave me a drink. I was a stranger, and you invited me into your home. ³⁶I was naked, and you gave me clothing. I was sick, and you cared for me. I was in prison, and you visited me.'

³⁷"Then these righteous ones will reply, 'Lord, when did we ever see you hungry and feed you? Or thirsty and give you something to drink? ³⁸Or a stranger and show you hospitality? Or naked and give you clothing? ³⁹When did we ever see you sick or in prison and visit you?'

⁴⁰"And the King will say, 'I tell you the truth, when you did it to one of the least of these my brothers and sisters,* you were doing it to me!'

⁴¹"Then the King will turn to those on the left and say, 'Away with you, you cursed ones, into the eternal fire prepared for the devil and his demons.* ⁴²For I was hungry, and you didn't feed me. I was thirsty, and you didn't give me a drink. ⁴³I was a stranger, and you didn't invite me into your home. I was naked, and you didn't give me clothing. I was sick and in prison, and you didn't visit me.'

⁴⁴"Then they will reply, 'Lord, when did we ever see you hungry or thirsty or a stranger or naked or sick or in prison, and not help you?'

⁴⁵"And he will answer, 'I tell you the truth, when you refused to help the least of these my brothers and sisters, you were refusing to help me.'

⁴⁶"And they will go away into eternal punishment, but the righteous will go into eternal life."

CHAPTER 26

The Plot to Kill Jesus

When Jesus had finished saying all these things, he said to his disciples, ²"As you know, Passover begins in two days, and the Son of Man* will be handed over to be crucified."

³At that same time the leading priests and elders were meeting at the residence of Caiaphas, the high priest, ⁴plotting how to capture Jesus secretly and kill him. ⁵"But not during the Passover celebration," they agreed, "or the people may riot."

25:31 "Son of Man" is a title Jesus used for himself.   25:32 Or peoples.   25:40 Greek my brothers.   25:41 Greek his angels.   26:2 "Son of Man" is a title Jesus used for himself.

Jesus Anointed at Bethany

⁶Meanwhile, Jesus was in Bethany at the home of Simon, a man who had previously had leprosy. ⁷While he was eating,* a woman came in with a beautiful alabaster jar of expensive perfume and poured it over his head.

⁸The disciples were indignant when they saw this. "What a waste!" they said. ⁹"It could have been sold for a high price and the money given to the poor."

¹⁰But Jesus, aware of this, replied, "Why criticize this woman for doing such a good thing to me? ¹¹You will always have the poor among you, but you will not always have me. ¹²She has poured this perfume on me to prepare my body for burial. ¹³I tell you the truth, wherever the Good News is preached throughout the world, this woman's deed will be remembered and discussed."

Judas Agrees to Betray Jesus

¹⁴Then Judas Iscariot, one of the twelve disciples, went to the leading priests ¹⁵and asked, "How much will you pay me to betray Jesus to you?" And they gave him thirty pieces of silver. ¹⁶From that time on, Judas began looking for an opportunity to betray Jesus.

The Last Supper

¹⁷On the first day of the Festival of Unleavened Bread, the disciples came to Jesus and asked, "Where do you want us to prepare the Passover meal for you?"

¹⁸"As you go into the city," he told them, "you will see a certain man. Tell him, 'The Teacher says: My time has come, and I will eat the Passover meal with my disciples at your house.'" ¹⁹So the disciples did as Jesus told them and prepared the Passover meal there.

²⁰When it was evening, Jesus sat down at the table* with the twelve disciples.* ²¹While they were eating, he said, "I tell you the truth, one of you will betray me."

²²Greatly distressed, each one asked in turn, "Am I the one, Lord?"

²³He replied, "One of you who has just eaten from this bowl with me will betray me. ²⁴For the Son of Man must die, as the Scriptures declared long ago. But how terrible it will be for the one who betrays him. It would be far better for that man if he had never been born!"

²⁵Judas, the one who would betray him, also asked, "Rabbi, am I the one?"

And Jesus told him, "You have said it."

²⁶As they were eating, Jesus took some bread and blessed it. Then he broke it in pieces and gave it to the disciples, saying, "Take this and eat it, for this is my body."

²⁷And he took a cup of wine and gave thanks to God for it. He gave it to them and said, "Each of you drink from it, ²⁸for this is my blood, which confirms the covenant* between God and his people. It is poured out as a sacrifice to forgive the sins of many. ²⁹Mark my words—I will not drink wine again until the day I drink it new with you in my Father's Kingdom."

³⁰Then they sang a hymn and went out to the Mount of Olives.

Jesus Predicts Peter's Denial

³¹On the way, Jesus told them, "Tonight all of you will desert me. For the Scriptures say,

'God will strike* the Shepherd,
    and the sheep of the flock will be scattered.'

³²But after I have been raised from the dead, I will go ahead of you to Galilee and meet you there."

³³Peter declared, "Even if everyone else deserts you, I will never desert you."

³⁴Jesus replied, "I tell you the truth, Peter—this very night, before the rooster crows, you will deny three times that you even know me."

³⁵"No!" Peter insisted. "Even if I have to die with you, I will never deny you!" And all the other disciples vowed the same.

26:7 Or reclining.   26:20a Or Jesus reclined.   26:20b Some manuscripts read the Twelve.   26:28 Some manuscripts read the new covenant.   26:31 Greek I will strike. Zech 13:7.

Jesus Prays in Gethsemane

³⁶Then Jesus went with them to the olive grove called Gethsemane, and he said, "Sit here while I go over there to pray." ³⁷He took Peter and Zebedee's two sons, James and John, and he became anguished and distressed. ³⁸He told them, "My soul is crushed with grief to the point of death. Stay here and keep watch with me."

³⁹He went on a little farther and bowed with his face to the ground, praying, "My Father! If it is possible, let this cup of suffering be taken away from me. Yet I want your will to be done, not mine."

⁴⁰Then he returned to the disciples and found them asleep. He said to Peter, "Couldn't you watch with me even one hour? ⁴¹Keep watch and pray, so that you will not give in to temptation. For the spirit is willing, but the body is weak!"

⁴²Then Jesus left them a second time and prayed, "My Father! If this cup cannot be taken away* unless I drink it, your will be done." ⁴³When he returned to them again, he found them sleeping, for they couldn't keep their eyes open.

⁴⁴So he went to pray a third time, saying the same things again. ⁴⁵Then he came to the disciples and said, "Go ahead and sleep. Have your rest. But look—the time has come. The Son of Man is betrayed into the hands of sinners. ⁴⁶Up, let's be going. Look, my betrayer is here!"

Jesus Is Betrayed and Arrested

⁴⁷And even as Jesus said this, Judas, one of the twelve disciples, arrived with a crowd of men armed with swords and clubs. They had been sent by the leading priests and elders of the people. ⁴⁸The traitor, Judas, had given them a prearranged signal: "You will know which one to arrest when I greet him with a kiss." ⁴⁹So Judas came straight to Jesus. "Greetings, Rabbi!" he exclaimed and gave him the kiss.

⁵⁰Jesus said, "My friend, go ahead and do what you have come for."

Then the others grabbed Jesus and arrested him. ⁵¹But one of the men with Jesus pulled out his sword and struck the high priest's slave, slashing off his ear.

⁵²"Put away your sword," Jesus told him. "Those who use the sword will die by the sword. ⁵³Don't you realize that I could ask my Father for thousands* of angels to protect us, and he would send them instantly? ⁵⁴But if I did, how would the Scriptures be fulfilled that describe what must happen now?"

⁵⁵Then Jesus said to the crowd, "Am I some dangerous revolutionary, that you come with swords and clubs to arrest me? Why didn't you arrest me in the Temple? I was there teaching every day. ⁵⁶But this is all happening to fulfill the words of the prophets as recorded in the Scriptures." At that point, all the disciples deserted him and fled.

Jesus before the Council

⁵⁷Then the people who had arrested Jesus led him to the home of Caiaphas, the high priest, where the teachers of religious law and the elders had gathered. ⁵⁸Meanwhile, Peter followed him at a distance and came to the high priest's courtyard. He went in and sat with the guards and waited to see how it would all end.

⁵⁹Inside, the leading priests and the entire high council* were trying to find witnesses who would lie about Jesus, so they could put him to death. ⁶⁰But even though they found many who agreed to give false witness, they could not use anyone's testimony. Finally, two men came forward ⁶¹who declared, "This man said, 'I am able to destroy the Temple of God and rebuild it in three days.'"

⁶²Then the high priest stood up and said to Jesus, "Well, aren't you going to answer these charges? What do you have to say for yourself?" ⁶³But Jesus remained silent. Then the high priest said to him, "I demand in the name of the living God—tell us if you are the Messiah, the Son of God."

⁶⁴Jesus replied, "You have said it. And in the future you

26:42 Greek *If this cannot pass.*   26:53 Greek *twelve legions.*   26:59 Greek *the Sanhedrin.*

will see the Son of Man seated in the place of power at God's right hand* and coming on the clouds of heaven."*

65Then the high priest tore his clothing to show his horror and said, "Blasphemy! Why do we need other witnesses? You have all heard his blasphemy. 66What is your verdict?"

"Guilty!" they shouted. "He deserves to die!"

67Then they began to spit in Jesus' face and beat him with their fists. And some slapped him, 68jeering, "Prophesy to us, you Messiah! Who hit you that time?"

Peter Denies Jesus

69Meanwhile, Peter was sitting outside in the courtyard. A servant girl came over and said to him, "You were one of those with Jesus the Galilean."

70But Peter denied it in front of everyone. "I don't know what you're talking about," he said.

71Later, out by the gate, another servant girl noticed him and said to those standing around, "This man was with Jesus of Nazareth.*"

72Again Peter denied it, this time with an oath. "I don't even know the man," he said.

73A little later some of the other bystanders came over to Peter and said, "You must be one of them; we can tell by your Galilean accent."

74Peter swore, "A curse on me if I'm lying—I don't know the man!" And immediately the rooster crowed.

75Suddenly, Jesus' words flashed through Peter's mind: "Before the rooster crows, you will deny three times that you even know me." And he went away, weeping bitterly.

CHAPTER 27

Judas Hangs Himself

Very early in the morning the leading priests and the elders of the people met again to lay plans for putting Jesus to death. 2Then they bound him, led him away, and took him to Pilate, the Roman governor.

3When Judas, who had betrayed him, realized that Jesus had been condemned to die, he was filled with remorse. So he took the thirty pieces of silver back to the leading priests and the elders. 4"I have sinned," he declared, "for I have betrayed an innocent man."

"What do we care?" they retorted. "That's your problem."

5Then Judas threw the silver coins down in the Temple and went out and hanged himself.

6The leading priests picked up the coins. "It wouldn't be right to put this money in the Temple treasury," they said, "since it was payment for murder."* 7After some discussion they finally decided to buy the potter's field, and they made it into a cemetery for foreigners. 8That is why the field is still called the Field of Blood. 9This fulfilled the prophecy of Jeremiah that says,

"They took* the thirty pieces of silver—
　　the price at which he was valued by the people
　　　　of Israel,
10 and purchased the potter's field,
　　as the LORD directed.*"

Jesus' Trial before Pilate

11Now Jesus was standing before Pilate, the Roman governor. "Are you the king of the Jews?" the governor asked him.

Jesus replied, "You have said it."

12But when the leading priests and the elders made their accusations against him, Jesus remained silent. 13"Don't you hear all these charges they are bringing against you?" Pilate demanded. 14But Jesus made no response to any of the charges, much to the governor's surprise.

15Now it was the governor's custom each year during the Passover celebration to release one prisoner to the crowd— anyone they wanted. 16This year there was a notorious

26:64a Greek *seated at the right hand of the power*. See Ps 110:1.　26:64b See Dan 7:13.　26:71 Or *Jesus the Nazarene*.　27:6 Greek *since it is the price for blood*.　27:9 Or *I took*.
27:9-10 Greek *as the LORD directed me*. Zech 11:12-13; Jer 32:6-9.

prisoner, a man named Barabbas.* ¹⁷As the crowds gathered before Pilate's house that morning, he asked them, "Which one do you want me to release to you—Barabbas, or Jesus who is called the Messiah?" ¹⁸(He knew very well that the religious leaders had arrested Jesus out of envy.)

¹⁹Just then, as Pilate was sitting on the judgment seat, his wife sent him this message: "Leave that innocent man alone. I suffered through a terrible nightmare about him last night."

²⁰Meanwhile, the leading priests and the elders persuaded the crowd to ask for Barabbas to be released and for Jesus to be put to death. ²¹So the governor asked again, "Which of these two do you want me to release to you?"

The crowd shouted back, "Barabbas!"

²²Pilate responded, "Then what should I do with Jesus who is called the Messiah?"

They shouted back, "Crucify him!"

²³"Why?" Pilate demanded. "What crime has he committed?"

But the mob roared even louder, "Crucify him!"

²⁴Pilate saw that he wasn't getting anywhere and that a riot was developing. So he sent for a bowl of water and washed his hands before the crowd, saying, "I am innocent of this man's blood. The responsibility is yours!"

²⁵And all the people yelled back, "We will take responsibility for his death—we and our children!"*

²⁶So Pilate released Barabbas to them. He ordered Jesus flogged with a lead-tipped whip, then turned him over to the Roman soldiers to be crucified.

The Soldiers Mock Jesus

²⁷Some of the governor's soldiers took Jesus into their headquarters* and called out the entire regiment. ²⁸They stripped him and put a scarlet robe on him. ²⁹They wove thorn branches into a crown and put it on his head, and they placed a reed stick in his right hand as a scepter. Then they knelt before him in mockery and taunted, "Hail! King of the Jews!" ³⁰And they spit on him and grabbed the stick and struck him on the head with it. ³¹When they were finally tired of mocking him, they took off the robe and put his own clothes on him again. Then they led him away to be crucified.

The Crucifixion

³²Along the way, they came across a man named Simon, who was from Cyrene,* and the soldiers forced him to carry Jesus' cross. ³³And they went out to a place called Golgotha (which means "Place of the Skull"). ³⁴The soldiers gave him wine mixed with bitter gall, but when he had tasted it, he refused to drink it.

³⁵After they had nailed him to the cross, the soldiers gambled for his clothes by throwing dice.* ³⁶Then they sat around and kept guard as he hung there. ³⁷A sign was fastened above Jesus' head, announcing the charge against him. It read: "This is Jesus, the King of the Jews." ³⁸Two revolutionaries* were crucified with him, one on his right and one on his left.

³⁹The people passing by shouted abuse, shaking their heads in mockery. ⁴⁰"Look at you now!" they yelled at him. "You said you were going to destroy the Temple and rebuild it in three days. Well then, if you are the Son of God, save yourself and come down from the cross!"

⁴¹The leading priests, the teachers of religious law, and the elders also mocked Jesus. ⁴²"He saved others," they scoffed, "but he can't save himself! So he is the King of Israel, is he? Let him come down from the cross right now, and we will believe in him! ⁴³He trusted God, so let God rescue him now if he wants him! For he said, 'I am the Son of God.'" ⁴⁴Even

27:16 Some manuscripts read *Jesus Barabbas;* also in 27:17.   27:25 Greek *"His blood be on us and on our children."*   27:27 Or *into the Praetorium.*   27:32 *Cyrene* was a city in northern Africa.   27:35 Greek *by casting lots.* A few late manuscripts add *This fulfilled the word of the prophet: "They divided my garments among themselves and cast lots for my robe."* See Ps 22:18.   27:38 Or *criminals;* also in 27:44.

the revolutionaries who were crucified with him ridiculed him in the same way.

The Death of Jesus

45At noon, darkness fell across the whole land until three o'clock. 46At about three o'clock, Jesus called out with a loud voice, *"Eli, Eli,* * *lema sabachthani?"* which means "My God, my God, why have you abandoned me?"*

47Some of the bystanders misunderstood and thought he was calling for the prophet Elijah. 48One of them ran and filled a sponge with sour wine, holding it up to him on a reed stick so he could drink. 49But the rest said, "Wait! Let's see whether Elijah comes to save him."*

50Then Jesus shouted out again, and he released his spirit. 51At that moment the curtain in the sanctuary of the Temple was torn in two, from top to bottom. The earth shook, rocks split apart, 52and tombs opened. The bodies of many godly men and women who had died were raised from the dead. 53They left the cemetery after Jesus' resurrection, went into the holy city of Jerusalem, and appeared to many people.

54The Roman officer* and the other soldiers at the crucifixion were terrified by the earthquake and all that had happened. They said, "This man truly was the Son of God!"

55And many women who had come from Galilee with Jesus to care for him were watching from a distance. 56Among them were Mary Magdalene, Mary (the mother of James and Joseph), and the mother of James and John, the sons of Zebedee.

The Burial of Jesus

57As evening approached, Joseph, a rich man from Arimathea who had become a follower of Jesus, 58went to Pilate and asked for Jesus' body. And Pilate issued an order to release it to him. 59Joseph took the body and wrapped it in a long sheet of clean linen cloth. 60He placed it in his own new tomb, which had been carved out of the rock. Then he rolled a great stone across the entrance and left. 61Both Mary Magdalene and the other Mary were sitting across from the tomb and watching.

The Guard at the Tomb

62The next day, on the Sabbath,* the leading priests and Pharisees went to see Pilate. 63They told him, "Sir, we remember what that deceiver once said while he was still alive: 'After three days I will rise from the dead.' 64So we request that you seal the tomb until the third day. This will prevent his disciples from coming and stealing his body and then telling everyone he was raised from the dead! If that happens, we'll be worse off than we were at first."

65Pilate replied, "Take guards and secure it the best you can." 66So they sealed the tomb and posted guards to protect it.

CHAPTER 28

The Resurrection

Early on Sunday morning,* as the new day was dawning, Mary Magdalene and the other Mary went out to visit the tomb.

2Suddenly there was a great earthquake! For an angel of the Lord came down from heaven, rolled aside the stone, and sat on it. 3His face shone like lightning, and his clothing was as white as snow. 4The guards shook with fear when they saw him, and they fell into a dead faint.

5Then the angel spoke to the women. "Don't be afraid!" he said. "I know you are looking for Jesus, who was crucified. 6He isn't here! He is risen from the dead, just as he said would happen. Come, see where his body was lying. 7And now, go quickly and tell his disciples that he has risen from the dead, and he is going ahead of you to Galilee. You will see him there. Remember what I have told you."

8The women ran quickly from the tomb. They were very

27:46a *Some manuscripts read Eloi, Eloi.*   27:46b Ps 22:1.   27:49 Some manuscripts add *And another took a spear and pierced his side, and out flowed water and blood.* Compare John 19:34.   27:54 Greek *The centurion.*   27:62 Or *On the next day, which is after the Preparation.*   28:1 Greek *After the Sabbath, on the first day of the week.*

frightened but also filled with great joy, and they rushed to give the disciples the angel's message. ⁹And as they went, Jesus met them and greeted them. And they ran to him, grasped his feet, and worshiped him. ¹⁰Then Jesus said to them, "Don't be afraid! Go tell my brothers to leave for Galilee, and they will see me there."

The Report of the Guard

¹¹As the women were on their way, some of the guards went into the city and told the leading priests what had happened. ¹²A meeting with the elders was called, and they decided to give the soldiers a large bribe. ¹³They told the soldiers, "You must say, 'Jesus' disciples came during the night while we were sleeping, and they stole his body.' ¹⁴If the governor hears about it, we'll stand up for you so you won't get in trouble." ¹⁵So the guards accepted the bribe and said what they were told to say. Their story spread widely among the Jews, and they still tell it today.

The Great Commission

¹⁶Then the eleven disciples left for Galilee, going to the mountain where Jesus had told them to go. ¹⁷When they saw him, they worshiped him—but some of them doubted!

¹⁸Jesus came and told his disciples, "I have been given all authority in heaven and on earth. ¹⁹Therefore, go and make disciples of all the nations,* baptizing them in the name of the Father and the Son and the Holy Spirit. ²⁰Teach these new disciples to obey all the commands I have given you. And be sure of this: I am with you always, even to the end of the age."

28:19 Or *all peoples.*

IF YOU WANT to cut to the chase and find out what Jesus is about, read the book of Mark. This dude Mark wasted no time in givin' a heads-up about Jesus' ministry. He didn't get into Jesus' birth or background; he came hard with in-your-face, do-or-die facts about Jesus' public ministry.

Mark did not actually hang with Jesus like Matthew and John. Mark hung out with his cousin Barnabas and with Peter, a brotha who always had Jesus' back. Mark was kinda like the rich kid from the burbs who hung out with the fellas on the block. You know, sorta like the boy you went to high school with that made it to the NBA—you might still catch him at the barbershop from time to time. When Mark started gettin' a taste of just how sweet Jesus' ministry was, he was simply blown away. He started preachin' and teachin' about Jesus to folks who would have otherwise never heard about the dude.

MARK

CHAPTER 1

John the Baptist Prepares the Way

This is the Good News about Jesus the Messiah, the Son of God.* It began ²just as the prophet Isaiah had written:

"Look, I am sending my messenger ahead of you,
and he will prepare your way.*
³ He is a voice shouting in the wilderness,
'Prepare the way for the LORD's coming!
Clear the road for him!'*"

⁴This messenger was John the Baptist. He was in the wilderness and preached that people should be baptized to show that they had repented of their sins and turned to God to be forgiven. ⁵All of Judea, including all the people of Jerusalem, went out to see and hear John. And when they confessed their sins, he baptized them in the Jordan River. ⁶His clothes were woven from coarse camel hair, and he wore a leather belt around his waist. For food he ate locusts and wild honey.

⁷John announced: "Someone is coming soon who is greater than I am—so much greater that I'm not even worthy to stoop down like a slave and untie the straps of his sandals. ⁸I baptize you with* water, but he will baptize you with the Holy Spirit!"

The Baptism and Temptation of Jesus

⁹One day Jesus came from Nazareth in Galilee, and John baptized him in the Jordan River. ¹⁰As Jesus came up out of the water, he saw the heavens splitting apart and the Holy Spirit descending on him* like a dove. ¹¹And a voice from heaven said, "You are my dearly loved Son, and you bring me great joy."

¹²The Spirit then compelled Jesus to go into the wilderness, ¹³where he was tempted by Satan for forty days. He was out among the wild animals, and angels took care of him.

¹⁴Later on, after John was arrested, Jesus went into Galilee, where he preached God's Good News.* ¹⁵"The time promised by God has come at last!" he announced. "The Kingdom of God is near! Repent of your sins and believe the Good News!"

The First Disciples

¹⁶One day as Jesus was walking along the shore of the Sea of Galilee, he saw Simon* and his brother Andrew throwing a net into the water, for they fished for a living. ¹⁷Jesus called out to them, "Come, follow me, and I will show you how to fish for people!" ¹⁸And they left their nets at once and followed him.

¹⁹A little farther up the shore Jesus saw Zebedee's sons, James and John, in a boat repairing their nets. ²⁰He called them at once, and they also followed him, leaving their father, Zebedee, in the boat with the hired men.

Jesus Casts Out an Evil Spirit

²¹Jesus and his companions went to the town of Capernaum. When the Sabbath day came, he went into the synagogue and began to teach. ²²The people were amazed at his teaching, for he taught with real authority—quite unlike the teachers of religious law.

²³Suddenly, a man in the synagogue who was possessed

1:1 Some manuscripts do not include *the Son of God.*   1:2 Mal 3:1.   1:3 Isa 40:3 (Greek version).   1:8 Or *in;* also in 1:8b.   1:10 Or *toward him,* or *into him.*   1:14 Some manuscripts read *the Good News of the Kingdom of God.*   1:16 *Simon* is called "Peter" in 3:16 and thereafter.

by an evil* spirit began shouting, ²⁴"Why are you interfering with us, Jesus of Nazareth? Have you come to destroy us? I know who you are—the Holy One of God!"

²⁵Jesus cut him short. "Be quiet! Come out of the man," he ordered. ²⁶At that, the evil spirit screamed, threw the man into a convulsion, and then came out of him.

²⁷Amazement gripped the audience, and they began to discuss what had happened. "What sort of new teaching is this?" they asked excitedly. "It has such authority! Even evil spirits obey his orders!" ²⁸The news about Jesus spread quickly throughout the entire region of Galilee.

Jesus Heals Many People

²⁹After Jesus left the synagogue with James and John, they went to Simon and Andrew's home. ³⁰Now Simon's mother-in-law was sick in bed with a high fever. They told Jesus about her right away. ³¹So he went to her bedside, took her by the hand, and helped her sit up. Then the fever left her, and she prepared a meal for them.

³²That evening after sunset, many sick and demon-possessed people were brought to Jesus. ³³The whole town gathered at the door to watch. ³⁴So Jesus healed many people who were sick with various diseases, and he cast out many demons. But because the demons knew who he was, he did not allow them to speak.

Jesus Preaches in Galilee

³⁵Before daybreak the next morning, Jesus got up and went out to an isolated place to pray. ³⁶Later Simon and the others went out to find him. ³⁷When they found him, they said, "Everyone is looking for you."

³⁸But Jesus replied, "We must go on to other towns as well, and I will preach to them, too. That is why I came." ³⁹So he traveled throughout the region of Galilee, preaching in the synagogues and casting out demons.

Jesus Heals a Man with Leprosy

⁴⁰A man with leprosy came and knelt in front of Jesus, begging to be healed. "If you are willing, you can heal me and make me clean," he said.

⁴¹Moved with compassion,* Jesus reached out and touched him. "I am willing," he said. "Be healed!" ⁴²Instantly the leprosy disappeared, and the man was healed. ⁴³Then Jesus sent him on his way with a stern warning: ⁴⁴"Don't tell anyone about this. Instead, go to the priest and let him examine you. Take along the offering required in the law of Moses for those who have been healed of leprosy.* This will be a public testimony that you have been cleansed."

⁴⁵But the man went and spread the word, proclaiming to everyone what had happened. As a result, large crowds soon surrounded Jesus, and he couldn't publicly enter a

1:23 Greek *unclean;* also in 1:26, 27.   **1:41** Some manuscripts read *Moved with anger.*   **1:44** See Lev 14:2-32.

THE POINT

Jesus is da Man. There's quite a few big ballers and shot callers out there today who sport a huge entourage. Can you imagine what would happen if Lebron James, Jay-Z, or Beyoncé visited a shopping mall or a college campus unannounced? There would be total chaos if a situation like this jumped off, but it would never happen because someone on Beyoncé's staff prepares the way; they call ahead to say, "Hey, get ready, 'cause Beyoncé is on her way!" Well, back in the day, Jesus was no different. Jesus' cuz, John the Baptist, told the people to get ready, 'cause Jesus—da Man—was on his way!

"Prepare the way for the Lord's coming! Clear the road for him!" (Mark 1:3)

Jesus' ministry was what was up. From the day Jesus' earthly ministry jumped off, it was on! Twenty-four/seven, non-stop castin' out demons, healin' lepers and cripples, and feedin' thousands of people with a small order of fish and bread. The brotha even walked on water (Mark 6:47-55)! Oh snap! That must have been awesome to see. People started following Jesus everywhere he went. Maybe this carpenter's son is on point after all.

town anywhere. He had to stay out in the secluded places, but people from everywhere kept coming to him.

CHAPTER 2

Jesus Heals a Paralyzed Man

When Jesus returned to Capernaum several days later, the news spread quickly that he was back home. [2]Soon the house where he was staying was so packed with visitors that there was no more room, even outside the door. While he was preaching God's word to them, [3]four men arrived carrying a paralyzed man on a mat. [4]They couldn't bring him to Jesus because of the crowd, so they dug a hole through the roof above his head. Then they lowered the man on his mat, right down in front of Jesus. [5]Seeing their faith, Jesus said to the paralyzed man, "My child, your sins are forgiven."

[6]But some of the teachers of religious law who were sitting there thought to themselves, [7]"What is he saying? This is blasphemy! Only God can forgive sins!"

[8]Jesus knew immediately what they were thinking, so he asked them, "Why do you question this in your hearts? [9]Is it easier to say to the paralyzed man 'Your sins are forgiven,' or 'Stand up, pick up your mat, and walk'? [10]So I will prove to you that the Son of Man* has the authority on earth to forgive sins." Then Jesus turned to the paralyzed man and said, [11]"Stand up, pick up your mat, and go home!"

[12]And the man jumped up, grabbed his mat, and walked out through the stunned onlookers. They were all amazed and praised God, exclaiming, "We've never seen anything like this before!"

Jesus Calls Levi (Matthew)

[13]Then Jesus went out to the lakeshore again and taught the crowds that were coming to him. [14]As he walked along, he saw Levi son of Alphaeus sitting at his tax collector's booth. "Follow me and be my disciple," Jesus said to him. So Levi got up and followed him.

[15]Later, Levi invited Jesus and his disciples to his home as dinner guests, along with many tax collectors and other disreputable sinners. (There were many people of this kind among Jesus' followers.) [16]But when the teachers of religious law who were Pharisees* saw him eating with tax collectors and other sinners, they asked his disciples, "Why does he eat with such scum?*"

[17]When Jesus heard this, he told them, "Healthy people don't need a doctor—sick people do. I have come to call not those who think they are righteous, but those who know they are sinners."

A Discussion about Fasting

[18]Once when John's disciples and the Pharisees were fasting, some people came to Jesus and asked, "Why don't your disciples fast like John's disciples and the Pharisees do?"

[19]Jesus replied, "Do wedding guests fast while celebrating with the groom? Of course not. They can't fast while the groom is with them. [20]But someday the groom will be taken away from them, and then they will fast.

[21]"Besides, who would patch old clothing with new cloth? For the new patch would shrink and rip away from the old cloth, leaving an even bigger tear than before.

[22]"And no one puts new wine into old wineskins. For the wine would burst the wineskins, and the wine and the skins would both be lost. New wine calls for new wineskins."

A Discussion about the Sabbath

[23]One Sabbath day as Jesus was walking through some grainfields, his disciples began breaking off heads of grain to eat. [24]But the Pharisees said to Jesus, "Look, why are they breaking the law by harvesting grain on the Sabbath?"

[25]Jesus said to them, "Haven't you ever read in the Scriptures what David did when he and his companions were hungry? [26]He went into the house of God (during the days when Abiathar was high priest) and broke the law by eating

2:10 "Son of Man" is a title Jesus used for himself.   2:16a Greek *the scribes of the Pharisees.*   2:16b Greek *with tax collectors and sinners?*

the sacred loaves of bread that only the priests are allowed to eat. He also gave some to his companions."

²⁷Then Jesus said to them, "The Sabbath was made to meet the needs of people, and not people to meet the requirements of the Sabbath. ²⁸So the Son of Man is Lord, even over the Sabbath!"

CHAPTER 3

Jesus Heals on the Sabbath

Jesus went into the synagogue again and noticed a man with a deformed hand. ²Since it was the Sabbath, Jesus' enemies watched him closely. If he healed the man's hand, they planned to accuse him of working on the Sabbath.

³Jesus said to the man with the deformed hand, "Come and stand in front of everyone." ⁴Then he turned to his critics and asked, "Does the law permit good deeds on the Sabbath, or is it a day for doing evil? Is this a day to save life or to destroy it?" But they wouldn't answer him.

⁵He looked around at them angrily and was deeply saddened by their hard hearts. Then he said to the man, "Hold out your hand." So the man held out his hand, and it was restored! ⁶At once the Pharisees went away and met with the supporters of Herod to plot how to kill Jesus.

Crowds Follow Jesus

⁷Jesus went out to the lake with his disciples, and a large crowd followed him. They came from all over Galilee, Judea, ⁸Jerusalem, Idumea, from east of the Jordan River, and even from as far north as Tyre and Sidon. The news about his miracles had spread far and wide, and vast numbers of people came to see him.

⁹Jesus instructed his disciples to have a boat ready so the crowd would not crush him. ¹⁰He had healed many people that day, so all the sick people eagerly pushed forward to touch him. ¹¹And whenever those possessed by evil* spirits caught sight of him, the spirits would throw them to the ground in front of him shrieking, "You are the Son of God!" ¹²But Jesus sternly commanded the spirits not to reveal who he was.

Jesus Chooses the Twelve Apostles

¹³Afterward Jesus went up on a mountain and called out the ones he wanted to go with him. And they came to him. ¹⁴Then he appointed twelve of them and called them his apostles.* They were to accompany him, and he would send them out to preach, ¹⁵giving them authority to cast out demons. ¹⁶These are the twelve he chose:

Simon (whom he named Peter),
¹⁷ James and John (the sons of Zebedee, but Jesus
    nicknamed them "Sons of Thunder"*),
¹⁸ Andrew,
    Philip,
    Bartholomew,
    Matthew,
    Thomas,
    James (son of Alphaeus),
    Thaddaeus,
    Simon (the zealot*),
¹⁹Judas Iscariot (who later betrayed him).

Jesus and the Prince of Demons

²⁰One time Jesus entered a house, and the crowds began to gather again. Soon he and his disciples couldn't even find time to eat. ²¹When his family heard what was happening, they tried to take him away. "He's out of his mind," they said.

²²But the teachers of religious law who had arrived from Jerusalem said, "He's possessed by Satan,* the prince of demons. That's where he gets the power to cast out demons."

²³Jesus called them over and responded with an illustration.

3:11 Greek *unclean;* also in 3:30.   3:14 Some manuscripts do not include *and called them his apostles.*   3:17 Greek *whom he named Boanerges, which means Sons of Thunder.*
3:18 Greek *the Cananean,* an Aramaic term for Jewish nationalists.   3:22 Greek *Beelzeboul;* other manuscripts read *Beezeboul;* Latin version reads *Beelzebub.*

"How can Satan cast out Satan?" he asked. ²⁴"A kingdom divided by civil war will collapse. ²⁵Similarly, a family splintered by feuding will fall apart. ²⁶And if Satan is divided and fights against himself, how can he stand? He would never survive. ²⁷Let me illustrate this further. Who is powerful enough to enter the house of a strong man like Satan and plunder his goods? Only someone even stronger—someone who could tie him up and then plunder his house.

²⁸"I tell you the truth, all sin and blasphemy can be forgiven, ²⁹but anyone who blasphemes the Holy Spirit will never be forgiven. This is a sin with eternal consequences." ³⁰He told them this because they were saying, "He's possessed by an evil spirit."

The True Family of Jesus

³¹Then Jesus' mother and brothers came to see him. They stood outside and sent word for him to come out and talk with them. ³²There was a crowd sitting around Jesus, and someone said, "Your mother and your brothers* are outside asking for you."

³³Jesus replied, "Who is my mother? Who are my brothers?" ³⁴Then he looked at those around him and said, "Look, these are my mother and brothers. ³⁵Anyone who does God's will is my brother and sister and mother."

CHAPTER **4**

Parable of the Farmer Scattering Seed

Once again Jesus began teaching by the lakeshore. A very large crowd soon gathered around him, so he got into a boat. Then he sat in the boat while all the people remained on the shore. ²He taught them by telling many stories in the form of parables, such as this one:

³"Listen! A farmer went out to plant some seed. ⁴As he scattered it across his field, some of the seed fell on a footpath, and the birds came and ate it. ⁵Other seed fell on shallow soil with underlying rock. The seed sprouted quickly because the soil was shallow. ⁶But the plant soon wilted under the hot sun, and since it didn't have deep roots, it died. ⁷Other seed fell among thorns that grew up and choked out the tender plants so they produced no grain. ⁸Still other seeds fell on fertile soil, and they sprouted, grew, and produced a crop that was thirty, sixty, and even a hundred times as much as had been planted!" ⁹Then he said, "Anyone with ears to hear should listen and understand."

¹⁰Later, when Jesus was alone with the twelve disciples and with the others who were gathered around, they asked him what the parables meant.

¹¹He replied, "You are permitted to understand the secret* of the Kingdom of God. But I use parables for everything I say to outsiders, ¹²so that the Scriptures might be fulfilled:

'When they see what I do,
    they will learn nothing.
When they hear what I say,
    they will not understand.
Otherwise, they will turn to me
    and be forgiven.'*"

¹³Then Jesus said to them, "If you can't understand the meaning of this parable, how will you understand all the other parables? ¹⁴The farmer plants seed by taking God's word to others. ¹⁵The seed that fell on the footpath represents those who hear the message, only to have Satan come at once and take it away. ¹⁶The seed on the rocky soil represents those who hear the message and immediately receive it with joy. ¹⁷But since they don't have deep roots, they don't last long. They fall away as soon as they have problems or are persecuted for believing God's word. ¹⁸The seed that fell among the thorns represents others who hear God's word, ¹⁹but all too quickly the message is crowded out by the worries of this life, the lure of wealth, and the desire for other things, so no fruit is produced. ²⁰And the seed that fell on

3:32 Some manuscripts add *and sisters.*   **4:11** Greek *mystery.*   **4:12** Isa 6:9-10 (Greek version).

good soil represents those who hear and accept God's word and produce a harvest of thirty, sixty, or even a hundred times as much as had been planted!"

Parable of the Lamp

²¹Then Jesus asked them, "Would anyone light a lamp and then put it under a basket or under a bed? Of course not! A lamp is placed on a stand, where its light will shine. ²²For everything that is hidden will eventually be brought into the open, and every secret will be brought to light. ²³Anyone with ears to hear should listen and understand."

²⁴Then he added, "Pay close attention to what you hear. The closer you listen, the more understanding you will be given*—and you will receive even more. ²⁵To those who listen to my teaching, more understanding will be given. But for those who are not listening, even what little understanding they have will be taken away from them."

Parable of the Growing Seed

²⁶Jesus also said, "The Kingdom of God is like a farmer who scatters seed on the ground. ²⁷Night and day, while he's asleep or awake, the seed sprouts and grows, but he does not understand how it happens. ²⁸The earth produces the crops on its own. First a leaf blade pushes through, then the heads of wheat are formed, and finally the grain ripens. ²⁹And as soon as the grain is ready, the farmer comes and harvests it with a sickle, for the harvest time has come."

Parable of the Mustard Seed

³⁰Jesus said, "How can I describe the Kingdom of God? What story should I use to illustrate it? ³¹It is like a mustard seed planted in the ground. It is the smallest of all seeds, ³²but it becomes the largest of all garden plants; it grows long branches, and birds can make nests in its shade."

³³Jesus used many similar stories and illustrations to teach the people as much as they could understand. ³⁴In fact, in his public ministry he never taught without using parables; but afterward, when he was alone with his disciples, he explained everything to them.

Jesus Calms the Storm

³⁵As evening came, Jesus said to his disciples, "Let's cross to the other side of the lake." ³⁶So they took Jesus in the boat and started out, leaving the crowds behind (although other boats followed). ³⁷But soon a fierce storm came up. High waves were breaking into the boat, and it began to fill with water.

³⁸Jesus was sleeping at the back of the boat with his head on a cushion. The disciples woke him up, shouting, "Teacher, don't you care that we're going to drown?"

³⁹When Jesus woke up, he rebuked the wind and said to the waves, "Silence! Be still!" Suddenly the wind stopped, and there was a great calm. ⁴⁰Then he asked them, "Why are you afraid? Do you still have no faith?"

⁴¹The disciples were absolutely terrified. "Who is this man?" they asked each other. "Even the wind and waves obey him!"

CHAPTER 5

Jesus Heals a Demon-Possessed Man

So they arrived at the other side of the lake, in the region of the Gerasenes.* ²When Jesus climbed out of the boat, a man possessed by an evil* spirit came out from a cemetery to meet him. ³This man lived among the burial caves and could no longer be restrained, even with a chain. ⁴Whenever he was put into chains and shackles—as he often was—he snapped the chains from his wrists and smashed the shackles. No one was strong enough to subdue him. ⁵Day and night he wandered among the burial caves and in the hills, howling and cutting himself with sharp stones.

4:24 Or *The measure you give will be the measure you get back.*   **5:1** Other manuscripts read *Gadarenes;* still others read *Gergesenes.* See Matt 8:28; Luke 8:26.   **5:2** Greek *unclean;* also in 5:8, 13.

⁶When Jesus was still some distance away, the man saw him, ran to meet him, and bowed low before him. ⁷With a shriek, he screamed, "Why are you interfering with me, Jesus, Son of the Most High God? In the name of God, I beg you, don't torture me!" ⁸For Jesus had already said to the spirit, "Come out of the man, you evil spirit."

⁹Then Jesus demanded, "What is your name?"

And he replied, "My name is Legion, because there are many of us inside this man." ¹⁰Then the evil spirits begged him again and again not to send them to some distant place.

¹¹There happened to be a large herd of pigs feeding on the hillside nearby. ¹²"Send us into those pigs," the spirits begged. "Let us enter them."

¹³So Jesus gave them permission. The evil spirits came out of the man and entered the pigs, and the entire herd of about 2,000 pigs plunged down the steep hillside into the lake and drowned in the water.

¹⁴The herdsmen fled to the nearby town and the surrounding countryside, spreading the news as they ran. People rushed out to see what had happened. ¹⁵A crowd soon gathered around Jesus, and they saw the man who had been possessed by the legion of demons. He was sitting there fully clothed and perfectly sane, and they were all afraid. ¹⁶Then those who had seen what happened told the others about the demon-possessed man and the pigs. ¹⁷And the crowd began pleading with Jesus to go away and leave them alone.

¹⁸As Jesus was getting into the boat, the man who had been demon possessed begged to go with him. ¹⁹But Jesus said, "No, go home to your family, and tell them everything the Lord has done for you and how merciful he has been." ²⁰So the man started off to visit the Ten Towns* of that region and began to proclaim the great things Jesus had done for him; and everyone was amazed at what he told them.

5:20 Greek *Decapolis.*

POWERCHOICES

WHAT HAPPENS WHEN YOU TRUST AND BELIEVE IN JESUS? ACCORDING TO MARK, JESUS WILL CHANGE YOUR LIFE. BACK IN BIBLE TIMES, PEOPLE FELT LIKE THEY HAD TO SEE IT TO BELIEVE IT. SO JESUS WENT AROUND PERFORMING MIRACLES AS A WAY OF LETTIN' PEOPLE KNOW HE WASN'T SOME FUGAZI. ¶ HOW WOULD YOU RESPOND TO JESUS IF HE WERE AROUND TODAY? WOULD YOU SHOW JESUS MAD LOVE BECAUSE HE HAD YOUR BACK AND PULLED YOU OUT OF SOME SERIOUS DRAMA? OR WOULD YOU BE LIKE THE FOLKS IN HIS HOMETOWN WHO TOTALLY MISSED OUT ON THEIR BLESSINGS BECAUSE THEY REFUSED TO BELIEVE THAT A CARPENTER'S SON WAS *ALL* THAT? MAYBE YOU'D BE LIKE THE RELIGIOUS FOLKS WHO WERE ALWAYS TRYIN' TO THROW JESUS OFF HIS GAME BY QUESTIONING HIM ON SOME THEOLOGICAL DRAMA. OR WOULD YOU TAKE A STAND FOR CHRIST IN THE FACE OF ALL THE HATERS? MAYBE YOU'D BE LIKE JUDAS AND SELL OUT YOUR BOY JESUS TO GET PAID; OR BE LIKE PETER AND DENY EVEN KNOWING HIM. ¶ *EITHER WAY, THE CHOICE TO TRUST JESUS AND FOLLOW HIM IS YOURS. HOW YOU GONNA REPRESENT?*

Jesus Heals in Response to Faith

²¹Jesus got into the boat again and went back to the other side of the lake, where a large crowd gathered around him on the shore. ²²Then a leader of the local synagogue, whose name was Jairus, arrived. When he saw Jesus, he fell at his feet, ²³pleading fervently with him. "My little daughter is dying," he said. "Please come and lay your hands on her; heal her so she can live."

²⁴Jesus went with him, and all the people followed, crowding around him. ²⁵A woman in the crowd had suffered for twelve years with constant bleeding. ²⁶She had suffered a

great deal from many doctors, and over the years she had spent everything she had to pay them, but she had gotten no better. In fact, she had gotten worse. ²⁷She had heard about Jesus, so she came up behind him through the crowd and touched his robe. ²⁸For she thought to herself, "If I can just touch his robe, I will be healed." ²⁹Immediately the bleeding stopped, and she could feel in her body that she had been healed of her terrible condition.

³⁰Jesus realized at once that healing power had gone out from him, so he turned around in the crowd and asked, "Who touched my robe?"

³¹His disciples said to him, "Look at this crowd pressing around you. How can you ask, 'Who touched me?'"

³²But he kept on looking around to see who had done it. ³³Then the frightened woman, trembling at the realization of what had happened to her, came and fell to her knees in front of him and told him what she had done. ³⁴And he said to her, "Daughter, your faith has made you well. Go in peace. Your suffering is over."

³⁵While he was still speaking to her, messengers arrived from the home of Jairus, the leader of the synagogue. They told him, "Your daughter is dead. There's no use troubling the Teacher now."

³⁶But Jesus overheard* them and said to Jairus, "Don't be afraid. Just have faith."

³⁷Then Jesus stopped the crowd and wouldn't let anyone go with him except Peter, James, and John (the brother of James). ³⁸When they came to the home of the synagogue leader, Jesus saw much commotion and weeping and wailing. ³⁹He went inside and asked, "Why all this commotion and weeping? The child isn't dead; she's only asleep."

⁴⁰The crowd laughed at him. But he made them all leave, and he took the girl's father and mother and his three disciples into the room where the girl was lying. ⁴¹Holding her hand, he said to her, *"Talitha koum,"* which means "Little girl, get up!" ⁴²And the girl, who was twelve years old, immediately stood up and walked around! They were overwhelmed and totally amazed. ⁴³Jesus gave them strict orders not to tell anyone what had happened, and then he told them to give her something to eat.

CHAPTER 6

Jesus Rejected at Nazareth

Jesus left that part of the country and returned with his disciples to Nazareth, his hometown. ²The next Sabbath he began teaching in the synagogue, and many who heard him were amazed. They asked, "Where did he get all this wisdom and the power to perform such miracles?" ³Then they scoffed, "He's just a carpenter, the son of Mary* and the brother of James, Joseph,* Judas, and Simon. And his sisters live right here among us." They were deeply offended and refused to believe in him.

⁴Then Jesus told them, "A prophet is honored everywhere except in his own hometown and among his relatives and his own family." ⁵And because of their unbelief, he couldn't do any miracles among them except to place his hands on a few sick people and heal them. ⁶And he was amazed at their unbelief.

Jesus Sends Out the Twelve Disciples

Then Jesus went from village to village, teaching the people. ⁷And he called his twelve disciples together and began sending them out two by two, giving them authority to cast out evil* spirits. ⁸He told them to take nothing for their journey except a walking stick—no food, no traveler's bag, no money.* ⁹He allowed them to wear sandals but not to take a change of clothes.

¹⁰"Wherever you go," he said, "stay in the same house until you leave town. ¹¹But if any place refuses to welcome you or listen to you, shake its dust from your feet as you

5:36 Or *ignored.*   **6:3a** Some manuscripts read *He's just the son of the carpenter and of Mary.*   **6:3b** Most manuscripts read *Joses;* see Matt 13:55.   **6:7** Greek *unclean.*   **6:8** Greek *no copper coins in their money belts.*

leave to show that you have abandoned those people to their fate."

¹²So the disciples went out, telling everyone they met to repent of their sins and turn to God. ¹³And they cast out many demons and healed many sick people, anointing them with olive oil.

The Death of John the Baptist

¹⁴Herod Antipas, the king, soon heard about Jesus, because everyone was talking about him. Some were saying,* "This must be John the Baptist raised from the dead. That is why he can do such miracles." ¹⁵Others said, "He's the prophet Elijah." Still others said, "He's a prophet like the other great prophets of the past."

¹⁶When Herod heard about Jesus, he said, "John, the man I beheaded, has come back from the dead."

¹⁷For Herod had sent soldiers to arrest and imprison John as a favor to Herodias. She had been his brother Philip's wife, but Herod had married her. ¹⁸John had been telling Herod, "It is against God's law for you to marry your brother's wife." ¹⁹So Herodias bore a grudge against John and wanted to kill him. But without Herod's approval she was powerless, ²⁰for Herod respected John; and knowing that he was a good and holy man, he protected him. Herod was greatly disturbed whenever he talked with John, but even so, he liked to listen to him.

²¹Herodias's chance finally came on Herod's birthday. He gave a party for his high government officials, army officers, and the leading citizens of Galilee. ²²Then his daughter, also named Herodias,* came in and performed a dance that greatly pleased Herod and his guests. "Ask me for anything you like," the king said to the girl, "and I will give it to you." ²³He even vowed, "I will give you whatever you ask, up to half my kingdom!"

²⁴She went out and asked her mother, "What should I ask for?"

Her mother told her, "Ask for the head of John the Baptist!"

²⁵So the girl hurried back to the king and told him, "I want the head of John the Baptist, right now, on a tray!"

²⁶Then the king deeply regretted what he had said; but because of the vows he had made in front of his guests, he couldn't refuse her. ²⁷So he immediately sent an executioner to the prison to cut off John's head and bring it to him. The soldier beheaded John in the prison, ²⁸brought his head on a tray, and gave it to the girl, who took it to her mother. ²⁹When John's disciples heard what had happened, they came to get his body and buried it in a tomb.

Jesus Feeds Five Thousand

³⁰The apostles returned to Jesus from their ministry tour and told him all they had done and taught. ³¹Then Jesus said, "Let's go off by ourselves to a quiet place and rest awhile." He said this because there were so many people coming and going that Jesus and his apostles didn't even have time to eat.

³²So they left by boat for a quiet place, where they could be alone. ³³But many people recognized them and saw them leaving, and people from many towns ran ahead along the shore and got there ahead of them. ³⁴Jesus saw the huge crowd as he stepped from the boat, and he had compassion on them because they were like sheep without a shepherd. So he began teaching them many things.

³⁵Late in the afternoon his disciples came to him and said, "This is a remote place, and it's already getting late. ³⁶Send the crowds away so they can go to the nearby farms and villages and buy something to eat."

³⁷But Jesus said, "You feed them."

"With what?" they asked. "We'd have to work for months to earn enough money* to buy food for all these people!"

³⁸"How much bread do you have?" he asked. "Go and find out."

6:14 Some manuscripts read *He was saying.*   6:22 Some manuscripts read *the daughter of Herodias herself.*   6:37 Greek *It would take 200 denarii.* A denarius was equivalent to a laborer's full day's wage.

keeping your swagger strong

BIBLICAL PRINCIPLES FOR SUCCESS AND LEADERSHIP

Leaders find solutions. That's what Jesus did. Even when he and his disciples left by boat in order to find a place to chill, thousands of people followed them despite their desire to get away from it all. It's like being a celebrity in today's media-frenzied society—they couldn't go anywhere or do anything without a crowd of fans or the paparazzi watching their every move. Even the biggest celebrities today don't have five thousand people constantly following them around—that would be more than a nuisance. But Jesus was different. He didn't turn the crowd away. He welcomed them. On several occasions he even fed them just to keep them satisfied while he preached!

You may not be able to turn five loaves of bread and two fish into a meal for five thousand, but you can find solutions to the things that are in your power to solve. Don't give up on a situation just because it seems too difficult. If you have been placed in a position of leadership, you have been given the power to find solutions. Ask God to give you the power, insight, and ability to change things for the better. Amazin' things can happen if you trust him.

They came back and reported, "We have five loaves of bread and two fish."

³⁹Then Jesus told the disciples to have the people sit down in groups on the green grass. ⁴⁰So they sat down in groups of fifty or a hundred.

⁴¹Jesus took the five loaves and two fish, looked toward heaven, and blessed them. Then, breaking the loaves into pieces, he kept giving the bread to the disciples so they could distribute it to the people. He also divided the fish for everyone to share. ⁴²They all ate as much as they wanted, ⁴³and afterward, the disciples picked up twelve baskets of leftover bread and fish. ⁴⁴A total of 5,000 men and their families were fed from those loaves!

Jesus Walks on Water

⁴⁵Immediately after this, Jesus insisted that his disciples get back into the boat and head across the lake to Bethsaida, while he sent the people home. ⁴⁶After telling everyone good-bye, he went up into the hills by himself to pray.

⁴⁷Late that night, the disciples were in their boat in the middle of the lake, and Jesus was alone on land. ⁴⁸He saw that they were in serious trouble, rowing hard and struggling against the wind and waves. About three o'clock in the morning* Jesus came toward them, walking on the water. He intended to go past them, ⁴⁹but when they saw him walking on the water, they cried out in terror, thinking he was a ghost. ⁵⁰They were all terrified when they saw him.

But Jesus spoke to them at once. "Don't be afraid," he said. "Take courage! I am here!*" ⁵¹Then he climbed into the boat, and the wind stopped. They were totally amazed, ⁵²for they still didn't understand the significance of the miracle of the loaves. Their hearts were too hard to take it in.

⁵³After they had crossed the lake, they landed at Gennesaret. They brought the boat to shore ⁵⁴and climbed out. The people recognized Jesus at once, ⁵⁵and they ran throughout the whole area, carrying sick people on mats to wherever they heard he was. ⁵⁶Wherever he went—in villages, cities, or the countryside—they brought the sick out to the marketplaces. They begged him to let the sick touch at least the fringe of his robe, and all who touched him were healed.

CHAPTER 7

Jesus Teaches about Inner Purity

One day some Pharisees and teachers of religious law arrived from Jerusalem to see Jesus. ²They noticed that some

6:48 Greek About the fourth watch of the night.　6:50 Or The 'I AM' is here; Greek reads I am. See Exod 3:14.

of his disciples failed to follow the Jewish ritual of hand washing before eating. ³(The Jews, especially the Pharisees, do not eat until they have poured water over their cupped hands,* as required by their ancient traditions. ⁴Similarly, they don't eat anything from the market until they immerse their hands* in water. This is but one of many traditions they have clung to—such as their ceremonial washing of cups, pitchers, and kettles.*)

⁵So the Pharisees and teachers of religious law asked him, "Why don't your disciples follow our age-old tradition? They eat without first performing the hand-washing ceremony."

⁶Jesus replied, "You hypocrites! Isaiah was right when he prophesied about you, for he wrote,

'These people honor me with their lips,
    but their hearts are far from me.
⁷ Their worship is a farce,
    for they teach man-made ideas as commands from
        God.'*

⁸For you ignore God's law and substitute your own tradition."

⁹Then he said, "You skillfully sidestep God's law in order to hold on to your own tradition. ¹⁰For instance, Moses gave you this law from God: 'Honor your father and mother,'* and 'Anyone who speaks disrespectfully of father or mother must be put to death.'* ¹¹But you say it is all right for people to say to their parents, 'Sorry, I can't help you. For I have vowed to give to God what I would have given to you.'* ¹²In this way, you let them disregard their needy parents. ¹³And so you cancel the word of God in order to hand down your own tradition. And this is only one example among many others."

¹⁴Then Jesus called to the crowd to come and hear. "All of you listen," he said, "and try to understand. ¹⁵It's not what goes into your body that defiles you; you are defiled by what comes from your heart.*"

¹⁷Then Jesus went into a house to get away from the crowd, and his disciples asked him what he meant by the parable he had just used. ¹⁸"Don't you understand either?" he asked. "Can't you see that the food you put into your body cannot defile you? ¹⁹Food doesn't go into your heart, but only passes through the stomach and then goes into the sewer." (By saying this, he declared that every kind of food is acceptable in God's eyes.)

²⁰And then he added, "It is what comes from inside that defiles you. ²¹For from within, out of a person's heart, come evil thoughts, sexual immorality, theft, murder, ²²adultery, greed, wickedness, deceit, lustful desires, envy, slander, pride, and foolishness. ²³All these vile things come from within; they are what defile you."

The Faith of a Gentile Woman

²⁴Then Jesus left Galilee and went north to the region of Tyre.* He didn't want anyone to know which house he was staying in, but he couldn't keep it a secret. ²⁵Right away a woman who had heard about him came and fell at his feet. Her little girl was possessed by an evil* spirit, ²⁶and she begged him to cast out the demon from her daughter.

Since she was a Gentile, born in Syrian Phoenicia, ²⁷Jesus told her, "First I should feed the children—my own family, the Jews.* It isn't right to take food from the children and throw it to the dogs."

²⁸She replied, "That's true, Lord, but even the dogs under the table are allowed to eat the scraps from the children's plates."

²⁹"Good answer!" he said. "Now go home, for the demon has left your daughter." ³⁰And when she arrived home, she found her little girl lying quietly in bed, and the demon was gone.

7:3 Greek *have washed with the fist.*   **7:4a** Some manuscripts read *sprinkle themselves.*   **7:4b** Some manuscripts add *and dining couches.*   **7:7** Isa 29:13 (Greek version).   **7:10a** Exod 20:12; Deut 5:16.   **7:10b** Exod 21:17 (Greek version); Lev 20:9 (Greek version).   **7:11** Greek *'What I would have given to you is Corban' (that is, a gift).*   **7:15** Some manuscripts add verse 16, *Anyone with ears to hear should listen and understand.* Compare 4:9, 23.   **7:24** Some manuscripts add *and Sidon.*   **7:25** Greek *unclean.*   **7:27** Greek *Let the children eat first.*

Jesus Heals a Deaf Man

³¹Jesus left Tyre and went up to Sidon before going back to the Sea of Galilee and the region of the Ten Towns.* ³²A deaf man with a speech impediment was brought to him, and the people begged Jesus to lay his hands on the man to heal him.

³³Jesus led him away from the crowd so they could be alone. He put his fingers into the man's ears. Then, spitting on his own fingers, he touched the man's tongue. ³⁴Looking up to heaven, he sighed and said, *"Ephphatha,"* which means, "Be opened!" ³⁵Instantly the man could hear perfectly, and his tongue was freed so he could speak plainly!

³⁶Jesus told the crowd not to tell anyone, but the more he told them not to, the more they spread the news. ³⁷They were completely amazed and said again and again, "Everything he does is wonderful. He even makes the deaf to hear and gives speech to those who cannot speak."

CHAPTER 8

Jesus Feeds Four Thousand

About this time another large crowd had gathered, and the people ran out of food again. Jesus called his disciples and told them, ²"I feel sorry for these people. They have been here with me for three days, and they have nothing left to eat. ³If I send them home hungry, they will faint along the way. For some of them have come a long distance."

⁴His disciples replied, "How are we supposed to find enough food to feed them out here in the wilderness?"

⁵Jesus asked, "How much bread do you have?"

"Seven loaves," they replied.

⁶So Jesus told all the people to sit down on the ground. Then he took the seven loaves, thanked God for them, and broke them into pieces. He gave them to his disciples, who distributed the bread to the crowd. ⁷A few small fish were found, too, so Jesus also blessed these and told the disciples to distribute them.

⁸They ate as much as they wanted. Afterward, the disciples picked up seven large baskets of leftover food. ⁹There were about 4,000 people in the crowd that day, and Jesus sent them home after they had eaten. ¹⁰Immediately after this, he got into a boat with his disciples and crossed over to the region of Dalmanutha.

Pharisees Demand a Miraculous Sign

¹¹When the Pharisees heard that Jesus had arrived, they came and started to argue with him. Testing him, they demanded that he show them a miraculous sign from heaven to prove his authority.

¹²When he heard this, he sighed deeply in his spirit and said, "Why do these people keep demanding a miraculous sign? I tell you the truth, I will not give this generation any such sign." ¹³So he got back into the boat and left them, and he crossed to the other side of the lake.

Yeast of the Pharisees and Herod

¹⁴But the disciples had forgotten to bring any food. They had only one loaf of bread with them in the boat. ¹⁵As they were crossing the lake, Jesus warned them, "Watch out! Beware of the yeast of the Pharisees and of Herod."

¹⁶At this they began to argue with each other because they hadn't brought any bread. ¹⁷Jesus knew what they were saying, so he said, "Why are you arguing about having no bread? Don't you know or understand even yet? Are your hearts too hard to take it in? ¹⁸'You have eyes—can't you see? You have ears—can't you hear?'* Don't you remember anything at all? ¹⁹When I fed the 5,000 with five loaves of bread, how many baskets of leftovers did you pick up afterward?"

"Twelve," they said.

²⁰"And when I fed the 4,000 with seven loaves, how many large baskets of leftovers did you pick up?"

"Seven," they said.

²¹"Don't you understand yet?" he asked them.

7:31 Greek *Decapolis.*   **8:18** Jer 5:21.

Jesus Heals a Blind Man

²²When they arrived at Bethsaida, some people brought a blind man to Jesus, and they begged him to touch the man and heal him. ²³Jesus took the blind man by the hand and led him out of the village. Then, spitting on the man's eyes, he laid his hands on him and asked, "Can you see anything now?"

²⁴The man looked around. "Yes," he said, "I see people, but I can't see them very clearly. They look like trees walking around."

²⁵Then Jesus placed his hands on the man's eyes again, and his eyes were opened. His sight was completely restored, and he could see everything clearly. ²⁶Jesus sent him away, saying, "Don't go back into the village on your way home."

Peter's Declaration about Jesus

²⁷Jesus and his disciples left Galilee and went up to the villages near Caesarea Philippi. As they were walking along, he asked them, "Who do people say I am?"

²⁸"Well," they replied, "some say John the Baptist, some say Elijah, and others say you are one of the other prophets."

²⁹Then he asked them, "But who do you say I am?"

Peter replied, "You are the Messiah.*"

³⁰But Jesus warned them not to tell anyone about him.

Jesus Predicts His Death

³¹Then Jesus began to tell them that the Son of Man* must suffer many terrible things and be rejected by the elders, the leading priests, and the teachers of religious law. He would be killed, but three days later he would rise from the dead. ³²As he talked about this openly with his disciples, Peter took him aside and began to reprimand him for saying such things.*

³³Jesus turned around and looked at his disciples, then reprimanded Peter. "Get away from me, Satan!" he said. "You are seeing things merely from a human point of view, not from God's."

³⁴Then, calling the crowd to join his disciples, he said, "If any of you wants to be my follower, you must turn

8:29 Or *the Christ. Messiah* (a Hebrew term) and *Christ* (a Greek term) both mean "the anointed one."   **8:31** "Son of Man" is a title Jesus used for himself.   **8:32** Or *began to correct him.*

THE POINT

Jesus was bout it, bout it. Jesus was all about spreadin' the Good News to the world. He didn't care where he had to go. Even when the people in Jesus' hometown couldn't get with his message because he was "just the carpenter's son," Jesus didn't trip. He was like: "My bad, if y'all don't want my help, me and mine can step." Next thing you know, Jesus divided the disciples up in pairs of two, gave them the juice to cast out demons, and sent them into the hood to help some folks who might appreciate it. Jesus told them,

"A prophet is honored everywhere except in his own hometown and among his relatives and his own family." And because of their unbelief, he couldn't do any miracles among them . . . [Jesus] called his twelve disciples together and sent them out two by two, giving them the authority to cast out evil spirits. . . . "Wherever you go," he said, "stay in the same house until you leave town. But if any place refuses to welcome you or listen to you, shake its dust from your feet as you leave." (Mark 6:4-11)

Then there was the time when Jesus and his boys were on their way to Caesarea, a town full of folks who didn't know about Jesus or his ministry. So Jesus asked the disciples a question to see if they really understood who it was they were hangin' with. Jesus asked, "Who do people say I am?" (8:27). Dude was deep. In effect, Jesus was tellin' the disciples "You better recognize, 'cause the next town we hit, they won't know about us or what we're tryin' to do. So, if don't nobody else recognize me, you, my disciples, better recognize that I AM who I say I AM, 'cause it might get rough."

from your selfish ways, take up your cross, and follow me. ³⁵If you try to hang on to your life, you will lose it. But if you give up your life for my sake and for the sake of the Good News, you will save it. ³⁶And what do you benefit if you gain the whole world but lose your own soul?* ³⁷Is anything worth more than your soul? ³⁸If anyone is ashamed of me and my message in these adulterous and sinful days, the Son of Man will be ashamed of that person when he returns in the glory of his Father with the holy angels."

CHAPTER 9

Jesus went on to say, "I tell you the truth, some standing here right now will not die before they see the Kingdom of God arrive in great power!"

The Transfiguration

²Six days later Jesus took Peter, James, and John, and led them up a high mountain to be alone. As the men watched, Jesus' appearance was transformed, ³and his clothes became dazzling white, far whiter than any earthly bleach could ever make them. ⁴Then Elijah and Moses appeared and began talking with Jesus.

⁵Peter exclaimed, "Rabbi, it's wonderful for us to be here! Let's make three shelters as memorials*—one for you, one for Moses, and one for Elijah." ⁶He said this because he didn't really know what else to say, for they were all terrified.

⁷Then a cloud overshadowed them, and a voice from the cloud said, "This is my dearly loved Son. Listen to him." ⁸Suddenly, when they looked around, Moses and Elijah were gone, and they saw only Jesus with them.

⁹As they went back down the mountain, he told them not to tell anyone what they had seen until the Son of Man* had risen from the dead. ¹⁰So they kept it to themselves, but they often asked each other what he meant by "rising from the dead."

¹¹Then they asked him, "Why do the teachers of religious law insist that Elijah must return before the Messiah comes?*"

¹²Jesus responded, "Elijah is indeed coming first to get everything ready. Yet why do the Scriptures say that the Son of Man must suffer greatly and be treated with utter contempt? ¹³But I tell you, Elijah has already come, and they chose to abuse him, just as the Scriptures predicted."

Jesus Heals a Demon-Possessed Boy

¹⁴When they returned to the other disciples, they saw a large crowd surrounding them, and some teachers of religious law were arguing with them. ¹⁵When the crowd saw Jesus, they were overwhelmed with awe, and they ran to greet him.

¹⁶"What is all this arguing about?" Jesus asked.

¹⁷One of the men in the crowd spoke up and said, "Teacher, I brought my son so you could heal him. He is possessed by an evil spirit that won't let him talk. ¹⁸And whenever this spirit seizes him, it throws him violently to the ground. Then he foams at the mouth and grinds his teeth and becomes rigid.* So I asked your disciples to cast out the evil spirit, but they couldn't do it."

¹⁹Jesus said to them,* "You faithless people! How long must I be with you? How long must I put up with you? Bring the boy to me."

²⁰So they brought the boy. But when the evil spirit saw Jesus, it threw the child into a violent convulsion, and he fell to the ground, writhing and foaming at the mouth.

²¹"How long has this been happening?" Jesus asked the boy's father.

He replied, "Since he was a little boy. ²²The spirit often

"If you try to hang on to your life, you will lose it. But if you give up your life for my sake and for the sake of the Good News, you will save it" (Mark 8:35).

You gotta lose your old self in order to live.

8:36 Or *your self?* also in 8:37.   **9:5** Greek *three tabernacles.*   **9:9** "Son of Man" is a title Jesus used for himself.   **9:11** Greek *that Elijah must come first?*   **9:18** Or *becomes weak.*
9:19 Or *said to his disciples.*

throws him into the fire or into water, trying to kill him. Have mercy on us and help us, if you can."

23"What do you mean, 'If I can'?" Jesus asked. "Anything is possible if a person believes."

24The father instantly cried out, "I do believe, but help me overcome my unbelief!"

25When Jesus saw that the crowd of onlookers was growing, he rebuked the evil* spirit. "Listen, you spirit that makes this boy unable to hear and speak," he said. "I command you to come out of this child and never enter him again!"

26Then the spirit screamed and threw the boy into another violent convulsion and left him. The boy appeared to be dead. A murmur ran through the crowd as people said, "He's dead." 27But Jesus took him by the hand and helped him to his feet, and he stood up.

28Afterward, when Jesus was alone in the house with his disciples, they asked him, "Why couldn't we cast out that evil spirit?"

29Jesus replied, "This kind can be cast out only by prayer.*"

Jesus Again Predicts His Death

30Leaving that region, they traveled through Galilee. Jesus didn't want anyone to know he was there, 31for he wanted to spend more time with his disciples and teach them. He said to them, "The Son of Man is going to be betrayed into the hands of his enemies. He will be killed, but three days later he will rise from the dead." 32They didn't understand what he was saying, however, and they were afraid to ask him what he meant.

The Greatest in the Kingdom

33After they arrived at Capernaum and settled in a house, Jesus asked his disciples, "What were you discussing out on the road?" 34But they didn't answer, because they had

been arguing about which of them was the greatest. 35He sat down, called the twelve disciples over to him, and said, "Whoever wants to be first must take last place and be the servant of everyone else."

36Then he put a little child among them. Taking the child in his arms, he said to them, 37"Anyone who welcomes a little child like this on my behalf* welcomes me, and anyone who welcomes me welcomes not only me but also my Father who sent me."

Using the Name of Jesus

38John said to Jesus, "Teacher, we saw someone using your name to cast out demons, but we told him to stop because he wasn't in our group."

39"Don't stop him!" Jesus said. "No one who performs a miracle in my name will soon be able to speak evil of me. 40Anyone who is not against us is for us. 41If anyone gives you even a cup of water because you belong to the Messiah, I tell you the truth, that person will surely be rewarded.

42"But if you cause one of these little ones who trusts in me to fall into sin, it would be better for you to be thrown into the sea with a large millstone hung around your neck. 43If your hand causes you to sin, cut it off. It's better to enter eternal life with only one hand than to go into the unquenchable fires of hell* with two hands.* 45If your foot causes you to sin, cut it off. It's better to enter eternal life with only one foot than to be thrown into hell with two feet.* 47And if your eye causes you to sin, gouge it out. It's better to enter the Kingdom of God with only one eye than to have two eyes and be thrown into hell, 48'where the maggots never die and the fire never goes out.'*

49"For everyone will be tested with fire.* 50Salt is good for seasoning. But if it loses its flavor, how do you make it salty again? You must have the qualities of salt among yourselves and live in peace with each other."

9:25 Greek *unclean.*   **9:29** Some manuscripts read *by prayer and fasting.*   **9:37** Greek *in my name.*   **9:43a** Greek *Gehenna; also in 9:45, 47.*   **9:43b** Some manuscripts add verse 44, *'where the maggots never die and the fire never goes out.'* See 9:48.   **9:45** Some manuscripts add verse 46, *'where the maggots never die and the fire never goes out.'* See 9:48.   **9:48** Isa 66:24.   **9:49** Greek *salted with fire;* other manuscripts add *and every sacrifice will be salted with salt.*

Discussion about Divorce and Marriage

Then Jesus left Capernaum and went down to the region of Judea and into the area east of the Jordan River. Once again crowds gathered around him, and as usual he was teaching them.

²Some Pharisees came and tried to trap him with this question: "Should a man be allowed to divorce his wife?"

³Jesus answered them with a question: "What did Moses say in the law about divorce?"

⁴"Well, he permitted it," they replied. "He said a man can give his wife a written notice of divorce and send her away."*

⁵But Jesus responded, "He wrote this commandment only as a concession to your hard hearts. ⁶But 'God made them male and female'* from the beginning of creation. ⁷'This explains why a man leaves his father and mother and is joined to his wife,* ⁸and the two are united into one.'* Since they are no longer two but one, ⁹let no one split apart what God has joined together."

¹⁰Later, when he was alone with his disciples in the house, they brought up the subject again. ¹¹He told them, "Whoever divorces his wife and marries someone else commits adultery against her. ¹²And if a woman divorces her husband and marries someone else, she commits adultery."

Jesus Blesses the Children

¹³One day some parents brought their children to Jesus so he could touch and bless them. But the disciples scolded the parents for bothering him.

¹⁴When Jesus saw what was happening, he was angry with his disciples. He said to them, "Let the children come to me. Don't stop them! For the Kingdom of God belongs to those who are like these children. ¹⁵I tell you the truth, anyone who doesn't receive the Kingdom of God like a child will never enter it." ¹⁶Then he took the children in his arms and placed his hands on their heads and blessed them.

The Rich Man

¹⁷As Jesus was starting out on his way to Jerusalem, a man came running up to him, knelt down, and asked, "Good Teacher, what must I do to inherit eternal life?"

¹⁸"Why do you call me good?" Jesus asked. "Only God is truly good. ¹⁹But to answer your question, you know the commandments: 'You must not murder. You must not commit adultery. You must not steal. You must not testify falsely. You must not cheat anyone. Honor your father and mother.'*"

²⁰"Teacher," the man replied, "I've obeyed all these commandments since I was young."

²¹Looking at the man, Jesus felt genuine love for him. "There is still one thing you haven't done," he told him. "Go and sell all your possessions and give the money to the poor, and you will have treasure in heaven. Then come, follow me."

²²At this the man's face fell, and he went away sad, for he had many possessions.

²³Jesus looked around and said to his disciples, "How hard it is for the rich to enter the Kingdom of God!" ²⁴This amazed them. But Jesus said again, "Dear children, it is very hard* to enter the Kingdom of God. ²⁵In fact, it is easier for a camel to go through the eye of a needle than for a rich person to enter the Kingdom of God!"

²⁶The disciples were astounded. "Then who in the world can be saved?" they asked.

²⁷Jesus looked at them intently and said, "Humanly speaking, it is impossible. But not with God. Everything is possible with God."

²⁸Then Peter began to speak up. "We've given up everything to follow you," he said.

"Jesus looked at them intently and said, 'Humanly speaking, it is impossible. But not with God. Everything is possible with God'" (Mark 10:27).

say what?

What seems impossible is always possible with God.

10:4 See Deut 24:1. **10:6** Gen 1:27; 5:2. **10:7** Some manuscripts do not include *and is joined to his wife.* **10:7-8** Gen 2:24. **10:19** Exod 20:12-16; Deut 5:16-20. **10:24** Some manuscripts read *very hard for those who trust in riches.*

29"Yes," Jesus replied, "and I assure you that everyone who has given up house or brothers or sisters or mother or father or children or property, for my sake and for the Good News, 30will receive now in return a hundred times as many houses, brothers, sisters, mothers, children, and property— along with persecution. And in the world to come that person will have eternal life. 31But many who are the greatest now will be least important then, and those who seem least important now will be the greatest then.*"

Jesus Again Predicts His Death

32They were now on the way up to Jerusalem, and Jesus was walking ahead of them. The disciples were filled with awe, and the people following behind were overwhelmed with fear. Taking the twelve disciples aside, Jesus once more began to describe everything that was about to happen to him. 33"Listen," he said, "we're going up to Jerusalem, where the Son of Man* will be betrayed to the leading priests and the teachers of religious law. They will sentence him to die and hand him over to the Romans.* 34They will mock him, spit on him, flog him with a whip, and kill him, but after three days he will rise again."

Jesus Teaches about Serving Others

35Then James and John, the sons of Zebedee, came over and spoke to him. "Teacher," they said, "we want you to do us a favor."

36"What is your request?" he asked.

37They replied, "When you sit on your glorious throne, we want to sit in places of honor next to you, one on your right and the other on your left."

38But Jesus said to them, "You don't know what you are asking! Are you able to drink from the bitter cup of suffering I am about to drink? Are you able to be baptized with the baptism of suffering I must be baptized with?"

39"Oh yes," they replied, "we are able!"

Then Jesus told them, "You will indeed drink from my bitter cup and be baptized with my baptism of suffering. 40But I have no right to say who will sit on my right or my left. God has prepared those places for the ones he has chosen."

41When the ten other disciples heard what James and John had asked, they were indignant. 42So Jesus called them together and said, "You know that the rulers in this world lord it over their people, and officials flaunt their authority over those under them. 43But among you it will be different. Who-

10:31 Greek *But many who are first will be last; and the last, first.*   **10:33a** "Son of Man" is a title Jesus used for himself.   **10:33b** Greek *the Gentiles.*

THE POINT

Jesus came to serve. Mark talks about several times when the disciples were left scratchin' their heads. Like the time Jesus told this rich dude to give away his house, his cash, his bling, and all his stuff to the poor before he could qualify for eternal life (10:17-27). Basically, Jesus told the dude if he wasn't ready to give up all he had, then he wasn't ready for the life Jesus offered.

"If any of you wants to be my follower, you must turn from your selfish ways, take up your cross, and follow me." (Mark 8:34)

Everybody was looking for some larger-than-life dude to show up and save them. So when Jesus showed up on the scene, a cool, sorta laid-back dude, no one thought he was all that. C'mon, he was just a carpenter's son! No way was he the promised Messiah! But then Jesus showed what he was all about. He even told his boys to make sure they wanted to roll with him cause living a life of serving others ain't an easy thing.

"Whoever wants to be a leader among you must be your servant, and whoever wants to

be first among you must be the slave of everyone else. For even the Son of Man came not to be served but to serve others and to give his life as a ransom for many." (Mark 10:43-45)

It was non-stop casting out demons, healing lepers and cripples, calming storms, and feeding thousands. People started following Jesus everywhere. This carpenter's son was all about takin' care of others before himself. And he was askin' the same of his boys.

ever wants to be a leader among you must be your servant, 44and whoever wants to be first among you must be the slave of everyone else. 45For even the Son of Man came not to be served but to serve others and to give his life as a ransom for many."

Jesus Heals Blind Bartimaeus

46Then they reached Jericho, and as Jesus and his disciples left town, a large crowd followed him. A blind beggar named Bartimaeus (son of Timaeus) was sitting beside the road. 47When Bartimaeus heard that Jesus of Nazareth was nearby, he began to shout, "Jesus, Son of David, have mercy on me!"

48"Be quiet!" many of the people yelled at him.

But he only shouted louder, "Son of David, have mercy on me!"

49When Jesus heard him, he stopped and said, "Tell him to come here."

So they called the blind man. "Cheer up," they said. "Come on, he's calling you!" 50Bartimaeus threw aside his coat, jumped up, and came to Jesus.

51"What do you want me to do for you?" Jesus asked.

"My rabbi,*" the blind man said, "I want to see!"

52And Jesus said to him, "Go, for your faith has healed you." Instantly the man could see, and he followed Jesus down the road.*

4The two disciples left and found the colt standing in the street, tied outside the front door. 5As they were untying it, some bystanders demanded, "What are you doing, untying that colt?" 6They said what Jesus had told them to say, and they were permitted to take it. 7Then they brought the colt to Jesus and threw their garments over it, and he sat on it.

8Many in the crowd spread their garments on the road ahead of him, and others spread leafy branches they had cut in the fields. 9Jesus was in the center of the procession, and the people all around him were shouting,

"Praise God!*
Blessings on the one who comes in the name of the
LORD!
10 Blessings on the coming Kingdom of our ancestor
David!
Praise God in highest heaven!"*

11So Jesus came to Jerusalem and went into the Temple. After looking around carefully at everything, he left because it was late in the afternoon. Then he returned to Bethany with the twelve disciples.

Jesus Curses the Fig Tree

12The next morning as they were leaving Bethany, Jesus was hungry. 13He noticed a fig tree in full leaf a little way off, so he went over to see if he could find any figs. But there were only leaves because it was too early in the season for fruit. 14Then Jesus said to the tree, "May no one ever eat your fruit again!" And the disciples heard him say it.

Jesus Clears the Temple

15When they arrived back in Jerusalem, Jesus entered the Temple and began to drive out the people buying and selling animals for sacrifices. He knocked over the tables of the money changers and the chairs of those selling doves, 16and

CHAPTER 11

Jesus' Triumphant Entry

As Jesus and his disciples approached Jerusalem, they came to the towns of Bethphage and Bethany on the Mount of Olives. Jesus sent two of them on ahead. 2"Go into that village over there," he told them. "As soon as you enter it, you will see a young donkey tied there that no one has ever ridden. Untie it and bring it here. 3If anyone asks, 'What are you doing?' just say, 'The Lord needs it and will return it soon.'"

10:51 Greek uses the Hebrew term Rabboni.   10:52 Or on the way.   11:9 Greek Hosanna, an exclamation of praise that literally means "save now"; also in 11:10.   11:9-10 Pss 118:25-26; 148:1.

he stopped everyone from using the Temple as a marketplace.* ¹⁷He said to them, "The Scriptures declare, 'My Temple will be called a house of prayer for all nations,' but you have turned it into a den of thieves."*

¹⁸When the leading priests and teachers of religious law heard what Jesus had done, they began planning how to kill him. But they were afraid of him because the people were so amazed at his teaching.

¹⁹That evening Jesus and the disciples left* the city.

²⁰The next morning as they passed by the fig tree he had cursed, the disciples noticed it had withered from the roots up. ²¹Peter remembered what Jesus had said to the tree on the previous day and exclaimed, "Look, Rabbi! The fig tree you cursed has withered and died!"

²²Then Jesus said to the disciples, "Have faith in God. ²³I tell you the truth, you can say to this mountain, 'May you be lifted up and thrown into the sea,' and it will happen. But you must really believe it will happen and have no doubt in your heart. ²⁴I tell you, you can pray for anything, and if you believe that you've received it, it will be yours. ²⁵But when you are praying, first forgive anyone you are holding a grudge against, so that your Father in heaven will forgive your sins, too.*"

The Authority of Jesus Challenged

²⁷Again they entered Jerusalem. As Jesus was walking through the Temple area, the leading priests, the teachers of religious law, and the elders came up to him. ²⁸They demanded, "By what authority are you doing all these things? Who gave you the right to do them?"

²⁹"I'll tell you by what authority I do these things if you answer one question," Jesus replied. ³⁰"Did John's authority to baptize come from heaven, or was it merely human? Answer me!"

³¹They talked it over among themselves. "If we say it was

from heaven, he will ask why we didn't believe John. ³²But do we dare say it was merely human?" For they were afraid of what the people would do, because everyone believed that John was a prophet. ³³So they finally replied, "We don't know."

And Jesus responded, "Then I won't tell you by what authority I do these things."

CHAPTER 12

Parable of the Evil Farmers

Then Jesus began teaching them with stories: "A man planted a vineyard. He built a wall around it, dug a pit for pressing out the grape juice, and built a lookout tower. Then he leased the vineyard to tenant farmers and moved to another country. ²At the time of the grape harvest, he sent one of his servants to collect his share of the crop. ³But the farmers grabbed the servant, beat him up, and sent him back empty-handed. ⁴The owner then sent another servant, but they insulted him and beat him over the head. ⁵The next servant he sent was killed. Others he sent were either beaten or killed, ⁶until there was only one left—his son whom he loved dearly. The owner finally sent him, thinking, 'Surely they will respect my son.'

⁷"But the tenant farmers said to one another, 'Here comes the heir to this estate. Let's kill him and get the estate for ourselves!' ⁸So they grabbed him and murdered him and threw his body out of the vineyard.

⁹"What do you suppose the owner of the vineyard will do?" Jesus asked. "I'll tell you—he will come and kill those farmers and lease the vineyard to others. ¹⁰Didn't you ever read this in the Scriptures?

'The stone that the builders rejected
    has now become the cornerstone.
¹¹ This is the LORD's doing,
    and it is wonderful to see.'*"

11:16 Or *from carrying merchandise through the Temple.*   11:17 Isa 56:7; Jer 7:11.   11:19 Greek *they left;* other manuscripts read *he left.*   11:25 Some manuscripts add verse 26, *But if you refuse to forgive, your Father in heaven will not forgive your sins.* Compare Matt 6:15.   12:10-11 Ps 118:22-23.

¹²The religious leaders* wanted to arrest Jesus because they realized he was telling the story against them—they were the wicked farmers. But they were afraid of the crowd, so they left him and went away.

Taxes for Caesar

¹³Later the leaders sent some Pharisees and supporters of Herod to trap Jesus into saying something for which he could be arrested. ¹⁴"Teacher," they said, "we know how honest you are. You are impartial and don't play favorites. You teach the way of God truthfully. Now tell us—is it right to pay taxes to Caesar or not? ¹⁵Should we pay them, or shouldn't we?"

Jesus saw through their hypocrisy and said, "Why are you trying to trap me? Show me a Roman coin,* and I'll tell you." ¹⁶When they handed it to him, he asked, "Whose picture and title are stamped on it?"

"Caesar's," they replied.

¹⁷"Well, then," Jesus said, "give to Caesar what belongs to Caesar, and give to God what belongs to God."

His reply completely amazed them.

Discussion about Resurrection

¹⁸Then Jesus was approached by some Sadducees—religious leaders who say there is no resurrection from the dead. They posed this question: ¹⁹"Teacher, Moses gave us a law that if a man dies, leaving a wife without children, his brother should marry the widow and have a child who will carry on the brother's name.* ²⁰Well, suppose there were seven brothers. The oldest one married and then died without children. ²¹So the second brother married the widow, but he also died without children. Then the third brother married her. ²²This continued with all seven of them, and still there were no children. Last of all, the woman also died. ²³So tell us, whose wife will she be in the resurrection? For all seven were married to her."

²⁴Jesus replied, "Your mistake is that you don't know the Scriptures, and you don't know the power of God. ²⁵For when the dead rise, they will neither marry nor be given in marriage. In this respect they will be like the angels in heaven.

²⁶"But now, as to whether the dead will be raised—haven't you ever read about this in the writings of Moses, in the story of the burning bush? Long after Abraham, Isaac, and Jacob had died, God said to Moses,* 'I am the God of Abraham, the God of Isaac, and the God of Jacob.'* ²⁷So he is the God of the living, not the dead. You have made a serious error."

The Most Important Commandment

²⁸One of the teachers of religious law was standing there listening to the debate. He realized that Jesus had answered well, so he asked, "Of all the commandments, which is the most important?"

²⁹Jesus replied, "The most important commandment is this: 'Listen, O Israel! The LORD our God is the one and only LORD. ³⁰And you must love the LORD your God with all your heart, all your soul, all your mind, and all your strength.'* ³¹The second is equally important: 'Love your neighbor as yourself.'* No other commandment is greater than these."

³²The teacher of religious law replied, "Well said, Teacher. You have spoken the truth by saying that there is only one God and no other. ³³And I know it is important to love him with all my heart and all my understanding and all my strength, and to love my neighbor as myself. This is more important than to offer all of the burnt offerings and sacrifices required in the law."

³⁴Realizing how much the man understood, Jesus said to him, "You are not far from the Kingdom of God." And after that, no one dared to ask him any more questions.

Whose Son Is the Messiah?

³⁵Later, as Jesus was teaching the people in the Temple, he asked, "Why do the teachers of religious law claim that the

12:12 Greek *They.* 12:15 Greek *a denarius.* 12:19 See Deut 25:5-6. 12:26a Greek *in the story of the bush? God said to him.* 12:26b Exod 3:6. 12:29-30 Deut 6:4-5. 12:31 Lev 19:18.

Messiah is the son of David? ³⁶For David himself, speaking under the inspiration of the Holy Spirit, said,

'The LORD said to my Lord,
Sit in the place of honor at my right hand
    until I humble your enemies beneath your feet.'*

³⁷Since David himself called the Messiah 'my Lord,' how can the Messiah be his son?" The large crowd listened to him with great delight.

³⁸Jesus also taught: "Beware of these teachers of religious law! For they like to parade around in flowing robes and receive respectful greetings as they walk in the marketplaces. ³⁹And how they love the seats of honor in the synagogues and the head table at banquets. ⁴⁰Yet they shamelessly cheat widows out of their property and then pretend to be pious by making long prayers in public. Because of this, they will be more severely punished."

The Widow's Offering

⁴¹Jesus sat down near the collection box in the Temple and watched as the crowds dropped in their money. Many rich people put in large amounts. ⁴²Then a poor widow came and dropped in two small coins.*

⁴³Jesus called his disciples to him and said, "I tell you the truth, this poor widow has given more than all the others who are making contributions. ⁴⁴For they gave a tiny part of their surplus, but she, poor as she is, has given everything she had to live on."

CHAPTER 13

Jesus Foretells the Future

As Jesus was leaving the Temple that day, one of his disciples said, "Teacher, look at these magnificent buildings! Look at the impressive stones in the walls."

²Jesus replied, "Yes, look at these great buildings. But they will be completely demolished. Not one stone will be left on top of another!"

³Later, Jesus sat on the Mount of Olives across the valley from the Temple. Peter, James, John, and Andrew came to him privately and asked him, ⁴"Tell us, when will all this happen? What sign will show us that these things are about to be fulfilled?"

⁵Jesus replied, "Don't let anyone mislead you, ⁶for many will come in my name, claiming, 'I am the Messiah.'* They will deceive many. ⁷And you will hear of wars and threats of wars, but don't panic. Yes, these things must take place, but the end won't follow immediately. ⁸Nation will go to war against nation, and kingdom against kingdom. There will be earthquakes in many parts of the world, as well as famines. But this is only the first of the birth pains, with more to come.

⁹"When these things begin to happen, watch out! You will be handed over to the local councils and beaten in the synagogues. You will stand trial before governors and kings because you are my followers. But this will be your opportunity to tell them about me.* ¹⁰For the Good News must first be preached to all nations.* ¹¹But when you are arrested and stand trial, don't worry in advance about what to say. Just say what God tells you at that time, for it is not you who will be speaking, but the Holy Spirit.

¹²"A brother will betray his brother to death, a father will betray his own child, and children will rebel against their parents and cause them to be killed. ¹³And everyone will hate you because you are my followers.* But the one who endures to the end will be saved.

¹⁴"The day is coming when you will see the sacrilegious object that causes desecration* standing where he* should not be." (Reader, pay attention!) "Then those in Judea must flee to the hills. ¹⁵A person out on the deck of a roof must not go down into the house to pack. ¹⁶A person out in the

12:36 Ps 110:1.   12:42 Greek *two lepta, which is a kodrantes* [i.e., a quadrans].   13:6 Greek *claiming, 'I am.'*   13:9 Or *But this will be your testimony against them.*   13:10 Or *all peoples.*   13:13 Greek *on account of my name.*   13:14a Greek *the abomination of desolation.* See Dan 9:27; 11:31; 12:11.   13:14b Or *it.*

field must not return even to get a coat. ¹⁷How terrible it will be for pregnant women and for nursing mothers in those days. ¹⁸And pray that your flight will not be in winter. ¹⁹For there will be greater anguish in those days than at any time since God created the world. And it will never be so great again. ²⁰In fact, unless the Lord shortens that time of calamity, not a single person will survive. But for the sake of his chosen ones he has shortened those days.

²¹"Then if anyone tells you, 'Look, here is the Messiah,' or 'There he is,' don't believe it. ²²For false messiahs and false prophets will rise up and perform signs and wonders so as to deceive, if possible, even God's chosen ones. ²³Watch out! I have warned you about this ahead of time!

²⁴"At that time, after the anguish of those days,

the sun will be darkened,
    the moon will give no light,
²⁵ the stars will fall from the sky,
    and the powers in the heavens will be shaken.*

²⁶Then everyone will see the Son of Man* coming on the clouds with great power and glory.* ²⁷And he will send out his angels to gather his chosen ones from all over the world*—from the farthest ends of the earth and heaven.

²⁸"Now learn a lesson from the fig tree. When its branches bud and its leaves begin to sprout, you know that summer is near. ²⁹In the same way, when you see all these things taking place, you can know that his return is very near, right at the door. ³⁰I tell you the truth, this generation* will not pass from the scene before all these things take place. ³¹Heaven and earth will disappear, but my words will never disappear.

³²"However, no one knows the day or hour when these things will happen, not even the angels in heaven or the Son himself. Only the Father knows. ³³And since you don't know when that time will come, be on guard! Stay alert*!

³⁴"The coming of the Son of Man can be illustrated by the story of a man going on a long trip. When he left home, he gave each of his slaves instructions about the work they were to do, and he told the gatekeeper to watch for his return. ³⁵You, too, must keep watch! For you don't know when the master of the household will return—in the evening, at midnight, before dawn, or at daybreak. ³⁶Don't let him find you sleeping when he arrives without warning. ³⁷I say to you what I say to everyone: Watch for him!"

CHAPTER **14**

Jesus Anointed at Bethany

It was now two days before Passover and the Festival of Unleavened Bread. The leading priests and the teachers of religious law were still looking for an opportunity to capture Jesus secretly and kill him. ²"But not during the Passover celebration," they agreed, "or the people may riot."

³Meanwhile, Jesus was in Bethany at the home of Simon, a man who had previously had leprosy. While he was eating,* a woman came in with a beautiful alabaster jar of expensive perfume made from essence of nard. She broke open the jar and poured the perfume over his head.

⁴Some of those at the table were indignant. "Why waste such expensive perfume?" they asked. ⁵"It could have been sold for a year's wages* and the money given to the poor!" So they scolded her harshly.

⁶But Jesus replied, "Leave her alone. Why criticize her for doing such a good thing to me? ⁷You will always have the poor among you, and you can help them whenever you want to. But you will not always have me. ⁸She has done what she could and has anointed my body for burial ahead of time. ⁹I tell you the truth, wherever the Good News is preached throughout the world, this woman's deed will be remembered and discussed."

13:24-25 See Isa 13:10; 34:4; Joel 2:10.   **13:26a** "Son of Man" is a title Jesus used for himself.   **13:26b** See Dan 7:13.   **13:27** Greek *from the four winds.*   **13:30** Or *this age,* or *this nation.*   **13:33** Some manuscripts add *and pray.*   **14:3** Or *reclining.*   **14:5** Greek *for 300 denarii.* A denarius was equivalent to a laborer's full day's wage.

Judas Agrees to Betray Jesus

¹⁰Then Judas Iscariot, one of the twelve disciples, went to the leading priests to arrange to betray Jesus to them. ¹¹They were delighted when they heard why he had come, and they promised to give him money. So he began looking for an opportunity to betray Jesus.

The Last Supper

¹²On the first day of the Festival of Unleavened Bread, when the Passover lamb is sacrificed, Jesus' disciples asked him, "Where do you want us to go to prepare the Passover meal for you?"

¹³So Jesus sent two of them into Jerusalem with these instructions: "As you go into the city, a man carrying a pitcher of water will meet you. Follow him. ¹⁴At the house he enters, say to the owner, 'The Teacher asks: Where is the guest room where I can eat the Passover meal with my disciples?' ¹⁵He will take you upstairs to a large room that is already set up. That is where you should prepare our meal." ¹⁶So the two disciples went into the city and found everything just as Jesus had said, and they prepared the Passover meal there.

¹⁷In the evening Jesus arrived with the twelve disciples.* ¹⁸As they were at the table* eating, Jesus said, "I tell you the truth, one of you eating with me here will betray me."

¹⁹Greatly distressed, each one asked in turn, "Am I the one?"

²⁰He replied, "It is one of you twelve who is eating from this bowl with me. ²¹For the Son of Man* must die, as the Scriptures declared long ago. But how terrible it will be for the one who betrays him. It would be far better for that man if he had never been born!"

²²As they were eating, Jesus took some bread and blessed it. Then he broke it in pieces and gave it to the disciples, saying, "Take it, for this is my body."

²³And he took a cup of wine and gave thanks to God for it. He gave it to them, and they all drank from it. ²⁴And he said to them, "This is my blood, which confirms the covenant* between God and his people. It is poured out as a sacrifice for many. ²⁵I tell you the truth, I will not drink wine again until the day I drink it new in the Kingdom of God."

²⁶Then they sang a hymn and went out to the Mount of Olives.

Jesus Predicts Peter's Denial

²⁷On the way, Jesus told them, "All of you will desert me. For the Scriptures say,

> 'God will strike* the Shepherd,
> and the sheep will be scattered.'

²⁸But after I am raised from the dead, I will go ahead of you to Galilee and meet you there."

²⁹Peter said to him, "Even if everyone else deserts you, I never will."

³⁰Jesus replied, "I tell you the truth, Peter—this very night, before the rooster crows twice, you will deny three times that you even know me."

³¹"No!" Peter declared emphatically. "Even if I have to die with you, I will never deny you!" And all the others vowed the same.

Jesus Prays in Gethsemane

³²They went to the olive grove called Gethsemane, and Jesus said, "Sit here while I go and pray." ³³He took Peter, James, and John with him, and he became deeply troubled and distressed. ³⁴He told them, "My soul is crushed with grief to the point of death. Stay here and keep watch with me."

³⁵He went on a little farther and fell to the ground. He prayed that, if it were possible, the awful hour awaiting him might pass him by. ³⁶"Abba, Father,"* he cried out, "everything is possible for you. Please take this cup of suffering away from me. Yet I want your will to be done, not mine."

14:17 Greek *the Twelve*.   14:18 Or *As they reclined*.   14:21 "Son of Man" is a title Jesus used for himself.   14:24 Some manuscripts read *the new covenant*.   14:27 Greek *I will strike*. Zech 13:7.   14:36 *Abba* is an Aramaic term for "father."

³⁷Then he returned and found the disciples asleep. He said to Peter, "Simon, are you asleep? Couldn't you watch with me even one hour? ³⁸Keep watch and pray, so that you will not give in to temptation. For the spirit is willing, but the body is weak."

³⁹Then Jesus left them again and prayed the same prayer as before. ⁴⁰When he returned to them again, he found them sleeping, for they couldn't keep their eyes open. And they didn't know what to say.

⁴¹When he returned to them the third time, he said, "Go ahead and sleep. Have your rest. But no—the time has come. The Son of Man is betrayed into the hands of sinners. ⁴²Up, let's be going. Look, my betrayer is here!"

Jesus Is Betrayed and Arrested

⁴³And immediately, even as Jesus said this, Judas, one of the twelve disciples, arrived with a crowd of men armed with swords and clubs. They had been sent by the leading priests, the teachers of religious law, and the elders. ⁴⁴The traitor, Judas, had given them a prearranged signal: "You will know which one to arrest when I greet him with a kiss. Then you can take him away under guard." ⁴⁵As soon as they arrived, Judas walked up to Jesus. "Rabbi!" he exclaimed, and gave him the kiss.

⁴⁶Then the others grabbed Jesus and arrested him. ⁴⁷But one of the men with Jesus pulled out his sword and struck the high priest's slave, slashing off his ear.

⁴⁸Jesus asked them, "Am I some dangerous revolutionary, that you come with swords and clubs to arrest me? ⁴⁹Why didn't you arrest me in the Temple? I was there among you teaching every day. But these things are happening to fulfill what the Scriptures say about me."

⁵⁰Then all his disciples deserted him and ran away. ⁵¹One young man following behind was clothed only in a long linen shirt. When the mob tried to grab him, ⁵²he slipped out of his shirt and ran away naked.

Jesus before the Council

⁵³They took Jesus to the high priest's home where the leading priests, the elders, and the teachers of religious law had gathered. ⁵⁴Meanwhile, Peter followed him at a distance and went right into the high priest's courtyard. There he sat with the guards, warming himself by the fire.

⁵⁵Inside, the leading priests and the entire high council* were trying to find evidence against Jesus, so they could put him to death. But they couldn't find any. ⁵⁶Many false witnesses spoke against him, but they contradicted each other. ⁵⁷Finally, some men stood up and gave this false testimony: ⁵⁸"We heard him say, 'I will destroy this Temple made with human hands, and in three days I will build another, made without human hands.'" ⁵⁹But even then they didn't get their stories straight!

⁶⁰Then the high priest stood up before the others and asked Jesus, "Well, aren't you going to answer these charges? What do you have to say for yourself?" ⁶¹But Jesus was silent and made no reply. Then the high priest asked him, "Are you the Messiah, the Son of the Blessed One?"

⁶²Jesus said, "I AM.* And you will see the Son of Man seated in the place of power at God's right hand* and coming on the clouds of heaven.*"

⁶³Then the high priest tore his clothing to show his horror and said, "Why do we need other witnesses? ⁶⁴You have all heard his blasphemy. What is your verdict?"

"Guilty!" they all cried. "He deserves to die!"

⁶⁵Then some of them began to spit at him, and they blindfolded him and beat him with their fists. "Prophesy to us," they jeered. And the guards slapped him as they took him away.

Peter Denies Jesus

⁶⁶Meanwhile, Peter was in the courtyard below. One of the servant girls who worked for the high priest came by ⁶⁷and noticed Peter warming himself at the fire. She looked at

14:55 Greek *the Sanhedrin.*   **14:62a** Or *The 'I AM' is here;* or *I am the LORD.* See Exod 3:14.   **14:62b** Greek *at the right hand of the power.* See Ps 110:1.   **14:62c** See Dan 7:13.

him closely and said, "You were one of those with Jesus of Nazareth.*"

⁶⁸But Peter denied it. "I don't know what you're talking about," he said, and he went out into the entryway. Just then, a rooster crowed.*

⁶⁹When the servant girl saw him standing there, she began telling the others, "This man is definitely one of them!" ⁷⁰But Peter denied it again.

A little later some of the other bystanders confronted Peter and said, "You must be one of them, because you are a Galilean."

⁷¹Peter swore, "A curse on me if I'm lying—I don't know this man you're talking about!" ⁷²And immediately the rooster crowed the second time.

Suddenly, Jesus' words flashed through Peter's mind: "Before the rooster crows twice, you will deny three times that you even know me." And he broke down and wept.

CHAPTER 15

Jesus' Trial before Pilate

Very early in the morning the leading priests, the elders, and the teachers of religious law—the entire high council*—met to discuss their next step. They bound Jesus, led him away, and took him to Pilate, the Roman governor.

²Pilate asked Jesus, "Are you the king of the Jews?"

Jesus replied, "You have said it."

³Then the leading priests kept accusing him of many crimes, ⁴and Pilate asked him, "Aren't you going to answer them? What about all these charges they are bringing against you?" ⁵But Jesus said nothing, much to Pilate's surprise.

⁶Now it was the governor's custom each year during the Passover celebration to release one prisoner—anyone the people requested. ⁷One of the prisoners at that time was Barabbas, a revolutionary who had committed murder in an uprising. ⁸The crowd went to Pilate and asked him to release a prisoner as usual.

⁹"Would you like me to release to you this 'King of the Jews'?" Pilate asked. ¹⁰(For he realized by now that the leading priests had arrested Jesus out of envy.) ¹¹But at this point the leading priests stirred up the crowd to demand the release of Barabbas instead of Jesus. ¹²Pilate asked them, "Then what should I do with this man you call the king of the Jews?"

¹³They shouted back, "Crucify him!"

¹⁴"Why?" Pilate demanded. "What crime has he committed?"

But the mob roared even louder, "Crucify him!"

¹⁵So to pacify the crowd, Pilate released Barabbas to them. He ordered Jesus flogged with a lead-tipped whip, then turned him over to the Roman soldiers to be crucified.

The Soldiers Mock Jesus

¹⁶The soldiers took Jesus into the courtyard of the governor's headquarters (called the Praetorium) and called out the entire regiment. ¹⁷They dressed him in a purple robe, and they wove thorn branches into a crown and put it on his head. ¹⁸Then they saluted him and taunted, "Hail! King of the Jews!" ¹⁹And they struck him on the head with a reed stick, spit on him, and dropped to their knees in mock worship. ²⁰When they were finally tired of mocking him, they took off the purple robe and put his own clothes on him again. Then they led him away to be crucified.

The Crucifixion

²¹A passerby named Simon, who was from Cyrene,* was coming in from the countryside just then, and the soldiers forced him to carry Jesus' cross. (Simon was the father of Alexander and Rufus.) ²²And they brought Jesus to a place called Golgotha (which means "Place of the Skull"). ²³They offered him wine drugged with myrrh, but he refused it.

14:67 Or *Jesus the Nazarene.* 14:68 Some manuscripts do not include *Just then, a rooster crowed.* 15:1 Greek *the Sanhedrin;* also in 15:43. 15:21 *Cyrene* was a city in northern Africa.

²⁴Then the soldiers nailed him to the cross. They divided his clothes and threw dice* to decide who would get each piece. ²⁵It was nine o'clock in the morning when they crucified him. ²⁶A sign announced the charge against him. It read, "The King of the Jews." ²⁷Two revolutionaries* were crucified with him, one on his right and one on his left.*

²⁹The people passing by shouted abuse, shaking their heads in mockery. "Ha! Look at you now!" they yelled at him. "You said you were going to destroy the Temple and rebuild it in three days. ³⁰Well then, save yourself and come down from the cross!"

³¹The leading priests and teachers of religious law also mocked Jesus. "He saved others," they scoffed, "but he can't save himself! ³²Let this Messiah, this King of Israel, come down from the cross so we can see it and believe him!" Even the men who were crucified with Jesus ridiculed him.

The Death of Jesus

³³At noon, darkness fell across the whole land until three o'clock. ³⁴Then at three o'clock Jesus called out with a loud voice, *"Eloi, Eloi, lema sabachthani?"* which means "My God, my God, why have you abandoned me?"*

³⁵Some of the bystanders misunderstood and thought he was calling for the prophet Elijah. ³⁶One of them ran and filled a sponge with sour wine, holding it up to him on a reed stick so he could drink. "Wait!" he said. "Let's see whether Elijah comes to take him down!"

³⁷Then Jesus uttered another loud cry and breathed his last. ³⁸And the curtain in the sanctuary of the Temple was torn in two, from top to bottom.

³⁹When the Roman officer* who stood facing him* saw how he had died, he exclaimed, "This man truly was the Son of God!"

⁴⁰Some women were there, watching from a distance, including Mary Magdalene, Mary (the mother of James the younger and of Joseph*), and Salome. ⁴¹They had been followers of Jesus and had cared for him while he was in Galilee. Many other women who had come with him to Jerusalem were also there.

The Burial of Jesus

⁴²This all happened on Friday, the day of preparation,* the day before the Sabbath. As evening approached, ⁴³Joseph of Arimathea took a risk and went to Pilate and asked for Jesus' body. (Joseph was an honored member of the high council, and he was waiting for the Kingdom of God to come.) ⁴⁴Pilate couldn't believe that Jesus was already dead, so he called for the Roman officer and asked if he had died yet. ⁴⁵The officer confirmed that Jesus was dead, so Pilate told Joseph he could have the body. ⁴⁶Joseph bought a long sheet of linen cloth. Then he took Jesus' body down from the cross, wrapped it in the cloth, and laid it in a tomb that had been carved out of the rock. Then he rolled a stone in front of the entrance. ⁴⁷Mary Magdalene and Mary the mother of Joseph saw where Jesus' body was laid.

CHAPTER 16

The Resurrection

Saturday evening, when the Sabbath ended, Mary Magdalene, Mary the mother of James, and Salome went out and purchased burial spices so they could anoint Jesus' body. ²Very early on Sunday morning,* just at sunrise, they went to the tomb. ³On the way they were asking each other, "Who will roll away the stone for us from the entrance to the tomb?" ⁴But as they arrived, they looked up and saw that the stone, which was very large, had already been rolled aside.

15:24 Greek *cast lots.* See Ps 22:18.   15:27a Or *Two criminals.*   15:27b Some manuscripts add verse 28, *And the Scripture was fulfilled that said, "He was counted among those who were rebels."* See Isa 53:12; also compare Luke 22:37.   15:34 Ps 22:1.   15:39a Greek *the centurion;* similarly in 15:44, 45.   15:39b Some manuscripts add *heard his cry and.*   15:40 Greek *Joses;* also in 15:47. See Matt 27:56.   15:42 Greek *It was the day of preparation.*   16:2 Greek *on the first day of the week;* also in 16:9.

"[Jesus] told them, 'Go into all the world and preach the Good News to everyone'" (Mark 16:15).

You got good news—now you gotta share it with everybody!

⁵When they entered the tomb, they saw a young man clothed in a white robe sitting on the right side. The women were shocked, ⁶but the angel said, "Don't be alarmed. You are looking for Jesus of Nazareth,* who was crucified. He isn't here! He is risen from the dead! Look, this is where they laid his body. ⁷Now go and tell his disciples, including Peter, that Jesus is going ahead of you to Galilee. You will see him there, just as he told you before he died."

⁸The women fled from the tomb, trembling and bewildered, and they said nothing to anyone because they were too frightened.*

[Shorter Ending of Mark]

Then they briefly reported all this to Peter and his companions. Afterward Jesus himself sent them out from east to west with the sacred and unfailing message of salvation that gives eternal life. Amen.

[Longer Ending of Mark]

⁹After Jesus rose from the dead early on Sunday morning, the first person who saw him was Mary Magdalene, the woman from whom he had cast out seven demons. ¹⁰She went to the disciples, who were grieving and weeping, and told them what had happened. ¹¹But when she told them that Jesus was alive and she had seen him, they didn't believe her.

¹²Afterward he appeared in a different form to two of his followers who were walking from Jerusalem into the country. ¹³They rushed back to tell the others, but no one believed them.

¹⁴Still later he appeared to the eleven disciples as they were eating together. He rebuked them for their stubborn unbelief because they refused to believe those who had seen him after he had been raised from the dead.*

¹⁵And then he told them, "Go into all the world and preach the Good News to everyone. ¹⁶Anyone who believes and is baptized will be saved. But anyone who refuses to believe will be condemned. ¹⁷These miraculous signs will accompany those who believe: They will cast out demons in my name, and they will speak in new languages.* ¹⁸They will be able to handle snakes with safety, and if they drink anything poisonous, it won't hurt them. They will be able to place their hands on the sick, and they will be healed."

¹⁹When the Lord Jesus had finished talking with them, he was taken up into heaven and sat down in the place of honor at God's right hand. ²⁰And the disciples went everywhere and preached, and the Lord worked through them, confirming what they said by many miraculous signs.

16:6 Or *Jesus the Nazarene.*   **16:8** The most reliable early manuscripts of the Gospel of Mark end at verse 8. Other manuscripts include various endings to the Gospel. A few include both the "shorter ending" and the "longer ending." The majority of manuscripts include the "longer ending" immediately after verse 8.   **16:14** Some early manuscripts add: *And they excused themselves, saying, "This age of lawlessness and unbelief is under Satan, who does not permit God's truth and power to conquer the evil [unclean] spirits. Therefore, reveal your justice now." This is what they said to Christ. And Christ replied to them, "The period of years of Satan's power has been fulfilled, but other dreadful things will happen soon. And I was handed over to death for those who have sinned, so that they may return to the truth and sin no more, and so they may inherit the spiritual, incorruptible, and righteous glory in heaven."*   **16:17** Or *new tongues;* some manuscripts do not include *new.*

JUST LIKE MATTHEW, MARK, AND JOHN, the Gospel of Luke is a remix of Jesus' life and ministry. What makes Luke's Gospel stand out from the rest is the details he uses. Luke was a doctor and approached Jesus' story like a meticulous surgeon. He started at the beginning of time with Adam's family and moved forward through Abraham's descendants, the Jews. This family line is completed with Jesus' birth. He carries the story from Jesus' birth to his death, burial, resurrection and eventually his return to his Father in heaven.

Even though Luke was not an apostle (a person who was with Jesus), he gives us the grimey details of Jesus' ministry not found in any of the other Gospels. He talks about the importance of prayer and lets us know that Jesus was a dude for all people not just the Jews. He focuses on Jesus' mad love for society's outcasts, including women, children, the sick and weak, and the poor.

LUKE

CHAPTER **1**

Introduction

Many people have set out to write accounts about the events that have been fulfilled among us. ²They used the eyewitness reports circulating among us from the early disciples.* ³Having carefully investigated everything from the beginning, I also have decided to write a careful account for you, most honorable Theophilus, ⁴so you can be certain of the truth of everything you were taught.

The Birth of John the Baptist Foretold

⁵When Herod was king of Judea, there was a Jewish priest named Zechariah. He was a member of the priestly order of Abijah, and his wife, Elizabeth, was also from the priestly line of Aaron. ⁶Zechariah and Elizabeth were righteous in God's eyes, careful to obey all of the Lord's commandments and regulations. ⁷They had no children because Elizabeth was unable to conceive, and they were both very old.

⁸One day Zechariah was serving God in the Temple, for his order was on duty that week. ⁹As was the custom of the priests, he was chosen by lot to enter the sanctuary of the Lord and burn incense. ¹⁰While the incense was being burned, a great crowd stood outside, praying.

¹¹While Zechariah was in the sanctuary, an angel of the Lord appeared to him, standing to the right of the incense altar. ¹²Zechariah was shaken and overwhelmed with fear when he saw him. ¹³But the angel said, "Don't be afraid, Zechariah! God has heard your prayer. Your wife, Elizabeth, will give you a son, and you are to name him John. ¹⁴You will have great joy and gladness, and many will rejoice at his birth, ¹⁵for he will be great in the eyes of the Lord. He must never touch wine or other alcoholic drinks. He will be filled with the Holy Spirit, even before his birth.* ¹⁶And he will turn many Israelites to the Lord their God. ¹⁷He will be a man with the spirit and power of Elijah. He will prepare the people for the coming of the Lord. He will turn the hearts of the fathers to their children,* and he will cause those who are rebellious to accept the wisdom of the godly."

¹⁸Zechariah said to the angel, "How can I be sure this will happen? I'm an old man now, and my wife is also well along in years."

¹⁹Then the angel said, "I am Gabriel! I stand in the very presence of God. It was he who sent me to bring you this good news! ²⁰But now, since you didn't believe what I said, you will be silent and unable to speak until the child is born. For my words will certainly be fulfilled at the proper time."

²¹Meanwhile, the people were waiting for Zechariah to come out of the sanctuary, wondering why he was taking so long. ²²When he finally did come out, he couldn't speak to them. Then they realized from his gestures and his silence that he must have seen a vision in the sanctuary.

²³When Zechariah's week of service in the Temple was over, he returned home. ²⁴Soon afterward his wife, Elizabeth, became pregnant and went into seclusion for five months. ²⁵"How kind the Lord is!" she exclaimed. "He has taken away my disgrace of having no children."

The Birth of Jesus Foretold

²⁶In the sixth month of Elizabeth's pregnancy, God sent the angel Gabriel to Nazareth, a village in Galilee, ²⁷to a vir-

1:2 Greek *from those who from the beginning were servants of the word.*   **1:15** Or *even from birth.*   **1:17** See Mal 4:5-6.

gin named Mary. She was engaged to be married to a man named Joseph, a descendant of King David. ²⁸Gabriel appeared to her and said, "Greetings, favored woman! The Lord is with you!*"

²⁹Confused and disturbed, Mary tried to think what the angel could mean. ³⁰"Don't be afraid, Mary," the angel told her, "for you have found favor with God! ³¹You will conceive and give birth to a son, and you will name him Jesus. ³²He will be very great and will be called the Son of the Most High. The Lord God will give him the throne of his ancestor David. ³³And he will reign over Israel* forever; his Kingdom will never end!"

³⁴Mary asked the angel, "But how can this happen? I am a virgin."

³⁵The angel replied, "The Holy Spirit will come upon you, and the power of the Most High will overshadow you. So the baby to be born will be holy, and he will be called the Son of God. ³⁶What's more, your relative Elizabeth has become pregnant in her old age! People used to say she was barren, but she has conceived a son and is now in her sixth month. ³⁷For nothing is impossible with God.*"

³⁸Mary responded, "I am the Lord's servant. May everything you have said about me come true." And then the angel left her.

Mary Visits Elizabeth

³⁹A few days later Mary hurried to the hill country of Judea, to the town ⁴⁰where Zechariah lived. She entered the house and greeted Elizabeth. ⁴¹At the sound of Mary's greeting, Elizabeth's child leaped within her, and Elizabeth was filled with the Holy Spirit.

⁴²Elizabeth gave a glad cry and exclaimed to Mary, "God has blessed you above all women, and your child is blessed. ⁴³Why am I so honored, that the mother of my Lord should visit me? ⁴⁴When I heard your greeting, the baby in my womb jumped for joy. ⁴⁵You are blessed because you believed that the Lord would do what he said."

The Magnificat: Mary's Song of Praise

⁴⁶Mary responded,

"Oh, how my soul praises the Lord.
⁴⁷   How my spirit rejoices in God my Savior!
⁴⁸ For he took notice of his lowly servant girl,
        and from now on all generations will call me blessed.
⁴⁹ For the Mighty One is holy,
        and he has done great things for me.
⁵⁰ He shows mercy from generation to generation
        to all who fear him.
⁵¹ His mighty arm has done tremendous things!
        He has scattered the proud and haughty ones.
⁵² He has brought down princes from their thrones
        and exalted the humble.
⁵³ He has filled the hungry with good things
        and sent the rich away with empty hands.
⁵⁴ He has helped his servant Israel
        and remembered to be merciful.
⁵⁵ For he made this promise to our ancestors,
        to Abraham and his children forever."

⁵⁶Mary stayed with Elizabeth about three months and then went back to her own home.

The Birth of John the Baptist

⁵⁷When it was time for Elizabeth's baby to be born, she gave birth to a son. ⁵⁸And when her neighbors and relatives heard that the Lord had been very merciful to her, everyone rejoiced with her.

⁵⁹When the baby was eight days old, they all came for the circumcision ceremony. They wanted to name him Zechariah, after his father. ⁶⁰But Elizabeth said, "No! His name is John!"

⁶¹"What?" they exclaimed. "There is no one in all your family by that name." ⁶²So they used gestures to ask the baby's father what he wanted to name him. ⁶³He motioned for a writing tablet, and to everyone's surprise he wrote, "His name

1:28 Some manuscripts add *Blessed are you among women.* **1:33** Greek *over the house of Jacob.* **1:37** Some manuscripts read *For the word of God will never fail.*

is John." [64]Instantly Zechariah could speak again, and he began praising God.

[65]Awe fell upon the whole neighborhood, and the news of what had happened spread throughout the Judean hills. [66]Everyone who heard about it reflected on these events and asked, "What will this child turn out to be?" For the hand of the Lord was surely upon him in a special way.

Zechariah's Prophecy

[67]Then his father, Zechariah, was filled with the Holy Spirit and gave this prophecy:

[68] "Praise the Lord, the God of Israel,
  because he has visited and redeemed his people.
[69] He has sent us a mighty Savior*
  from the royal line of his servant David,
[70] just as he promised
  through his holy prophets long ago.
[71] Now we will be saved from our enemies
  and from all who hate us.
[72] He has been merciful to our ancestors
  by remembering his sacred covenant—
[73] the covenant he swore with an oath
  to our ancestor Abraham.
[74] We have been rescued from our enemies
  so we can serve God without fear,
[75] in holiness and righteousness
  for as long as we live.

[76] "And you, my little son,
  will be called the prophet of the Most High,
  because you will prepare the way for the Lord.
[77] You will tell his people how to find salvation
  through forgiveness of their sins.
[78] Because of God's tender mercy,
  the morning light from heaven is about to break
  upon us,*

[79] to give light to those who sit in darkness and in the
  shadow of death,
  and to guide us to the path of peace."

[80]John grew up and became strong in spirit. And he lived in the wilderness until he began his public ministry to Israel.

CHAPTER 2

The Birth of Jesus

At that time the Roman emperor, Augustus, decreed that a census should be taken throughout the Roman Empire. [2](This was the first census taken when Quirinius was governor of Syria.) [3]All returned to their own ancestral towns to register for this census. [4]And because Joseph was a descendant of King David, he had to go to Bethlehem in Judea, David's ancient home. He traveled there from the village of Nazareth in Galilee. [5]He took with him Mary, his fiancée, who was now obviously pregnant.

[6]And while they were there, the time came for her baby to be born. [7]She gave birth to her first child, a son. She wrapped him snugly in strips of cloth and laid him in a manger, because there was no lodging available for them.

The Shepherds and Angels

[8]That night there were shepherds staying in the fields nearby, guarding their flocks of sheep. [9]Suddenly, an angel of the Lord appeared among them, and the radiance of the Lord's glory surrounded them. They were terrified, [10]but the angel reassured them. "Don't be afraid!" he said. "I bring you good news that will bring great joy to all people. [11]The Savior—yes, the Messiah, the Lord—has been born today in Bethlehem, the city of David! [12]And you will recognize him by this sign: You will find a baby wrapped snugly in strips of cloth, lying in a manger."

[13]Suddenly, the angel was joined by a vast host of others—the armies of heaven—praising God and saying,

1:69 Greek *has raised up a horn of salvation for us.*   1:78 Or *the Morning Light from Heaven is about to visit us.*

14 "Glory to God in highest heaven,
and peace on earth to those with whom God is pleased."

15When the angels had returned to heaven, the shepherds said to each other, "Let's go to Bethlehem! Let's see this thing that has happened, which the Lord has told us about."

16They hurried to the village and found Mary and Joseph. And there was the baby, lying in the manger. 17After seeing him, the shepherds told everyone what had happened and what the angel had said to them about this child. 18All who heard the shepherds' story were astonished, 19but Mary kept all these things in her heart and thought about them often. 20The shepherds went back to their flocks, glorifying and praising God for all they had heard and seen. It was just as the angel had told them.

Jesus Is Presented in the Temple

21Eight days later, when the baby was circumcised, he was named Jesus, the name given him by the angel even before he was conceived.

22Then it was time for their purification offering, as required by the law of Moses after the birth of a child; so his parents took him to Jerusalem to present him to the Lord. 23The law of the Lord says, "If a woman's first child is a boy, he must be dedicated to the LORD."* 24So they offered the sacrifice required in the law of the Lord—"either a pair of turtledoves or two young pigeons."*

The Prophecy of Simeon

25At that time there was a man in Jerusalem named Simeon. He was righteous and devout and was eagerly waiting for the Messiah to come and rescue Israel. The Holy Spirit was upon him 26and had revealed to him that he would not die until he had seen the Lord's Messiah. 27That day the Spirit led him to the Temple. So when Mary and Joseph came to present the baby Jesus to the Lord as the law required, 28Simeon was there. He took the child in his arms and praised God, saying,

29 "Sovereign Lord, now let your servant die in peace,
as you have promised.
30 I have seen your salvation,
31   which you have prepared for all people.
32 He is a light to reveal God to the nations,
and he is the glory of your people Israel!"

33Jesus' parents were amazed at what was being said about him. 34Then Simeon blessed them, and he said to Mary, the baby's mother, "This child is destined to cause many in Israel to fall, but he will be a joy to many others. He has been sent as a sign from God, but many will oppose him. 35As a result, the deepest thoughts of many hearts will be revealed. And a sword will pierce your very soul."

The Prophecy of Anna

36Anna, a prophet, was also there in the Temple. She was the daughter of Phanuel from the tribe of Asher, and she was very old. Her husband died when they had been married only seven years. 37Then she lived as a widow to the age of eighty-four.* She never left the Temple but stayed there day and night, worshiping God with fasting and prayer. 38She came along just as Simeon was talking with Mary and Joseph, and she began praising God. She talked about the child to everyone who had been waiting expectantly for God to rescue Jerusalem.

39When Jesus' parents had fulfilled all the requirements of the law of the Lord, they returned home to Nazareth in Galilee. 40There the child grew up healthy and strong. He was filled with wisdom, and God's favor was on him.

Jesus Speaks with the Teachers

41Every year Jesus' parents went to Jerusalem for the Passover festival. 42When Jesus was twelve years old, they

2:23 Exod 13:2. 2:24 Lev 12:8. 2:37 Or She had been a widow for eighty-four years.

attended the festival as usual. [43]After the celebration was over, they started home to Nazareth, but Jesus stayed behind in Jerusalem. His parents didn't miss him at first, [44]because they assumed he was among the other travelers. But when he didn't show up that evening, they started looking for him among their relatives and friends.

[45]When they couldn't find him, they went back to Jerusalem to search for him there. [46]Three days later they finally discovered him in the Temple, sitting among the religious teachers, listening to them and asking questions. [47]All who heard him were amazed at his understanding and his answers.

[48]His parents didn't know what to think. "Son," his mother said to him, "why have you done this to us? Your father and I have been frantic, searching for you everywhere."

[49]"But why did you need to search?" he asked. "Didn't you know that I must be in my Father's house?"* [50]But they didn't understand what he meant.

[51]Then he returned to Nazareth with them and was obedient to them. And his mother stored all these things in her heart.

[52]Jesus grew in wisdom and in stature and in favor with God and all the people.

CHAPTER 3
John the Baptist Prepares the Way
It was now the fifteenth year of the reign of Tiberius, the Roman emperor. Pontius Pilate was governor over Judea; Herod Antipas was ruler* over Galilee; his brother Philip was ruler* over Iturea and Traconitis; Lysanias was ruler over Abilene. [2]Annas and Caiaphas were the high priests. At this time a message from God came to John son of Zechariah, who was living in the wilderness. [3]Then John went from place to place on both sides of the Jordan River, preaching that people should be baptized to show that they had repented of their sins and turned to God to be forgiven. [4]Isaiah had spoken of John when he said,

"He is a voice shouting in the wilderness,
'Prepare the way for the LORD's coming!
    Clear the road for him!
[5] The valleys will be filled,
    and the mountains and hills made level.
The curves will be straightened,
    and the rough places made smooth.
[6] And then all people will see
    the salvation sent from God.'"*

2:49 Or *"Didn't you realize that I should be involved with my Father's affairs?"*   **3:1a** Greek *Herod was tetrarch.* Herod Antipas was a son of King Herod.   **3:1b** Greek *tetrarch;* also in 3:1c. **3:4-6** Isa 40:3-5 (Greek version).

THE POINT

God's Son was Son of Man. A'right, we know from readin' the other Gospels that Jesus was a good look. He was out there handlin' his business, performin' miracles, healin' people, and reppin' God's ministry. But one point of Luke's Gospel was to show the human side of Jesus—the Son of Man. Luke wanted everyone to know that even though Jesus was God's Son, he was also human. Like any other newborn Jewish baby boy at this time, he was circumcised (Luke 2:21), he was dedicated to the Lord (2:22-23), and he had to mind his parents:

He returned to Nazareth with them [Mary and Joseph] and was obedient to them. . . . Jesus grew in wisdom and in stature and in favor with God and all the people. (Luke 2:51-52)

On more than one occasion the devil got it twisted and tried to catch Jesus up in some drama that he wasn't even vouching for.

[Jesus] was led by the Spirit in the wilderness, where he was tempted by the devil for forty days. . . . "I will give you the glory of these kingdoms and authority over them," the devil said, "because they are mine to give to anyone I please. I will give it all to you if you will worship me." (Luke 4:2-7)

But Jesus knew what to do and dropped some Word on him and told him to fall back: "The Scriptures say, 'You must worship the LORD your God and serve only him'" (Luke 4:8).

7When the crowds came to John for baptism, he said, "You brood of snakes! Who warned you to flee God's coming wrath? 8Prove by the way you live that you have repented of your sins and turned to God. Don't just say to each other, 'We're safe, for we are descendants of Abraham.' That means nothing, for I tell you, God can create children of Abraham from these very stones. 9Even now the ax of God's judgment is poised, ready to sever the roots of the trees. Yes, every tree that does not produce good fruit will be chopped down and thrown into the fire."

10The crowds asked, "What should we do?"

11John replied, "If you have two shirts, give one to the poor. If you have food, share it with those who are hungry."

12Even corrupt tax collectors came to be baptized and asked, "Teacher, what should we do?"

13He replied, "Collect no more taxes than the government requires."

14"What should we do?" asked some soldiers.

John replied, "Don't extort money or make false accusations. And be content with your pay."

15Everyone was expecting the Messiah to come soon, and they were eager to know whether John might be the Messiah. 16John answered their questions by saying, "I baptize you with* water; but someone is coming soon who is greater than I am—so much greater that I'm not even worthy to be his slave and untie the straps of his sandals. He will baptize you with the Holy Spirit and with fire.* 17He is ready to separate the chaff from the wheat with his winnowing fork. Then he will clean up the threshing area, gathering the wheat into his barn but burning the chaff with never-ending fire."

18John used many such warnings as he announced the Good News to the people.

19John also publicly criticized Herod Antipas, the ruler of Galilee,* for marrying Herodias, his brother's wife, and for many other wrongs he had done. 20So Herod put John in prison, adding this sin to his many others.

The Baptism of Jesus

21One day when the crowds were being baptized, Jesus himself was baptized. As he was praying, the heavens opened, 22and the Holy Spirit, in bodily form, descended on him like a dove. And a voice from heaven said, "You are my dearly loved Son, and you bring me great joy.*"

The Ancestors of Jesus

23Jesus was about thirty years old when he began his public ministry.

Jesus was known as the son of Joseph.
Joseph was the son of Heli.
24 Heli was the son of Matthat.
Matthat was the son of Levi.
Levi was the son of Melki.
Melki was the son of Jannai.
Jannai was the son of Joseph.
25 Joseph was the son of Mattathias.
Mattathias was the son of Amos.
Amos was the son of Nahum.
Nahum was the son of Esli.
Esli was the son of Naggai.
26 Naggai was the son of Maath.
Maath was the son of Mattathias.
Mattathias was the son of Semein.
Semein was the son of Josech.
Josech was the son of Joda.
27 Joda was the son of Joanan.
Joanan was the son of Rhesa.
Rhesa was the son of Zerubbabel.
Zerubbabel was the son of Shealtiel.
Shealtiel was the son of Neri.
28 Neri was the son of Melki.
Melki was the son of Addi.
Addi was the son of Cosam.

3:16a Or in.   3:16b Or in the Holy Spirit and in fire.   3:19 Greek Herod the tetrarch.   3:22 Some manuscripts read my Son, and today I have become your Father.

Cosam was the son of Elmadam.
Elmadam was the son of Er.
29 Er was the son of Joshua.
Joshua was the son of Eliezer.
Eliezer was the son of Jorim.
Jorim was the son of Matthat.
Matthat was the son of Levi.
30 Levi was the son of Simeon.
Simeon was the son of Judah.
Judah was the son of Joseph.
Joseph was the son of Jonam.
Jonam was the son of Eliakim.
31 Eliakim was the son of Melea.
Melea was the son of Menna.
Menna was the son of Mattatha.
Mattatha was the son of Nathan.
Nathan was the son of David.
32 David was the son of Jesse.
Jesse was the son of Obed.
Obed was the son of Boaz.
Boaz was the son of Salmon.*
Salmon was the son of Nahshon.
33 Nahshon was the son of Amminadab.
Amminadab was the son of Admin.
Admin was the son of Arni.*
Arni was the son of Hezron.
Hezron was the son of Perez.
Perez was the son of Judah.
34 Judah was the son of Jacob.
Jacob was the son of Isaac.
Isaac was the son of Abraham.
Abraham was the son of Terah.
Terah was the son of Nahor.
35 Nahor was the son of Serug.
Serug was the son of Reu.

Reu was the son of Peleg.
Peleg was the son of Eber.
Eber was the son of Shelah.
36 Shelah was the son of Cainan.
Cainan was the son of Arphaxad.
Arphaxad was the son of Shem.
Shem was the son of Noah.
Noah was the son of Lamech.
37 Lamech was the son of Methuselah.
Methuselah was the son of Enoch.
Enoch was the son of Jared.
Jared was the son of Mahalalel.
Mahalalel was the son of Kenan.
38 Kenan was the son of Enosh.*
Enosh was the son of Seth.
Seth was the son of Adam.
Adam was the son of God.

CHAPTER 4

The Temptation of Jesus

Then Jesus, full of the Holy Spirit, returned from the Jordan River. He was led by the Spirit in the wilderness,* 2where he was tempted by the devil for forty days. Jesus ate nothing all that time and became very hungry.

3Then the devil said to him, "If you are the Son of God, tell this stone to become a loaf of bread."

4But Jesus told him, "No! The Scriptures say, 'People do not live by bread alone.'*"

5Then the devil took him up and revealed to him all the kingdoms of the world in a moment of time. 6"I will give you the glory of these kingdoms and authority over them," the devil said, "because they are mine to give to anyone I please. 7I will give it all to you if you will worship me."

8Jesus replied, "The Scriptures say,

3:32 Greek Sala, a variant spelling of Salmon; also in 3:32b. See Ruth 4:22.   3:33 Some manuscripts read Amminadab was the son of Aram. Arni and Aram are alternate spellings of Ram. See 1 Chr 2:9-10.   3:38 Greek Enos, a variant spelling of Enosh; also in 3:38b. See Gen 5:6.   4:1 Some manuscripts read into the wilderness.   4:4 Deut 8:3.

'You must worship the LORD your God
and serve only him.'*"

⁹Then the devil took him to Jerusalem, to the highest point of the Temple, and said, "If you are the Son of God, jump off! ¹⁰For the Scriptures say,

'He will order his angels to protect and guard you.
¹¹ And they will hold you up with their hands
so you won't even hurt your foot on a stone.'*"

¹²Jesus responded, "The Scriptures also say, 'You must not test the LORD your God.'*"

¹³When the devil had finished tempting Jesus, he left him until the next opportunity came.

Jesus Rejected at Nazareth

¹⁴Then Jesus returned to Galilee, filled with the Holy Spirit's power. Reports about him spread quickly through the whole region. ¹⁵He taught regularly in their synagogues and was praised by everyone.

¹⁶When he came to the village of Nazareth, his boyhood home, he went as usual to the synagogue on the Sabbath and stood up to read the Scriptures. ¹⁷The scroll of Isaiah the prophet was handed to him. He unrolled the scroll and found the place where this was written:

¹⁸ "The Spirit of the LORD is upon me,
for he has anointed me to bring Good News to the poor.
He has sent me to proclaim that captives will be released,
that the blind will see,
that the oppressed will be set free,
¹⁹ and that the time of the LORD's favor has come.*"

²⁰He rolled up the scroll, handed it back to the attendant, and sat down. All eyes in the synagogue looked at him intently. ²¹Then he began to speak to them. "The Scripture you've just heard has been fulfilled this very day!"

²²Everyone spoke well of him and was amazed by the gracious words that came from his lips. "How can this be?" they asked. "Isn't this Joseph's son?"

²³Then he said, "You will undoubtedly quote me this proverb: 'Physician, heal yourself'—meaning, 'Do miracles here in your hometown like those you did in Capernaum.' ²⁴But I tell you the truth, no prophet is accepted in his own hometown.

²⁵"Certainly there were many needy widows in Israel in Elijah's time, when the heavens were closed for three and a half years, and a severe famine devastated the land. ²⁶Yet Elijah was not sent to any of them. He was sent instead to a foreigner—a widow of Zarephath in the land of Sidon. ²⁷And there were many lepers in Israel in the time of the prophet Elisha, but the only one healed was Naaman, a Syrian."

²⁸When they heard this, the people in the synagogue were furious. ²⁹Jumping up, they mobbed him and forced him to the edge of the hill on which the town was built. They intended to push him over the cliff, ³⁰but he passed right through the crowd and went on his way.

Jesus Casts Out a Demon

³¹Then Jesus went to Capernaum, a town in Galilee, and taught there in the synagogue every Sabbath day. ³²There, too, the people were amazed at his teaching, for he spoke with authority.

³³Once when he was in the synagogue, a man possessed by a demon—an evil* spirit—began shouting at Jesus, ³⁴"Go away! Why are you interfering with us, Jesus of Nazareth? Have you come to destroy us? I know who you are—the Holy One of God!"

³⁵Jesus cut him short. "Be quiet! Come out of the man," he ordered. At that, the demon threw the man to the floor as

4:8 Deut 6:13. 4:10-11 Ps 91:11-12. 4:12 Deut 6:16. 4:18-19 Or *and to proclaim the acceptable year of the LORD.* Isa 61:1-2 (Greek version); 58:6. 4:33 Greek *unclean;* also in 4:36.

the crowd watched; then it came out of him without hurting him further.

³⁶Amazed, the people exclaimed, "What authority and power this man's words possess! Even evil spirits obey him, and they flee at his command!" ³⁷The news about Jesus spread through every village in the entire region.

Jesus Heals Many People

³⁸After leaving the synagogue that day, Jesus went to Simon's home, where he found Simon's mother-in-law very sick with a high fever. "Please heal her," everyone begged. ³⁹Standing at her bedside, he rebuked the fever, and it left her. And she got up at once and prepared a meal for them.

⁴⁰As the sun went down that evening, people throughout the village brought sick family members to Jesus. No matter what their diseases were, the touch of his hand healed every one. ⁴¹Many were possessed by demons; and the demons came out at his command, shouting, "You are the Son of God!" But because they knew he was the Messiah, he rebuked them and refused to let them speak.

Jesus Continues to Preach

⁴²Early the next morning Jesus went out to an isolated place. The crowds searched everywhere for him, and when they finally found him, they begged him not to leave them. ⁴³But he replied, "I must preach the Good News of the Kingdom of God in other towns, too, because that is why I was sent." ⁴⁴So he continued to travel around, preaching in synagogues throughout Judea.*

CHAPTER 5

The First Disciples

One day as Jesus was preaching on the shore of the Sea of Galilee,* great crowds pressed in on him to listen to the word of God. ²He noticed two empty boats at the water's edge, for the fishermen had left them and were washing their nets. ³Stepping into one of the boats, Jesus asked Simon,* its owner, to push it out into the water. So he sat in the boat and taught the crowds from there.

⁴When he had finished speaking, he said to Simon, "Now go out where it is deeper, and let down your nets to catch some fish."

⁵"Master," Simon replied, "we worked hard all last night and didn't catch a thing. But if you say so, I'll let the nets down again." ⁶And this time their nets were so full of fish they began to tear! ⁷A shout for help brought their partners in the other boat, and soon both boats were filled with fish and on the verge of sinking.

⁸When Simon Peter realized what had happened, he fell to his knees before Jesus and said, "Oh, Lord, please leave me—I'm too much of a sinner to be around you." ⁹For he was awestruck by the number of fish they had caught, as were the others with him. ¹⁰His partners, James and John, the sons of Zebedee, were also amazed.

Jesus replied to Simon, "Don't be afraid! From now on you'll be fishing for people!" ¹¹And as soon as they landed, they left everything and followed Jesus.

Jesus Heals a Man with Leprosy

¹²In one of the villages, Jesus met a man with an advanced case of leprosy. When the man saw Jesus, he bowed with his face to the ground, begging to be healed. "Lord," he said, "if you are willing, you can heal me and make me clean."

¹³Jesus reached out and touched him. "I am willing," he said. "Be healed!" And instantly the leprosy disappeared. ¹⁴Then Jesus instructed him not to tell anyone what had happened. He said, "Go to the priest and let him examine you. Take along the offering required in the law of Moses for those who have been healed of leprosy.* This will be a public testimony that you have been cleansed."

¹⁵But despite Jesus' instructions, the report of his power spread even faster, and vast crowds came to hear him

4:44 Some manuscripts read *Galilee.*   **5:1** Greek *Lake Gennesaret,* another name for the Sea of Galilee.   **5:3** *Simon* is called "Peter" in 6:14 and thereafter.   **5:14** See Lev 14:2-32.

preach and to be healed of their diseases. [16]But Jesus often withdrew to the wilderness for prayer.

Jesus Heals a Paralyzed Man

[17]One day while Jesus was teaching, some Pharisees and teachers of religious law were sitting nearby. (It seemed that these men showed up from every village in all Galilee and Judea, as well as from Jerusalem.) And the Lord's healing power was strongly with Jesus. [18]Some men came carrying a paralyzed man on a sleeping mat. They tried to take him inside to Jesus, [19]but they couldn't reach him because of the crowd. So they went up to the roof and took off some tiles. Then they lowered the sick man on his mat down into the crowd, right in front of Jesus. [20]Seeing their faith, Jesus said to the man, "Young man, your sins are forgiven."

[21]But the Pharisees and teachers of religious law said to themselves, "Who does he think he is? That's blasphemy! Only God can forgive sins!"

[22]Jesus knew what they were thinking, so he asked them, "Why do you question this in your hearts? [23]Is it easier to say 'Your sins are forgiven,' or 'Stand up and walk'? [24]So I will prove to you that the Son of Man* has the authority on earth to forgive sins." Then Jesus turned to the paralyzed man and said, "Stand up, pick up your mat, and go home!"

[25]And immediately, as everyone watched, the man jumped up, picked up his mat, and went home praising God. [26]Everyone was gripped with great wonder and awe, and they praised God, exclaiming, "We have seen amazing things today!"

Jesus Calls Levi (Matthew)

[27]Later, as Jesus left the town, he saw a tax collector named Levi sitting at his tax collector's booth. "Follow me and be my disciple," Jesus said to him. [28]So Levi got up, left everything, and followed him.

[29]Later, Levi held a banquet in his home with Jesus as the guest of honor. Many of Levi's fellow tax collectors and other guests also ate with them. [30]But the Pharisees and their teachers of religious law complained bitterly to Jesus' disciples, "Why do you eat and drink with such scum?*"

[31]Jesus answered them, "Healthy people don't need a doctor—sick people do. [32]I have come to call not those who think they are righteous, but those who know they are sinners and need to repent."

A Discussion about Fasting

[33]One day some people said to Jesus, "John the Baptist's disciples fast and pray regularly, and so do the disciples of the Pharisees. Why are your disciples always eating and drinking?"

[34]Jesus responded, "Do wedding guests fast while celebrating with the groom? Of course not. [35]But someday the groom will be taken away from them, and then they will fast."

[36]Then Jesus gave them this illustration: "No one tears a piece of cloth from a new garment and uses it to patch an old garment. For then the new garment would be ruined, and the new patch wouldn't even match the old garment.

[37]"And no one puts new wine into old wineskins. For the new wine would burst the wineskins, spilling the wine and ruining the skins. [38]New wine must be stored in new wineskins. [39]But no one who drinks the old wine seems to want the new wine. 'The old is just fine,' they say."

CHAPTER 6

A Discussion about the Sabbath

One Sabbath day as Jesus was walking through some grainfields, his disciples broke off heads of grain, rubbed off the husks in their hands, and ate the grain. [2]But some Pharisees said, "Why are you breaking the law by harvesting grain on the Sabbath?"

[3]Jesus replied, "Haven't you read in the Scriptures what

5:24 "Son of Man" is a title Jesus used for himself.   5:30 Greek *with tax collectors and sinners?*

David did when he and his companions were hungry? ⁴He went into the house of God and broke the law by eating the sacred loaves of bread that only the priests can eat. He also gave some to his companions." ⁵And Jesus added, "The Son of Man* is Lord, even over the Sabbath."

Jesus Heals on the Sabbath

⁶On another Sabbath day, a man with a deformed right hand was in the synagogue while Jesus was teaching. ⁷The teachers of religious law and the Pharisees watched Jesus closely. If he healed the man's hand, they planned to accuse him of working on the Sabbath.

⁸But Jesus knew their thoughts. He said to the man with the deformed hand, "Come and stand in front of everyone." So the man came forward. ⁹Then Jesus said to his critics, "I have a question for you. Does the law permit good deeds on the Sabbath, or is it a day for doing evil? Is this a day to save life or to destroy it?"

¹⁰He looked around at them one by one and then said to the man, "Hold out your hand." So the man held out his hand, and it was restored! ¹¹At this, the enemies of Jesus were wild with rage and began to discuss what to do with him.

Jesus Chooses the Twelve Apostles

¹²One day soon afterward Jesus went up on a mountain to pray, and he prayed to God all night. ¹³At daybreak he called together all of his disciples and chose twelve of them to be apostles. Here are their names:

¹⁴ Simon (whom he named Peter),
Andrew (Peter's brother),
James,
John,
Philip,
Bartholomew,
¹⁵ Matthew,
Thomas,
James (son of Alphaeus),

6:5 "Son of Man" is a title Jesus used for himself.

THE POINT

Hangin' with outcasts. Just like today, back in Bible days a person could get beat down for being seen on the block with the wrong people. Folks like lepers (people with a disease with kinda the same stereotypes that people with AIDS experience), unwed mothers, hookers, the handicapped, dope fiends—you know, outcasts—were kept at a distance. Good, religious folks wouldn't be seen hangin' out with such hoodlums. Luke pointed out that hangin' with outcasts was Jesus' favorite pastime. Jesus showed mad love and compassion for the sick, the poor, and the beat down. Matter of fact, that was the reason he showed up on the set in the first place.

"The Spirit of the Lord is upon me, for he has anointed me to bring Good News to the poor.

He has sent me to proclaim that captives will be released, that the blind will see, that the oppressed will be set free." (Luke 4:18)

Jesus told his disciples they needed to recognize the difference between religion and relationship. Truth be told, Jesus said the poor, the hungry, and the sick stood a better chance of getting into God's Kingdom than the rich and famous who only value cars, clothes, houses, and bling. In the Bible, this passage of Scripture is called "The Beatitudes"; check it out:

"God blesses you who are poor, for the Kingdom of God is yours. God blesses you who are hungry now, for you will be satisfied. God

blesses you who weep now, for in due time you will laugh. . . . What sorrow awaits you who are rich, for you have your only happiness now. What sorrow awaits you who are fat and prosperous now, for a time of awful hunger awaits you. What sorrow awaits you who laugh now, for your laughing will turn to mourning and sorrow." (Luke 6:20-21, 24-25)

Deep, right? Now that doesn't mean you are supposed to stay poor, broke, hungry, or dissatisfied. It just means if you find yourself in that place, God is your way out. And because you've been there, done that, you'll be able to reach back and help someone else once you get your act together.

Simon (who was called the zealot),
16 Judas (son of James),
Judas Iscariot (who later betrayed him).

Crowds Follow Jesus
17When they came down from the mountain, the disciples stood with Jesus on a large, level area, surrounded by many of his followers and by the crowds. There were people from all over Judea and from Jerusalem and from as far north as the seacoasts of Tyre and Sidon. 18They had come to hear him and to be healed of their diseases; and those troubled by evil* spirits were healed. 19Everyone tried to touch him, because healing power went out from him, and he healed everyone.

The Beatitudes
20Then Jesus turned to his disciples and said,

"God blesses you who are poor,
   for the Kingdom of God is yours.
21 God blesses you who are hungry now,
   for you will be satisfied.
God blesses you who weep now,
   for in due time you will laugh.

22What blessings await you when people hate you and exclude you and mock you and curse you as evil because you follow the Son of Man. 23When that happens, be happy! Yes, leap for joy! For a great reward awaits you in heaven. And remember, their ancestors treated the ancient prophets that same way.

Sorrows Foretold
24 "What sorrow awaits you who are rich,
   for you have your only happiness now.
25 What sorrow awaits you who are fat and prosperous now,
   for a time of awful hunger awaits you.

What sorrow awaits you who laugh now,
   for your laughing will turn to mourning and sorrow.
26 What sorrow awaits you who are praised by the crowds,
   for their ancestors also praised false prophets.

Love for Enemies
27"But to you who are willing to listen, I say, love your enemies! Do good to those who hate you. 28Bless those who curse you. Pray for those who hurt you. 29If someone slaps you on one cheek, offer the other cheek also. If someone demands your coat, offer your shirt also. 30Give to anyone who asks; and when things are taken away from you, don't try to get them back. 31Do to others as you would like them to do to you.

32"If you love only those who love you, why should you get credit for that? Even sinners love those who love them! 33And if you do good only to those who do good to you, why should you get credit? Even sinners do that much! 34And if you lend money only to those who can repay you, why should you get credit? Even sinners will lend to other sinners for a full return.

35"Love your enemies! Do good to them. Lend to them without expecting to be repaid. Then your reward from heaven will be very great, and you will truly be acting as children of the Most High, for he is kind to those who are unthankful and wicked. 36You must be compassionate, just as your Father is compassionate.

Do Not Judge Others
37"Do not judge others, and you will not be judged. Do not condemn others, or it will all come back against you. Forgive others, and you will be forgiven. 38Give, and you will receive. Your gift will return to you in full—pressed down, shaken together to make room for more, running over, and poured into your lap. The amount you give will determine the amount you get back.*"

6:18 Greek *unclean.*   6:38 Or *The measure you give will be the measure you get back.*

"If you love only those who love you, why should you get credit for that? Even sinners love those who love them! . . . Love your enemies! Do good to them. Lend to them without expecting to be repaid" (Luke 6:32, 35).

If you only have love for those who love you, you can't get points for that! Even the illest people love those who love them! It sounds crazy, but love your enemies! Let them borrow from you without expecting anything back.

³⁹Then Jesus gave the following illustration: "Can one blind person lead another? Won't they both fall into a ditch? ⁴⁰Students* are not greater than their teacher. But the student who is fully trained will become like the teacher.

⁴¹"And why worry about a speck in your friend's eye* when you have a log in your own? ⁴²How can you think of saying, 'Friend,* let me help you get rid of that speck in your eye,' when you can't see past the log in your own eye? Hypocrite! First get rid of the log in your own eye; then you will see well enough to deal with the speck in your friend's eye.

The Tree and Its Fruit

⁴³"A good tree can't produce bad fruit, and a bad tree can't produce good fruit. ⁴⁴A tree is identified by its fruit. Figs are never gathered from thornbushes, and grapes are not picked from bramble bushes. ⁴⁵A good person produces good things from the treasury of a good heart, and an evil person produces evil things from the treasury of an evil heart. What you say flows from what is in your heart.

Building on a Solid Foundation

⁴⁶"So why do you keep calling me 'Lord, Lord!' when you don't do what I say? ⁴⁷I will show you what it's like when someone comes to me, listens to my teaching, and then follows it. ⁴⁸It is like a person building a house who digs deep and lays the foundation on solid rock. When the floodwaters rise and break against that house, it stands firm because it is well built. ⁴⁹But anyone who hears and doesn't obey is like a person who builds a house without a foundation. When the floods sweep down against that house, it will collapse into a heap of ruins."

CHAPTER 7

The Faith of a Roman Officer

When Jesus had finished saying all this to the people, he returned to Capernaum. ²At that time the highly valued slave of a Roman officer* was sick and near death. ³When the officer heard about Jesus, he sent some respected Jewish elders to ask him to come and heal his slave. ⁴So they earnestly begged Jesus to help the man. "If anyone deserves your help, he does," they said, ⁵"for he loves the Jewish people and even built a synagogue for us."

⁶So Jesus went with them. But just before they arrived at the house, the officer sent some friends to say, "Lord, don't trouble yourself by coming to my home, for I am not worthy of such an honor. ⁷I am not even worthy to come and meet you. Just say the word from where you are, and my servant will be healed. ⁸I know this because I am under the authority of my superior officers, and I have authority over my soldiers. I only need to say, 'Go,' and they go, or 'Come,' and they come. And if I say to my slaves, 'Do this,' they do it."

⁹When Jesus heard this, he was amazed. Turning to the crowd that was following him, he said, "I tell you, I haven't seen faith like this in all Israel!" ¹⁰And when the officer's friends returned to his house, they found the slave completely healed.

Jesus Raises a Widow's Son

¹¹Soon afterward Jesus went with his disciples to the village of Nain, and a large crowd followed him. ¹²A funeral procession was coming out as he approached the village gate. The young man who had died was a widow's only son, and a large crowd from the village was with her. ¹³When the Lord saw her, his heart overflowed with compassion. "Don't cry!" he said. ¹⁴Then he walked over to the coffin and touched it, and the bearers stopped. "Young man," he said, "I tell you, get up." ¹⁵Then the dead boy sat up and began to talk! And Jesus gave him back to his mother.

¹⁶Great fear swept the crowd, and they praised God, saying, "A mighty prophet has risen among us," and "God has visited his people today." ¹⁷And the news about Jesus spread throughout Judea and the surrounding countryside.

6:40 Or *Disciples.*   **6:41** Greek *your brother's eye;* also in 6:42.   **6:42** Greek *Brother.*   **7:2** Greek *a centurion;* similarly in 7:6.

Jesus and John the Baptist

¹⁸The disciples of John the Baptist told John about everything Jesus was doing. So John called for two of his disciples, ¹⁹and he sent them to the Lord to ask him, "Are you the Messiah we've been expecting,* or should we keep looking for someone else?"

²⁰John's two disciples found Jesus and said to him, "John the Baptist sent us to ask, 'Are you the Messiah we've been expecting, or should we keep looking for someone else?'"

²¹At that very time, Jesus cured many people of their diseases, illnesses, and evil spirits, and he restored sight to many who were blind. ²²Then he told John's disciples, "Go back to John and tell him what you have seen and heard—the blind see, the lame walk, the lepers are cured, the deaf hear, the dead are raised to life, and the Good News is being preached to the poor. ²³And tell him, 'God blesses those who do not turn away because of me.*'"

²⁴After John's disciples left, Jesus began talking about him to the crowds. "What kind of man did you go into the wilderness to see? Was he a weak reed, swayed by every breath of wind? ²⁵Or were you expecting to see a man dressed in expensive clothes? No, people who wear beautiful clothes and live in luxury are found in palaces. ²⁶Were you looking for a prophet? Yes, and he is more than a prophet. ²⁷John is the man to whom the Scriptures refer when they say,

'Look, I am sending my messenger ahead of you,
    and he will prepare your way before you.'*

²⁸I tell you, of all who have ever lived, none is greater than John. Yet even the least person in the Kingdom of God is greater than he is!"

²⁹When they heard this, all the people—even the tax collectors—agreed that God's way was right,* for they had been baptized by John. ³⁰But the Pharisees and experts in religious law rejected God's plan for them, for they had refused John's baptism.

³¹"To what can I compare the people of this generation?" Jesus asked. "How can I describe them? ³²They are like children playing a game in the public square. They complain to their friends,

'We played wedding songs,
    and you didn't dance,
so we played funeral songs,
    and you didn't weep.'

³³For John the Baptist didn't spend his time eating bread or drinking wine, and you say, 'He's possessed by a demon.' ³⁴The Son of Man,* on the other hand, feasts and drinks, and you say, 'He's a glutton and a drunkard, and a friend of tax collectors and other sinners!' ³⁵But wisdom is shown to be right by the lives of those who follow it.*"

Jesus Anointed by a Sinful Woman

³⁶One of the Pharisees asked Jesus to have dinner with him, so Jesus went to his home and sat down to eat.* ³⁷When a certain immoral woman from that city heard he was eating there, she brought a beautiful alabaster jar filled with expensive perfume. ³⁸Then she knelt behind him at his feet, weeping. Her tears fell on his feet, and she wiped them off with her hair. Then she kept kissing his feet and putting perfume on them.

³⁹When the Pharisee who had invited him saw this, he said to himself, "If this man were a prophet, he would know what kind of woman is touching him. She's a sinner!"

⁴⁰Then Jesus answered his thoughts. "Simon," he said to the Pharisee, "I have something to say to you."

"Go ahead, Teacher," Simon replied.

⁴¹Then Jesus told him this story: "A man loaned money

7:19 Greek *Are you the one who is coming?* Also in 7:20. **7:23** Or *who are not offended by me.* **7:27** Mal 3:1. **7:29** Or *praised God for his justice.* **7:34** "Son of Man" is a title Jesus used for himself. **7:35** Or *But wisdom is justified by all her children.* **7:36** Or *and reclined.*

to two people—500 pieces of silver* to one and 50 pieces to the other. ⁴²But neither of them could repay him, so he kindly forgave them both, canceling their debts. Who do you suppose loved him more after that?"

⁴³Simon answered, "I suppose the one for whom he canceled the larger debt."

"That's right," Jesus said. ⁴⁴Then he turned to the woman and said to Simon, "Look at this woman kneeling here. When I entered your home, you didn't offer me water to wash the dust from my feet, but she has washed them with her tears and wiped them with her hair. ⁴⁵You didn't greet me with a kiss, but from the time I first came in, she has not stopped kissing my feet. ⁴⁶You neglected the courtesy of olive oil to anoint my head, but she has anointed my feet with rare perfume.

⁴⁷"I tell you, her sins—and they are many—have been forgiven, so she has shown me much love. But a person who is forgiven little shows only little love." ⁴⁸Then Jesus said to the woman, "Your sins are forgiven."

⁴⁹The men at the table said among themselves, "Who is this man, that he goes around forgiving sins?"

⁵⁰And Jesus said to the woman, "Your faith has saved you; go in peace."

CHAPTER 8

Women Who Followed Jesus

Soon afterward Jesus began a tour of the nearby towns and villages, preaching and announcing the Good News about the Kingdom of God. He took his twelve disciples with him, ²along with some women who had been cured of evil spirits and diseases. Among them were Mary Magdalene, from whom he had cast out seven demons; ³Joanna, the wife of Chuza, Herod's business manager; Susanna; and many others who were contributing from their own resources to support Jesus and his disciples.

Parable of the Farmer Scattering Seed

⁴One day Jesus told a story in the form of a parable to a large crowd that had gathered from many towns to hear him: ⁵"A farmer went out to plant his seed. As he scattered it across his field, some seed fell on a footpath, where it was stepped on, and the birds ate it. ⁶Other seed fell among rocks. It began to grow, but the plant soon wilted and died for lack of moisture. ⁷Other seed fell among thorns that grew up with it and choked out the tender plants. ⁸Still other seed fell on fertile soil. This seed grew and produced a crop that was a hundred times as much as had been planted!" When he had said this, he called out, "Anyone with ears to hear should listen and understand."

⁹His disciples asked him what this parable meant. ¹⁰He replied, "You are permitted to understand the secrets* of the Kingdom of God. But I use parables to teach the others so that the Scriptures might be fulfilled:

'When they look, they won't really see.
When they hear, they won't understand.'*

¹¹"This is the meaning of the parable: The seed is God's word. ¹²The seeds that fell on the footpath represent those who hear the message, only to have the devil come and take it away from their hearts and prevent them from believing and being saved. ¹³The seeds on the rocky soil represent those who hear the message and receive it with joy. But since they don't have deep roots, they believe for a while, then they fall away when they face temptation. ¹⁴The seeds that fell among the thorns represent those who hear the message, but all too quickly the message is crowded out by the cares and riches and pleasures of this life. And so they never grow into maturity. ¹⁵And the seeds that fell on the good soil represent honest, good-hearted people who hear God's word, cling to it, and patiently produce a huge harvest.

7:41 Greek *500 denarii.* A denarius was equivalent to a laborer's full day's wage.   **8:10a** Greek *mysteries.*   **8:10b** Isa 6:9 (Greek version).

Parable of the Lamp

16"No one lights a lamp and then covers it with a bowl or hides it under a bed. A lamp is placed on a stand, where its light can be seen by all who enter the house. 17For all that is secret will eventually be brought into the open, and everything that is concealed will be brought to light and made known to all.

18"So pay attention to how you hear. To those who listen to my teaching, more understanding will be given. But for those who are not listening, even what they think they understand will be taken away from them."

The True Family of Jesus

19Then Jesus' mother and brothers came to see him, but they couldn't get to him because of the crowd. 20Someone told Jesus, "Your mother and your brothers are outside, and they want to see you."

21Jesus replied, "My mother and my brothers are all those who hear God's word and obey it."

Jesus Calms the Storm

22One day Jesus said to his disciples, "Let's cross to the other side of the lake." So they got into a boat and started out. 23As they sailed across, Jesus settled down for a nap. But soon a fierce storm came down on the lake. The boat was filling with water, and they were in real danger.

24The disciples went and woke him up, shouting, "Master, Master, we're going to drown!"

When Jesus woke up, he rebuked the wind and the raging waves. Suddenly the storm stopped and all was calm. 25Then he asked them, "Where is your faith?"

The disciples were terrified and amazed. "Who is this man?" they asked each other. "When he gives a command, even the wind and waves obey him!"

Jesus Heals a Demon-Possessed Man

26So they arrived in the region of the Gerasenes,* across the lake from Galilee. 27As Jesus was climbing out of the boat, a man who was possessed by demons came out to meet him. For a long time he had been homeless and naked, living in a cemetery outside the town.

28As soon as he saw Jesus, he shrieked and fell down in front of him. Then he screamed, "Why are you interfering with me, Jesus, Son of the Most High God? Please, I beg you, don't torture me!" 29For Jesus had already commanded the evil* spirit to come out of him. This spirit had often taken

8:26 Other manuscripts read *Gadarenes;* still others read *Gergesenes;* also in 8:37. See Matt 8:28; Mark 5:1.   8:29 Greek *unclean.*

THE POINT

Women are part of God's entourage. Luke is the only Gospel that points out that Jesus showed mad love for the women in his life. Jesus had the utmost respect for women. During a time when women were treated real bad, Jesus was a brotha who treated women with respect, compassion, and care. He healed the woman who'd suffered from bleeding for twelve years (Luke 8:43-48). Women were present at the cross (23:49), and it was a woman who first discovered Jesus' body was missing from the tomb (24:1-10). Jesus even had some women as part of his entourage.

Jesus began a tour of the nearby towns and villages. . . . He took his twelve disciples with him, along with some women who had been cured of evil spirits and diseases. Among them were Mary Magdalene, . . . Joanna, . . . Susanna; and many others who were contributing from their own resources to support Jesus and his disciples. (Luke 8:1-3)

At the end of the day, Luke's Gospel is about showing others that Jesus came to save the lost, no matter who they were: "For the Son of Man came to seek and save those who are lost" (Luke 19:10).

control of the man. Even when he was placed under guard and put in chains and shackles, he simply broke them and rushed out into the wilderness, completely under the demon's power.

³⁰Jesus demanded, "What is your name?"

"Legion," he replied, for he was filled with many demons. ³¹The demons kept begging Jesus not to send them into the bottomless pit.*

³²There happened to be a large herd of pigs feeding on the hillside nearby, and the demons begged him to let them enter into the pigs.

So Jesus gave them permission. ³³Then the demons came out of the man and entered the pigs, and the entire herd plunged down the steep hillside into the lake and drowned.

³⁴When the herdsmen saw it, they fled to the nearby town and the surrounding countryside, spreading the news as they ran. ³⁵People rushed out to see what had happened. A crowd soon gathered around Jesus, and they saw the man who had been freed from the demons. He was sitting at Jesus' feet, fully clothed and perfectly sane, and they were all afraid. ³⁶Then those who had seen what happened told the others how the demon-possessed man had been healed. ³⁷And all the people in the region of the Gerasenes begged Jesus to go away and leave them alone, for a great wave of fear swept over them.

So Jesus returned to the boat and left, crossing back to the other side of the lake. ³⁸The man who had been freed from the demons begged to go with him. But Jesus sent him home, saying, ³⁹"No, go back to your family, and tell them everything God has done for you." So he went all through the town proclaiming the great things Jesus had done for him.

Jesus Heals in Response to Faith

⁴⁰On the other side of the lake the crowds welcomed Jesus, because they had been waiting for him. ⁴¹Then a man named Jairus, a leader of the local synagogue, came and fell at Jesus' feet, pleading with him to come home with him. ⁴²His only daughter,* who was about twelve years old, was dying.

As Jesus went with him, he was surrounded by the crowds. ⁴³A woman in the crowd had suffered for twelve years with constant bleeding,* and she could find no cure. ⁴⁴Coming up behind Jesus, she touched the fringe of his robe. Immediately, the bleeding stopped.

⁴⁵"Who touched me?" Jesus asked.

Everyone denied it, and Peter said, "Master, this whole crowd is pressing up against you."

⁴⁶But Jesus said, "Someone deliberately touched me, for I felt healing power go out from me." ⁴⁷When the woman realized that she could not stay hidden, she began to tremble and fell to her knees in front of him. The whole crowd heard her explain why she had touched him and that she had been immediately healed. ⁴⁸"Daughter," he said to her, "your faith has made you well. Go in peace."

⁴⁹While he was still speaking to her, a messenger arrived from the home of Jairus, the leader of the synagogue. He told him, "Your daughter is dead. There's no use troubling the Teacher now."

⁵⁰But when Jesus heard what had happened, he said to Jairus, "Don't be afraid. Just have faith, and she will be healed."

⁵¹When they arrived at the house, Jesus wouldn't let anyone go in with him except Peter, John, James, and the little girl's father and mother. ⁵²The house was filled with people weeping and wailing, but he said, "Stop the weeping! She isn't dead; she's only asleep."

⁵³But the crowd laughed at him because they all knew she had died. ⁵⁴Then Jesus took her by the hand and said in a loud voice, "My child, get up!" ⁵⁵And at that moment her life* returned, and she immediately stood up! Then Jesus told them to give her something to eat. ⁵⁶Her parents were

8:31 Or *the abyss,* or *the underworld.*   8:42 Or *His only child, a daughter.*   8:43 Some manuscripts add *having spent everything she had on doctors.*   8:55 Or *her spirit.*

overwhelmed, but Jesus insisted that they not tell anyone what had happened.

CHAPTER 9

Jesus Sends Out the Twelve Disciples

One day Jesus called together his twelve disciples* and gave them power and authority to cast out all demons and to heal all diseases. ²Then he sent them out to tell everyone about the Kingdom of God and to heal the sick. ³"Take nothing for your journey," he instructed them. "Don't take a walking stick, a traveler's bag, food, money,* or even a change of clothes. ⁴Wherever you go, stay in the same house until you leave town. ⁵And if a town refuses to welcome you, shake its dust from your feet as you leave to show that you have abandoned those people to their fate."

⁶So they began their circuit of the villages, preaching the Good News and healing the sick.

Herod's Confusion

⁷When Herod Antipas, the ruler of Galilee,* heard about everything Jesus was doing, he was puzzled. Some were saying that John the Baptist had been raised from the dead. ⁸Others thought Jesus was Elijah or one of the other prophets risen from the dead.

⁹"I beheaded John," Herod said, "so who is this man about whom I hear such stories?" And he kept trying to see him.

Jesus Feeds Five Thousand

¹⁰When the apostles returned, they told Jesus everything they had done. Then he slipped quietly away with them toward the town of Bethsaida. ¹¹But the crowds found out where he was going, and they followed him. He welcomed them and taught them about the Kingdom of God, and he healed those who were sick.

¹²Late in the afternoon the twelve disciples came to him and said, "Send the crowds away to the nearby villages and farms, so they can find food and lodging for the night. There is nothing to eat here in this remote place."

¹³But Jesus said, "You feed them."

"But we have only five loaves of bread and two fish," they answered. "Or are you expecting us to go and buy enough food for this whole crowd?" ¹⁴For there were about 5,000 men there.

Jesus replied, "Tell them to sit down in groups of about fifty each." ¹⁵So the people all sat down. ¹⁶Jesus took the five loaves and two fish, looked up toward heaven, and blessed them. Then, breaking the loaves into pieces, he kept giving the bread and fish to the disciples so they could distribute it to the people. ¹⁷They all ate as much as they wanted, and afterward, the disciples picked up twelve baskets of leftovers!

Peter's Declaration about Jesus

¹⁸One day Jesus left the crowds to pray alone. Only his disciples were with him, and he asked them, "Who do people say I am?"

¹⁹"Well," they replied, "some say John the Baptist, some say Elijah, and others say you are one of the other ancient prophets risen from the dead."

²⁰Then he asked them, "But who do you say I am?"

Peter replied, "You are the Messiah* sent from God!"

Jesus Predicts His Death

²¹Jesus warned his disciples not to tell anyone who he was. ²²"The Son of Man* must suffer many terrible things," he said. "He will be rejected by the elders, the leading priests, and the teachers of religious law. He will be killed, but on the third day he will be raised from the dead."

²³Then he said to the crowd, "If any of you wants to be my follower, you must turn from your selfish ways, take up

9:1 Greek *the Twelve*; other manuscripts read *the twelve apostles*. 9:3 Or *silver coins*. 9:7 Greek *Herod the tetrarch*. Herod Antipas was a son of King Herod and was ruler over Galilee. 9:20 Or *the Christ. Messiah* (a Hebrew term) and *Christ* (a Greek term) both mean "the anointed one." 9:22 "Son of Man" is a title Jesus used for himself.

your cross daily, and follow me. 24If you try to hang on to your life, you will lose it. But if you give up your life for my sake, you will save it. 25And what do you benefit if you gain the whole world but are yourself lost or destroyed? 26If anyone is ashamed of me and my message, the Son of Man will be ashamed of that person when he returns in his glory and in the glory of the Father and the holy angels. 27I tell you the truth, some standing here right now will not die before they see the Kingdom of God."

The Transfiguration

28About eight days later Jesus took Peter, John, and James up on a mountain to pray. 29And as he was praying, the appearance of his face was transformed, and his clothes became dazzling white. 30Suddenly, two men, Moses and Elijah, appeared and began talking with Jesus. 31They were glorious to see. And they were speaking about his exodus from this world, which was about to be fulfilled in Jerusalem.

32Peter and the others had fallen asleep. When they woke up, they saw Jesus' glory and the two men standing with him. 33As Moses and Elijah were starting to leave, Peter, not even knowing what he was saying, blurted out, "Master, it's wonderful for us to be here! Let's make three shelters as memorials*—one for you, one for Moses, and one for Elijah." 34But even as he was saying this, a cloud overshadowed them, and terror gripped them as the cloud covered them.

35Then a voice from the cloud said, "This is my Son, my Chosen One.* Listen to him." 36When the voice finished, Jesus was there alone. They didn't tell anyone at that time what they had seen.

Jesus Heals a Demon-Possessed Boy

37The next day, after they had come down the mountain, a large crowd met Jesus. 38A man in the crowd called out to him, "Teacher, I beg you to look at my son, my only child. 39An evil spirit keeps seizing him, making him scream. It throws him into convulsions so that he foams at the mouth. It batters him and hardly ever leaves him alone. 40I begged your disciples to cast out the spirit, but they couldn't do it."

41Jesus said, "You faithless and corrupt people! How long must I be with you and put up with you?" Then he said to the man, "Bring your son here."

42As the boy came forward, the demon knocked him to the ground and threw him into a violent convulsion. But Jesus rebuked the evil* spirit and healed the boy. Then he gave him back to his father. 43Awe gripped the people as they saw this majestic display of God's power.

Jesus Again Predicts His Death

While everyone was marveling at everything he was doing, Jesus said to his disciples, 44"Listen to me and remember what I say. The Son of Man is going to be betrayed into the hands of his enemies." 45But they didn't know what he meant. Its significance was hidden from them, so they couldn't understand it, and they were afraid to ask him about it.

The Greatest in the Kingdom

46Then his disciples began arguing about which of them was the greatest. 47But Jesus knew their thoughts, so he brought a little child to his side. 48Then he said to them, "Anyone who welcomes a little child like this on my behalf* welcomes me, and anyone who welcomes me also welcomes my Father who sent me. Whoever is the least among you is the greatest."

Using the Name of Jesus

49John said to Jesus, "Master, we saw someone using your name to cast out demons, but we told him to stop because he isn't in our group."

50But Jesus said, "Don't stop him! Anyone who is not against you is for you."

9:33 Greek three tabernacles.   9:35 Some manuscripts read This is my dearly loved Son.   9:42 Greek unclean.   9:48 Greek in my name.

Opposition from Samaritans

⁵¹As the time drew near for him to ascend to heaven, Jesus resolutely set out for Jerusalem. ⁵²He sent messengers ahead to a Samaritan village to prepare for his arrival. ⁵³But the people of the village did not welcome Jesus because he was on his way to Jerusalem. ⁵⁴When James and John saw this, they said to Jesus, "Lord, should we call down fire from heaven to burn them up*?" ⁵⁵But Jesus turned and rebuked them.* ⁵⁶So they went on to another village.

The Cost of Following Jesus

⁵⁷As they were walking along, someone said to Jesus, "I will follow you wherever you go."

⁵⁸But Jesus replied, "Foxes have dens to live in, and birds have nests, but the Son of Man has no place even to lay his head."

⁵⁹He said to another person, "Come, follow me."

The man agreed, but he said, "Lord, first let me return home and bury my father."

⁶⁰But Jesus told him, "Let the spiritually dead bury their own dead!* Your duty is to go and preach about the Kingdom of God."

⁶¹Another said, "Yes, Lord, I will follow you, but first let me say good-bye to my family."

⁶²But Jesus told him, "Anyone who puts a hand to the plow and then looks back is not fit for the Kingdom of God."

CHAPTER 10

Jesus Sends Out His Disciples

The Lord now chose seventy-two* other disciples and sent them ahead in pairs to all the towns and places he planned to visit. ²These were his instructions to them: "The harvest is great, but the workers are few. So pray to the Lord who is in charge of the harvest; ask him to send more workers into his fields. ³Now go, and remember that I am sending you out as lambs among wolves. ⁴Don't take any money with you, nor a traveler's bag, nor an extra pair of sandals. And don't stop to greet anyone on the road.

⁵"Whenever you enter someone's home, first say, 'May God's peace be on this house.' ⁶If those who live there are peaceful, the blessing will stand; if they are not, the blessing will return to you. ⁷Don't move around from home to home. Stay in one place, eating and drinking what they provide. Don't hesitate to accept hospitality, because those who work deserve their pay.

⁸"If you enter a town and it welcomes you, eat whatever is set before you. ⁹Heal the sick, and tell them, 'The Kingdom of God is near you now.' ¹⁰But if a town refuses to welcome you, go out into its streets and say, ¹¹'We wipe even the dust of your town from our feet to show that we have abandoned you to your fate. And know this—the Kingdom of God is near!' ¹²I assure you, even wicked Sodom will be better off than such a town on judgment day.

¹³"What sorrow awaits you, Korazin and Bethsaida! For if the miracles I did in you had been done in wicked Tyre and Sidon, their people would have repented of their sins long ago, clothing themselves in burlap and throwing ashes on their heads to show their remorse. ¹⁴Yes, Tyre and Sidon will be better off on judgment day than you. ¹⁵And you people of Capernaum, will you be honored in heaven? No, you will go down to the place of the dead.*"

¹⁶Then he said to the disciples, "Anyone who accepts your message is also accepting me. And anyone who rejects you is rejecting me. And anyone who rejects me is rejecting God, who sent me."

¹⁷When the seventy-two disciples returned, they joyfully reported to him, "Lord, even the demons obey us when we use your name!"

9:54 Some manuscripts add *as Elijah did.*   **9:55** Some manuscripts add an expanded conclusion to verse 55 and an additional sentence in verse 56: *And he said, "You don't realize what your hearts are like. ⁵⁶For the Son of Man has not come to destroy people's lives, but to save them."*   **9:60** Greek *Let the dead bury their own dead.*   **10:1** Some manuscripts read *seventy;* also in 10:17.   **10:15** Greek *to Hades.*

¹⁸"Yes," he told them, "I saw Satan fall from heaven like lightning! ¹⁹Look, I have given you authority over all the power of the enemy, and you can walk among snakes and scorpions and crush them. Nothing will injure you. ²⁰But don't rejoice because evil spirits obey you; rejoice because your names are registered in heaven."

Jesus' Prayer of Thanksgiving

²¹At that same time Jesus was filled with the joy of the Holy Spirit, and he said, "O Father, Lord of heaven and earth, thank you for hiding these things from those who think themselves wise and clever, and for revealing them to the childlike. Yes, Father, it pleased you to do it this way.

²²"My Father has entrusted everything to me. No one truly knows the Son except the Father, and no one truly knows the Father except the Son and those to whom the Son chooses to reveal him."

²³Then when they were alone, he turned to the disciples and said, "Blessed are the eyes that see what you have seen. ²⁴I tell you, many prophets and kings longed to see what you see, but they didn't see it. And they longed to hear what you hear, but they didn't hear it."

The Most Important Commandment

²⁵One day an expert in religious law stood up to test Jesus by asking him this question: "Teacher, what should I do to inherit eternal life?"

²⁶Jesus replied, "What does the law of Moses say? How do you read it?"

²⁷The man answered, "'You must love the LORD your God with all your heart, all your soul, all your strength, and all your mind.' And, 'Love your neighbor as yourself.'"*

²⁸"Right!" Jesus told him. "Do this and you will live!"

²⁹The man wanted to justify his actions, so he asked Jesus, "And who is my neighbor?"

Parable of the Good Samaritan

³⁰Jesus replied with a story: "A Jewish man was traveling from Jerusalem down to Jericho, and he was attacked by bandits. They stripped him of his clothes, beat him up, and left him half dead beside the road.

³¹"By chance a priest came along. But when he saw the man lying there, he crossed to the other side of the road and passed him by. ³²A Temple assistant* walked over and looked at him lying there, but he also passed by on the other side.

³³"Then a despised Samaritan came along, and when he saw the man, he felt compassion for him. ³⁴Going over to him, the Samaritan soothed his wounds with olive oil and wine and bandaged them. Then he put the man on his own donkey and took him to an inn, where he took care of him. ³⁵The next day he handed the innkeeper two silver coins,* telling him, 'Take care of this man. If his bill runs higher than this, I'll pay you the next time I'm here.'

³⁶"Now which of these three would you say was a neighbor to the man who was attacked by bandits?" Jesus asked.

³⁷The man replied, "The one who showed him mercy."

Then Jesus said, "Yes, now go and do the same."

Jesus Visits Martha and Mary

³⁸As Jesus and the disciples continued on their way to Jerusalem, they came to a certain village where a woman named Martha welcomed him into her home. ³⁹Her sister, Mary, sat at the Lord's feet, listening to what he taught. ⁴⁰But Martha was distracted by the big dinner she was preparing. She came to Jesus and said, "Lord, doesn't it seem unfair to you that my sister just sits here while I do all the work? Tell her to come and help me."

⁴¹But the Lord said to her, "My dear Martha, you are worried and upset over all these details! ⁴²There is only one thing worth being concerned about. Mary has discovered it, and it will not be taken away from her."

10:27 Deut 6:5; Lev 19:18.   **10:32** Greek *A Levite.*   **10:35** Greek *two denarii.* A denarius was equivalent to a laborer's full day's wage.

CHAPTER 11

Teaching about Prayer

Once Jesus was in a certain place praying. As he finished, one of his disciples came to him and said, "Lord, teach us to pray, just as John taught his disciples."

²Jesus said, "This is how you should pray:*

"Father, may your name be kept holy.
    May your Kingdom come soon.
³ Give us each day the food we need,*
⁴ and forgive us our sins,
    as we forgive those who sin against us.
    And don't let us yield to temptation.*"

⁵Then, teaching them more about prayer, he used this story: "Suppose you went to a friend's house at midnight, wanting to borrow three loaves of bread. You say to him, ⁶'A friend of mine has just arrived for a visit, and I have nothing for him to eat.' ⁷And suppose he calls out from his bedroom, 'Don't bother me. The door is locked for the night, and my family and I are all in bed. I can't help you.' ⁸But I tell you this—though he won't do it for friendship's sake, if you keep knocking long enough, he will get up and give you whatever you need because of your shameless persistence.*

⁹"And so I tell you, keep on asking, and you will receive what you ask for. Keep on seeking, and you will find. Keep on knocking, and the door will be opened to you. ¹⁰For everyone who asks, receives. Everyone who seeks, finds. And to everyone who knocks, the door will be opened.

¹¹"You fathers—if your children ask* for a fish, do you give them a snake instead? ¹²Or if they ask for an egg, do you give them a scorpion? Of course not! ¹³So if you sinful people know how to give good gifts to your children, how much more will your heavenly Father give the Holy Spirit to those who ask him."

Jesus and the Prince of Demons

¹⁴One day Jesus cast out a demon from a man who couldn't speak, and when the demon was gone, the man began to speak. The crowds were amazed, ¹⁵but some of them said, "No wonder he can cast out demons. He gets his power from Satan,* the prince of demons." ¹⁶Others, trying to test Jesus, demanded that he show them a miraculous sign from heaven to prove his authority.

¹⁷He knew their thoughts, so he said, "Any kingdom divided by civil war is doomed. A family splintered by feuding will fall apart. ¹⁸You say I am empowered by Satan. But

11:2 Some manuscripts add additional phrases from the Lord's Prayer as it reads in Matt 6:9-13. 11:3 Or *Give us each day our food for the day;* or *Give us each day our food for tomorrow.* 11:4 Or *And keep us from being tested.* 11:8 Or *in order to avoid shame,* or *so his reputation won't be damaged.* 11:11 Some manuscripts add *for bread, do you give them a stone? Or [if they ask].* 11:15 Greek *Beelzeboul;* also in 11:18, 19. Other manuscripts read *Beezeboul;* Latin version reads *Beelzebub.*

THE POINT

Not a prayer without prayer. More than any of the other Gospels, Luke points to the importance of prayer. He shows that Jesus prayed on a regular basis and got results. Jesus prayed after he was baptized and the heavens opened up (Luke 3:21). He prayed after healing ole boy with the jacked-up hand (5:16). He prayed before he recruited the twelve brothas who became his apostles (6:12-16). He went up in the mountains to pray, and Moses and Elijah showed up on the set for conversation (9:28-31). He prayed before he ate a meal (9:16; 22:17-19). Jesus even taught his boys how to pray. Get it? Jesus prayed. That's what the Lord's prayer thing is all about—fo' sho:

"Father, may your name be kept holy. May your Kingdom come soon. Give us each day the food we need, and forgive us our sins, as we forgive those who sin against us. And don't let us yield to temptation." (Luke 11:2-4)

Luke doesn't always tell us the exact words Jesus used when he prayed, but the point is that when Jesus prayed to his Father, things happened. To quote Steve Harvey, "Don't be afraid to pray, don't be too shamed to pray, don't be too proud to pray, 'cause prayer changes things."

if Satan is divided and fighting against himself, how can his kingdom survive? ¹⁹And if I am empowered by Satan, what about your own exorcists? They cast out demons, too, so they will condemn you for what you have said. ²⁰But if I am casting out demons by the power of God,* then the Kingdom of God has arrived among you. ²¹For when a strong man like Satan is fully armed and guards his palace, his possessions are safe—²²until someone even stronger attacks and overpowers him, strips him of his weapons, and carries off his belongings.

²³"Anyone who isn't with me opposes me, and anyone who isn't working with me is actually working against me.

²⁴"When an evil* spirit leaves a person, it goes into the desert, searching for rest. But when it finds none, it says, 'I will return to the person I came from.' ²⁵So it returns and finds that its former home is all swept and in order. ²⁶Then the spirit finds seven other spirits more evil than itself, and they all enter the person and live there. And so that person is worse off than before."

²⁷As he was speaking, a woman in the crowd called out, "God bless your mother—the womb from which you came, and the breasts that nursed you!"

²⁸Jesus replied, "But even more blessed are all who hear the word of God and put it into practice."

The Sign of Jonah

²⁹As the crowd pressed in on Jesus, he said, "This evil generation keeps asking me to show them a miraculous sign. But the only sign I will give them is the sign of Jonah. ³⁰What happened to him was a sign to the people of Nineveh that God had sent him. What happens to the Son of Man* will be a sign to these people that he was sent by God.

³¹"The queen of Sheba* will stand up against this generation on judgment day and condemn it, for she came from a distant land to hear the wisdom of Solomon. Now some-

one greater than Solomon is here—but you refuse to listen. ³²The people of Nineveh will also stand up against this generation on judgment day and condemn it, for they repented of their sins at the preaching of Jonah. Now someone greater than Jonah is here—but you refuse to repent.

Receiving the Light

³³"No one lights a lamp and then hides it or puts it under a basket.* Instead, a lamp is placed on a stand, where its light can be seen by all who enter the house.

³⁴"Your eye is a lamp that provides light for your body. When your eye is good, your whole body is filled with light. But when it is bad, your body is filled with darkness. ³⁵Make sure that the light you think you have is not actually darkness. ³⁶If you are filled with light, with no dark corners, then your whole life will be radiant, as though a floodlight were filling you with light."

Jesus Criticizes the Religious Leaders

³⁷As Jesus was speaking, one of the Pharisees invited him home for a meal. So he went in and took his place at the table.* ³⁸His host was amazed to see that he sat down to eat without first performing the hand-washing ceremony required by Jewish custom. ³⁹Then the Lord said to him, "You Pharisees are so careful to clean the outside of the cup and the dish, but inside you are filthy—full of greed and wickedness! ⁴⁰Fools! Didn't God make the inside as well as the outside? ⁴¹So clean the inside by giving gifts to the poor, and you will be clean all over.

⁴²"What sorrow awaits you Pharisees! For you are careful to tithe even the tiniest income from your herb gardens,* but you ignore justice and the love of God. You should tithe, yes, but do not neglect the more important things.

⁴³"What sorrow awaits you Pharisees! For you love to sit in the seats of honor in the synagogues and receive respect-

11:20 Greek *by the finger of God.*   11:24 Greek *unclean.*   11:30 "Son of Man" is a title Jesus used for himself.   11:31 Greek *The queen of the south.*   11:33 Some manuscripts do not include *or puts it under a basket.*   11:37 Or *and reclined.*   11:42 Greek *tithe the mint, the rue, and every herb.*

ful greetings as you walk in the marketplaces. ⁴⁴Yes, what sorrow awaits you! For you are like hidden graves in a field. People walk over them without knowing the corruption they are stepping on."

⁴⁵"Teacher," said an expert in religious law, "you have insulted us, too, in what you just said."

⁴⁶"Yes," said Jesus, "what sorrow also awaits you experts in religious law! For you crush people with unbearable religious demands, and you never lift a finger to ease the burden. ⁴⁷What sorrow awaits you! For you build monuments for the prophets your own ancestors killed long ago. ⁴⁸But in fact, you stand as witnesses who agree with what your ancestors did. They killed the prophets, and you join in their crime by building the monuments! ⁴⁹This is what God in his wisdom said about you:* 'I will send prophets and apostles to them, but they will kill some and persecute the others.'

⁵⁰"As a result, this generation will be held responsible for the murder of all God's prophets from the creation of the world—⁵¹from the murder of Abel to the murder of Zechariah, who was killed between the altar and the sanctuary. Yes, it will certainly be charged against this generation.

⁵²"What sorrow awaits you experts in religious law! For you remove the key to knowledge from the people. You don't enter the Kingdom yourselves, and you prevent others from entering."

⁵³As Jesus was leaving, the teachers of religious law and the Pharisees became hostile and tried to provoke him with many questions. ⁵⁴They wanted to trap him into saying something they could use against him.

CHAPTER 12

A Warning against Hypocrisy

Meanwhile, the crowds grew until thousands were milling about and stepping on each other. Jesus turned first to his disciples and warned them, "Beware of the yeast of the Pharisees—their hypocrisy. ²The time is coming when everything that is covered up will be revealed, and all that is secret will be made known to all. ³Whatever you have said in the dark will be heard in the light, and what you have whispered behind closed doors will be shouted from the housetops for all to hear!

⁴"Dear friends, don't be afraid of those who want to kill your body; they cannot do any more to you after that. ⁵But I'll tell you whom to fear. Fear God, who has the power to kill you and then throw you into hell.* Yes, he's the one to fear.

⁶"What is the price of five sparrows—two copper coins*? Yet God does not forget a single one of them. ⁷And the very hairs on your head are all numbered. So don't be afraid; you are more valuable to God than a whole flock of sparrows.

⁸"I tell you the truth, everyone who acknowledges me publicly here on earth, the Son of Man* will also acknowledge in the presence of God's angels. ⁹But anyone who denies me here on earth will be denied before God's angels. ¹⁰Anyone who speaks against the Son of Man can be forgiven, but anyone who blasphemes the Holy Spirit will not be forgiven.

¹¹"And when you are brought to trial in the synagogues and before rulers and authorities, don't worry about how to defend yourself or what to say, ¹²for the Holy Spirit will teach you at that time what needs to be said."

Parable of the Rich Fool

¹³Then someone called from the crowd, "Teacher, please tell my brother to divide our father's estate with me."

¹⁴Jesus replied, "Friend, who made me a judge over you to decide such things as that?" ¹⁵Then he said, "Beware! Guard against every kind of greed. Life is not measured by how much you own."

¹⁶Then he told them a story: "A rich man had a fertile farm that produced fine crops. ¹⁷He said to himself, 'What

"Beware! Guard against every kind of greed. Life is not measured by how much you own" (Luke 12:15).

Don't be greedy! God ain't keepin' score based on what you got.

11:49 Greek *Therefore, the wisdom of God said.*   **12:5** Greek *Gehenna.*   **12:6** Greek *two assaria* [Roman coins equal to ¹⁄₁₆ of a denarius].   **12:8** "Son of Man" is a title Jesus used for himself.

should I do? I don't have room for all my crops.' ¹⁸Then he said, 'I know! I'll tear down my barns and build bigger ones. Then I'll have room enough to store all my wheat and other goods. ¹⁹And I'll sit back and say to myself, "My friend, you have enough stored away for years to come. Now take it easy! Eat, drink, and be merry!"'

²⁰"But God said to him, 'You fool! You will die this very night. Then who will get everything you worked for?'

²¹"Yes, a person is a fool to store up earthly wealth but not have a rich relationship with God."

Teaching about Money and Possessions

²²Then, turning to his disciples, Jesus said, "That is why I tell you not to worry about everyday life—whether you have enough food to eat or enough clothes to wear. ²³For life is more than food, and your body more than clothing. ²⁴Look at the ravens. They don't plant or harvest or store food in barns, for God feeds them. And you are far more valuable to him than any birds! ²⁵Can all your worries add a single moment to your life? ²⁶And if worry can't accomplish a little thing like that, what's the use of worrying over bigger things?

²⁷"Look at the lilies and how they grow. They don't work or make their clothing, yet Solomon in all his glory was not dressed as beautifully as they are. ²⁸And if God cares so wonderfully for flowers that are here today and thrown into the fire tomorrow, he will certainly care for you. Why do you have so little faith?

²⁹"And don't be concerned about what to eat and what to drink. Don't worry about such things. ³⁰These things dominate the thoughts of unbelievers all over the world, but your Father already knows your needs. ³¹Seek the Kingdom of God above all else, and he will give you everything you need.

³²"So don't be afraid, little flock. For it gives your Father great happiness to give you the Kingdom.

³³"Sell your possessions and give to those in need. This will store up treasure for you in heaven! And the purses of heaven never get old or develop holes. Your treasure will be safe; no thief can steal it and no moth can destroy it. ³⁴Wherever your treasure is, there the desires of your heart will also be.

Be Ready for the Lord's Coming

³⁵"Be dressed for service and keep your lamps burning, ³⁶as though you were waiting for your master to return from the wedding feast. Then you will be ready to open the door and let him in the moment he arrives and knocks. ³⁷The servants who are ready and waiting for his return will be rewarded. I tell you the truth, he himself will seat them, put on an apron, and serve them as they sit and eat! ³⁸He may come in the middle of the night or just before dawn.* But whenever he comes, he will reward the servants who are ready.

³⁹"Understand this: If a homeowner knew exactly when a burglar was coming, he would not permit his house to be broken into. ⁴⁰You also must be ready all the time, for the Son of Man will come when least expected."

⁴¹Peter asked, "Lord, is that illustration just for us or for everyone?"

⁴²And the Lord replied, "A faithful, sensible servant is one to whom the master can give the responsibility of managing his other household servants and feeding them. ⁴³If the master returns and finds that the servant has done a good job, there will be a reward. ⁴⁴I tell you the truth, the master will put that servant in charge of all he owns. ⁴⁵But what if the servant thinks, 'My master won't be back for a while,' and he begins beating the other servants, partying, and getting drunk? ⁴⁶The master will return unannounced and unexpected, and he will cut the servant in pieces and banish him with the unfaithful.

⁴⁷"And a servant who knows what the master wants, but

12:38 Greek *in the second or third watch.*

keeping your swagger strong

BIBLICAL PRINCIPLES FOR SUCCESS AND LEADERSHIP

The good life is a life spent storing up treasures in heaven. A lot of people think that living the good life means having lots of stuff—cars, homes, jewelry, etc., but Jesus said life is far more than food and clothing (Luke 12:23). In other words, the old saying, "The best things in life are free" really is true. Livin' the good life means you don't get hyped up about material stuff. God ain't concerned about your stuff anyway. He wants to see how much or how well others benefit from your stuff. And if you playin' it right, God will keep giving you stuff so you can continue to bless others.

If you're storing things away 'cause you're afraid of what's around the corner, stop worryin' yourself. God's got you covered.

"What is the price of five sparrows—two copper coins? Yet God does not forget a single one of them. And the very hairs on your head are all numbered. So don't be afraid; you are more valuable to God than a whole flock of sparrows." (Luke 12:6-7)

earth? No, I have come to divide people against each other! ⁵²From now on families will be split apart, three in favor of me, and two against—or two in favor and three against.

⁵³ 'Father will be divided against son
and son against father;
mother against daughter
and daughter against mother;
and mother-in-law against daughter-in-law
and daughter-in-law against mother-in-law.'*"

⁵⁴Then Jesus turned to the crowd and said, "When you see clouds beginning to form in the west, you say, 'Here comes a shower.' And you are right. ⁵⁵When the south wind blows, you say, 'Today will be a scorcher.' And it is. ⁵⁶You fools! You know how to interpret the weather signs of the earth and sky, but you don't know how to interpret the present times.

⁵⁷"Why can't you decide for yourselves what is right? ⁵⁸When you are on the way to court with your accuser, try to settle the matter before you get there. Otherwise, your accuser may drag you before the judge, who will hand you over to an officer, who will throw you into prison. ⁵⁹And if that happens, you won't be free again until you have paid the very last penny.*"

isn't prepared and doesn't carry out those instructions, will be severely punished. ⁴⁸But someone who does not know, and then does something wrong, will be punished only lightly. When someone has been given much, much will be required in return; and when someone has been entrusted with much, even more will be required.

Jesus Causes Division

⁴⁹"I have come to set the world on fire, and I wish it were already burning! ⁵⁰I have a terrible baptism of suffering ahead of me, and I am under a heavy burden until it is accomplished. ⁵¹Do you think I have come to bring peace to the

CHAPTER **13**

A Call to Repentance

About this time Jesus was informed that Pilate had murdered some people from Galilee as they were offering sacrifices at the Temple. ²"Do you think those Galileans were worse sinners than all the other people from Galilee?" Jesus asked. "Is that why they suffered? ³Not at all! And you will perish, too, unless you repent of your sins and turn to God. ⁴And what about the eighteen people who died when the tower in Siloam fell on them? Were they the worst sinners in Jerusalem? ⁵No, and I tell you again that unless you repent, you will perish, too."

12:53 Mic 7:6.   **12:59** Greek *last lepton* [the smallest Jewish coin].

Parable of the Barren Fig Tree

⁶Then Jesus told this story: "A man planted a fig tree in his garden and came again and again to see if there was any fruit on it, but he was always disappointed. ⁷Finally, he said to his gardener, 'I've waited three years, and there hasn't been a single fig! Cut it down. It's just taking up space in the garden.'

⁸"The gardener answered, 'Sir, give it one more chance. Leave it another year, and I'll give it special attention and plenty of fertilizer. ⁹If we get figs next year, fine. If not, then you can cut it down.'"

Jesus Heals on the Sabbath

¹⁰One Sabbath day as Jesus was teaching in a synagogue, ¹¹he saw a woman who had been crippled by an evil spirit. She had been bent double for eighteen years and was unable to stand up straight. ¹²When Jesus saw her, he called her over and said, "Dear woman, you are healed of your sickness!" ¹³Then he touched her, and instantly she could stand straight. How she praised God!

¹⁴But the leader in charge of the synagogue was indignant that Jesus had healed her on the Sabbath day. "There are six days of the week for working," he said to the crowd. "Come on those days to be healed, not on the Sabbath."

¹⁵But the Lord replied, "You hypocrites! Each of you works on the Sabbath day! Don't you untie your ox or your donkey from its stall on the Sabbath and lead it out for water? ¹⁶This dear woman, a daughter of Abraham, has been held in bondage by Satan for eighteen years. Isn't it right that she be released, even on the Sabbath?"

¹⁷This shamed his enemies, but all the people rejoiced at the wonderful things he did.

Parable of the Mustard Seed

¹⁸Then Jesus said, "What is the Kingdom of God like? How can I illustrate it? ¹⁹It is like a tiny mustard seed that a man planted in a garden; it grows and becomes a tree, and the birds make nests in its branches."

Parable of the Yeast

²⁰He also asked, "What else is the Kingdom of God like? ²¹It is like the yeast a woman used in making bread. Even though she put only a little yeast in three measures of flour, it permeated every part of the dough."

The Narrow Door

²²Jesus went through the towns and villages, teaching as he went, always pressing on toward Jerusalem. ²³Someone asked him, "Lord, will only a few be saved?"

He replied, ²⁴"Work hard to enter the narrow door to God's Kingdom, for many will try to enter but will fail. ²⁵When the master of the house has locked the door, it will be too late. You will stand outside knocking and pleading, 'Lord, open the door for us!' But he will reply, 'I don't know you or where you come from.' ²⁶Then you will say, 'But we ate and drank with you, and you taught in our streets.' ²⁷And he will reply, 'I tell you, I don't know you or where you come from. Get away from me, all you who do evil.'

²⁸"There will be weeping and gnashing of teeth, for you will see Abraham, Isaac, Jacob, and all the prophets in the Kingdom of God, but you will be thrown out. ²⁹And people will come from all over the world—from east and west, north and south—to take their places in the Kingdom of God. ³⁰And note this: Some who seem least important now will be the greatest then, and some who are the greatest now will be least important then.*"

Jesus Grieves over Jerusalem

³¹At that time some Pharisees said to him, "Get away from here if you want to live! Herod Antipas wants to kill you!"

³²Jesus replied, "Go tell that fox that I will keep on cast-

13:30 Greek *Some are last who will be first, and some are first who will be last.*

POWERCHOICES

IMAGE IS EVERYTHING! OR SO WE ARE TOLD BY THE MEDIA AND POPU-LAR CULTURE. WE CURRENTLY LIVE IN A CULTURE WHERE BIG CARS, BIG HOUSES, DESIGNER CLOTHES, DESIGNER HANDBAGS, AND LOTS AND LOTS OF BLING ARE STATUS SYMBOLS THAT REPRESENT POWER, MONEY, AND PRESTIGE. THE PERCEPTION IS YOU'RE LIVIN' LARGE IF YOU HAVE ALL THIS STUFF. IT'S ALL ABOUT A STATUS SYMBOL, HAVING SOMETHING THAT REPRESENTS AN OVER-THE-TOP LIFESTYLE.

¶ IT'S IN OUR FACES EVERY DAY. REALITY TV SHOWS THAT DEPICT THE LIFESTYLE OF THE RICH AND FAMOUS HAVE RESULTED IN A CUL-TURE OF CELEBRITY WANNABES THAT FLOCK TO RETAIL STORES. THEY PURCHASE THE LATEST GYM SHOE, HANDBAG, CAR, OR PAIR OF JEANS ASSOCIATED WITH THEIR FAVORITE HOLLYWOOD CELEB. BUT WHAT DOES IT ALL MEAN? DOES OUR GROWING APPETITE FOR ALL THINGS LUXURIOUS HAVE A PRICE? WELL, JESUS EXPLAINS IT LIKE THIS:

¶ ONE DAY THIS RICH GUY HAD A FARM GROWING LOTS OF VEGE-TABLES—THE CROPS WERE QUALITY FOOD—NOT THE CHEAP STUFF. HE HAD SO MUCH LAND AND SO MUCH FOOD STORED UP THAT HE DECIDED TO BUILD BIGGER BARNS TO STORE EVEN MORE FOOD SO HE COULD JUST KICK BACK AND CHILL FOR YEARS TO COME. JESUS BROKE IT DOWN LIKE THIS: HE CALLED THE MAN A FOOL. WHAT IF THE RICH MAN WERE TO DIE THAT SAME NIGHT? WHO WOULD GET ALL THAT STUFF HE HAD SELFISHLY STORED AWAY? WHAT WAS THE POINT OF STORING UP ALL THAT FOOD IF HE WAS NOT AROUND TO EAT IT (LUKE 12:15-21)? ¶ *WHAT ABOUT YOU? ARE YOU USING YOUR PERSONAL TREASURE TO SERVE OTHERS?*

---

ing out demons and healing people today and tomorrow; and the third day I will accomplish my purpose. ³³Yes, to-day, tomorrow, and the next day I must proceed on my way. For it wouldn't do for a prophet of God to be killed ex-cept in Jerusalem!

³⁴"O Jerusalem, Jerusalem, the city that kills the prophets and stones God's messengers! How often I have wanted to gather your children together as a hen protects her chicks beneath her wings, but you wouldn't let me. ³⁵And now, look, your house is abandoned. And you will never see me again until you say, 'Blessings on the one who comes in the name of the LORD!'*"

CHAPTER 14

Jesus Heals on the Sabbath

One Sabbath day Jesus went to eat dinner in the home of a leader of the Pharisees, and the people were watching him closely. ²There was a man there whose arms and legs were swollen.* ³Jesus asked the Pharisees and experts in religious law, "Is it permitted in the law to heal people on the Sabbath day, or not?" ⁴When they refused to answer, Jesus touched the sick man and healed him and sent him away. ⁵Then he turned to them and said, "Which of you doesn't work on the Sabbath? If your son* or your cow falls into a pit, don't you rush to get him out?" ⁶Again they could not answer.

Jesus Teaches about Humility

⁷When Jesus noticed that all who had come to the dinner were trying to sit in the seats of honor near the head of the table, he gave them this advice: ⁸"When you are invited to a wedding feast, don't sit in the seat of honor. What if some-one who is more distinguished than you has also been in-vited? ⁹The host will come and say, 'Give this person your seat.' Then you will be embarrassed, and you will have to take whatever seat is left at the foot of the table!

¹⁰"Instead, take the lowest place at the foot of the ta-ble. Then when your host sees you, he will come and say, 'Friend, we have a better place for you!' Then you will be honored in front of all the other guests. ¹¹For those who

---

13:35 Ps 118:26.   **14:2** Or *who had dropsy.*   **14:5** Some manuscripts read *donkey.*

exalt themselves will be humbled, and those who humble themselves will be exalted."

¹²Then he turned to his host. "When you put on a luncheon or a banquet," he said, "don't invite your friends, brothers, relatives, and rich neighbors. For they will invite you back, and that will be your only reward. ¹³Instead, invite the poor, the crippled, the lame, and the blind. ¹⁴Then at the resurrection of the righteous, God will reward you for inviting those who could not repay you."

Parable of the Great Feast

¹⁵Hearing this, a man sitting at the table with Jesus exclaimed, "What a blessing it will be to attend a banquet* in the Kingdom of God!"

¹⁶Jesus replied with this story: "A man prepared a great feast and sent out many invitations. ¹⁷When the banquet was ready, he sent his servant to tell the guests, 'Come, the banquet is ready.' ¹⁸But they all began making excuses. One said, 'I have just bought a field and must inspect it. lease excuse me.' ¹⁹Another said, 'I have just bought five pairs of oxen, and I want to try them out. Please excuse me.' ²⁰Another said, 'I now have a wife, so I can't come.'

²¹"The servant returned and told his master what they had said. His master was furious and said, 'Go quickly into the streets and alleys of the town and invite the poor, the crippled, the blind, and the lame.' ²²After the servant had done this, he reported, 'There is still room for more.' ²³So his master said, 'Go out into the country lanes and behind the hedges and urge anyone you find to come, so that the house will be full. ²⁴For none of those I first invited will get even the smallest taste of my banquet.'"

The Cost of Being a Disciple

²⁵A large crowd was following Jesus. He turned around and said to them, ²⁶"If you want to be my disciple, you must hate everyone else by comparison—your father and mother, wife and children, brothers and sisters—yes, even your own life. Otherwise, you cannot be my disciple. ²⁷And if you do not carry your own cross and follow me, you cannot be my disciple.

²⁸"But don't begin until you count the cost. For who would begin construction of a building without first calculating the cost to see if there is enough money to finish it? ²⁹Otherwise, you might complete only the foundation before running out of money, and then everyone would laugh at you. ³⁰They would say, 'There's the person who started that building and couldn't afford to finish it!'

³¹"Or what king would go to war against another king without first sitting down with his counselors to discuss whether his army of 10,000 could defeat the 20,000 soldiers marching against him? ³²And if he can't, he will send a delegation to discuss terms of peace while the enemy is still far away. ³³So you cannot become my disciple without giving up everything you own.

³⁴"Salt is good for seasoning. But if it loses its flavor, how do you make it salty again? ³⁵Flavorless salt is good neither for the soil nor for the manure pile. It is thrown away. Anyone with ears to hear should listen and understand!"

CHAPTER 15

Parable of the Lost Sheep

Tax collectors and other notorious sinners often came to listen to Jesus teach. ²This made the Pharisees and teachers of religious law complain that he was associating with such sinful people—even eating with them!

³So Jesus told them this story: ⁴"If a man has a hundred sheep and one of them gets lost, what will he do? Won't he leave the ninety-nine others in the wilderness and go to search for the one that is lost until he finds it? ⁵And when he has found it, he will joyfully carry it home on his shoulders. ⁶When he arrives, he will call together his friends and neigh-

14:15 Greek *to eat bread.*

bors, saying, 'Rejoice with me because I have found my lost sheep.' ⁷In the same way, there is more joy in heaven over one lost sinner who repents and returns to God than over ninety-nine others who are righteous and haven't strayed away!

Parable of the Lost Coin

⁸"Or suppose a woman has ten silver coins* and loses one. Won't she light a lamp and sweep the entire house and search carefully until she finds it? ⁹And when she finds it, she will call in her friends and neighbors and say, 'Rejoice with me because I have found my lost coin.' ¹⁰In the same way, there is joy in the presence of God's angels when even one sinner repents."

Parable of the Lost Son

¹¹To illustrate the point further, Jesus told them this story: "A man had two sons. ¹²The younger son told his father, 'I want my share of your estate now before you die.' So his father agreed to divide his wealth between his sons.

¹³"A few days later this younger son packed all his belongings and moved to a distant land, and there he wasted all his money in wild living. ¹⁴About the time his money ran out, a great famine swept over the land, and he began to starve. ¹⁵He persuaded a local farmer to hire him, and the man sent him into his fields to feed the pigs. ¹⁶The young man became so hungry that even the pods he was feeding the pigs looked good to him. But no one gave him anything.

¹⁷"When he finally came to his senses, he said to himself, 'At home even the hired servants have food enough to spare, and here I am dying of hunger! ¹⁸I will go home to my father and say, "Father, I have sinned against both heaven and you, ¹⁹and I am no longer worthy of being called your son. Please take me on as a hired servant."'

²⁰"So he returned home to his father. And while he was still a long way off, his father saw him coming. Filled with love and compassion, he ran to his son, embraced him, and kissed him. ²¹His son said to him, 'Father, I have sinned against both heaven and you, and I am no longer worthy of being called your son.*'

²²"But his father said to the servants, 'Quick! Bring the finest robe in the house and put it on him. Get a ring for his finger and sandals for his feet. ²³And kill the calf we have been fattening. We must celebrate with a feast, ²⁴for this son of mine was dead and has now returned to life. He was lost, but now he is found.' So the party began.

²⁵"Meanwhile, the older son was in the fields working. When he returned home, he heard music and dancing in the house, ²⁶and he asked one of the servants what was going on. ²⁷'Your brother is back,' he was told, 'and your father has killed the fattened calf. We are celebrating because of his safe return.'

²⁸"The older brother was angry and wouldn't go in. His father came out and begged him, ²⁹but he replied, 'All these years I've slaved for you and never once refused to do a single thing you told me to. And in all that time you never gave me even one young goat for a feast with my friends. ³⁰Yet when this son of yours comes back after squandering your money on prostitutes, you celebrate by killing the fattened calf!'

³¹"His father said to him, 'Look, dear son, you have always stayed by me, and everything I have is yours. ³²We had to celebrate this happy day. For your brother was dead and has come back to life! He was lost, but now he is found!'"

CHAPTER **16**

Parable of the Shrewd Manager

Jesus told this story to his disciples: "There was a certain rich man who had a manager handling his affairs. One day a report came that the manager was wasting his employer's money. ²So the employer called him in and said, 'What's this I hear about you? Get your report in order, because you are going to be fired.'

15:8 Greek *ten drachmas.* A drachma was the equivalent of a full day's wage.   **15:21** Some manuscripts add *Please take me on as a hired servant.*

³"The manager thought to himself, 'Now what? My boss has fired me. I don't have the strength to dig ditches, and I'm too proud to beg. ⁴Ah, I know how to ensure that I'll have plenty of friends who will give me a home when I am fired.'

⁵"So he invited each person who owed money to his employer to come and discuss the situation. He asked the first one, 'How much do you owe him?' ⁶The man replied, 'I owe him 800 gallons of olive oil.' So the manager told him, 'Take the bill and quickly change it to 400 gallons.*'

⁷"'And how much do you owe my employer?' he asked the next man. 'I owe him 1,000 bushels of wheat,' was the reply. 'Here,' the manager said, 'take the bill and change it to 800 bushels.*'

⁸"The rich man had to admire the dishonest rascal for being so shrewd. And it is true that the children of this world are more shrewd in dealing with the world around them than are the children of the light. ⁹Here's the lesson: Use your worldly resources to benefit others and make friends. Then, when your earthly possessions are gone, they will welcome you to an eternal home.*

¹⁰"If you are faithful in little things, you will be faithful in large ones. But if you are dishonest in little things, you won't be honest with greater responsibilities. ¹¹And if you are untrustworthy about worldly wealth, who will trust you with the true riches of heaven? ¹²And if you are not faithful with other people's things, why should you be trusted with things of your own?

¹³"No one can serve two masters. For you will hate one and love the other; you will be devoted to one and despise the other. You cannot serve both God and money."

¹⁴The Pharisees, who dearly loved their money, heard all this and scoffed at him. ¹⁵Then he said to them, "You like to appear righteous in public, but God knows your hearts. What this world honors is detestable in the sight of God.

"If you are faithful in little things, you will be faithful in large ones. But if you are dishonest in little things, you won't be honest with greater responsibilities. And if you are untrustworthy about worldly wealth, who will trust you with the true riches of heaven?" (Luke 16:10-11).

say what?

The way you handle the "little things" will be the way you handle the "bigger things."

¹⁶"Until John the Baptist, the law of Moses and the messages of the prophets were your guides. But now the Good News of the Kingdom of God is preached, and everyone is eager to get in.* ¹⁷But that doesn't mean that the law has lost its force. It is easier for heaven and earth to disappear than for the smallest point of God's law to be overturned.

¹⁸"For example, a man who divorces his wife and marries someone else commits adultery. And anyone who marries a woman divorced from her husband commits adultery."

Parable of the Rich Man and Lazarus

¹⁹Jesus said, "There was a certain rich man who was splendidly clothed in purple and fine linen and who lived each day in luxury. ²⁰At his gate lay a poor man named Lazarus who was covered with sores. ²¹As Lazarus lay there longing for scraps from the rich man's table, the dogs would come and lick his open sores.

²²"Finally, the poor man died and was carried by the angels to be with Abraham.* The rich man also died and was buried, ²³and his soul went to the place of the dead.* There, in torment, he saw Abraham in the far distance with Lazarus at his side.

²⁴"The rich man shouted, 'Father Abraham, have some pity! Send Lazarus over here to dip the tip of his finger in water and cool my tongue. I am in anguish in these flames.'

²⁵"But Abraham said to him, 'Son, remember that during your lifetime you had everything you wanted, and Lazarus had nothing. So now he is here being comforted, and you are in anguish. ²⁶And besides, there is a great chasm separating us. No one can cross over to you from here, and no one can cross over to us from there.'

²⁷"Then the rich man said, 'Please, Father Abraham, at least send him to my father's home. ²⁸For I have five brothers, and I want him to warn them so they don't end up in this place of torment.'

16:6 Greek *100 baths . . . 50 [baths]*.   16:7 Greek *100 korous . . . 80 [korous]*.   16:9 Or *you will be welcomed into eternal homes*.   16:16 Or *everyone is urged to enter in*.   16:22 Greek *into Abraham's bosom*.   16:23 Greek *to Hades*.

²⁹"But Abraham said, 'Moses and the prophets have warned them. Your brothers can read what they wrote.'

³⁰"The rich man replied, 'No, Father Abraham! But if someone is sent to them from the dead, then they will repent of their sins and turn to God.'

³¹"But Abraham said, 'If they won't listen to Moses and the prophets, they won't listen even if someone rises from the dead.'"

CHAPTER 17

Teachings about Forgiveness and Faith

One day Jesus said to his disciples, "There will always be temptations to sin, but what sorrow awaits the person who does the tempting! ²It would be better to be thrown into the sea with a millstone hung around your neck than to cause one of these little ones to fall into sin. ³So watch yourselves!

"If another believer* sins, rebuke that person; then if there is repentance, forgive. ⁴Even if that person wrongs you seven times a day and each time turns again and asks forgiveness, you must forgive."

⁵The apostles said to the Lord, "Show us how to increase our faith."

⁶The Lord answered, "If you had faith even as small as a mustard seed, you could say to this mulberry tree, 'May you be uprooted and thrown into the sea,' and it would obey you!

⁷"When a servant comes in from plowing or taking care of sheep, does his master say, 'Come in and eat with me'? ⁸No, he says, 'Prepare my meal, put on your apron, and serve me while I eat. Then you can eat later.' ⁹And does the master thank the servant for doing what he was told to do? Of course not. ¹⁰In the same way, when you obey me you should say, 'We are unworthy servants who have simply done our duty.'"

Ten Healed of Leprosy

¹¹As Jesus continued on toward Jerusalem, he reached the border between Galilee and Samaria. ¹²As he entered a village there, ten lepers stood at a distance, ¹³crying out, "Jesus, Master, have mercy on us!"

¹⁴He looked at them and said, "Go show yourselves to the priests."* And as they went, they were cleansed of their leprosy.

¹⁵One of them, when he saw that he was healed, came back to Jesus, shouting, "Praise God!" ¹⁶He fell to the ground at Jesus' feet, thanking him for what he had done. This man was a Samaritan.

¹⁷Jesus asked, "Didn't I heal ten men? Where are the other nine? ¹⁸Has no one returned to give glory to God except this foreigner?" ¹⁹And Jesus said to the man, "Stand up and go. Your faith has healed you.*"

The Coming of the Kingdom

²⁰One day the Pharisees asked Jesus, "When will the Kingdom of God come?"

Jesus replied, "The Kingdom of God can't be detected by visible signs.* ²¹You won't be able to say, 'Here it is!' or 'It's over there!' For the Kingdom of God is already among you.*"

²²Then he said to his disciples, "The time is coming when you will long to see the day when the Son of Man returns,* but you won't see it. ²³People will tell you, 'Look, there is the Son of Man,' or 'Here he is,' but don't go out and follow them. ²⁴For as the lightning flashes and lights up the sky from one end to the other, so it will be on the day when the Son of Man comes. ²⁵But first the Son of Man must suffer terribly* and be rejected by this generation.

²⁶"When the Son of Man returns, it will be like it was in Noah's day. ²⁷In those days, the people enjoyed

---

17:3 Greek *If your brother.*   17:14 See Lev 14:2-32.   17:19 Or *Your faith has saved you.*   17:20 Or *by your speculations.*   17:21 Or *is within you,* or *is in your grasp.*   17:22 Or *long for even one day with the Son of Man.* "Son of Man" is a title Jesus used for himself.   17:25 Or *suffer many things.*

banquets and parties and weddings right up to the time Noah entered his boat and the flood came and destroyed them all.

28"And the world will be as it was in the days of Lot. People went about their daily business—eating and drinking, buying and selling, farming and building—29until the morning Lot left Sodom. Then fire and burning sulfur rained down from heaven and destroyed them all. 30Yes, it will be 'business as usual' right up to the day when the Son of Man is revealed. 31On that day a person out on the deck of a roof must not go down into the house to pack. A person out in the field must not return home. 32Remember what happened to Lot's wife! 33If you cling to your life, you will lose it, and if you let your life go, you will save it. 34That night two people will be asleep in one bed; one will be taken, the other left. 35Two women will be grinding flour together at the mill; one will be taken, the other left.*"

37"Where will this happen, Lord?"* the disciples asked.

Jesus replied, "Just as the gathering of vultures shows there is a carcass nearby, so these signs indicate that the end is near."*

CHAPTER 18

Parable of the Persistent Widow

One day Jesus told his disciples a story to show that they should always pray and never give up. 2"There was a judge in a certain city," he said, "who neither feared God nor cared about people. 3A widow of that city came to him repeatedly, saying, 'Give me justice in this dispute with my enemy.' 4The judge ignored her for a while, but finally he said to himself, 'I don't fear God or care about people, 5but this woman is driving me crazy. I'm going to see that she gets justice, because she is wearing me out with her constant requests!'"

6Then the Lord said, "Learn a lesson from this unjust judge. 7Even he rendered a just decision in the end. So don't you think God will surely give justice to his chosen people who cry out to him day and night? Will he keep putting them off? 8I tell you, he will grant justice to them quickly! But when the Son of Man* returns, how many will he find on the earth who have faith?"

Parable of the Pharisee and Tax Collector

9Then Jesus told this story to some who had great confidence in their own righteousness and scorned everyone else: 10"Two men went to the Temple to pray. One was a Pharisee, and the other was a despised tax collector. 11The Pharisee stood by himself and prayed this prayer*: 'I thank you, God, that I am not a sinner like everyone else. For I don't cheat, I don't sin, and I don't commit adultery. I'm certainly not like that tax collector! 12I fast twice a week, and I give you a tenth of my income.'

13"But the tax collector stood at a distance and dared not even lift his eyes to heaven as he prayed. Instead, he beat his chest in sorrow, saying, 'O God, be merciful to me, for I am a sinner.' 14I tell you, this sinner, not the Pharisee, returned home justified before God. For those who exalt themselves will be humbled, and those who humble themselves will be exalted."

Jesus Blesses the Children

15One day some parents brought their little children to Jesus so he could touch and bless them. But when the disciples saw this, they scolded the parents for bothering him.

16Then Jesus called for the children and said to the disciples, "Let the children come to me. Don't stop them! For the Kingdom of God belongs to those who are like these children. 17I tell you the truth, anyone who doesn't receive the Kingdom of God like a child will never enter it."

17:35 Some manuscripts add verse 36, *Two men will be working in the field; one will be taken, the other left.* Compare Matt 24:40.   17:37a Greek *"Where, Lord?"*   17:37b Greek *"Wherever the carcass is, the vultures gather."*   18:8 "Son of Man" is a title Jesus used for himself.   18:11 Some manuscripts read *stood and prayed this prayer to himself.*

The Rich Man

¹⁸Once a religious leader asked Jesus this question: "Good Teacher, what should I do to inherit eternal life?"

¹⁹"Why do you call me good?" Jesus asked him. "Only God is truly good. ²⁰But to answer your question, you know the commandments: 'You must not commit adultery. You must not murder. You must not steal. You must not testify falsely. Honor your father and mother.'*"

²¹The man replied, "I've obeyed all these commandments since I was young."

²²When Jesus heard his answer, he said, "There is still one thing you haven't done. Sell all your possessions and give the money to the poor, and you will have treasure in heaven. Then come, follow me."

²³But when the man heard this he became very sad, for he was very rich.

²⁴When Jesus saw this,* he said, "How hard it is for the rich to enter the Kingdom of God! ²⁵In fact, it is easier for a camel to go through the eye of a needle than for a rich person to enter the Kingdom of God!"

²⁶Those who heard this said, "Then who in the world can be saved?"

²⁷He replied, "What is impossible for people is possible with God."

²⁸Peter said, "We've left our homes to follow you."

²⁹"Yes," Jesus replied, "and I assure you that everyone who has given up house or wife or brothers or parents or children, for the sake of the Kingdom of God, ³⁰will be repaid many times over in this life, and will have eternal life in the world to come."

Jesus Again Predicts His Death

³¹Taking the twelve disciples aside, Jesus said, "Listen, we're going up to Jerusalem, where all the predictions of the prophets concerning the Son of Man will come true. ³²He will be handed over to the Romans,* and he will be mocked, treated shamefully, and spit upon. ³³They will flog him with a whip and kill him, but on the third day he will rise again."

³⁴But they didn't understand any of this. The significance of his words was hidden from them, and they failed to grasp what he was talking about.

Jesus Heals a Blind Beggar

³⁵As Jesus approached Jericho, a blind beggar was sitting beside the road. ³⁶When he heard the noise of a crowd going past, he asked what was happening. ³⁷They told him that Jesus the Nazarene* was going by. ³⁸So he began shouting, "Jesus, Son of David, have mercy on me!"

³⁹"Be quiet!" the people in front yelled at him.

But he only shouted louder, "Son of David, have mercy on me!"

⁴⁰When Jesus heard him, he stopped and ordered that the man be brought to him. As the man came near, Jesus asked him, ⁴¹"What do you want me to do for you?"

"Lord," he said, "I want to see!"

⁴²And Jesus said, "All right, receive your sight! Your faith has healed you." ⁴³Instantly the man could see, and he followed Jesus, praising God. And all who saw it praised God, too.

CHAPTER 19

Jesus and Zacchaeus

Jesus entered Jericho and made his way through the town. ²There was a man there named Zacchaeus. He was the chief tax collector in the region, and he had become very rich. ³He tried to get a look at Jesus, but he was too short to see over the crowd. ⁴So he ran ahead and climbed a sycamore-fig tree beside the road, for Jesus was going to pass that way.

⁵When Jesus came by, he looked up at Zacchaeus and called him by name. "Zacchaeus!" he said. "Quick, come down! I must be a guest in your home today."

18:20 Exod 20:12-16; Deut 5:16-20.   18:24 Some manuscripts read *When Jesus saw how sad the man was.*   18:32 Greek *the Gentiles.*   18:37 Or *Jesus of Nazareth.*

⁶Zacchaeus quickly climbed down and took Jesus to his house in great excitement and joy. ⁷But the people were displeased. "He has gone to be the guest of a notorious sinner," they grumbled.

⁸Meanwhile, Zacchaeus stood before the Lord and said, "I will give half my wealth to the poor, Lord, and if I have cheated people on their taxes, I will give them back four times as much!"

⁹Jesus responded, "Salvation has come to this home today, for this man has shown himself to be a true son of Abraham. ¹⁰For the Son of Man* came to seek and save those who are lost."

Parable of the Ten Servants

¹¹The crowd was listening to everything Jesus said. And because he was nearing Jerusalem, he told them a story to correct the impression that the Kingdom of God would begin right away. ¹²He said, "A nobleman was called away to a distant empire to be crowned king and then return. ¹³Before he left, he called together ten of his servants and divided among them ten pounds of silver,* saying, 'Invest this for me while I am gone.' ¹⁴But his people hated him and sent a delegation after him to say, 'We do not want him to be our king.'

¹⁵"After he was crowned king, he returned and called in the servants to whom he had given the money. He wanted to find out what their profits were. ¹⁶The first servant reported, 'Master, I invested your money and made ten times the original amount!'

¹⁷"'Well done!' the king exclaimed. 'You are a good servant. You have been faithful with the little I entrusted to you, so you will be governor of ten cities as your reward.'

¹⁸"The next servant reported, 'Master, I invested your money and made five times the original amount.'

¹⁹"'Well done!' the king said. 'You will be governor over five cities.'

²⁰"But the third servant brought back only the original amount of money and said, 'Master, I hid your money and kept it safe. ²¹I was afraid because you are a hard man to deal with, taking what isn't yours and harvesting crops you didn't plant.'

²²"'You wicked servant!' the king roared. 'Your own words condemn you. If you knew that I'm a hard man who takes what isn't mine and harvests crops I didn't plant, ²³why didn't you deposit my money in the bank? At least I could have gotten some interest on it.'

²⁴"Then, turning to the others standing nearby, the king ordered, 'Take the money from this servant, and give it to the one who has ten pounds.'

²⁵"'But, master,' they said, 'he already has ten pounds!'

²⁶"'Yes,' the king replied, 'and to those who use well what they are given, even more will be given. But from those who do nothing, even what little they have will be taken away. ²⁷And as for these enemies of mine who didn't want me to be their king—bring them in and execute them right here in front of me.'"

Jesus' Triumphant Entry

²⁸After telling this story, Jesus went on toward Jerusalem, walking ahead of his disciples. ²⁹As he came to the towns of Bethphage and Bethany on the Mount of Olives, he sent two disciples ahead. ³⁰"Go into that village over there," he told them. "As you enter it, you will see a young donkey tied there that no one has ever ridden. Untie it and bring it here. ³¹If anyone asks, 'Why are you untying that colt?' just say, 'The Lord needs it.'"

³²So they went and found the colt, just as Jesus had said. ³³And sure enough, as they were untying it, the owners asked them, "Why are you untying that colt?"

³⁴And the disciples simply replied, "The Lord needs it." ³⁵So they brought the colt to Jesus and threw their garments over it for him to ride on.

19:10 "Son of Man" is a title Jesus used for himself.   19:13 Greek *ten minas;* one mina was worth about three months' wages.

³⁶As he rode along, the crowds spread out their garments on the road ahead of him. ³⁷When he reached the place where the road started down the Mount of Olives, all of his followers began to shout and sing as they walked along, praising God for all the wonderful miracles they had seen.

³⁸ "Blessings on the King who comes in the name of the
     LORD!
     Peace in heaven, and glory in highest heaven!"*

³⁹But some of the Pharisees among the crowd said, "Teacher, rebuke your followers for saying things like that!"

⁴⁰He replied, "If they kept quiet, the stones along the road would burst into cheers!"

Jesus Weeps over Jerusalem

⁴¹But as he came closer to Jerusalem and saw the city ahead, he began to weep. ⁴²"How I wish today that you of all people would understand the way to peace. But now it is too late, and peace is hidden from your eyes. ⁴³Before long your enemies will build ramparts against your walls and encircle you and close in on you from every side. ⁴⁴They will crush you into the ground, and your children with you. Your enemies will not leave a single stone in place, because you did not accept your opportunity for salvation."

Jesus Clears the Temple

⁴⁵Then Jesus entered the Temple and began to drive out the people selling animals for sacrifices. ⁴⁶He said to them, "The Scriptures declare, 'My Temple will be a house of prayer,' but you have turned it into a den of thieves."*

⁴⁷After that, he taught daily in the Temple, but the leading priests, the teachers of religious law, and the other leaders of the people began planning how to kill him. ⁴⁸But they could think of nothing, because all the people hung on every word he said.

CHAPTER **20**

The Authority of Jesus Challenged

One day as Jesus was teaching the people and preaching the Good News in the Temple, the leading priests, the teachers of religious law, and the elders came up to him. ²They demanded, "By what authority are you doing all these things? Who gave you the right?"

³"Let me ask you a question first," he replied. ⁴"Did John's authority to baptize come from heaven, or was it merely human?"

⁵They talked it over among themselves. "If we say it was from heaven, he will ask why we didn't believe John. ⁶But if we say it was merely human, the people will stone us because they are convinced John was a prophet." ⁷So they finally replied that they didn't know.

⁸And Jesus responded, "Then I won't tell you by what authority I do these things."

Parable of the Evil Farmers

⁹Now Jesus turned to the people again and told them this story: "A man planted a vineyard, leased it to tenant farmers, and moved to another country to live for several years. ¹⁰At the time of the grape harvest, he sent one of his servants to collect his share of the crop. But the farmers attacked the servant, beat him up, and sent him back empty-handed. ¹¹So the owner sent another servant, but they also insulted him, beat him up, and sent him away empty-handed. ¹²A third man was sent, and they wounded him and chased him away.

¹³"'What will I do?' the owner asked himself. 'I know! I'll send my cherished son. Surely they will respect him.'

¹⁴"But when the tenant farmers saw his son, they said to each other, 'Here comes the heir to this estate. Let's kill him and get the estate for ourselves!' ¹⁵So they dragged him out of the vineyard and murdered him.

"What do you suppose the owner of the vineyard will do

to them?" Jesus asked. [16]"I'll tell you—he will come and kill those farmers and lease the vineyard to others."

"How terrible that such a thing should ever happen," his listeners protested.

[17]Jesus looked at them and said, "Then what does this Scripture mean?

'The stone that the builders rejected
has now become the cornerstone.'*

[18]Everyone who stumbles over that stone will be broken to pieces, and it will crush anyone it falls on."

[19]The teachers of religious law and the leading priests wanted to arrest Jesus immediately because they realized he was telling the story against them—they were the wicked farmers. But they were afraid of the people's reaction.

Taxes for Caesar

[20]Watching for their opportunity, the leaders sent spies pretending to be honest men. They tried to get Jesus to say something that could be reported to the Roman governor so he would arrest Jesus. [21]"Teacher," they said, "we know that you speak and teach what is right and are not influenced by what others think. You teach the way of God truthfully. [22]Now tell us—is it right for us to pay taxes to Caesar or not?"

[23]He saw through their trickery and said, [24]"Show me a Roman coin.* Whose picture and title are stamped on it?"

"Caesar's," they replied.

[25]"Well then," he said, "give to Caesar what belongs to Caesar, and give to God what belongs to God."

[26]So they failed to trap him by what he said in front of the people. Instead, they were amazed by his answer, and they became silent.

Discussion about Resurrection

[27]Then Jesus was approached by some Sadducees—religious leaders who say there is no resurrection from the dead.

[28]They posed this question: "Teacher, Moses gave us a law that if a man dies, leaving a wife but no children, his brother should marry the widow and have a child who will carry on the brother's name.* [29]Well, suppose there were seven brothers. The oldest one married and then died without children. [30]So the second brother married the widow, but he also died. [31]Then the third brother married her. This continued with all seven of them, who died without children. [32]Finally, the woman also died. [33]So tell us, whose wife will she be in the resurrection? For all seven were married to her!"

[34]Jesus replied, "Marriage is for people here on earth. [35]But in the age to come, those worthy of being raised from the dead will neither marry nor be given in marriage. [36]And they will never die again. In this respect they will be like angels. They are children of God and children of the resurrection.

[37]"But now, as to whether the dead will be raised—even Moses proved this when he wrote about the burning bush. Long after Abraham, Isaac, and Jacob had died, he referred to the Lord* as 'the God of Abraham, the God of Isaac, and the God of Jacob.'* [38]So he is the God of the living, not the dead, for they are all alive to him."

[39]"Well said, Teacher!" remarked some of the teachers of religious law who were standing there. [40]And then no one dared to ask him any more questions.

Whose Son Is the Messiah?

[41]Then Jesus presented them with a question. "Why is it," he asked, "that the Messiah is said to be the son of David? [42]For David himself wrote in the book of Psalms:

'The LORD said to my Lord,
Sit in the place of honor at my right hand
[43] until I humble your enemies,
making them a footstool under your feet.'*

[44]Since David called the Messiah 'Lord,' how can the Messiah be his son?"

20:17 Ps 118:22.   20:24 Greek *a denarius.*   20:28 See Deut 25:5-6.   20:37a Greek *when he wrote about the bush. He referred to the Lord.*   20:37b Exod 3:6.   20:42-43 Ps 110:1.

⁴⁵Then, with the crowds listening, he turned to his disciples and said, ⁴⁶"Beware of these teachers of religious law! For they like to parade around in flowing robes and love to receive respectful greetings as they walk in the marketplaces. And how they love the seats of honor in the synagogues and the head table at banquets. ⁴⁷Yet they shamelessly cheat widows out of their property and then pretend to be pious by making long prayers in public. Because of this, they will be severely punished."

CHAPTER 21

The Widow's Offering

While Jesus was in the Temple, he watched the rich people dropping their gifts in the collection box. ²Then a poor widow came by and dropped in two small coins.*

³"I tell you the truth," Jesus said, "this poor widow has given more than all the rest of them. ⁴For they have given a tiny part of their surplus, but she, poor as she is, has given everything she has."

Jesus Foretells the Future

⁵Some of his disciples began talking about the majestic stonework of the Temple and the memorial decorations on the walls. But Jesus said, ⁶"The time is coming when all these things will be completely demolished. Not one stone will be left on top of another!"

⁷"Teacher," they asked, "when will all this happen? What sign will show us that these things are about to take place?"

⁸He replied, "Don't let anyone mislead you, for many will come in my name, claiming, 'I am the Messiah,'* and saying, 'The time has come!' But don't believe them. ⁹And when you hear of wars and insurrections, don't panic. Yes, these things must take place first, but the end won't follow immediately." ¹⁰Then he added, "Nation will go to war against nation, and kingdom against kingdom. ¹¹There will be great earthquakes, and there will be famines and plagues in many lands, and there will be terrifying things and great miraculous signs from heaven.

¹²"But before all this occurs, there will be a time of great persecution. You will be dragged into synagogues and prisons, and you will stand trial before kings and governors because you are my followers. ¹³But this will be your opportunity to tell them about me.* ¹⁴So don't worry in advance about how to answer the charges against you, ¹⁵for I will give you the right words and such wisdom that none of your opponents will be able to reply or refute you! ¹⁶Even those closest to you—your parents, brothers, relatives, and friends—will betray you. They will even kill some of you. ¹⁷And everyone will hate you because you are my followers.* ¹⁸But not a hair of your head will perish! ¹⁹By standing firm, you will win your souls.

²⁰"And when you see Jerusalem surrounded by armies, then you will know that the time of its destruction has arrived. ²¹Then those in Judea must flee to the hills. Those in Jerusalem must get out, and those out in the country should not return to the city. ²²For those will be days of God's vengeance, and the prophetic words of the Scriptures will be fulfilled. ²³How terrible it will be for pregnant women and for nursing mothers in those days. For there will be disaster in the land and great anger against this people. ²⁴They will be killed by the sword or sent away as captives to all the nations of the world. And Jerusalem will be trampled down by the Gentiles until the period of the Gentiles comes to an end.

²⁵"And there will be strange signs in the sun, moon, and stars. And here on earth the nations will be in turmoil, perplexed by the roaring seas and strange tides. ²⁶People will be terrified at what they see coming upon the earth, for the powers in the heavens will be shaken. ²⁷Then everyone will see the Son of Man* coming on a cloud with power and great glory.*

21:2 Greek *two lepta* [the smallest of Jewish coins]. 21:8 Greek *claiming, 'I am.'* 21:13 Or *This will be your testimony against them.* 21:17 Greek *on account of my name.* 21:27a "Son of Man" is a title Jesus used for himself. 21:27b See Dan 7:13.

²⁸So when all these things begin to happen, stand and look up, for your salvation is near!"

²⁹Then he gave them this illustration: "Notice the fig tree, or any other tree. ³⁰When the leaves come out, you know without being told that summer is near. ³¹In the same way, when you see all these things taking place, you can know that the Kingdom of God is near. ³²I tell you the truth, this generation will not pass from the scene until all these things have taken place. ³³Heaven and earth will disappear, but my words will never disappear.

³⁴"Watch out! Don't let your hearts be dulled by carousing and drunkenness, and by the worries of this life. Don't let that day catch you unaware, ³⁵like a trap. For that day will come upon everyone living on the earth. ³⁶Keep alert at all times. And pray that you might be strong enough to escape these coming horrors and stand before the Son of Man."

³⁷Every day Jesus went to the Temple to teach, and each evening he returned to spend the night on the Mount of Olives. ³⁸The crowds gathered at the Temple early each morning to hear him.

CHAPTER 22

Judas Agrees to Betray Jesus

The Festival of Unleavened Bread, which is also called Passover, was approaching. ²The leading priests and teachers of religious law were plotting how to kill Jesus, but they were afraid of the people's reaction.

³Then Satan entered into Judas Iscariot, who was one of the twelve disciples, ⁴and he went to the leading priests and captains of the Temple guard to discuss the best way to betray Jesus to them. ⁵They were delighted, and they promised to give him money. ⁶So he agreed and began looking for an opportunity to betray Jesus so they could arrest him when the crowds weren't around.

"Watch out! Don't let your hearts be dulled by carousing and drunkenness, and by the worries of this life" (Luke 21:34).

Heads up! Don't get hung up by gettin' drunk and by the things that make you worry.

The Last Supper

⁷Now the Festival of Unleavened Bread arrived, when the Passover lamb is sacrificed. ⁸Jesus sent Peter and John ahead and said, "Go and prepare the Passover meal, so we can eat it together."

⁹"Where do you want us to prepare it?" they asked him.

¹⁰He replied, "As soon as you enter Jerusalem, a man carrying a pitcher of water will meet you. Follow him. At the house he enters, ¹¹say to the owner, 'The Teacher asks: Where is the guest room where I can eat the Passover meal with my disciples?' ¹²He will take you upstairs to a large room that is already set up. That is where you should prepare our meal." ¹³They went off to the city and found everything just as Jesus had said, and they prepared the Passover meal there.

¹⁴When the time came, Jesus and the apostles sat down together at the table.* ¹⁵Jesus said, "I have been very eager to eat this Passover meal with you before my suffering begins. ¹⁶For I tell you now that I won't eat this meal again until its meaning is fulfilled in the Kingdom of God."

¹⁷Then he took a cup of wine and gave thanks to God for it. Then he said, "Take this and share it among yourselves. ¹⁸For I will not drink wine again until the Kingdom of God has come."

¹⁹He took some bread and gave thanks to God for it. Then he broke it in pieces and gave it to the disciples, saying, "This is my body, which is given for you. Do this to remember me."

²⁰After supper he took another cup of wine and said, "This cup is the new covenant between God and his people—an agreement confirmed with my blood, which is poured out as a sacrifice for you.*

²¹"But here at this table, sitting among us as a friend, is the man who will betray me. ²²For it has been determined that the Son of Man* must die. But what sorrow awaits the

22:14 Or *reclined together.* **22:19-20** Some manuscripts do not include 22:19b-20, *which is given for you . . . which is poured out as a sacrifice for you.* **22:22** "Son of Man" is a title Jesus used for himself.

one who betrays him." [23]The disciples began to ask each other which of them would ever do such a thing.

[24]Then they began to argue among themselves about who would be the greatest among them. [25]Jesus told them, "In this world the kings and great men lord it over their people, yet they are called 'friends of the people.' [26]But among you it will be different. Those who are the greatest among you should take the lowest rank, and the leader should be like a servant. [27]Who is more important, the one who sits at the table or the one who serves? The one who sits at the table, of course. But not here! For I am among you as one who serves.

[28]"You have stayed with me in my time of trial. [29]And just as my Father has granted me a Kingdom, I now grant you the right [30]to eat and drink at my table in my Kingdom. And you will sit on thrones, judging the twelve tribes of Israel.

Jesus Predicts Peter's Denial

[31]"Simon, Simon, Satan has asked to sift each of you like wheat. [32]But I have pleaded in prayer for you, Simon, that your faith should not fail. So when you have repented and turned to me again, strengthen your brothers."

[33]Peter said, "Lord, I am ready to go to prison with you, and even to die with you."

[34]But Jesus said, "Peter, let me tell you something. Before the rooster crows tomorrow morning, you will deny three times that you even know me."

[35]Then Jesus asked them, "When I sent you out to preach the Good News and you did not have money, a traveler's bag, or an extra pair of sandals, did you need anything?"

"No," they replied.

[36]"But now," he said, "take your money and a traveler's bag. And if you don't have a sword, sell your cloak and buy one! [37]For the time has come for this prophecy about me to be fulfilled: 'He was counted among the rebels.'* Yes, everything written about me by the prophets will come true."

[38]"Look, Lord," they replied, "we have two swords among us."

"That's enough," he said.

Jesus Prays on the Mount of Olives

[39]Then, accompanied by the disciples, Jesus left the upstairs room and went as usual to the Mount of Olives. [40]There he told them, "Pray that you will not give in to temptation."

[41]He walked away, about a stone's throw, and knelt down and prayed, [42]"Father, if you are willing, please take this cup of suffering away from me. Yet I want your will to be done, not mine." [43]Then an angel from heaven appeared and strengthened him. [44]He prayed more fervently, and he was in such agony of spirit that his sweat fell to the ground like great drops of blood.*

[45]At last he stood up again and returned to the disciples, only to find them asleep, exhausted from grief. [46]"Why are you sleeping?" he asked them. "Get up and pray, so that you will not give in to temptation."

Jesus Is Betrayed and Arrested

[47]But even as Jesus said this, a crowd approached, led by Judas, one of the twelve disciples. Judas walked over to Jesus to greet him with a kiss. [48]But Jesus said, "Judas, would you betray the Son of Man with a kiss?"

[49]When the other disciples saw what was about to happen, they exclaimed, "Lord, should we fight? We brought the swords!" [50]And one of them struck at the high priest's slave, slashing off his right ear.

[51]But Jesus said, "No more of this." And he touched the man's ear and healed him.

[52]Then Jesus spoke to the leading priests, the captains of the Temple guard, and the elders who had come for him. "Am I some dangerous revolutionary," he asked, "that you come with swords and clubs to arrest me? [53]Why didn't you arrest me in the Temple? I was there every day. But

22:37 Isa 53:12.   22:43-44 Verses 43 and 44 are not included in many ancient manuscripts.

this is your moment, the time when the power of darkness reigns."

Peter Denies Jesus

⁵⁴So they arrested him and led him to the high priest's home. And Peter followed at a distance. ⁵⁵The guards lit a fire in the middle of the courtyard and sat around it, and Peter joined them there. ⁵⁶A servant girl noticed him in the firelight and began staring at him. Finally she said, "This man was one of Jesus' followers!"

⁵⁷But Peter denied it. "Woman," he said, "I don't even know him!"

⁵⁸After a while someone else looked at him and said, "You must be one of them!"

"No, man, I'm not!" Peter retorted.

⁵⁹About an hour later someone else insisted, "This must be one of them, because he is a Galilean, too."

⁶⁰But Peter said, "Man, I don't know what you are talking about." And immediately, while he was still speaking, the rooster crowed. ⁶¹At that moment the Lord turned and looked at Peter. Suddenly, the Lord's words flashed through Peter's mind: "Before the rooster crows tomorrow morning, you will deny three times that you even know me." ⁶²And Peter left the courtyard, weeping bitterly.

⁶³The guards in charge of Jesus began mocking and beating him. ⁶⁴They blindfolded him and said, "Prophesy to us! Who hit you that time?" ⁶⁵And they hurled all sorts of terrible insults at him.

Jesus before the Council

⁶⁶At daybreak all the elders of the people assembled, including the leading priests and the teachers of religious law. Jesus was led before this high council,* ⁶⁷and they said, "Tell us, are you the Messiah?"

But he replied, "If I tell you, you won't believe me. ⁶⁸And if I ask you a question, you won't answer. ⁶⁹But from now on the Son of Man will be seated in the place of power at God's right hand.*"

⁷⁰They all shouted, "So, are you claiming to be the Son of God?"

And he replied, "You say that I am."

⁷¹"Why do we need other witnesses?" they said. "We ourselves heard him say it."

CHAPTER 23

Jesus' Trial before Pilate

Then the entire council took Jesus to Pilate, the Roman governor. ²They began to state their case: "This man has been leading our people astray by telling them not to pay their taxes to the Roman government and by claiming he is the Messiah, a king."

³So Pilate asked him, "Are you the king of the Jews?"

Jesus replied, "You have said it."

⁴Pilate turned to the leading priests and to the crowd and said, "I find nothing wrong with this man!"

⁵Then they became insistent. "But he is causing riots by his teaching wherever he goes—all over Judea, from Galilee to Jerusalem!"

⁶"Oh, is he a Galilean?" Pilate asked. ⁷When they said that he was, Pilate sent him to Herod Antipas, because Galilee was under Herod's jurisdiction, and Herod happened to be in Jerusalem at the time.

⁸Herod was delighted at the opportunity to see Jesus, because he had heard about him and had been hoping for a long time to see him perform a miracle. ⁹He asked Jesus question after question, but Jesus refused to answer. ¹⁰Meanwhile, the leading priests and the teachers of religious law stood there shouting their accusations. ¹¹Then Herod and his soldiers began mocking and ridiculing Jesus. Finally, they put a royal robe on him and sent him back to Pilate. ¹²(Herod and Pilate, who had been enemies before, became friends that day.)

22:66 Greek *before their Sanhedrin.*   22:69 See Ps 110:1.

¹³Then Pilate called together the leading priests and other religious leaders, along with the people, ¹⁴and he announced his verdict. "You brought this man to me, accusing him of leading a revolt. I have examined him thoroughly on this point in your presence and find him innocent. ¹⁵Herod came to the same conclusion and sent him back to us. Nothing this man has done calls for the death penalty. ¹⁶So I will have him flogged, and then I will release him."*

¹⁸Then a mighty roar rose from the crowd, and with one voice they shouted, "Kill him, and release Barabbas to us!" ¹⁹(Barabbas was in prison for taking part in an insurrection in Jerusalem against the government, and for murder.) ²⁰Pilate argued with them, because he wanted to release Jesus. ²¹But they kept shouting, "Crucify him! Crucify him!"

²²For the third time he demanded, "Why? What crime has he committed? I have found no reason to sentence him to death. So I will have him flogged, and then I will release him."

²³But the mob shouted louder and louder, demanding that Jesus be crucified, and their voices prevailed. ²⁴So Pilate sentenced Jesus to die as they demanded. ²⁵As they had requested, he released Barabbas, the man in prison for insurrection and murder. But he turned Jesus over to them to do as they wished.

The Crucifixion

²⁶As they led Jesus away, a man named Simon, who was from Cyrene,* happened to be coming in from the countryside. The soldiers seized him and put the cross on him and made him carry it behind Jesus. ²⁷A large crowd trailed behind, including many grief-stricken women. ²⁸But Jesus turned and said to them, "Daughters of Jerusalem, don't weep for me, but weep for yourselves and for your children. ²⁹For the days are coming when they will say, 'Fortunate indeed are the women who are childless, the wombs that have not borne a child and the breasts that have never nursed.' ³⁰People will beg the mountains, 'Fall on us,' and plead with the hills, 'Bury us.'* ³¹For if these things are done when the tree is green, what will happen when it is dry?*"

³²Two others, both criminals, were led out to be executed with him. ³³When they came to a place called The Skull,* they nailed him to the cross. And the criminals were also crucified—one on his right and one on his left.

³⁴Jesus said, "Father, forgive them, for they don't know what they are doing."* And the soldiers gambled for his clothes by throwing dice.*

³⁵The crowd watched and the leaders scoffed. "He saved others," they said, "let him save himself if he is really God's Messiah, the Chosen One." ³⁶The soldiers mocked him, too, by offering him a drink of sour wine. ³⁷They called out to him, "If you are the King of the Jews, save yourself!" ³⁸A sign was fastened above him with these words: "This is the King of the Jews."

³⁹One of the criminals hanging beside him scoffed, "So you're the Messiah, are you? Prove it by saving yourself— and us, too, while you're at it!"

⁴⁰But the other criminal protested, "Don't you fear God even when you have been sentenced to die? ⁴¹We deserve to die for our crimes, but this man hasn't done anything wrong." ⁴²Then he said, "Jesus, remember me when you come into your Kingdom."

⁴³And Jesus replied, "I assure you, today you will be with me in paradise."

The Death of Jesus

⁴⁴By this time it was about noon, and darkness fell across the whole land until three o'clock. ⁴⁵The light from the sun was gone. And suddenly, the curtain in the sanctuary of the Temple was torn down the middle. ⁴⁶Then Jesus shouted,

---

23:16 Some manuscripts add verse 17, *Now it was necessary for him to release one prisoner to them during the Passover celebration.* Compare Matt 27:15; Mark 15:6; John 18:39.
23:26 *Cyrene* was a city in northern Africa.   **23:30** Hos 10:8.   **23:31** Or *If these things are done to me, the living tree, what will happen to you, the dry tree?*   **23:33** Sometimes rendered *Calvary,* which comes from the Latin word for "skull."   **23:34a** This sentence is not included in many ancient manuscripts.   **23:34b** Greek *by casting lots.* See Ps 22:18.

"Father, I entrust my spirit into your hands!"* And with those words he breathed his last.

47When the Roman officer* overseeing the execution saw what had happened, he worshiped God and said, "Surely this man was innocent.*" 48And when all the crowd that came to see the crucifixion saw what had happened, they went home in deep sorrow.* 49But Jesus' friends, including the women who had followed him from Galilee, stood at a distance watching.

The Burial of Jesus

50Now there was a good and righteous man named Joseph. He was a member of the Jewish high council, 51but he had not agreed with the decision and actions of the other religious leaders. He was from the town of Arimathea in Judea, and he was waiting for the Kingdom of God to come. 52He went to Pilate and asked for Jesus' body. 53Then he took the body down from the cross and wrapped it in a long sheet of linen cloth and laid it in a new tomb that had been carved out of rock. 54This was done late on Friday afternoon, the day of preparation,* as the Sabbath was about to begin.

55As his body was taken away, the women from Galilee followed and saw the tomb where his body was placed. 56Then they went home and prepared spices and ointments to anoint his body. But by the time they were finished the Sabbath had begun, so they rested as required by the law.

CHAPTER 24

The Resurrection

But very early on Sunday morning* the women went to the tomb, taking the spices they had prepared. 2They found that the stone had been rolled away from the entrance. 3So they went in, but they didn't find the body of the Lord Jesus. 4As they stood there puzzled, two men suddenly appeared to them, clothed in dazzling robes.

5The women were terrified and bowed with their faces to the ground. Then the men asked, "Why are you looking among the dead for someone who is alive? 6He isn't here! He is risen from the dead! Remember what he told you back in Galilee, 7that the Son of Man* must be betrayed into the hands of sinful men and be crucified, and that he would rise again on the third day."

8Then they remembered that he had said this. 9So they rushed back from the tomb to tell his eleven disciples—and everyone else—what had happened. 10It was Mary Magdalene, Joanna, Mary the mother of James, and several other women who told the apostles what had happened. 11But the story sounded like nonsense to the men, so they didn't believe it. 12However, Peter jumped up and ran to the tomb to look. Stooping, he peered in and saw the empty linen wrappings; then he went home again, wondering what had happened.

The Walk to Emmaus

13That same day two of Jesus' followers were walking to the village of Emmaus, seven miles* from Jerusalem. 14As they walked along they were talking about everything that had happened. 15As they talked and discussed these things, Jesus himself suddenly came and began walking with them. 16But God kept them from recognizing him.

17He asked them, "What are you discussing so intently as you walk along?"

They stopped short, sadness written across their faces. 18Then one of them, Cleopas, replied, "You must be the only person in Jerusalem who hasn't heard about all the things that have happened there the last few days."

19"What things?" Jesus asked.

"The things that happened to Jesus, the man from Nazareth," they said. "He was a prophet who did powerful miracles, and he was a mighty teacher in the eyes of God and

23:46 Ps 31:5. 23:47a Greek the centurion. 23:47b Or righteous. 23:48 Greek went home beating their breasts. 23:54 Greek It was the day of preparation. 24:1 Greek But on the first day of the week, very early in the morning. 24:7 "Son of Man" is a title Jesus used for himself. 24:13 Greek 60 stadia [11.1 kilometers].

all the people. [20]But our leading priests and other religious leaders handed him over to be condemned to death, and they crucified him. [21]We had hoped he was the Messiah who had come to rescue Israel. This all happened three days ago.

[22]"Then some women from our group of his followers were at his tomb early this morning, and they came back with an amazing report. [23]They said his body was missing, and they had seen angels who told them Jesus is alive! [24]Some of our men ran out to see, and sure enough, his body was gone, just as the women had said."

[25]Then Jesus said to them, "You foolish people! You find it so hard to believe all that the prophets wrote in the Scriptures. [26]Wasn't it clearly predicted that the Messiah would have to suffer all these things before entering his glory?" [27]Then Jesus took them through the writings of Moses and all the prophets, explaining from all the Scriptures the things concerning himself.

[28]By this time they were nearing Emmaus and the end of their journey. Jesus acted as if he were going on, [29]but they begged him, "Stay the night with us, since it is getting late." So he went home with them. [30]As they sat down to eat,* he took the bread and blessed it. Then he broke it and gave it to them. [31]Suddenly, their eyes were opened, and they recognized him. And at that moment he disappeared!

[32]They said to each other, "Didn't our hearts burn within us as he talked with us on the road and explained the Scriptures to us?" [33]And within the hour they were on their way back to Jerusalem. There they found the eleven disciples and the others who had gathered with them, [34]who said, "The Lord has really risen! He appeared to Peter.*"

Jesus Appears to the Disciples

[35]Then the two from Emmaus told their story of how Jesus had appeared to them as they were walking along the road, and how they had recognized him as he was breaking the bread. [36]And just as they were telling about it, Jesus himself was suddenly standing there among them. "Peace be with you," he said. [37]But the whole group was startled and frightened, thinking they were seeing a ghost!

[38]"Why are you frightened?" he asked. "Why are your hearts filled with doubt? [39]Look at my hands. Look at my feet. You can see that it's really me. Touch me and make sure that I am not a ghost, because ghosts don't have bodies, as you see that I do." [40]As he spoke, he showed them his hands and his feet.

[41]Still they stood there in disbelief, filled with joy and wonder. Then he asked them, "Do you have anything here to eat?" [42]They gave him a piece of broiled fish, [43]and he ate it as they watched.

[44]Then he said, "When I was with you before, I told you that everything written about me in the law of Moses and the prophets and in the Psalms must be fulfilled." [45]Then he opened their minds to understand the Scriptures. [46]And he said, "Yes, it was written long ago that the Messiah would suffer and die and rise from the dead on the third day. [47]It was also written that this message would be proclaimed in the authority of his name to all the nations,* beginning in Jerusalem: 'There is forgiveness of sins for all who repent.' [48]You are witnesses of all these things.

[49]"And now I will send the Holy Spirit, just as my Father promised. But stay here in the city until the Holy Spirit comes and fills you with power from heaven."

The Ascension

[50]Then Jesus led them to Bethany, and lifting his hands to heaven, he blessed them. [51]While he was blessing them, he left them and was taken up to heaven. [52]So they worshiped him and then returned to Jerusalem filled with great joy. [53]And they spent all of their time in the Temple, praising God.

24:30 Or *As they reclined.*   **24:34** Greek *Simon.*   **24:47** Or *all peoples.*

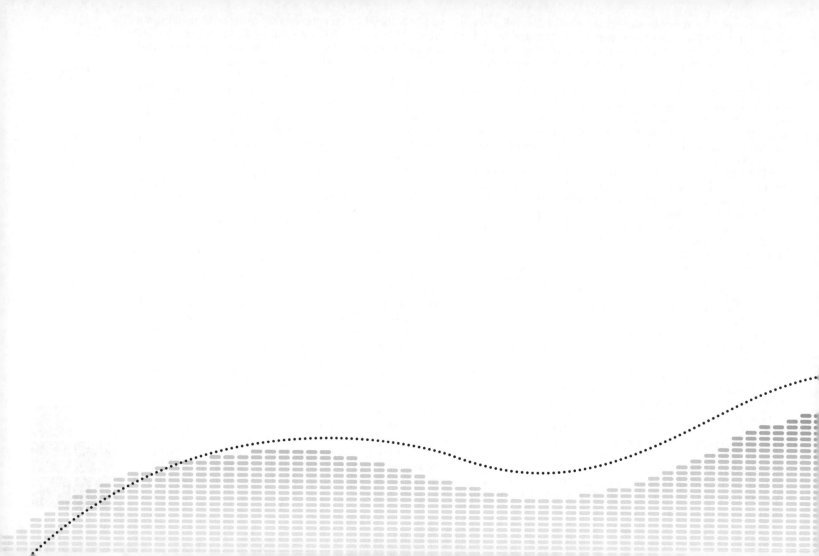

IN MANY WAYS, John's Gospel is very different from the others. His purpose for writing the book was to connect the human side of Jesus with his divine nature. Like the other Gospels, John talks about Jesus' ministry on Earth. But while the other Gospels talk about Jesus as the Son of Man, John played up the fact that Jesus was the Son of God. You know how people always say, "Don't believe the hype"? Well, when it came to Jesus, John wanted everyone to know that Jesus wasn't some fake preacher from Nazareth. From jump, he was and still is the real thing. And if you want to make it out here, you need to holla at him. John himself said that he wrote the book so that people would believe Jesus is the Messiah, the Son of God (John 20:31).

John calls Jesus' miracles "signs"—signs that should leave no doubt in people's minds that Jesus was special. John was out to prove that Jesus was not just some ordinary brotha hangin' on the set. Wanna read about it? Check out John 2:1-11, where Jesus turned water to wine; John 4:46-51, when Jesus healed Five-O's son. Read John 5:1-9, where Jesus healed a brotha lampin' at the pool, or 6:1-14, when he fed five thousand people with a small order of fish and bread. And in John 6:16-21, the brotha walked on water! Then he restored this blind guy's eyesight with a mud pie (John 9:1-11) and raised Lazarus from the dead (John 11:1-46). Cuz was off the chain! Each and every time, John says, Jesus performed these signs to prove he was special— he was and is and continues to be the Son of God.

JOHN

CHAPTER 1

Prologue: Christ, the Eternal Word

¹ In the beginning the Word already existed.
The Word was with God,
and the Word was God.
² He existed in the beginning with God.
³ God created everything through him,
and nothing was created except through him.
⁴ The Word gave life to everything that was created,*
and his life brought light to everyone.
⁵ The light shines in the darkness,
and the darkness can never extinguish it.*

⁶God sent a man, John the Baptist,* ⁷to tell about the light so that everyone might believe because of his testimony. ⁸John himself was not the light; he was simply a witness to tell about the light. ⁹The one who is the true light, who gives light to everyone, was coming into the world.

¹⁰He came into the very world he created, but the world didn't recognize him. ¹¹He came to his own people, and even they rejected him. ¹²But to all who believed him and accepted him, he gave the right to become children of God. ¹³They are reborn—not with a physical birth resulting from human passion or plan, but a birth that comes from God.

¹⁴So the Word became human* and made his home among us. He was full of unfailing love and faithfulness.* And we have seen his glory, the glory of the Father's one and only Son.

¹⁵John testified about him when he shouted to the crowds, "This is the one I was talking about when I said, 'Someone is coming after me who is far greater than I am, for he existed long before me.'"

¹⁶From his abundance we have all received one gracious blessing after another.* ¹⁷For the law was given through Moses, but God's unfailing love and faithfulness came through Jesus Christ. ¹⁸No one has ever seen God. But the

1:3-4 Or *and nothing that was created was created except through him. The Word gave life to everything.*   **1:5** Or *and the darkness has not understood it.*   **1:6** Greek *a man named John.*   **1:14a** Greek *became flesh.*   **1:14b** Or *grace and truth; also in 1:17.*   **1:16** Or *received the grace of Christ rather than the grace of the law;* Greek reads *received grace upon grace.*

THE POINT

Jesus is God in the hood. For centuries the Jewish teachers had been talkin' about prophecies of a Messiah who would come and make everything right, but nothin' ever seemed to happen. People were tired of hearin' these old dudes talkin' about this "Messiah"—that is, until Jesus showed up. And John made it clear—this Messiah, Jesus, is God himself. Booyah! It was that simple. Jesus came

to hang out in the hood, puttin' God right here with us. John put it down like this:

In the beginning the Word already existed. The Word was with God, and the Word was God. He existed in the beginning with God. God created everything through him, and nothing was created except through him. . . . So the

Word became human and made his home among us. (John 1:1-3, 14)

And John went through the trouble of backing up his claim. He not only told us Jesus was God; he also told us about all Jesus' miracles—all his signs and wonders—to prove that his claims were true.

unique One, who is himself God,* is near to the Father's heart. He has revealed God to us.

The Testimony of John the Baptist

¹⁹This was John's testimony when the Jewish leaders sent priests and Temple assistants* from Jerusalem to ask John, "Who are you?" ²⁰He came right out and said, "I am not the Messiah."

²¹"Well then, who are you?" they asked. "Are you Elijah?"

"No," he replied.

"Are you the Prophet we are expecting?"*

"No."

²²"Then who are you? We need an answer for those who sent us. What do you have to say about yourself?"

²³John replied in the words of the prophet Isaiah:

"I am a voice shouting in the wilderness,
  'Clear the way for the LORD's coming!'"*

²⁴Then the Pharisees who had been sent ²⁵asked him, "If you aren't the Messiah or Elijah or the Prophet, what right do you have to baptize?"

²⁶John told them, "I baptize with* water, but right here in the crowd is someone you do not recognize. ²⁷Though his ministry follows mine, I'm not even worthy to be his slave and untie the straps of his sandal."

²⁸This encounter took place in Bethany, an area east of the Jordan River, where John was baptizing.

Jesus, the Lamb of God

²⁹The next day John saw Jesus coming toward him and said, "Look! The Lamb of God who takes away the sin of the world! ³⁰He is the one I was talking about when I said, 'A man is coming after me who is far greater than I am, for he existed long before me.' ³¹I did not recognize him as the Messiah, but I have been baptizing with water so that he might be revealed to Israel."

³²Then John testified, "I saw the Holy Spirit descending like a dove from heaven and resting upon him. ³³I didn't know he was the one, but when God sent me to baptize with water, he told me, 'The one on whom you see the Spirit descend and rest is the one who will baptize with the Holy Spirit.' ³⁴I saw this happen to Jesus, so I testify that he is the Chosen One of God.*"

The First Disciples

³⁵The following day John was again standing with two of his disciples. ³⁶As Jesus walked by, John looked at him and declared, "Look! There is the Lamb of God!" ³⁷When John's two disciples heard this, they followed Jesus.

³⁸Jesus looked around and saw them following. "What do you want?" he asked them.

They replied, "Rabbi" (which means "Teacher"), "where are you staying?"

³⁹"Come and see," he said. It was about four o'clock in the afternoon when they went with him to the place where he was staying, and they remained with him the rest of the day.

⁴⁰Andrew, Simon Peter's brother, was one of these men who heard what John said and then followed Jesus. ⁴¹Andrew went to find his brother, Simon, and told him, "We have found the Messiah" (which means "Christ"*).

⁴²Then Andrew brought Simon to meet Jesus. Looking intently at Simon, Jesus said, "Your name is Simon, son of John—but you will be called Cephas" (which means "Peter"*).

⁴³The next day Jesus decided to go to Galilee. He found Philip and said to him, "Come, follow me." ⁴⁴Philip was from Bethsaida, Andrew and Peter's hometown.

⁴⁵Philip went to look for Nathanael and told him, "We

"No one has ever seen God. But the unique One, who is himself God, is near to the Father's heart. He has revealed God to us" (John 1:18).

No one except for his Son has ever seen God. His Son has shown us who God is.

1:18 Some manuscripts read *But the one and only Son.* 1:19 Greek *and Levites.* 1:21 Greek *Are you the Prophet?* See Deut 18:15, 18; Mal 4:5-6. 1:23 Isa 40:3. 1:26 Or *in;* also in 1:31, 33. 1:34 Some manuscripts read *the Son of God.* 1:41 *Messiah* (a Hebrew term) and *Christ* (a Greek term) both mean "the anointed one." 1:42 The names *Cephas* (from Aramaic) and *Peter* (from Greek) both mean "rock."

have found the very person Moses* and the prophets wrote about! His name is Jesus, the son of Joseph from Nazareth."

⁴⁶"Nazareth!" exclaimed Nathanael. "Can anything good come from Nazareth?"

"Come and see for yourself," Philip replied.

⁴⁷As they approached, Jesus said, "Now here is a genuine son of Israel—a man of complete integrity."

⁴⁸"How do you know about me?" Nathanael asked.

Jesus replied, "I could see you under the fig tree before Philip found you."

⁴⁹Then Nathanael exclaimed, "Rabbi, you are the Son of God—the King of Israel!"

⁵⁰Jesus asked him, "Do you believe this just because I told you I had seen you under the fig tree? You will see greater things than this." ⁵¹Then he said, "I tell you the truth, you will all see heaven open and the angels of God going up and down on the Son of Man, the one who is the stairway between heaven and earth.*"

CHAPTER **2**

The Wedding at Cana

The next day* there was a wedding celebration in the village of Cana in Galilee. Jesus' mother was there, ²and Jesus and his disciples were also invited to the celebration. ³The wine supply ran out during the festivities, so Jesus' mother told him, "They have no more wine."

⁴"Dear woman, that's not our problem," Jesus replied. "My time has not yet come."

⁵But his mother told the servants, "Do whatever he tells you."

⁶Standing nearby were six stone water jars, used for Jewish ceremonial washing. Each could hold twenty to thirty gallons.* ⁷Jesus told the servants, "Fill the jars with water." When the jars had been filled, ⁸he said, "Now dip some out,

and take it to the master of ceremonies." So the servants followed his instructions.

⁹When the master of ceremonies tasted the water that was now wine, not knowing where it had come from (though, of course, the servants knew), he called the bridegroom over. ¹⁰"A host always serves the best wine first," he said. "Then, when everyone has had a lot to drink, he brings out the less expensive wine. But you have kept the best until now!"

¹¹This miraculous sign at Cana in Galilee was the first time Jesus revealed his glory. And his disciples believed in him.

¹²After the wedding he went to Capernaum for a few days with his mother, his brothers, and his disciples.

Jesus Clears the Temple

¹³It was nearly time for the Jewish Passover celebration, so Jesus went to Jerusalem. ¹⁴In the Temple area he saw merchants selling cattle, sheep, and doves for sacrifices; he also saw dealers at tables exchanging foreign money. ¹⁵Jesus made a whip from some ropes and chased them all out of the Temple. He drove out the sheep and cattle, scattered the money changers' coins over the floor, and turned over their tables. ¹⁶Then, going over to the people who sold doves, he told them, "Get these things out of here. Stop turning my Father's house into a marketplace!"

¹⁷Then his disciples remembered this prophecy from the Scriptures: "Passion for God's house will consume me."*

¹⁸But the Jewish leaders demanded, "What are you doing? If God gave you authority to do this, show us a miraculous sign to prove it."

¹⁹"All right," Jesus replied. "Destroy this temple, and in three days I will raise it up."

²⁰"What!" they exclaimed. "It has taken forty-six years to build this Temple, and you can rebuild it in three days?" ²¹But when Jesus said "this temple," he meant his own body.

1:45 Greek *Moses in the law.*   1:51 Greek *going up and down on the Son of Man;* see Gen 28:10-17. "Son of Man" is a title Jesus used for himself.   2:1 Greek *On the third day;* see 1:35, 43.   2:6 Greek *2 or 3 measures* [75 to 113 liters].   2:17 Or *"Concern for God's house will be my undoing."* Ps 69:9.

²²After he was raised from the dead, his disciples remembered he had said this, and they believed both the Scriptures and what Jesus had said.

Jesus and Nicodemus

²³Because of the miraculous signs Jesus did in Jerusalem at the Passover celebration, many began to trust in him. ²⁴But Jesus didn't trust them, because he knew human nature. ²⁵No one needed to tell him what mankind is really like.

CHAPTER 3

There was a man named Nicodemus, a Jewish religious leader who was a Pharisee. ²After dark one evening, he came to speak with Jesus. "Rabbi," he said, "we all know that God has sent you to teach us. Your miraculous signs are evidence that God is with you."

³Jesus replied, "I tell you the truth, unless you are born again,* you cannot see the Kingdom of God."

⁴"What do you mean?" exclaimed Nicodemus. "How can an old man go back into his mother's womb and be born again?"

⁵Jesus replied, "I assure you, no one can enter the Kingdom of God without being born of water and the Spirit.* ⁶Humans can reproduce only human life, but the Holy Spirit gives birth to spiritual life.* ⁷So don't be surprised when I say, 'You* must be born again.' ⁸The wind blows wherever it wants. Just as you can hear the wind but can't tell where it comes from or where it is going, so you can't explain how people are born of the Spirit."

⁹"How are these things possible?" Nicodemus asked.

¹⁰Jesus replied, "You are a respected Jewish teacher, and yet you don't understand these things? ¹¹I assure you, we tell you what we know and have seen, and yet you won't believe our testimony. ¹²But if you don't believe me when I tell you about earthly things, how can you possibly believe if I tell you about heavenly things? ¹³No one has ever gone to heaven and returned. But the Son of Man* has come down from heaven. ¹⁴And as Moses lifted up the bronze snake on a pole in the wilderness, so the Son of Man must be lifted up, ¹⁵so that everyone who believes in him will have eternal life.*

¹⁶"For God loved the world so much that he gave his one and only Son, so that everyone who believes in him will not perish but have eternal life. ¹⁷God sent his Son into the world not to judge the world, but to save the world through him.

¹⁸"There is no judgment against anyone who believes in him. But anyone who does not believe in him has already been judged for not believing in God's one and only Son. ¹⁹And the judgment is based on this fact: God's light came

---

3:3 Or born from above; also in 3:7. 3:5 Or and spirit. The Greek word for Spirit can also be translated wind; see 3:8. 3:6 Greek what is born of the Spirit is spirit. 3:7 The Greek word for you is plural; also in 3:12. 3:13 Some manuscripts add who lives in heaven. "Son of Man" is a title Jesus used for himself. 3:15 Or everyone who believes will have eternal life in him.

THE POINT

Jesus gave it to fix it. It's not hard to see that something's wrong in the hood. Things have gone crazy. We've been cut off from family and neighbors, separated from the Maker and his Word. And without an act of mad love from God, there's no hope for eternal life. Here's one of the most familiar passages in the Bible:

"For God loved the world so much that he gave his one and only Son, so that everyone who believes in him will not perish but have eternal life." (John 3:16)

There it is. God came to earth in human form so that (1) we would believe he's here and cares about us, and (2) we would get the chance for eternal life. God knew we were messed up and out of touch. He wanted us to get back in contact. So he reached out, dressed up like us, and paid the price to patch things up. Now we can live with him forever.

into the world, but people loved the darkness more than the light, for their actions were evil. ²⁰All who do evil hate the light and refuse to go near it for fear their sins will be exposed. ²¹But those who do what is right come to the light so others can see that they are doing what God wants.*"

John the Baptist Exalts Jesus

²²Then Jesus and his disciples left Jerusalem and went into the Judean countryside. Jesus spent some time with them there, baptizing people.

²³At this time John the Baptist was baptizing at Aenon, near Salim, because there was plenty of water there; and people kept coming to him for baptism. ²⁴(This was before John was thrown into prison.) ²⁵A debate broke out between John's disciples and a certain Jew* over ceremonial cleansing. ²⁶So John's disciples came to him and said, "Rabbi, the man you met on the other side of the Jordan River, the one you identified as the Messiah, is also baptizing people. And everybody is going to him instead of coming to us."

²⁷John replied, "No one can receive anything unless God gives it from heaven. ²⁸You yourselves know how plainly I told you, 'I am not the Messiah. I am only here to prepare the way for him.' ²⁹It is the bridegroom who marries the bride, and the best man is simply glad to stand with him and hear his vows. Therefore, I am filled with joy at his success. ³⁰He must become greater and greater, and I must become less and less.

³¹"He has come from above and is greater than anyone else. We are of the earth, and we speak of earthly things, but he has come from heaven and is greater than anyone else.* ³²He testifies about what he has seen and heard, but how few believe what he tells them! ³³Anyone who accepts his testimony can affirm that God is true. ³⁴For he is sent by God. He speaks God's words, for God gives him the Spirit without limit. ³⁵The Father loves his Son and has put everything into his hands. ³⁶And anyone who believes in God's Son has eternal life. Anyone who doesn't obey the Son will never experience eternal life but remains under God's angry judgment."

CHAPTER 4

Jesus and the Samaritan Woman

Jesus* knew the Pharisees had heard that he was baptizing and making more disciples than John ²(though Jesus himself didn't baptize them—his disciples did). ³So he left Judea and returned to Galilee.

⁴He had to go through Samaria on the way. ⁵Eventually he came to the Samaritan village of Sychar, near the field that Jacob gave to his son Joseph. ⁶Jacob's well was there; and Jesus, tired from the long walk, sat wearily beside the well about noontime. ⁷Soon a Samaritan woman came to draw water, and Jesus said to her, "Please give me a drink." ⁸He was alone at the time because his disciples had gone into the village to buy some food.

⁹The woman was surprised, for Jews refuse to have anything to do with Samaritans.* She said to Jesus, "You are a Jew, and I am a Samaritan woman. Why are you asking me for a drink?"

¹⁰Jesus replied, "If you only knew the gift God has for you and who you are speaking to, you would ask me, and I would give you living water."

¹¹"But sir, you don't have a rope or a bucket," she said, "and this well is very deep. Where would you get this living water? ¹²And besides, do you think you're greater than our ancestor Jacob, who gave us this well? How can you offer better water than he and his sons and his animals enjoyed?"

¹³Jesus replied, "Anyone who drinks this water will soon become thirsty again. ¹⁴But those who drink the water I give will never be thirsty again. It becomes a fresh, bubbling spring within them, giving them eternal life."

¹⁵"Please, sir," the woman said, "give me this water! Then

3:21 Or *can see God at work in what he is doing.* 3:25 Some manuscripts read *some Jews.* 3:31 Some manuscripts do not include *and is greater than anyone else.* 4:1 Some manuscripts read *The Lord.* 4:9 Some manuscripts do not include this sentence.

I'll never be thirsty again, and I won't have to come here to get water."

16"Go and get your husband," Jesus told her.

17"I don't have a husband," the woman replied.

Jesus said, "You're right! You don't have a husband—18for you have had five husbands, and you aren't even married to the man you're living with now. You certainly spoke the truth!"

19"Sir," the woman said, "you must be a prophet. 20So tell me, why is it that you Jews insist that Jerusalem is the only place of worship, while we Samaritans claim it is here at Mount Gerizim,* where our ancestors worshiped?"

21Jesus replied, "Believe me, dear woman, the time is coming when it will no longer matter whether you worship the Father on this mountain or in Jerusalem. 22You Samaritans know very little about the one you worship, while we Jews know all about him, for salvation comes through the Jews. 23But the time is coming—indeed it's here now—when true worshipers will worship the Father in spirit and in truth. The Father is looking for those who will worship him that way. 24For God is Spirit, so those who worship him must worship in spirit and in truth."

25The woman said, "I know the Messiah is coming—the one who is called Christ. When he comes, he will explain everything to us."

26Then Jesus told her, "I AM the Messiah!"*

27Just then his disciples came back. They were shocked to find him talking to a woman, but none of them had the nerve to ask, "What do you want with her?" or "Why are you talking to her?" 28The woman left her water jar beside the well and ran back to the village, telling everyone, 29"Come and see a man who told me everything I ever did! Could he possibly be the Messiah?" 30So the people came streaming from the village to see him.

31Meanwhile, the disciples were urging Jesus, "Rabbi, eat something."

32But Jesus replied, "I have a kind of food you know nothing about."

33"Did someone bring him food while we were gone?" the disciples asked each other.

34Then Jesus explained: "My nourishment comes from doing the will of God, who sent me, and from finishing his work. 35You know the saying, 'Four months between planting and harvest.' But I say, wake up and look around. The fields are already ripe* for harvest. 36The harvesters are paid good wages, and the fruit they harvest is people brought to eternal life. What joy awaits both the planter and the harvester alike! 37You know the saying, 'One plants and another harvests.' And it's true. 38I sent you to harvest where you didn't plant; others had already done the work, and now you will get to gather the harvest."

Many Samaritans Believe

39Many Samaritans from the village believed in Jesus because the woman had said, "He told me everything I ever did!" 40When they came out to see him, they begged him to stay in their village. So he stayed for two days, 41long enough for many more to hear his message and believe. 42Then they said to the woman, "Now we believe, not just because of what you told us, but because we have heard him ourselves. Now we know that he is indeed the Savior of the world."

Jesus Heals an Official's Son

43At the end of the two days, Jesus went on to Galilee. 44He himself had said that a prophet is not honored in his own hometown. 45Yet the Galileans welcomed him, for they had been in Jerusalem at the Passover celebration and had seen everything he did there.

46As he traveled through Galilee, he came to Cana, where he had turned the water into wine. There was a government official in nearby Capernaum whose son was very sick. 47When he heard that Jesus had come from Judea to Galilee,

"But the time is coming—indeed it's here now—when true worshipers will worship the Father in spirit and in truth. The Father is looking for those who will worship him that way" (John 4:23).

say what?

Worship isn't about a special place or time of day. It's about what's goin' on in your heart. This type of worship is pleasing to God.

4:20 Greek on this mountain.   4:26 Or "The 'I AM' is here"; or "I am the LORD"; Greek reads "I am, the one speaking to you." See Exod 3:14.   4:35 Greek white.

he went and begged Jesus to come to Capernaum to heal his son, who was about to die.

[48]Jesus asked, "Will you never believe in me unless you see miraculous signs and wonders?"

[49]The official pleaded, "Lord, please come now before my little boy dies."

[50]Then Jesus told him, "Go back home. Your son will live!" And the man believed what Jesus said and started home.

[51]While the man was on his way, some of his servants met him with the news that his son was alive and well. [52]He asked them when the boy had begun to get better, and they replied, "Yesterday afternoon at one o'clock his fever suddenly disappeared!" [53]Then the father realized that that was the very time Jesus had told him, "Your son will live." And he and his entire household believed in Jesus. [54]This was the second miraculous sign Jesus did in Galilee after coming from Judea.

CHAPTER 5

Jesus Heals a Lame Man

Afterward Jesus returned to Jerusalem for one of the Jewish holy days. [2]Inside the city, near the Sheep Gate, was the pool of Bethesda,* with five covered porches. [3]Crowds of sick people—blind, lame, or paralyzed—lay on the porches.* [5]One of the men lying there had been sick for thirty-eight years. [6]When Jesus saw him and knew he had been ill for a long time, he asked him, "Would you like to get well?"

[7]"I can't, sir," the sick man said, "for I have no one to put me into the pool when the water bubbles up. Someone else always gets there ahead of me."

[8]Jesus told him, "Stand up, pick up your mat, and walk!"

[9]Instantly, the man was healed! He rolled up his sleeping mat and began walking! But this miracle happened on the Sabbath, [10]so the Jewish leaders objected. They said to the man who was cured, "You can't work on the Sabbath! The law doesn't allow you to carry that sleeping mat!"

[11]But he replied, "The man who healed me told me, 'Pick up your mat and walk.'"

[12]"Who said such a thing as that?" they demanded.

[13]The man didn't know, for Jesus had disappeared into the crowd. [14]But afterward Jesus found him in the Temple and told him, "Now you are well; so stop sinning, or something even worse may happen to you." [15]Then the man went and told the Jewish leaders that it was Jesus who had healed him.

Jesus Claims to Be the Son of God

[16]So the Jewish leaders began harassing* Jesus for breaking the Sabbath rules. [17]But Jesus replied, "My Father is always working, and so am I." [18]So the Jewish leaders tried all the harder to find a way to kill him. For he not only broke the Sabbath, he called God his Father, thereby making himself equal with God.

[19]So Jesus explained, "I tell you the truth, the Son can do nothing by himself. He does only what he sees the Father doing. Whatever the Father does, the Son also does. [20]For the Father loves the Son and shows him everything he is doing. In fact, the Father will show him how to do even greater works than healing this man. Then you will truly be astonished. [21]For just as the Father gives life to those he raises from the dead, so the Son gives life to anyone he wants. [22]In addition, the Father judges no one. Instead, he has given the Son absolute authority to judge, [23]so that everyone will honor the Son, just as they honor the Father. Anyone who does not honor the Son is certainly not honoring the Father who sent him.

[24]"I tell you the truth, those who listen to my message and believe in God who sent me have eternal life. They will

5:2 Other manuscripts read *Beth-zatha;* still others read *Bethsaida.* 5:3 Some manuscripts add an expanded conclusion to verse 3 and all of verse 4: *waiting for a certain movement of the water,* [4]*for an angel of the Lord came from time to time and stirred up the water. And the first person to step in after the water was stirred was healed of whatever disease he had.* 5:16 Or *persecuting.*

never be condemned for their sins, but they have already passed from death into life.

25"And I assure you that the time is coming, indeed it's here now, when the dead will hear my voice—the voice of the Son of God. And those who listen will live. 26The Father has life in himself, and he has granted that same life-giving power to his Son. 27And he has given him authority to judge everyone because he is the Son of Man.* 28Don't be so surprised! Indeed, the time is coming when all the dead in their graves will hear the voice of God's Son, 29and they will rise again. Those who have done good will rise to experience eternal life, and those who have continued in evil will rise to experience judgment. 30I can do nothing on my own. I judge as God tells me. Therefore, my judgment is just, because I carry out the will of the one who sent me, not my own will.

Witnesses to Jesus

31"If I were to testify on my own behalf, my testimony would not be valid. 32But someone else is also testifying about me, and I assure you that everything he says about me is true. 33In fact, you sent investigators to listen to John the Baptist, and his testimony about me was true. 34Of course, I have no need of human witnesses, but I say these things so you might be saved. 35John was like a burning and shining lamp, and you were excited for a while about his message. 36But I have a greater witness than John—my teachings and my miracles. The Father gave me these works to accomplish, and they prove that he sent me. 37And the Father who sent me has testified about me himself. You have never heard his voice or seen him face to face, 38and you do not have his message in your hearts, because you do not believe me— the one he sent to you.

39"You search the Scriptures because you think they give you eternal life. But the Scriptures point to me! 40Yet you refuse to come to me to receive this life.

41"Your approval means nothing to me, 42because I know you don't have God's love within you. 43For I have come to you in my Father's name, and you have rejected me. Yet if others come in their own name, you gladly welcome them. 44No wonder you can't believe! For you gladly honor each other, but you don't care about the honor that comes from the one who alone is God.*

45"Yet it isn't I who will accuse you before the Father. Moses will accuse you! Yes, Moses, in whom you put your hopes. 46If you really believed Moses, you would believe me, because he wrote about me. 47But since you don't believe what he wrote, how will you believe what I say?"

CHAPTER 6

Jesus Feeds Five Thousand

After this, Jesus crossed over to the far side of the Sea of Galilee, also known as the Sea of Tiberias. 2A huge crowd kept following him wherever he went, because they saw his miraculous signs as he healed the sick. 3Then Jesus climbed a hill and sat down with his disciples around him. 4(It was nearly time for the Jewish Passover celebration.) 5Jesus soon saw a huge crowd of people coming to look for him. Turning to Philip, he asked, "Where can we buy bread to feed all these people?" 6He was testing Philip, for he already knew what he was going to do.

7Philip replied, "Even if we worked for months, we wouldn't have enough money* to feed them!"

8Then Andrew, Simon Peter's brother, spoke up. 9"There's a young boy here with five barley loaves and two fish. But what good is that with this huge crowd?"

10"Tell everyone to sit down," Jesus said. So they all sat down on the grassy slopes. (The men alone numbered about 5,000.) 11Then Jesus took the loaves, gave thanks to God, and distributed them to the people. Afterward he did the same with the fish. And they all ate as much as they wanted. 12After

---

5:27 "Son of Man" is a title Jesus used for himself.   5:44 Some manuscripts read *from the only One*.   6:7 Greek *Two hundred denarii would not be enough*. A denarius was equivalent to a laborer's full day's wage.

everyone was full, Jesus told his disciples, "Now gather the leftovers, so that nothing is wasted." ¹³So they picked up the pieces and filled twelve baskets with scraps left by the people who had eaten from the five barley loaves.

¹⁴When the people saw him* do this miraculous sign, they exclaimed, "Surely, he is the Prophet we have been expecting!"* ¹⁵When Jesus saw that they were ready to force him to be their king, he slipped away into the hills by himself.

Jesus Walks on Water

¹⁶That evening Jesus' disciples went down to the shore to wait for him. ¹⁷But as darkness fell and Jesus still hadn't come back, they got into the boat and headed across the lake toward Capernaum. ¹⁸Soon a gale swept down upon them, and the sea grew very rough. ¹⁹They had rowed three or four miles* when suddenly they saw Jesus walking on the water toward the boat. They were terrified, ²⁰but he called out to them, "Don't be afraid. I am here!*" ²¹Then they were eager to let him in the boat, and immediately they arrived at their destination!

Jesus, the Bread of Life

²²The next day the crowd that had stayed on the far shore saw that the disciples had taken the only boat, and they realized Jesus had not gone with them. ²³Several boats from Tiberias landed near the place where the Lord had blessed the bread and the people had eaten. ²⁴So when the crowd saw that neither Jesus nor his disciples were there, they got into the boats and went across to Capernaum to look for him. ²⁵They found him on the other side of the lake and asked, "Rabbi, when did you get here?"

²⁶Jesus replied, "I tell you the truth, you want to be with me because I fed you, not because you understood the miraculous signs. ²⁷But don't be so concerned about perishable things like food. Spend your energy seeking the eternal life that the Son of Man* can give you. For God the Father has given me the seal of his approval."

²⁸They replied, "We want to perform God's works, too. What should we do?"

²⁹Jesus told them, "This is the only work God wants from you: Believe in the one he has sent."

³⁰They answered, "Show us a miraculous sign if you want us to believe in you. What can you do? ³¹After all, our ancestors ate manna while they journeyed through the wilderness! The Scriptures say, 'Moses gave them bread from heaven to eat.'*"

³²Jesus said, "I tell you the truth, Moses didn't give you bread from heaven. My Father did. And now he offers you the true bread from heaven. ³³The true bread of God is the one who comes down from heaven and gives life to the world."

³⁴"Sir," they said, "give us that bread every day."

³⁵Jesus replied, "I am the bread of life. Whoever comes to me will never be hungry again. Whoever believes in me will never be thirsty. ³⁶But you haven't believed in me even though you have seen me. ³⁷However, those the Father has given me will come to me, and I will never reject them. ³⁸For I have come down from heaven to do the will of God who sent me, not to do my own will. ³⁹And this is the will of God, that I should not lose even one of all those he has given me, but that I should raise them up at the last day. ⁴⁰For it is my Father's will that all who see his Son and believe in him should have eternal life. I will raise them up at the last day."

⁴¹Then the people* began to murmur in disagreement because he had said, "I am the bread that came down from heaven." ⁴²They said, "Isn't this Jesus, the son of Joseph? We know his father and mother. How can he say, 'I came down from heaven'?"

⁴³But Jesus replied, "Stop complaining about what I said. ⁴⁴For no one can come to me unless the Father who sent me draws them to me, and at the last day I will raise them up.

"I am the bread of life. Whoever comes to me will never be hungry again. Whoever believes in me will never be thirsty" (John 6:35).

say what?

Only Jesus has the stuff to feed a thirsty, starvin' soul.

6:14a Some manuscripts read *Jesus*.   **6:14b** See Deut 18:15, 18; Mal 4:5-6.   **6:19** Greek *25 or 30 stadia* [4.6 or 5.5 kilometers].   **6:20** Or *The 'I AM' is here*; Greek reads *I am*. See Exod 3:14.   **6:27** "Son of Man" is a title Jesus used for himself.   **6:31** Exod 16:4; Ps 78:24.   **6:41** Greek *Jewish people*; also in 6:52.

⁴⁵As it is written in the Scriptures,* 'They will all be taught by God.' Everyone who listens to the Father and learns from him comes to me. ⁴⁶(Not that anyone has ever seen the Father; only I, who was sent from God, have seen him.)

⁴⁷"I tell you the truth, anyone who believes has eternal life. ⁴⁸Yes, I am the bread of life! ⁴⁹Your ancestors ate manna in the wilderness, but they all died. ⁵⁰Anyone who eats the bread from heaven, however, will never die. ⁵¹I am the living bread that came down from heaven. Anyone who eats this bread will live forever; and this bread, which I will offer so the world may live, is my flesh."

⁵²Then the people began arguing with each other about what he meant. "How can this man give us his flesh to eat?" they asked.

⁵³So Jesus said again, "I tell you the truth, unless you eat the flesh of the Son of Man and drink his blood, you cannot have eternal life within you. ⁵⁴But anyone who eats my flesh and drinks my blood has eternal life, and I will raise that person at the last day. ⁵⁵For my flesh is true food, and my blood is true drink. ⁵⁶Anyone who eats my flesh and drinks my blood remains in me, and I in him. ⁵⁷I live because of the living Father who sent me; in the same way, anyone who feeds on me will live because of me. ⁵⁸I am the true bread that came down from heaven. Anyone who eats this bread will not die as your ancestors did (even though they ate the manna) but will live forever."

⁵⁹He said these things while he was teaching in the synagogue in Capernaum.

Many Disciples Desert Jesus

⁶⁰Many of his disciples said, "This is very hard to understand. How can anyone accept it?"

⁶¹Jesus was aware that his disciples were complaining, so he said to them, "Does this offend you? ⁶²Then what will you think if you see the Son of Man ascend to heaven again?

⁶³The Spirit alone gives eternal life. Human effort accomplishes nothing. And the very words I have spoken to you are spirit and life. ⁶⁴But some of you do not believe me." (For Jesus knew from the beginning which ones didn't believe, and he knew who would betray him.) ⁶⁵Then he said, "That is why I said that people can't come to me unless the Father gives them to me."

⁶⁶At this point many of his disciples turned away and deserted him. ⁶⁷Then Jesus turned to the Twelve and asked, "Are you also going to leave?"

⁶⁸Simon Peter replied, "Lord, to whom would we go? You have the words that give eternal life. ⁶⁹We believe, and we know you are the Holy One of God.*"

⁷⁰Then Jesus said, "I chose the twelve of you, but one is a devil." ⁷¹He was speaking of Judas, son of Simon Iscariot, one of the Twelve, who would later betray him.

CHAPTER 7

Jesus and His Brothers

After this, Jesus traveled around Galilee. He wanted to stay out of Judea, where the Jewish leaders were plotting his death. ²But soon it was time for the Jewish Festival of Shelters, ³and Jesus' brothers said to him, "Leave here and go to Judea, where your followers can see your miracles! ⁴You can't become famous if you hide like this! If you can do such wonderful things, show yourself to the world!" ⁵For even his brothers didn't believe in him.

⁶Jesus replied, "Now is not the right time for me to go, but you can go anytime. ⁷The world can't hate you, but it does hate me because I accuse it of doing evil. ⁸You go on. I'm not going* to this festival, because my time has not yet come." ⁹After saying these things, Jesus remained in Galilee.

Jesus Teaches Openly at the Temple

¹⁰But after his brothers left for the festival, Jesus also went, though secretly, staying out of public view. ¹¹The Jewish

6:45 Greek *in the prophets.* Isa 54:13.   **6:69** Other manuscripts read *you are the Christ, the Holy One of God;* still others read *you are the Christ, the Son of God;* and still others read *you are the Christ, the Son of the living God.*   **7:8** Some manuscripts read *not yet going.*

leaders tried to find him at the festival and kept asking if anyone had seen him. [12]There was a lot of grumbling about him among the crowds. Some argued, "He's a good man," but others said, "He's nothing but a fraud who deceives the people." [13]But no one had the courage to speak favorably about him in public, for they were afraid of getting in trouble with the Jewish leaders.

[14]Then, midway through the festival, Jesus went up to the Temple and began to teach. [15]The people* were surprised when they heard him. "How does he know so much when he hasn't been trained?" they asked.

[16]So Jesus told them, "My message is not my own; it comes from God who sent me. [17]Anyone who wants to do the will of God will know whether my teaching is from God or is merely my own. [18]Those who speak for themselves want glory only for themselves, but a person who seeks to honor the one who sent him speaks truth, not lies. [19]Moses gave you the law, but none of you obeys it! In fact, you are trying to kill me."

[20]The crowd replied, "You're demon possessed! Who's trying to kill you?"

[21]Jesus replied, "I did one miracle on the Sabbath, and you were amazed. [22]But you work on the Sabbath, too, when you obey Moses' law of circumcision. (Actually, this tradition of circumcision began with the patriarchs, long before the law of Moses.) [23]For if the correct time for circumcising your son falls on the Sabbath, you go ahead and do it so as not to break the law of Moses. So why should you be angry with me for healing a man on the Sabbath? [24]Look beneath the surface so you can judge correctly."

Is Jesus the Messiah?

[25]Some of the people who lived in Jerusalem started to ask each other, "Isn't this the man they are trying to kill? [26]But here he is, speaking in public, and they say nothing to him. Could our leaders possibly believe that he is the Messiah? [27]But how could he be? For we know where this man comes from. When the Messiah comes, he will simply appear; no one will know where he comes from."

[28]While Jesus was teaching in the Temple, he called out, "Yes, you know me, and you know where I come from. But I'm not here on my own. The one who sent me is true, and you don't know him. [29]But I know him because I come from him, and he sent me to you." [30]Then the leaders tried to arrest him; but no one laid a hand on him, because his time* had not yet come.

[31]Many among the crowds at the Temple believed in him. "After all," they said, "would you expect the Messiah to do more miraculous signs than this man has done?"

[32]When the Pharisees heard that the crowds were whispering such things, they and the leading priests sent Temple guards to arrest Jesus. [33]But Jesus told them, "I will be with you only a little longer. Then I will return to the one who sent me. [34]You will search for me but not find me. And you cannot go where I am going."

[35]The Jewish leaders were puzzled by this statement. "Where is he planning to go?" they asked. "Is he thinking of leaving the country and going to the Jews in other lands?* Maybe he will even teach the Greeks! [36]What does he mean when he says, 'You will search for me but not find me,' and 'You cannot go where I am going'?"

Jesus Promises Living Water

[37]On the last day, the climax of the festival, Jesus stood and shouted to the crowds, "Anyone who is thirsty may come to me! [38]Anyone who believes in me may come and drink! For the Scriptures declare, 'Rivers of living water will flow from his heart.'"* [39](When he said "living water," he was speaking of the Spirit, who would be given to everyone believing in him. But the Spirit had not yet been given,* because Jesus had not yet entered into his glory.)

7:15 Greek *Jewish people.*   **7:30** Greek *his hour.*   **7:35** Or *the Jews who live among the Greeks?*   **7:37-38** Or *"Let anyone who is thirsty come to me and drink.* **38***For the Scriptures declare,* *'Rivers of living water will flow from the heart of anyone who believes in me.'"*   **7:39** Some manuscripts read *But as yet there was no Spirit.* Still others read *But as yet there was no Holy Spirit.*

Division and Unbelief

40When the crowds heard him say this, some of them declared, "Surely this man is the Prophet we've been expecting."* 41Others said, "He is the Messiah." Still others said, "But he can't be! Will the Messiah come from Galilee? 42For the Scriptures clearly state that the Messiah will be born of the royal line of David, in Bethlehem, the village where King David was born."* 43So the crowd was divided about him. 44Some even wanted him arrested, but no one laid a hand on him.

45When the Temple guards returned without having arrested Jesus, the leading priests and Pharisees demanded, "Why didn't you bring him in?"

46"We have never heard anyone speak like this!" the guards responded.

47"Have you been led astray, too?" the Pharisees mocked. 48"Is there a single one of us rulers or Pharisees who believes in him? 49This foolish crowd follows him, but they are ignorant of the law. God's curse is on them!"

50Then Nicodemus, the leader who had met with Jesus earlier, spoke up. 51"Is it legal to convict a man before he is given a hearing?" he asked.

52They replied, "Are you from Galilee, too? Search the Scriptures and see for yourself—no prophet ever comes* from Galilee!"

[*The most ancient Greek manuscripts do not include John 7:53–8:11.*]

53Then the meeting broke up, and everybody went home.

CHAPTER 8

A Woman Caught in Adultery

Jesus returned to the Mount of Olives, 2but early the next morning he was back again at the Temple. A crowd soon gathered, and he sat down and taught them. 3As he was speaking, the teachers of religious law and the Pharisees brought a woman who had been caught in the act of adultery. They put her in front of the crowd.

4"Teacher," they said to Jesus, "this woman was caught in the act of adultery. 5The law of Moses says to stone her. What do you say?"

6They were trying to trap him into saying something they could use against him, but Jesus stooped down and wrote in the dust with his finger. 7They kept demanding an answer, so he stood up again and said, "All right, but let the one who has never sinned throw the first stone!" 8Then he stooped down again and wrote in the dust.

9When the accusers heard this, they slipped away one by one, beginning with the oldest, until only Jesus was left in the middle of the crowd with the woman. 10Then Jesus stood up again and said to the woman, "Where are your accusers? Didn't even one of them condemn you?"

11"No, Lord," she said.

And Jesus said, "Neither do I. Go and sin no more."

Jesus, the Light of the World

12Jesus spoke to the people once more and said, "I am the light of the world. If you follow me, you won't have to walk in darkness, because you will have the light that leads to life."

13The Pharisees replied, "You are making those claims about yourself! Such testimony is not valid."

14Jesus told them, "These claims are valid even though I make them about myself. For I know where I came from and where I am going, but you don't know this about me. 15You judge me by human standards, but I do not judge anyone. 16And if I did, my judgment would be correct in every respect because I am not alone. The Father* who

"I am the light of the world. If you follow me, you won't have to walk in darkness, because you will have the light that leads to life" (John 8:12).

say what?

I am the light of the world, and if you choose to follow me, you won't have to walk in darkness 'cause I light up everything. If you follow me, I will lead you to eternal life.

7:40 See Deut 18:15, 18; Mal 4:5-6. **7:42** See Mic 5:2. **7:52** Some manuscripts read *the prophet does not come.* **8:16** Some manuscripts read *The One.*

sent me is with me. [17]Your own law says that if two people agree about something, their witness is accepted as fact.* [18]I am one witness, and my Father who sent me is the other."

[19]"Where is your father?" they asked.

Jesus answered, "Since you don't know who I am, you don't know who my Father is. If you knew me, you would also know my Father." [20]Jesus made these statements while he was teaching in the section of the Temple known as the Treasury. But he was not arrested, because his time* had not yet come.

The Unbelieving People Warned

[21]Later Jesus said to them again, "I am going away. You will search for me but will die in your sin. You cannot come where I am going."

[22]The people* asked, "Is he planning to commit suicide? What does he mean, 'You cannot come where I am going'?"

[23]Jesus continued, "You are from below; I am from above. You belong to this world; I do not. [24]That is why I said that you will die in your sins; for unless you believe that I AM who I claim to be,* you will die in your sins."

[25]"Who are you?" they demanded.

Jesus replied, "The one I have always claimed to be.* [26]I have much to say about you and much to condemn, but I won't. For I say only what I have heard from the one who sent me, and he is completely truthful." [27]But they still didn't understand that he was talking about his Father.

[28]So Jesus said, "When you have lifted up the Son of Man on the cross, then you will understand that I AM he.* I do nothing on my own but say only what the Father taught me. [29]And the one who sent me is with me—he has not deserted me. For I always do what pleases him." [30]Then many who heard him say these things believed in him.

Jesus and Abraham

[31]Jesus said to the people who believed in him, "You are truly my disciples if you remain faithful to my teachings. [32]And you will know the truth, and the truth will set you free."

[33]"But we are descendants of Abraham," they said. "We have never been slaves to anyone. What do you mean, 'You will be set free'?"

[34]Jesus replied, "I tell you the truth, everyone who sins is a slave of sin. [35]A slave is not a permanent member of the family, but a son is part of the family forever. [36]So if the Son sets you free, you are truly free. [37]Yes, I realize that you are descendants of Abraham. And yet some of you are trying to kill me because there's no room in your hearts for my message. [38]I am telling you what I saw when I was with my Father. But you are following the advice of your father."

[39]"Our father is Abraham!" they declared.

"No," Jesus replied, "for if you were really the children of Abraham, you would follow his example.* [40]Instead, you are trying to kill me because I told you the truth, which I heard from God. Abraham never did such a thing. [41]No, you are imitating your real father."

They replied, "We aren't illegitimate children! God himself is our true Father."

[42]Jesus told them, "If God were your Father, you would love me, because I have come to you from God. I am not here on my own, but he sent me. [43]Why can't you understand what I am saying? It's because you can't even hear me! [44]For you are the children of your father the devil, and you love to do the evil things he does. He was a murderer from the beginning. He has always hated the truth, because there is no truth in him. When he lies, it is consistent with his character; for he is a liar and the father of lies. [45]So when I tell the truth, you just naturally don't believe me! [46]Which of you can truthfully accuse me of sin? And since I am tell-

8:17 See Deut 19:15.   **8:20** Greek *his hour.*   **8:22** Greek *Jewish people;* also in 8:31, 48, 52, 57.   **8:24** Greek *unless you believe that I am.* See Exod 3:14.   **8:25** Or *Why do I speak to you at all?*   **8:28** Greek *When you have lifted up the Son of Man, then you will know that I am.* "Son of Man" is a title Jesus used for himself.   **8:39** Some manuscripts read *if you are really the children of Abraham, follow his example.*

ing you the truth, why don't you believe me? [47]Anyone who belongs to God listens gladly to the words of God. But you don't listen because you don't belong to God."

[48]The people retorted, "You Samaritan devil! Didn't we say all along that you were possessed by a demon?"

[49]"No," Jesus said, "I have no demon in me. For I honor my Father—and you dishonor me. [50]And though I have no wish to glorify myself, God is going to glorify me. He is the true judge. [51]I tell you the truth, anyone who obeys my teaching will never die!"

[52]The people said, "Now we know you are possessed by a demon. Even Abraham and the prophets died, but you say, 'Anyone who obeys my teaching will never die!' [53]Are you greater than our father Abraham? He died, and so did the prophets. Who do you think you are?"

[54]Jesus answered, "If I want glory for myself, it doesn't count. But it is my Father who will glorify me. You say, 'He is our God,'* [55]but you don't even know him. I know him. If I said otherwise, I would be as great a liar as you! But I do know him and obey him. [56]Your father Abraham rejoiced as he looked forward to my coming. He saw it and was glad."

[57]The people said, "You aren't even fifty years old. How can you say you have seen Abraham?*"

[58]Jesus answered, "I tell you the truth, before Abraham was even born, I AM!*" [59]At that point they picked up stones to throw at him. But Jesus was hidden from them and left the Temple.

CHAPTER 9

Jesus Heals a Man Born Blind

As Jesus was walking along, he saw a man who had been blind from birth. [2]"Rabbi," his disciples asked him, "why was this man born blind? Was it because of his own sins or his parents' sins?"

[3]"It was not because of his sins or his parents' sins," Jesus answered. "This happened so the power of God could be seen in him. [4]We must quickly carry out the tasks assigned us by the one who sent us.* The night is coming, and then no one can work. [5]But while I am here in the world, I am the light of the world."

[6]Then he spit on the ground, made mud with the saliva, and spread the mud over the blind man's eyes. [7]He told him, "Go wash yourself in the pool of Siloam" (Siloam means "sent"). So the man went and washed and came back seeing!

[8]His neighbors and others who knew him as a blind beggar asked each other, "Isn't this the man who used to sit and beg?" [9]Some said he was, and others said, "No, he just looks like him!"

But the beggar kept saying, "Yes, I am the same one!"

[10]They asked, "Who healed you? What happened?"

[11]He told them, "The man they call Jesus made mud and spread it over my eyes and told me, 'Go to the pool of Siloam and wash yourself.' So I went and washed, and now I can see!"

[12]"Where is he now?" they asked.

"I don't know," he replied.

[13]Then they took the man who had been blind to the Pharisees, [14]because it was on the Sabbath that Jesus had made the mud and healed him. [15]The Pharisees asked the man all about it. So he told them, "He put the mud over my eyes, and when I washed it away, I could see!"

[16]Some of the Pharisees said, "This man Jesus is not from God, for he is working on the Sabbath." Others said, "But how could an ordinary sinner do such miraculous signs?" So there was a deep division of opinion among them.

[17]Then the Pharisees again questioned the man who had been blind and demanded, "What's your opinion about this man who healed you?"

8:54 Some manuscripts read *your God.* **8:57** Some manuscripts read *How can you say Abraham has seen you?* **8:58** Or *before Abraham was even born, I have always been alive;* Greek reads *before Abraham was, I am.* See Exod 3:14. **9:4** Other manuscripts read *I must quickly carry out the tasks assigned me by the one who sent me;* still others read *We must quickly carry out the tasks assigned us by the one who sent me.*

The man replied, "I think he must be a prophet."

18The Jewish leaders still refused to believe the man had been blind and could now see, so they called in his parents. 19They asked them, "Is this your son? Was he born blind? If so, how can he now see?"

20His parents replied, "We know this is our son and that he was born blind, 21but we don't know how he can see or who healed him. Ask him. He is old enough to speak for himself." 22His parents said this because they were afraid of the Jewish leaders, who had announced that anyone saying Jesus was the Messiah would be expelled from the synagogue. 23That's why they said, "He is old enough. Ask him."

24So for the second time they called in the man who had been blind and told him, "God should get the glory for this,* because we know this man Jesus is a sinner."

25"I don't know whether he is a sinner," the man replied. "But I know this: I was blind, and now I can see!"

26"But what did he do?" they asked. "How did he heal you?"

27"Look!" the man exclaimed. "I told you once. Didn't you listen? Why do you want to hear it again? Do you want to become his disciples, too?"

28Then they cursed him and said, "You are his disciple, but we are disciples of Moses! 29We know God spoke to Moses, but we don't even know where this man comes from."

30"Why, that's very strange!" the man replied. "He healed my eyes, and yet you don't know where he comes from? 31We know that God doesn't listen to sinners, but he is ready to hear those who worship him and do his will. 32Ever since the world began, no one has been able to open the eyes of someone born blind. 33If this man were not from God, he couldn't have done it."

34"You were born a total sinner!" they answered. "Are you trying to teach us?" And they threw him out of the synagogue.

Spiritual Blindness

35When Jesus heard what had happened, he found the man and asked, "Do you believe in the Son of Man?*"

36The man answered, "Who is he, sir? I want to believe in him."

37"You have seen him," Jesus said, "and he is speaking to you!"

38"Yes, Lord, I believe!" the man said. And he worshiped Jesus.

39Then Jesus told him,* "I entered this world to render judgment—to give sight to the blind and to show those who think they see* that they are blind."

40Some Pharisees who were standing nearby heard him and asked, "Are you saying we're blind?"

41"If you were blind, you wouldn't be guilty," Jesus replied. "But you remain guilty because you claim you can see.

CHAPTER 10

The Good Shepherd and His Sheep

"I tell you the truth, anyone who sneaks over the wall of a sheepfold, rather than going through the gate, must surely be a thief and a robber! 2But the one who enters through the gate is the shepherd of the sheep. 3The gatekeeper opens the gate for him, and the sheep recognize his voice and come to him. He calls his own sheep by name and leads them out. 4After he has gathered his own flock, he walks ahead of them, and they follow him because they know his voice. 5They won't follow a stranger; they will run from him because they don't know his voice."

6Those who heard Jesus use this illustration didn't understand what he meant, 7so he explained it to them: "I tell you the truth, I am the gate for the sheep. 8All who came before me* were thieves and robbers. But the true sheep did not listen to them. 9Yes, I am the gate. Those who come in through

9:24 Or *Give glory to God, not to Jesus;* Greek reads *Give glory to God.* 9:35 Some manuscripts read *the Son of God?* "Son of Man" is a title Jesus used for himself. 9:38-39a Some manuscripts do not include "*Yes, Lord, I believe!" the man said. And he worshiped Jesus. Then Jesus told him.* 9:39b Greek *those who see.* 10:8 Some manuscripts do not include *before me.*

me will be saved.* They will come and go freely and will find good pastures. ¹⁰The thief's purpose is to steal and kill and destroy. My purpose is to give them a rich and satisfying life.

¹¹"I am the good shepherd. The good shepherd sacrifices his life for the sheep. ¹²A hired hand will run when he sees a wolf coming. He will abandon the sheep because they don't belong to him and he isn't their shepherd. And so the wolf attacks them and scatters the flock. ¹³The hired hand runs away because he's working only for the money and doesn't really care about the sheep.

¹⁴"I am the good shepherd; I know my own sheep, and they know me, ¹⁵just as my Father knows me and I know the Father. So I sacrifice my life for the sheep. ¹⁶I have other sheep, too, that are not in this sheepfold. I must bring them also. They will listen to my voice, and there will be one flock with one shepherd.

¹⁷"The Father loves me because I sacrifice my life so I may take it back again. ¹⁸No one can take my life from me. I sacrifice it voluntarily. For I have the authority to lay it down when I want to and also to take it up again. For this is what my Father has commanded."

¹⁹When he said these things, the people* were again divided in their opinions about him. ²⁰Some said, "He's demon possessed and out of his mind. Why listen to a man like that?"

²¹Others said, "This doesn't sound like a man possessed by a demon! Can a demon open the eyes of the blind?"

Jesus Claims to Be the Son of God

²²It was now winter, and Jesus was in Jerusalem at the time of Hanukkah, the Festival of Dedication. ²³He was in the Temple, walking through the section known as Solomon's Colonnade. ²⁴The people surrounded him and asked, "How long are you going to keep us in suspense? If you are the Messiah, tell us plainly."

²⁵Jesus replied, "I have already told you, and you don't believe me. The proof is the work I do in my Father's name. ²⁶But you don't believe me because you are not my sheep. ²⁷My sheep listen to my voice; I know them, and they follow me. ²⁸I give them eternal life, and they will never perish. No one can snatch them away from me, ²⁹for my Father has given them to me, and he is more powerful than anyone else.* No one can snatch them from the Father's hand. ³⁰The Father and I are one."

³¹Once again the people picked up stones to kill him. ³²Jesus said, "At my Father's direction I have done many good works. For which one are you going to stone me?"

³³They replied, "We're stoning you not for any good work, but for blasphemy! You, a mere man, claim to be God."

10:9 Or *will find safety.* 10:19 Greek *Jewish people;* also in 10:24, 31. 10:29 Other manuscripts read *for what my Father has given me is more powerful than anything;* still others read *for regarding that which my Father has given me, he is greater than all.*

THE POINT

Jesus is all that—and more. John is the only Gospel that records Jesus' seven "I Am" statements. To help us get to know who he is, Jesus compared himself to things people back in the day knew about. We know something about most of these things, too. Look at this list:

"I am the bread of life" (John 6:35); "I am the light of the world" (8:12); "I am the gate for the sheep" (10:7); "I am the good shepherd" (10:11, 14); "I am the resurrection and the life" (11:25); "I am the way, the truth, and the life" (14:6); and "I am the true grapevine" (15:1).

John wanted to make sure we got who Jesus was. Jesus was on point, and John knew it. John got his witness firsthand. He was there when Jesus turned water into wine and raised Lazarus from the dead. John made it his business to point out that Jesus was, and is, the promised Messiah—the one true Savior.

³⁴Jesus replied, "It is written in your own Scriptures* that God said to certain leaders of the people, 'I say, you are gods!'* ³⁵And you know that the Scriptures cannot be altered. So if those people who received God's message were called 'gods,' ³⁶why do you call it blasphemy when I say, 'I am the Son of God'? After all, the Father set me apart and sent me into the world. ³⁷Don't believe me unless I carry out my Father's work. ³⁸But if I do his work, believe in the evidence of the miraculous works I have done, even if you don't believe me. Then you will know and understand that the Father is in me, and I am in the Father."

³⁹Once again they tried to arrest him, but he got away and left them. ⁴⁰He went beyond the Jordan River near the place where John was first baptizing and stayed there awhile. ⁴¹And many followed him. "John didn't perform miraculous signs," they remarked to one another, "but everything he said about this man has come true." ⁴²And many who were there believed in Jesus.

CHAPTER 11

The Raising of Lazarus

A man named Lazarus was sick. He lived in Bethany with his sisters, Mary and Martha. ²This is the Mary who later poured the expensive perfume on the Lord's feet and wiped them with her hair.* Her brother, Lazarus, was sick. ³So the two sisters sent a message to Jesus telling him, "Lord, your dear friend is very sick."

⁴But when Jesus heard about it he said, "Lazarus's sickness will not end in death. No, it happened for the glory of God so that the Son of God will receive glory from this." ⁵So although Jesus loved Martha, Mary, and Lazarus, ⁶he stayed where he was for the next two days. ⁷Finally, he said to his disciples, "Let's go back to Judea."

⁸But his disciples objected. "Rabbi," they said, "only a few days ago the people* in Judea were trying to stone you. Are you going there again?"

⁹Jesus replied, "There are twelve hours of daylight every day. During the day people can walk safely. They can see because they have the light of this world. ¹⁰But at night there is danger of stumbling because they have no light." ¹¹Then he said, "Our friend Lazarus has fallen asleep, but now I will go and wake him up."

¹²The disciples said, "Lord, if he is sleeping, he will soon get better!" ¹³They thought Jesus meant Lazarus was simply sleeping, but Jesus meant Lazarus had died.

¹⁴So he told them plainly, "Lazarus is dead. ¹⁵And for your sakes, I'm glad I wasn't there, for now you will really believe. Come, let's go see him."

¹⁶Thomas, nicknamed the Twin,* said to his fellow disciples, "Let's go, too—and die with Jesus."

¹⁷When Jesus arrived at Bethany, he was told that Lazarus had already been in his grave for four days. ¹⁸Bethany was only a few miles* down the road from Jerusalem, ¹⁹and many of the people had come to console Martha and Mary in their loss. ²⁰When Martha got word that Jesus was coming, she went to meet him. But Mary stayed in the house. ²¹Martha said to Jesus, "Lord, if only you had been here, my brother would not have died. ²²But even now I know that God will give you whatever you ask."

²³Jesus told her, "Your brother will rise again."

²⁴"Yes," Martha said, "he will rise when everyone else rises, at the last day."

²⁵Jesus told her, "I am the resurrection and the life.* Anyone who believes in me will live, even after dying. ²⁶Everyone who lives in me and believes in me will never ever die. Do you believe this, Martha?"

²⁷"Yes, Lord," she told him. "I have always believed you are the Messiah, the Son of God, the one who has come into the world from God." ²⁸Then she returned to Mary. She

"I am the resurrection and the life. Anyone who believes in me will live, even after dying" (John 11:25).

I am life, and if you die, I'm the comeback. If you believe in me, you'll live even after death.

10:34a Greek *your own law.* **10:34b** Ps 82:6. **11:2** This incident is recorded in chapter 12. **11:8** Greek *Jewish people;* also in 11:19, 31, 33, 36, 45, 54. **11:16** Greek *Thomas, who was called Didymus.* **11:18** Greek *was about 15 stadia* [about 2.8 kilometers]. **11:25** Some manuscripts do not include *and the life.*

called Mary aside from the mourners and told her, "The Teacher is here and wants to see you." 29So Mary immediately went to him.

30Jesus had stayed outside the village, at the place where Martha met him. 31When the people who were at the house consoling Mary saw her leave so hastily, they assumed she was going to Lazarus's grave to weep. So they followed her there. 32When Mary arrived and saw Jesus, she fell at his feet and said, "Lord, if only you had been here, my brother would not have died."

33When Jesus saw her weeping and saw the other people wailing with her, a deep anger welled up within him,* and he was deeply troubled. 34"Where have you put him?" he asked them.

They told him, "Lord, come and see." 35Then Jesus wept. 36The people who were standing nearby said, "See how much he loved him!" 37But some said, "This man healed a blind man. Couldn't he have kept Lazarus from dying?"

38Jesus was still angry as he arrived at the tomb, a cave with a stone rolled across its entrance. 39"Roll the stone aside," Jesus told them.

But Martha, the dead man's sister, protested, "Lord, he has been dead for four days. The smell will be terrible."

40Jesus responded, "Didn't I tell you that you would see God's glory if you believe?" 41So they rolled the stone aside. Then Jesus looked up to heaven and said, "Father, thank you for hearing me. 42You always hear me, but I said it out loud for the sake of all these people standing here, so that they will believe you sent me." 43Then Jesus shouted, "Lazarus, come out!" 44And the dead man came out, his hands and feet bound in graveclothes, his face wrapped in a headcloth. Jesus told them, "Unwrap him and let him go!"

The Plot to Kill Jesus

45Many of the people who were with Mary believed in Jesus when they saw this happen. 46But some went to the Pharisees and told them what Jesus had done. 47Then the leading priests and Pharisees called the high council* together. "What are we going to do?" they asked each other. "This man certainly performs many miraculous signs. 48If we allow him to go on like this, soon everyone will believe in him. Then the Roman army will come and destroy both our Temple* and our nation."

49Caiaphas, who was high priest at that time,* said, "You don't know what you're talking about! 50You don't realize that it's better for you that one man should die for the people than for the whole nation to be destroyed."

51He did not say this on his own; as high priest at that time he was led to prophesy that Jesus would die for the entire nation. 52And not only for that nation, but to bring together and unite all the children of God scattered around the world.

53So from that time on, the Jewish leaders began to plot Jesus' death. 54As a result, Jesus stopped his public ministry among the people and left Jerusalem. He went to a place near the wilderness, to the village of Ephraim, and stayed there with his disciples.

55It was now almost time for the Jewish Passover celebration, and many people from all over the country arrived in Jerusalem several days early so they could go through the purification ceremony before Passover began. 56They kept looking for Jesus, but as they stood around in the Temple, they said to each other, "What do you think? He won't come for Passover, will he?" 57Meanwhile, the leading priests and Pharisees had publicly ordered that anyone seeing Jesus must report it immediately so they could arrest him.

CHAPTER 12

Jesus Anointed at Bethany

Six days before the Passover celebration began, Jesus arrived in Bethany, the home of Lazarus—the man he had raised from the dead. 2A dinner was prepared in Jesus'

11:33 Or he was angry in his spirit.   11:47 Greek the Sanhedrin.   11:48 Or our position; Greek reads our place.   11:49 Greek that year; also in 11:51.

honor. Martha served, and Lazarus was among those who ate* with him. ³Then Mary took a twelve-ounce jar* of expensive perfume made from essence of nard, and she anointed Jesus' feet with it, wiping his feet with her hair. The house was filled with the fragrance.

⁴But Judas Iscariot, the disciple who would soon betray him, said, ⁵"That perfume was worth a year's wages.* It should have been sold and the money given to the poor." ⁶Not that he cared for the poor—he was a thief, and since he was in charge of the disciples' money, he often stole some for himself.

⁷Jesus replied, "Leave her alone. She did this in preparation for my burial. ⁸You will always have the poor among you, but you will not always have me."

⁹When all the people* heard of Jesus' arrival, they flocked to see him and also to see Lazarus, the man Jesus had raised from the dead. ¹⁰Then the leading priests decided to kill Lazarus, too, ¹¹for it was because of him that many of the people had deserted them* and believed in Jesus.

Jesus' Triumphant Entry

¹²The next day, the news that Jesus was on the way to Jerusalem swept through the city. A large crowd of Passover visitors ¹³took palm branches and went down the road to meet him. They shouted,

> "Praise God!*
> Blessings on the one who comes in the name of the LORD!
> Hail to the King of Israel!"*

¹⁴Jesus found a young donkey and rode on it, fulfilling the prophecy that said:

¹⁵ "Don't be afraid, people of Jerusalem.*
Look, your King is coming,
  riding on a donkey's colt."*

¹⁶His disciples didn't understand at the time that this was a fulfillment of prophecy. But after Jesus entered into his glory, they remembered what had happened and realized that these things had been written about him.

¹⁷Many in the crowd had seen Jesus call Lazarus from the tomb, raising him from the dead, and they were telling others* about it. ¹⁸That was the reason so many went out to meet him—because they had heard about this miraculous sign. ¹⁹Then the Pharisees said to each other, "There's nothing we can do. Look, everyone* has gone after him!"

Jesus Predicts His Death

²⁰Some Greeks who had come to Jerusalem for the Passover celebration ²¹paid a visit to Philip, who was from Bethsaida in Galilee. They said, "Sir, we want to meet Jesus." ²²Philip told Andrew about it, and they went together to ask Jesus.

²³Jesus replied, "Now the time has come for the Son of Man* to enter into his glory. ²⁴I tell you the truth, unless a kernel of wheat is planted in the soil and dies, it remains alone. But its death will produce many new kernels—a plentiful harvest of new lives. ²⁵Those who love their life in this world will lose it. Those who care nothing for their life in this world will keep it for eternity. ²⁶Anyone who wants to be my disciple must follow me, because my servants must be where I am. And the Father will honor anyone who serves me.

²⁷"Now my soul is deeply troubled. Should I pray, 'Father, save me from this hour'? But this is the very reason I came! ²⁸Father, bring glory to your name."

Then a voice spoke from heaven, saying, "I have already brought glory to my name, and I will do so again." ²⁹When the crowd heard the voice, some thought it was thunder, while others declared an angel had spoken to him.

³⁰Then Jesus told them, "The voice was for your benefit,

12:2 Or *who reclined.*   **12:3** Greek *took 1 litra* [327 grams].   **12:5** Greek *worth 300 denarii.* A denarius was equivalent to a laborer's full day's wage.   **12:9** Greek *Jewish people;* also in 12:11.   **12:11** Or *had deserted their traditions;* Greek reads *had deserted.*   **12:13a** Greek *Hosanna,* an exclamation of praise adapted from a Hebrew expression that means "save now."   **12:13b** Ps 118:25-26; Zeph 3:15.   **12:15a** Greek *daughter of Zion.*   **12:15b** Zech 9:9.   **12:17** Greek *were testifying.*   **12:19** Greek *the world.*   **12:23** "Son of Man" is a title Jesus used for himself.

not mine. ³¹The time for judging this world has come, when Satan, the ruler of this world, will be cast out. ³²And when I am lifted up from the earth, I will draw everyone to myself." ³³He said this to indicate how he was going to die.

³⁴The crowd responded, "We understood from Scripture* that the Messiah would live forever. How can you say the Son of Man will die? Just who is this Son of Man, anyway?"

³⁵Jesus replied, "My light will shine for you just a little longer. Walk in the light while you can, so the darkness will not overtake you. Those who walk in the darkness cannot see where they are going. ³⁶Put your trust in the light while there is still time; then you will become children of the light."

After saying these things, Jesus went away and was hidden from them.

The Unbelief of the People

³⁷But despite all the miraculous signs Jesus had done, most of the people still did not believe in him. ³⁸This is exactly what Isaiah the prophet had predicted:

"LORD, who has believed our message?
  To whom has the LORD revealed his powerful arm?"*

³⁹But the people couldn't believe, for as Isaiah also said,

⁴⁰ "The Lord has blinded their eyes
    and hardened their hearts—
so that their eyes cannot see,
    and their hearts cannot understand,
and they cannot turn to me
    and have me heal them."*

⁴¹Isaiah was referring to Jesus when he said this, because he saw the future and spoke of the Messiah's glory. ⁴²Many people did believe in him, however, including some of the Jewish leaders. But they wouldn't admit it for fear that the Pharisees would expel them from the synagogue. ⁴³For they loved human praise more than the praise of God.

⁴⁴Jesus shouted to the crowds, "If you trust me, you are trusting not only me, but also God who sent me. ⁴⁵For when you see me, you are seeing the one who sent me. ⁴⁶I have come as a light to shine in this dark world, so that all who put their trust in me will no longer remain in the dark. ⁴⁷I will not judge those who hear me but don't obey me, for I have come to save the world and not to judge it. ⁴⁸But all who reject me and my message will be judged on the day of judgment by the truth I have spoken. ⁴⁹I don't speak on my own authority. The Father who sent me has commanded me what to say and how to say it. ⁵⁰And I know his commands lead to eternal life; so I say whatever the Father tells me to say."

CHAPTER 13

Jesus Washes His Disciples' Feet

Before the Passover celebration, Jesus knew that his hour had come to leave this world and return to his Father. He had loved his disciples during his ministry on earth, and now he loved them to the very end.* ²It was time for supper, and the devil had already prompted Judas,* son of Simon Iscariot, to betray Jesus. ³Jesus knew that the Father had given him authority over everything and that he had come from God and would return to God. ⁴So he got up from the table, took off his robe, wrapped a towel around his waist, ⁵and poured water into a basin. Then he began to wash the disciples' feet, drying them with the towel he had around him.

⁶When Jesus came to Simon Peter, Peter said to him, "Lord, are you going to wash my feet?"

⁷Jesus replied, "You don't understand now what I am doing, but someday you will."

⁸"No," Peter protested, "you will never ever wash my feet!"
Jesus replied, "Unless I wash you, you won't belong to me."

⁹Simon Peter exclaimed, "Then wash my hands and head as well, Lord, not just my feet!"

¹⁰Jesus replied, "A person who has bathed all over does

flo

"Despite all the miraculous signs Jesus had done, most of the people still did not believe in him" (John 12:37).

say wut?

Even though Jesus was a show-and-prove dude, most cats didn't believe in him.

12:34 Greek *from the law.* **12:38** Isa 53:1. **12:40** Isa 6:10. **13:1** Or *he showed them the full extent of his love.* **13:2** Or *the devil had already intended for Judas.*

not need to wash, except for the feet,* to be entirely clean. And you disciples are clean, but not all of you." ¹¹For Jesus knew who would betray him. That is what he meant when he said, "Not all of you are clean."

¹²After washing their feet, he put on his robe again and sat down and asked, "Do you understand what I was doing? ¹³You call me 'Teacher' and 'Lord,' and you are right, because that's what I am. ¹⁴And since I, your Lord and Teacher, have washed your feet, you ought to wash each other's feet. ¹⁵I have given you an example to follow. Do as I have done to you. ¹⁶I tell you the truth, slaves are not greater than their master. Nor is the messenger more important than the one who sends the message. ¹⁷Now that you know these things, God will bless you for doing them.

Jesus Predicts His Betrayal

¹⁸"I am not saying these things to all of you; I know the ones I have chosen. But this fulfills the Scripture that says, 'The one who eats my food has turned against me.'* ¹⁹I tell you this beforehand, so that when it happens you will believe that I AM the Messiah.* ²⁰I tell you the truth, anyone who welcomes my messenger is welcoming me, and anyone who welcomes me is welcoming the Father who sent me."

²¹Now Jesus was deeply troubled,* and he exclaimed, "I tell you the truth, one of you will betray me!"

²²The disciples looked at each other, wondering whom he could mean. ²³The disciple Jesus loved was sitting next to Jesus at the table.* ²⁴Simon Peter motioned to him to ask, "Who's he talking about?" ²⁵So that disciple leaned over to Jesus and asked, "Lord, who is it?"

²⁶Jesus responded, "It is the one to whom I give the bread I dip in the bowl." And when he had dipped it, he gave it to Judas, son of Simon Iscariot. ²⁷When Judas had eaten the bread, Satan entered into him. Then Jesus told him, "Hurry and do what you're going to do." ²⁸None of the others at the table knew what Jesus meant. ²⁹Since Judas was their treasurer, some thought Jesus was telling him to go and pay for the food or to give some money to the poor. ³⁰So Judas left at once, going out into the night.

Jesus Predicts Peter's Denial

³¹As soon as Judas left the room, Jesus said, "The time has come for the Son of Man* to enter into his glory, and God will be glorified because of him. ³²And since God receives glory because of the Son,* he will soon give glory to the Son. ³³Dear children, I will be with you only a little longer. And as I told the Jewish leaders, you will search for me, but you can't come where I am going. ³⁴So now I am giving you a new commandment: Love each other. Just as I have loved you, you should love each other. ³⁵Your love for one another will prove to the world that you are my disciples."

³⁶Simon Peter asked, "Lord, where are you going?"

And Jesus replied, "You can't go with me now, but you will follow me later."

³⁷"But why can't I come now, Lord?" he asked. "I'm ready to die for you."

³⁸Jesus answered, "Die for me? I tell you the truth, Peter—before the rooster crows tomorrow morning, you will deny three times that you even know me.

CHAPTER 14

Jesus, the Way to the Father

"Don't let your hearts be troubled. Trust in God, and trust also in me. ²There is more than enough room in my Father's home.* If this were not so, would I have told you that I am going to prepare a place for you?* ³When everything is ready, I will come and get you, so that you will always be with me where I am. ⁴And you know the way to where I am going."

13:10 Some manuscripts do not include *except for the feet.* **13:18** Ps 41:9. **13:19** Or *that the 'I AM' has come;* or *that I am the LORD;* Greek reads *that I am.* See Exod 3:14. **13:21** Greek *was troubled in his spirit.* **13:23** Greek *was reclining on Jesus' bosom.* The "disciple Jesus loved" was probably John. **13:31** "Son of Man" is a title Jesus used for himself. **13:32** Some manuscripts do not include *And since God receives glory because of the Son.* **14:2a** Or *There are many rooms in my Father's house.* **14:2b** Or *If this were not so, I would have told you that I am going to prepare a place for you.* Some manuscripts read *If this were not so, I would have told you. I am going to prepare a place for you.*

[5]"No, we don't know, Lord," Thomas said. "We have no idea where you are going, so how can we know the way?"

[6]Jesus told him, "I am the way, the truth, and the life. No one can come to the Father except through me. [7]If you had really known me, you would know who my Father is.* From now on, you do know him and have seen him!"

[8]Philip said, "Lord, show us the Father, and we will be satisfied."

[9]Jesus replied, "Have I been with you all this time, Philip, and yet you still don't know who I am? Anyone who has seen me has seen the Father! So why are you asking me to show him to you? [10]Don't you believe that I am in the Father and the Father is in me? The words I speak are not my own, but my Father who lives in me does his work through me. [11]Just believe that I am in the Father and the Father is in me. Or at least believe because of the work you have seen me do.

[12]"I tell you the truth, anyone who believes in me will do the same works I have done, and even greater works, because I am going to be with the Father. [13]You can ask for anything in my name, and I will do it, so that the Son can bring glory to the Father. [14]Yes, ask me for anything in my name, and I will do it!

Jesus Promises the Holy Spirit

[15]"If you love me, obey* my commandments. [16]And I will ask the Father, and he will give you another Advocate,* who will never leave you. [17]He is the Holy Spirit, who leads into all truth. The world cannot receive him, because it isn't looking for him and doesn't recognize him. But you know him, because he lives with you now and later will be in you.* [18]No, I will not abandon you as orphans—I will come to you. [19]Soon the world will no longer see me, but you will see me. Since I live, you also will live. [20]When I am raised to life again, you will know that I am in my Father, and you are in me, and I am in you. [21]Those who accept my command-ments and obey them are the ones who love me. And because they love me, my Father will love them. And I will love them and reveal myself to each of them."

[22]Judas (not Judas Iscariot, but the other disciple with that name) said to him, "Lord, why are you going to reveal yourself only to us and not to the world at large?"

[23]Jesus replied, "All who love me will do what I say. My Father will love them, and we will come and make our home with each of them. [24]Anyone who doesn't love me will not obey me. And remember, my words are not my own. What I am telling you is from the Father who sent me. [25]I am telling you these things now while I am still with you. [26]But when the Father sends the Advocate as my representative—that is, the Holy Spirit—he will teach you everything and will remind you of everything I have told you.

[27]"I am leaving you with a gift—peace of mind and heart. And the peace I give is a gift the world cannot give. So don't be troubled or afraid. [28]Remember what I told you: I am going away, but I will come back to you again. If you really loved me, you would be happy that I am going to the Father, who is greater than I am. [29]I have told you these things before they happen so that when they do happen, you will believe.

[30]"I don't have much more time to talk to you, because the ruler of this world approaches. He has no power over me, [31]but I will do what the Father requires of me, so that the world will know that I love the Father. Come, let's be going.

CHAPTER 15

Jesus, the True Vine

"I am the true grapevine, and my Father is the gardener. [2]He cuts off every branch of mine that doesn't produce fruit, and he prunes the branches that do bear fruit so they will produce even more. [3]You have already been pruned and

"I am the way, the truth, and the life. No one can come to the Father except through me" (John 14:6).

Jesus is the one-way street to God.

14:7 Some manuscripts read *If you have really known me, you will know who my Father is.*   **14:15** Other manuscripts read *you will obey;* still others read *you should obey.*   **14:16** Or *Comforter,* or *Encourager,* or *Counselor.* Greek reads *Paraclete;* also in 14:26.   **14:17** Some manuscripts read *and is in you.*

purified by the message I have given you. ⁴Remain in me, and I will remain in you. For a branch cannot produce fruit if it is severed from the vine, and you cannot be fruitful unless you remain in me.

⁵"Yes, I am the vine; you are the branches. Those who remain in me, and I in them, will produce much fruit. For apart from me you can do nothing. ⁶Anyone who does not remain in me is thrown away like a useless branch and withers. Such branches are gathered into a pile to be burned. ⁷But if you remain in me and my words remain in you, you may ask for anything you want, and it will be granted! ⁸When you produce much fruit, you are my true disciples. This brings great glory to my Father.

⁹"I have loved you even as the Father has loved me. Remain in my love. ¹⁰When you obey my commandments, you remain in my love, just as I obey my Father's commandments and remain in his love. ¹¹I have told you these things so that you will be filled with my joy. Yes, your joy will overflow! ¹²This is my commandment: Love each other in the same way I have loved you. ¹³There is no greater love than to lay down one's life for one's friends. ¹⁴You are my friends if you do what I command. ¹⁵I no longer call you slaves, because a master doesn't confide in his slaves. Now you are my friends, since I have told you everything the Father told me. ¹⁶You didn't choose me. I chose you. I appointed you to go and produce lasting fruit, so that the Father will give you whatever you ask for, using my name. ¹⁷This is my command: Love each other.

The World's Hatred

¹⁸"If the world hates you, remember that it hated me first. ¹⁹The world would love you as one of its own if you belonged to it, but you are no longer part of the world. I chose you to come out of the world, so it hates you. ²⁰Do you remember what I told you? 'A slave is not greater than the master.' Since they persecuted me, naturally they will persecute you. And if they had listened to me, they would listen to you. ²¹They

will do all this to you because of me, for they have rejected the one who sent me. ²²They would not be guilty if I had not come and spoken to them. But now they have no excuse for their sin. ²³Anyone who hates me also hates my Father. ²⁴If I hadn't done such miraculous signs among them that no one else could do, they would not be guilty. But as it is, they have seen everything I did, yet they still hate me and my Father. ²⁵This fulfills what is written in their Scriptures*: 'They hated me without cause.'

²⁶"But I will send you the Advocate*—the Spirit of truth. He will come to you from the Father and will testify all about me. ²⁷And you must also testify about me because you have been with me from the beginning of my ministry.

CHAPTER 16

"I have told you these things so that you won't abandon your faith. ²For you will be expelled from the synagogues, and the time is coming when those who kill you will think they are doing a holy service for God. ³This is because they have never known the Father or me. ⁴Yes, I'm telling you these things now, so that when they happen, you will remember my warning. I didn't tell you earlier because I was going to be with you for a while longer.

The Work of the Holy Spirit

⁵"But now I am going away to the one who sent me, and not one of you is asking where I am going. ⁶Instead, you grieve because of what I've told you. ⁷But in fact, it is best for you that I go away, because if I don't, the Advocate* won't come. If I do go away, then I will send him to you. ⁸And when he comes, he will convict the world of its sin, and of God's righteousness, and of the coming judgment. ⁹The world's sin is that it refuses to believe in me. ¹⁰Righteousness is available because I go to the Father, and you will see me no more. ¹¹Judgment will come because the ruler of this world has already been judged.

15:25 Greek in their law. Pss 35:19; 69:4.   **15:26** Or Comforter, or Encourager, or Counselor. Greek reads Paraclete.   **16:7** Or Comforter, or Encourager, or Counselor. Greek reads Paraclete.

¹²"There is so much more I want to tell you, but you can't bear it now. ¹³When the Spirit of truth comes, he will guide you into all truth. He will not speak on his own but will tell you what he has heard. He will tell you about the future. ¹⁴He will bring me glory by telling you whatever he receives from me. ¹⁵All that belongs to the Father is mine; this is why I said, 'The Spirit will tell you whatever he receives from me.'

Sadness Will Be Turned to Joy

¹⁶"In a little while you won't see me anymore. But a little while after that, you will see me again."

¹⁷Some of the disciples asked each other, "What does he mean when he says, 'In a little while you won't see me, but then you will see me,' and 'I am going to the Father'? ¹⁸And what does he mean by 'a little while'? We don't understand."

¹⁹Jesus realized they wanted to ask him about it, so he said, "Are you asking yourselves what I meant? I said in a little while you won't see me, but a little while after that you will see me again. ²⁰I tell you the truth, you will weep and mourn over what is going to happen to me, but the world will rejoice. You will grieve, but your grief will suddenly turn to wonderful joy. ²¹It will be like a woman suffering the pains of labor. When her child is born, her anguish gives way to joy because she has brought a new baby into the world. ²²So you have sorrow now, but I will see you again; then you will rejoice, and no one can rob you of that joy. ²³At that time you won't need to ask me for anything. I tell you the truth, you will ask the Father directly, and he will grant your request because you use my name. ²⁴You haven't done this before. Ask, using my name, and you will receive, and you will have abundant joy.

²⁵"I have spoken of these matters in figures of speech, but soon I will stop speaking figuratively and will tell you plainly all about the Father. ²⁶Then you will ask in my name. I'm not saying I will ask the Father on your behalf, ²⁷for the Father himself loves you dearly because you love me and believe that I came from God.* ²⁸Yes, I came from the Father into the world, and now I will leave the world and return to the Father."

²⁹Then his disciples said, "At last you are speaking plainly and not figuratively. ³⁰Now we understand that you know everything, and there's no need to question you. From this we believe that you came from God."

³¹Jesus asked, "Do you finally believe? ³²But the time is coming—indeed it's here now—when you will be scattered, each one going his own way, leaving me alone. Yet I am not alone because the Father is with me. ³³I have told you all this so that you may have peace in me. Here on earth you will have many trials and sorrows. But take heart, because I have overcome the world."

CHAPTER 17

The Prayer of Jesus

After saying all these things, Jesus looked up to heaven and said, "Father, the hour has come. Glorify your Son so he can give glory back to you. ²For you have given him authority over everyone. He gives eternal life to each one you have given him. ³And this is the way to have eternal life—to know you, the only true God, and Jesus Christ, the one you sent to earth. ⁴I brought glory to you here on earth by completing the work you gave me to do. ⁵Now, Father, bring me into the glory we shared before the world began.

⁶"I have revealed you* to the ones you gave me from this world. They were always yours. You gave them to me, and they have kept your word. ⁷Now they know that everything I have is a gift from you, ⁸for I have passed on to them the message you gave me. They accepted it and know that I came from you, and they believe you sent me.

⁹"My prayer is not for the world, but for those you have given me, because they belong to you. ¹⁰All who are mine belong to you, and you have given them to me, so they

bring me glory. ¹¹Now I am departing from the world; they are staying in this world, but I am coming to you. Holy Father, you have given me your name;* now protect them by the power of your name so that they will be united just as we are. ¹²During my time here, I protected them by the power of the name you gave me.* I guarded them so that not one was lost, except the one headed for destruction, as the Scriptures foretold.

¹³"Now I am coming to you. I told them many things while I was with them in this world so they would be filled with my joy. ¹⁴I have given them your word. And the world hates them because they do not belong to the world, just as I do not belong to the world. ¹⁵I'm not asking you to take them out of the world, but to keep them safe from the evil one. ¹⁶They do not belong to this world any more than I do. ¹⁷Make them holy by your truth; teach them your word, which is truth. ¹⁸Just as you sent me into the world, I am sending them into the world. ¹⁹And I give myself as a holy sacrifice for them so they can be made holy by your truth.

²⁰"I am praying not only for these disciples but also for all who will ever believe in me through their message. ²¹I pray that they will all be one, just as you and I are one—as you are in me, Father, and I am in you. And may they be in us so that the world will believe you sent me.

²²"I have given them the glory you gave me, so they may be one as we are one. ²³I am in them and you are in me. May they experience such perfect unity that the world will know that you sent me and that you love them as much as you love me. ²⁴Father, I want these whom you have given me to be with me where I am. Then they can see all the glory you gave me because you loved me even before the world began!

²⁵"O righteous Father, the world doesn't know you, but I do; and these disciples know you sent me. ²⁶I have revealed you to them, and I will continue to do so. Then your love for me will be in them, and I will be in them."

CHAPTER 18

Jesus Is Betrayed and Arrested

After saying these things, Jesus crossed the Kidron Valley with his disciples and entered a grove of olive trees. ²Judas, the betrayer, knew this place, because Jesus had often gone there with his disciples. ³The leading priests and Pharisees had given Judas a contingent of Roman soldiers and Temple guards to accompany him. Now with blazing torches, lanterns, and weapons, they arrived at the olive grove.

⁴Jesus fully realized all that was going to happen to him, so he stepped forward to meet them. "Who are you looking for?" he asked.

⁵"Jesus the Nazarene,"* they replied.

"I AM he,"* Jesus said. (Judas, who betrayed him, was standing with them.) ⁶As Jesus said "I AM he," they all drew back and fell to the ground! ⁷Once more he asked them, "Who are you looking for?"

And again they replied, "Jesus the Nazarene."

⁸"I told you that I AM he," Jesus said. "And since I am the one you want, let these others go." ⁹He did this to fulfill his own statement: "I did not lose a single one of those you have given me."*

¹⁰Then Simon Peter drew a sword and slashed off the right ear of Malchus, the high priest's slave. ¹¹But Jesus said to Peter, "Put your sword back into its sheath. Shall I not drink from the cup of suffering the Father has given me?"

Jesus at the High Priest's House

¹²So the soldiers, their commanding officer, and the Temple guards arrested Jesus and tied him up. ¹³First they took him to Annas, the father-in-law of Caiaphas, the high priest at that time.* ¹⁴Caiaphas was the one who had told the other Jewish leaders, "It's better that one man should die for the people."

17:11 Some manuscripts read *you have given me these [disciples].*   **17:12** Some manuscripts read *I protected those you gave me, by the power of your name.*   **18:5a** Or *Jesus of Nazarene;* also in 18:7.   **18:5b** Or *"The 'I AM' is here";* or *"I am the LORD";* Greek reads *I am;* also in 18:6, 8. See Exod 3:14.   **18:9** See John 6:39 and 17:12.   **18:13** Greek *that year.*

Peter's First Denial

15Simon Peter followed Jesus, as did another of the disciples. That other disciple was acquainted with the high priest, so he was allowed to enter the high priest's courtyard with Jesus. 16Peter had to stay outside the gate. Then the disciple who knew the high priest spoke to the woman watching at the gate, and she let Peter in. 17The woman asked Peter, "You're not one of that man's disciples, are you?"

"No," he said, "I am not."

18Because it was cold, the household servants and the guards had made a charcoal fire. They stood around it, warming themselves, and Peter stood with them, warming himself.

The High Priest Questions Jesus

19Inside, the high priest began asking Jesus about his followers and what he had been teaching them. 20Jesus replied, "Everyone knows what I teach. I have preached regularly in the synagogues and the Temple, where the people* gather. I have not spoken in secret. 21Why are you asking me this question? Ask those who heard me. They know what I said."

22Then one of the Temple guards standing nearby slapped Jesus across the face. "Is that the way to answer the high priest?" he demanded.

23Jesus replied, "If I said anything wrong, you must prove it. But if I'm speaking the truth, why are you beating me?"

24Then Annas bound Jesus and sent him to Caiaphas, the high priest.

Peter's Second and Third Denials

25Meanwhile, as Simon Peter was standing by the fire warming himself, they asked him again, "You're not one of his disciples, are you?"

He denied it, saying, "No, I am not."

26But one of the household slaves of the high priest, a relative of the man whose ear Peter had cut off, asked, "Didn't I see you out there in the olive grove with Jesus?" 27Again Peter denied it. And immediately a rooster crowed.

Jesus' Trial before Pilate

28Jesus' trial before Caiaphas ended in the early hours of the morning. Then he was taken to the headquarters of the Roman governor.* His accusers didn't go inside because it would defile them, and they wouldn't be allowed to celebrate the Passover. 29So Pilate, the governor, went out to them and asked, "What is your charge against this man?"

30"We wouldn't have handed him over to you if he weren't a criminal!" they retorted.

31"Then take him away and judge him by your own law," Pilate told them.

"Only the Romans are permitted to execute someone," the Jewish leaders replied. 32(This fulfilled Jesus' prediction about the way he would die.*)

33Then Pilate went back into his headquarters and called for Jesus to be brought to him. "Are you the king of the Jews?" he asked him.

34Jesus replied, "Is this your own question, or did others tell you about me?"

35"Am I a Jew?" Pilate retorted. "Your own people and their leading priests brought you to me for trial. Why? What have you done?"

36Jesus answered, "My Kingdom is not an earthly kingdom. If it were, my followers would fight to keep me from being handed over to the Jewish leaders. But my Kingdom is not of this world."

37Pilate said, "So you are a king?"

Jesus responded, "You say I am a king. Actually, I was born and came into the world to testify to the truth. All who love the truth recognize that what I say is true."

38"What is truth?" Pilate asked. Then he went out again to the people and told them, "He is not guilty of any crime.

18:20 Greek *Jewish people;* also in 18:38.   **18:28** Greek *to the Praetorium;* also in 18:33.   **18:32** See John 12:32-33.

³⁹But you have a custom of asking me to release one prisoner each year at Passover. Would you like me to release this 'King of the Jews'?"

⁴⁰But they shouted back, "No! Not this man. We want Barabbas!" (Barabbas was a revolutionary.)

CHAPTER 19

Jesus Sentenced to Death

Then Pilate had Jesus flogged with a lead-tipped whip. ²The soldiers wove a crown of thorns and put it on his head, and they put a purple robe on him. ³"Hail! King of the Jews!" they mocked, as they slapped him across the face.

⁴Pilate went outside again and said to the people, "I am going to bring him out to you now, but understand clearly that I find him not guilty." ⁵Then Jesus came out wearing the crown of thorns and the purple robe. And Pilate said, "Look, here is the man!"

⁶When they saw him, the leading priests and Temple guards began shouting, "Crucify him! Crucify him!"

"Take him yourselves and crucify him," Pilate said. "I find him not guilty."

⁷The Jewish leaders replied, "By our law he ought to die because he called himself the Son of God."

⁸When Pilate heard this, he was more frightened than ever. ⁹He took Jesus back into the headquarters* again and asked him, "Where are you from?" But Jesus gave no answer. ¹⁰"Why don't you talk to me?" Pilate demanded. "Don't you realize that I have the power to release you or crucify you?"

¹¹Then Jesus said, "You would have no power over me at all unless it were given to you from above. So the one who handed me over to you has the greater sin."

¹²Then Pilate tried to release him, but the Jewish leaders shouted, "If you release this man, you are no 'friend of Caesar.'* Anyone who declares himself a king is a rebel against Caesar."

¹³When they said this, Pilate brought Jesus out to them again. Then Pilate sat down on the judgment seat on the platform that is called the Stone Pavement (in Hebrew, *Gabbatha*). ¹⁴It was now about noon on the day of preparation for the Passover. And Pilate said to the people,* "Look, here is your king!"

¹⁵"Away with him," they yelled. "Away with him! Crucify him!"

"What? Crucify your king?" Pilate asked.

"We have no king but Caesar," the leading priests shouted back.

¹⁶Then Pilate turned Jesus over to them to be crucified.

The Crucifixion

So they took Jesus away. ¹⁷Carrying the cross by himself, he went to the place called Place of the Skull (in Hebrew, *Golgotha*). ¹⁸There they nailed him to the cross. Two others were crucified with him, one on either side, with Jesus between them. ¹⁹And Pilate posted a sign on the cross that read, "Jesus of Nazareth,* the King of the Jews." ²⁰The place where Jesus was crucified was near the city, and the sign was written in Hebrew, Latin, and Greek, so that many people could read it.

²¹Then the leading priests objected and said to Pilate, "Change it from 'The King of the Jews' to 'He said, I am King of the Jews.'"

²²Pilate replied, "No, what I have written, I have written."

²³When the soldiers had crucified Jesus, they divided his clothes among the four of them. They also took his robe, but it was seamless, woven in one piece from top to bottom. ²⁴So they said, "Rather than tearing it apart, let's throw dice* for it." This fulfilled the Scripture that says, "They divided my garments among themselves and threw dice for my clothing."* So that is what they did.

²⁵Standing near the cross were Jesus' mother, and his moth-

19:9 Greek *the Praetorium.* **19:12** "Friend of Caesar" is a technical term that refers to an ally of the emperor. **19:14** Greek *Jewish people;* also in 19:20. **19:19** Or *Jesus the Nazarene.* **19:24a** Greek *cast lots.* **19:24b** Ps 22:18.

er's sister, Mary (the wife of Clopas), and Mary Magdalene. ²⁶When Jesus saw his mother standing there beside the disciple he loved, he said to her, "Dear woman, here is your son." ²⁷And he said to this disciple, "Here is your mother." And from then on this disciple took her into his home.

The Death of Jesus

²⁸Jesus knew that his mission was now finished, and to fulfill Scripture he said, "I am thirsty."* ²⁹A jar of sour wine was sitting there, so they soaked a sponge in it, put it on a hyssop branch, and held it up to his lips. ³⁰When Jesus had tasted it, he said, "It is finished!" Then he bowed his head and released his spirit.

³¹It was the day of preparation, and the Jewish leaders didn't want the bodies hanging there the next day, which was the Sabbath (and a very special Sabbath, because it was the Passover). So they asked Pilate to hasten their deaths by ordering that their legs be broken. Then their bodies could be taken down. ³²So the soldiers came and broke the legs of the two men crucified with Jesus. ³³But when they came to Jesus, they saw that he was already dead, so they didn't break his legs. ³⁴One of the soldiers, however, pierced his side with a spear, and immediately blood and water flowed out. ³⁵(This report is from an eyewitness giving an accurate account. He speaks the truth so that you also can believe.*) ³⁶These things happened in fulfillment of the Scriptures that say, "Not one of his bones will be broken,"* ³⁷and "They will look on the one they pierced."*

The Burial of Jesus

³⁸Afterward Joseph of Arimathea, who had been a secret disciple of Jesus (because he feared the Jewish leaders), asked Pilate for permission to take down Jesus' body. When Pilate gave permission, Joseph came and took the body away. ³⁹With him came Nicodemus, the man who had come to Jesus at night. He brought about seventy-five pounds* of perfumed ointment made from myrrh and aloes. ⁴⁰Following Jewish burial custom, they wrapped Jesus' body with the spices in long sheets of linen cloth. ⁴¹The place of crucifixion was near a garden, where there was a new tomb, never used before. ⁴²And so, because it was the day of preparation for the Jewish Passover* and since the tomb was close at hand, they laid Jesus there.

CHAPTER 20

The Resurrection

Early on Sunday morning,* while it was still dark, Mary Magdalene came to the tomb and found that the stone had been rolled away from the entrance. ²She ran and found Simon Peter and the other disciple, the one whom Jesus loved. She said, "They have taken the Lord's body out of the tomb, and we don't know where they have put him!"

³Peter and the other disciple started out for the tomb. ⁴They were both running, but the other disciple outran Peter and reached the tomb first. ⁵He stooped and looked in and saw the linen wrappings lying there, but he didn't go in. ⁶Then Simon Peter arrived and went inside. He also noticed the linen wrappings lying there, ⁷while the cloth that had covered Jesus' head was folded up and lying apart from the other wrappings. ⁸Then the disciple who had reached the tomb first also went in, and he saw and believed—⁹for until then they still hadn't understood the Scriptures that said Jesus must rise from the dead. ¹⁰Then they went home.

Jesus Appears to Mary Magdalene

¹¹Mary was standing outside the tomb crying, and as she wept, she stooped and looked in. ¹²She saw two white-robed angels, one sitting at the head and the other at the foot of the place where the body of Jesus had been lying. ¹³"Dear woman, why are you crying?" the angels asked her.

19:28 See Pss 22:15; 69:21. 19:35 Some manuscripts read *can continue to believe.* 19:36 Exod 12:46; Num 9:12; Ps 34:20. 19:37 Zech 12:10. 19:39 Greek *100 litras* [32.7 kilograms]. 19:42 Greek *because of the Jewish day of preparation.* 20:1 Greek *On the first day of the week.*

"Because they have taken away my Lord," she replied, "and I don't know where they have put him."

¹⁴She turned to leave and saw someone standing there. It was Jesus, but she didn't recognize him. ¹⁵"Dear woman, why are you crying?" Jesus asked her. "Who are you looking for?"

She thought he was the gardener. "Sir," she said, "if you have taken him away, tell me where you have put him, and I will go and get him."

¹⁶"Mary!" Jesus said.

She turned to him and cried out, "Rabboni!" (which is Hebrew for "Teacher").

¹⁷"Don't cling to me," Jesus said, "for I haven't yet ascended to the Father. But go find my brothers and tell them, 'I am ascending to my Father and your Father, to my God and your God.'"

¹⁸Mary Magdalene found the disciples and told them, "I have seen the Lord!" Then she gave them his message.

Jesus Appears to His Disciples

¹⁹That Sunday evening* the disciples were meeting behind locked doors because they were afraid of the Jewish leaders. Suddenly, Jesus was standing there among them! "Peace be with you," he said. ²⁰As he spoke, he showed them the wounds in his hands and his side. They were filled with joy when they saw the Lord! ²¹Again he said, "Peace be with you. As the Father has sent me, so I am sending you." ²²Then he breathed on them and said, "Receive the Holy Spirit. ²³If you forgive anyone's sins, they are forgiven. If you do not forgive them, they are not forgiven."

Jesus Appears to Thomas

²⁴One of the twelve disciples, Thomas (nicknamed the Twin),* was not with the others when Jesus came. ²⁵They told him, "We have seen the Lord!"

But he replied, "I won't believe it unless I see the nail

POWERCHOICES

BACK IN BIBLE DAYS PEOPLE WERE IN A SPECIAL SITUATION. WITH JESUS ON THE BLOCK, THEY DIDN'T REALLY NEED TO HAVE A SERIOUS PRAYER LIFE BECAUSE HE WAS THERE WITH THEM, HOLDIN' IT DOWN. WHEN CRAZY THINGS HAPPENED OR PEOPLE HAD ISSUES, THEY WERE ABLE TO CATCH JESUS ROLLIN' THROUGH TOWN, AND JESUS OR ONE OF HIS BOYS COULD DEAL WITH THE SITUATION RIGHT THERE ON THE SPOT. ¶ NOWADAYS, JESUS IS NOT WALKING AROUND PERFORMING MIRACLES FOR EVERYONE TO SEE. SO HOW ARE YOU SUPPOSED TO HAVE FAITH IN SOMETHING YOU CANNOT SEE, HEAR, OR TOUCH? TO HAVE FAITH, YOU HAVE TO DO LIKE THE FOLKS BACK IN THE BIBLE DID AFTER JESUS VAMPED. YOU HAVE TO GET INTO THE WORD, DEVELOP A SERIOUS PRAYER LIFE, AND THEN LET THE HOLY SPIRIT DEAL WITH YOUR ISSUES. ¶ CONSIDER THIS FROM THE PEN OF THE INFAMOUS RAPPER 2PAC SHAKUR: ¶ *"I SEE MOTHERS IN BLACK CRYIN', BROTHERS IN PACKS DYIN' / PLUS EVERYBODY'S HIGH, TOO DOPED UP TO ASK WHY / WATCHIN' OUR OWN DOWNFALL, WITNESS THE END / IT'S LIKE WE DON'T BELIEVE IN GOD CAUSE WE LIVIN' IN SIN . . . / WHO DO YOU BELIEVE IN? / I PUT MY FAITH IN GOD, BLESSED AND STILL BREATHIN' / AND EVEN THOUGH IT'S HARD, THAT'S WHO I BELIEVE IN / BEFORE I'M LEAVIN' I'M ASKIN' THE GRIEVIN'—WHO DO YOU BELIEVE IN?" —"WHO DO YOU BELIEVE IN,"* BETTER DAYZ, © 2002

wounds in his hands, put my fingers into them, and place my hand into the wound in his side."

²⁶Eight days later the disciples were together again, and this time Thomas was with them. The doors were locked; but suddenly, as before, Jesus was standing among them. "Peace be with you," he said. ²⁷Then he said to Thomas, "Put your finger here, and look at my hands. Put your hand

20:19 Greek *In the evening of that day, the first day of the week.*   20:24 Greek *Thomas, who was called Didymus.*

into the wound in my side. Don't be faithless any longer. Believe!"

²⁸"My Lord and my God!" Thomas exclaimed.

²⁹Then Jesus told him, "You believe because you have seen me. Blessed are those who believe without seeing me."

Purpose of the Book

³⁰The disciples saw Jesus do many other miraculous signs in addition to the ones recorded in this book. ³¹But these are written so that you may continue to believe* that Jesus is the Messiah, the Son of God, and that by believing in him you will have life by the power of his name.

CHAPTER 21

Epilogue: Jesus Appears to Seven Disciples

Later, Jesus appeared again to the disciples beside the Sea of Galilee.* This is how it happened. ²Several of the disciples were there—Simon Peter, Thomas (nicknamed the Twin),* Nathanael from Cana in Galilee, the sons of Zebedee, and two other disciples.

³Simon Peter said, "I'm going fishing."

"We'll come, too," they all said. So they went out in the boat, but they caught nothing all night.

⁴At dawn Jesus was standing on the beach, but the disciples couldn't see who he was. ⁵He called out, "Fellows,* have you caught any fish?"

"No," they replied.

⁶Then he said, "Throw out your net on the right-hand side of the boat, and you'll get some!" So they did, and they couldn't haul in the net because there were so many fish in it.

⁷Then the disciple Jesus loved said to Peter, "It's the Lord!" When Simon Peter heard that it was the Lord, he put on his tunic (for he had stripped for work), jumped into the water, and headed to shore. ⁸The others stayed with the boat and pulled the loaded net to the shore, for they were only about a hundred yards* from shore. ⁹When they got there, they found breakfast waiting for them—fish cooking over a charcoal fire, and some bread.

¹⁰"Bring some of the fish you've just caught," Jesus said. ¹¹So Simon Peter went aboard and dragged the net to the shore. There were 153 large fish, and yet the net hadn't torn.

¹²"Now come and have some breakfast!" Jesus said. None of the disciples dared to ask him, "Who are you?" They knew it was the Lord. ¹³Then Jesus served them the bread and the fish. ¹⁴This was the third time Jesus had appeared to his disciples since he had been raised from the dead.

¹⁵After breakfast Jesus asked Simon Peter, "Simon son of John, do you love me more than these?*"

"Yes, Lord," Peter replied, "you know I love you."

"Then feed my lambs," Jesus told him.

¹⁶Jesus repeated the question: "Simon son of John, do you love me?"

"Yes, Lord," Peter said, "you know I love you."

"Then take care of my sheep," Jesus said.

¹⁷A third time he asked him, "Simon son of John, do you love me?"

Peter was hurt that Jesus asked the question a third time. He said, "Lord, you know everything. You know that I love you."

Jesus said, "Then feed my sheep.

¹⁸"I tell you the truth, when you were young, you were able to do as you liked; you dressed yourself and went wherever you wanted to go. But when you are old, you will stretch out your hands, and others* will dress you and take you where you don't want to go." ¹⁹Jesus said this to let him know by what kind of death he would glorify God. Then Jesus told him, "Follow me."

²⁰Peter turned around and saw behind them the disciple Jesus loved—the one who had leaned over to Jesus during supper and asked, "Lord, who will betray you?" ²¹Peter asked Jesus, "What about him, Lord?"

20:31 Some manuscripts read *that you may believe.*   **21:1** Greek *Sea of Tiberias,* another name for the Sea of Galilee.   **21:2** Greek *Thomas, who was called Didymus.*   **21:5** Greek *Children.*   **21:8** Greek *200 cubits* [90 meters].   **21:15** Or *more than these others do?*   **21:18** Some manuscripts read *and another one.*

"Jesus also did many other things. If they were all written down, I suppose the whole world could not contain the books that would be written" (John 21:25).

Jesus did a lot of good stuff. He changed so many lives that the world couldn't hold the books if the stories were written down.

²²Jesus replied, "If I want him to remain alive until I return, what is that to you? As for you, follow me." ²³So the rumor spread among the community of believers* that this disciple wouldn't die. But that isn't what Jesus said at all. He only said, "If I want him to remain alive until I return, what is that to you?"

21:23 Greek *the brothers.*

²⁴This disciple is the one who testifies to these events and has recorded them here. And we know that his account of these things is accurate.

²⁵Jesus also did many other things. If they were all written down, I suppose the whole world could not contain the books that would be written.

THE BOOK OF ACTS was written by Luke, the same dude who wrote the Gospel of Luke. This book is also called the Acts of the Apostles because it records important things the apostles did and said after the death and resurrection of Jesus. (The apostles were the dudes who followed Jesus and took over his work after he went back to heaven.) Think of Luke as a newscaster, giving an accurate account of the things happenin' on the block. In this book he focused on the things that happened after Jesus left things to his boys, the apostles. Think of this book as the sequel to the Gospels.

ACTS

CHAPTER 1

The Promise of the Holy Spirit

In my first book* I told you, Theophilus, about everything Jesus began to do and teach ²until the day he was taken up to heaven after giving his chosen apostles further instructions through the Holy Spirit. ³During the forty days after his crucifixion, he appeared to the apostles from time to time, and he proved to them in many ways that he was actually alive. And he talked to them about the Kingdom of God.

⁴Once when he was eating with them, he commanded them, "Do not leave Jerusalem until the Father sends you the gift he promised, as I told you before. ⁵John baptized with* water, but in just a few days you will be baptized with the Holy Spirit."

The Ascension of Jesus

⁶So when the apostles were with Jesus, they kept asking him, "Lord, has the time come for you to free Israel and restore our kingdom?"

⁷He replied, "The Father alone has the authority to set those dates and times, and they are not for you to know. ⁸But you will receive power when the Holy Spirit comes upon you. And you will be my witnesses, telling people about me everywhere—in Jerusalem, throughout Judea, in Samaria, and to the ends of the earth."

⁹After saying this, he was taken up into a cloud while they were watching, and they could no longer see him. ¹⁰As they strained to see him rising into heaven, two white-robed men suddenly stood among them. ¹¹"Men of Galilee," they said, "why are you standing here staring into heaven? Jesus has been taken from you into heaven, but someday he will return from heaven in the same way you saw him go!"

Matthias Replaces Judas

¹²Then the apostles returned to Jerusalem from the Mount of Olives, a distance of half a mile.* ¹³When they arrived, they went to the upstairs room of the house where they were staying.

Here are the names of those who were present: Peter, John, James, Andrew, Philip, Thomas, Bartholomew, Matthew, James (son of Alphaeus), Simon (the Zealot), and Judas (son of James). ¹⁴They all met together and were constantly united in prayer, along with Mary the mother of Jesus, several other women, and the brothers of Jesus.

¹⁵During this time, when about 120 believers* were together in one place, Peter stood up and addressed them. ¹⁶"Brothers," he said, "the Scriptures had to be fulfilled concerning Judas, who guided those who arrested Jesus. This was predicted long ago by the Holy Spirit, speaking through King David. ¹⁷Judas was one of us and shared in the ministry with us."

¹⁸(Judas had bought a field with the money he received for his treachery. Falling headfirst there, his body split open, spilling out all his intestines. ¹⁹The news of his death spread to all the people of Jerusalem, and they gave the place the Aramaic name *Akeldama*, which means "Field of Blood.")

²⁰Peter continued, "This was written in the book of Psalms, where it says, 'Let his home become desolate, with no one living in it.' It also says, 'Let someone else take his position.'*

1:1 The reference is to the Gospel of Luke.   1:5 Or *in*; also in 1:5b.   1:12 Greek *a Sabbath day's journey.*   1:15 Greek *brothers.*   1:20 Pss 69:25; 109:8.

²¹"So now we must choose a replacement for Judas from among the men who were with us the entire time we were traveling with the Lord Jesus—²²from the time he was baptized by John until the day he was taken from us. Whoever is chosen will join us as a witness of Jesus' resurrection."

²³So they nominated two men: Joseph called Barsabbas (also known as Justus) and Matthias. ²⁴Then they all prayed, "O Lord, you know every heart. Show us which of these men you have chosen ²⁵as an apostle to replace Judas in this ministry, for he has deserted us and gone where he belongs." ²⁶Then they cast lots, and Matthias was selected to become an apostle with the other eleven.

CHAPTER 2

The Holy Spirit Comes

On the day of Pentecost* all the believers were meeting together in one place. ²Suddenly, there was a sound from heaven like the roaring of a mighty windstorm, and it filled the house where they were sitting. ³Then, what looked like flames or tongues of fire appeared and settled on each of them. ⁴And everyone present was filled with the Holy Spirit and began speaking in other languages,* as the Holy Spirit gave them this ability.

⁵At that time there were devout Jews from every nation living in Jerusalem. ⁶When they heard the loud noise, everyone came running, and they were bewildered to hear their own languages being spoken by the believers.

⁷They were completely amazed. "How can this be?" they exclaimed. "These people are all from Galilee, ⁸and yet we hear them speaking in our own native languages! ⁹Here we are—Parthians, Medes, Elamites, people from Mesopotamia, Judea, Cappadocia, Pontus, the province of Asia, ¹⁰Phrygia, Pamphylia, Egypt, and the areas of Libya around Cyrene, visitors from Rome ¹¹(both Jews and converts to Judaism), Cretans, and Arabs. And we all hear these people speaking in our own languages about the wonderful things

God has done!" ¹²They stood there amazed and perplexed. "What can this mean?" they asked each other.

¹³But others in the crowd ridiculed them, saying, "They're just drunk, that's all!"

Peter Preaches to the Crowd

¹⁴Then Peter stepped forward with the eleven other apostles and shouted to the crowd, "Listen carefully, all of you, fellow Jews and residents of Jerusalem! Make no mistake about this. ¹⁵These people are not drunk, as some of you are assuming. Nine o'clock in the morning is much too early for that. ¹⁶No, what you see was predicted long ago by the prophet Joel:

¹⁷ 'In the last days,' God says,
　　'I will pour out my Spirit upon all people.
　Your sons and daughters will prophesy.
　　Your young men will see visions,
　　and your old men will dream dreams.
¹⁸ In those days I will pour out my Spirit
　　even on my servants—men and women alike—
　　and they will prophesy.
¹⁹ And I will cause wonders in the heavens above
　　and signs on the earth below—
　　blood and fire and clouds of smoke.
²⁰ The sun will become dark,
　　and the moon will turn blood red
　　before that great and glorious day of the LORD arrives.
²¹ But everyone who calls on the name of the LORD
　　will be saved.'*

²²"People of Israel, listen! God publicly endorsed Jesus the Nazarene* by doing powerful miracles, wonders, and signs through him, as you well know. ²³But God knew what would happen, and his prearranged plan was carried out when Jesus was betrayed. With the help of lawless Gentiles, you nailed him to a cross and killed him. ²⁴But God released

2:1 The Festival of Pentecost came 50 days after Passover (when Jesus was crucified).　**2:4** Or *in other tongues.*　**2:17-21** Joel 2:28-32.　**2:22** Or *Jesus of Nazareth.*

"But Peter said,
'I don't have any
silver or gold for
you. But I'll give you
what I have. In the
name of Jesus
Christ the Nazarene,
get up and walk!'
. . . He jumped up,
stood on his feet,
and began to walk!
Then, walking, leap-
ing, and praising
God, he went into
the Temple with
them" (Acts 3:6, 8).

*But Peter said, "I
ain't got no money,
but I can let you
have what I have.
In the name of
Jesus Christ, get
up and walk!" . . .
He jumped up, was
able to stand on
both feet, and then
he started to walk!
Then, walking,
jumping, and prais-
ing God, he rolled to
church with them.*

him from the horrors of death and raised him back to life, for death could not keep him in its grip. ²⁵King David said this about him:

'I see that the LORD is always with me.
I will not be shaken, for he is right beside me.
²⁶ No wonder my heart is glad,
and my tongue shouts his praises!
My body rests in hope.
²⁷ For you will not leave my soul among the dead*
or allow your Holy One to rot in the grave.
²⁸ You have shown me the way of life,
and you will fill me with the joy of your presence.'*

²⁹"Dear brothers, think about this! You can be sure that the patriarch David wasn't referring to himself, for he died and was buried, and his tomb is still here among us. ³⁰But he was a prophet, and he knew God had promised with an oath that one of David's own descendants would sit on his throne. ³¹David was looking into the future and speaking of the Messiah's resurrection. He was saying that God would not leave him among the dead or allow his body to rot in the grave.

³²"God raised Jesus from the dead, and we are all witnesses of this. ³³Now he is exalted to the place of highest honor in heaven, at God's right hand. And the Father, as he had promised, gave him the Holy Spirit to pour out upon us, just as you see and hear today. ³⁴For David himself never ascended into heaven, yet he said,

'The LORD said to my Lord,
"Sit in the place of honor at my right hand
³⁵ until I humble your enemies,
making them a footstool under your feet."'*

³⁶"So let everyone in Israel know for certain that God has made this Jesus, whom you crucified, to be both Lord and Messiah!"

³⁷Peter's words pierced their hearts, and they said to him and to the other apostles, "Brothers, what should we do?"

³⁸Peter replied, "Each of you must repent of your sins and turn to God, and be baptized in the name of Jesus Christ for the forgiveness of your sins. Then you will receive the gift of the Holy Spirit. ³⁹This promise is to you, and to your children, and even to the Gentiles*—all who have been called by the Lord our God." ⁴⁰Then Peter continued preaching for a long time, strongly urging all his listeners, "Save yourselves from this crooked generation!"

⁴¹Those who believed what Peter said were baptized and added to the church that day—about 3,000 in all.

The Believers Form a Community

⁴²All the believers devoted themselves to the apostles' teaching, and to fellowship, and to sharing in meals (including the Lord's Supper*), and to prayer.

⁴³A deep sense of awe came over them all, and the apostles performed many miraculous signs and wonders. ⁴⁴And all the believers met together in one place and shared everything they had. ⁴⁵They sold their property and possessions and shared the money with those in need. ⁴⁶They worshiped together at the Temple each day, met in homes for the Lord's Supper, and shared their meals with great joy and generosity*—⁴⁷all the while praising God and enjoying the goodwill of all the people. And each day the Lord added to their fellowship those who were being saved.

CHAPTER 3

Peter Heals a Crippled Beggar

Peter and John went to the Temple one afternoon to take part in the three o'clock prayer service. ²As they approached the Temple, a man lame from birth was being carried in. Each day he was put beside the Temple gate, the one called the Beautiful Gate, so he could beg from the people going

2:27 Greek *in Hades;* also in 2:31.   2:25-28 Ps 16:8-11 (Greek version).   2:34-35 Ps 110:1.   2:39 Or *and to people far in the future;* Greek reads *and to those far away.*   2:42 Greek *the breaking of bread;* also in 2:46.   2:46 Or *and sincere hearts.*

into the Temple. ³When he saw Peter and John about to enter, he asked them for some money.

⁴Peter and John looked at him intently, and Peter said, "Look at us!" ⁵The lame man looked at them eagerly, expecting some money. ⁶But Peter said, "I don't have any silver or gold for you. But I'll give you what I have. In the name of Jesus Christ the Nazarene,* get up and* walk!"

⁷Then Peter took the lame man by the right hand and helped him up. And as he did, the man's feet and ankles were instantly healed and strengthened. ⁸He jumped up, stood on his feet, and began to walk! Then, walking, leaping, and praising God, he went into the Temple with them.

⁹All the people saw him walking and heard him praising God. ¹⁰When they realized he was the lame beggar they had seen so often at the Beautiful Gate, they were absolutely astounded! ¹¹They all rushed out in amazement to Solomon's Colonnade, where the man was holding tightly to Peter and John.

Peter Preaches in the Temple

¹²Peter saw his opportunity and addressed the crowd. "People of Israel," he said, "what is so surprising about this? And why stare at us as though we had made this man walk by our own power or godliness? ¹³For it is the God of Abraham, Isaac, and Jacob—the God of all our ancestors—who has brought glory to his servant Jesus by doing this. This is the same Jesus whom you handed over and rejected before Pilate, despite Pilate's decision to release him. ¹⁴You rejected this holy, righteous one and instead demanded the release of a murderer. ¹⁵You killed the author of life, but God raised him from the dead. And we are witnesses of this fact!

¹⁶"Through faith in the name of Jesus, this man was healed—and you know how crippled he was before. Faith in Jesus' name has healed him before your very eyes.

¹⁷"Friends,* I realize that what you and your leaders did to Jesus was done in ignorance. ¹⁸But God was fulfilling what all the prophets had foretold about the Messiah—that he must suffer these things. ¹⁹Now repent of your sins and turn to God, so that your sins may be wiped away. ²⁰Then times of refreshment will come from the presence of the Lord, and he will again send you Jesus, your appointed Messiah. ²¹For he must remain in heaven until the time for the final restoration of all things, as God promised long ago through his holy prophets. ²²Moses said, 'The LORD your God will raise up for you a Prophet like me from among your own people. Listen carefully to everything he tells you.'* ²³Then Moses said, 'Anyone who will not listen to that Prophet will be completely cut off from God's people.'*

²⁴"Starting with Samuel, every prophet spoke about what is happening today. ²⁵You are the children of those prophets, and you are included in the covenant God promised to your ancestors. For God said to Abraham, 'Through your descendants* all the families on earth will be blessed.' ²⁶When God raised up his servant, Jesus, he sent him first to you people of Israel, to bless you by turning each of you back from your sinful ways."

CHAPTER 4

Peter and John before the Council

While Peter and John were speaking to the people, they were confronted by the priests, the captain of the Temple guard, and some of the Sadducees. ²These leaders were very disturbed that Peter and John were teaching the people that through Jesus there is a resurrection of the dead. ³They arrested them and, since it was already evening, put them in jail until morning. ⁴But many of the people who heard their message believed it, so the number of believers now totaled about 5,000 men, not counting women and children.*

⁵The next day the council of all the rulers and elders and teachers of religious law met in Jerusalem. ⁶Annas the high

---

3:6a Or *Jesus Christ of Nazareth.*   **3:6b** Some manuscripts do not include *get up and.*   **3:17** Greek *Brothers.*   **3:22** Deut 18:15.   **3:23** Deut 18:19; Lev 23:29.   **3:25** Greek *your seed;* see Gen 12:3; 22:18.   **4:4** Greek *5,000 adult males.*

priest was there, along with Caiaphas, John, Alexander, and other relatives of the high priest. [7]They brought in the two disciples and demanded, "By what power, or in whose name, have you done this?"

[8]Then Peter, filled with the Holy Spirit, said to them, "Rulers and elders of our people, [9]are we being questioned today because we've done a good deed for a crippled man? Do you want to know how he was healed? [10]Let me clearly state to all of you and to all the people of Israel that he was healed by the powerful name of Jesus Christ the Nazarene,* the man you crucified but whom God raised from the dead. [11]For Jesus is the one referred to in the Scriptures, where it says,

'The stone that you builders rejected
has now become the cornerstone.'*

[12]There is salvation in no one else! God has given no other name under heaven by which we must be saved."

[13]The members of the council were amazed when they saw the boldness of Peter and John, for they could see that they were ordinary men with no special training in the Scriptures. They also recognized them as men who had been with Jesus. [14]But since they could see the man who had been healed standing right there among them, there was nothing the council could say. [15]So they ordered Peter and John out of the council chamber* and conferred among themselves.

[16]"What should we do with these men?" they asked each other. "We can't deny that they have performed a miraculous sign, and everybody in Jerusalem knows about it. [17]But to keep them from spreading their propaganda any further, we must warn them not to speak to anyone in Jesus' name again." [18]So they called the apostles back in and commanded them never again to speak or teach in the name of Jesus.

[19]But Peter and John replied, "Do you think God wants us to obey you rather than him? [20]We cannot stop telling about everything we have seen and heard."

[21]The council then threatened them further, but they finally let them go because they didn't know how to punish them without starting a riot. For everyone was praising God [22]for this miraculous sign—the healing of a man who had been lame for more than forty years.

The Believers Pray for Courage

[23]As soon as they were freed, Peter and John returned to the other believers and told them what the leading priests and elders had said. [24]When they heard the report, all the believers lifted their voices together in prayer to God: "O Sovereign Lord, Creator of heaven and earth, the sea, and everything in them—[25]you spoke long ago by the Holy Spirit through our ancestor David, your servant, saying,

'Why were the nations so angry?
Why did they waste their time with futile plans?
[26] The kings of the earth prepared for battle;
the rulers gathered together
against the LORD
and against his Messiah.'*

[27]"In fact, this has happened here in this very city! For Herod Antipas, Pontius Pilate the governor, the Gentiles, and the people of Israel were all united against Jesus, your holy servant, whom you anointed. [28]But everything they did was determined beforehand according to your will. [29]And now, O Lord, hear their threats, and give us, your servants, great boldness in preaching your word. [30]Stretch out your hand with healing power; may miraculous signs and wonders be done through the name of your holy servant Jesus."

[31]After this prayer, the meeting place shook, and they were all filled with the Holy Spirit. Then they preached the word of God with boldness.

4:10 Or *Jesus Christ of Nazareth.*   4:11 Ps 118:22.   4:15 Greek *the Sanhedrin.*   4:25-26 Or *his anointed one;* or *his Christ.* Ps 2:1-2.

The Believers Share Their Possessions

³²All the believers were united in heart and mind. And they felt that what they owned was not their own, so they shared everything they had. ³³The apostles testified powerfully to the resurrection of the Lord Jesus, and God's great blessing was upon them all. ³⁴There were no needy people among them, because those who owned land or houses would sell them ³⁵and bring the money to the apostles to give to those in need.

³⁶For instance, there was Joseph, the one the apostles nicknamed Barnabas (which means "Son of Encouragement"). He was from the tribe of Levi and came from the island of Cyprus. ³⁷He sold a field he owned and brought the money to the apostles.

CHAPTER 5

Ananias and Sapphira

But there was a certain man named Ananias who, with his wife, Sapphira, sold some property. ²He brought part of the money to the apostles, claiming it was the full amount. With his wife's consent, he kept the rest.

³Then Peter said, "Ananias, why have you let Satan fill your heart? You lied to the Holy Spirit, and you kept some of the money for yourself. ⁴The property was yours to sell or not sell, as you wished. And after selling it, the money was also yours to give away. How could you do a thing like this? You weren't lying to us but to God!"

⁵As soon as Ananias heard these words, he fell to the floor and died. Everyone who heard about it was terrified. ⁶Then some young men got up, wrapped him in a sheet, and took him out and buried him.

⁷About three hours later his wife came in, not knowing what had happened. ⁸Peter asked her, "Was this the price you and your husband received for your land?"

"Yes," she replied, "that was the price."

⁹And Peter said, "How could the two of you even think of conspiring to test the Spirit of the Lord like this? The young men who buried your husband are just outside the door, and they will carry you out, too."

¹⁰Instantly, she fell to the floor and died. When the young men came in and saw that she was dead, they carried her out and buried her beside her husband. ¹¹Great fear gripped the entire church and everyone else who heard what had happened.

The Apostles Heal Many

¹²The apostles were performing many miraculous signs and wonders among the people. And all the believers were meeting regularly at the Temple in the area known as Solomon's Colonnade. ¹³But no one else dared to join them, even though all the people had high regard for them. ¹⁴Yet more and more people believed and were brought to the Lord—crowds of both men and women. ¹⁵As a result of the apostles' work, sick people were brought out into the streets on beds and mats so that Peter's shadow might fall across some of them as he went by. ¹⁶Crowds came from the villages around Jerusalem, bringing their sick and those possessed by evil* spirits, and they were all healed.

The Apostles Meet Opposition

¹⁷The high priest and his officials, who were Sadducees, were filled with jealousy. ¹⁸They arrested the apostles and put them in the public jail. ¹⁹But an angel of the Lord came at night, opened the gates of the jail, and brought them out. Then he told them, ²⁰"Go to the Temple and give the people this message of life!"

²¹So at daybreak the apostles entered the Temple, as they were told, and immediately began teaching.

When the high priest and his officials arrived, they convened the high council*—the full assembly of the elders of Israel. Then they sent for the apostles to be brought from the jail for trial. ²²But when the Temple guards went to the

---

5:16 Greek *unclean.*   **5:21** Greek *Sanhedrin;* also in 5:27, 41.

jail, the men were gone. So they returned to the council and reported, ²³"The jail was securely locked, with the guards standing outside, but when we opened the gates, no one was there!"

²⁴When the captain of the Temple guard and the leading priests heard this, they were perplexed, wondering where it would all end. ²⁵Then someone arrived with startling news: "The men you put in jail are standing in the Temple, teaching the people!"

²⁶The captain went with his Temple guards and arrested the apostles, but without violence, for they were afraid the people would stone them. ²⁷Then they brought the apostles before the high council, where the high priest confronted them. ²⁸"Didn't we tell you never again to teach in this man's name?" he demanded. "Instead, you have filled all Jerusalem with your teaching about him, and you want to make us responsible for his death!"

²⁹But Peter and the apostles replied, "We must obey God rather than any human authority. ³⁰The God of our ancestors raised Jesus from the dead after you killed him by hanging him on a cross.* ³¹Then God put him in the place of honor at his right hand as Prince and Savior. He did this so the people of Israel would repent of their sins and be forgiven. ³²We are witnesses of these things and so is the Holy Spirit, who is given by God to those who obey him."

³³When they heard this, the high council was furious and decided to kill them. ³⁴But one member, a Pharisee named Gamaliel, who was an expert in religious law and respected by all the people, stood up and ordered that the men be sent outside the council chamber for a while. ³⁵Then he said to his colleagues, "Men of Israel, take care what you are planning to do to these men! ³⁶Some time ago there was that fellow Theudas, who pretended to be someone great. About 400 others joined him, but he was killed, and all his followers went their various ways. The whole movement came to nothing. ³⁷After him, at the time of the census, there was

Judas of Galilee. He got people to follow him, but he was killed, too, and all his followers were scattered.

³⁸"So my advice is, leave these men alone. Let them go. If they are planning and doing these things merely on their own, it will soon be overthrown. ³⁹But if it is from God, you will not be able to overthrow them. You may even find yourselves fighting against God!"

⁴⁰The others accepted his advice. They called in the apostles and had them flogged. Then they ordered them never again to speak in the name of Jesus, and they let them go.

⁴¹The apostles left the high council rejoicing that God had counted them worthy to suffer disgrace for the name of Jesus.* ⁴²And every day, in the Temple and from house to house, they continued to teach and preach this message: "Jesus is the Messiah."

CHAPTER 6

Seven Men Chosen to Serve

But as the believers* rapidly multiplied, there were rumblings of discontent. The Greek-speaking believers complained about the Hebrew-speaking believers, saying that their widows were being discriminated against in the daily distribution of food.

²So the Twelve called a meeting of all the believers. They said, "We apostles should spend our time teaching the word of God, not running a food program. ³And so, brothers, select seven men who are well respected and are full of the Spirit and wisdom. We will give them this responsibility. ⁴Then we apostles can spend our time in prayer and teaching the word."

⁵Everyone liked this idea, and they chose the following: Stephen (a man full of faith and the Holy Spirit), Philip, Procorus, Nicanor, Timon, Parmenas, and Nicolas of Antioch (an earlier convert to the Jewish faith). ⁶These seven were presented to the apostles, who prayed for them as they laid their hands on them.

5:30 Greek *on a tree.*   **5:41** Greek *for the name.*   **6:1** Greek *disciples;* also in 6:2, 7.

keeping your swagger strong

BIBLICAL PRINCIPLES FOR SUCCESS AND LEADERSHIP

Stephen was "a man full of God's grace" (Acts 6:8). Isn't the grace of God what we need today? He "performed amazing miracles and signs among the people." I would imagine that people looked up to him and trusted him because he exhibited so many of God's characteristics.

What will people say about you? As a leader, are you full of godly grace? Do your actions prove that God is truly with you? Think about these questions and answer them honestly. Your success is linked to God's influence in your life.

[7]So God's message continued to spread. The number of believers greatly increased in Jerusalem, and many of the Jewish priests were converted, too.

Stephen Is Arrested

[8]Stephen, a man full of God's grace and power, performed amazing miracles and signs among the people. [9]But one day some men from the Synagogue of Freed Slaves, as it was called, started to debate with him. They were Jews from Cyrene, Alexandria, Cilicia, and the province of Asia. [10]None of them could stand against the wisdom and the Spirit with which Stephen spoke.

[11]So they persuaded some men to lie about Stephen, saying, "We heard him blaspheme Moses, and even God." [12]This roused the people, the elders, and the teachers of religious law. So they arrested Stephen and brought him before the high council.*

[13]The lying witnesses said, "This man is always speaking against the holy Temple and against the law of Moses. [14]We have heard him say that this Jesus of Nazareth* will destroy the Temple and change the customs Moses handed down to us."

[15]At this point everyone in the high council stared at Stephen, because his face became as bright as an angel's.

CHAPTER 7

Stephen Addresses the Council

Then the high priest asked Stephen, "Are these accusations true?"

[2]This was Stephen's reply: "Brothers and fathers, listen to me. Our glorious God appeared to our ancestor Abraham in Mesopotamia before he settled in Haran.* [3]God told him, 'Leave your native land and your relatives, and come into the land that I will show you.'* [4]So Abraham left the land of the Chaldeans and lived in Haran until his father died. Then God brought him here to the land where you now live.

[5]"But God gave him no inheritance here, not even one square foot of land. God did promise, however, that eventually the whole land would belong to Abraham and his descendants—even though he had no children yet. [6]God also told him that his descendants would live in a foreign land, where they would be oppressed as slaves for 400 years. [7]'But I will punish the nation that enslaves them,' God said, 'and in the end they will come out and worship me here in this place.'*

[8]"God also gave Abraham the covenant of circumcision at that time. So when Abraham became the father of Isaac, he circumcised him on the eighth day. And the practice was continued when Isaac became the father of Jacob, and when Jacob became the father of the twelve patriarchs of the Israelite nation.

[9]"These patriarchs were jealous of their brother Joseph, and they sold him to be a slave in Egypt. But God was with him [10]and rescued him from all his troubles. And God gave him favor before Pharaoh, king of Egypt. God also gave

6:12 Greek *Sanhedrin;* also in 6:15.   **6:14** Or *Jesus the Nazarene.*   **7:2** *Mesopotamia* was the region now called Iraq. *Haran* was a city in what is now called Syria.   **7:3** Gen 12:1.
7:5-7 Gen 12:7; 15:13-14; Exod 3:12.

Joseph unusual wisdom, so that Pharaoh appointed him governor over all of Egypt and put him in charge of the palace.

¹¹"But a famine came upon Egypt and Canaan. There was great misery, and our ancestors ran out of food. ¹²Jacob heard that there was still grain in Egypt, so he sent his sons—our ancestors—to buy some. ¹³The second time they went, Joseph revealed his identity to his brothers,* and they were introduced to Pharaoh. ¹⁴Then Joseph sent for his father, Jacob, and all his relatives to come to Egypt, seventy-five persons in all. ¹⁵So Jacob went to Egypt. He died there, as did our ancestors. ¹⁶Their bodies were taken to Shechem and buried in the tomb Abraham had bought for a certain price from Hamor's sons in Shechem.

¹⁷"As the time drew near when God would fulfill his promise to Abraham, the number of our people in Egypt greatly increased. ¹⁸But then a new king came to the throne of Egypt who knew nothing about Joseph. ¹⁹This king exploited our people and oppressed them, forcing parents to abandon their newborn babies so they would die.

²⁰"At that time Moses was born—a beautiful child in God's eyes. His parents cared for him at home for three months. ²¹When they had to abandon him, Pharaoh's daughter adopted him and raised him as her own son. ²²Moses was taught all the wisdom of the Egyptians, and he was powerful in both speech and action.

²³"One day when Moses was forty years old, he decided to visit his relatives, the people of Israel. ²⁴He saw an Egyptian mistreating an Israelite. So Moses came to the man's defense and avenged him, killing the Egyptian. ²⁵Moses assumed his fellow Israelites would realize that God had sent him to rescue them, but they didn't.

²⁶"The next day he visited them again and saw two men of Israel fighting. He tried to be a peacemaker. 'Men,' he said, 'you are brothers. Why are you fighting each other?'

²⁷"But the man in the wrong pushed Moses aside. 'Who made you a ruler and judge over us?' he asked. ²⁸'Are you going to kill me as you killed that Egyptian yesterday?' ²⁹When Moses heard that, he fled the country and lived as a foreigner in the land of Midian. There his two sons were born.

³⁰"Forty years later, in the desert near Mount Sinai, an angel appeared to Moses in the flame of a burning bush. ³¹When Moses saw it, he was amazed at the sight. As he went to take a closer look, the voice of the LORD called out to him, ³²'I am the God of your ancestors—the God of Abraham, Isaac, and Jacob.' Moses shook with terror and did not dare to look.

³³"Then the LORD said to him, 'Take off your sandals, for you are standing on holy ground. ³⁴I have certainly seen the oppression of my people in Egypt. I have heard their groans and have come down to rescue them. Now go, for I am sending you back to Egypt.'*

³⁵"So God sent back the same man his people had previously rejected when they demanded, 'Who made you a ruler and judge over us?' Through the angel who appeared to him in the burning bush, God sent Moses to be their ruler and savior. ³⁶And by means of many wonders and miraculous signs, he led them out of Egypt, through the Red Sea, and through the wilderness for forty years.

³⁷"Moses himself told the people of Israel, 'God will raise up for you a Prophet like me from among your own people.'* ³⁸Moses was with our ancestors, the assembly of God's people in the wilderness, when the angel spoke to him at Mount Sinai. And there Moses received life-giving words to pass on to us.*

³⁹"But our ancestors refused to listen to Moses. They rejected him and wanted to return to Egypt. ⁴⁰They told Aaron, 'Make us some gods who can lead us, for we don't know what has become of this Moses, who brought us out of Egypt.' ⁴¹So they made an idol shaped like a calf, and they sacrificed to it and celebrated over this thing they had

7:13 Other manuscripts read *Joseph was recognized by his brothers.* 7:31-34 Exod 3:5-10. 7:37 Deut 18:15. 7:38 Some manuscripts read *to you.*

made. [42]Then God turned away from them and abandoned them to serve the stars of heaven as their gods! In the book of the prophets it is written,

'Was it to me you were bringing sacrifices and offerings
during those forty years in the wilderness, Israel?
[43] No, you carried your pagan gods—
the shrine of Molech,
the star of your god Rephan,
and the images you made to worship them.
So I will send you into exile
as far away as Babylon.'*

[44]"Our ancestors carried the Tabernacle* with them through the wilderness. It was constructed according to the plan God had shown to Moses. [45]Years later, when Joshua led our ancestors in battle against the nations that God drove out of this land, the Tabernacle was taken with them into their new territory. And it stayed there until the time of King David.

[46]"David found favor with God and asked for the privilege of building a permanent Temple for the God of Jacob.* [47]But it was Solomon who actually built it. [48]However, the Most High doesn't live in temples made by human hands. As the prophet says,

[49] 'Heaven is my throne,
and the earth is my footstool.
Could you build me a temple as good as that?'
asks the LORD.
'Could you build me such a resting place?
[50] Didn't my hands make both heaven and earth?'*

[51]"You stubborn people! You are heathen* at heart and deaf to the truth. Must you forever resist the Holy Spirit? That's what your ancestors did, and so do you! [52]Name one prophet your ancestors didn't persecute! They even killed the ones who predicted the coming of the Righteous One— the Messiah whom you betrayed and murdered. [53]You deliberately disobeyed God's law, even though you received it from the hands of angels."

[54]The Jewish leaders were infuriated by Stephen's accusation, and they shook their fists at him in rage.* [55]But Stephen, full of the Holy Spirit, gazed steadily into heaven and saw the glory of God, and he saw Jesus standing in the place of honor at God's right hand. [56]And he told them, "Look, I see the heavens opened and the Son of Man standing in the place of honor at God's right hand!"

[57]Then they put their hands over their ears and began shouting. They rushed at him [58]and dragged him out of the city and began to stone him. His accusers took off their coats and laid them at the feet of a young man named Saul.* [59]As they stoned him, Stephen prayed, "Lord Jesus, receive my spirit." [60]He fell to his knees, shouting, "Lord, don't charge them with this sin!" And with that, he died.

CHAPTER 8

Saul was one of the witnesses, and he agreed completely with the killing of Stephen.

Persecution Scatters the Believers

A great wave of persecution began that day, sweeping over the church in Jerusalem; and all the believers except the apostles were scattered through the regions of Judea and Samaria. [2](Some devout men came and buried Stephen with great mourning.) [3]But Saul was going everywhere to destroy the church. He went from house to house, dragging out both men and women to throw them into prison.

Philip Preaches in Samaria

[4]But the believers who were scattered preached the Good News about Jesus wherever they went. [5]Philip, for

7:42-43 Amos 5:25-27 (Greek version).   7:44 Greek *the tent of witness.*   7:46 Some manuscripts read *the house of Jacob.*   7:49-50 Isa 66:1-2.   7:51 Greek *uncircumcised.*   7:54 Greek *they were grinding their teeth against him.*   7:58 *Saul* is later called Paul; see 13:9.

example, went to the city of Samaria and told the people there about the Messiah. 6Crowds listened intently to Philip because they were eager to hear his message and see the miraculous signs he did. 7Many evil* spirits were cast out, screaming as they left their victims. And many who had been paralyzed or lame were healed. 8So there was great joy in that city.

9A man named Simon had been a sorcerer there for many years, amazing the people of Samaria and claiming to be someone great. 10Everyone, from the least to the greatest, often spoke of him as "the Great One—the Power of God." 11They listened closely to him because for a long time he had astounded them with his magic.

12But now the people believed Philip's message of Good News concerning the Kingdom of God and the name of Jesus Christ. As a result, many men and women were baptized. 13Then Simon himself believed and was baptized. He began following Philip wherever he went, and he was amazed by the signs and great miracles Philip performed.

14When the apostles in Jerusalem heard that the people of Samaria had accepted God's message, they sent Peter and John there. 15As soon as they arrived, they prayed for these new believers to receive the Holy Spirit. 16The Holy Spirit had not yet come upon any of them, for they had only been baptized in the name of the Lord Jesus. 17Then Peter and John laid their hands upon these believers, and they received the Holy Spirit.

18When Simon saw that the Spirit was given when the apostles laid their hands on people, he offered them money to buy this power. 19"Let me have this power, too," he exclaimed, "so that when I lay my hands on people, they will receive the Holy Spirit!"

20But Peter replied, "May your money be destroyed with you for thinking God's gift can be bought! 21You can have no part in this, for your heart is not right with God. 22Repent of your wickedness and pray to the Lord. Perhaps he will forgive your evil thoughts, 23for I can see that you are full of bitter jealousy and are held captive by sin."

24"Pray to the Lord for me," Simon exclaimed, "that these terrible things you've said won't happen to me!"

25After testifying and preaching the word of the Lord in Samaria, Peter and John returned to Jerusalem. And they stopped in many Samaritan villages along the way to preach the Good News.

Philip and the Ethiopian Eunuch

26As for Philip, an angel of the Lord said to him, "Go south* down the desert road that runs from Jerusalem to Gaza." 27So he started out, and he met the treasurer of Ethiopia, a eunuch of great authority under the Kandake, the queen of Ethiopia. The eunuch had gone to Jerusalem to worship, 28and he was now returning. Seated in his carriage, he was reading aloud from the book of the prophet Isaiah.

29The Holy Spirit said to Philip, "Go over and walk along beside the carriage."

30Philip ran over and heard the man reading from the prophet Isaiah. Philip asked, "Do you understand what you are reading?"

31The man replied, "How can I, unless someone instructs me?" And he urged Philip to come up into the carriage and sit with him.

32The passage of Scripture he had been reading was this:

"He was led like a sheep to the slaughter.
    And as a lamb is silent before the shearers,
        he did not open his mouth.
33 He was humiliated and received no justice.
    Who can speak of his descendants?
        For his life was taken from the earth."*

34The eunuch asked Philip, "Tell me, was the prophet talking about himself or someone else?" 35So beginning with this same Scripture, Philip told him the Good News about Jesus.

8:7 Greek *unclean*.   8:26 Or *Go at noon*.   8:32-33 Isa 53:7-8 (Greek version).

³⁶As they rode along, they came to some water, and the eunuch said, "Look! There's some water! Why can't I be baptized?"* ³⁸He ordered the carriage to stop, and they went down into the water, and Philip baptized him.

³⁹When they came up out of the water, the Spirit of the Lord snatched Philip away. The eunuch never saw him again but went on his way rejoicing. ⁴⁰Meanwhile, Philip found himself farther north at the town of Azotus. He preached the Good News there and in every town along the way until he came to Caesarea.

CHAPTER 9

Saul's Conversion

Meanwhile, Saul was uttering threats with every breath and was eager to kill the Lord's followers.* So he went to the high priest. ²He requested letters addressed to the synagogues in Damascus, asking for their cooperation in the arrest of any followers of the Way he found there. He wanted to bring them—both men and women—back to Jerusalem in chains.

³As he was approaching Damascus on this mission, a light from heaven suddenly shone down around him. ⁴He fell to the ground and heard a voice saying to him, "Saul! Saul! Why are you persecuting me?"

⁵"Who are you, lord?" Saul asked.

And the voice replied, "I am Jesus, the one you are persecuting! ⁶Now get up and go into the city, and you will be told what you must do."

⁷The men with Saul stood speechless, for they heard the sound of someone's voice but saw no one! ⁸Saul picked himself up off the ground, but when he opened his eyes he was blind. So his companions led him by the hand to Damascus. ⁹He remained there blind for three days and did not eat or drink.

¹⁰Now there was a believer* in Damascus named Ananias. The Lord spoke to him in a vision, calling, "Ananias!"

"Yes, Lord!" he replied.

¹¹The Lord said, "Go over to Straight Street, to the house of Judas. When you get there, ask for a man from Tarsus named Saul. He is praying to me right now. ¹²I have shown him a vision of a man named Ananias coming in and laying hands on him so he can see again."

¹³"But Lord," exclaimed Ananias, "I've heard many people talk about the terrible things this man has done to the believers* in Jerusalem! ¹⁴And he is authorized by the leading priests to arrest everyone who calls upon your name."

¹⁵But the Lord said, "Go, for Saul is my chosen instrument to take my message to the Gentiles and to kings, as well as to the people of Israel. ¹⁶And I will show him how much he must suffer for my name's sake."

¹⁷So Ananias went and found Saul. He laid his hands on him and said, "Brother Saul, the Lord Jesus, who appeared to you on the road, has sent me so that you might regain your sight and be filled with the Holy Spirit." ¹⁸Instantly something like scales fell from Saul's eyes, and he regained his sight. Then he got up and was baptized. ¹⁹Afterward he ate some food and regained his strength.

Saul in Damascus and Jerusalem

Saul stayed with the believers* in Damascus for a few days. ²⁰And immediately he began preaching about Jesus in the synagogues, saying, "He is indeed the Son of God!"

²¹All who heard him were amazed. "Isn't this the same man who caused such devastation among Jesus' followers in Jerusalem?" they asked. "And didn't he come here to arrest them and take them in chains to the leading priests?"

²²Saul's preaching became more and more powerful, and the Jews in Damascus couldn't refute his proofs that Jesus was indeed the Messiah. ²³After a while some of the Jews plotted together to kill him. ²⁴They were watching for him

8:36 Some manuscripts add verse 37, *"You can," Philip answered, "if you believe with all your heart." And the eunuch replied, "I believe that Jesus Christ is the Son of God."* 9:1 Greek *disciples.* 9:10 Greek *disciple;* also in 9:26, 36. 9:13 Greek *God's holy people;* also in 9:32, 41. 9:19 Greek *disciples;* also in 9:26, 38.

day and night at the city gate so they could murder him, but Saul was told about their plot. ²⁵So during the night, some of the other believers* lowered him in a large basket through an opening in the city wall.

²⁶When Saul arrived in Jerusalem, he tried to meet with the believers, but they were all afraid of him. They did not believe he had truly become a believer! ²⁷Then Barnabas brought him to the apostles and told them how Saul had seen the Lord on the way to Damascus and how the Lord had spoken to Saul. He also told them that Saul had preached boldly in the name of Jesus in Damascus. ²⁸So Saul stayed with the apostles and went all around Jerusalem with them, preaching boldly in the name of the Lord. ²⁹He debated with some Greek-speaking Jews, but they tried to murder him. ³⁰When the believers* heard about this, they took him down to Caesarea and sent him away to Tarsus, his hometown.

³¹The church then had peace throughout Judea, Galilee, and Samaria, and it became stronger as the believers lived in the fear of the Lord. And with the encouragement of the Holy Spirit, it also grew in numbers.

Peter Heals Aeneas and Raises Dorcas

³²Meanwhile, Peter traveled from place to place, and he came down to visit the believers in the town of Lydda. ³³There he met a man named Aeneas, who had been paralyzed and bedridden for eight years. ³⁴Peter said to him, "Aeneas, Jesus Christ heals you! Get up, and roll up your sleeping mat!" And he was healed instantly. ³⁵Then the whole population of Lydda and Sharon saw Aeneas walking around, and they turned to the Lord.

³⁶There was a believer in Joppa named Tabitha (which in Greek is Dorcas*). She was always doing kind things for others and helping the poor. ³⁷About this time she became ill and died. Her body was washed for burial and laid in an upstairs room. ³⁸But the believers had heard that Peter was nearby at Lydda, so they sent two men to beg him, "Please come as soon as possible!"

³⁹So Peter returned with them; and as soon as he arrived, they took him to the upstairs room. The room was filled with widows who were weeping and showing him the coats and other clothes Dorcas had made for them. ⁴⁰But Peter asked them all to leave the room; then he knelt and prayed. Turning to the body he said, "Get up, Tabitha." And she opened her eyes! When she saw Peter, she sat up! ⁴¹He gave her his hand and helped her up. Then he called in the widows and all the believers, and he presented her to them alive.

⁴²The news spread through the whole town, and many believed in the Lord. ⁴³And Peter stayed a long time in Joppa, living with Simon, a tanner of hides.

CHAPTER 10

Cornelius Calls for Peter

In Caesarea there lived a Roman army officer* named Cornelius, who was a captain of the Italian Regiment. ²He was a devout, God-fearing man, as was everyone in his household. He gave generously to the poor and prayed regularly to God. ³One afternoon about three o'clock, he had a vision in which he saw an angel of God coming toward him. "Cornelius!" the angel said.

⁴Cornelius stared at him in terror. "What is it, sir?" he asked the angel.

And the angel replied, "Your prayers and gifts to the poor have been received by God as an offering! ⁵Now send some men to Joppa, and summon a man named Simon Peter. ⁶He is staying with Simon, a tanner who lives near the seashore."

⁷As soon as the angel was gone, Cornelius called two of his household servants and a devout soldier, one of his personal attendants. ⁸He told them what had happened and sent them off to Joppa.

9:25 Greek *his disciples.*   9:30 Greek *brothers.*   9:36 The names *Tabitha* in Aramaic and *Dorcas* in Greek both mean "gazelle."   10:1 Greek *a centurion;* similarly in 10:22.

Peter Visits Cornelius

9The next day as Cornelius's messengers were nearing the town, Peter went up on the flat roof to pray. It was about noon, 10and he was hungry. But while a meal was being prepared, he fell into a trance. 11He saw the sky open, and something like a large sheet was let down by its four corners. 12In the sheet were all sorts of animals, reptiles, and birds. 13Then a voice said to him, "Get up, Peter; kill and eat them."

14"No, Lord," Peter declared. "I have never eaten anything that our Jewish laws have declared impure and unclean.*"

15But the voice spoke again: "Do not call something unclean if God has made it clean." 16The same vision was repeated three times. Then the sheet was suddenly pulled up to heaven.

17Peter was very perplexed. What could the vision mean? Just then the men sent by Cornelius found Simon's house. Standing outside the gate, 18they asked if a man named Simon Peter was staying there.

19Meanwhile, as Peter was puzzling over the vision, the Holy Spirit said to him, "Three men have come looking for you. 20Get up, go downstairs, and go with them without hesitation. Don't worry, for I have sent them."

21So Peter went down and said, "I'm the man you are looking for. Why have you come?"

22They said, "We were sent by Cornelius, a Roman officer. He is a devout and God-fearing man, well respected by all the Jews. A holy angel instructed him to summon you to his house so that he can hear your message." 23So Peter invited the men to stay for the night. The next day he went with them, accompanied by some of the brothers from Joppa.

24They arrived in Caesarea the following day. Cornelius was waiting for them and had called together his relatives and close friends. 25As Peter entered his home, Cornelius fell at his feet and worshiped him. 26But Peter pulled him up and said, "Stand up! I'm a human being just like you!"

27So they talked together and went inside, where many others were assembled.

28Peter told them, "You know it is against our laws for a Jewish man to enter a Gentile home like this or to associate with you. But God has shown me that I should no longer think of anyone as impure or unclean. 29So I came without objection as soon as I was sent for. Now tell me why you sent for me."

30Cornelius replied, "Four days ago I was praying in my house about this same time, three o'clock in the afternoon. Suddenly, a man in dazzling clothes was standing in front of me. 31He told me, 'Cornelius, your prayer has been heard, and your gifts to the poor have been noticed by God! 32Now send messengers to Joppa, and summon a man named Simon Peter. He is staying in the home of Simon, a tanner who lives near the seashore.' 33So I sent for you at once, and it was good of you to come. Now we are all here, waiting before God to hear the message the Lord has given you."

The Gentiles Hear the Good News

34Then Peter replied, "I see very clearly that God shows no favoritism. 35In every nation he accepts those who fear him and do what is right. 36This is the message of Good News for the people of Israel—that there is peace with God through Jesus Christ, who is Lord of all. 37You know what happened throughout Judea, beginning in Galilee, after John began preaching his message of baptism. 38And you know that God anointed Jesus of Nazareth with the Holy Spirit and with power. Then Jesus went around doing good and healing all who were oppressed by the devil, for God was with him.

39"And we apostles are witnesses of all he did throughout Judea and in Jerusalem. They put him to death by hanging him on a cross,* 40but God raised him to life on the third day. Then God allowed him to appear, 41not to the general public,* but to us whom God had chosen in advance to be his

"Then Peter replied, 'I see very clearly that God shows no favoritism. In every nation he accepts those who fear him and do what is right'" (Acts 10:34-35).

Then Peter hollered back and said, "I see fo' sho God ain't about playin' favorites. He's down with everybody, everywhere who's down with him and doing the right thing."

witnesses. We were those who ate and drank with him after he rose from the dead. ⁴²And he ordered us to preach everywhere and to testify that Jesus is the one appointed by God to be the judge of all—the living and the dead. ⁴³He is the one all the prophets testified about, saying that everyone who believes in him will have their sins forgiven through his name."

The Gentiles Receive the Holy Spirit

⁴⁴Even as Peter was saying these things, the Holy Spirit fell upon all who were listening to the message. ⁴⁵The Jewish believers* who came with Peter were amazed that the gift of the Holy Spirit had been poured out on the Gentiles, too. ⁴⁶For they heard them speaking in other tongues* and praising God.

Then Peter asked, ⁴⁷"Can anyone object to their being baptized, now that they have received the Holy Spirit just as we did?" ⁴⁸So he gave orders for them to be baptized in the name of Jesus Christ. Afterward Cornelius asked him to stay with them for several days.

CHAPTER 11

Peter Explains His Actions

Soon the news reached the apostles and other believers* in Judea that the Gentiles had received the word of God. ²But when Peter arrived back in Jerusalem, the Jewish believers* criticized him. ³"You entered the home of Gentiles* and even ate with them!" they said.

⁴Then Peter told them exactly what had happened. ⁵"I was in the town of Joppa," he said, "and while I was praying, I went into a trance and saw a vision. Something like a large sheet was let down by its four corners from the sky. And it came right down to me. ⁶When I looked inside the sheet, I saw all sorts of tame and wild animals, reptiles, and birds. ⁷And I heard a voice say, 'Get up, Peter; kill and eat them.'

⁸"'No, Lord,' I replied. 'I have never eaten anything that our Jewish laws have declared impure or unclean.*'

⁹"But the voice from heaven spoke again: 'Do not call something unclean if God has made it clean.' ¹⁰This happened three times before the sheet and all it contained was pulled back up to heaven.

¹¹"Just then three men who had been sent from Caesarea arrived at the house where we were staying. ¹²The Holy Spirit told me to go with them and not to worry that they were Gentiles. These six brothers here accompanied me, and we soon entered the home of the man who had sent for us. ¹³He told us how an angel had appeared to him in his home and had told him, 'Send messengers to Joppa, and summon a man named Simon Peter. ¹⁴He will tell you how you and everyone in your household can be saved!'

¹⁵"As I began to speak," Peter continued, "the Holy Spirit fell on them, just as he fell on us at the beginning. ¹⁶Then I thought of the Lord's words when he said, 'John baptized with* water, but you will be baptized with the Holy Spirit.' ¹⁷And since God gave these Gentiles the same gift he gave us when we believed in the Lord Jesus Christ, who was I to stand in God's way?"

¹⁸When the others heard this, they stopped objecting and began praising God. They said, "We can see that God has also given the Gentiles the privilege of repenting of their sins and receiving eternal life."

The Church in Antioch of Syria

¹⁹Meanwhile, the believers who had been scattered during the persecution after Stephen's death traveled as far as Phoenicia, Cyprus, and Antioch of Syria. They preached the word of God, but only to Jews. ²⁰However, some of the believers who went to Antioch from Cyprus and Cyrene began preaching to the Gentiles* about the Lord Jesus. ²¹The power of the Lord was with them, and a large

10:45 Greek *The faithful ones of the circumcision.* 10:46 Or *in other languages.* 11:1 Greek *brothers.* 11:2 Greek *those of the circumcision.* 11:3 Greek *of uncircumcised men.* 11:8 Greek *anything common or unclean.* 11:16 Or *in;* also in 11:16b. 11:20 Greek *the Hellenists* (i.e., those who speak Greek); other manuscripts read *the Greeks.*

number of these Gentiles believed and turned to the Lord.

²²When the church at Jerusalem heard what had happened, they sent Barnabas to Antioch. ²³When he arrived and saw this evidence of God's blessing, he was filled with joy, and he encouraged the believers to stay true to the Lord. ²⁴Barnabas was a good man, full of the Holy Spirit and strong in faith. And many people were brought to the Lord.

²⁵Then Barnabas went on to Tarsus to look for Saul. ²⁶When he found him, he brought him back to Antioch. Both of them stayed there with the church for a full year, teaching large crowds of people. (It was at Antioch that the believers* were first called Christians.)

²⁷During this time some prophets traveled from Jerusalem to Antioch. ²⁸One of them named Agabus stood up in one of the meetings and predicted by the Spirit that a great famine was coming upon the entire Roman world. (This was fulfilled during the reign of Claudius.) ²⁹So the believers in Antioch decided to send relief to the brothers and sisters* in Judea, everyone giving as much as they could. ³⁰This they did, entrusting their gifts to Barnabas and Saul to take to the elders of the church in Jerusalem.

CHAPTER 12

James Is Killed and Peter Is Imprisoned

About that time King Herod Agrippa* began to persecute some believers in the church. ²He had the apostle James (John's brother) killed with a sword. ³When Herod saw how much this pleased the Jewish people, he also arrested Peter. (This took place during the Passover celebration.*) ⁴Then he imprisoned him, placing him under the guard of four squads of four soldiers each. Herod intended to bring Peter out for public trial after the Passover. ⁵But while Peter was in prison, the church prayed very earnestly for him.

Peter's Miraculous Escape from Prison

⁶The night before Peter was to be placed on trial, he was asleep, fastened with two chains between two soldiers. Others stood guard at the prison gate. ⁷Suddenly, there was a bright light in the cell, and an angel of the Lord stood before Peter. The angel struck him on the side to awaken him and said, "Quick! Get up!" And the chains fell off his wrists. ⁸Then the angel told him, "Get dressed and put on your sandals." And he did. "Now put on your coat and follow me," the angel ordered.

⁹So Peter left the cell, following the angel. But all the time he thought it was a vision. He didn't realize it was actually happening. ¹⁰They passed the first and second guard posts and came to the iron gate leading to the city, and this opened for them all by itself. So they passed through and started walking down the street, and then the angel suddenly left him.

¹¹Peter finally came to his senses. "It's really true!" he said. "The Lord has sent his angel and saved me from Herod and from what the Jewish leaders* had planned to do to me!"

¹²When he realized this, he went to the home of Mary, the mother of John Mark, where many were gathered for prayer. ¹³He knocked at the door in the gate, and a servant girl named Rhoda came to open it. ¹⁴When she recognized Peter's voice, she was so overjoyed that, instead of opening the door, she ran back inside and told everyone, "Peter is standing at the door!"

¹⁵"You're out of your mind!" they said. When she insisted, they decided, "It must be his angel."

¹⁶Meanwhile, Peter continued knocking. When they finally opened the door and saw him, they were amazed. ¹⁷He motioned for them to quiet down and told them how the Lord had led him out of prison. "Tell James and the other brothers what happened," he said. And then he went to another place.

11:26 Greek disciples; also in 11:29.   11:29 Greek the brothers.   12:1 Greek Herod the king. He was the nephew of Herod Antipas and a grandson of Herod the Great.   12:3 Greek the days of unleavened bread.   12:11 Or the Jewish people.

¹⁸At dawn there was a great commotion among the soldiers about what had happened to Peter. ¹⁹Herod Agrippa ordered a thorough search for him. When he couldn't be found, Herod interrogated the guards and sentenced them to death. Afterward Herod left Judea to stay in Caesarea for a while.

The Death of Herod Agrippa

²⁰Now Herod was very angry with the people of Tyre and Sidon. So they sent a delegation to make peace with him because their cities were dependent upon Herod's country for food. The delegates won the support of Blastus, Herod's personal assistant, ²¹and an appointment with Herod was granted. When the day arrived, Herod put on his royal robes, sat on his throne, and made a speech to them. ²²The people gave him a great ovation, shouting, "It's the voice of a god, not of a man!"

²³Instantly, an angel of the Lord struck Herod with a sickness, because he accepted the people's worship instead of giving the glory to God. So he was consumed with worms and died.

²⁴Meanwhile, the word of God continued to spread, and there were many new believers.

²⁵When Barnabas and Saul had finished their mission to Jerusalem, they returned,* taking John Mark with them.

CHAPTER 13

Barnabas and Saul Are Commissioned

Among the prophets and teachers of the church at Antioch of Syria were Barnabas, Simeon (called "the black man"*), Lucius (from Cyrene), Manaen (the childhood companion of King Herod Antipas*), and Saul. ²One day as these men were worshiping the Lord and fasting, the Holy Spirit said, "Dedicate Barnabas and Saul for the special work to which I have called them." ³So after more fasting and prayer, the men laid their hands on them and sent them on their way.

Paul's First Missionary Journey

⁴So Barnabas and Saul were sent out by the Holy Spirit. They went down to the seaport of Seleucia and then sailed for the island of Cyprus. ⁵There, in the town of Salamis, they went to the Jewish synagogues and preached the word of God. John Mark went with them as their assistant.

⁶Afterward they traveled from town to town across the entire island until finally they reached Paphos, where they met a Jewish sorcerer, a false prophet named Bar-Jesus. ⁷He had attached himself to the governor, Sergius Paulus, who was an intelligent man. The governor invited Barnabas and Saul to visit him, for he wanted to hear the word of God. ⁸But Elymas, the sorcerer (as his name means in Greek), interfered and urged the governor to pay no attention to what Barnabas and Saul said. He was trying to keep the governor from believing.

⁹Saul, also known as Paul, was filled with the Holy Spirit, and he looked the sorcerer in the eye. ¹⁰Then he said, "You son of the devil, full of every sort of deceit and fraud, and enemy of all that is good! Will you never stop perverting the true ways of the Lord? ¹¹Watch now, for the Lord has laid his hand of punishment upon you, and you will be struck blind. You will not see the sunlight for some time." Instantly mist and darkness came over the man's eyes, and he began groping around begging for someone to take his hand and lead him.

¹²When the governor saw what had happened, he became a believer, for he was astonished at the teaching about the Lord.

Paul Preaches in Antioch of Pisidia

¹³Paul and his companions then left Paphos by ship for Pamphylia, landing at the port town of Perga. There John Mark left them and returned to Jerusalem. ¹⁴But Paul and Barnabas traveled inland to Antioch of Pisidia.*

12:25 Or *mission, they returned to Jerusalem.* Other manuscripts read *mission, they returned from Jerusalem;* still others read *mission, they returned from Jerusalem to Antioch.*   13:1a Greek *who was called Niger.*   13:1b Greek *Herod the tetrarch.*   13:13-14 *Pamphylia* and *Pisidia* were districts in what is now Turkey.

On the Sabbath they went to the synagogue for the services. [15]After the usual readings from the books of Moses* and the prophets, those in charge of the service sent them this message: "Brothers, if you have any word of encouragement for the people, come and give it."

[16]So Paul stood, lifted his hand to quiet them, and started speaking. "Men of Israel," he said, "and you God-fearing Gentiles, listen to me.

[17]"The God of this nation of Israel chose our ancestors and made them multiply and grow strong during their stay in Egypt. Then with a powerful arm he led them out of their slavery. [18]He put up with them* through forty years of wandering in the wilderness. [19]Then he destroyed seven nations in Canaan and gave their land to Israel as an inheritance. [20]All this took about 450 years.

"After that, God gave them judges to rule until the time of Samuel the prophet. [21]Then the people begged for a king, and God gave them Saul son of Kish, a man of the tribe of Benjamin, who reigned for forty years. [22]But God removed Saul and replaced him with David, a man about whom God said, 'I have found David son of Jesse, a man after my own heart. He will do everything I want him to do.'*

[23]"And it is one of King David's descendants, Jesus, who is God's promised Savior of Israel! [24]Before he came, John the Baptist preached that all the people of Israel needed to repent of their sins and turn to God and be baptized. [25]As John was finishing his ministry he asked, 'Do you think I am the Messiah? No, I am not! But he is coming soon—and I'm not even worthy to be his slave and untie the sandals on his feet.'

[26]"Brothers—you sons of Abraham, and also you God-fearing Gentiles—this message of salvation has been sent to us! [27]The people in Jerusalem and their leaders did not recognize Jesus as the one the prophets had spoken about. Instead, they condemned him, and in doing this they fulfilled the prophets' words that are read every Sabbath. [28]They found no legal reason to execute him, but they asked Pilate to have him killed anyway.

[29]"When they had done all that the prophecies said about him, they took him down from the cross* and placed him in a tomb. [30]But God raised him from the dead! [31]And over a period of many days he appeared to those who had gone with him from Galilee to Jerusalem. They are now his witnesses to the people of Israel.

[32]"And now we are here to bring you this Good News. The promise was made to our ancestors, [33]and God has now fulfilled it for us, their descendants, by raising Jesus. This is what the second psalm says about Jesus:

'You are my Son.
  Today I have become your Father.*'

[34]For God had promised to raise him from the dead, not leaving him to rot in the grave. He said, 'I will give you the sacred blessings I promised to David.'* [35]Another psalm explains it more fully: 'You will not allow your Holy One to rot in the grave.'* [36]This is not a reference to David, for after David had done the will of God in his own generation, he died and was buried with his ancestors, and his body decayed. [37]No, it was a reference to someone else—someone whom God raised and whose body did not decay.

[38]*"Brothers, listen! We are here to proclaim that through this man Jesus there is forgiveness for your sins. [39]Everyone who believes in him is declared right with God—something the law of Moses could never do. [40]Be careful! Don't let the prophets' words apply to you. For they said,

[41] 'Look, you mockers,
  be amazed and die!
For I am doing something in your own day,
  something you wouldn't believe
  even if someone told you about it.'*"

13:15 Greek *from the law.* **13:18** Some manuscripts read *He cared for them;* compare Deut 1:31. **13:22** 1 Sam 13:14. **13:29** Greek *from the tree.* **13:33** Or *Today I reveal you as my Son.* Ps 2:7. **13:34** Isa 55:3. **13:35** Ps 16:10. **13:38** English translations divide verses 38 and 39 in various ways. **13:41** Hab 1:5 (Greek version).

⁴²As Paul and Barnabas left the synagogue that day, the people begged them to speak about these things again the next week. ⁴³Many Jews and devout converts to Judaism followed Paul and Barnabas, and the two men urged them to continue to rely on the grace of God.

Paul Turns to the Gentiles

⁴⁴The following week almost the entire city turned out to hear them preach the word of the Lord. ⁴⁵But when some of the Jews saw the crowds, they were jealous; so they slandered Paul and argued against whatever he said.

⁴⁶Then Paul and Barnabas spoke out boldly and declared, "It was necessary that we first preach the word of God to you Jews. But since you have rejected it and judged yourselves unworthy of eternal life, we will offer it to the Gentiles. ⁴⁷For the Lord gave us this command when he said,

'I have made you a light to the Gentiles,
   to bring salvation to the farthest corners of the
   earth.'*"

⁴⁸When the Gentiles heard this, they were very glad and thanked the Lord for his message; and all who were chosen for eternal life became believers. ⁴⁹So the Lord's message spread throughout that region.

⁵⁰Then the Jews stirred up the influential religious women and the leaders of the city, and they incited a mob against Paul and Barnabas and ran them out of town. ⁵¹So they shook the dust from their feet as a sign of rejection and went to the town of Iconium. ⁵²And the believers* were filled with joy and with the Holy Spirit.

CHAPTER 14

Paul and Barnabas in Iconium

The same thing happened in Iconium.* Paul and Barnabas went to the Jewish synagogue and preached with such power that a great number of both Jews and Greeks became believers. ²Some of the Jews, however, spurned God's message and poisoned the minds of the Gentiles against Paul and Barnabas. ³But the apostles stayed there a long time, preaching boldly about the grace of the Lord. And the Lord proved their message was true by giving them power to do miraculous signs and wonders. ⁴But the people of the town were divided in their opinion about them. Some sided with the Jews, and some with the apostles.

⁵Then a mob of Gentiles and Jews, along with their leaders, decided to attack and stone them. ⁶When the apostles learned of it, they fled to the region of Lycaonia—to the towns of Lystra and Derbe and the surrounding area. ⁷And there they preached the Good News.

Paul and Barnabas in Lystra and Derbe

⁸While they were at Lystra, Paul and Barnabas came upon a man with crippled feet. He had been that way from birth, so he had never walked. He was sitting ⁹and listening as Paul preached. Looking straight at him, Paul realized he had faith to be healed. ¹⁰So Paul called to him in a loud voice, "Stand up!" And the man jumped to his feet and started walking.

¹¹When the crowd saw what Paul had done, they shouted in their local dialect, "These men are gods in human form!" ¹²They decided that Barnabas was the Greek god Zeus and that Paul was Hermes, since he was the chief speaker. ¹³Now the temple of Zeus was located just outside the town. So the priest of the temple and the crowd brought bulls and wreaths of flowers to the town gates, and they prepared to offer sacrifices to the apostles.

¹⁴But when the apostles Barnabas and Paul heard what was happening, they tore their clothing in dismay and ran out among the people, shouting, ¹⁵"Friends,* why are you doing this? We are merely human beings—just like you! We have come to bring you the Good News that you should turn from these worthless things and turn to the living God, who made heaven and earth, the sea, and everything in them.

13:47 Isa 49:6.   13:52 Greek *the disciples*.   14:1 *Iconium*, as well as *Lystra* and *Derbe* (14:6), were towns in what is now Turkey.   14:15 Greek *Men*.

[16]In the past he permitted all the nations to go their own ways, [17]but he never left them without evidence of himself and his goodness. For instance, he sends you rain and good crops and gives you food and joyful hearts." [18]But even with these words, Paul and Barnabas could scarcely restrain the people from sacrificing to them.

[19]Then some Jews arrived from Antioch and Iconium and won the crowds to their side. They stoned Paul and dragged him out of town, thinking he was dead. [20]But as the believers* gathered around him, he got up and went back into the town. The next day he left with Barnabas for Derbe.

Paul and Barnabas Return to Antioch of Syria

[21]After preaching the Good News in Derbe and making many disciples, Paul and Barnabas returned to Lystra, Iconium, and Antioch of Pisidia, [22]where they strengthened the believers. They encouraged them to continue in the faith, reminding them that we must suffer many hardships to enter the Kingdom of God. [23]Paul and Barnabas also appointed elders in every church. With prayer and fasting, they turned the elders over to the care of the Lord, in whom they had put their trust. [24]Then they traveled back through Pisidia to Pamphylia. [25]They preached the word in Perga, then went down to Attalia.

[26]Finally, they returned by ship to Antioch of Syria, where their journey had begun. The believers there had entrusted them to the grace of God to do the work they had now completed. [27]Upon arriving in Antioch, they called the church together and reported everything God had done through them and how he had opened the door of faith to the Gentiles, too. [28]And they stayed there with the believers for a long time.

CHAPTER 15

The Council at Jerusalem

While Paul and Barnabas were at Antioch of Syria, some men from Judea arrived and began to teach the believers*: "Unless you are circumcised as required by the law of Moses, you cannot be saved." [2]Paul and Barnabas disagreed with them, arguing vehemently. Finally, the church decided to send Paul and Barnabas to Jerusalem, accompanied by some local believers, to talk to the apostles and elders about this question. [3]The church sent the delegates to Jerusalem, and they stopped along the way in Phoenicia and Samaria to visit the believers. They told them—much to everyone's joy—that the Gentiles, too, were being converted.

[4]When they arrived in Jerusalem, Barnabas and Paul were welcomed by the whole church, including the apostles and elders. They reported everything God had done through them. [5]But then some of the believers who belonged to the sect of the Pharisees stood up and insisted, "The Gentile converts must be circumcised and required to follow the law of Moses."

[6]So the apostles and elders met together to resolve this issue. [7]At the meeting, after a long discussion, Peter stood and addressed them as follows: "Brothers, you all know that God chose me from among you some time ago to preach to the Gentiles so that they could hear the Good News and believe. [8]God knows people's hearts, and he confirmed that he accepts Gentiles by giving them the Holy Spirit, just as he did to us. [9]He made no distinction between us and them, for he cleansed their hearts through faith. [10]So why are you now challenging God by burdening the Gentile believers* with a yoke that neither we nor our ancestors were able to bear? [11]We believe that we are all saved the same way, by the undeserved grace of the Lord Jesus."

[12]Everyone listened quietly as Barnabas and Paul told about the miraculous signs and wonders God had done through them among the Gentiles.

[13]When they had finished, James stood and said, "Brothers, listen to me. [14]Peter* has told you about the time God first visited the Gentiles to take from them a people for

14:20 Greek disciples; also in 14:22, 28.   15:1 Greek brothers; also in 15:3, 23, 32, 33, 36, 40.   15:10 Greek disciples.   15:14 Greek Symeon.

himself. 15And this conversion of Gentiles is exactly what the prophets predicted. As it is written:

16 'Afterward I will return
    and restore the fallen house* of David.
  I will rebuild its ruins
    and restore it,
17 so that the rest of humanity might seek the LORD,
    including the Gentiles—
    all those I have called to be mine.
  The LORD has spoken—
18 he who made these things known so long ago.'*

19"And so my judgment is that we should not make it difficult for the Gentiles who are turning to God. 20Instead, we should write and tell them to abstain from eating food offered to idols, from sexual immorality, from eating the meat of strangled animals, and from consuming blood. 21For these laws of Moses have been preached in Jewish synagogues in every city on every Sabbath for many generations."

The Letter for Gentile Believers

22Then the apostles and elders together with the whole church in Jerusalem chose delegates, and they sent them to Antioch of Syria with Paul and Barnabas to report on this decision. The men chosen were two of the church leaders*—Judas (also called Barsabbas) and Silas. 23This is the letter they took with them:

"This letter is from the apostles and elders, your brothers in Jerusalem. It is written to the Gentile believers in Antioch, Syria, and Cilicia. Greetings!

24"We understand that some men from here have troubled you and upset you with their teaching, but we did not send them! 25So we decided, having come to complete agreement, to send you official representatives, along with our beloved Barnabas and Paul, 26who have risked their lives for the name of our Lord Jesus Christ. 27We are sending Judas and Silas to confirm what we have decided concerning your question.

28"For it seemed good to the Holy Spirit and to us to lay no greater burden on you than these few requirements: 29You must abstain from eating food offered to idols, from consuming blood or the meat of strangled animals, and from sexual immorality. If you do this, you will do well. Farewell."

30The messengers went at once to Antioch, where they called a general meeting of the believers and delivered the letter. 31And there was great joy throughout the church that day as they read this encouraging message.

32Then Judas and Silas, both being prophets, spoke at length to the believers, encouraging and strengthening their faith. 33They stayed for a while, and then the believers sent them back to the church in Jerusalem with a blessing of peace.* 35Paul and Barnabas stayed in Antioch. They and many others taught and preached the word of the Lord there.

Paul and Barnabas Separate

36After some time Paul said to Barnabas, "Let's go back and visit each city where we previously preached the word of the Lord, to see how the new believers are doing." 37Barnabas agreed and wanted to take along John Mark. 38But Paul disagreed strongly, since John Mark had deserted them in Pamphylia and had not continued with them in their work. 39Their disagreement was so sharp that they separated. Barnabas took John Mark with him and sailed for Cyprus. 40Paul chose Silas, and as he left, the believers entrusted him to the Lord's gracious care. 41Then he traveled throughout Syria and Cilicia, strengthening the churches there.

15:16 Or *kingdom;* Greek reads *tent.*   15:16-18 Amos 9:11-12 (Greek version); Isa 45:21.   15:22 Greek *were leaders among the brothers.*   15:33 Some manuscripts add verse 34, *But Silas decided to stay there.*

CHAPTER 16

Paul's Second Missionary Journey

Paul went first to Derbe and then to Lystra, where there was a young disciple named Timothy. His mother was a Jewish believer, but his father was a Greek. ²Timothy was well thought of by the believers* in Lystra and Iconium, ³so Paul wanted him to join them on their journey. In deference to the Jews of the area, he arranged for Timothy to be circumcised before they left, for everyone knew that his father was a Greek. ⁴Then they went from town to town, instructing the believers to follow the decisions made by the apostles and elders in Jerusalem. ⁵So the churches were strengthened in their faith and grew larger every day.

A Call from Macedonia

⁶Next Paul and Silas traveled through the area of Phrygia and Galatia, because the Holy Spirit had prevented them from preaching the word in the province of Asia at that time. ⁷Then coming to the borders of Mysia, they headed north for the province of Bithynia,* but again the Spirit of Jesus did not allow them to go there. ⁸So instead, they went on through Mysia to the seaport of Troas.

⁹That night Paul had a vision: A man from Macedonia in northern Greece was standing there, pleading with him, "Come over to Macedonia and help us!" ¹⁰So we* decided to leave for Macedonia at once, having concluded that God was calling us to preach the Good News there.

Lydia of Philippi Believes in Jesus

¹¹We boarded a boat at Troas and sailed straight across to the island of Samothrace, and the next day we landed at Neapolis. ¹²From there we reached Philippi, a major city of that district of Macedonia and a Roman colony. And we stayed there several days.

¹³On the Sabbath we went a little way outside the city to a riverbank, where we thought people would be meeting for prayer, and we sat down to speak with some women who had gathered there. ¹⁴One of them was Lydia from Thyatira, a merchant of expensive purple cloth, who worshiped God. As she listened to us, the Lord opened her heart, and she accepted what Paul was saying. ¹⁵She was baptized along with other members of her household, and she asked us to be her guests. "If you agree that I am a true believer in the Lord," she said, "come and stay at my home." And she urged us until we agreed.

16:2 Greek *brothers;* also in 16:40.   **16:6-7** *Phrygia, Galatia, Asia, Mysia,* and *Bithynia* were all districts in what is now Turkey.   **16:10** Luke, the writer of this book, here joined Paul and accompanied him on his journey.

THE POINT

Praisin' in pain. So maybe you haven't heard the story of what happened when Paul and Silas were in prison. Just in case you haven't, this is how it all went down:

Around midnight Paul and Silas were praying and singing hymns to God, and the other prisoners were listening. Suddenly, there was a massive earthquake, and the prison was shaken to its foundations. All the doors immediately flew open, and the chains of every prisoner fell off! (Acts 16:25-26)

Paul and Silas were in prison because they had upset some men who hoped to become wealthy by selling the services of a fortune-tellin' demon-possessed girl. But her demonic possession frustrated Paul and Silas, who had to pass by her every day in order to reach their place of prayer. Paul cast the demon out, and that's where their trouble began. The government officials had Paul and Silas stripped and beaten. Afterward, they were thrown in prison. Despite this bad situation, they prayed and sang to the

Lord. Soon, the prisoners were freed from their chains and prison cells.

Life is rough, and sometimes unfair things happen to us. No matter what happens, learn to pray and praise God. Pray and sing. Sing and pray. Continue to talk to God until he makes somethin' happen for you. And like with Paul and Silas, along the way you may get a chance to change someone else's life.

Paul and Silas in Prison

¹⁶One day as we were going down to the place of prayer, we met a demon-possessed slave girl. She was a fortune-teller who earned a lot of money for her masters. ¹⁷She followed Paul and the rest of us, shouting, "These men are servants of the Most High God, and they have come to tell you how to be saved."

¹⁸This went on day after day until Paul got so exasperated that he turned and said to the demon within her, "I command you in the name of Jesus Christ to come out of her." And instantly it left her.

¹⁹Her masters' hopes of wealth were now shattered, so they grabbed Paul and Silas and dragged them before the authorities at the marketplace. ²⁰"The whole city is in an uproar because of these Jews!" they shouted to the city officials. ²¹"They are teaching customs that are illegal for us Romans to practice."

²²A mob quickly formed against Paul and Silas, and the city officials ordered them stripped and beaten with wooden rods. ²³They were severely beaten, and then they were thrown into prison. The jailer was ordered to make sure they didn't escape. ²⁴So the jailer put them into the inner dungeon and clamped their feet in the stocks.

²⁵Around midnight Paul and Silas were praying and singing hymns to God, and the other prisoners were listening. ²⁶Suddenly, there was a massive earthquake, and the prison was shaken to its foundations. All the doors immediately flew open, and the chains of every prisoner fell off! ²⁷The jailer woke up to see the prison doors wide open. He assumed the prisoners had escaped, so he drew his sword to kill himself. ²⁸But Paul shouted to him, "Stop! Don't kill yourself! We are all here!"

²⁹The jailer called for lights and ran to the dungeon and fell down trembling before Paul and Silas. ³⁰Then he brought them out and asked, "Sirs, what must I do to be saved?"

³¹They replied, "Believe in the Lord Jesus and you will be saved, along with everyone in your household." ³²And they shared the word of the Lord with him and with all who lived in his household. ³³Even at that hour of the night, the jailer cared for them and washed their wounds. Then he and everyone in his household were immediately baptized. ³⁴He brought them into his house and set a meal before them, and he and his entire household rejoiced because they all believed in God.

³⁵The next morning the city officials sent the police to tell the jailer, "Let those men go!" ³⁶So the jailer told Paul, "The city officials have said you and Silas are free to leave. Go in peace."

³⁷But Paul replied, "They have publicly beaten us without a trial and put us in prison—and we are Roman citizens. So now they want us to leave secretly? Certainly not! Let them come themselves to release us!"

³⁸When the police reported this, the city officials were alarmed to learn that Paul and Silas were Roman citizens. ³⁹So they came to the jail and apologized to them. Then they brought them out and begged them to leave the city. ⁴⁰When Paul and Silas left the prison, they returned to the home of Lydia. There they met with the believers and encouraged them once more. Then they left town.

CHAPTER 17

Paul Preaches in Thessalonica

Paul and Silas then traveled through the towns of Amphipolis and Apollonia and came to Thessalonica, where there was a Jewish synagogue. ²As was Paul's custom, he went to the synagogue service, and for three Sabbaths in a row he used the Scriptures to reason with the people. ³He explained the prophecies and proved that the Messiah must suffer and rise from the dead. He said, "This Jesus I'm telling you about is the Messiah." ⁴Some of the Jews who listened were persuaded and joined Paul and Silas, along with many God-fearing Greek men and quite a few prominent women.*

⁵But some of the Jews were jealous, so they gathered some

17:4 Some manuscripts read quite a few of the wives of the leading men.

troublemakers from the marketplace to form a mob and start a riot. They attacked the home of Jason, searching for Paul and Silas so they could drag them out to the crowd.* ⁶Not finding them there, they dragged out Jason and some of the other believers* instead and took them before the city council. "Paul and Silas have caused trouble all over the world," they shouted, "and now they are here disturbing our city, too. ⁷And Jason has welcomed them into his home. They are all guilty of treason against Caesar, for they profess allegiance to another king, named Jesus."

⁸The people of the city, as well as the city council, were thrown into turmoil by these reports. ⁹So the officials forced Jason and the other believers to post bond, and then they released them.

Paul and Silas in Berea

¹⁰That very night the believers sent Paul and Silas to Berea. When they arrived there, they went to the Jewish synagogue. ¹¹And the people of Berea were more open-minded than those in Thessalonica, and they listened eagerly to Paul's message. They searched the Scriptures day after day to see if Paul and Silas were teaching the truth. ¹²As a result, many Jews believed, as did many of the prominent Greek women and men.

¹³But when some Jews in Thessalonica learned that Paul was preaching the word of God in Berea, they went there and stirred up trouble. ¹⁴The believers acted at once, sending Paul on to the coast, while Silas and Timothy remained behind. ¹⁵Those escorting Paul went with him all the way to Athens; then they returned to Berea with instructions for Silas and Timothy to hurry and join him.

Paul Preaches in Athens

¹⁶While Paul was waiting for them in Athens, he was deeply troubled by all the idols he saw everywhere in the city. ¹⁷He went to the synagogue to reason with the Jews and the God-fearing Gentiles, and he spoke daily in the public square to all who happened to be there.

¹⁸He also had a debate with some of the Epicurean and Stoic philosophers. When he told them about Jesus and his resurrection, they said, "What's this babbler trying to say with these strange ideas he's picked up?" Others said, "He seems to be preaching about some foreign gods."

¹⁹Then they took him to the high council of the city.* "Come and tell us about this new teaching," they said. ²⁰"You are saying some rather strange things, and we want to know what it's all about." ²¹(It should be explained that all the Athenians as well as the foreigners in Athens seemed to spend all their time discussing the latest ideas.)

²²So Paul, standing before the council,* addressed them as follows: "Men of Athens, I notice that you are very religious in every way, ²³for as I was walking along I saw your many shrines. And one of your altars had this inscription on it: 'To an Unknown God.' This God, whom you worship without knowing, is the one I'm telling you about.

²⁴"He is the God who made the world and everything in it. Since he is Lord of heaven and earth, he doesn't live in man-made temples, ²⁵and human hands can't serve his needs—for he has no needs. He himself gives life and breath to everything, and he satisfies every need. ²⁶From one man* he created all the nations throughout the whole earth. He decided beforehand when they should rise and fall, and he determined their boundaries.

²⁷"His purpose was for the nations to seek after God and perhaps feel their way toward him and find him—though he is not far from any one of us. ²⁸For in him we live and move and exist. As some of your* own poets have said, 'We are his offspring.' ²⁹And since this is true, we shouldn't think of God as an idol designed by craftsmen from gold or silver or stone.

"And the people of Berea were more open-minded than those in Thessalonica, and they listened eagerly to Paul's message. They searched the Scriptures day after day to see if Paul and Silas were teaching the truth" (Acts 17:11).

And the homies in Berea were more open-minded than the homies in Thessolonica, and they listened to the jewels Paul was droppin' with their ears wide open. They looked up what he was sayin' each day in the Bible to make sure Paul and Silas was spittin' the truth.

17:5 Or *the city council.* 17:6 Greek *brothers;* also in 17:10, 14. 17:19 Or *the most learned society of philosophers in the city,* Greek reads *the Areopagus.* 17:22 Traditionally rendered *standing in the middle of Mars Hill;* Greek reads *standing in the middle of the Areopagus.* 17:26 Greek *From one;* other manuscripts read *From one blood.* 17:28 Some manuscripts read *our.*

³⁰"God overlooked people's ignorance about these things in earlier times, but now he commands everyone everywhere to repent of their sins and turn to him. ³¹For he has set a day for judging the world with justice by the man he has appointed, and he proved to everyone who this is by raising him from the dead."

³²When they heard Paul speak about the resurrection of the dead, some laughed in contempt, but others said, "We want to hear more about this later." ³³That ended Paul's discussion with them, ³⁴but some joined him and became believers. Among them were Dionysius, a member of the council,* a woman named Damaris, and others with them.

CHAPTER 18

Paul Meets Priscilla and Aquila in Corinth

Then Paul left Athens and went to Corinth.* ²There he became acquainted with a Jew named Aquila, born in Pontus, who had recently arrived from Italy with his wife, Priscilla. They had left Italy when Claudius Caesar deported all Jews from Rome. ³Paul lived and worked with them, for they were tentmakers* just as he was.

⁴Each Sabbath found Paul at the synagogue, trying to convince the Jews and Greeks alike. ⁵And after Silas and Timothy came down from Macedonia, Paul spent all his time preaching the word. He testified to the Jews that Jesus was the Messiah. ⁶But when they opposed and insulted him, Paul shook the dust from his clothes and said, "Your blood is upon your own heads—I am innocent. From now on I will go preach to the Gentiles."

⁷Then he left and went to the home of Titius Justus, a Gentile who worshiped God and lived next door to the synagogue. ⁸Crispus, the leader of the synagogue, and everyone in his household believed in the Lord. Many others in Corinth also heard Paul, became believers, and were baptized.

⁹One night the Lord spoke to Paul in a vision and told him, "Don't be afraid! Speak out! Don't be silent! ¹⁰For I am with you, and no one will attack and harm you, for many people in this city belong to me." ¹¹So Paul stayed there for the next year and a half, teaching the word of God.

¹²But when Gallio became governor of Achaia, some Jews rose up together against Paul and brought him before the governor for judgment. ¹³They accused Paul of "persuading people to worship God in ways that are contrary to our law."

¹⁴But just as Paul started to make his defense, Gallio turned to Paul's accusers and said, "Listen, you Jews, if this were a case involving some wrongdoing or a serious crime, I would have a reason to accept your case. ¹⁵But since it is merely a question of words and names and your Jewish law, take care of it yourselves. I refuse to judge such matters." ¹⁶And he threw them out of the courtroom.

¹⁷The crowd* then grabbed Sosthenes, the leader of the synagogue, and beat him right there in the courtroom. But Gallio paid no attention.

Paul Returns to Antioch of Syria

¹⁸Paul stayed in Corinth for some time after that, then said good-bye to the brothers and sisters* and went to nearby Cenchrea. There he shaved his head according to Jewish custom, marking the end of a vow. Then he set sail for Syria, taking Priscilla and Aquila with him.

¹⁹They stopped first at the port of Ephesus, where Paul left the others behind. While he was there, he went to the synagogue to reason with the Jews. ²⁰They asked him to stay longer, but he declined. ²¹As he left, however, he said, "I will come back later,* God willing." Then he set sail from Ephesus. ²²The next stop was at the port of Caesarea. From there he went up and visited the church at Jerusalem* and then went back to Antioch.

17:34 Greek *an Areopagite.* **18:1** *Athens* and *Corinth* were major cities in Achaia, the region in the southern portion of the Greek peninsula. **18:3** Or *leatherworkers.* **18:17** Greek *Everyone;* other manuscripts read *All the Greeks.* **18:18** Greek *brothers;* also in 18:27. **18:21** Some manuscripts read *"I must by all means be at Jerusalem for the upcoming festival, but I will come back later."* **18:22** Greek *the church.*

²³After spending some time in Antioch, Paul went back through Galatia and Phrygia, visiting and strengthening all the believers.*

Apollos Instructed at Ephesus

²⁴Meanwhile, a Jew named Apollos, an eloquent speaker who knew the Scriptures well, had arrived in Ephesus from Alexandria in Egypt. ²⁵He had been taught the way of the Lord, and he taught others about Jesus with an enthusiastic spirit* and with accuracy. However, he knew only about John's baptism. ²⁶When Priscilla and Aquila heard him preaching boldly in the synagogue, they took him aside and explained the way of God even more accurately.

²⁷Apollos had been thinking about going to Achaia, and the brothers and sisters in Ephesus encouraged him to go. They wrote to the believers in Achaia, asking them to welcome him. When he arrived there, he proved to be of great benefit to those who, by God's grace, had believed. ²⁸He refuted the Jews with powerful arguments in public debate. Using the Scriptures, he explained to them that Jesus was the Messiah.

CHAPTER 19

Paul's Third Missionary Journey

While Apollos was in Corinth, Paul traveled through the interior regions until he reached Ephesus, on the coast, where he found several believers.* ²"Did you receive the Holy Spirit when you believed?" he asked them.

"No," they replied, "we haven't even heard that there is a Holy Spirit."

³"Then what baptism did you experience?" he asked.

And they replied, "The baptism of John."

⁴Paul said, "John's baptism called for repentance from sin. But John himself told the people to believe in the one who would come later, meaning Jesus."

⁵As soon as they heard this, they were baptized in the name of the Lord Jesus. ⁶Then when Paul laid his hands on them, the Holy Spirit came on them, and they spoke in other tongues* and prophesied. ⁷There were about twelve men in all.

Paul Ministers in Ephesus

⁸Then Paul went to the synagogue and preached boldly for the next three months, arguing persuasively about the Kingdom of God. ⁹But some became stubborn, rejecting his message and publicly speaking against the Way. So Paul left the synagogue and took the believers with him. Then he held daily discussions at the lecture hall of Tyrannus. ¹⁰This went on for the next two years, so that people throughout the province of Asia—both Jews and Greeks—heard the word of the Lord.

¹¹God gave Paul the power to perform unusual miracles. ¹²When handkerchiefs or aprons that had merely touched his skin were placed on sick people, they were healed of their diseases, and evil spirits were expelled.

¹³A group of Jews was traveling from town to town casting out evil spirits. They tried to use the name of the Lord Jesus in their incantation, saying, "I command you in the name of Jesus, whom Paul preaches, to come out!" ¹⁴Seven sons of Sceva, a leading priest, were doing this. ¹⁵But one time when they tried it, the evil spirit replied, "I know Jesus, and I know Paul, but who are you?" ¹⁶Then the man with the evil spirit leaped on them, overpowered them, and attacked them with such violence that they fled from the house, naked and battered.

¹⁷The story of what happened spread quickly all through Ephesus, to Jews and Greeks alike. A solemn fear descended on the city, and the name of the Lord Jesus was greatly honored. ¹⁸Many who became believers confessed their sinful practices. ¹⁹A number of them who had been practicing sorcery brought their incantation books and burned them at a public bonfire. The value of the books was several million

18:23 Greek *disciples;* also in 18:27.   18:25 Or *with enthusiasm in the Spirit.*   19:1 Greek *disciples;* also in 19:9, 30.   19:6 Or *in other languages.*

dollars.* ²⁰So the message about the Lord spread widely and had a powerful effect.

²¹Afterward Paul felt compelled by the Spirit* to go over to Macedonia and Achaia before going to Jerusalem. "And after that," he said, "I must go on to Rome!" ²²He sent his two assistants, Timothy and Erastus, ahead to Macedonia while he stayed awhile longer in the province of Asia.

The Riot in Ephesus

²³About that time, serious trouble developed in Ephesus concerning the Way. ²⁴It began with Demetrius, a silversmith who had a large business manufacturing silver shrines of the Greek goddess Artemis.* He kept many craftsmen busy. ²⁵He called them together, along with others employed in similar trades, and addressed them as follows:

"Gentlemen, you know that our wealth comes from this business. ²⁶But as you have seen and heard, this man Paul has persuaded many people that handmade gods aren't really gods at all. And he's done this not only here in Ephesus but throughout the entire province! ²⁷Of course, I'm not just talking about the loss of public respect for our business. I'm also concerned that the temple of the great goddess Artemis will lose its influence and that Artemis—this magnificent goddess worshiped throughout the province of Asia and all around the world—will be robbed of her great prestige!"

²⁸At this their anger boiled, and they began shouting, "Great is Artemis of the Ephesians!" ²⁹Soon the whole city was filled with confusion. Everyone rushed to the amphitheater, dragging along Gaius and Aristarchus, who were Paul's traveling companions from Macedonia. ³⁰Paul wanted to go in, too, but the believers wouldn't let him. ³¹Some of the officials of the province, friends of Paul, also sent a message to him, begging him not to risk his life by entering the amphitheater.

³²Inside, the people were all shouting, some one thing and some another. Everything was in confusion. In fact, most of them didn't even know why they were there. ³³The Jews in the crowd pushed Alexander forward and told him to explain the situation. He motioned for silence and tried to speak. ³⁴But when the crowd realized he was a Jew, they started shouting again and kept it up for about two hours: "Great is Artemis of the Ephesians! Great is Artemis of the Ephesians!"

³⁵At last the mayor was able to quiet them down enough to speak. "Citizens of Ephesus," he said. "Everyone knows that Ephesus is the official guardian of the temple of the great Artemis, whose image fell down to us from heaven. ³⁶Since this is an undeniable fact, you should stay calm and not do anything rash. ³⁷You have brought these men here, but they have stolen nothing from the temple and have not spoken against our goddess.

³⁸"If Demetrius and the craftsmen have a case against them, the courts are in session and the officials can hear the case at once. Let them make formal charges. ³⁹And if there are complaints about other matters, they can be settled in a legal assembly. ⁴⁰I am afraid we are in danger of being charged with rioting by the Roman government, since there is no cause for all this commotion. And if Rome demands an explanation, we won't know what to say." ⁴¹*Then he dismissed them, and they dispersed.

CHAPTER 20

Paul Goes to Macedonia and Greece

When the uproar was over, Paul sent for the believers* and encouraged them. Then he said good-bye and left for Macedonia. ²While there, he encouraged the believers in all the towns he passed through. Then he traveled down to Greece, ³where he stayed for three months. He was preparing to sail back to Syria when he discovered a plot by

19:19 Greek *50,000 pieces of silver,* each of which was the equivalent of a day's wage.   19:21 Or *decided in his spirit.*   19:24 *Artemis* is otherwise known as Diana.   19:41 Some translations include verse 41 as part of verse 40.   20:1 Greek *disciples.*

some Jews against his life, so he decided to return through Macedonia.

[4] Several men were traveling with him. They were Sopater son of Pyrrhus from Berea; Aristarchus and Secundus from Thessalonica; Gaius from Derbe; Timothy; and Tychicus and Trophimus from the province of Asia. [5] They went on ahead and waited for us at Troas. [6] After the Passover* ended, we boarded a ship at Philippi in Macedonia and five days later joined them in Troas, where we stayed a week.

Paul's Final Visit to Troas

[7] On the first day of the week, we gathered with the local believers to share in the Lord's Supper.* Paul was preaching to them, and since he was leaving the next day, he kept talking until midnight. [8] The upstairs room where we met was lighted with many flickering lamps. [9] As Paul spoke on and on, a young man named Eutychus, sitting on the windowsill, became very drowsy. Finally, he fell sound asleep and dropped three stories to his death below. [10] Paul went down, bent over him, and took him into his arms. "Don't worry," he said, "he's alive!" [11] Then they all went back upstairs, shared in the Lord's Supper,* and ate together. Paul continued talking to them until dawn, and then he left. [12] Meanwhile, the young man was taken home unhurt, and everyone was greatly relieved.

Paul Meets the Ephesian Elders

[13] Paul went by land to Assos, where he had arranged for us to join him, while we traveled by ship. [14] He joined us there, and we sailed together to Mitylene. [15] The next day we sailed past the island of Kios. The following day we crossed to the island of Samos, and* a day later we arrived at Miletus.

[16] Paul had decided to sail on past Ephesus, for he didn't want to spend any more time in the province of Asia. He was hurrying to get to Jerusalem, if possible, in time for the Festival of Pentecost. [17] But when we landed at Miletus, he sent a message to the elders of the church at Ephesus, asking them to come and meet him.

[18] When they arrived he declared, "You know that from the day I set foot in the province of Asia until now [19] I have done the Lord's work humbly and with many tears. I have endured the trials that came to me from the plots of the Jews. [20] I never shrank back from telling you what you needed to hear, either publicly or in your homes. [21] I have had one message for Jews and Greeks alike—the necessity of repenting from sin and turning to God, and of having faith in our Lord Jesus.

[22] "And now I am bound by the Spirit* to go to Jerusalem. I don't know what awaits me, [23] except that the Holy Spirit tells me in city after city that jail and suffering lie ahead. [24] But my life is worth nothing to me unless I use it for finishing the work assigned me by the Lord Jesus—the work of telling others the Good News about the wonderful grace of God.

[25] "And now I know that none of you to whom I have preached the Kingdom will ever see me again. [26] I declare today that I have been faithful. If anyone suffers eternal death, it's not my fault,* [27] for I didn't shrink from declaring all that God wants you to know.

[28] "So guard yourselves and God's people. Feed and shepherd God's flock—his church, purchased with his own blood*—over which the Holy Spirit has appointed you as elders.* [29] I know that false teachers, like vicious wolves, will come in among you after I leave, not sparing the flock. [30] Even some men from your own group will rise up and distort the truth in order to draw a following. [31] Watch out! Remember the three years I was with you—my constant watch and care over you night and day, and my many tears for you.

[32] "And now I entrust you to God and the message of his grace that is able to build you up and give you an inheritance with all those he has set apart for himself.

"But my life is worth nothing to me unless I use it for finishing the work assigned me by the Lord Jesus—the work of telling others the Good News about the wonderful grace of God" (Acts 20:24).

say what?

"My life ain't worth a thing unless I use it to work for Jesus—to finish all the stuff he wants me to do. That means I gotta tell everybody around me—the homies, my fam, even people I don't know. They all need to be schooled on God's favor."

20:6 Greek *the days of unleavened bread.*   **20:7** Greek *to break bread.*   **20:11** Greek *broke the bread.*   **20:15** Some manuscripts read *and having stayed at Trogyllium.*   **20:22** Or *by my spirit,* or *by an inner compulsion;* Greek reads *by the spirit.*   **20:26** Greek *I am innocent of the blood of all.*   **20:28a** Or *with the blood of his own [Son].*   **20:28b** Greek *overseers.*

³³"I have never coveted anyone's silver or gold or fine clothes. ³⁴You know that these hands of mine have worked to supply my own needs and even the needs of those who were with me. ³⁵And I have been a constant example of how you can help those in need by working hard. You should remember the words of the Lord Jesus: 'It is more blessed to give than to receive.'"

³⁶When he had finished speaking, he knelt and prayed with them. ³⁷They all cried as they embraced and kissed him good-bye. ³⁸They were sad most of all because he had said that they would never see him again. Then they escorted him down to the ship.

CHAPTER 21

Paul's Journey to Jerusalem

After saying farewell to the Ephesian elders, we sailed straight to the island of Cos. The next day we reached Rhodes and then went to Patara. ²There we boarded a ship sailing for Phoenicia. ³We sighted the island of Cyprus, passed it on our left, and landed at the harbor of Tyre, in Syria, where the ship was to unload its cargo.

⁴We went ashore, found the local believers,* and stayed with them a week. These believers prophesied through the Holy Spirit that Paul should not go on to Jerusalem. ⁵When we returned to the ship at the end of the week, the entire congregation, including women* and children, left the city and came down to the shore with us. There we knelt, prayed, ⁶and said our farewells. Then we went aboard, and they returned home.

⁷The next stop after leaving Tyre was Ptolemais, where we greeted the brothers and sisters* and stayed for one day. ⁸The next day we went on to Caesarea and stayed at the home of Philip the Evangelist, one of the seven men who had been chosen to distribute food. ⁹He had four unmarried daughters who had the gift of prophecy.

¹⁰Several days later a man named Agabus, who also had the gift of prophecy, arrived from Judea. ¹¹He came over, took Paul's belt, and bound his own feet and hands with it. Then he said, "The Holy Spirit declares, 'So shall the owner of this belt be bound by the Jewish leaders in Jerusalem and turned over to the Gentiles.'" ¹²When we heard this, we and the local believers all begged Paul not to go on to Jerusalem.

¹³But he said, "Why all this weeping? You are breaking my heart! I am ready not only to be jailed at Jerusalem but even to die for the sake of the Lord Jesus." ¹⁴When it was clear that we couldn't persuade him, we gave up and said, "The Lord's will be done."

Paul Arrives at Jerusalem

¹⁵After this we packed our things and left for Jerusalem. ¹⁶Some believers from Caesarea accompanied us, and they took us to the home of Mnason, a man originally from Cyprus and one of the early believers. ¹⁷When we arrived, the brothers and sisters in Jerusalem welcomed us warmly.

¹⁸The next day Paul went with us to meet with James, and all the elders of the Jerusalem church were present. ¹⁹After greeting them, Paul gave a detailed account of the things God had accomplished among the Gentiles through his ministry.

²⁰After hearing this, they praised God. And then they said, "You know, dear brother, how many thousands of Jews have also believed, and they all follow the law of Moses very seriously. ²¹But the Jewish believers here in Jerusalem have been told that you are teaching all the Jews who live among the Gentiles to turn their backs on the laws of Moses. They've heard that you teach them not to circumcise their children or follow other Jewish customs. ²²What should we do? They will certainly hear that you have come.

²³"Here's what we want you to do. We have four men here who have completed their vow. ²⁴Go with them to the Temple and join them in the purification ceremony, paying for

21:4 Greek *disciples;* also in 21:16.   21:5 Or *wives.*   21:7 Greek *brothers;* also in 21:17.

them to have their heads ritually shaved. Then everyone will know that the rumors are all false and that you yourself observe the Jewish laws.

²⁵"As for the Gentile believers, they should do what we already told them in a letter: They should abstain from eating food offered to idols, from consuming blood or the meat of strangled animals, and from sexual immorality."

Paul Is Arrested

²⁶So Paul went to the Temple the next day with the other men. They had already started the purification ritual, so he publicly announced the date when their vows would end and sacrifices would be offered for each of them.

²⁷The seven days were almost ended when some Jews from the province of Asia saw Paul in the Temple and roused a mob against him. They grabbed him, ²⁸yelling, "Men of Israel, help us! This is the man who preaches against our people everywhere and tells everybody to disobey the Jewish laws. He speaks against the Temple—and even defiles this holy place by bringing in Gentiles.*" ²⁹(For earlier that day they had seen him in the city with Trophimus, a Gentile from Ephesus,* and they assumed Paul had taken him into the Temple.)

³⁰The whole city was rocked by these accusations, and a great riot followed. Paul was grabbed and dragged out of the Temple, and immediately the gates were closed behind him. ³¹As they were trying to kill him, word reached the commander of the Roman regiment that all Jerusalem was in an uproar. ³²He immediately called out his soldiers and officers* and ran down among the crowd. When the mob saw the commander and the troops coming, they stopped beating Paul.

³³Then the commander arrested him and ordered him bound with two chains. He asked the crowd who he was and what he had done. ³⁴Some shouted one thing and some another. Since he couldn't find out the truth in all the up-roar and confusion, he ordered that Paul be taken to the fortress. ³⁵As Paul reached the stairs, the mob grew so violent the soldiers had to lift him to their shoulders to protect him. ³⁶And the crowd followed behind, shouting, "Kill him, kill him!"

Paul Speaks to the Crowd

³⁷As Paul was about to be taken inside, he said to the commander, "May I have a word with you?"

"Do you know Greek?" the commander asked, surprised. ³⁸"Aren't you the Egyptian who led a rebellion some time ago and took 4,000 members of the Assassins out into the desert?"

³⁹"No," Paul replied, "I am a Jew and a citizen of Tarsus in Cilicia, which is an important city. Please, let me talk to these people." ⁴⁰The commander agreed, so Paul stood on the stairs and motioned to the people to be quiet. Soon a deep silence enveloped the crowd, and he addressed them in their own language, Aramaic.*

CHAPTER **22**

"Brothers and esteemed fathers," Paul said, "listen to me as I offer my defense." ²When they heard him speaking in their own language,* the silence was even greater.

³Then Paul said, "I am a Jew, born in Tarsus, a city in Cilicia, and I was brought up and educated here in Jerusalem under Gamaliel. As his student, I was carefully trained in our Jewish laws and customs. I became very zealous to honor God in everything I did, just like all of you today. ⁴And I persecuted the followers of the Way, hounding some to death, arresting both men and women and throwing them in prison. ⁵The high priest and the whole council of elders can testify that this is so. For I received letters from them to our Jewish brothers in Damascus, authorizing me to bring the Christians from there to Jerusalem, in chains, to be punished.

21:28 Greek *Greeks.*   **21:29** Greek *Trophimus, the Ephesian.*   **21:32** Greek *centurions.*   **21:40** Or *Hebrew.*   **22:2** Greek *in Aramaic,* or *in Hebrew.*

⁶"As I was on the road, approaching Damascus about noon, a very bright light from heaven suddenly shone down around me. ⁷I fell to the ground and heard a voice saying to me, 'Saul, Saul, why are you persecuting me?'

⁸"'Who are you, lord?' I asked.

"And the voice replied, 'I am Jesus the Nazarene,* the one you are persecuting.' ⁹The people with me saw the light but didn't understand the voice speaking to me.

¹⁰"I asked, 'What should I do, Lord?'

"And the Lord told me, 'Get up and go into Damascus, and there you will be told everything you are to do.'

¹¹"I was blinded by the intense light and had to be led by the hand to Damascus by my companions. ¹²A man named Ananias lived there. He was a godly man, deeply devoted to the law, and well regarded by all the Jews of Damascus. ¹³He came and stood beside me and said, 'Brother Saul, regain your sight.' And that very moment I could see him!

¹⁴"Then he told me, 'The God of our ancestors has chosen you to know his will and to see the Righteous One and hear him speak. ¹⁵For you are to be his witness, telling everyone what you have seen and heard. ¹⁶What are you waiting for? Get up and be baptized. Have your sins washed away by calling on the name of the Lord.'

¹⁷"After I returned to Jerusalem, I was praying in the Temple and fell into a trance. ¹⁸I saw a vision of Jesus* saying to me, 'Hurry! Leave Jerusalem, for the people here won't accept your testimony about me.'

¹⁹"'But Lord,' I argued, 'they certainly know that in every synagogue I imprisoned and beat those who believed in you. ²⁰And I was in complete agreement when your witness Stephen was killed. I stood by and kept the coats they took off when they stoned him.'

²¹"But the Lord said to me, 'Go, for I will send you far away to the Gentiles!'"

²²The crowd listened until Paul said that word. Then they all began to shout, "Away with such a fellow! He isn't fit to live!" ²³They yelled, threw off their coats, and tossed handfuls of dust into the air.

Paul Reveals His Roman Citizenship

²⁴The commander brought Paul inside and ordered him lashed with whips to make him confess his crime. He wanted to find out why the crowd had become so furious. ²⁵When they tied Paul down to lash him, Paul said to the officer* standing there, "Is it legal for you to whip a Roman citizen who hasn't even been tried?"

²⁶When the officer heard this, he went to the commander and asked, "What are you doing? This man is a Roman citizen!"

²⁷So the commander went over and asked Paul, "Tell me, are you a Roman citizen?"

"Yes, I certainly am," Paul replied.

²⁸"I am, too," the commander muttered, "and it cost me plenty!"

Paul answered, "But I am a citizen by birth!"

²⁹The soldiers who were about to interrogate Paul quickly withdrew when they heard he was a Roman citizen, and the commander was frightened because he had ordered him bound and whipped.

Paul before the High Council

³⁰The next day the commander ordered the leading priests into session with the Jewish high council.* He wanted to find out what the trouble was all about, so he released Paul to have him stand before them.

CHAPTER 23

Gazing intently at the high council,* Paul began: "Brothers, I have always lived before God with a clear conscience!"

²Instantly Ananias the high priest commanded those close to Paul to slap him on the mouth. ³But Paul said to

22:8 Or *Jesus of Nazareth.*   22:18 Greek *him.*   22:25 Greek *the centurion;* also in 22:26.   22:30 Greek *Sanhedrin.*   23:1 Greek *Sanhedrin;* also in 23:6, 15, 20, 28.

him, "God will slap you, you corrupt hypocrite!* What kind of judge are you to break the law yourself by ordering me struck like that?"

⁴Those standing near Paul said to him, "Do you dare to insult God's high priest?"

⁵"I'm sorry, brothers. I didn't realize he was the high priest," Paul replied, "for the Scriptures say, 'You must not speak evil of any of your rulers.'*"

⁶Paul realized that some members of the high council were Sadducees and some were Pharisees, so he shouted, "Brothers, I am a Pharisee, as were my ancestors! And I am on trial because my hope is in the resurrection of the dead!"

⁷This divided the council—the Pharisees against the Sadducees—⁸for the Sadducees say there is no resurrection or angels or spirits, but the Pharisees believe in all of these. ⁹So there was a great uproar. Some of the teachers of religious law who were Pharisees jumped up and began to argue forcefully. "We see nothing wrong with him," they shouted. "Perhaps a spirit or an angel spoke to him." ¹⁰As the conflict grew more violent, the commander was afraid they would tear Paul apart. So he ordered his soldiers to go and rescue him by force and take him back to the fortress.

¹¹That night the Lord appeared to Paul and said, "Be encouraged, Paul. Just as you have been a witness to me here in Jerusalem, you must preach the Good News in Rome as well."

The Plan to Kill Paul

¹²The next morning a group of Jews* got together and bound themselves with an oath not to eat or drink until they had killed Paul. ¹³There were more than forty of them in the conspiracy. ¹⁴They went to the leading priests and elders and told them, "We have bound ourselves with an oath to eat nothing until we have killed Paul. ¹⁵So you and the high council should ask the commander to bring Paul back

to the council again. Pretend you want to examine his case more fully. We will kill him on the way."

¹⁶But Paul's nephew—his sister's son—heard of their plan and went to the fortress and told Paul. ¹⁷Paul called for one of the Roman officers* and said, "Take this young man to the commander. He has something important to tell him."

¹⁸So the officer did, explaining, "Paul, the prisoner, called me over and asked me to bring this young man to you because he has something to tell you."

¹⁹The commander took his hand, led him aside, and asked, "What is it you want to tell me?"

²⁰Paul's nephew told him, "Some Jews are going to ask you to bring Paul before the high council tomorrow, pretending they want to get some more information. ²¹But don't do it! There are more than forty men hiding along the way ready to ambush him. They have vowed not to eat or drink anything until they have killed him. They are ready now, just waiting for your consent."

²²"Don't let anyone know you told me this," the commander warned the young man.

Paul Is Sent to Caesarea

²³Then the commander called two of his officers and ordered, "Get 200 soldiers ready to leave for Caesarea at nine o'clock tonight. Also take 200 spearmen and 70 mounted troops. ²⁴Provide horses for Paul to ride, and get him safely to Governor Felix." ²⁵Then he wrote this letter to the governor:

²⁶"From Claudius Lysias, to his Excellency, Governor Felix: Greetings!

²⁷"This man was seized by some Jews, and they were about to kill him when I arrived with the troops. When I learned that he was a Roman citizen, I removed him to safety. ²⁸Then I took him to their high council to try to learn the basis of the accusations against him. ²⁹I soon

"The next morning a group of Jews got together and bound themselves with an oath not to eat or drink until they had killed Paul. There were more than forty of them in the conspiracy" (Acts 23:12-13).

The next morning some Jewish peeps got together and made a pact. They decided not to eat or drink until Paul had been taken out. About forty of 'em decided they would get in on the deal to kill him.

23:3 Greek *you whitewashed wall.* 23:5 Exod 22:28. 23:12 Greek *the Jews.* 23:17 Greek *centurions;* also in 23:23.

discovered the charge was something regarding their religious law—certainly nothing worthy of imprisonment or death. ³⁰But when I was informed of a plot to kill him, I immediately sent him on to you. I have told his accusers to bring their charges before you."

³¹So that night, as ordered, the soldiers took Paul as far as Antipatris. ³²They returned to the fortress the next morning, while the mounted troops took him on to Caesarea. ³³When they arrived in Caesarea, they presented Paul and the letter to Governor Felix. ³⁴He read it and then asked Paul what province he was from. "Cilicia," Paul answered.

³⁵"I will hear your case myself when your accusers arrive," the governor told him. Then the governor ordered him kept in the prison at Herod's headquarters.*

CHAPTER **24**

Paul Appears before Felix

Five days later Ananias, the high priest, arrived with some of the Jewish elders and the lawyer* Tertullus, to present their case against Paul to the governor. ²When Paul was called in, Tertullus presented the charges against Paul in the following address to the governor:

"You have provided a long period of peace for us Jews and with foresight have enacted reforms for us. ³For all of this, Your Excellency, we are very grateful to you. ⁴But I don't want to bore you, so please give me your attention for only a moment. ⁵We have found this man to be a troublemaker who is constantly stirring up riots among the Jews all over the world. He is a ringleader of the cult known as the Nazarenes. ⁶Furthermore, he was trying to desecrate the Temple when we arrested him.* ⁸You can find out the truth of our accusations by examining him yourself." ⁹Then the other Jews chimed in, declaring that everything Tertullus said was true.

¹⁰The governor then motioned for Paul to speak. Paul said, "I know, sir, that you have been a judge of Jewish affairs for many years, so I gladly present my defense before you. ¹¹You can quickly discover that I arrived in Jerusalem no more than twelve days ago to worship at the Temple. ¹²My accusers never found me arguing with anyone in the Temple, nor stirring up a riot in any synagogue or on the streets of the city. ¹³These men cannot prove the things they accuse me of doing.

¹⁴"But I admit that I follow the Way, which they call a cult. I worship the God of our ancestors, and I firmly believe the Jewish law and everything written in the prophets. ¹⁵I have the same hope in God that these men have, that he will raise both the righteous and the unrighteous. ¹⁶Because of this, I always try to maintain a clear conscience before God and all people.

¹⁷"After several years away, I returned to Jerusalem with money to aid my people and to offer sacrifices to God. ¹⁸My accusers saw me in the Temple as I was completing a purification ceremony. There was no crowd around me and no rioting. ¹⁹But some Jews from the province of Asia were there—and they ought to be here to bring charges if they have anything against me! ²⁰Ask these men here what crime the Jewish high council* found me guilty of, ²¹except for the one time I shouted out, 'I am on trial before you today because I believe in the resurrection of the dead!'"

²²At that point Felix, who was quite familiar with the Way, adjourned the hearing and said, "Wait until Lysias, the garrison commander, arrives. Then I will decide the case." ²³He ordered an officer* to keep Paul in custody but to give him some freedom and allow his friends to visit him and take care of his needs.

²⁴A few days later Felix came back with his wife, Drusilla, who was Jewish. Sending for Paul, they listened as he told

23:35 Greek *Herod's Praetorium.*   24:1 Greek *some elders and an orator.*   24:6 Some manuscripts add an expanded conclusion to verse 6, all of verse 7, and an additional phrase in verse 8: *We would have judged him by our law, ⁷but Lysias, the commander of the garrison, came and violently took him away from us, ⁸commanding his accusers to come before you.*   24:20 Greek *Sanhedrin.*   24:23 Greek *a centurion.*

them about faith in Christ Jesus. ²⁵As he reasoned with them about righteousness and self-control and the coming day of judgment, Felix became frightened. "Go away for now," he replied. "When it is more convenient, I'll call for you again." ²⁶He also hoped that Paul would bribe him, so he sent for him quite often and talked with him.

²⁷After two years went by in this way, Felix was succeeded by Porcius Festus. And because Felix wanted to gain favor with the Jewish people, he left Paul in prison.

CHAPTER 25

Paul Appears before Festus

Three days after Festus arrived in Caesarea to take over his new responsibilities, he left for Jerusalem, ²where the leading priests and other Jewish leaders met with him and made their accusations against Paul. ³They asked Festus as a favor to transfer Paul to Jerusalem (planning to ambush and kill him on the way). ⁴But Festus replied that Paul was at Caesarea and he himself would be returning there soon. ⁵So he said, "Those of you in authority can return with me. If Paul has done anything wrong, you can make your accusations."

⁶About eight or ten days later Festus returned to Caesarea, and on the following day he took his seat in court and ordered that Paul be brought in. ⁷When Paul arrived, the Jewish leaders from Jerusalem gathered around and made many serious accusations they couldn't prove.

⁸Paul denied the charges. "I am not guilty of any crime against the Jewish laws or the Temple or the Roman government," he said.

⁹Then Festus, wanting to please the Jews, asked him, "Are you willing to go to Jerusalem and stand trial before me there?"

¹⁰But Paul replied, "No! This is the official Roman court, so I ought to be tried right here. You know very well I am not guilty of harming the Jews. ¹¹If I have done something worthy of death, I don't refuse to die. But if I am innocent, no one has a right to turn me over to these men to kill me. I appeal to Caesar!"

¹²Festus conferred with his advisers and then replied, "Very well! You have appealed to Caesar, and to Caesar you will go!"

¹³A few days later King Agrippa arrived with his sister, Bernice,* to pay their respects to Festus. ¹⁴During their stay of several days, Festus discussed Paul's case with the king. "There is a prisoner here," he told him, "whose case was left for me by Felix. ¹⁵When I was in Jerusalem, the leading priests and Jewish elders pressed charges against him and asked me to condemn him. ¹⁶I pointed out to them that Roman law does not convict people without a trial. They must be given an opportunity to confront their accusers and defend themselves.

¹⁷"When his accusers came here for the trial, I didn't delay. I called the case the very next day and ordered Paul brought in. ¹⁸But the accusations made against him weren't any of the crimes I expected. ¹⁹Instead, it was something about their religion and a dead man named Jesus, who Paul insists is alive. ²⁰I was at a loss to know how to investigate these things, so I asked him whether he would be willing to stand trial on these charges in Jerusalem. ²¹But Paul appealed to have his case decided by the emperor. So I ordered that he be held in custody until I could arrange to send him to Caesar."

²²"I'd like to hear the man myself," Agrippa said.

And Festus replied, "You will—tomorrow!"

Paul Speaks to Agrippa

²³So the next day Agrippa and Bernice arrived at the auditorium with great pomp, accompanied by military officers and prominent men of the city. Festus ordered that Paul be brought in. ²⁴Then Festus said, "King Agrippa and all who are here, this is the man whose death is demanded by all the Jews, both here and in Jerusalem. ²⁵But in my opinion

25:13 Greek *Agrippa the king and Bernice arrived.*

he has done nothing deserving death. However, since he appealed his case to the emperor, I have decided to send him to Rome.

²⁶"But what shall I write the emperor? For there is no clear charge against him. So I have brought him before all of you, and especially you, King Agrippa, so that after we examine him, I might have something to write. ²⁷For it makes no sense to send a prisoner to the emperor without specifying the charges against him!"

CHAPTER 26

Then Agrippa said to Paul, "You may speak in your defense."

So Paul, gesturing with his hand, started his defense: ²"I am fortunate, King Agrippa, that you are the one hearing my defense today against all these accusations made by the Jewish leaders, ³for I know you are an expert on all Jewish customs and controversies. Now please listen to me patiently!

⁴"As the Jewish leaders are well aware, I was given a thorough Jewish training from my earliest childhood among my own people and in Jerusalem. ⁵If they would admit it, they know that I have been a member of the Pharisees, the strictest sect of our religion. ⁶Now I am on trial because of my hope in the fulfillment of God's promise made to our ancestors. ⁷In fact, that is why the twelve tribes of Israel zealously worship God night and day, and they share the same hope I have. Yet, Your Majesty, they accuse me for having this hope! ⁸Why does it seem incredible to any of you that God can raise the dead?

⁹"I used to believe that I ought to do everything I could to oppose the very name of Jesus the Nazarene.* ¹⁰Indeed, I did just that in Jerusalem. Authorized by the leading priests, I caused many believers* there to be sent to prison. And I cast my vote against them when they were condemned to death. ¹¹Many times I had them punished in the synagogues to get them to curse Jesus.* I was so violently opposed to them that I even chased them down in foreign cities.

¹²"One day I was on such a mission to Damascus, armed with the authority and commission of the leading priests. ¹³About noon, Your Majesty, as I was on the road, a light from heaven brighter than the sun shone down on me and my companions. ¹⁴We all fell down, and I heard a voice saying to me in Aramaic,* 'Saul, Saul, why are you persecuting me? It is useless for you to fight against my will.*'

¹⁵"'Who are you, lord?' I asked.

"And the Lord replied, 'I am Jesus, the one you are persecuting. ¹⁶Now get to your feet! For I have appeared to you to appoint you as my servant and witness. You are to tell the world what you have seen and what I will show you in the future. ¹⁷And I will rescue you from both your own people and the Gentiles. Yes, I am sending you to the Gentiles ¹⁸to open their eyes, so they may turn from darkness to light and from the power of Satan to God. Then they will receive forgiveness for their sins and be given a place among God's people, who are set apart by faith in me.'

¹⁹"And so, King Agrippa, I obeyed that vision from heaven. ²⁰I preached first to those in Damascus, then in Jerusalem and throughout all Judea, and also to the Gentiles, that all must repent of their sins and turn to God—and prove they have changed by the good things they do. ²¹Some Jews arrested me in the Temple for preaching this, and they tried to kill me. ²²But God has protected me right up to this present time so I can testify to everyone, from the least to the greatest. I teach nothing except what the prophets and Moses said would happen—²³that the Messiah would suffer and be the first to rise from the dead, and in this way announce God's light to Jews and Gentiles alike."

²⁴Suddenly, Festus shouted, "Paul, you are insane. Too much study has made you crazy!"

²⁵But Paul replied, "I am not insane, Most Excellent Fes-

26:9 Or *Jesus of Nazareth.* **26:10** Greek *many of God's holy people.* **26:11** Greek *to blaspheme.* **26:14a** Or *Hebrew.* **26:14b** Greek *It is hard for you to kick against the oxgoads.*

tus. What I am saying is the sober truth. ²⁶And King Agrippa knows about these things. I speak boldly, for I am sure these events are all familiar to him, for they were not done in a corner! ²⁷King Agrippa, do you believe the prophets? I know you do—"

²⁸Agrippa interrupted him. "Do you think you can persuade me to become a Christian so quickly?"*

²⁹Paul replied, "Whether quickly or not, I pray to God that both you and everyone here in this audience might become the same as I am, except for these chains."

³⁰Then the king, the governor, Bernice, and all the others stood and left. ³¹As they went out, they talked it over and agreed, "This man hasn't done anything to deserve death or imprisonment."

³²And Agrippa said to Festus, "He could have been set free if he hadn't appealed to Caesar."

CHAPTER 27

Paul Sails for Rome

When the time came, we set sail for Italy. Paul and several other prisoners were placed in the custody of a Roman officer* named Julius, a captain of the Imperial Regiment. ²Aristarchus, a Macedonian from Thessalonica, was also with us. We left on a ship whose home port was Adramyttium on the northwest coast of the province of Asia;* it was scheduled to make several stops at ports along the coast of the province.

³The next day when we docked at Sidon, Julius was very kind to Paul and let him go ashore to visit with friends so they could provide for his needs. ⁴Putting out to sea from there, we encountered strong headwinds that made it difficult to keep the ship on course, so we sailed north of Cyprus between the island and the mainland. ⁵Keeping to the open sea, we passed along the coast of Cilicia

and Pamphylia, landing at Myra, in the province of Lycia. ⁶There the commanding officer found an Egyptian ship from Alexandria that was bound for Italy, and he put us on board.

⁷We had several days of slow sailing, and after great difficulty we finally neared Cnidus. But the wind was against us, so we sailed across to Crete and along the sheltered coast of the island, past the cape of Salmone. ⁸We struggled along the coast with great difficulty and finally arrived at Fair Havens, near the town of Lasea. ⁹We had lost a lot of time. The weather was becoming dangerous for sea travel because it was so late in the fall,* and Paul spoke to the ship's officers about it.

¹⁰"Men," he said, "I believe there is trouble ahead if we go on—shipwreck, loss of cargo, and danger to our lives as well." ¹¹But the officer in charge of the prisoners listened more to the ship's captain and the owner than to Paul. ¹²And since Fair Havens was an exposed harbor—a poor place to spend the winter—most of the crew wanted to go on to Phoenix, farther up the coast of Crete, and spend the winter there. Phoenix was a good harbor with only a southwest and northwest exposure.

The Storm at Sea

¹³When a light wind began blowing from the south, the sailors thought they could make it. So they pulled up anchor and sailed close to the shore of Crete. ¹⁴But the weather changed abruptly, and a wind of typhoon strength (called a "northeaster") burst across the island and blew us out to sea. ¹⁵The sailors couldn't turn the ship into the wind, so they gave up and let it run before the gale.

¹⁶We sailed along the sheltered side of a small island named Cauda,* where with great difficulty we hoisted aboard the lifeboat being towed behind us. ¹⁷Then the sailors bound

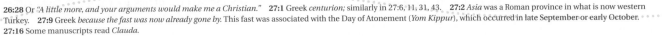

26:28 Or "A little more, and your arguments would make me a Christian."   27:1 Greek centurion; similarly in 27:6, 11, 31, 43.   27:2 Asia was a Roman province in what is now western Turkey.   27:9 Greek because the fast was now already gone by. This fast was associated with the Day of Atonement (Yom Kippur), which occurred in late September or early October.   27:16 Some manuscripts read Clauda.

ropes around the hull of the ship to strengthen it. They were afraid of being driven across to the sandbars of Syrtis off the African coast, so they lowered the sea anchor to slow the ship and were driven before the wind.

¹⁸The next day, as gale-force winds continued to batter the ship, the crew began throwing the cargo overboard. ¹⁹The following day they even took some of the ship's gear and threw it overboard. ²⁰The terrible storm raged for many days, blotting out the sun and the stars, until at last all hope was gone.

²¹No one had eaten for a long time. Finally, Paul called the crew together and said, "Men, you should have listened to me in the first place and not left Crete. You would have avoided all this damage and loss. ²²But take courage! None of you will lose your lives, even though the ship will go down. ²³For last night an angel of the God to whom I belong and whom I serve stood beside me, ²⁴and he said, 'Don't be afraid, Paul, for you will surely stand trial before Caesar! What's more, God in his goodness has granted safety to everyone sailing with you.' ²⁵So take courage! For I believe God. It will be just as he said. ²⁶But we will be shipwrecked on an island."

The Shipwreck

²⁷About midnight on the fourteenth night of the storm, as we were being driven across the Sea of Adria,* the sailors sensed land was near. ²⁸They dropped a weighted line and found that the water was 120 feet deep. But a little later they measured again and found it was only 90 feet deep.* ²⁹At this rate they were afraid we would soon be driven against the rocks along the shore, so they threw out four anchors from the back of the ship and prayed for daylight.

³⁰Then the sailors tried to abandon the ship; they lowered the lifeboat as though they were going to put out anchors from the front of the ship. ³¹But Paul said to the commanding officer and the soldiers, "You will all die unless the sailors stay aboard." ³²So the soldiers cut the ropes to the lifeboat and let it drift away.

³³Just as day was dawning, Paul urged everyone to eat. "You have been so worried that you haven't touched food for two weeks," he said. ³⁴"Please eat something now for your own good. For not a hair of your heads will perish." ³⁵Then he took some bread, gave thanks to God before them all, and broke off a piece and ate it. ³⁶Then everyone was encouraged and began to eat—³⁷all 276 of us who were on board. ³⁸After eating, the crew lightened the ship further by throwing the cargo of wheat overboard.

³⁹When morning dawned, they didn't recognize the coastline, but they saw a bay with a beach and wondered if they could get to shore by running the ship aground. ⁴⁰So they cut off the anchors and left them in the sea. Then they lowered the rudders, raised the foresail, and headed toward shore. ⁴¹But they hit a shoal and ran the ship aground too soon. The bow of the ship stuck fast, while the stern was repeatedly smashed by the force of the waves and began to break apart.

⁴²The soldiers wanted to kill the prisoners to make sure they didn't swim ashore and escape. ⁴³But the commanding officer wanted to spare Paul, so he didn't let them carry out their plan. Then he ordered all who could swim to jump overboard first and make for land. ⁴⁴The others held on to planks or debris from the broken ship.* So everyone escaped safely to shore.

CHAPTER 28

Paul on the Island of Malta

Once we were safe on shore, we learned that we were on the island of Malta. ²The people of the island were very kind to us. It was cold and rainy, so they built a fire on the shore to welcome us.

³As Paul gathered an armful of sticks and was laying them

27:27 The *Sea of Adria* includes the central portion of the Mediterranean.   27:28 Greek *20 fathoms . . . 15 fathoms* [37 meters . . . 27 meters].   27:44 Or *or were helped by members of the ship's crew.*

on the fire, a poisonous snake, driven out by the heat, bit him on the hand. ⁴The people of the island saw it hanging from his hand and said to each other, "A murderer, no doubt! Though he escaped the sea, justice will not permit him to live." ⁵But Paul shook off the snake into the fire and was unharmed. ⁶The people waited for him to swell up or suddenly drop dead. But when they had waited a long time and saw that he wasn't harmed, they changed their minds and decided he was a god.

⁷Near the shore where we landed was an estate belonging to Publius, the chief official of the island. He welcomed us and treated us kindly for three days. ⁸As it happened, Publius's father was ill with fever and dysentery. Paul went in and prayed for him, and laying his hands on him, he healed him. ⁹Then all the other sick people on the island came and were healed. ¹⁰As a result we were showered with honors, and when the time came to sail, people supplied us with everything we would need for the trip.

Paul Arrives at Rome

¹¹It was three months after the shipwreck that we set sail on another ship that had wintered at the island—an Alexandrian ship with the twin gods* as its figurehead. ¹²Our first stop was Syracuse,* where we stayed three days. ¹³From there we sailed across to Rhegium.* A day later a south wind began blowing, so the following day we sailed up the coast to Puteoli. ¹⁴There we found some believers,* who invited us to spend a week with them. And so we came to Rome.

¹⁵The brothers and sisters* in Rome had heard we were coming, and they came to meet us at the Forum* on the Appian Way. Others joined us at The Three Taverns.* When Paul saw them, he was encouraged and thanked God.

¹⁶When we arrived in Rome, Paul was permitted to have his own private lodging, though he was guarded by a soldier.

Paul Preaches at Rome under Guard

¹⁷Three days after Paul's arrival, he called together the local Jewish leaders. He said to them, "Brothers, I was arrested in Jerusalem and handed over to the Roman government, even though I had done nothing against our people or the customs of our ancestors. ¹⁸The Romans tried me and wanted to release me, because they found no cause for the death sentence. ¹⁹But when the Jewish leaders protested the decision, I felt it necessary to appeal to Caesar, even though I had no desire to press charges against my own people. ²⁰I asked you to come here today so we could get acquainted and so I could explain to you that I am bound with this chain because I believe that the hope of Israel—the Messiah—has already come."

²¹They replied, "We have had no letters from Judea or reports against you from anyone who has come here. ²²But we want to hear what you believe, for the only thing we know about this movement is that it is denounced everywhere."

²³So a time was set, and on that day a large number of people came to Paul's lodging. He explained and testified about the Kingdom of God and tried to persuade them about Jesus from the Scriptures. Using the law of Moses and the books of the prophets, he spoke to them from morning until evening. ²⁴Some were persuaded by the things he said, but others did not believe. ²⁵And after they had argued back and forth among themselves, they left with this final word from Paul: "The Holy Spirit was right when he said to your ancestors through Isaiah the prophet,

²⁶ 'Go and say to this people:
When you hear what I say,
    you will not understand.
When you see what I do,
    you will not comprehend.
²⁷ For the hearts of these people are hardened,
    and their ears cannot hear,

28:11 The *twin gods* were the Roman gods Castor and Pollux.   **28:12** *Syracuse* was on the island of Sicily.   **28:13** *Rhegium* was on the southern tip of Italy.   **28:14** Greek *brothers.*
28:15a Greek *brothers.*   **28:15b** *The Forum* was about 43 miles (70 kilometers) from Rome.   **28:15c** *The Three Taverns* was about 35 miles (57 kilometers) from Rome.

and they have closed their eyes—
so their eyes cannot see,
and their ears cannot hear,
and their hearts cannot understand,
and they cannot turn to me
and let me heal them.'*

[28]So I want you to know that this salvation from God has also been offered to the Gentiles, and they will accept it."*

[30]For the next two years, Paul lived in Rome at his own expense.* He welcomed all who visited him, [31]boldly proclaiming the Kingdom of God and teaching about the Lord Jesus Christ. And no one tried to stop him.

28:26-27 Isa 6:9-10 (Greek version).   **28:28** Some manuscripts add verse 29, *And when he had said these words, the Jews departed, greatly disagreeing with each other.*   **28:30** Or *in his own rented quarters.*

THE BOOK OF ROMANS was written by Paul (formerly called Saul). Paul was a Jew and was also a Roman citizen. Before he converted to Christianity, he persecuted those who believed in Jesus. In the modern sense, Paul would've been considered a hardcore thug. He had no love for God's people, and he had no problem letting them know how he felt. Paul had an experience with God on his way to up the cal on some fools in the city of Damascus, and he quickly became a faithful believer in Christ. Paul is credited with writing much of the New Testament.

Paul wrote this letter to the Christians in the city of Rome, summarizing the essential beliefs of the Christian faith. If you want the story without commercials, Paul gives it to us here. He comes first with the bad news: We are all guilty and deserve to be punished—forever. But there's good news, too: We can be freed from the power of sin by God's grace and forgiveness. We're all broken down and in need of help, but there's hope for us all.

ROMANS

CHAPTER 1

Greetings from Paul

This letter is from Paul, a slave of Christ Jesus, chosen by God to be an apostle and sent out to preach his Good News. ²God promised this Good News long ago through his prophets in the holy Scriptures. ³The Good News is about his Son. In his earthly life he was born into King David's family line, ⁴and he was shown to be* the Son of God when he was raised from the dead by the power of the Holy Spirit.* He is Jesus Christ our Lord. ⁵Through Christ, God has given us the privilege* and authority as apostles to tell Gentiles everywhere what God has done for them, so that they will believe and obey him, bringing glory to his name.

⁶And you are included among those Gentiles who have been called to belong to Jesus Christ. ⁷I am writing to all of you in Rome who are loved by God and are called to be his own holy people.

May God our Father and the Lord Jesus Christ give you grace and peace.

God's Good News

⁸Let me say first that I thank my God through Jesus Christ for all of you, because your faith in him is being talked about all over the world. ⁹God knows how often I pray for you. Day and night I bring you and your needs in prayer to God, whom I serve with all my heart* by spreading the Good News about his Son.

¹⁰One of the things I always pray for is the opportunity, God willing, to come at last to see you. ¹¹For I long to visit you so I can bring you some spiritual gift that will help you grow strong in the Lord. ¹²When we get together, I want to encourage you in your faith, but I also want to be encouraged by yours.

¹³I want you to know, dear brothers and sisters,* that I planned many times to visit you, but I was prevented until now. I want to work among you and see spiritual fruit, just as I have seen among other Gentiles. ¹⁴For I have a great sense of obligation to people in both the civilized world and the rest of the world,* to the educated and uneducated alike. ¹⁵So I am eager to come to you in Rome, too, to preach the Good News.

¹⁶For I am not ashamed of this Good News about Christ. It is the power of God at work, saving everyone who believes—the Jew first and also the Gentile.* ¹⁷This Good News tells us how God makes us right in his sight. This is accomplished from start to finish by faith. As the Scriptures say, "It is through faith that a righteous person has life."*

God's Anger at Sin

¹⁸But God shows his anger from heaven against all sinful, wicked people who suppress the truth by their wickedness.* ¹⁹They know the truth about God because he has made it obvious to them. ²⁰For ever since the world was created, people have seen the earth and sky. Through everything God made, they can clearly see his invisible qualities—his eternal power and divine nature. So they have no excuse for not knowing God.

²¹Yes, they knew God, but they wouldn't worship him as

1:4a Or *and was designated.*   1:4b Or *by the Spirit of holiness;* or *in the new realm of the Spirit.*   1:5 Or *the grace.*   1:9 Or *in my spirit.*   1:13 Greek *brothers.*   1:14 Greek *to Greeks and barbarians.*   1:16 Greek *also the Greek.*   1:17 Or *"The righteous will live by faith."* Hab 2:4.   1:18 Or *who, by their wickedness, prevent the truth from being known.*

God or even give him thanks. And they began to think up foolish ideas of what God was like. As a result, their minds became dark and confused. 22Claiming to be wise, they instead became utter fools. 23And instead of worshiping the glorious, ever-living God, they worshiped idols made to look like mere people and birds and animals and reptiles.

24So God abandoned them to do whatever shameful things their hearts desired. As a result, they did vile and degrading things with each other's bodies. 25They traded the truth about God for a lie. So they worshiped and served the things God created instead of the Creator himself, who is worthy of eternal praise! Amen. 26That is why God abandoned them to their shameful desires. Even the women turned against the natural way to have sex and instead indulged in sex with each other. 27And the men, instead of having normal sexual relations with women, burned with lust for each other. Men did shameful things with other men, and as a result of this sin, they suffered within themselves the penalty they deserved.

28Since they thought it foolish to acknowledge God, he abandoned them to their foolish thinking and let them do things that should never be done. 29Their lives became full of every kind of wickedness, sin, greed, hate, envy, murder, quarreling, deception, malicious behavior, and gossip. 30They are backstabbers, haters of God, insolent, proud, and boastful. They invent new ways of sinning, and they disobey their parents. 31They refuse to understand, break their promises, are heartless, and have no mercy. 32They know God's justice requires that those who do these things deserve to die, yet they do them anyway. Worse yet, they encourage others to do them, too.

CHAPTER 2
God's Judgment of Sin

You may think you can condemn such people, but you are just as bad, and you have no excuse! When you say they are wicked and should be punished, you are condemning yourself, for you who judge others do these very same things. 2And we know that God, in his justice, will punish anyone who does such things. 3Since you judge others for doing these things, why do you think you can avoid God's judgment when you do the same things? 4Don't you see how wonderfully kind, tolerant, and patient God is with you? Does this mean nothing to you? Can't you see that his kindness is intended to turn you from your sin?

5But because you are stubborn and refuse to turn from your sin, you are storing up terrible punishment for yourself. For a day of anger is coming, when God's righteous judgment will be revealed. 6He will judge everyone according to what they have done. 7He will give eternal life to those who keep on doing good, seeking after the glory and honor and immortality that God offers. 8But he will pour out his anger and wrath on those who live for themselves, who refuse to obey the truth and instead live lives of wickedness. 9There will be trouble and calamity for everyone who keeps on doing what is evil—for the Jew first and also for the Gentile.* 10But there will be glory and honor and peace from God for all who do good—for the Jew first and also for the Gentile. 11For God does not show favoritism.

12When the Gentiles sin, they will be destroyed, even though they never had God's written law. And the Jews, who do have God's law, will be judged by that law when they fail to obey it. 13For merely listening to the law doesn't make us right with God. It is obeying the law that makes us right in his sight. 14Even Gentiles, who do not have God's written law, show that they know his law when they instinctively obey it, even without having heard it. 15They demonstrate that God's law is written in their hearts, for their own conscience and thoughts either accuse them or tell them they are doing right. 16And this is the message I proclaim—that the day is coming when God, through Christ Jesus, will judge everyone's secret life.

2:9 Greek also for the Greek; also in 2:10.

The Jews and the Law

¹⁷You who call yourselves Jews are relying on God's law, and you boast about your special relationship with him. ¹⁸You know what he wants; you know what is right because you have been taught his law. ¹⁹You are convinced that you are a guide for the blind and a light for people who are lost in darkness. ²⁰You think you can instruct the ignorant and teach children the ways of God. For you are certain that God's law gives you complete knowledge and truth.

²¹Well then, if you teach others, why don't you teach yourself? You tell others not to steal, but do you steal? ²²You say it is wrong to commit adultery, but do you commit adultery? You condemn idolatry, but do you use items stolen from pagan temples?* ²³You are so proud of knowing the law, but you dishonor God by breaking it. ²⁴No wonder the Scriptures say, "The Gentiles blaspheme the name of God because of you."*

²⁵The Jewish ceremony of circumcision has value only if you obey God's law. But if you don't obey God's law, you are no better off than an uncircumcised Gentile. ²⁶And if the Gentiles obey God's law, won't God declare them to be his own people? ²⁷In fact, uncircumcised Gentiles who keep God's law will condemn you Jews who are circumcised and possess God's law but don't obey it.

²⁸For you are not a true Jew just because you were born of Jewish parents or because you have gone through the ceremony of circumcision. ²⁹No, a true Jew is one whose heart is right with God. And true circumcision is not merely obeying the letter of the law; rather, it is a change of heart produced by God's Spirit. And a person with a changed heart seeks praise* from God, not from people.

"No one is righteous—not even one" (Romans 3:10).

Only God is perfect.

CHAPTER 3

God Remains Faithful

Then what's the advantage of being a Jew? Is there any value in the ceremony of circumcision? ²Yes, there are great benefits! First of all, the Jews were entrusted with the whole revelation of God.*

³True, some of them were unfaithful; but just because they were unfaithful, does that mean God will be unfaithful? ⁴Of course not! Even if everyone else is a liar, God is true. As the Scriptures say about him,

> "You will be proved right in what you say,
>   and you will win your case in court."*

⁵"But," some might say, "our sinfulness serves a good purpose, for it helps people see how righteous God is. Isn't it unfair, then, for him to punish us?" (This is merely a human point of view.) ⁶Of course not! If God were not entirely fair, how would he be qualified to judge the world? ⁷"But," someone might still argue, "how can God condemn me as a sinner if my dishonesty highlights his truthfulness and brings him more glory?" ⁸And some people even slander us by claiming that we say, "The more we sin, the better it is!" Those who say such things deserve to be condemned.

All People Are Sinners

⁹Well then, should we conclude that we Jews are better than others? No, not at all, for we have already shown that all people, whether Jews or Gentiles,* are under the power of sin. ¹⁰As the Scriptures say,

> "No one is righteous—
>   not even one.
> ¹¹ No one is truly wise;
>   no one is seeking God.
> ¹² All have turned away;
>   all have become useless.
> No one does good,
>   not a single one."*
> ¹³ "Their talk is foul, like the stench from an open grave.

2:22 Greek *do you steal from temples?* 2:24 Isa 52:5 (Greek version). 2:29 Or *receives praise.* 3:2 Greek *the oracles of God.* 3:4 Ps 51:4 (Greek version). 3:9 Greek *or Greeks.*
3:10-12 Pss 14:1-3; 53:1-3 (Greek version).

Their tongues are filled with lies."
"Snake venom drips from their lips."*
14 "Their mouths are full of cursing and bitterness."*
15 "They rush to commit murder.
16 Destruction and misery always follow them.
17 They don't know where to find peace."*
18 "They have no fear of God at all."*

19Obviously, the law applies to those to whom it was given, for its purpose is to keep people from having excuses, and to show that the entire world is guilty before God. 20For no one can ever be made right with God by doing what the law commands. The law simply shows us how sinful we are.

Christ Took Our Punishment

21But now God has shown us a way to be made right with him without keeping the requirements of the law, as was promised in the writings of Moses* and the prophets long ago. 22We are made right with God by placing our faith in Jesus Christ. And this is true for everyone who believes, no matter who we are.

23For everyone has sinned; we all fall short of God's glorious standard. 24Yet God, with undeserved kindness, declares that we are righteous. He did this through Christ Jesus when he freed us from the penalty for our sins. 25For God presented Jesus as the sacrifice for sin. People are made right with God when they believe that Jesus sacrificed his life, shedding his blood. This sacrifice shows that God was being fair when he held back and did not punish those who sinned in times past, 26for he was looking ahead and including them in what he would do in this present time. God did this to demonstrate his righteousness, for he himself is fair and just, and he declares sinners to be right in his sight when they believe in Jesus.

27Can we boast, then, that we have done anything to be accepted by God? No, because our acquittal is not based on obeying the law. It is based on faith. 28So we are made right with God through faith and not by obeying the law.

29After all, is God the God of the Jews only? Isn't he also the God of the Gentiles? Of course he is. 30There is only one God, and he makes people right with himself only by faith, whether they are Jews or Gentiles.* 31Well then, if we emphasize faith, does this mean that we can forget about the law? Of course not! In fact, only when we have faith do we truly fulfill the law.

3:13 Pss 5:9 (Greek version); 140:3.   3:14 Ps 10:7 (Greek version).   3:15-17 Isa 59:7-8.   3:18 Ps 36:1.   3:21 Greek in the law.   3:30 Greek whether they are circumcised or uncircumcised.

THE POINT

Salvation for everyone. So maybe you don't know that even those who seem perfect are not perfect at all and that everyone is in need of God's help. Just in case you've never read Romans 3:23, here it is: "For everyone has sinned; we all fall short of God's glorious standard" (Romans 3:23).

Paul had a challenging job. He had to tell the Jewish people and the Gentiles (non-Jews) that salvation was meant for everyone. I'll bet some of them had difficulty believing him. It's like being in your neighborhood and stumbling upon a box filled with everything you've ever wanted in life. The plan of salvation seemed too good to be true, and the idea that you didn't have to work for it was even harder to believe. Some people probably felt that they had done too many wrong things in their lifetime. I imagine some of them thought that the lies they had told, the things they had stolen, or the time they'd spent in prison would disqualify them.

Pause for a moment and think of the worst thing you've ever done. Now take a moment and realize that God's plan for salvation includes forgiveness for that very thing. We all have sinned; none of us are perfect in any way. Yet Jesus still died for us. Even though we are sinners and we all have sinned, we can all be saved.

CHAPTER 4

The Faith of Abraham

Abraham was, humanly speaking, the founder of our Jewish nation. What did he discover about being made right with God? [2]If his good deeds had made him acceptable to God, he would have had something to boast about. But that was not God's way. [3]For the Scriptures tell us, "Abraham believed God, and God counted him as righteous because of his faith."*

[4]When people work, their wages are not a gift, but something they have earned. [5]But people are counted as righteous, not because of their work, but because of their faith in God who forgives sinners. [6]David also spoke of this when he described the happiness of those who are declared righteous without working for it:

[7] "Oh, what joy for those
   whose disobedience is forgiven,
   whose sins are put out of sight.
[8] Yes, what joy for those
   whose record the LORD has cleared of sin."*

[9]Now, is this blessing only for the Jews, or is it also for uncircumcised Gentiles?* Well, we have been saying that Abraham was counted as righteous by God because of his faith. [10]But how did this happen? Was he counted as righteous only after he was circumcised, or was it before he was circumcised? Clearly, God accepted Abraham before he was circumcised!

[11]Circumcision was a sign that Abraham already had faith and that God had already accepted him and declared him to be righteous—even before he was circumcised. So Abraham is the spiritual father of those who have faith but have not been circumcised. They are counted as righteous because of their faith. [12]And Abraham is also the spiritual father of those who have been circumcised, but only if they have the same kind of faith Abraham had before he was circumcised.

[13]Clearly, God's promise to give the whole earth to Abraham and his descendants was based not on his obedience to God's law, but on a right relationship with God that comes by faith. [14]If God's promise is only for those who obey the law, then faith is not necessary and the promise is pointless. [15]For the law always brings punishment on those who try to obey it. (The only way to avoid breaking the law is to have no law to break!)

[16]So the promise is received by faith. It is given as a free gift. And we are all certain to receive it, whether or not we live according to the law of Moses, if we have faith like Abraham's. For Abraham is the father of all who believe. [17]That is what the Scriptures mean when God told him, "I have made you the father of many nations."* This happened because Abraham believed in the God who brings the dead back to life and who creates new things out of nothing.

[18]Even when there was no reason for hope, Abraham kept hoping—believing that he would become the father of many nations. For God had said to him, "That's how many descendants you will have!"* [19]And Abraham's faith did not weaken, even though, at about 100 years of age, he figured his body was as good as dead—and so was Sarah's womb.

[20]Abraham never wavered in believing God's promise. In fact, his faith grew stronger, and in this he brought glory to God. [21]He was fully convinced that God is able to do whatever he promises. [22]And because of Abraham's faith, God counted him as righteous. [23]And when God counted him as righteous, it wasn't just for Abraham's benefit. It was recorded [24]for our benefit, too, assuring us that God will also count us as righteous if we believe in him, the one who raised Jesus our Lord from the dead. [25]He was handed over to die because of our sins, and he was raised to life to make us right with God.

CHAPTER 5

Faith Brings Joy

Therefore, since we have been made right in God's sight by faith, we have peace with God because of what Jesus Christ our Lord has done for us. [2]Because of our faith, Christ has

4:3 Gen 15:6.   **4:7-8** Ps 32:1-2 (Greek version).   **4:9** Greek *is this blessing only for the circumcised, or is it also for the uncircumcised?*   **4:17** Gen 17:5.   **4:18** Gen 15:5.

brought us into this place of undeserved privilege where we now stand, and we confidently and joyfully look forward to sharing God's glory.

³We can rejoice, too, when we run into problems and trials, for we know that they help us develop endurance. ⁴And endurance develops strength of character, and character strengthens our confident hope of salvation. ⁵And this hope will not lead to disappointment. For we know how dearly God loves us, because he has given us the Holy Spirit to fill our hearts with his love.

⁶When we were utterly helpless, Christ came at just the right time and died for us sinners. ⁷Now, most people would not be willing to die for an upright person, though someone might perhaps be willing to die for a person who is especially good. ⁸But God showed his great love for us by sending Christ to die for us while we were still sinners. ⁹And since we have been made right in God's sight by the blood of Christ, he will certainly save us from God's condemnation. ¹⁰For since our friendship with God was restored by the death of his Son while we were still his enemies, we will certainly be saved through the life of his Son. ¹¹So now we can rejoice in our wonderful new relationship with God because our Lord Jesus Christ has made us friends of God.

Adam and Christ Contrasted

¹²When Adam sinned, sin entered the world. Adam's sin brought death, so death spread to everyone, for everyone sinned. ¹³Yes, people sinned even before the law was given. But it was not counted as sin because there was not yet any law to break. ¹⁴Still, everyone died—from the time of Adam to the time of Moses—even those who did not disobey an explicit commandment of God, as Adam did. Now Adam is a symbol, a representation of Christ, who was yet to come. ¹⁵But there is a great difference between Adam's sin and God's gracious gift. For the sin of this one man, Adam, brought death to many. But even greater is God's wonderful grace and his gift of forgiveness to many through this other man, Jesus Christ. ¹⁶And the result of God's gracious gift is very different from the result of that one man's sin. For Adam's sin led to condemnation, but God's free gift leads to our being made right with God, even though we are guilty of many sins. ¹⁷For the sin of this one man, Adam, caused death to rule over many. But even greater is God's wonderful grace and his gift of righteousness, for all who receive it will live in triumph over sin and death through this one man, Jesus Christ.

¹⁸Yes, Adam's one sin brings condemnation for everyone, but Christ's one act of righteousness brings a right relationship with God and new life for everyone. ¹⁹Because one person disobeyed God, many became sinners. But because one other person obeyed God, many will be made righteous.

²⁰God's law was given so that all people could see how sinful they were. But as people sinned more and more, God's wonderful grace became more abundant. ²¹So just as sin ruled over all people and brought them to death, now God's wonderful grace rules instead, giving us right standing with God and resulting in eternal life through Jesus Christ our Lord.

CHAPTER **6**

Sin's Power Is Broken

Well then, should we keep on sinning so that God can show us more and more of his wonderful grace? ²Of course not! Since we have died to sin, how can we continue to live in it? ³Or have you forgotten that when we were joined with Christ Jesus in baptism, we joined him in his death? ⁴For we died and were buried with Christ by baptism. And just as Christ was raised from the dead by the glorious power of the Father, now we also may live new lives.

⁵Since we have been united with him in his death, we will also be raised to life as he was. ⁶We know that our old sinful selves were crucified with Christ so that sin might lose its power in our lives. We are no longer slaves to sin. ⁷For when we died with Christ we were set free from the power of sin.

8And since we died with Christ, we know we will also live with him. 9We are sure of this because Christ was raised from the dead, and he will never die again. Death no longer has any power over him. 10When he died, he died once to break the power of sin. But now that he lives, he lives for the glory of God. 11So you also should consider yourselves to be dead to the power of sin and alive to God through Christ Jesus.

12Do not let sin control the way you live;* do not give in to sinful desires. 13Do not let any part of your body become an instrument of evil to serve sin. Instead, give yourselves completely to God, for you were dead, but now you have new life. So use your whole body as an instrument to do what is right for the glory of God. 14Sin is no longer your master, for you no longer live under the requirements of the law. Instead, you live under the freedom of God's grace.

15Well then, since God's grace has set us free from the law, does that mean we can go on sinning? Of course not! 16Don't you realize that you become the slave of whatever you choose to obey? You can be a slave to sin, which leads to death, or you can choose to obey God, which leads to righteous living. 17Thank God! Once you were slaves of sin, but now you wholeheartedly obey this teaching we have given you. 18Now you are free from your slavery to sin, and you have become slaves to righteous living.

19Because of the weakness of your human nature, I am using the illustration of slavery to help you understand all this. Previously, you let yourselves be slaves to impurity and lawlessness, which led ever deeper into sin. Now you must give yourselves to be slaves to righteous living so that you will become holy.

20When you were slaves to sin, you were free from the obligation to do right. 21And what was the result? You are now ashamed of the things you used to do, things that end in eternal doom. 22But now you are free from the power of sin and have become slaves of God. Now you do those things that lead to holiness and result in eternal life. 23For the wages of sin is death, but the free gift of God is eternal life through Christ Jesus our Lord.

CHAPTER 7

No Longer Bound to the Law

Now, dear brothers and sisters*—you who are familiar with the law—don't you know that the law applies only while a person is living? 2For example, when a woman marries, the law binds her to her husband as long as he is alive. But if he dies, the laws of marriage no longer apply to her. 3So while her husband is alive, she would be committing adultery if she married another man. But if her husband dies, she is free from that law and does not commit adultery when she remarries.

4So, my dear brothers and sisters, this is the point: You died to the power of the law when you died with Christ. And now you are united with the one who was raised from the dead. As a result, we can produce a harvest of good deeds for God. 5When we were controlled by our old nature,* sinful desires were at work within us, and the law aroused these evil desires that produced a harvest of sinful deeds, resulting in death. 6But now we have been released from the law, for we died to it and are no longer captive to its power. Now we can serve God, not in the old way of obeying the letter of the law, but in the new way of living in the Spirit.

God's Law Reveals Our Sin

7Well then, am I suggesting that the law of God is sinful? Of course not! In fact, it was the law that showed me my sin. I would never have known that coveting is wrong if the law had not said, "You must not covet."* 8But sin used this command to arouse all kinds of covetous desires within me! If there were no law, sin would not have that power. 9At one time I lived without understanding the law. But when I learned the command not to covet, for instance, the power of sin came to life, 10and I died. So I discovered that the law's

6:12 Or Do not let sin reign in your body, which is subject to death.   7:1 Greek brothers; also in 7:4.   7:5 Greek When we were in the flesh.   7:7 Exod 20:17; Deut 5:21.

keeping your swagger strong

BIBLICAL PRINCIPLES FOR SUCCESS AND LEADERSHIP

Sometimes we can get things so twisted that it can only be described as—you guessed it—a hot mess! We often become consumed with how our bad choices, poor judgment, or even lack of greenbacks can impact the things and the people we're responsible for. As we journey through life, it would help us to remember that nothing can separate any of us from God's love (Romans 8:35-37). Nothing—it's that simple.

The eighth chapter of Romans has a wealth of information that lets us see that God is truly down for us. When things go wrong or when we're wildin' out, it doesn't make him love us any less. As people with tremendous responsibilities, we should be able to go easy on ourselves when trouble comes our way. No matter what goes down, God will always be there. As current and future leaders this is something we should know.

what is right, but I don't do it. Instead, I do what I hate. ¹⁶But if I know that what I am doing is wrong, this shows that I agree that the law is good. ¹⁷So I am not the one doing wrong; it is sin living in me that does it.

¹⁸And I know that nothing good lives in me, that is, in my sinful nature.* I want to do what is right, but I can't. ¹⁹I want to do what is good, but I don't. I don't want to do what is wrong, but I do it anyway. ²⁰But if I do what I don't want to do, I am not really the one doing wrong; it is sin living in me that does it.

²¹I have discovered this principle of life—that when I want to do what is right, I inevitably do what is wrong. ²²I love God's law with all my heart. ²³But there is another power* within me that is at war with my mind. This power makes me a slave to the sin that is still within me. ²⁴Oh, what a miserable person I am! Who will free me from this life that is dominated by sin and death? ²⁵Thank God! The answer is in Jesus Christ our Lord. So you see how it is: In my mind I really want to obey God's law, but because of my sinful nature I am a slave to sin.

CHAPTER 8

Life in the Spirit

So now there is no condemnation for those who belong to Christ Jesus. ²And because you belong to him, the power* of the life-giving Spirit has freed you* from the power of sin that leads to death. ³The law of Moses was unable to save us because of the weakness of our sinful nature.* So God did what the law could not do. He sent his own Son in a body like the bodies we sinners have. And in that body God declared an end to sin's control over us by giving his Son as a sacrifice for our sins. ⁴He did this so that the just requirement of the law would be fully satisfied for us, who no longer follow our sinful nature but instead follow the Spirit.

⁵Those who are dominated by the sinful nature think about sinful things, but those who are controlled by the Holy Spirit

commands, which were supposed to bring life, brought spiritual death instead. ¹¹Sin took advantage of those commands and deceived me; it used the commands to kill me. ¹²But still, the law itself is holy, and its commands are holy and right and good.

¹³But how can that be? Did the law, which is good, cause my death? Of course not! Sin used what was good to bring about my condemnation to death. So we can see how terrible sin really is. It uses God's good commands for its own evil purposes.

Struggling with Sin

¹⁴So the trouble is not with the law, for it is spiritual and good. The trouble is with me, for I am all too human, a slave to sin. ¹⁵I don't really understand myself, for I want to do

7:18 Greek *my flesh;* also in 7:25.   **7:23** Greek *law;* also in 7:23b.   **8:2a** Greek *the law;* also in 8:2b.   **8:2b** Some manuscripts read *me.*   **8:3** Greek *our flesh;* similarly in 8:4, 5, 6, 7, 8, 9, 12.

think about things that please the Spirit. ⁶So letting your sinful nature control your mind leads to death. But letting the Spirit control your mind leads to life and peace. ⁷For the sinful nature is always hostile to God. It never did obey God's laws, and it never will. ⁸That's why those who are still under the control of their sinful nature can never please God.

⁹But you are not controlled by your sinful nature. You are controlled by the Spirit if you have the Spirit of God living in you. (And remember that those who do not have the Spirit of Christ living in them do not belong to him at all.) ¹⁰And Christ lives within you, so even though your body will die because of sin, the Spirit gives you life* because you have been made right with God. ¹¹The Spirit of God, who raised Jesus from the dead, lives in you. And just as God raised Christ Jesus from the dead, he will give life to your mortal bodies by this same Spirit living within you.

¹²Therefore, dear brothers and sisters,* you have no obligation to do what your sinful nature urges you to do. ¹³For if you live by its dictates, you will die. But if through the power of the Spirit you put to death the deeds of your sinful nature,* you will live. ¹⁴For all who are led by the Spirit of God are children* of God.

¹⁵So you have not received a spirit that makes you fearful slaves. Instead, you received God's Spirit when he adopted you as his own children.* Now we call him, "Abba, Father."* ¹⁶For his Spirit joins with our spirit to affirm that we are God's children. ¹⁷And since we are his children, we are his heirs. In fact, together with Christ we are heirs of God's glory. But if we are to share his glory, we must also share his suffering.

The Future Glory

¹⁸Yet what we suffer now is nothing compared to the glory he will reveal to us later. ¹⁹For all creation is waiting eagerly for that future day when God will reveal who his children really are. ²⁰Against its will, all creation was subjected to God's curse. But with eager hope, ²¹the creation looks forward to the day when it will join God's children in glorious freedom from death and decay. ²²For we know that all creation has been groaning as in the pains of childbirth right up to the present time. ²³And we believers also groan, even though we have the Holy Spirit within us as a foretaste of future glory, for we long for our bodies to be released from sin and suffering. We, too, wait with eager hope for the day when God will give us our full rights as his adopted children,* including the new bodies he has promised us. ²⁴We were given this hope when we were saved. (If we already have something, we don't need to hope* for it. ²⁵But if we look forward to something we don't yet have, we must wait patiently and confidently.)

²⁶And the Holy Spirit helps us in our weakness. For example, we don't know what God wants us to pray for. But the Holy Spirit prays for us with groanings that cannot be expressed in words. ²⁷And the Father who knows all hearts knows what the Spirit is saying, for the Spirit pleads for us believers* in harmony with God's own will. ²⁸And we know that God causes everything to work together* for the good of those who love God and are called according to his purpose for them. ²⁹For God knew his people in advance, and he chose them to become like his Son, so that his Son would be the firstborn* among many brothers and sisters. ³⁰And having chosen them, he called them to come to him. And having called them, he gave them right standing with himself. And having given them right standing, he gave them his glory.

Nothing Can Separate Us from God's Love

³¹What shall we say about such wonderful things as these? If God is for us, who can ever be against us? ³²Since he did not spare even his own Son but gave him up for us all, won't he also give us everything else? ³³Who dares accuse us whom God has chosen for his own? No one—for God himself has

---

8:10 Or *your spirit is alive.* **8:12** Greek *brothers;* also in 8:29. **8:13** Greek *deeds of the body.* **8:14** Greek *sons;* also in 8:19. **8:15a** Greek *you received a spirit of sonship.* **8:15b** *Abba* is an Aramaic term for "father." **8:23** Greek *wait anxiously for sonship.* **8:24** Some manuscripts read *wait.* **8:27** Greek *for God's holy people.* **8:28** Some manuscripts read *And we know that everything works together.* **8:29** Or *would be supreme.*

given us right standing with himself. ³⁴Who then will condemn us? No one—for Christ Jesus died for us and was raised to life for us, and he is sitting in the place of honor at God's right hand, pleading for us.

³⁵Can anything ever separate us from Christ's love? Does it mean he no longer loves us if we have trouble or calamity, or are persecuted, or hungry, or destitute, or in danger, or threatened with death? ³⁶(As the Scriptures say, "For your sake we are killed every day; we are being slaughtered like sheep."*) ³⁷No, despite all these things, overwhelming victory is ours through Christ, who loved us.

³⁸And I am convinced that nothing can ever separate us from God's love. Neither death nor life, neither angels nor demons,* neither our fears for today nor our worries about tomorrow—not even the powers of hell can separate us from God's love. ³⁹No power in the sky above or in the earth below—indeed, nothing in all creation will ever be able to separate us from the love of God that is revealed in Christ Jesus our Lord.

CHAPTER 9

God's Selection of Israel

With Christ as my witness, I speak with utter truthfulness. My conscience and the Holy Spirit confirm it. ²My heart is filled with bitter sorrow and unending grief ³for my people, my Jewish brothers and sisters.* I would be willing to be forever cursed—cut off from Christ!—if that would save them. ⁴They are the people of Israel, chosen to be God's adopted children.* God revealed his glory to them. He made covenants with them and gave them his law. He gave them the privilege of worshiping him and receiving his wonderful promises. ⁵Abraham, Isaac, and Jacob are their ancestors, and Christ himself was an Israelite as far as his human nature is concerned. And he is God, the one who rules over everything and is worthy of eternal praise! Amen.*

⁶Well then, has God failed to fulfill his promise to Israel? No, for not all who are born into the nation of Israel are truly members of God's people! ⁷Being descendants of Abraham doesn't make them truly Abraham's children. For the Scriptures say, "Isaac is the son through whom your descendants will be counted,"* though Abraham had other children, too. ⁸This means that Abraham's physical descendants are not necessarily children of God. Only the children of the promise are considered to be Abraham's children. ⁹For God had promised, "I will return about this time next year, and Sarah will have a son."*

¹⁰This son was our ancestor Isaac. When he married Rebekah, she gave birth to twins.* ¹¹But before they were born, before they had done anything good or bad, she received a message from God. (This message shows that God chooses people according to his own purposes; ¹²he calls people, but not according to their good or bad works.) She was told, "Your older son will serve your younger son."* ¹³In the words of the Scriptures, "I loved Jacob, but I rejected Esau."*

¹⁴Are we saying, then, that God was unfair? Of course not! ¹⁵For God said to Moses,

"I will show mercy to anyone I choose,
and I will show compassion to anyone I choose."*

¹⁶So it is God who decides to show mercy. We can neither choose it nor work for it.

¹⁷For the Scriptures say that God told Pharaoh, "I have appointed you for the very purpose of displaying my power in you and to spread my fame throughout the earth."* ¹⁸So you see, God chooses to show mercy to some, and he chooses to harden the hearts of others so they refuse to listen.

¹⁹Well then, you might say, "Why does God blame people for not responding? Haven't they simply done what he makes them do?"

²⁰No, don't say that. Who are you, a mere human being,

"I will show mercy to anyone I choose, and I will show compassion to anyone I choose" (Romans 9:15).

"I created mercy and compassion, and I will shower it on my people whenever I want to."

8:36 Ps 44:22.   **8:38** Greek *nor rulers.*   **9:3** Greek *my brothers.*   **9:4** Greek *chosen for sonship.*   **9:5** Or *May God, the one who rules over everything, be praised forever. Amen.*
9:7 Gen 21:12.   **9:9** Gen 18:10, 14.   **9:10** Greek *she conceived children through this one man.*   **9:12** Gen 25:23.   **9:13** Mal 1:2-3.   **9:15** Exod 33:19.   **9:17** Exod 9:16 (Greek version).

"Who are you, a mere human being, to argue with God? Should the thing that was created say to the one who created it, 'Why have you made me like this?'" (Romans 9:20).

Who are you to argue with God? You are human, created by him. Should the creation question the creator by asking, "Why'd you make me wild out like this?"

to argue with God? Should the thing that was created say to the one who created it, "Why have you made me like this?" ²¹When a potter makes jars out of clay, doesn't he have a right to use the same lump of clay to make one jar for decoration and another to throw garbage into? ²²In the same way, even though God has the right to show his anger and his power, he is very patient with those on whom his anger falls, who are destined for destruction. ²³He does this to make the riches of his glory shine even brighter on those to whom he shows mercy, who were prepared in advance for glory. ²⁴And we are among those whom he selected, both from the Jews and from the Gentiles.

²⁵Concerning the Gentiles, God says in the prophecy of Hosea,

"Those who were not my people,
    I will now call my people.
And I will love those
    whom I did not love before."*

²⁶And,

"Then, at the place where they were told,
    'You are not my people,'
there they will be called
    'children of the living God.'"*

²⁷And concerning Israel, Isaiah the prophet cried out,

"Though the people of Israel are as numerous as the
        sand of the seashore,
    only a remnant will be saved.
²⁸ For the LORD will carry out his sentence upon the earth
        quickly and with finality."*

²⁹And Isaiah said the same thing in another place:

"If the LORD of Heaven's Armies
        had not spared a few of our children,

we would have been wiped out like Sodom,
        destroyed like Gomorrah."*

Israel's Unbelief

³⁰What does all this mean? Even though the Gentiles were not trying to follow God's standards, they were made right with God. And it was by faith that this took place. ³¹But the people of Israel, who tried so hard to get right with God by keeping the law, never succeeded. ³²Why not? Because they were trying to get right with God by keeping the law* instead of by trusting in him. They stumbled over the great rock in their path. ³³God warned them of this in the Scriptures when he said,

"I am placing a stone in Jerusalem* that makes people
        stumble,
    a rock that makes them fall.
But anyone who trusts in him
    will never be disgraced."*

CHAPTER 10

Dear brothers and sisters,* the longing of my heart and my prayer to God is for the people of Israel to be saved. ²I know what enthusiasm they have for God, but it is misdirected zeal. ³For they don't understand God's way of making people right with himself. Refusing to accept God's way, they cling to their own way of getting right with God by trying to keep the law. ⁴For Christ has already accomplished the purpose for which the law was given.* As a result, all who believe in him are made right with God.

Salvation Is for Everyone

⁵For Moses writes that the law's way of making a person right with God requires obedience to all of its commands.* ⁶But faith's way of getting right with God says, "Don't say in your heart, 'Who will go up to heaven?' (to bring Christ

9:25 Hos 2:23. 9:26 Greek *sons of the living God.* Hos 1:10. 9:27-28 Isa 10:22-23 (Greek version). 9:29 Isa 1:9. 9:32 Greek *by works.* 9:33a Greek *in Zion.* 9:33b Isa 8:14; 28:16 (Greek version). 10:1 Greek *Brothers.* 10:4 Or *For Christ is the end of the law.* 10:5 See Lev 18:5.

down to earth). 7And don't say, 'Who will go down to the place of the dead?' (to bring Christ back to life again)." 8In fact, it says,

> "The message is very close at hand;
>   it is on your lips and in your heart."*

And that message is the very message about faith that we preach: 9If you confess with your mouth that Jesus is Lord and believe in your heart that God raised him from the dead, you will be saved. 10For it is by believing in your heart that you are made right with God, and it is by confessing with your mouth that you are saved. 11As the Scriptures tell us, "Anyone who trusts in him will never be disgraced."* 12Jew and Gentile* are the same in this respect. They have the same Lord, who gives generously to all who call on him. 13For "Everyone who calls on the name of the LORD will be saved."*

14But how can they call on him to save them unless they believe in him? And how can they believe in him if they have never heard about him? And how can they hear about him unless someone tells them? 15And how will anyone go and tell them without being sent? That is why the Scriptures say, "How beautiful are the feet of messengers who bring good news!"*

16But not everyone welcomes the Good News, for Isaiah the prophet said, "LORD, who has believed our message?"* 17So faith comes from hearing, that is, hearing the Good News about Christ. 18But I ask, have the people of Israel actually heard the message? Yes, they have:

> "The message has gone throughout the earth,
>   and the words to all the world."*

19But I ask, did the people of Israel really understand? Yes, they did, for even in the time of Moses, God said,

> "I will rouse your jealousy through people who are not
>   even a nation.
>   I will provoke your anger through the foolish
>   Gentiles."*

20And later Isaiah spoke boldly for God, saying,

> "I was found by people who were not looking for me.
>   I showed myself to those who were not asking for
>   me."*

21But regarding Israel, God said,

> "All day long I opened my arms to them,
>   but they were disobedient and rebellious."*

CHAPTER 11

God's Mercy on Israel

I ask, then, has God rejected his own people, the nation of Israel? Of course not! I myself am an Israelite, a descendant of Abraham and a member of the tribe of Benjamin.

2No, God has not rejected his own people, whom he chose from the very beginning. Do you realize what the Scriptures say about this? Elijah the prophet complained to God about the people of Israel and said, 3"LORD, they have killed your prophets and torn down your altars. I am the only one left, and now they are trying to kill me, too."*

4And do you remember God's reply? He said, "No, I have 7,000 others who have never bowed down to Baal!"*

5It is the same today, for a few of the people of Israel* have remained faithful because of God's grace—his undeserved kindness in choosing them. 6And since it is through God's kindness, then it is not by their good works. For in that case, God's grace would not be what it really is—free and undeserved.

7So this is the situation: Most of the people of Israel have not found the favor of God they are looking for so earnestly. A few have—the ones God has chosen—but the hearts of the rest were hardened. 8As the Scriptures say,

10:6-8 Deut 30:12-14.   10:11 Isa 28:16 (Greek version).   10:12 Greek *and Greek*.   10:13 Joel 2:32.   10:15 Isa 52:7.   10:16 Isa 53:1.   10:18 Ps 19:4.   10:19 Deut 32:21.   10:20 Isa 65:1 (Greek version).   10:21 Isa 65:2 (Greek version).   11:3 1 Kgs 19:10, 14.   11:4 1 Kgs 19:18.   11:5 Greek *for a remnant*.

"God has put them into a deep sleep.
To this day he has shut their eyes so they do not see,
and closed their ears so they do not hear."*

[9]Likewise, David said,

"Let their bountiful table become a snare,
a trap that makes them think all is well.
Let their blessings cause them to stumble,
and let them get what they deserve.
[10] Let their eyes go blind so they cannot see,
and let their backs be bent forever."*

[11]Did God's people stumble and fall beyond recovery? Of course not! They were disobedient, so God made salvation available to the Gentiles. But he wanted his own people to become jealous and claim it for themselves. [12]Now if the Gentiles were enriched because the people of Israel turned down God's offer of salvation, think how much greater a blessing the world will share when they finally accept it.

[13]I am saying all this especially for you Gentiles. God has appointed me as the apostle to the Gentiles. I stress this, [14]for I want somehow to make the people of Israel jealous of what you Gentiles have, so I might save some of them. [15]For since their rejection meant that God offered salvation to the rest of the world, their acceptance will be even more wonderful. It will be life for those who were dead! [16]And since Abraham and the other patriarchs were holy, their descendants will also be holy—just as the entire batch of dough is holy because the portion given as an offering is holy. For if the roots of the tree are holy, the branches will be, too.

[17]But some of these branches from Abraham's tree—some of the people of Israel—have been broken off. And you Gentiles, who were branches from a wild olive tree, have been grafted in. So now you also receive the blessing God has promised Abraham and his children, sharing in the rich nourishment from the root of God's special olive tree. [18]But you must not brag about being grafted in to replace the branches that were broken off. You are just a branch, not the root.

[19]"Well," you may say, "those branches were broken off to make room for me." [20]Yes, but remember—those branches were broken off because they didn't believe in Christ, and you are there because you do believe. So don't think highly of yourself, but fear what could happen. [21]For if God did not spare the original branches, he won't* spare you either.

[22]Notice how God is both kind and severe. He is severe toward those who disobeyed, but kind to you if you continue to trust in his kindness. But if you stop trusting, you also will be cut off. [23]And if the people of Israel turn from their unbelief, they will be grafted in again, for God has the power to graft them back into the tree. [24]You, by nature, were a branch cut from a wild olive tree. So if God was willing to do something contrary to nature by grafting you into his cultivated tree, he will be far more eager to graft the original branches back into the tree where they belong.

God's Mercy Is for Everyone

[25]I want you to understand this mystery, dear brothers and sisters,* so that you will not feel proud about yourselves. Some of the people of Israel have hard hearts, but this will last only until the full number of Gentiles comes to Christ. [26]And so all Israel will be saved. As the Scriptures say,

"The one who rescues will come from Jerusalem,*
and he will turn Israel* away from ungodliness.
[27] And this is my covenant with them,
that I will take away their sins."*

[28]Many of the people of Israel are now enemies of the Good News, and this benefits you Gentiles. Yet they are still the people he loves because he chose their ancestors Abraham, Isaac, and Jacob. [29]For God's gifts and his call can never

11:8 Isa 29:10; Deut 29:4.   11:9-10 Ps 69:22-23 (Greek version).   11:21 Some manuscripts read *perhaps he won't*.   11:25 Greek *brothers*.   11:26a Greek *from Zion*.   11:26b Greek *Jacob*.   11:26-27 Isa 59:20-21; 27:9 (Greek version).

be withdrawn. ³⁰Once, you Gentiles were rebels against God, but when the people of Israel rebelled against him, God was merciful to you instead. ³¹Now they are the rebels, and God's mercy has come to you so that they, too, will share* in God's mercy. ³²For God has imprisoned everyone in disobedience so he could have mercy on everyone.

³³Oh, how great are God's riches and wisdom and knowledge! How impossible it is for us to understand his decisions and his ways!

³⁴ For who can know the LORD's thoughts?
    Who knows enough to give him advice?*
³⁵ And who has given him so much
    that he needs to pay it back?*

³⁶For everything comes from him and exists by his power and is intended for his glory. All glory to him forever! Amen.

CHAPTER 12

A Living Sacrifice to God

And so, dear brothers and sisters,* I plead with you to give your bodies to God because of all he has done for you. Let them be a living and holy sacrifice—the kind he will find acceptable. This is truly the way to worship him.* ²Don't copy the behavior and customs of this world, but let God transform you into a new person by changing the way you think. Then you will learn to know God's will for you, which is good and pleasing and perfect.

³Because of the privilege and authority* God has given me, I give each of you this warning: Don't think you are better than you really are. Be honest in your evaluation of yourselves, measuring yourselves by the faith God has given us.* ⁴Just as our bodies have many parts and each part has a special function, ⁵so it is with Christ's body. We are many parts of one body, and we all belong to each other.

⁶In his grace, God has given us different gifts for doing certain things well. So if God has given you the ability to prophesy, speak out with as much faith as God has given you. ⁷If your gift is serving others, serve them well. If you are a teacher, teach well. ⁸If your gift is to encourage others, be encouraging. If it is giving, give generously. If God has given you leadership ability, take the responsibility seriously. And if you have a gift for showing kindness to others, do it gladly.

⁹Don't just pretend to love others. Really love them. Hate what is wrong. Hold tightly to what is good. ¹⁰Love each other with genuine affection,* and take delight in honoring each other. ¹¹Never be lazy, but work hard and serve the Lord enthusiastically.* ¹²Rejoice in our confident hope. Be patient in trouble, and keep on praying. ¹³When God's people are in need, be ready to help them. Always be eager to practice hospitality.

¹⁴Bless those who persecute you. Don't curse them; pray that God will bless them. ¹⁵Be happy with those who are happy, and weep with those who weep. ¹⁶Live in harmony with each other. Don't be too proud to enjoy the company of ordinary people. And don't think you know it all!

¹⁷Never pay back evil with more evil. Do things in such a way that everyone can see you are honorable. ¹⁸Do all that you can to live in peace with everyone.

¹⁹Dear friends, never take revenge. Leave that to the righteous anger of God. For the Scriptures say,

"I will take revenge;
    I will pay them back,"*
    says the LORD.

²⁰Instead,

"If your enemies are hungry, feed them.
    If they are thirsty, give them something to drink.

"Don't copy the behavior and customs of this world, but let God transform you into a new person by changing the way you think. Then you will learn to know God's will for you, which is good and pleasing and perfect" (Romans 12:2).

say what?

Don't try to be like the people of this world. When God transforms you, he'll change the way you think. Then you'll learn that his plan for you is perfect.

11:31 Other manuscripts read *will now share;* still others read *will someday share.*   **11:34** Isa 40:13 (Greek version).   **11:35** See Job 41:11.   **12:1a** Greek *brothers.*   **12:1b** Or *This is your spiritual worship;* or *This is your reasonable service.*   **12:3a** Or *Because of the grace;* compare 1:5.   **12:3b** Or *by the faith God has given you;* or *by the standard of our God-given faith.*   **12:10** Greek *with brotherly love.*   **12:11** Or *but serve the Lord with a zealous spirit;* or *but let the Spirit excite you as you serve the Lord.*   **12:19** Deut 32:35.

In doing this, you will heap
    burning coals of shame on their heads."*

²¹Don't let evil conquer you, but conquer evil by doing good.

CHAPTER 13

Respect for Authority

Everyone must submit to governing authorities. For all authority comes from God, and those in positions of authority have been placed there by God. ²So anyone who rebels against authority is rebelling against what God has instituted, and they will be punished. ³For the authorities do not strike fear in people who are doing right, but in those who are doing wrong. Would you like to live without fear of the authorities? Do what is right, and they will honor you. ⁴The authorities are God's servants, sent for your good. But if you are doing wrong, of course you should be afraid, for they have the power to punish you. They are God's servants, sent for the very purpose of punishing those who do what is wrong. ⁵So you must submit to them, not only to avoid punishment, but also to keep a clear conscience.

⁶Pay your taxes, too, for these same reasons. For government workers need to be paid. They are serving God in what they do. ⁷Give to everyone what you owe them: Pay your taxes and government fees to those who collect them, and give respect and honor to those who are in authority.

Love Fulfills God's Requirements

⁸Owe nothing to anyone—except for your obligation to love one another. If you love your neighbor, you will fulfill the requirements of God's law. ⁹For the commandments say, "You must not commit adultery. You must not murder. You must not steal. You must not covet."* These—and other such commandments—are summed up in this one commandment: "Love your neighbor as yourself."* ¹⁰Love does no wrong to others, so love fulfills the requirements of God's law.

¹¹This is all the more urgent, for you know how late it is; time is running out. Wake up, for our salvation is nearer now than when we first believed. ¹²The night is almost gone; the day of salvation will soon be here. So remove your dark deeds like dirty clothes, and put on the shining armor of right living. ¹³Because we belong to the day, we must live decent lives for all to see. Don't participate in the darkness of wild parties and drunkenness, or in sexual promiscuity and immoral living, or in quarreling and jealousy. ¹⁴Instead, clothe yourself with the presence of the Lord Jesus Christ. And don't let yourself think about ways to indulge your evil desires.

CHAPTER 14

The Danger of Criticism

Accept other believers who are weak in faith, and don't argue with them about what they think is right or wrong. ²For instance, one person believes it's all right to eat anything. But another believer with a sensitive conscience will eat only vegetables. ³Those who feel free to eat anything must not look down on those who don't. And those who don't eat certain foods must not condemn those who do, for God has accepted them. ⁴Who are you to condemn someone else's servants? Their own master will judge whether they stand or fall. And with the Lord's help, they will stand and receive his approval.

⁵In the same way, some think one day is more holy than another day, while others think every day is alike. You should each be fully convinced that whichever day you choose is acceptable. ⁶Those who worship the Lord on a special day do it to honor him. Those who eat any kind of food do so to honor the Lord, since they give thanks to God before eating. And those who refuse to eat certain foods also want to please the Lord and give thanks to God. ⁷For we don't live for ourselves or die for ourselves. ⁸If we live, it's to honor the Lord. And if we die, it's to honor the Lord. So whether

12:20 Prov 25:21-22.   13:9a Exod 20:13-15, 17.   13:9b Lev 19:18.

we live or die, we belong to the Lord. ⁹Christ died and rose again for this very purpose—to be Lord both of the living and of the dead.

¹⁰So why do you condemn another believer*? Why do you look down on another believer? Remember, we will all stand before the judgment seat of God. ¹¹For the Scriptures say,

"'As surely as I live,' says the LORD,
'every knee will bend to me,
    and every tongue will confess and give praise to
    God.*'"

¹²Yes, each of us will give a personal account to God. ¹³So let's stop condemning each other. Decide instead to live in such a way that you will not cause another believer to stumble and fall.

¹⁴I know and am convinced on the authority of the Lord Jesus that no food, in and of itself, is wrong to eat. But if someone believes it is wrong, then for that person it is wrong. ¹⁵And if another believer is distressed by what you eat, you are not acting in love if you eat it. Don't let your eating ruin someone for whom Christ died. ¹⁶Then you will not be criticized for doing something you believe is good. ¹⁷For the Kingdom of God is not a matter of what we eat or drink, but of living a life of goodness and peace and joy in the Holy Spirit. ¹⁸If you serve Christ with this attitude, you will please God, and others will approve of you, too. ¹⁹So then, let us aim for harmony in the church and try to build each other up.

²⁰Don't tear apart the work of God over what you eat. Remember, all foods are acceptable, but it is wrong to eat something if it makes another person stumble. ²¹It is better not to eat meat or drink wine or do anything else if it might cause another believer to stumble. ²²You may believe there's nothing wrong with what you are doing, but keep it between yourself and God. Blessed are those who don't feel guilty for doing something they have decided is right. ²³But if you have doubts about whether or not you should eat something, you are sinning if you go ahead and do it. For you are not following your convictions. If you do anything you believe is not right, you are sinning.

CHAPTER 15

Living to Please Others

We who are strong must be considerate of those who are sensitive about things like this. We must not just please ourselves. ²We should help others do what is right and build them up in the Lord. ³For even Christ didn't live to please himself. As the Scriptures say, "The insults of those who insult you, O God, have fallen on me."* ⁴Such things were written in the Scriptures long ago to teach us. And the Scriptures give us hope and encouragement as we wait patiently for God's promises to be fulfilled.

⁵May God, who gives this patience and encouragement, help you live in complete harmony with each other, as is fitting for followers of Christ Jesus. ⁶Then all of you can join together with one voice, giving praise and glory to God, the Father of our Lord Jesus Christ.

⁷Therefore, accept each other just as Christ has accepted you so that God will be given glory. ⁸Remember that Christ came as a servant to the Jews* to show that God is true to the promises he made to their ancestors. ⁹He also came so that the Gentiles might give glory to God for his mercies to them. That is what the psalmist meant when he wrote:

"For this, I will praise you among the Gentiles;
    I will sing praises to your name."*

¹⁰And in another place it is written,

"Rejoice with his people,
    you Gentiles."*

14:10 Greek *your brother;* also in 14:10b, 13, 15, 21.   14:11 Or *confess allegiance to God.* Isa 49:18; 45:23 (Greek version).   15:3 Greek *who insult you have fallen on me.* Ps 69:9.
15:8 Greek *servant of circumcision.*   15:9 Ps 18:49.   15:10 Deut 32:43.

[11]And yet again,

"Praise the LORD, all you Gentiles.
Praise him, all you people of the earth."*

[12]And in another place Isaiah said,

"The heir to David's throne* will come,
and he will rule over the Gentiles.
They will place their hope on him."*

[13]I pray that God, the source of hope, will fill you completely with joy and peace because you trust in him. Then you will overflow with confident hope through the power of the Holy Spirit.

Paul's Reason for Writing

[14]I am fully convinced, my dear brothers and sisters,* that you are full of goodness. You know these things so well you can teach each other all about them. [15]Even so, I have been bold enough to write about some of these points, knowing that all you need is this reminder. For by God's grace, [16]I am a special messenger from Christ Jesus to you Gentiles. I bring you the Good News so that I might present you as an acceptable offering to God, made holy by the Holy Spirit. [17]So I have reason to be enthusiastic about all Christ Jesus has done through me in my service to God. [18]Yet I dare not boast about anything except what Christ has done through me, bringing the Gentiles to God by my message and by the way I worked among them. [19]They were convinced by the power of miraculous signs and wonders and by the power of God's Spirit.* In this way, I have fully presented the Good News of Christ from Jerusalem all the way to Illyricum.*

[20]My ambition has always been to preach the Good News where the name of Christ has never been heard, rather than where a church has already been started by someone else.

[21]I have been following the plan spoken of in the Scriptures, where it says,

"Those who have never been told about him will see,
and those who have never heard of him will understand."*

[22]In fact, my visit to you has been delayed so long because I have been preaching in these places.

Paul's Travel Plans

[23]But now I have finished my work in these regions, and after all these long years of waiting, I am eager to visit you. [24]I am planning to go to Spain, and when I do, I will stop off in Rome. And after I have enjoyed your fellowship for a little while, you can provide for my journey.

[25]But before I come, I must go to Jerusalem to take a gift to the believers* there. [26]For you see, the believers in Macedonia and Achaia* have eagerly taken up an offering for the poor among the believers in Jerusalem. [27]They were glad to do this because they feel they owe a real debt to them. Since the Gentiles received the spiritual blessings of the Good News from the believers in Jerusalem, they feel the least they can do in return is to help them financially. [28]As soon as I have delivered this money and completed this good deed of theirs, I will come to see you on my way to Spain. [29]And I am sure that when I come, Christ will richly bless our time together.

[30]Dear brothers and sisters, I urge you in the name of our Lord Jesus Christ to join in my struggle by praying to God for me. Do this because of your love for me, given to you by the Holy Spirit. [31]Pray that I will be rescued from those in Judea who refuse to obey God. Pray also that the believers there will be willing to accept the donation* I am taking to Jerusalem. [32]Then, by the will of God, I will be able to come to you with a joyful heart, and we will be an encouragement to each other.

15:11 Ps 117:1. 15:12a Greek *The root of Jesse.* David was the son of Jesse. 15:12b Isa 11:10 (Greek version). 15:14 Greek *brothers;* also in 15:30. 15:19a Other manuscripts read *the Spirit;* still others read *the Holy Spirit.* 15:19b *Illyricum* was a region northeast of Italy. 15:21 Isa 52:15 (Greek version). 15:25 Greek *God's holy people;* also in 15:26, 31. 15:26 *Macedonia* and *Achaia* were the northern and southern regions of Greece. 15:31 Greek *the ministry;* other manuscripts read *the gift.*

[33]And now may God, who gives us his peace, be with you all. Amen.*

CHAPTER 16

Paul Greets His Friends

I commend to you our sister Phoebe, who is a deacon in the church in Cenchrea. [2]Welcome her in the Lord as one who is worthy of honor among God's people. Help her in whatever she needs, for she has been helpful to many, and especially to me.

[3]Give my greetings to Priscilla and Aquila, my co-workers in the ministry of Christ Jesus. [4]In fact, they once risked their lives for me. I am thankful to them, and so are all the Gentile churches. [5]Also give my greetings to the church that meets in their home.

Greet my dear friend Epenetus. He was the first person from the province of Asia to become a follower of Christ. [6]Give my greetings to Mary, who has worked so hard for your benefit. [7]Greet Andronicus and Junia,* my fellow Jews,* who were in prison with me. They are highly respected among the apostles and became followers of Christ before I did. [8]Greet Ampliatus, my dear friend in the Lord. [9]Greet Urbanus, our co-worker in Christ, and my dear friend Stachys.

[10]Greet Apelles, a good man whom Christ approves. And give my greetings to the believers from the household of Aristobulus. [11]Greet Herodion, my fellow Jew.* Greet the Lord's people from the household of Narcissus. [12]Give my greetings to Tryphena and Tryphosa, the Lord's workers, and to dear Persis, who has worked so hard for the Lord. [13]Greet Rufus, whom the Lord picked out to be his very own; and also his dear mother, who has been a mother to me.

[14]Give my greetings to Asyncritus, Phlegon, Hermes, Patrobas, Hermas, and the brothers and sisters* who meet with them. [15]Give my greetings to Philologus, Julia, Nereus and his sister, and to Olympas and all the believers* who meet with them. [16]Greet each other in Christian love.* All the churches of Christ send you their greetings.

Paul's Final Instructions

[17]And now I make one more appeal, my dear brothers and sisters. Watch out for people who cause divisions and upset people's faith by teaching things contrary to what you have been taught. Stay away from them. [18]Such people are not serving Christ our Lord; they are serving their own personal interests. By smooth talk and glowing words they deceive innocent people. [19]But everyone knows that you are obedient to the Lord. This makes me very happy. I want you to be wise in doing right and to stay innocent of any wrong. [20]The God of peace will soon crush Satan under your feet. May the grace of our Lord Jesus* be with you.

[21]Timothy, my fellow worker, sends you his greetings, as do Lucius, Jason, and Sosipater, my fellow Jews.

[22]I, Tertius, the one writing this letter for Paul, send my greetings, too, as one of the Lord's followers.

[23]Gaius says hello to you. He is my host and also serves as host to the whole church. Erastus, the city treasurer, sends you his greetings, and so does our brother Quartus.*

[25]Now all glory to God, who is able to make you strong, just as my Good News says. This message about Jesus Christ has revealed his plan for you Gentiles, a plan kept secret from the beginning of time. [26]But now as the prophets* foretold and as the eternal God has commanded, this message is made known to all Gentiles everywhere, so that they too might believe and obey him. [27]All glory to the only wise God, through Jesus Christ, forever. Amen.

15:33 Some manuscripts do not include *Amen.* One very early manuscript places 16:25-27 here. *Junias,* a masculine name; still others read *Julia* (feminine). **16:7a** *Junia* is a feminine name. Some late manuscripts accent the word so it reads *Junias,* a masculine name; still others read *Julia* (feminine).   **16:7b** Or *compatriots;* also in 16:21.   **16:11** Or *compatriot.*   **16:14** Greek *brothers;* also in 16:17.   **16:15** Greek *all of God's holy people.*   **16:16** Greek *with a sacred kiss.*   **16:20** Some manuscripts read *Lord Jesus Christ.*   **16:23** Some manuscripts add verse 24, *May the grace of our Lord Jesus Christ be with you all. Amen.* Still others add this sentence after verse 27.   **16:26** Greek *the prophetic writings.*

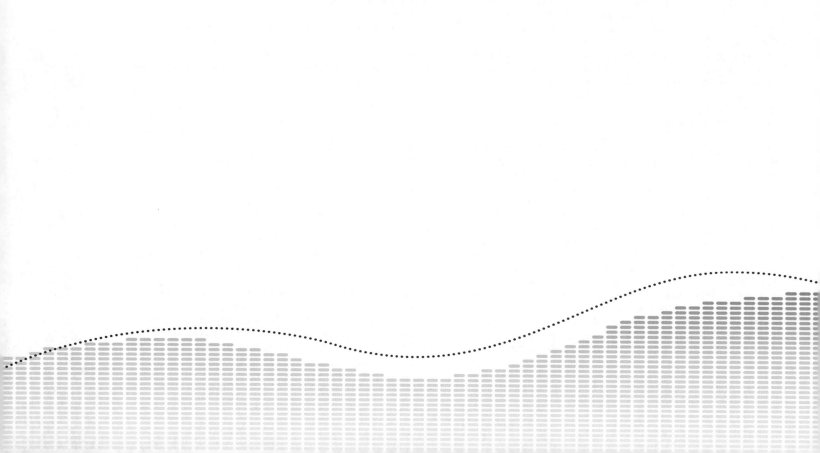

THE APOSTLE PAUL WROTE this letter to a church in the city of Corinth (in Greece). The people of Corinth had a lot of bling-bling, but very few morals. They had no shame. Not only did they "bring sexy back," they also started dividin' the community over the wrong kinda things. Some people started thinkin' they were better than everybody else. So Paul wrote this letter to the Corinthians to straighten out their off-the-chain thinking and behavior. He wanted them to remember that true love is all about thinkin' about the brothas and sistas first and then lookin' to take care of our own needs later. It's not about lookin' out for *numero uno*.

1 CORINTHIANS

CHAPTER **1**

Greetings from Paul

This letter is from Paul, chosen by the will of God to be an apostle of Christ Jesus, and from our brother Sosthenes.

²I am writing to God's church in Corinth,* to you who have been called by God to be his own holy people. He made you holy by means of Christ Jesus,* just as he did for all people everywhere who call on the name of our Lord Jesus Christ, their Lord and ours.

³May God our Father and the Lord Jesus Christ give you grace and peace.

Paul Gives Thanks to God

⁴I always thank my God for you and for the gracious gifts he has given you, now that you belong to Christ Jesus. ⁵Through him, God has enriched your church in every way—with all of your eloquent words and all of your knowledge. ⁶This confirms that what I told you about Christ is true. ⁷Now you have every spiritual gift you need as you eagerly wait for the return of our Lord Jesus Christ. ⁸He will keep you strong to the end so that you will be free from all blame on the day when our Lord Jesus Christ returns. ⁹God will do this, for he is faithful to do what he says, and he has invited you into partnership with his Son, Jesus Christ our Lord.

Divisions in the Church

¹⁰I appeal to you, dear brothers and sisters,* by the authority of our Lord Jesus Christ, to live in harmony with each other. Let there be no divisions in the church. Rather, be of one mind, united in thought and purpose. ¹¹For some members of Chloe's household have told me about your quarrels, my dear brothers and sisters. ¹²Some of you are saying, "I am a follower of Paul." Others are saying, "I follow Apollos," or "I follow Peter,*" or "I follow only Christ."

¹³Has Christ been divided into factions? Was I, Paul, crucified for you? Were any of you baptized in the name of Paul? Of course not! ¹⁴I thank God that I did not baptize any of you except Crispus and Gaius, ¹⁵for now no one can say they were baptized in my name. ¹⁶(Oh yes, I also baptized the household of Stephanas, but I don't remember baptizing anyone else.) ¹⁷For Christ didn't send me to baptize, but to preach the Good News—and not with clever speech, for fear that the cross of Christ would lose its power.

The Wisdom of God

¹⁸The message of the cross is foolish to those who are headed for destruction! But we who are being saved know it is the very power of God. ¹⁹As the Scriptures say,

"I will destroy the wisdom of the wise
    and discard the intelligence of the intelligent."*

²⁰So where does this leave the philosophers, the scholars, and the world's brilliant debaters? God has made the wisdom of this world look foolish. ²¹Since God in his wisdom saw to it that the world would never know him through human wisdom, he has used our foolish preaching to save those who believe. ²²It is foolish to the Jews, who ask for signs from heaven. And it is foolish to the Greeks, who seek human wis-

1:2a *Corinth* was the capital city of Achaia, the southern region of the Greek peninsula.   1:2b Or *because you belong to Christ Jesus.*   1:10 Greek *brothers;* also in 1:11, 26.   1:12 Greek *Cephas.*   1:19 Isa 29:14.

dom. ²³So when we preach that Christ was crucified, the Jews are offended and the Gentiles say it's all nonsense.

²⁴But to those called by God to salvation, both Jews and Gentiles,* Christ is the power of God and the wisdom of God. ²⁵This foolish plan of God is wiser than the wisest of human plans, and God's weakness is stronger than the greatest of human strength.

²⁶Remember, dear brothers and sisters, that few of you were wise in the world's eyes or powerful or wealthy* when God called you. ²⁷Instead, God chose things the world considers foolish in order to shame those who think they are wise. And he chose things that are powerless to shame those who are powerful. ²⁸God chose things despised by the world,* things counted as nothing at all, and used them to bring to nothing what the world considers important. ²⁹As a result, no one can ever boast in the presence of God.

³⁰God has united you with Christ Jesus. For our benefit God made him to be wisdom itself. Christ made us right with God; he made us pure and holy, and he freed us from sin. ³¹Therefore, as the Scriptures say, "If you want to boast, boast only about the LORD."*

CHAPTER 2
Paul's Message of Wisdom

When I first came to you, dear brothers and sisters,* I didn't use lofty words and impressive wisdom to tell you God's secret plan.* ²For I decided that while I was with you I would forget everything except Jesus Christ, the one who was crucified. ³I came to you in weakness—timid and trembling. ⁴And my message and my preaching were very plain. Rather than using clever and persuasive speeches, I relied only on the power of the Holy Spirit. ⁵I did this so you would trust not in human wisdom but in the power of God.

⁶Yet when I am among mature believers, I do speak with words of wisdom, but not the kind of wisdom that belongs to this world or to the rulers of this world, who are soon forgotten. ⁷No, the wisdom we speak of is the mystery of God*—his plan that was previously hidden, even though he made it for our ultimate glory before the world began. ⁸But the rulers of this world have not understood it; if they had, they would not have crucified our glorious Lord. ⁹That is what the Scriptures mean when they say,

> "No eye has seen, no ear has heard,
>   and no mind has imagined
> what God has prepared
>   for those who love him."*

¹⁰But* it was to us that God revealed these things by his Spirit. For his Spirit searches out everything and shows us God's deep secrets. ¹¹No one can know a person's thoughts except that person's own spirit, and no one can know God's thoughts except God's own Spirit. ¹²And we have received God's Spirit (not the world's spirit), so we can know the wonderful things God has freely given us.

¹³When we tell you these things, we do not use words that come from human wisdom. Instead, we speak words given to us by the Spirit, using the Spirit's words to explain spiritual truths.* ¹⁴But people who aren't spiritual* can't receive these truths from God's Spirit. It all sounds foolish to them and they can't understand it, for only those who are spiritual can understand what the Spirit means. ¹⁵Those who are spiritual can evaluate all things, but they themselves cannot be evaluated by others. ¹⁶For,

> "Who can know the LORD's thoughts?
>   Who knows enough to teach him?"*

But we understand these things, for we have the mind of Christ.

"This foolish plan of God is wiser than the wisest of human plans, and God's weakness is stronger than the greatest of human strength" (1 Corinthians 1:25).

say wyat?

God's craziest plan is way smarter than the wisest plan anybody can come up with, and God's weakness is stronger than a million brolic dudes.

1:24 Greek *and Greeks.*   **1:26** Or *high born.*   **1:28** Or *God chose those who are low born.*   **1:31** Jer 9:24.   **2:1a** Greek *brothers.*   **2:1b** Greek *God's mystery;* other manuscripts read *God's testimony.*   **2:7** Greek *But we speak God's wisdom in a mystery.*   **2:9** Isa 64:4.   **2:10** Some manuscripts read *For.*   **2:13** Or *explaining spiritual truths in spiritual language,* or *explaining spiritual truths to spiritual people.*   **2:14** Or *who don't have the Spirit;* or *who have only physical life.*   **2:16** Isa 40:13 (Greek version).

Don't you know that the crew—as a whole—is the place where God and the Holy Spirit live? They live in you! God will take out people who try to come against his house. God's temple is holy, and you are that temple!

CHAPTER 3

Paul and Apollos, Servants of Christ

Dear brothers and sisters,* when I was with you I couldn't talk to you as I would to spiritual people.* I had to talk as though you belonged to this world or as though you were infants in the Christian life.* ²I had to feed you with milk, not with solid food, because you weren't ready for anything stronger. And you still aren't ready, ³for you are still controlled by your sinful nature. You are jealous of one another and quarrel with each other. Doesn't that prove you are controlled by your sinful nature? Aren't you living like people of the world? ⁴When one of you says, "I am a follower of Paul," and another says, "I follow Apollos," aren't you acting just like people of the world?

⁵After all, who is Apollos? Who is Paul? We are only God's servants through whom you believed the Good News. Each of us did the work the Lord gave us. ⁶I planted the seed in your hearts, and Apollos watered it, but it was God who made it grow. ⁷It's not important who does the planting, or who does the watering. What's important is that God makes the seed grow. ⁸The one who plants and the one who waters work together with the same purpose. And both will be rewarded for their own hard work. ⁹For we are both God's workers. And you are God's field. You are God's building.

¹⁰Because of God's grace to me, I have laid the foundation like an expert builder. Now others are building on it. But whoever is building on this foundation must be very careful. ¹¹For no one can lay any foundation other than the one we already have—Jesus Christ.

¹²Anyone who builds on that foundation may use a variety of materials—gold, silver, jewels, wood, hay, or straw. ¹³But on the judgment day, fire will reveal what kind of work each builder has done. The fire will show if a person's work has any value. ¹⁴If the work survives, that builder will receive a reward. ¹⁵But if the work is burned up, the builder will suffer great loss. The builder will be saved, but like someone barely escaping through a wall of flames.

¹⁶Don't you realize that all of you together are the temple of God and that the Spirit of God lives in* you? ¹⁷God will destroy anyone who destroys this temple. For God's temple is holy, and you are that temple.

¹⁸Stop deceiving yourselves. If you think you are wise by this world's standards, you need to become a fool to be truly wise. ¹⁹For the wisdom of this world is foolishness to God. As the Scriptures say,

"He traps the wise
  in the snare of their own cleverness."*

²⁰And again,

"The LORD knows the thoughts of the wise;
  he knows they are worthless."*

²¹So don't boast about following a particular human leader. For everything belongs to you—²²whether Paul or Apollos or Peter,* or the world, or life and death, or the present and the future. Everything belongs to you, ²³and you belong to Christ, and Christ belongs to God.

CHAPTER 4

Paul's Relationship with the Corinthians

So look at Apollos and me as mere servants of Christ who have been put in charge of explaining God's mysteries. ²Now, a person who is put in charge as a manager must be faithful. ³As for me, it matters very little how I might be evaluated by you or by any human authority. I don't even trust my own judgment on this point. ⁴My conscience is clear, but that doesn't prove I'm right. It is the Lord himself who will examine me and decide.

⁵So don't make judgments about anyone ahead of time—before the Lord returns. For he will bring our darkest secrets

3:1a Greek *Brothers.*   3:1b Or *to people who have the Spirit.*   3:1c Greek *in Christ.*   3:16 Or *among.*   3:19 Job 5:13.   3:20 Ps 94:11.   3:22 Greek *Cephas.*

to light and will reveal our private motives. Then God will give to each one whatever praise is due.

[6]Dear brothers and sisters,* I have used Apollos and myself to illustrate what I've been saying. If you pay attention to what I have quoted from the Scriptures,* you won't be proud of one of your leaders at the expense of another. [7]For what gives you the right to make such a judgment? What do you have that God hasn't given you? And if everything you have is from God, why boast as though it were not a gift?

[8]You think you already have everything you need. You think you are already rich. You have begun to reign in God's kingdom without us! I wish you really were reigning already, for then we would be reigning with you. [9]Instead, I sometimes think God has put us apostles on display, like prisoners of war at the end of a victor's parade, condemned to die. We have become a spectacle to the entire world—to people and angels alike.

[10]Our dedication to Christ makes us look like fools, but you claim to be so wise in Christ! We are weak, but you are so powerful! You are honored, but we are ridiculed. [11]Even now we go hungry and thirsty, and we don't have enough clothes to keep warm. We are often beaten and have no home. [12]We work wearily with our own hands to earn our living. We bless those who curse us. We are patient with those who abuse us. [13]We appeal gently when evil things are said about us. Yet we are treated like the world's garbage, like everybody's trash—right up to the present moment.

[14]I am not writing these things to shame you, but to warn you as my beloved children. [15]For even if you had ten thousand others to teach you about Christ, you have only one spiritual father. For I became your father in Christ Jesus when I preached the Good News to you. [16]So I urge you to imitate me.

[17]That's why I have sent Timothy, my beloved and faithful child in the Lord. He will remind you of how I follow Christ Jesus, just as I teach in all the churches wherever I go.

[18]Some of you have become arrogant, thinking I will not visit you again. [19]But I will come—and soon—if the Lord lets me, and then I'll find out whether these arrogant people just give pretentious speeches or whether they really have God's power. [20]For the Kingdom of God is not just a lot of talk; it is living by God's power. [21]Which do you choose? Should I come with a rod to punish you, or should I come with love and a gentle spirit?

CHAPTER 5

Paul Condemns Spiritual Pride

I can hardly believe the report about the sexual immorality going on among you—something that even pagans don't do. I am told that a man in your church is living in sin with his stepmother.* [2]You are so proud of yourselves, but you should be mourning in sorrow and shame. And you should remove this man from your fellowship.

[3]Even though I am not with you in person, I am with you in the Spirit.* And as though I were there, I have already passed judgment on this man [4]in the name of the Lord Jesus. You must call a meeting of the church.* I will be present with you in spirit, and so will the power of our Lord Jesus. [5]Then you must throw this man out and hand him over to Satan so that his sinful nature will be destroyed* and he himself* will be saved on the day the Lord* returns.

[6]Your boasting about this is terrible. Don't you realize that this sin is like a little yeast that spreads through the whole batch of dough? [7]Get rid of the old "yeast" by removing this wicked person from among you. Then you will be like a fresh batch of dough made without yeast, which is what you really are. Christ, our Passover Lamb, has been sacrificed for us.* [8]So let us celebrate the festival, not with the

4:6a Greek *Brothers.*   **4:6b** Or *If you learn not to go beyond "what is written."*   **5:1** Greek *his father's wife.*   **5:3** Or *in spirit.*   **5:4** Or *In the name of the Lord Jesus, you must call a meeting of the church.*   **5:5a** Or *so that his body will be destroyed;* Greek reads *for the destruction of the flesh.*   **5:5b** Greek *and the spirit.*   **5:5c** Other manuscripts read *the Lord Jesus;* still others read *our Lord Jesus Christ.*   **5:7** Greek *has been sacrificed.*

old bread* of wickedness and evil, but with the new bread* of sincerity and truth.

⁹When I wrote to you before, I told you not to associate with people who indulge in sexual sin. ¹⁰But I wasn't talking about unbelievers who indulge in sexual sin, or are greedy, or cheat people, or worship idols. You would have to leave this world to avoid people like that. ¹¹I meant that you are not to associate with anyone who claims to be a believer* yet indulges in sexual sin, or is greedy, or worships idols, or is abusive, or is a drunkard, or cheats people. Don't even eat with such people.

¹²It isn't my responsibility to judge outsiders, but it certainly is your responsibility to judge those inside the church who are sinning. ¹³God will judge those on the outside; but as the Scriptures say, "You must remove the evil person from among you."*

CHAPTER 6

Avoiding Lawsuits with Christians

When one of you has a dispute with another believer, how dare you file a lawsuit and ask a secular court to decide the matter instead of taking it to other believers*! ²Don't you realize that someday we believers will judge the world? And since you are going to judge the world, can't you decide even these little things among yourselves? ³Don't you realize that we will judge angels? So you should surely be able to resolve ordinary disputes in this life. ⁴If you have legal disputes about such matters, why go to outside judges who are not respected by the church? ⁵I am saying this to shame you. Isn't there anyone in all the church who is wise enough to decide these issues? ⁶But instead, one believer* sues another—right in front of unbelievers!

⁷Even to have such lawsuits with one another is a defeat for you. Why not just accept the injustice and leave it at that? Why not let yourselves be cheated? ⁸Instead, you yourselves are the ones who do wrong and cheat even your fellow believers.*

⁹Don't you realize that those who do wrong will not inherit the Kingdom of God? Don't fool yourselves. Those who indulge in sexual sin, or who worship idols, or commit adultery, or are male prostitutes, or practice homosexuality, ¹⁰or are thieves, or greedy people, or drunkards, or are abusive, or cheat people—none of these will inherit the Kingdom of God. ¹¹Some of you were once like that. But you were cleansed; you were made holy; you were made right with God by calling on the name of the Lord Jesus Christ and by the Spirit of our God.

Avoiding Sexual Sin

¹²You say, "I am allowed to do anything"—but not everything is good for you. And even though "I am allowed to do anything," I must not become a slave to anything. ¹³You say, "Food was made for the stomach, and the stomach for food." (This is true, though someday God will do away with both of them.) But you can't say that our bodies were made for sexual immorality. They were made for the Lord, and the Lord cares about our bodies. ¹⁴And God will raise us from the dead by his power, just as he raised our Lord from the dead.

¹⁵Don't you realize that your bodies are actually parts of Christ? Should a man take his body, which is part of Christ, and join it to a prostitute? Never! ¹⁶And don't you realize that if a man joins himself to a prostitute, he becomes one body with her? For the Scriptures say, "The two are united into one."* ¹⁷But the person who is joined to the Lord is one spirit with him.

¹⁸Run from sexual sin! No other sin so clearly affects the body as this one does. For sexual immorality is a sin against your own body. ¹⁹Don't you realize that your body is the temple of the Holy Spirit, who lives in you and was given to you

5:8a Greek *not with old leaven.*   5:8b Greek *but with unleavened [bread].*   5:11 Greek *a brother.*   5:13 Deut 17:7.   6:1 Greek *God's holy people;* also in 6:2.   6:6 Greek *one brother.*
6:8 Greek *even the brothers.*   6:16 Gen 2:24.

by God? You do not belong to yourself, [20]for God bought you with a high price. So you must honor God with your body.

CHAPTER 7

Instruction on Marriage

Now regarding the questions you asked in your letter. Yes, it is good to abstain from sexual relations.* [2]But because there is so much sexual immorality, each man should have his own wife, and each woman should have her own husband.

[3]The husband should fulfill his wife's sexual needs, and the wife should fulfill her husband's needs. [4]The wife gives authority over her body to her husband, and the husband gives authority over his body to his wife.

[5]Do not deprive each other of sexual relations, unless you both agree to refrain from sexual intimacy for a limited time so you can give yourselves more completely to prayer. Afterward, you should come together again so that Satan won't be able to tempt you because of your lack of self-control. [6]I say this as a concession, not as a command. [7]But I wish everyone were single, just as I am. Yet each person has a special gift from God, of one kind or another.

[8]So I say to those who aren't married and to widows—it's better to stay unmarried, just as I am. [9]But if they can't control themselves, they should go ahead and marry. It's better to marry than to burn with lust.

[10]But for those who are married, I have a command that comes not from me, but from the Lord.* A wife must not leave her husband. [11]But if she does leave him, let her remain single or else be reconciled to him. And the husband must not leave his wife.

[12]Now, I will speak to the rest of you, though I do not have a direct command from the Lord. If a Christian man* has a wife who is not a believer and she is willing to continue living with him, he must not leave her. [13]And if a Christian woman has a husband who is not a believer and he is willing to continue living with her, she must not leave him. [14]For the Christian wife brings holiness to her marriage, and the Christian husband* brings holiness to his marriage. Otherwise, your children would not be holy, but now they are holy. [15](But if the husband or wife who isn't a believer insists on leaving, let them go. In such cases the Christian husband or wife* is no longer bound to the other, for God has called you* to live in peace.) [16]Don't you wives realize that your husbands might be saved because of you? And don't you husbands realize that your wives might be saved because of you?

[17]Each of you should continue to live in whatever situation the Lord has placed you, and remain as you were when God first called you. This is my rule for all the churches. [18]For instance, a man who was circumcised before he became a

---

7:1 Or *to live a celibate life*; Greek reads *It is good for a man not to touch a woman.*   **7:10** See Matt 5:32; 19:9; Mark 10:11-12; Luke 16:18.   **7:12** Greek *a brother.*   **7:14** Greek *the brother.*
7:15a Greek *the brother or sister.*   **7:15b** Some manuscripts read *us.*

THE POINT

Single and servin'. So maybe you've heard somethin' or read about 1 Corinthians 7, where Paul talks about marriage, but you want to know a li'l more. Maybe you haven't read it or heard about it at all. Don't sweat it. Keep reading—you'll soon get the point.

The apostle Paul was single, and he wasn't havin' sex—*at all*. Still, Paul wasn't trippin' on married people who did have sex (emphasis on *married*). He had hoped that people could stay single and celibate like him. He looked at singleness as a gift—he knew all people weren't going to get married. For Paul, being single was something to value.

In our world, provocative videos and high-profile hustlas and playas make it hard for us to believe that people are actually single and not havin' sex.

It's even more difficult to believe that single people can cherish their singleness, not for the purposes of runnin' game, but strictly because they enjoy bein' both single and a Christian. Bein' single is not a curse or an excuse to get busy. It's a time for total commitment to God and livin' a life focused on him.

believer should not try to reverse it. And the man who was uncircumcised when he became a believer should not be circumcised now. ¹⁹For it makes no difference whether or not a man has been circumcised. The important thing is to keep God's commandments.

²⁰Yes, each of you should remain as you were when God called you. ²¹Are you a slave? Don't let that worry you—but if you get a chance to be free, take it. ²²And remember, if you were a slave when the Lord called you, you are now free in the Lord. And if you were free when the Lord called you, you are now a slave of Christ. ²³God paid a high price for you, so don't be enslaved by the world.* ²⁴Each of you, dear brothers and sisters,* should remain as you were when God first called you.

²⁵Now regarding your question about the young women who are not yet married. I do not have a command from the Lord for them. But the Lord in his mercy has given me wisdom that can be trusted, and I will share it with you. ²⁶Because of the present crisis,* I think it is best to remain as you are. ²⁷If you have a wife, do not seek to end the marriage. If you do not have a wife, do not seek to get married. ²⁸But if you do get married, it is not a sin. And if a young woman gets married, it is not a sin. However, those who get married at this time will have troubles, and I am trying to spare you those problems.

²⁹But let me say this, dear brothers and sisters: The time that remains is very short. So from now on, those with wives should not focus only on their marriage. ³⁰Those who weep or who rejoice or who buy things should not be absorbed by their weeping or their joy or their possessions. ³¹Those who use the things of the world should not become attached to them. For this world as we know it will soon pass away.

³²I want you to be free from the concerns of this life. An unmarried man can spend his time doing the Lord's work and thinking how to please him. ³³But a married man has to think about his earthly responsibilities and how to please his wife. ³⁴His interests are divided. In the same way, a woman who is no longer married or has never been married can be devoted to the Lord and holy in body and in spirit. But a married woman has to think about her earthly responsibilities and how to please her husband. ³⁵I am saying this for your benefit, not to place restrictions on you. I want you to do whatever will help you serve the Lord best, with as few distractions as possible.

³⁶But if a man thinks that he's treating his fiancée improperly and will inevitably give in to his passion, let him marry her as he wishes. It is not a sin. ³⁷But if he has decided firmly not to marry and there is no urgency and he can control his passion, he does well not to marry. ³⁸So the person who marries his fiancée does well, and the person who doesn't marry does even better.

³⁹A wife is bound to her husband as long as he lives. If her husband dies, she is free to marry anyone she wishes, but only if he loves the Lord.* ⁴⁰But in my opinion it would be better for her to stay single, and I think I am giving you counsel from God's Spirit when I say this.

CHAPTER 8

Food Sacrificed to Idols

Now regarding your question about food that has been offered to idols. Yes, we know that "we all have knowledge" about this issue. But while knowledge makes us feel important, it is love that strengthens the church. ²Anyone who claims to know all the answers doesn't really know very much. ³But the person who loves God is the one whom God recognizes.*

⁴So, what about eating meat that has been offered to idols? Well, we all know that an idol is not really a god and that there is only one God. ⁵There may be so-called gods both in heaven and on earth, and some people actually worship

7:23 Greek *don't become slaves of people.*   7:24 Greek *brothers;* also in 7:29.   7:26 Or *the pressures of life.*   7:39 Greek *but only in the Lord.*   8:3 Some manuscripts read *the person who loves has full knowledge.*

many gods and many lords. ⁶But we know that there is only one God, the Father, who created everything, and we live for him. And there is only one Lord, Jesus Christ, through whom God made everything and through whom we have been given life.

⁷However, not all believers know this. Some are accustomed to thinking of idols as being real, so when they eat food that has been offered to idols, they think of it as the worship of real gods, and their weak consciences are violated. ⁸It's true that we can't win God's approval by what we eat. We don't lose anything if we don't eat it, and we don't gain anything if we do.

⁹But you must be careful so that your freedom does not cause others with a weaker conscience to stumble. ¹⁰For if others see you—with your "superior knowledge"—eating in the temple of an idol, won't they be encouraged to violate their conscience by eating food that has been offered to an idol? ¹¹So because of your superior knowledge, a weak believer* for whom Christ died will be destroyed. ¹²And when you sin against other believers* by encouraging them to do something they believe is wrong, you are sinning against Christ. ¹³So if what I eat causes another believer to sin, I will never eat meat again as long as I live—for I don't want to cause another believer to stumble.

CHAPTER 9

Paul Gives Up His Rights

Am I not as free as anyone else? Am I not an apostle? Haven't I seen Jesus our Lord with my own eyes? Isn't it because of my work that you belong to the Lord? ²Even if others think I am not an apostle, I certainly am to you. You yourselves are proof that I am the Lord's apostle.

³This is my answer to those who question my authority.* ⁴Don't we have the right to live in your homes and share your meals? ⁵Don't we have the right to bring a Christian wife with us as the other apostles and the Lord's brothers do, and as Peter* does? ⁶Or is it only Barnabas and I who have to work to support ourselves?

⁷What soldier has to pay his own expenses? What farmer plants a vineyard and doesn't have the right to eat some of its fruit? What shepherd cares for a flock of sheep and isn't allowed to drink some of the milk? ⁸Am I expressing merely a human opinion, or does the law say the same thing? ⁹For the law of Moses says, "You must not muzzle an ox to keep it from eating as it treads out the grain."* Was God thinking only about oxen when he said this? ¹⁰Wasn't he actually speaking to us? Yes, it was written for us, so that the one who plows and the one who threshes the grain might both expect a share of the harvest.

¹¹Since we have planted spiritual seed among you, aren't we entitled to a harvest of physical food and drink? ¹²If you support others who preach to you, shouldn't we have an even greater right to be supported? But we have never used this right. We would rather put up with anything than be an obstacle to the Good News about Christ.

¹³Don't you realize that those who work in the temple get their meals from the offerings brought to the temple? And those who serve at the altar get a share of the sacrificial offerings. ¹⁴In the same way, the Lord ordered that those who preach the Good News should be supported by those who benefit from it. ¹⁵Yet I have never used any of these rights. And I am not writing this to suggest that I want to start now. In fact, I would rather die than lose my right to boast about preaching without charge. ¹⁶Yet preaching the Good News is not something I can boast about. I am compelled by God to do it. How terrible for me if I didn't preach the Good News!

¹⁷If I were doing this on my own initiative, I would deserve payment. But I have no choice, for God has given me this sacred trust. ¹⁸What then is my pay? It is the opportunity to preach the Good News without charging anyone. That's why I never demand my rights when I preach the Good News.

¹⁹Even though I am a free man with no master, I have

8:11 Greek brother; also in 8:13.   8:12 Greek brothers.   9:3 Greek those who examine me.   9:5 Greek Cephas.   9:9 Deut 25:4.

become a slave to all people to bring many to Christ. ²⁰When I was with the Jews, I lived like a Jew to bring the Jews to Christ. When I was with those who follow the Jewish law, I too lived under that law. Even though I am not subject to the law, I did this so I could bring to Christ those who are under the law. ²¹When I am with the Gentiles who do not follow the Jewish law,* I too live apart from that law so I can bring them to Christ. But I do not ignore the law of God; I obey the law of Christ.

²²When I am with those who are weak, I share their weakness, for I want to bring the weak to Christ. Yes, I try to find common ground with everyone, doing everything I can to save some. ²³I do everything to spread the Good News and share in its blessings.

²⁴Don't you realize that in a race everyone runs, but only one person gets the prize? So run to win! ²⁵All athletes are disciplined in their training. They do it to win a prize that will fade away, but we do it for an eternal prize. ²⁶So I run with purpose in every step. I am not just shadowboxing. ²⁷I discipline my body like an athlete, training it to do what it should. Otherwise, I fear that after preaching to others I myself might be disqualified.

CHAPTER 10

Lessons from Israel's Idolatry

I don't want you to forget, dear brothers and sisters,* about our ancestors in the wilderness long ago. All of them were guided by a cloud that moved ahead of them, and all of them walked through the sea on dry ground. ²In the cloud and in the sea, all of them were baptized as followers of Moses. ³All of them ate the same spiritual food, ⁴and all of them drank the same spiritual water. For they drank from the spiritual rock that traveled with them, and that rock was Christ. ⁵Yet God was not pleased with most of them, and their bodies were scattered in the wilderness.

⁶These things happened as a warning to us, so that we would not crave evil things as they did, ⁷or worship idols as some of them did. As the Scriptures say, "The people celebrated with feasting and drinking, and they indulged in pagan revelry."* ⁸And we must not engage in sexual immorality as some of them did, causing 23,000 of them to die in one day.

⁹Nor should we put Christ* to the test, as some of them did and then died from snakebites. ¹⁰And don't grumble as some of them did, and then were destroyed by the angel of death. ¹¹These things happened to them as examples for us. They were written down to warn us who live at the end of the age.

¹²If you think you are standing strong, be careful not to fall. ¹³The temptations in your life are no different from what others experience. And God is faithful. He will not allow the temptation to be more than you can stand. When you are tempted, he will show you a way out so that you can endure.

¹⁴So, my dear friends, flee from the worship of idols. ¹⁵You are reasonable people. Decide for yourselves if what I am saying is true. ¹⁶When we bless the cup at the Lord's Table, aren't we sharing in the blood of Christ? And when we break the bread, aren't we sharing in the body of Christ? ¹⁷And though we are many, we all eat from one loaf of bread, showing that we are one body. ¹⁸Think about the people of Israel. Weren't they united by eating the sacrifices at the altar?

¹⁹What am I trying to say? Am I saying that food offered to idols has some significance, or that idols are real gods? ²⁰No, not at all. I am saying that these sacrifices are offered to demons, not to God. And I don't want you to participate with demons. ²¹You cannot drink from the cup of the Lord and from the cup of demons, too. You cannot eat at the Lord's Table and at the table of demons, too. ²²What? Do we dare to rouse the Lord's jealousy? Do you think we are stronger than he is?

²³You say, "I am allowed to do anything"*—but not everything is good for you. You say, "I am allowed to do anything"— but not everything is beneficial. ²⁴Don't be concerned for your own good but for the good of others.

9:21 Greek *those without the law.*   10:1 Greek *brothers.*   10:7 Exod 32:6.   10:9 Some manuscripts read *the Lord.*   10:23 Greek *All things are lawful;* also in 10:23b.

²⁵So you may eat any meat that is sold in the marketplace without raising questions of conscience. ²⁶For "the earth is the LORD's, and everything in it."*

²⁷If someone who isn't a believer asks you home for dinner, accept the invitation if you want to. Eat whatever is offered to you without raising questions of conscience. ²⁸(But suppose someone tells you, "This meat was offered to an idol." Don't eat it, out of consideration for the conscience of the one who told you. ²⁹It might not be a matter of conscience for you, but it is for the other person.) For why should my freedom be limited by what someone else thinks? ³⁰If I can thank God for the food and enjoy it, why should I be condemned for eating it?

³¹So whether you eat or drink, or whatever you do, do it all for the glory of God. ³²Don't give offense to Jews or Gentiles* or the church of God. ³³I, too, try to please everyone in everything I do. I don't just do what is best for me; I do what is best for others so that many may be saved. ¹¹:¹And you should imitate me, just as I imitate Christ.

CHAPTER 11

Instructions for Public Worship

²I am so glad that you always keep me in your thoughts, and that you are following the teachings I passed on to you. ³But there is one thing I want you to know: The head of every man is Christ, the head of woman is man, and the head of Christ is God.* ⁴A man dishonors his head* if he covers his head while praying or prophesying. ⁵But a woman dishonors her head* if she prays or prophesies without a covering on her head, for this is the same as shaving her head. ⁶Yes, if she refuses to wear a head covering, she should cut off all her hair! But since it is shameful for a woman to have her hair cut or her head shaved, she should wear a covering.*

⁷A man should not wear anything on his head when worshiping, for man is made in God's image and reflects God's glory. And woman reflects man's glory. ⁸For the first man didn't come from woman, but the first woman came from man. ⁹And man was not made for woman, but woman was made for man. ¹⁰For this reason, and because the angels are watching, a woman should wear a covering on her head to show she is under authority.*

¹¹But among the Lord's people, women are not independent of men, and men are not independent of women. ¹²For although the first woman came from man, every other man was born from a woman, and everything comes from God.

¹³Judge for yourselves. Is it right for a woman to pray to God in public without covering her head? ¹⁴Isn't it obvious that it's disgraceful for a man to have long hair? ¹⁵And isn't long hair a woman's pride and joy? For it has been given to her as a covering. ¹⁶But if anyone wants to argue about this, I simply say that we have no other custom than this, and neither do God's other churches.

Order at the Lord's Supper

¹⁷But in the following instructions, I cannot praise you. For it sounds as if more harm than good is done when you meet together. ¹⁸First, I hear that there are divisions among you when you meet as a church, and to some extent I believe it. ¹⁹But, of course, there must be divisions among you so that you who have God's approval will be recognized!

²⁰When you meet together, you are not really interested in the Lord's Supper. ²¹For some of you hurry to eat your own meal without sharing with others. As a result, some go hungry while others get drunk. ²²What? Don't you have your own homes for eating and drinking? Or do you really want to disgrace God's church and shame the poor? What am I supposed to say? Do you want me to praise you? Well, I certainly will not praise you for this!

10:26 Ps 24:1. 10:32 Greek or Greeks. 11:3 Or to know: The source of every man is Christ, the source of woman is man, and the source of Christ is God. Or to know: Every man is responsible to Christ, a woman is responsible to her husband, and Christ is responsible to God. 11:4 Or dishonors Christ. 11:5 Or dishonors her husband. 11:6 Or should have long hair. 11:10 Greek should have an authority on her head.

fYo

"For every time you eat this bread and drink this cup, you are announcing the Lord's death until he comes again" (1 Corinthians 11:26).

Every time you grub on this bread and turn up this cup, you are reppin' the Lord's death until he comes back.

²³For I pass on to you what I received from the Lord himself. On the night when he was betrayed, the Lord Jesus took some bread ²⁴and gave thanks to God for it. Then he broke it in pieces and said, "This is my body, which is given for you.* Do this to remember me." ²⁵In the same way, he took the cup of wine after supper, saying, "This cup is the new covenant between God and his people—an agreement confirmed with my blood. Do this to remember me as often as you drink it." ²⁶For every time you eat this bread and drink this cup, you are announcing the Lord's death until he comes again.

²⁷So anyone who eats this bread or drinks this cup of the Lord unworthily is guilty of sinning against* the body and blood of the Lord. ²⁸That is why you should examine yourself before eating the bread and drinking the cup. ²⁹For if you eat the bread or drink the cup without honoring the body of Christ,* you are eating and drinking God's judgment upon yourself. ³⁰That is why many of you are weak and sick and some have even died.

³¹But if we would examine ourselves, we would not be judged by God in this way. ³²Yet when we are judged by the Lord, we are being disciplined so that we will not be condemned along with the world.

³³So, my dear brothers and sisters,* when you gather for the Lord's Supper, wait for each other. ³⁴If you are really hungry, eat at home so you won't bring judgment upon yourselves when you meet together. I'll give you instructions about the other matters after I arrive.

CHAPTER 12

Spiritual Gifts

Now, dear brothers and sisters,* regarding your question about the special abilities the Spirit gives us. I don't want you to misunderstand this. ²You know that when you were still pagans, you were led astray and swept along in wor-shiping speechless idols. ³So I want you to know that no one speaking by the Spirit of God will curse Jesus, and no one can say Jesus is Lord, except by the Holy Spirit.

⁴There are different kinds of spiritual gifts, but the same Spirit is the source of them all. ⁵There are different kinds of service, but we serve the same Lord. ⁶God works in different ways, but it is the same God who does the work in all of us.

⁷A spiritual gift is given to each of us so we can help each other. ⁸To one person the Spirit gives the ability to give wise advice*; to another the same Spirit gives a message of special knowledge.* ⁹The same Spirit gives great faith to another, and to someone else the one Spirit gives the gift of healing. ¹⁰He gives one person the power to perform miracles, and another the ability to prophesy. He gives someone else the ability to discern whether a message is from the Spirit of God or from another spirit. Still another person is given the ability to speak in unknown languages,* while another is given the ability to interpret what is being said. ¹¹It is the one and only Spirit who distributes all these gifts. He alone decides which gift each person should have.

One Body with Many Parts

¹²The human body has many parts, but the many parts make up one whole body. So it is with the body of Christ. ¹³Some of us are Jews, some are Gentiles,* some are slaves, and some are free. But we have all been baptized into one body by one Spirit, and we all share the same Spirit.*

¹⁴Yes, the body has many different parts, not just one part. ¹⁵If the foot says, "I am not a part of the body because I am not a hand," that does not make it any less a part of the body. ¹⁶And if the ear says, "I am not part of the body because I am not an eye," would that make it any less a part of the body? ¹⁷If the whole body were an eye, how would you hear? Or if your whole body were an ear, how would you smell anything?

11:24 Greek *which is for you;* other manuscripts read *which is broken for you.*   **11:27** Or *is responsible for.*   **11:29** Greek *the body;* other manuscripts read *the Lord's body.*   **11:33** Greek *brothers.*   **12:1** Greek *brothers.*   **12:8a** Or *gives a word of wisdom.*   **12:8b** Or *gives a word of knowledge.*   **12:10** Or *in various tongues;* also in 12:28, 30.   **12:13a** Greek *some are Greeks.* **12:13b** Greek *we were all given one Spirit to drink.*

[18]But our bodies have many parts, and God has put each part just where he wants it. [19]How strange a body would be if it had only one part! [20]Yes, there are many parts, but only one body. [21]The eye can never say to the hand, "I don't need you." The head can't say to the feet, "I don't need you."

[22]In fact, some parts of the body that seem weakest and least important are actually the most necessary. [23]And the parts we regard as less honorable are those we clothe with the greatest care. So we carefully protect those parts that should not be seen, [24]while the more honorable parts do not require this special care. So God has put the body together such that extra honor and care are given to those parts that have less dignity. [25]This makes for harmony among the members, so that all the members care for each other. [26]If one part suffers, all the parts suffer with it, and if one part is honored, all the parts are glad.

[27]All of you together are Christ's body, and each of you is a part of it. [28]Here are some of the parts God has appointed for the church:

first are apostles,
second are prophets,
third are teachers,
then those who do miracles,
those who have the gift of healing,
those who can help others,
those who have the gift of leadership,
those who speak in unknown languages.

[29]Are we all apostles? Are we all prophets? Are we all teachers? Do we all have the power to do miracles? [30]Do we all have the gift of healing? Do we all have the ability to speak in unknown languages? Do we all have the ability to interpret unknown languages? Of course not! [31]So you should earnestly desire the most helpful gifts.

But now let me show you a way of life that is best of all.

CHAPTER 13

Love Is the Greatest

If I could speak all the languages of earth and of angels, but didn't love others, I would only be a noisy gong or a clanging cymbal. [2]If I had the gift of prophecy, and if I understood all of God's secret plans and possessed all knowledge, and if I had such faith that I could move mountains, but didn't love others, I would be nothing. [3]If I gave everything I have to the poor and even sacrificed my body, I could boast about it;* but if I didn't love others, I would have gained nothing.

[4]Love is patient and kind. Love is not jealous or boastful or proud [5]or rude. It does not demand its own way. It is not irritable, and it keeps no record of being wronged. [6]It does not rejoice about injustice but rejoices whenever the truth wins out. [7]Love never gives up, never loses faith, is always hopeful, and endures through every circumstance.

[8]Prophecy and speaking in unknown languages* and special knowledge will become useless. But love will last forever! [9]Now our knowledge is partial and incomplete, and even the gift of prophecy reveals only part of the whole picture! [10]But when the time of perfection comes, these partial things will become useless.

[11]When I was a child, I spoke and thought and reasoned as a child. But when I grew up, I put away childish things. [12]Now we see things imperfectly, like puzzling reflections in a mirror, but then we will see everything with perfect clarity.* All that I know now is partial and incomplete, but then I will know everything completely, just as God now knows me completely.

[13]Three things will last forever—faith, hope, and love—and the greatest of these is love.

CHAPTER 14

Tongues and Prophecy

Let love be your highest goal! But you should also desire the special abilities the Spirit gives—especially the

"Three things will last forever—faith, hope, and love—and the greatest of these is love" (1 Corinthians 13:13).

Faith, hope, and love last forever, and love is the most important. So focus on lovin' others.

13:3 Some manuscripts read *sacrificed my body to be burned.*   **13:8** Or *in tongues.*   **13:12** Greek *see face to face.*

ability to prophesy. [2]For if you have the ability to speak in tongues,* you will be talking only to God, since people won't be able to understand you. You will be speaking by the power of the Spirit,* but it will all be mysterious. [3]But one who prophesies strengthens others, encourages them, and comforts them. [4]A person who speaks in tongues is strengthened personally, but one who speaks a word of prophecy strengthens the entire church.

[5]I wish you could all speak in tongues, but even more I wish you could all prophesy. For prophecy is greater than speaking in tongues, unless someone interprets what you are saying so that the whole church will be strengthened.

[6]Dear brothers and sisters,* if I should come to you speaking in an unknown language,* how would that help you? But if I bring you a revelation or some special knowledge or prophecy or teaching, that will be helpful. [7]Even lifeless instruments like the flute or the harp must play the notes clearly, or no one will recognize the melody. [8]And if the bugler doesn't sound a clear call, how will the soldiers know they are being called to battle?

[9]It's the same for you. If you speak to people in words they don't understand, how will they know what you are saying? You might as well be talking into empty space.

[10]There are many different languages in the world, and every language has meaning. [11]But if I don't understand a language, I will be a foreigner to someone who speaks it, and the one who speaks it will be a foreigner to me. [12]And the same is true for you. Since you are so eager to have the special abilities the Spirit gives, seek those that will strengthen the whole church.

[13]So anyone who speaks in tongues should pray also for the ability to interpret what has been said. [14]For if I pray in tongues, my spirit is praying, but I don't understand what I am saying.

[15]Well then, what shall I do? I will pray in the spirit,* and I will also pray in words I understand. I will sing in the spirit, and I will also sing in words I understand. [16]For if you praise God only in the spirit, how can those who don't understand you praise God along with you? How can they join you in giving thanks when they don't understand what you are saying? [17]You will be giving thanks very well, but it won't strengthen the people who hear you.

[18]I thank God that I speak in tongues more than any of you. [19]But in a church meeting I would rather speak five understandable words to help others than ten thousand words in an unknown language.

[20]Dear brothers and sisters, don't be childish in your understanding of these things. Be innocent as babies when it comes to evil, but be mature in understanding matters of this kind. [21]It is written in the Scriptures*:

"I will speak to my own people
   through strange languages
   and through the lips of foreigners.
But even then, they will not listen to me,"*
   says the LORD.

[22]So you see that speaking in tongues is a sign, not for believers, but for unbelievers. Prophecy, however, is for the benefit of believers, not unbelievers. [23]Even so, if unbelievers or people who don't understand these things come into your church meeting and hear everyone speaking in an unknown language, they will think you are crazy. [24]But if all of you are prophesying, and unbelievers or people who don't understand these things come into your meeting, they will be convicted of sin and judged by what you say. [25]As they listen, their secret thoughts will be exposed, and they will fall to their knees and worship God, declaring, "God is truly here among you."

14:2a Or *in unknown languages;* also in 14:4, 5, 13, 14, 18, 22, 26, 27, 28, 39.   14:2b Or *speaking in your spirit.*   14:6a Greek *brothers;* also in 14:20, 26, 39.   14:6b Or *in tongues;* also in 14:19, 23.   14:15 Or *in the Spirit;* also in 14:15b, 16.   14:21a Greek *in the law.*   14:21b Isa 28:11-12.

²⁶Well, my brothers and sisters, let's summarize. When you meet together, one will sing, another will teach, another will tell some special revelation God has given, one will speak in tongues, and another will interpret what is said. But everything that is done must strengthen all of you.

²⁷No more than two or three should speak in tongues. They must speak one at a time, and someone must interpret what they say. ²⁸But if no one is present who can interpret, they must be silent in your church meeting and speak in tongues to God privately.

²⁹Let two or three people prophesy, and let the others evaluate what is said. ³⁰But if someone is prophesying and another person receives a revelation from the Lord, the one who is speaking must stop. ³¹In this way, all who prophesy will have a turn to speak, one after the other, so that everyone will learn and be encouraged. ³²Remember that people who prophesy are in control of their spirit and can take turns. ³³For God is not a God of disorder but of peace, as in all the meetings of God's holy people.*

³⁴Women should be silent during the church meetings. It is not proper for them to speak. They should be submissive, just as the law says. ³⁵If they have any questions, they should ask their husbands at home, for it is improper for women to speak in church meetings.*

³⁶Or do you think God's word originated with you Corinthians? Are you the only ones to whom it was given? ³⁷If you claim to be a prophet or think you are spiritual, you should recognize that what I am saying is a command from the Lord himself. ³⁸But if you do not recognize this, you yourself will not be recognized.*

³⁹So, my dear brothers and sisters, be eager to prophesy, and don't forbid speaking in tongues. ⁴⁰But be sure that everything is done properly and in order.

The Resurrection of Christ

Let me now remind you, dear brothers and sisters,* of the Good News I preached to you before. You welcomed it then, and you still stand firm in it. ²It is this Good News that saves you if you continue to believe the message I told you—unless, of course, you believed something that was never true in the first place.*

³I passed on to you what was most important and what had also been passed on to me. Christ died for our sins, just as the Scriptures said. ⁴He was buried, and he was raised from the dead on the third day, just as the Scriptures said. ⁵He was seen by Peter* and then by the Twelve. ⁶After that, he was seen by more than 500 of his followers* at one time, most of whom are still alive, though some have died. ⁷Then he was seen by James and later by all the apostles. ⁸Last of all, as though I had been born at the wrong time, I also saw him. ⁹For I am the least of all the apostles. In fact, I'm not even worthy to be called an apostle after the way I persecuted God's church.

¹⁰But whatever I am now, it is all because God poured out his special favor on me—and not without results. For I have worked harder than any of the other apostles; yet it was not I but God who was working through me by his grace. ¹¹So it makes no difference whether I preach or they preach, for we all preach the same message you have already believed.

The Resurrection of the Dead

¹²But tell me this—since we preach that Christ rose from the dead, why are some of you saying there will be no resurrection of the dead? ¹³For if there is no resurrection of the dead, then Christ has not been raised either. ¹⁴And if Christ has not been raised, then all our preaching is useless, and your faith is useless. ¹⁵And we apostles would all be lying

---

14:33 The phrase *as in all the meetings of God's holy people* could instead be joined to the beginning of 14:34. **14:35** Some manuscripts place verses 34-35 after 14:40. **14:38** Some manuscripts read *If you are ignorant of this, stay in your ignorance.* **15:1** Greek *brothers*; also in 15:31, 50, 58. **15:2** Or *unless you never believed it in the first place.* **15:5** Greek *Cephas.* **15:6** Greek *the brothers.*

about God—for we have said that God raised Christ from the grave. But that can't be true if there is no resurrection of the dead. ¹⁶And if there is no resurrection of the dead, then Christ has not been raised. ¹⁷And if Christ has not been raised, then your faith is useless and you are still guilty of your sins. ¹⁸In that case, all who have died believing in Christ are lost! ¹⁹And if our hope in Christ is only for this life, we are more to be pitied than anyone in the world.

²⁰But in fact, Christ has been raised from the dead. He is the first of a great harvest of all who have died.

²¹So you see, just as death came into the world through a man, now the resurrection from the dead has begun through another man. ²²Just as everyone dies because we all belong to Adam, everyone who belongs to Christ will be given new life. ²³But there is an order to this resurrection: Christ was raised as the first of the harvest; then all who belong to Christ will be raised when he comes back.

²⁴After that the end will come, when he will turn the Kingdom over to God the Father, having destroyed every ruler and authority and power. ²⁵For Christ must reign until he humbles all his enemies beneath his feet. ²⁶And the last enemy to be destroyed is death. ²⁷For the Scriptures say, "God has put all things under his authority."* (Of course, when it says "all things are under his authority," that does not include God himself, who gave Christ his authority.) ²⁸Then, when all things are under his authority, the Son will put himself under God's authority, so that God, who gave his Son authority over all things, will be utterly supreme over everything everywhere.

²⁹If the dead will not be raised, what point is there in people being baptized for those who are dead? Why do it unless the dead will someday rise again?

³⁰And why should we ourselves risk our lives hour by hour? ³¹For I swear, dear brothers and sisters, that I face death daily. This is as certain as my pride in what Christ Jesus our Lord has done in you. ³²And what value was there in fighting wild beasts—those people of Ephesus*—if there will be no resurrection from the dead? And if there is no resurrection, "Let's feast and drink, for tomorrow we die!"* ³³Don't be fooled by those who say such things, for "bad company corrupts good character." ³⁴Think carefully about what is right, and stop sinning. For to your shame I say that some of you don't know God at all.

The Resurrection Body

³⁵But someone may ask, "How will the dead be raised? What kind of bodies will they have?" ³⁶What a foolish question! When you put a seed into the ground, it doesn't grow into a plant unless it dies first. ³⁷And what you put in the ground is not the plant that will grow, but only a bare seed of wheat or whatever you are planting. ³⁸Then God gives it the new body he wants it to have. A different plant grows from each kind of seed. ³⁹Similarly there are different kinds of flesh—one kind for humans, another for animals, another for birds, and another for fish.

⁴⁰There are also bodies in the heavens and bodies on the earth. The glory of the heavenly bodies is different from the glory of the earthly bodies. ⁴¹The sun has one kind of glory, while the moon and stars each have another kind. And even the stars differ from each other in their glory.

⁴²It is the same way with the resurrection of the dead. Our earthly bodies are planted in the ground when we die, but they will be raised to live forever. ⁴³Our bodies are buried in brokenness, but they will be raised in glory. They are buried in weakness, but they will be raised in strength. ⁴⁴They are buried as natural human bodies, but they will be raised as spiritual bodies. For just as there are natural bodies, there are also spiritual bodies.

⁴⁵The Scriptures tell us, "The first man, Adam, became a living person."* But the last Adam—that is, Christ—is a life-giving Spirit. ⁴⁶What comes first is the natural body, then the spiritual body comes later. ⁴⁷Adam, the first man, was made

15:27 Ps 8:6.   15:32a Greek *fighting wild beasts in Ephesus.*   15:32b Isa 22:13.   15:45 Gen 2:7.

from the dust of the earth, while Christ, the second man, came from heaven. [48]Earthly people are like the earthly man, and heavenly people are like the heavenly man. [49]Just as we are now like the earthly man, we will someday be like* the heavenly man.

[50]What I am saying, dear brothers and sisters, is that our physical bodies cannot inherit the Kingdom of God. These dying bodies cannot inherit what will last forever. [51]But let me reveal to you a wonderful secret. We will not all die, but we will all be transformed! [52]It will happen in a moment, in the blink of an eye, when the last trumpet is blown. For when the trumpet sounds, those who have died will be raised to live forever. And we who are living will also be transformed. [53]For our dying bodies must be transformed into bodies that will never die; our mortal bodies must be transformed into immortal bodies. [54]Then, when our dying bodies have been transformed into bodies that will never die,* this Scripture will be fulfilled:

"Death is swallowed up in victory.*
[55] O death, where is your victory?
    O death, where is your sting?*"

[56]For sin is the sting that results in death, and the law gives sin its power. [57]But thank God! He gives us victory over sin and death through our Lord Jesus Christ.

[58]So, my dear brothers and sisters, be strong and immovable. Always work enthusiastically for the Lord, for you know that nothing you do for the Lord is ever useless.

CHAPTER 16

The Collection for Jerusalem

Now regarding your question about the money being collected for God's people in Jerusalem. You should follow the same procedure I gave to the churches in Galatia. [2]On the first day of each week, you should each put aside a portion of the money you have earned. Don't wait until I get there and then try to collect it all at once. [3]When I come, I will write letters of recommendation for the messengers you choose to deliver your gift to Jerusalem. [4]And if it seems appropriate for me to go along, they can travel with me.

Paul's Final Instructions

[5]I am coming to visit you after I have been to Macedonia,* for I am planning to travel through Macedonia. [6]Perhaps I will stay awhile with you, possibly all winter, and then you can send me on my way to my next destination. [7]This time I don't want to make just a short visit and then go right on. I want to come and stay awhile, if the Lord will let me. [8]In the meantime, I will be staying here at Ephesus until the Festival of Pentecost. [9]There is a wide-open door for a great work here, although many oppose me.

[10]When Timothy comes, don't intimidate him. He is doing the Lord's work, just as I am. [11]Don't let anyone treat him with contempt. Send him on his way with your blessing when he returns to me. I expect him to come with the other believers.*

[12]Now about our brother Apollos—I urged him to visit you with the other believers, but he was not willing to go right now. He will see you later when he has the opportunity.

[13]Be on guard. Stand firm in the faith. Be courageous.* Be strong. [14]And do everything with love.

[15]You know that Stephanas and his household were the first of the harvest of believers in Greece,* and they are spending their lives in service to God's people. I urge you, dear brothers and sisters,* [16]to submit to them and others like them who serve with such devotion. [17]I am very glad that Stephanas, Fortunatus, and Achaicus have come here.

15:49 Some manuscripts read *let us be like.*   **15:54a** Some manuscripts add *and our mortal bodies have been transformed into immortal bodies.*   **15:54b** Isa 25:8.   **15:55** Hos 13:14 (Greek version).   **16:5** *Macedonia* was in the northern region of Greece.   **16:11** Greek *with the brothers;* also in 16:12.   **16:13** Greek *Be men.*   **16:15a** Greek *in Achaia,* the southern region of the Greek peninsula.   **16:15b** Greek *brothers;* also in 16:20.

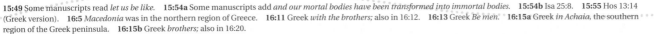

They have been providing the help you weren't here to give me. [18]They have been a wonderful encouragement to me, as they have been to you. You must show your appreciation to all who serve so well.

Paul's Final Greetings

[19]The churches here in the province of Asia* send greetings in the Lord, as do Aquila and Priscilla* and all the others who gather in their home for church meetings. [20]All the brothers and sisters here send greetings to you. Greet each other with Christian love.*

[21]HERE IS MY GREETING IN MY OWN HANDWRITING—PAUL.

[22]If anyone does not love the Lord, that person is cursed. Our Lord, come!*

[23]May the grace of the Lord Jesus be with you.

[24]My love to all of you in Christ Jesus.*

16:19a *Asia* was a Roman province in what is now western Turkey.   16:19b Greek *Prisca*.   16:20 Greek *with a sacred kiss*.   16:22 From Aramaic, *Marana tha*. Some manuscripts read *Maran atha*, "Our Lord has come."   16:24 Some manuscripts add *Amen*.

PAUL WASN'T NECESSARILY the man. He had some difficulties convincing people that Jesus was the real deal. He even found it difficult to roll with some of the same guys that hung with Jesus back in the day. Before he became a Christian he had been with the crew that stoned Stephen to death (see Acts 7:57–8:1). They had a hard time feeling Paul because of his past thug mentality. Second Corinthians is really about God's comfort, but some of it is just Paul defendin' himself against his critics. He was tryin' to earn some street credibility. He wanted people to know he wasn't a fake—and neither was Jesus.

2 CORINTHIANS

CHAPTER 1

Greetings from Paul

This letter is from Paul, chosen by the will of God to be an apostle of Christ Jesus, and from our brother Timothy.

I am writing to God's church in Corinth and to all of his holy people throughout Greece.*

²May God our Father and the Lord Jesus Christ give you grace and peace.

God Offers Comfort to All

³All praise to God, the Father of our Lord Jesus Christ. God is our merciful Father and the source of all comfort. ⁴He comforts us in all our troubles so that we can comfort others. When they are troubled, we will be able to give them the same comfort God has given us. ⁵For the more we suffer for Christ, the more God will shower us with his comfort through Christ. ⁶Even when we are weighed down with troubles, it is for your comfort and salvation! For when we ourselves are comforted, we will certainly comfort you. Then you can patiently endure the same things we suffer. ⁷We are confident that as you share in our sufferings, you will also share in the comfort God gives us.

⁸We think you ought to know, dear brothers and sisters,* about the trouble we went through in the province of Asia. We were crushed and overwhelmed beyond our ability to endure, and we thought we would never live through it. ⁹In fact, we expected to die. But as a result, we stopped relying on ourselves and learned to rely only on God, who raises the dead. ¹⁰And he did rescue us from mortal danger, and he will rescue us again. We have placed our confidence in him, and he will continue to rescue us. ¹¹And you are helping us by praying for us. Then many people will give thanks because God has graciously answered so many prayers for our safety.

Paul's Change of Plans

¹²We can say with confidence and a clear conscience that we have lived with a God-given holiness* and sincerity in all our dealings. We have depended on God's grace, not on our own human wisdom. That is how we have conducted ourselves before the world, and especially toward you. ¹³Our letters have been straightforward, and there is nothing written between the lines and nothing you can't understand. I hope someday you will fully understand us, ¹⁴even if you don't understand us now. Then on the day when the Lord Jesus* returns, you will be proud of us in the same way we are proud of you.

¹⁵Since I was so sure of your understanding and trust, I wanted to give you a double blessing by visiting you twice—¹⁶first on my way to Macedonia and again when I returned from Macedonia.* Then you could send me on my way to Judea.

¹⁷You may be asking why I changed my plan. Do you think I make my plans carelessly? Do you think I am like people of the world who say "Yes" when they really mean "No"? ¹⁸As surely as God is faithful, our word to you does not waver between "Yes" and "No." ¹⁹For Jesus Christ, the Son of God, does not waver between "Yes" and "No." He is

1:1 Greek *Achaia,* the southern region of the Greek peninsula.   1:8 Greek *brothers.*   1:12 Some manuscripts read *honesty.*   1:14 Some manuscripts read *our Lord Jesus.*
1:16 *Macedonia* was in the northern region of Greece.

the one whom Silas,* Timothy, and I preached to you, and as God's ultimate "Yes," he always does what he says. 20For all of God's promises have been fulfilled in Christ with a resounding "Yes!" And through Christ, our "Amen" (which means "Yes") ascends to God for his glory.

21It is God who enables us, along with you, to stand firm for Christ. He has commissioned us, 22and he has identified us as his own by placing the Holy Spirit in our hearts as the first installment that guarantees everything he has promised us.

23Now I call upon God as my witness that I am telling the truth. The reason I didn't return to Corinth was to spare you from a severe rebuke. 24But that does not mean we want to dominate you by telling you how to put your faith into practice. We want to work together with you so you will be full of joy, for it is by your own faith that you stand firm.

CHAPTER 2

So I decided that I would not bring you grief with another painful visit. 2For if I cause you grief, who will make me glad? Certainly not someone I have grieved. 3That is why I wrote to you as I did, so that when I do come, I won't be grieved by the very ones who ought to give me the greatest joy. Surely you all know that my joy comes from your being joyful. 4I wrote that letter in great anguish, with a troubled heart and many tears. I didn't want to grieve you, but I wanted to let you know how much love I have for you.

Forgiveness for the Sinner

5I am not overstating it when I say that the man who caused all the trouble hurt all of you more than he hurt me. 6Most of you opposed him, and that was punishment enough. 7Now, however, it is time to forgive and comfort him. Otherwise he may be overcome by discouragement. 8So I urge you now to reaffirm your love for him.

9I wrote to you as I did to test you and see if you would fully comply with my instructions. 10When you forgive this man, I forgive him, too. And when I forgive whatever needs to be forgiven, I do so with Christ's authority for your benefit, 11so that Satan will not outsmart us. For we are familiar with his evil schemes.

12When I came to the city of Troas to preach the Good News of Christ, the Lord opened a door of opportunity for me. 13But I had no peace of mind because my dear brother Titus hadn't yet arrived with a report from you. So I said good-bye and went on to Macedonia to find him.

Ministers of the New Covenant

14But thank God! He has made us his captives and continues to lead us along in Christ's triumphal procession. Now he uses us to spread the knowledge of Christ everywhere, like a sweet perfume. 15Our lives are a Christ-like fragrance rising up to God. But this fragrance is perceived differently by those who are being saved and by those who are perishing. 16To those who are perishing, we are a dreadful smell of death and doom. But to those who are being saved, we are a life-giving perfume. And who is adequate for such a task as this?

17You see, we are not like the many hucksters* who preach for personal profit. We preach the word of God with sincerity and with Christ's authority, knowing that God is watching us.

CHAPTER 3

Are we beginning to praise ourselves again? Are we like others, who need to bring you letters of recommendation, or who ask you to write such letters on their behalf? Surely not! 2The only letter of recommendation we need is you yourselves. Your lives are a letter written in our* hearts; everyone can read it and recognize our good work among you. 3Clearly, you are a letter from Christ showing the result of our ministry among you. This "letter" is written not with

"Our letters have been straightforward, and there is nothing written between the lines and nothing you can't understand. I hope someday you will fully understand us, even if you don't understand us now. Then on the day when the Lord Jesus returns, you will be proud of us in the same way we are proud of you" (2 Corinthians 1:13-14).

Our letters ain't full of fugazi! What we wrote, you should understand. I hope you'll get the picture someday, even if you don't feel us now. When Jesus returns, you'll rep for us the same way we repped for you.

1:19 Greek *Silvanus.*   2:17 Some manuscripts read *the rest of the hucksters.*   3:2 Some manuscripts read *your.*

pen and ink, but with the Spirit of the living God. It is carved not on tablets of stone, but on human hearts.

⁴We are confident of all this because of our great trust in God through Christ. ⁵It is not that we think we are qualified to do anything on our own. Our qualification comes from God. ⁶He has enabled us to be ministers of his new covenant. This is a covenant not of written laws, but of the Spirit. The old written covenant ends in death; but under the new covenant, the Spirit gives life.

The Glory of the New Covenant

⁷The old way,* with laws etched in stone, led to death, though it began with such glory that the people of Israel could not bear to look at Moses' face. For his face shone with the glory of God, even though the brightness was already fading away. ⁸Shouldn't we expect far greater glory under the new way, now that the Holy Spirit is giving life? ⁹If the old way, which brings condemnation, was glorious, how much more glorious is the new way, which makes us right with God! ¹⁰In fact, that first glory was not glorious at all compared with the overwhelming glory of the new way. ¹¹So if the old way, which has been replaced, was glorious, how much more glorious is the new, which remains forever!

¹²Since this new way gives us such confidence, we can be very bold. ¹³We are not like Moses, who put a veil over his face so the people of Israel would not see the glory, even though it was destined to fade away. ¹⁴But the people's minds were hardened, and to this day whenever the old covenant is being read, the same veil covers their minds so they cannot understand the truth. And this veil can be removed only by believing in Christ. ¹⁵Yes, even today when they read Moses' writings, their hearts are covered with that veil, and they do not understand.

¹⁶But whenever someone turns to the Lord, the veil is taken away. ¹⁷For the Lord is the Spirit, and wherever the Spirit of the Lord is, there is freedom. ¹⁸So all of us who have had that veil removed can see and reflect the glory of the Lord. And the Lord—who is the Spirit—makes us more and more like him as we are changed into his glorious image.

CHAPTER 4

Treasure in Fragile Clay Jars

Therefore, since God in his mercy has given us this new way,* we never give up. ²We reject all shameful deeds and underhanded methods. We don't try to trick anyone or distort the word of God. We tell the truth before God, and all who are honest know this.

³If the Good News we preach is hidden behind a veil, it is hidden only from people who are perishing. ⁴Satan, who is the god of this world, has blinded the minds of those who don't believe. They are unable to see the glorious light of the Good News. They don't understand this message about the glory of Christ, who is the exact likeness of God.

⁵You see, we don't go around preaching about ourselves. We preach that Jesus Christ is Lord, and we ourselves are your servants for Jesus' sake. ⁶For God, who said, "Let there be light in the darkness," has made this light shine in our hearts so we could know the glory of God that is seen in the face of Jesus Christ.

⁷We now have this light shining in our hearts, but we ourselves are like fragile clay jars containing this great treasure.* This makes it clear that our great power is from God, not from ourselves.

⁸We are pressed on every side by troubles, but we are not crushed. We are perplexed, but not driven to despair. ⁹We are hunted down, but never abandoned by God. We get knocked down, but we are not destroyed. ¹⁰Through suffering, our bodies continue to share in the death of Jesus so that the life of Jesus may also be seen in our bodies.

¹¹Yes, we live under constant danger of death because we serve Jesus, so that the life of Jesus will be evident in our

3:7 Or *ministry*; also in 3:8, 9, 10, 11, 12.   4:1 Or *ministry*.   4:7 Greek *We now have this treasure in clay jars.*

the way it is

RETELLING A BIBLICAL STORY: 2 CORINTHIANS 5:1-5

We know for a fact that when we're dead and buried—when we leave this earth for good—we'll have a crib in heaven. Not a crib like what we see being built down here, where the construction workers put it together brick by brick, but the kind of house only God can build. Sometimes life is ill and everything makes us ache for the comfortable bodies we'll have in heaven. It'll be like getting a new outfit, an outfit so fresh we'll wish we'd had it all along.

In heaven we'll still have bodies—we won't be like Casper, floatin' around lookin' spooky. It's true, while we're here on earth we might get sick and tired, workin' double shifts, tryin' hard to make ends. It's not that we want to die—it's just that our heavenly bodies will be so fresh and clean, full of life. God has prepared us for this sort of thing. And just so that we wouldn't think he was sellin' us out, he gave us his Holy Spirit to be with us until we make it to heaven.

---

dying bodies. ¹²So we live in the face of death, but this has resulted in eternal life for you.

¹³But we continue to preach because we have the same kind of faith the psalmist had when he said, "I believed in God, so I spoke."* ¹⁴We know that God, who raised the Lord Jesus,* will also raise us with Jesus and present us to himself together with you. ¹⁵All of this is for your benefit. And as God's grace reaches more and more people, there will be great thanksgiving, and God will receive more and more glory.

¹⁶That is why we never give up. Though our bodies are dying, our spirits are* being renewed every day. ¹⁷For our present troubles are small and won't last very long. Yet they produce for us a glory that vastly outweighs them and will last forever! ¹⁸So we don't look at the troubles we can see now; rather, we fix our gaze on things that cannot be seen. For the things we see now will soon be gone, but the things we cannot see will last forever.

CHAPTER 5

New Bodies

For we know that when this earthly tent we live in is taken down (that is, when we die and leave this earthly body), we will have a house in heaven, an eternal body made for us by God himself and not by human hands. ²We grow weary in our present bodies, and we long to put on our heavenly bodies like new clothing. ³For we will put on heavenly bodies; we will not be spirits without bodies.* ⁴While we live in these earthly bodies, we groan and sigh, but it's not that we want to die and get rid of these bodies that clothe us. Rather, we want to put on our new bodies so that these dying bodies will be swallowed up by life. ⁵God himself has prepared us for this, and as a guarantee he has given us his Holy Spirit.

⁶So we are always confident, even though we know that as long as we live in these bodies we are not at home with the Lord. ⁷For we live by believing and not by seeing. ⁸Yes, we are fully confident, and we would rather be away from these earthly bodies, for then we will be at home with the Lord. ⁹So whether we are here in this body or away from this body, our goal is to please him. ¹⁰For we must all stand before Christ to be judged. We will each receive whatever we deserve for the good or evil we have done in this earthly body.

We Are God's Ambassadors

¹¹Because we understand our fearful responsibility to the Lord, we work hard to persuade others. God knows we are sincere, and I hope you know this, too. ¹²Are we commending ourselves to you again? No, we are giving you a reason to be proud of us,* so you can answer those who brag about

---

4:13 Ps 116:10. **4:14** Some manuscripts read *who raised Jesus.* **4:16** Greek *our inner being is.* **5:3** Greek *we will not be naked.* **5:12** Some manuscripts read *proud of yourselves.*

having a spectacular ministry rather than having a sincere heart. [13]If it seems we are crazy, it is to bring glory to God. And if we are in our right minds, it is for your benefit. [14]Either way, Christ's love controls us.* Since we believe that Christ died for all, we also believe that we have all died to our old life.* [15]He died for everyone so that those who receive his new life will no longer live for themselves. Instead, they will live for Christ, who died and was raised for them.

[16]So we have stopped evaluating others from a human point of view. At one time we thought of Christ merely from a human point of view. How differently we know him now! [17]This means that anyone who belongs to Christ has become a new person. The old life is gone; a new life has begun!

[18]And all of this is a gift from God, who brought us back to himself through Christ. And God has given us this task of reconciling people to him. [19]For God was in Christ, reconciling the world to himself, no longer counting people's sins against them. And he gave us this wonderful message of reconciliation. [20]So we are Christ's ambassadors; God is making his appeal through us. We speak for Christ when we plead, "Come back to God!" [21]For God made Christ, who never sinned, to be the offering for our sin,* so that we could be made right with God through Christ.

CHAPTER 6

As God's partners,* we beg you not to accept this marvelous gift of God's kindness and then ignore it. [2]For God says,

"At just the right time, I heard you.
   On the day of salvation, I helped you."*

Indeed, the "right time" is now. Today is the day of salvation.

Paul's Hardships

[3]We live in such a way that no one will stumble because of us, and no one will find fault with our ministry. [4]In everything we do, we show that we are true ministers of God. We patiently endure troubles and hardships and calamities of every kind. [5]We have been beaten, been put in prison, faced angry mobs, worked to exhaustion, endured sleepless nights, and gone without food. [6]We prove ourselves by our purity, our understanding, our patience, our kindness, by the Holy Spirit within us,* and by our sincere love. [7]We faithfully preach the truth. God's power is working in us. We use the weapons of righteousness in the right hand for attack and the left hand for defense. [8]We serve God whether people honor us or despise us, whether they slander us or praise us. We are honest, but they call us impostors. [9]We are ignored, even though we are well known. We live close to death, but we are still alive. We have been beaten, but we have not been killed. [10]Our hearts ache, but we always have joy. We are poor, but we give spiritual riches to others. We own nothing, and yet we have everything.

[11]Oh, dear Corinthian friends! We have spoken honestly with you, and our hearts are open to you. [12]There is no lack of love on our part, but you have withheld your love from us. [13]I am asking you to respond as if you were my own children. Open your hearts to us!

The Temple of the Living God

[14]Don't team up with those who are unbelievers. How can righteousness be a partner with wickedness? How can light live with darkness? [15]What harmony can there be between Christ and the devil*? How can a believer be a partner with an unbeliever? [16]And what union can there be between God's temple and idols? For we are the temple of the living God. As God said:

"I will live in them
   and walk among them.
I will be their God,
   and they will be my people."*

5:14a Or *urges us on.*   **5:14b** Greek *Since one died for all, then all died.*   **5:21** Or *to become sin itself.*   **6:1** Or *As we work together.*   **6:2** Isa 49:8 (Greek version).   **6:6** Or *by our holiness of spirit.*   **6:15** Greek *Beliar;* various other manuscripts render this proper name of the devil as *Belian, Beliab,* or *Belial.*   **6:16** Lev 26:12; Ezek 37:27.

¹⁷ Therefore, come out from among unbelievers,
   and separate yourselves from them, says the LORD.
Don't touch their filthy things,
   and I will welcome you.*
¹⁸ And I will be your Father,
   and you will be my sons and daughters,
   says the LORD Almighty.*"

CHAPTER 7

Because we have these promises, dear friends, let us cleanse ourselves from everything that can defile our body or spirit. And let us work toward complete holiness because we fear God.

²Please open your hearts to us. We have not done wrong to anyone, nor led anyone astray, nor taken advantage of anyone. ³I'm not saying this to condemn you. I said before that you are in our hearts, and we live or die together with you. ⁴I have the highest confidence in you, and I take great pride in you. You have greatly encouraged me and made me happy despite all our troubles.

Paul's Joy at the Church's Repentance

⁵When we arrived in Macedonia, there was no rest for us. We faced conflict from every direction, with battles on the outside and fear on the inside. ⁶But God, who encourages those who are discouraged, encouraged us by the arrival of Titus. ⁷His presence was a joy, but so was the news he brought of the encouragement he received from you. When he told us how much you long to see me, and how sorry you are for what happened, and how loyal you are to me, I was filled with joy!

⁸I am not sorry that I sent that severe letter to you, though I was sorry at first, for I know it was painful to you for a little while. ⁹Now I am glad I sent it, not because it hurt you, but because the pain caused you to repent and change your ways. It was the kind of sorrow God wants his people to have, so you were not harmed by us in any way. ¹⁰For the kind of sorrow God wants us to experience leads us away from sin and results in salvation. There's no regret for that kind of sorrow. But worldly sorrow, which lacks repentance, results in spiritual death.

¹¹Just see what this godly sorrow produced in you! Such earnestness, such concern to clear yourselves, such indignation, such alarm, such longing to see me, such zeal, and such a readiness to punish wrong. You showed that you have done everything necessary to make things right. ¹²My purpose, then, was not to write about who did the wrong or who was wronged. I wrote to you so that in the sight of God you could see for yourselves how loyal you are to us. ¹³We have been greatly encouraged by this.

In addition to our own encouragement, we were especially delighted to see how happy Titus was about the way all of you welcomed him and set his mind* at ease. ¹⁴I had told him how proud I was of you—and you didn't disappoint me. I have always told you the truth, and now my boasting to Titus has also proved true! ¹⁵Now he cares for you more than ever when he remembers the way all of you obeyed him and welcomed him with such fear and deep respect. ¹⁶I am very happy now because I have complete confidence in you.

CHAPTER 8

A Call to Generous Giving

Now I want you to know, dear brothers and sisters,* what God in his kindness has done through the churches in Macedonia. ²They are being tested by many troubles, and they are very poor. But they are also filled with abundant joy, which has overflowed in rich generosity.

³For I can testify that they gave not only what they could afford, but far more. And they did it of their own free will. ⁴They begged us again and again for the privilege of sharing in the gift for the believers* in Jerusalem. ⁵They even

"Don't team up with those who are unbelievers. How can righteousness be a partner with wickedness? How can light live with darkness?" (2 Corinthians 6:14).

say wyat?

Be careful who you roll with. Righteous people and wicked people are like oil and water—they shouldn't mix. How can light live in the presence of darkness?

6:17 Isa 52:11; Ezek 20:34 (Greek version).   **6:18** 2 Sam 7:14.   **7:13** Greek *his spirit*.   **8:1** Greek *brothers*.   **8:4** Greek *for God's holy people*.

did more than we had hoped, for their first action was to give themselves to the Lord and to us, just as God wanted them to do.

⁶So we have urged Titus, who encouraged your giving in the first place, to return to you and encourage you to finish this ministry of giving. ⁷Since you excel in so many ways— in your faith, your gifted speakers, your knowledge, your enthusiasm, and your love from us*—I want you to excel also in this gracious act of giving.

⁸I am not commanding you to do this. But I am testing how genuine your love is by comparing it with the eagerness of the other churches.

⁹You know the generous grace of our Lord Jesus Christ. Though he was rich, yet for your sakes he became poor, so that by his poverty he could make you rich.

¹⁰Here is my advice: It would be good for you to finish what you started a year ago. Last year you were the first who wanted to give, and you were the first to begin doing it. ¹¹Now you should finish what you started. Let the eagerness you showed in the beginning be matched now by your giving. Give in proportion to what you have. ¹²Whatever you give is acceptable if you give it eagerly. And give according to what you have, not what you don't have. ¹³Of course, I don't mean your giving should make life easy for others and hard for yourselves. I only mean that there should be some equality. ¹⁴Right now you have plenty and can help those who are in need. Later, they will have plenty and can share with you when you need it. In this way, things will be equal. ¹⁵As the Scriptures say,

"Those who gathered a lot had nothing left over,
    and those who gathered only a little had enough."*

Titus and His Companions

¹⁶But thank God! He has given Titus the same enthusiasm for you that I have. ¹⁷Titus welcomed our request that he visit you again. In fact, he himself was very eager to go and

POWERCHOICES

IN THE FOURTH CHAPTER OF 2 CORINTHIANS, PAUL EXPLAINS THAT HE HAS BEEN PUT IN CHARGE OF EXPLAINING WHAT'S REALLY UP WITH GOD. THAT IS, THINGS THAT MIGHT OTHERWISE BE CONFUSIN' AND HARD TO TAKE IN. PAUL'S LIKE A TRUE LYRICIST—SPITTIN' KNOWLEDGE AND TRUTH TO PEOPLE—SOME WANT TO HEAR, AND SOME DON'T. ¶ LIKE SOME OF THE GREATEST EMCEES AND ARTISTS OF ALL TIME, PAUL GAVE VERY LITTLE THOUGHT TO HOW PEOPLE MIGHT LOOK AT HIM OR FEEL ABOUT HIS VERSE. HE JUST SAID WHAT HE HAD TO SAY, AND THAT WAS IT. HE WAS KINDA TELLIN' THEM NOT TO JUDGE HIM—JUST TO RECEIVE THE TRUTH HE WAS SPEAKIN' ABOUT GOD. QUESTION: CAN YOU HANDLE THE TRUTH? ¶ *JESUS IS REAL. HE DIED FOR OUR MESS-UPS AND SHORTCOMINGS. HE IS COMING BACK. DO YOU FEEL ME ON THAT?*

see you. ¹⁸We are also sending another brother with Titus. All the churches praise him as a preacher of the Good News. ¹⁹He was appointed by the churches to accompany us as we take the offering to Jerusalem*—a service that glorifies the Lord and shows our eagerness to help.

²⁰We are traveling together to guard against any criticism for the way we are handling this generous gift. ²¹We are careful to be honorable before the Lord, but we also want everyone else to see that we are honorable.

²²We are also sending with them another of our brothers who has proven himself many times and has shown on many occasions how eager he is. He is now even more enthusiastic because of his great confidence in you. ²³If anyone asks about Titus, say that he is my partner who works with me to help you. And the brothers with him have been sent by the churches,* and they bring honor to Christ. ²⁴So show them your love, and prove to all the churches that our boasting about you is justified.

8:7 Some manuscripts read *your love for us.*   8:15 Exod 16:18.   8:19 See 1 Cor 16:3-4.   8:23 Greek *are apostles of the churches.*

CHAPTER 9

The Collection for Christians in Jerusalem

I really don't need to write to you about this ministry of giving for the believers in Jerusalem.* ²For I know how eager you are to help, and I have been boasting to the churches in Macedonia that you in Greece* were ready to send an offering a year ago. In fact, it was your enthusiasm that stirred up many of the Macedonian believers to begin giving.

³But I am sending these brothers to be sure you really are ready, as I have been telling them, and that your money is all collected. I don't want to be wrong in my boasting about you. ⁴We would be embarrassed—not to mention your own embarrassment—if some Macedonian believers came with me and found that you weren't ready after all I had told them! ⁵So I thought I should send these brothers ahead of me to make sure the gift you promised is ready. But I want it to be a willing gift, not one given grudgingly.

⁶Remember this—a farmer who plants only a few seeds will get a small crop. But the one who plants generously will get a generous crop. ⁷You must each decide in your heart how much to give. And don't give reluctantly or in response to pressure. "For God loves a person who gives cheerfully."* ⁸And God will generously provide all you need. Then you will always have everything you need and plenty left over to share with others. ⁹As the Scriptures say,

"They share freely and give generously to the poor.
    Their good deeds will be remembered forever."*

¹⁰For God is the one who provides seed for the farmer and then bread to eat. In the same way, he will provide and increase your resources and then produce a great harvest of generosity* in you.

¹¹Yes, you will be enriched in every way so that you can always be generous. And when we take your gifts to those who need them, they will thank God. ¹²So two good things will result from this ministry of giving—the needs of the believers in Jerusalem* will be met, and they will joyfully express their thanks to God.

¹³As a result of your ministry, they will give glory to God. For your generosity to them and to all believers will prove that you are obedient to the Good News of Christ. ¹⁴And they will pray for you with deep affection because of the overflowing grace God has given to you. ¹⁵Thank God for this gift* too wonderful for words!

CHAPTER 10

Paul Defends His Authority

Now I, Paul, appeal to you with the gentleness and kindness of Christ—though I realize you think I am timid in person and bold only when I write from far away. ²Well, I am begging you now so that when I come I won't have to be bold with those who think we act from human motives.

³We are human, but we don't wage war as humans do. ⁴*We use God's mighty weapons, not worldly weapons, to knock down the strongholds of human reasoning and to destroy false arguments. ⁵We destroy every proud obstacle that keeps people from knowing God. We capture their rebellious thoughts and teach them to obey Christ. ⁶And after you have become fully obedient, we will punish everyone who remains disobedient.

⁷Look at the obvious facts.* Those who say they belong to Christ must recognize that we belong to Christ as much as they do. ⁸I may seem to be boasting too much about the authority given to us by the Lord. But our authority builds you up; it doesn't tear you down. So I will not be ashamed of using my authority.

⁹I'm not trying to frighten you by my letters. ¹⁰For some say, "Paul's letters are demanding and forceful, but in person

9:1 Greek *about the offering for God's holy people.* 9:2 Greek *in Achaia,* the southern region of the Greek peninsula. *Macedonia* was in the northern region of Greece. 9:7 See footnote on Prov 22:8. 9:9 Ps 112:9. 9:10 Greek *righteousness.* 9:12 Greek *of God's holy people.* 9:15 Greek *his gift.* 10:4 English translations divide verses 4 and 5 in various ways. 10:7 Or *You look at things only on the basis of appearance.*

he is weak, and his speeches are worthless!" ¹¹Those people should realize that our actions when we arrive in person will be as forceful as what we say in our letters from far away.

¹²Oh, don't worry; we wouldn't dare say that we are as wonderful as these other men who tell you how important they are! But they are only comparing themselves with each other, using themselves as the standard of measurement. How ignorant!

¹³We will not boast about things done outside our area of authority. We will boast only about what has happened within the boundaries of the work God has given us, which includes our working with you. ¹⁴We are not reaching beyond these boundaries when we claim authority over you, as if we had never visited you. For we were the first to travel all the way to Corinth with the Good News of Christ.

¹⁵Nor do we boast and claim credit for the work someone else has done. Instead, we hope that your faith will grow so that the boundaries of our work among you will be extended. ¹⁶Then we will be able to go and preach the Good News in other places far beyond you, where no one else is working. Then there will be no question of our boasting about work done in someone else's territory. ¹⁷As the Scriptures say, "If you want to boast, boast only about the LORD."*

¹⁸When people commend themselves, it doesn't count for much. The important thing is for the Lord to commend them.

CHAPTER **11**

Paul and the False Apostles

I hope you will put up with a little more of my foolishness. Please bear with me. ²For I am jealous for you with the jealousy of God himself. I promised you as a pure bride* to one husband—Christ. ³But I fear that somehow your pure and undivided devotion to Christ will be corrupted, just as Eve was deceived by the cunning ways of the serpent. ⁴You hap-

pily put up with whatever anyone tells you, even if they preach a different Jesus than the one we preach, or a different kind of Spirit than the one you received, or a different kind of gospel than the one you believed.

⁵But I don't consider myself inferior in any way to these "super apostles" who teach such things. ⁶I may be unskilled as a speaker, but I'm not lacking in knowledge. We have made this clear to you in every possible way.

⁷Was I wrong when I humbled myself and honored you by preaching God's Good News to you without expecting anything in return? ⁸I "robbed" other churches by accepting their contributions so I could serve you at no cost. ⁹And when I was with you and didn't have enough to live on, I did not become a financial burden to anyone. For the brothers who came from Macedonia brought me all that I needed. I have never been a burden to you, and I never will be. ¹⁰As surely as the truth of Christ is in me, no one in all of Greece* will ever stop me from boasting about this. ¹¹Why? Because I don't love you? God knows that I do.

¹²But I will continue doing what I have always done. This will undercut those who are looking for an opportunity to boast that their work is just like ours. ¹³These people are false apostles. They are deceitful workers who disguise themselves as apostles of Christ. ¹⁴But I am not surprised! Even Satan disguises himself as an angel of light. ¹⁵So it is no wonder that his servants also disguise themselves as servants of righteousness. In the end they will get the punishment their wicked deeds deserve.

Paul's Many Trials

¹⁶Again I say, don't think that I am a fool to talk like this. But even if you do, listen to me, as you would to a foolish person, while I also boast a little. ¹⁷Such boasting is not from the Lord, but I am acting like a fool. ¹⁸And since others boast about their human achievements, I will, too. ¹⁹After all, you think you are so wise, but you enjoy putting up with fools!

10:17 Jer 9:24.   11:2 Greek *a virgin*.   11:10 Greek *Achaia*, the southern region of the Greek peninsula.

²⁰You put up with it when someone enslaves you, takes everything you have, takes advantage of you, takes control of everything, and slaps you in the face. ²¹I'm ashamed to say that we've been too "weak" to do that!

But whatever they dare to boast about—I'm talking like a fool again—I dare to boast about it, too. ²²Are they Hebrews? So am I. Are they Israelites? So am I. Are they descendants of Abraham? So am I. ²³Are they servants of Christ? I know I sound like a madman, but I have served him far more! I have worked harder, been put in prison more often, been whipped times without number, and faced death again and again. ²⁴Five different times the Jewish leaders gave me thirty-nine lashes. ²⁵Three times I was beaten with rods. Once I was stoned. Three times I was shipwrecked. Once I spent a whole night and a day adrift at sea. ²⁶I have traveled on many long journeys. I have faced danger from rivers and from robbers. I have faced danger from my own people, the Jews, as well as from the Gentiles. I have faced danger in the cities, in the deserts, and on the seas. And I have faced danger from men who claim to be believers but are not.* ²⁷I have worked hard and long, enduring many sleepless nights. I have been hungry and thirsty and have often gone without food. I have shivered in the cold, without enough clothing to keep me warm.

²⁸Then, besides all this, I have the daily burden of my concern for all the churches. ²⁹Who is weak without my feeling that weakness? Who is led astray, and I do not burn with anger?

³⁰If I must boast, I would rather boast about the things that show how weak I am. ³¹God, the Father of our Lord Jesus, who is worthy of eternal praise, knows I am not lying. ³²When I was in Damascus, the governor under King Aretas kept guards at the city gates to catch me. ³³I had to be lowered in a basket through a window in the city wall to escape from him.

CHAPTER 12

Paul's Vision and His Thorn in the Flesh

This boasting will do no good, but I must go on. I will reluctantly tell about visions and revelations from the Lord. ²I* was caught up to the third heaven fourteen years ago. Whether I was in my body or out of my body, I don't know—only God knows. ³Yes, only God knows whether I was in my body or outside my body. But I do know ⁴that I was caught up* to paradise and heard things so astounding that they cannot be expressed in words, things no human is allowed to tell.

⁵That experience is worth boasting about, but I'm not going to do it. I will boast only about my weaknesses. ⁶If I wanted to boast, I would be no fool in doing so, because I would be telling the truth. But I won't do it, because I don't want anyone to give me credit beyond what they can see in my life or hear in my message, ⁷even though I have received such wonderful revelations from God. So to keep me from becoming proud, I was given a thorn in my flesh, a messenger from Satan to torment me and keep me from becoming proud.

⁸Three different times I begged the Lord to take it away. ⁹Each time he said, "My grace is all you need. My power works best in weakness." So now I am glad to boast about my weaknesses, so that the power of Christ can work through me. ¹⁰That's why I take pleasure in my weaknesses, and in the insults, hardships, persecutions, and troubles that I suffer for Christ. For when I am weak, then I am strong.

Paul's Concern for the Corinthians

¹¹You have made me act like a fool—boasting like this.* You ought to be writing commendations for me, for I am not at all inferior to these "super apostles," even though I am nothing at all. ¹²When I was with you, I certainly gave you proof that I am an apostle. For I patiently did many signs and wonders and miracles among you. ¹³The only thing I failed to do, which I do in the other churches, was to become a financial burden to you. Please forgive me for this wrong!

"Three different times I begged the Lord to take [my weakness] away. Each time he said, 'My grace is all you need. My power works best in weakness.' So now I am glad to boast about my weaknesses, so that the power of Christ can work through me" (2 Corinthians 12:8-9).

Say what?

I asked God to take my weakness away, but he wanted me to have it for a reason. He wants me to remember that I can't go it alone—that I can't do it without God. That's why I thank him now for my weaknesses.

11:26 Greek *from false brothers.*   **12:2** Greek *I know a man in Christ who.*   **12:3-4** Greek *But I know such a man, ⁴that he was caught up.*   **12:11** Some manuscripts do not include *boasting like this.*

[14]Now I am coming to you for the third time, and I will not be a burden to you. I don't want what you have—I want you. After all, children don't provide for their parents. Rather, parents provide for their children. [15]I will gladly spend myself and all I have for you, even though it seems that the more I love you, the less you love me.

[16]Some of you admit I was not a burden to you. But others still think I was sneaky and took advantage of you by trickery. [17]But how? Did any of the men I sent to you take advantage of you? [18]When I urged Titus to visit you and sent our other brother with him, did Titus take advantage of you? No! For we have the same spirit and walk in each other's steps, doing things the same way.

[19]Perhaps you think we're saying these things just to defend ourselves. No, we tell you this as Christ's servants, and with God as our witness. Everything we do, dear friends, is to strengthen you. [20]For I am afraid that when I come I won't like what I find, and you won't like my response. I am afraid that I will find quarreling, jealousy, anger, selfishness, slander, gossip, arrogance, and disorderly behavior. [21]Yes, I am afraid that when I come again, God will humble me in your presence. And I will be grieved because many of you have not given up your old sins. You have not repented of your impurity, sexual immorality, and eagerness for lustful pleasure.

CHAPTER 13
Paul's Final Advice

This is the third time I am coming to visit you (and as the Scriptures say, "The facts of every case must be established by the testimony of two or three witnesses"*). [2]I have already warned those who had been sinning when I was there on my second visit. Now I again warn them and all others, just as I did before, that next time I will not spare them.

[3]I will give you all the proof you want that Christ speaks through me. Christ is not weak when he deals with you; he is powerful among you. [4]Although he was crucified in weakness, he now lives by the power of God. We, too, are weak, just as Christ was, but when we deal with you we will be alive with him and will have God's power.

[5]Examine yourselves to see if your faith is genuine. Test yourselves. Surely you know that Jesus Christ is among you*; if not, you have failed the test of genuine faith. [6]As you test yourselves, I hope you will recognize that we have not failed the test of apostolic authority.

[7]We pray to God that you will not do what is wrong by refusing our correction. I hope we won't need to demonstrate our authority when we arrive. Do the right thing before we come—even if that makes it look like we have failed to demonstrate our authority. [8]For we cannot oppose the truth, but must always stand for the truth. [9]We are glad to seem weak if it helps show that you are actually strong. We pray that you will become mature.

[10]I am writing this to you before I come, hoping that I won't need to deal severely with you when I do come. For I want to use the authority the Lord has given me to strengthen you, not to tear you down.

Paul's Final Greetings

[11]Dear brothers and sisters,* I close my letter with these last words: Be joyful. Grow to maturity. Encourage each other. Live in harmony and peace. Then the God of love and peace will be with you.

[12]Greet each other with Christian love.* [13]All of God's people here send you their greetings.

[14]*May the grace of the Lord Jesus Christ, the love of God, and the fellowship of the Holy Spirit be with you all.

13:1 Deut 19:15.   **13:5** Or *in you.*   **13:11** Greek *Brothers.*   **13:12** Greek *with a sacred kiss.*   **13:14** Some English translations include verse 13 as part of verse 12, and then verse 14 becomes verse 13.

WHAT'S THE WORD on Galatians? The name might seem kind of wild. No one I know has ever been to Galatia on vacay. Here's the deal: The apostle Paul wrote this letter to the people in Galatia (somewhere not far from Greece) because they had become really uptight. They were the type of folks who would mean-mug you if you weren't doin' what they considered correct at all times.

Paul wanted to straighten them out. He wanted to help them remember it's not followin' a long list of dos and don'ts that makes us right with God; it's in receiving his gift of forgiveness and the payment he made through Jesus on the cross. Paul also took some time in this letter to tell the story about how Jesus' boys finally accepted Paul into the family.

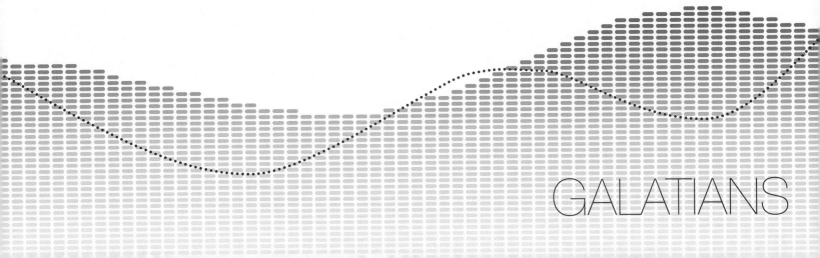

GALATIANS

CHAPTER **1**

Greetings from Paul

This letter is from Paul, an apostle. I was not appointed by any group of people or any human authority, but by Jesus Christ himself and by God the Father, who raised Jesus from the dead.

²All the brothers and sisters* here join me in sending this letter to the churches of Galatia.

³May God our Father and the Lord Jesus Christ* give you grace and peace. ⁴Jesus gave his life for our sins, just as God our Father planned, in order to rescue us from this evil world in which we live. ⁵All glory to God forever and ever! Amen.

There Is Only One Good News

⁶I am shocked that you are turning away so soon from God, who called you to himself through the loving mercy of Christ.* You are following a different way that pretends to be the Good News ⁷but is not the Good News at all. You are being fooled by those who deliberately twist the truth concerning Christ.

⁸Let God's curse fall on anyone, including us or even an angel from heaven, who preaches a different kind of Good News than the one we preached to you. ⁹I say again what we have said before: If anyone preaches any other Good News than the one you welcomed, let that person be cursed.

¹⁰Obviously, I'm not trying to win the approval of people, but of God. If pleasing people were my goal, I would not be Christ's servant.

Paul's Message Comes from Christ

¹¹Dear brothers and sisters, I want you to understand that the gospel message I preach is not based on mere human reasoning. ¹²I received my message from no human source, and no one taught me. Instead, I received it by direct revelation from Jesus Christ.*

¹³You know what I was like when I followed the Jewish religion—how I violently persecuted God's church. I did my best to destroy it. ¹⁴I was far ahead of my fellow Jews in my zeal for the traditions of my ancestors.

¹⁵But even before I was born, God chose me and called me by his marvelous grace. Then it pleased him ¹⁶to reveal his Son to me* so that I would proclaim the Good News about Jesus to the Gentiles.

When this happened, I did not rush out to consult with any human being.* ¹⁷Nor did I go up to Jerusalem to consult with those who were apostles before I was. Instead, I went away into Arabia, and later I returned to the city of Damascus.

¹⁸Then three years later I went to Jerusalem to get to know Peter,* and I stayed with him for fifteen days. ¹⁹The only other apostle I met at that time was James, the Lord's brother. ²⁰I declare before God that what I am writing to you is not a lie.

²¹After that visit I went north into the provinces of Syria and Cilicia. ²²And still the Christians in the churches in Judea didn't know me personally. ²³All they knew was that people were saying, "The one who used to persecute us is now preaching the very faith he tried to destroy!" ²⁴And they praised God because of me.

1:2 Greek *brothers;* also in 1:11.   **1:3** Some manuscripts read *God the Father and our Lord Jesus Christ.*   **1:6** Some manuscripts read *through loving mercy.*   **1:12** Or *by the revelation of Jesus Christ.*   **1:16a** Or *in me.*   **1:16b** Greek *with flesh and blood.*   **1:18** Greek *Cephas.*

CHAPTER 2

The Apostles Accept Paul

Then fourteen years later I went back to Jerusalem again, this time with Barnabas; and Titus came along, too. ²I went there because God revealed to me that I should go. While I was there I met privately with those considered to be leaders of the church and shared with them the message I had been preaching to the Gentiles. I wanted to make sure that we were in agreement, for fear that all my efforts had been wasted and I was running the race for nothing. ³And they supported me and did not even demand that my companion Titus be circumcised, though he was a Gentile.*

⁴Even that question came up only because of some so-called Christians there—false ones, really*—who were secretly brought in. They sneaked in to spy on us and take away the freedom we have in Christ Jesus. They wanted to enslave us and force us to follow their Jewish regulations. ⁵But we refused to give in to them for a single moment. We wanted to preserve the truth of the gospel message for you.

⁶And the leaders of the church had nothing to add to what I was preaching. (By the way, their reputation as great leaders made no difference to me, for God has no favorites.) ⁷Instead, they saw that God had given me the responsibility of preaching the gospel to the Gentiles, just as he had given Peter the responsibility of preaching to the Jews. ⁸For the same God who worked through Peter as the apostle to the Jews also worked through me as the apostle to the Gentiles.

⁹In fact, James, Peter,* and John, who were known as pillars of the church, recognized the gift God had given me, and they accepted Barnabas and me as their co-workers. They encouraged us to keep preaching to the Gentiles, while they continued their work with the Jews. ¹⁰Their only suggestion was that we keep on helping the poor, which I have always been eager to do.

Paul Confronts Peter

¹¹But when Peter came to Antioch, I had to oppose him to his face, for what he did was very wrong. ¹²When he first arrived, he ate with the Gentile Christians, who were not circumcised. But afterward, when some friends of James came, Peter wouldn't eat with the Gentiles anymore. He was afraid of criticism from these people who insisted on the necessity of circumcision. ¹³As a result, other Jewish Christians followed Peter's hypocrisy, and even Barnabas was led astray by their hypocrisy.

¹⁴When I saw that they were not following the truth of the gospel message, I said to Peter in front of all the others, "Since you, a Jew by birth, have discarded the Jewish laws and are living like a Gentile, why are you now trying to make these Gentiles follow the Jewish traditions?

¹⁵"You and I are Jews by birth, not 'sinners' like the Gentiles. ¹⁶Yet we know that a person is made right with God by faith in Jesus Christ, not by obeying the law. And we have believed in Christ Jesus, so that we might be made right with God because of our faith in Christ, not because we have obeyed the law. For no one will ever be made right with God by obeying the law."*

¹⁷But suppose we seek to be made right with God through faith in Christ and then we are found guilty because we have abandoned the law. Would that mean Christ has led us into sin? Absolutely not! ¹⁸Rather, I am a sinner if I rebuild the old system of law I already tore down. ¹⁹For when I tried to keep the law, it condemned me. So I died to the law—I stopped trying to meet all its requirements—so that I might live for God. ²⁰My old self has been crucified with Christ.* It is no longer I who live, but Christ lives in me. So I live in this earthly body by trusting in the Son of God, who loved me and gave himself for me. ²¹I do not treat the grace of God as meaningless. For if keeping the law could make us right with God, then there was no need for Christ to die.

2:3 Greek *a Greek.*   **2:4** Greek *some false brothers.*   **2:9** Greek *Cephas;* also in 2:11, 14.   **2:16** Some translators hold that the quotation extends through verse 14; others through verse 16; and still others through verse 21.   **2:20** Some English translations put this sentence in verse 19.

CHAPTER 3

The Law and Faith in Christ

Oh, foolish Galatians! Who has cast an evil spell on you? For the meaning of Jesus Christ's death was made as clear to you as if you had seen a picture of his death on the cross. ²Let me ask you this one question: Did you receive the Holy Spirit by obeying the law of Moses? Of course not! You received the Spirit because you believed the message you heard about Christ. ³How foolish can you be? After starting your Christian lives in the Spirit, why are you now trying to become perfect by your own human effort? ⁴Have you experienced* so much for nothing? Surely it was not in vain, was it?

⁵I ask you again, does God give you the Holy Spirit and work miracles among you because you obey the law? Of course not! It is because you believe the message you heard about Christ.

⁶In the same way, "Abraham believed God, and God counted him as righteous because of his faith."* ⁷The real children of Abraham, then, are those who put their faith in God.

⁸What's more, the Scriptures looked forward to this time when God would declare the Gentiles to be righteous because of their faith. God proclaimed this good news to Abraham long ago when he said, "All nations will be blessed through you."* ⁹So all who put their faith in Christ share the same blessing Abraham received because of his faith.

¹⁰But those who depend on the law to make them right with God are under his curse, for the Scriptures say, "Cursed is everyone who does not observe and obey all the commands that are written in God's Book of the Law."* ¹¹So it is clear that no one can be made right with God by trying to keep the law. For the Scriptures say, "It is through faith that a righteous person has life."* ¹²This way of faith is very different from the way of law, which says, "It is through obeying the law that a person has life."*

¹³But Christ has rescued us from the curse pronounced by the law. When he was hung on the cross, he took upon himself the curse for our wrongdoing. For it is written in the Scriptures, "Cursed is everyone who is hung on a tree."* ¹⁴Through Christ Jesus, God has blessed the Gentiles with the same blessing he promised to Abraham, so that we who are believers might receive the promised* Holy Spirit through faith.

The Law and God's Promise

¹⁵Dear brothers and sisters,* here's an example from everyday life. Just as no one can set aside or amend an irrevocable agreement, so it is in this case. ¹⁶God gave the promises to Abraham and his child.* And notice that the Scripture doesn't say "to his children,*" as if it meant many descendants. Rather, it says "to his child"—and that, of course, means Christ. ¹⁷This is what I am trying to say: The agreement God made with Abraham could not be canceled 430 years later when God gave the law to Moses. God would be breaking his promise. ¹⁸For if the inheritance could be received by keeping the law, then it would not be the result of accepting God's promise. But God graciously gave it to Abraham as a promise.

¹⁹Why, then, was the law given? It was given alongside the promise to show people their sins. But the law was designed to last only until the coming of the child who was promised. God gave his law through angels to Moses, who was the mediator between God and the people. ²⁰Now a mediator is helpful if more than one party must reach an agreement. But God, who is one, did not use a mediator when he gave his promise to Abraham.

²¹Is there a conflict, then, between God's law and God's promises?* Absolutely not! If the law could give us new life, we could be made right with God by obeying it. ²²But the Scriptures declare that we are all prisoners of sin, so we receive God's promise of freedom only by believing in Jesus Christ.

3:4 Or *Have you suffered.* 3:6 Gen 15:6. 3:8 Gen 12:3; 18:18; 22:18. 3:10 Deut 27:26. 3:11 Hab 2:4. 3:12 Lev 18:5. 3:13 Deut 21:23 (Greek version). 3:14 Some manuscripts read *the blessing of the.* 3:15 Greek *Brothers.* 3:16a Greek *seed;* also in 3:16c, 19. See notes on Gen 12:7 and 13:15. 3:16b Greek *seeds.* 3:21 Some manuscripts read *and the promises?*

God's Children through Faith

²³Before the way of faith in Christ was available to us, we were placed under guard by the law. We were kept in protective custody, so to speak, until the way of faith was revealed.

²⁴Let me put it another way. The law was our guardian until Christ came; it protected us until we could be made right with God through faith. ²⁵And now that the way of faith has come, we no longer need the law as our guardian.

²⁶For you are all children* of God through faith in Christ Jesus. ²⁷And all who have been united with Christ in baptism have put on Christ, like putting on new clothes.* ²⁸There is no longer Jew or Gentile,* slave or free, male and female. For you are all one in Christ Jesus. ²⁹And now that you belong to Christ, you are the true children* of Abraham. You are his heirs, and God's promise to Abraham belongs to you.

CHAPTER 4

Think of it this way. If a father dies and leaves an inheritance for his young children, those children are not much better off than slaves until they grow up, even though they actually own everything their father had. ²They have to obey their guardians until they reach whatever age their father set. ³And that's the way it was with us before Christ came. We were like children; we were slaves to the basic spiritual principles* of this world.

⁴But when the right time came, God sent his Son, born of a woman, subject to the law. ⁵God sent him to buy freedom for us who were slaves to the law, so that he could adopt us as his very own children.* ⁶And because we* are his children, God has sent the Spirit of his Son into our hearts, prompting us to call out, "Abba, Father."* ⁷Now you are no longer a slave but God's own child.* And since you are his child, God has made you his heir.

Paul's Concern for the Galatians

⁸Before you Gentiles knew God, you were slaves to so-called gods that do not even exist. ⁹So now that you know God (or should I say, now that God knows you), why do you want to go back again and become slaves once more to the weak and useless spiritual principles of this world? ¹⁰You are trying to earn favor with God by observing certain days or months or seasons or years. ¹¹I fear for you. Perhaps all my hard work with you was for nothing. ¹²Dear brothers and sisters,* I plead with you to live as I do in freedom from these things, for I have become like you Gentiles—free from those laws.

You did not mistreat me when I first preached to you. ¹³Surely you remember that I was sick when I first brought you the Good News. ¹⁴But even though my condition tempted you to reject me, you did not despise me or turn me away. No, you took me in and cared for me as though I were an angel from God or even Christ Jesus himself. ¹⁵Where is that joyful and grateful spirit you felt then? I am sure you would have taken out your own eyes and given them to me if it had been possible. ¹⁶Have I now become your enemy because I am telling you the truth?

¹⁷Those false teachers are so eager to win your favor, but their intentions are not good. They are trying to shut you off from me so that you will pay attention only to them. ¹⁸If someone is eager to do good things for you, that's all right; but let them do it all the time, not just when I'm with you.

¹⁹Oh, my dear children! I feel as if I'm going through labor pains for you again, and they will continue until Christ is fully developed in your lives. ²⁰I wish I were with you right now so I could change my tone. But at this distance I don't know how else to help you.

Abraham's Two Children

²¹Tell me, you who want to live under the law, do you know what the law actually says? ²²The Scriptures say that

"And all who have been united with Christ in baptism have put on Christ, like putting on new clothes. There is no longer Jew or Gentile, slave or free, male and female. For you are all one in Christ Jesus" (Galatians 3:27-28).

say what?

Putting on Jesus is like puttin' on a new 'fit. You got a brand new look and feel. And in Christ, there's no dividing lines—race, class, or sex. When we've got him on, we're all the same.

3:26 Greek *sons.* **3:27** Greek *have put on Christ.* **3:28** Greek *Jew or Greek.* **3:29** Greek *seed.* **4:3** Or *powers;* also in 4:9. **4:5** Greek *sons;* also in 4:6. **4:6a** Greek *you.* **4:6b** *Abba* is an Aramaic term for "father." **4:7** Greek *son;* also in 4:7b. **4:12** Greek *brothers;* also in 4:28, 31.

Abraham had two sons, one from his slave wife and one from his freeborn wife.* ²³The son of the slave wife was born in a human attempt to bring about the fulfillment of God's promise. But the son of the freeborn wife was born as God's own fulfillment of his promise.

²⁴These two women serve as an illustration of God's two covenants. The first woman, Hagar, represents Mount Sinai where people received the law that enslaved them. ²⁵And now Jerusalem is just like Mount Sinai in Arabia,* because she and her children live in slavery to the law. ²⁶But the other woman, Sarah, represents the heavenly Jerusalem. She is the free woman, and she is our mother. ²⁷As Isaiah said,

"Rejoice, O childless woman,
    you who have never given birth!
Break into a joyful shout,
    you who have never been in labor!
For the desolate woman now has more children
    than the woman who lives with her husband!"*

²⁸And you, dear brothers and sisters, are children of the promise, just like Isaac. ²⁹But you are now being persecuted by those who want you to keep the law, just as Ishmael, the child born by human effort, persecuted Isaac, the child born by the power of the Spirit. ³⁰But what do the Scriptures say about that? "Get rid of the slave and her son, for the son of the slave woman will not share the inheritance with the free woman's son."* ³¹So, dear brothers and sisters, we are not children of the slave woman; we are children of the free woman.

CHAPTER 5

Freedom in Christ

So Christ has truly set us free. Now make sure that you stay free, and don't get tied up again in slavery to the law.

²Listen! I, Paul, tell you this: If you are counting on circumcision to make you right with God, then Christ will be of no benefit to you. ³I'll say it again. If you are trying to find favor with God by being circumcised, you must obey every regulation in the whole law of Moses. ⁴For if you are trying to make yourselves right with God by keeping the law, you have been cut off from Christ! You have fallen away from God's grace.

⁵But we who live by the Spirit eagerly wait to receive by faith the righteousness God has promised to us. ⁶For when we place our faith in Christ Jesus, there is no benefit in being circumcised or being uncircumcised. What is important is faith expressing itself in love.

⁷You were running the race so well. Who has held you back from following the truth? ⁸It certainly isn't God, for he is the one who called you to freedom. ⁹This false teaching is like a little yeast that spreads through the whole batch of dough! ¹⁰I am trusting the Lord to keep you from believing

4:22 See Gen 16:15; 21:2-3.   4:25 Greek *And Hagar, which is Mount Sinai in Arabia, is now like Jerusalem;* other manuscripts read *And Mount Sinai in Arabia is now like Jerusalem.* 4:27 Isa 54:1.   4:30 Gen 21:10.

THE POINT

Fruits to live by. If you've heard about the fruit of the Spirit, but didn't really get the point behind the whole thing, be easy—don't stress. I gotcha. Check this out:

But the Holy Spirit produces this kind of fruit in our lives: love, joy, peace, patience, kindness,

goodness, faithfulness, gentleness, and self-control. There is no law against these things! (Galatians 5:22-23)

When people talk about the fruit of the Spirit, they are talking about the kind of behavior or action that is brought about by the Holy Spirit.

Think about your favorite dessert—it's ill, right? The fruit of the Spirit is like everything that goes into a good dessert recipe. It's everything that goes into making us more like God.

false teachings. God will judge that person, whoever he is, who has been confusing you.

¹¹Dear brothers and sisters,* if I were still preaching that you must be circumcised—as some say I do—why am I still being persecuted? If I were no longer preaching salvation through the cross of Christ, no one would be offended. ¹²I just wish that those troublemakers who want to mutilate you by circumcision would mutilate themselves.*

¹³For you have been called to live in freedom, my brothers and sisters. But don't use your freedom to satisfy your sinful nature. Instead, use your freedom to serve one another in love. ¹⁴For the whole law can be summed up in this one command: "Love your neighbor as yourself."* ¹⁵But if you are always biting and devouring one another, watch out! Beware of destroying one another.

Living by the Spirit's Power

¹⁶So I say, let the Holy Spirit guide your lives. Then you won't be doing what your sinful nature craves. ¹⁷The sinful nature wants to do evil, which is just the opposite of what the Spirit wants. And the Spirit gives us desires that are the opposite of what the sinful nature desires. These two forces are constantly fighting each other, so you are not free to carry out your good intentions. ¹⁸But when you are directed by the Spirit, you are not under obligation to the law of Moses.

¹⁹When you follow the desires of your sinful nature, the results are very clear: sexual immorality, impurity, lustful pleasures, ²⁰idolatry, sorcery, hostility, quarreling, jealousy, outbursts of anger, selfish ambition, dissension, division, ²¹envy, drunkenness, wild parties, and other sins like these. Let me tell you again, as I have before, that anyone living that sort of life will not inherit the Kingdom of God.

²²But the Holy Spirit produces this kind of fruit in our lives: love, joy, peace, patience, kindness, goodness, faithfulness,

"When you follow the desires of your sinful nature, the results are very clear: sexual immorality, impurity, lustful pleasures, idolatry, sorcery, hostility, quarreling, jealousy, outbursts of anger, selfish ambition, dissension, division, envy, drunkenness, wild parties, and other sins like these. Let me tell you again, as I have before, that anyone living that sort of life will not inherit the Kingdom of God" (Galatians 5:19-21).

say wyat?

You might feel like you're livin' it up, but bed-hopping, lookin' at porn, worshiping cars and cash, playing with Ouija boards, bein' hot-headed, fussing, cussing, and fighting, only lookin' out for yourself, bein' jealous, gettin' drunk, throwin' and goin' to wild parties (or other things like these) is not what's up. Doin' these things does not make you better in the long run. For those who might've missed it the first time I said it, it's mad crazy to think that you can go to heaven and still wild out like that.

²³gentleness, and self-control. There is no law against these things!

²⁴Those who belong to Christ Jesus have nailed the passions and desires of their sinful nature to his cross and crucified them there. ²⁵Since we are living by the Spirit, let us follow the Spirit's leading in every part of our lives. ²⁶Let us not become conceited, or provoke one another, or be jealous of one another.

CHAPTER 6

We Harvest What We Plant

Dear brothers and sisters, if another believer* is overcome by some sin, you who are godly* should gently and humbly help that person back onto the right path. And be careful not to fall into the same temptation yourself. ²Share each other's burdens, and in this way obey the law of Christ. ³If you think you are too important to help someone, you are only fooling yourself. You are not that important.

5:11 Greek *Brothers;* similarly in 5:13. **5:12** Or *castrate themselves,* or *cut themselves off from you;* Greek reads *cut themselves off.* **5:14** Lev 19:18. **6:1a** Greek *Brothers, if a man.* **6:1b** Greek *spiritual.*

⁴Pay careful attention to your own work, for then you will get the satisfaction of a job well done, and you won't need to compare yourself to anyone else. ⁵For we are each responsible for our own conduct.

⁶Those who are taught the word of God should provide for their teachers, sharing all good things with them.

⁷Don't be misled—you cannot mock the justice of God. You will always harvest what you plant. ⁸Those who live only to satisfy their own sinful nature will harvest decay and death from that sinful nature. But those who live to please the Spirit will harvest everlasting life from the Spirit. ⁹So let's not get tired of doing what is good. At just the right time we will reap a harvest of blessing if we don't give up. ¹⁰Therefore, whenever we have the opportunity, we should do good to everyone—especially to those in the family of faith.

Paul's Final Advice

¹¹NOTICE WHAT LARGE LETTERS I USE AS I WRITE THESE CLOSING WORDS IN MY OWN HANDWRITING.

¹²Those who are trying to force you to be circumcised want to look good to others. They don't want to be persecuted for teaching that the cross of Christ alone can save. ¹³And even those who advocate circumcision don't keep the whole law themselves. They only want you to be circumcised so they can boast about it and claim you as their disciples.

¹⁴As for me, may I never boast about anything except the cross of our Lord Jesus Christ. Because of that cross,* my interest in this world has been crucified, and the world's interest in me has also died. ¹⁵It doesn't matter whether we have been circumcised or not. What counts is whether we have been transformed into a new creation. ¹⁶May God's peace and mercy be upon all who live by this principle; they are the new people of God.*

¹⁷From now on, don't let anyone trouble me with these things. For I bear on my body the scars that show I belong to Jesus.

¹⁸Dear brothers and sisters,* may the grace of our Lord Jesus Christ be with your spirit. Amen.

6:14 Or *Because of him.*   **6:16** Greek *this principle, and upon the Israel of God.*   **6:18** Greek *Brothers.*

THE BOOK OF EPHESIANS was written by the apostle Paul, and it's the first letter he wrote while he was locked up. He thought the Ephesians were decent people—the kind of people you don't mind hangin' with. I can picture Paul chillin' with his crew, gettin' ready for a game of 4-on-4. Get the picture? Paul also talked a lot about Christians bein' a family and the blessings that get tossed at us because of God's love.

EPHESIANS

CHAPTER 1

Greetings from Paul

This letter is from Paul, chosen by the will of God to be an apostle of Christ Jesus.

I am writing to God's holy people in Ephesus,* who are faithful followers of Christ Jesus.

²May God our Father and the Lord Jesus Christ give you grace and peace.

Spiritual Blessings

³All praise to God, the Father of our Lord Jesus Christ, who has blessed us with every spiritual blessing in the heavenly realms because we are united with Christ. ⁴Even before he made the world, God loved us and chose us in Christ to be holy and without fault in his eyes. ⁵God decided in advance to adopt us into his own family by bringing us to himself through Jesus Christ. This is what he wanted to do, and it gave him great pleasure. ⁶So we praise God for the glorious grace he has poured out on us who belong to his dear Son.* ⁷He is so rich in kindness and grace that he purchased our freedom with the blood of his Son and forgave our sins. ⁸He has showered his kindness on us, along with all wisdom and understanding.

⁹God has now revealed to us his mysterious plan regarding Christ, a plan to fulfill his own good pleasure. ¹⁰And this is the plan: At the right time he will bring everything together under the authority of Christ—everything in heaven and on earth. ¹¹Furthermore, because we are united with Christ, we have received an inheritance from God,* for he chose us in advance, and he makes everything work out according to his plan.

¹²God's purpose was that we Jews who were the first to trust in Christ would bring praise and glory to God. ¹³And now you Gentiles have also heard the truth, the Good News that God saves you. And when you believed in Christ, he identified you as his own* by giving you the Holy Spirit, whom he promised long ago. ¹⁴The Spirit is God's guarantee that he will give us the inheritance he promised and that he has purchased us to be his own people. He did this so we would praise and glorify him.

Paul's Prayer for Spiritual Wisdom

¹⁵Ever since I first heard of your strong faith in the Lord Jesus and your love for God's people everywhere,* ¹⁶I have not stopped thanking God for you. I pray for you constantly, ¹⁷asking God, the glorious Father of our Lord Jesus Christ, to give you spiritual wisdom* and insight so that you might grow in your knowledge of God. ¹⁸I pray that your hearts will be flooded with light so that you can understand the confident hope he has given to those he called—his holy people who are his rich and glorious inheritance.*

¹⁹I also pray that you will understand the incredible greatness of God's power for us who believe him. This is the same mighty power ²⁰that raised Christ from the dead and seated him in the place of honor at God's right hand in the heavenly realms. ²¹Now he is far above any ruler or authority or

---

1:1 The most ancient manuscripts do not include *in Ephesus*. **1:6** Greek *to us in the beloved*. **1:11** Or *we have become God's inheritance*. **1:13** Or *he put his seal on you*. **1:15** Some manuscripts read *your faithfulness to the Lord Jesus and to God's people everywhere*. **1:17** Or *to give you the Spirit of wisdom*. **1:18** Or *called, and the rich and glorious inheritance he has given to his holy people*.

power or leader or anything else—not only in this world but also in the world to come. ²²God has put all things under the authority of Christ and has made him head over all things for the benefit of the church. ²³And the church is his body; it is made full and complete by Christ, who fills all things everywhere with himself.

CHAPTER 2
Made Alive with Christ

Once you were dead because of your disobedience and your many sins. ²You used to live in sin, just like the rest of the world, obeying the devil—the commander of the powers in the unseen world.* He is the spirit at work in the hearts of those who refuse to obey God. ³All of us used to live that way, following the passionate desires and inclinations of our sinful nature. By our very nature we were subject to God's anger, just like everyone else.

⁴But God is so rich in mercy, and he loved us so much, ⁵that even though we were dead because of our sins, he gave us life when he raised Christ from the dead. (It is only by God's grace that you have been saved!) ⁶For he raised us from the dead along with Christ and seated us with him in the heavenly realms because we are united with Christ Jesus. ⁷So God can point to us in all future ages as examples of the incredible wealth of his grace and kindness toward us, as shown in all he has done for us who are united with Christ Jesus.

⁸God saved you by his grace when you believed. And you can't take credit for this; it is a gift from God. ⁹Salvation is not a reward for the good things we have done, so none of us can boast about it. ¹⁰For we are God's masterpiece. He has created us anew in Christ Jesus, so we can do the good things he planned for us long ago.

Oneness and Peace in Christ

¹¹Don't forget that you Gentiles used to be outsiders. You were called "uncircumcised heathens" by the Jews, who were proud of their circumcision, even though it affected only their bodies and not their hearts. ¹²In those days you were living apart from Christ. You were excluded from citizenship among the people of Israel, and you did not know the covenant promises God had made to them. You lived in this world without God and without hope. ¹³But now you have been united with Christ Jesus. Once you were far away from God, but now you have been brought near to him through the blood of Christ.

¹⁴For Christ himself has brought peace to us. He united Jews and Gentiles into one people when, in his own body on the cross, he broke down the wall of hostility that separated us. ¹⁵He did this by ending the system of law with its commandments and regulations. He made peace between Jews and Gentiles by creating in himself one new people from the two groups. ¹⁶Together as one body, Christ reconciled both groups to God by means of his death on the cross, and our hostility toward each other was put to death.

¹⁷He brought this Good News of peace to you Gentiles who were far away from him, and peace to the Jews who were near. ¹⁸Now all of us can come to the Father through the same Holy Spirit because of what Christ has done for us.

A Temple for the Lord

¹⁹So now you Gentiles are no longer strangers and foreigners. You are citizens along with all of God's holy people. You are members of God's family. ²⁰Together, we are his house, built on the foundation of the apostles and the prophets. And the cornerstone is Christ Jesus himself. ²¹We are carefully joined together in him, becoming a holy temple for the Lord. ²²Through him you Gentiles are also being made part of this dwelling where God lives by his Spirit.

CHAPTER 3
God's Mysterious Plan Revealed

When I think of all this, I, Paul, a prisoner of Christ Jesus for the benefit of you Gentiles* . . . . ²assuming, by the way, that

"God saved you by his grace when you believed. And you can't take credit for this; it is a gift from God. Salvation is not a reward for the good things we have done, so none of us can boast about it" (Ephesians 2:8-9).

say what?

God saved you by his grace because you believed. But you can't take credit for it—it's a gift from him, so don't go braggin' about it.

2:2 Greek *obeying the commander of the power of the air.* **3:1** Paul resumes this thought in verse 14: "When I think of all this, I fall to my knees and pray to the Father."

you know God gave me the special responsibility of extending his grace to you Gentiles. ³As I briefly wrote earlier, God himself revealed his mysterious plan to me. ⁴As you read what I have written, you will understand my insight into this plan regarding Christ. ⁵God did not reveal it to previous generations, but now by his Spirit he has revealed it to his holy apostles and prophets.

⁶And this is God's plan: Both Gentiles and Jews who believe the Good News share equally in the riches inherited by God's children. Both are part of the same body, and both enjoy the promise of blessings because they belong to Christ Jesus.* ⁷By God's grace and mighty power, I have been given the privilege of serving him by spreading this Good News.

⁸Though I am the least deserving of all God's people, he graciously gave me the privilege of telling the Gentiles about the endless treasures available to them in Christ. ⁹I was chosen to explain to everyone* this mysterious plan that God, the Creator of all things, had kept secret from the beginning.

¹⁰God's purpose in all this was to use the church to display his wisdom in its rich variety to all the unseen rulers and authorities in the heavenly places. ¹¹This was his eternal plan, which he carried out through Christ Jesus our Lord.

¹²Because of Christ and our faith in him,* we can now come boldly and confidently into God's presence. ¹³So please don't lose heart because of my trials here. I am suffering for you, so you should feel honored.

Paul's Prayer for Spiritual Growth

¹⁴When I think of all this, I fall to my knees and pray to the Father,* ¹⁵the Creator of everything in heaven and on earth.* ¹⁶I pray that from his glorious, unlimited resources he will empower you with inner strength through his Spirit. ¹⁷Then Christ will make his home in your hearts as you trust in him. Your roots will grow down into God's love and keep you strong. ¹⁸And may you have the power to understand, as all God's people should, how wide, how long, how high, and how deep his love is. ¹⁹May you experience the love of Christ, though it is too great to understand fully. Then you will be made complete with all the fullness of life and power that comes from God.

²⁰Now all glory to God, who is able, through his mighty power at work within us, to accomplish infinitely more than we might ask or think. ²¹Glory to him in the church and in Christ Jesus through all generations forever and ever! Amen.

CHAPTER 4

Unity in the Body

Therefore I, a prisoner for serving the Lord, beg you to lead a life worthy of your calling, for you have been called by God. ²Always be humble and gentle. Be patient with each other, making allowance for each other's faults because of your love. ³Make every effort to keep yourselves united in the Spirit, binding yourselves together with peace. ⁴For there is one body and one Spirit, just as you have been called to one glorious hope for the future. ⁵There is one Lord, one faith, one baptism, ⁶and one God and Father, who is over all and in all and living through all.

⁷However, he has given each one of us a special gift* through the generosity of Christ. ⁸That is why the Scriptures say,

"When he ascended to the heights,
  he led a crowd of captives
  and gave gifts to his people."*

⁹Notice that it says "he ascended." This clearly means that Christ also descended to our lowly world.* ¹⁰And the same one who descended is the one who ascended higher than

---

3:6 Or because they are united with Christ Jesus. **3:9** Some manuscripts do not include to everyone. **3:12** Or Because of Christ's faithfulness. **3:14** Some manuscripts read the Father of our Lord Jesus Christ. **3:15** Or from whom every family in heaven and on earth takes its name. **4:7** Greek a grace. **4:8** Ps 68:18. **4:9** Or to the lowest parts of the earth.

all the heavens, so that he might fill the entire universe with himself.

¹¹Now these are the gifts Christ gave to the church: the apostles, the prophets, the evangelists, and the pastors and teachers. ¹²Their responsibility is to equip God's people to do his work and build up the church, the body of Christ. ¹³This will continue until we all come to such unity in our faith and knowledge of God's Son that we will be mature in the Lord, measuring up to the full and complete standard of Christ.

¹⁴Then we will no longer be immature like children. We won't be tossed and blown about by every wind of new teaching. We will not be influenced when people try to trick us with lies so clever they sound like the truth. ¹⁵Instead, we will speak the truth in love, growing in every way more and more like Christ, who is the head of his body, the church. ¹⁶He makes the whole body fit together perfectly. As each part does its own special work, it helps the other parts grow, so that the whole body is healthy and growing and full of love.

Living as Children of Light

¹⁷With the Lord's authority I say this: Live no longer as the Gentiles do, for they are hopelessly confused. ¹⁸Their minds are full of darkness; they wander far from the life God gives because they have closed their minds and hardened their hearts against him. ¹⁹They have no sense of shame. They live for lustful pleasure and eagerly practice every kind of impurity.

²⁰But that isn't what you learned about Christ. ²¹Since you have heard about Jesus and have learned the truth that comes from him, ²²throw off your old sinful nature and your former way of life, which is corrupted by lust and deception. ²³Instead, let the Spirit renew your thoughts and attitudes. ²⁴Put on your new nature, created to be like God—truly righteous and holy.

²⁵So stop telling lies. Let us tell our neighbors the truth, for we are all parts of the same body. ²⁶And "don't sin by letting anger control you."* Don't let the sun go down while you are still angry, ²⁷for anger gives a foothold to the devil.

²⁸If you are a thief, quit stealing. Instead, use your hands for good hard work, and then give generously to others in need. ²⁹Don't use foul or abusive language. Let everything you say be good and helpful, so that your words will be an encouragement to those who hear them.

³⁰And do not bring sorrow to God's Holy Spirit by the way you live. Remember, he has identified you as his own,* guaranteeing that you will be saved on the day of redemption.

³¹Get rid of all bitterness, rage, anger, harsh words, and slander, as well as all types of evil behavior. ³²Instead, be kind to each other, tenderhearted, forgiving one another, just as God through Christ has forgiven you.

CHAPTER 5

Living in the Light

Imitate God, therefore, in everything you do, because you are his dear children. ²Live a life filled with love, following the example of Christ. He loved us* and offered himself as a sacrifice for us, a pleasing aroma to God.

³Let there be no sexual immorality, impurity, or greed among you. Such sins have no place among God's people. ⁴Obscene stories, foolish talk, and coarse jokes—these are not for you. Instead, let there be thankfulness to God. ⁵You can be sure that no immoral, impure, or greedy person will inherit the Kingdom of Christ and of God. For a greedy person is an idolater, worshiping the things of this world.

⁶Don't be fooled by those who try to excuse these sins, for the anger of God will fall on all who disobey him. ⁷Don't participate in the things these people do. ⁸For once you were full of darkness, but now you have light from the

---

4:26 Ps 4:4.   **4:30** Or *has put his seal on you.*   **5:2** Some manuscripts read *loved you.*

Lord. So live as people of light! [9]For this light within you produces only what is good and right and true.

[10]Carefully determine what pleases the Lord. [11]Take no part in the worthless deeds of evil and darkness; instead, expose them. [12]It is shameful even to talk about the things that ungodly people do in secret. [13]But their evil intentions will be exposed when the light shines on them, [14]for the light makes everything visible. This is why it is said,

"Awake, O sleeper,
    rise up from the dead,
    and Christ will give you light."

Living by the Spirit's Power

[15]So be careful how you live. Don't live like fools, but like those who are wise. [16]Make the most of every opportunity in these evil days. [17]Don't act thoughtlessly, but understand what the Lord wants you to do. [18]Don't be drunk with wine, because that will ruin your life. Instead, be filled with the Holy Spirit, [19]singing psalms and hymns and spiritual songs among yourselves, and making music to the Lord in your hearts. [20]And give thanks for everything to God the Father in the name of our Lord Jesus Christ.

5:26 Greek *washed by water with the word.*   **5:31** Gen 2:24.

Spirit-Guided Relationships: Wives and Husbands

[21]And further, submit to one another out of reverence for Christ.

[22]For wives, this means submit to your husbands as to the Lord. [23]For a husband is the head of his wife as Christ is the head of the church. He is the Savior of his body, the church. [24]As the church submits to Christ, so you wives should submit to your husbands in everything.

[25]For husbands, this means love your wives, just as Christ loved the church. He gave up his life for her [26]to make her holy and clean, washed by the cleansing of God's word.* [27]He did this to present her to himself as a glorious church without a spot or wrinkle or any other blemish. Instead, she will be holy and without fault. [28]In the same way, husbands ought to love their wives as they love their own bodies. For a man who loves his wife actually shows love for himself. [29]No one hates his own body but feeds and cares for it, just as Christ cares for the church. [30]And we are members of his body.

[31]As the Scriptures say, "A man leaves his father and mother and is joined to his wife, and the two are united into one."* [32]This is a great mystery, but it is an illustration of the

---

THE POINT

Suiting up. So maybe you've heard about "putting on the armor of God," but didn't really get the meaning behind it. It's just the same as getting geared up for a basketball game or putting on your freshest clothes for an event or outing. Here's the Bible verse below; check it out and see for yourself:

Therefore, put on every piece of God's armor so you will be able to resist the enemy in the time of evil. Then after the battle you will still be standing firm. Stand your ground, putting on the belt of truth and the body armor of God's righteousness. For shoes, put on the peace that comes from the Good News so that you will be fully prepared. In addition to all of these, hold up the shield of faith to stop the fiery arrows of the devil. Put on salvation as your helmet, and take the sword of the Spirit, which is the word of God. (Ephesians 6:13-17)

The armor of God is like a superhero's suit. Every single part of the 'fit works to our benefit. If you were in a war, body armor would protect you from even the illest artillery. Sometimes it's like that in life. The devil throws some wild stuff at us, and we've got to get him off our backs. You can devastate the devil with a knockout by putting on God's armor: truth, peace, faith, and salvation. Even more, you become better equipped to fight the enemy when your Word-game is on point—the Bible you're readin' right now is also a weapon against the enemy.

way Christ and the church are one. ³³So again I say, each man must love his wife as he loves himself, and the wife must respect her husband.

CHAPTER 6

Children and Parents

Children, obey your parents because you belong to the Lord,* for this is the right thing to do. ²"Honor your father and mother." This is the first commandment with a promise: ³If you honor your father and mother, "things will go well for you, and you will have a long life on the earth."*

⁴Fathers, do not provoke your children to anger by the way you treat them. Rather, bring them up with the discipline and instruction that comes from the Lord.

Slaves and Masters

⁵Slaves, obey your earthly masters with deep respect and fear. Serve them sincerely as you would serve Christ. ⁶Try to please them all the time, not just when they are watching you. As slaves of Christ, do the will of God with all your heart. ⁷Work with enthusiasm, as though you were working for the Lord rather than for people. ⁸Remember that the Lord will reward each one of us for the good we do, whether we are slaves or free.

⁹Masters, treat your slaves in the same way. Don't threaten them; remember, you both have the same Master in heaven, and he has no favorites.

The Whole Armor of God

¹⁰A final word: Be strong in the Lord and in his mighty power. ¹¹Put on all of God's armor so that you will be able to stand firm against all strategies of the devil. ¹²For we* are not fighting against flesh-and-blood enemies, but against evil rulers and authorities of the unseen world, against mighty powers in this dark world, and against evil spirits in the heavenly places.

¹³Therefore, put on every piece of God's armor so you will be able to resist the enemy in the time of evil. Then after the battle you will still be standing firm. ¹⁴Stand your ground, putting on the belt of truth and the body armor of God's righteousness. ¹⁵For shoes, put on the peace that comes from the Good News so that you will be fully prepared.* ¹⁶In addition to all of these, hold up the shield of faith to stop the fiery arrows of the devil.* ¹⁷Put on salvation as your helmet, and take the sword of the Spirit, which is the word of God.

¹⁸Pray in the Spirit at all times and on every occasion. Stay alert and be persistent in your prayers for all believers everywhere.*

¹⁹And pray for me, too. Ask God to give me the right words so I can boldly explain God's mysterious plan that the Good News is for Jews and Gentiles alike.* ²⁰I am in chains now, still preaching this message as God's ambassador. So pray that I will keep on speaking boldly for him, as I should.

Final Greetings

²¹To bring you up to date, Tychicus will give you a full report about what I am doing and how I am getting along. He is a beloved brother and faithful helper in the Lord's work. ²²I have sent him to you for this very purpose—to let you know how we are doing and to encourage you.

²³Peace be with you, dear brothers and sisters,* and may God the Father and the Lord Jesus Christ give you love with faithfulness. ²⁴May God's grace be eternally upon all who love our Lord Jesus Christ.

6:1 Or *Children, obey your parents who belong to the Lord;* some manuscripts read simply *Children, obey your parents.*   6:2-3 Exod 20:12; Deut 5:16.   6:12 Some manuscripts read *you.*   6:15 Or *For shoes, put on the readiness to preach the Good News of peace with God.*   6:16 Greek *the evil one.*   6:18 Greek *all of God's holy people.*   6:19 Greek *explain the mystery of the Good News;* some manuscripts read simply *explain the mystery.*   6:23 Greek *brothers.*

"Children, obey your parents because you belong to the Lord, for this is the right thing to do. 'Honor your father and mother.' This is the first commandment with a promise: If you honor your father and mother, 'things will go well for you, and you will have a long life on the earth' " (Ephesians 6:1-3).

"Honor your father and mother." It's the first commandment with a promise attached to it. If you follow it, good stuff will come.

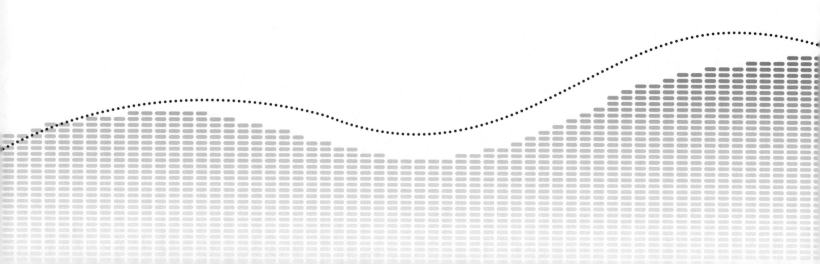

PAUL GOT MAD LOVE from the Philippians, and he wrote them this letter, not just as a shout-out, but also as a way to give them props. They had looked out for and refused to let people come at him in a foul way—things you would only do for people who were like family to you. Although the Philippians looked out for Paul, they still had a problem with looking out for each other. It's kind of like what happens between friends, or even in corporate America—sometimes you're left wondering who really has your back. He wanted them to unify—that's why he wrote them this letter while he was locked up.

PHILIPPIANS

CHAPTER 1

Greetings from Paul

This letter is from Paul and Timothy, slaves of Christ Jesus.

I am writing to all of God's holy people in Philippi who belong to Christ Jesus, including the elders* and deacons.

²May God our Father and the Lord Jesus Christ give you grace and peace.

Paul's Thanksgiving and Prayer

³Every time I think of you, I give thanks to my God. ⁴Whenever I pray, I make my requests for all of you with joy, ⁵for you have been my partners in spreading the Good News about Christ from the time you first heard it until now. ⁶And I am certain that God, who began the good work within you, will continue his work until it is finally finished on the day when Christ Jesus returns.

⁷So it is right that I should feel as I do about all of you, for you have a special place in my heart. You share with me the special favor of God, both in my imprisonment and in defending and confirming the truth of the Good News. ⁸God knows how much I love you and long for you with the tender compassion of Christ Jesus.

⁹I pray that your love will overflow more and more, and that you will keep on growing in knowledge and understanding. ¹⁰For I want you to understand what really matters, so that you may live pure and blameless lives until the day of Christ's return. ¹¹May you always be filled with the fruit of your salvation—the righteous character produced in your life by Jesus Christ*—for this will bring much glory and praise to God.

Paul's Joy That Christ Is Preached

¹²And I want you to know, my dear brothers and sisters,* that everything that has happened to me here has helped to spread the Good News. ¹³For everyone here, including the whole palace guard,* knows that I am in chains because of Christ. ¹⁴And because of my imprisonment, most of the believers* here have gained confidence and boldly speak God's message* without fear.

¹⁵It's true that some are preaching out of jealousy and rivalry. But others preach about Christ with pure motives. ¹⁶They preach because they love me, for they know I have been appointed to defend the Good News. ¹⁷Those others do not have pure motives as they preach about Christ. They preach with selfish ambition, not sincerely, intending to make my chains more painful to me. ¹⁸But that doesn't matter. Whether their motives are false or genuine, the message about Christ is being preached either way, so I rejoice. And I will continue to rejoice. ¹⁹For I know that as you pray for me and the Spirit of Jesus Christ helps me, this will lead to my deliverance.

Paul's Life for Christ

²⁰For I fully expect and hope that I will never be ashamed, but that I will continue to be bold for Christ, as I have been in the past. And I trust that my life will bring honor to Christ, whether I live or die. ²¹For to me, living means living for Christ, and dying is even better. ²²But if I live, I can do more fruitful work for Christ. So I really don't know which is better. ²³I'm torn between two desires: I long to go and be

1:1 Or overseers; or bishops.　1:11 Greek with the fruit of righteousness through Jesus Christ.　1:12 Greek brothers.　1:13 Greek including all the Praetorium.　1:14a Greek brothers in the Lord.　1:14b Some manuscripts read speak the message.

keeping your swagger strong

BIBLICAL PRINCIPLES FOR SUCCESS AND LEADERSHIP

Good leaders don't just look out for themselves and leave everybody else out there bogus! They assess a situation and figure out how it can work out in everybody's best interest. I know it seems kind of wack to ask what Jesus might do in any given situation, but it really is how things should go down. We should try to be cool with everyone as much as we can—not just so they like us, but so they can see the love of God in us.

> *Don't be selfish; don't try to impress others. Be humble, thinking of others as better than yourselves. Don't look out only for your own interests, but take an interest in others, too. You must have the same attitude that Christ Jesus had.*
> (Philippians 2:3-5)

It's hard to be respected as a leader if people don't know that you genuinely care about them. Frontin' and tryin' to impress others is not the way to go. Chill and think for a minute. Then ask yourself, "Would Jesus vouch for this?" If the answer is no, rethink the action.

Christ. Then, whether I come and see you again or only hear about you, I will know that you are standing together with one spirit and one purpose, fighting together for the faith, which is the Good News. ²⁸Don't be intimidated in any way by your enemies. This will be a sign to them that they are going to be destroyed, but that you are going to be saved, even by God himself. ²⁹For you have been given not only the privilege of trusting in Christ but also the privilege of suffering for him. ³⁰We are in this struggle together. You have seen my struggle in the past, and you know that I am still in the midst of it.

CHAPTER 2

Have the Attitude of Christ

Is there any encouragement from belonging to Christ? Any comfort from his love? Any fellowship together in the Spirit? Are your hearts tender and compassionate? ²Then make me truly happy by agreeing wholeheartedly with each other, loving one another, and working together with one mind and purpose.

³Don't be selfish; don't try to impress others. Be humble, thinking of others as better than yourselves. ⁴Don't look out only for your own interests, but take an interest in others, too.

⁵You must have the same attitude that Christ Jesus had.

⁶ Though he was God,*
    he did not think of equality with God
    as something to cling to.
⁷ Instead, he gave up his divine privileges*;
    he took the humble position of a slave*
    and was born as a human being.
  When he appeared in human form,*
⁸   he humbled himself in obedience to God
    and died a criminal's death on a cross.

⁹ Therefore, God elevated him to the place of highest
    honor
    and gave him the name above all other names,

with Christ, which would be far better for me. ²⁴But for your sakes, it is better that I continue to live.

²⁵Knowing this, I am convinced that I will remain alive so I can continue to help all of you grow and experience the joy of your faith. ²⁶And when I come to you again, you will have even more reason to take pride in Christ Jesus because of what he is doing through me.

Live as Citizens of Heaven

²⁷Above all, you must live as citizens of heaven, conducting yourselves in a manner worthy of the Good News about

2:6 Or *Being in the form of God.*   2:7a Greek *he emptied himself.*   2:7b Or *the form of a slave.*   2:7c Some English translations put this phrase in verse 8.

¹⁰ that at the name of Jesus every knee should bow,
   in heaven and on earth and under the earth,
¹¹ and every tongue confess that Jesus Christ is Lord,
   to the glory of God the Father.

Shine Brightly for Christ

¹²Dear friends, you always followed my instructions when I was with you. And now that I am away, it is even more important. Work hard to show the results of your salvation, obeying God with deep reverence and fear. ¹³For God is working in you, giving you the desire and the power to do what pleases him.

¹⁴Do everything without complaining and arguing, ¹⁵so that no one can criticize you. Live clean, innocent lives as children of God, shining like bright lights in a world full of crooked and perverse people. ¹⁶Hold firmly to the word of life; then, on the day of Christ's return, I will be proud that I did not run the race in vain and that my work was not useless. ¹⁷But I will rejoice even if I lose my life, pouring it out like a liquid offering to God,* just like your faithful service is an offering to God. And I want all of you to share that joy. ¹⁸Yes, you should rejoice, and I will share your joy.

Paul Commends Timothy

¹⁹If the Lord Jesus is willing, I hope to send Timothy to you soon for a visit. Then he can cheer me up by telling me how you are getting along. ²⁰I have no one else like Timothy, who genuinely cares about your welfare. ²¹All the others care only for themselves and not for what matters to Jesus Christ. ²²But you know how Timothy has proved himself. Like a son with his father, he has served with me in preaching the Good News. ²³I hope to send him to you just as soon as I find out what is going to happen to me here. ²⁴And I have confidence from the Lord that I myself will come to see you soon.

POWERCHOICES

AS MANAGERS, LEADERS, OR JUST FRIENDS, IT'S SOMETIMES HARD TO SEE THE FOREST FOR THE TREES. WE GET SO BOGGED DOWN WITH THE DETAILS OF LIFE OR BUSINESS OR TRYING TO GET THINGS DONE THAT WE FORGET TO SAY THANK YOU—THANK YOU TO GOD (FIRST AND FOREMOST) AND THANK YOU TO THE PEOPLE WHO HAVE HELPED US TO GET THE BALL ROLLING. DEALING WITH PEOPLE IS HARD WORK, AND EVERY NOW AND THEN, THEY JUST WANT TO HEAR, "IT'S ALL GOOD; I REALLY JUST WANTED TO SAY THANK YOU." ¶ SAYING THANKS IS SOMETHING PAUL DOES PRETTY WELL IN HIS LETTER TO THE PHILIPPIANS. IT'S LIKE HE'S GIVING PEOPLE A LITTLE DAP WITHOUT EVEN BEING IN THE ROOM. IT'S EASIER TO MAKE THINGS HAPPEN WHEN YOU REMEMBER THOSE TWO SIMPLE WORDS: THANK YOU.
¶ *ARE THERE PEOPLE CLOSE TO YOU WHO DESERVE A WORD OF THANKS? GIVE IT TO 'EM!*

Paul Commends Epaphroditus

²⁵Meanwhile, I thought I should send Epaphroditus back to you. He is a true brother, co-worker, and fellow soldier. And he was your messenger to help me in my need. ²⁶I am sending him because he has been longing to see you, and he was very distressed that you heard he was ill. ²⁷And he certainly was ill; in fact, he almost died. But God had mercy on him—and also on me, so that I would not have one sorrow after another.

²⁸So I am all the more anxious to send him back to you, for I know you will be glad to see him, and then I will not be so worried about you. ²⁹Welcome him with Christian love* and with great joy, and give him the honor that people like him deserve. ³⁰For he risked his life for the work of Christ, and he was at the point of death while doing for me what you couldn't do from far away.

2:17 Greek *I will rejoice even if I am to be poured out as a liquid offering.* • 2:29 Greek *in the Lord.*

CHAPTER 3

The Priceless Value of Knowing Christ

Whatever happens, my dear brothers and sisters,* rejoice in the Lord. I never get tired of telling you these things, and I do it to safeguard your faith.

²Watch out for those dogs, those people who do evil, those mutilators who say you must be circumcised to be saved. ³For we who worship by the Spirit of God* are the ones who are truly circumcised. We rely on what Christ Jesus has done for us. We put no confidence in human effort, ⁴though I could have confidence in my own effort if anyone could. Indeed, if others have reason for confidence in their own efforts, I have even more!

⁵I was circumcised when I was eight days old. I am a pure-blooded citizen of Israel and a member of the tribe of Benjamin—a real Hebrew if there ever was one! I was a member of the Pharisees, who demand the strictest obedience to the Jewish law. ⁶I was so zealous that I harshly persecuted the church. And as for righteousness, I obeyed the law without fault.

⁷I once thought these things were valuable, but now I consider them worthless because of what Christ has done. ⁸Yes, everything else is worthless when compared with the infinite value of knowing Christ Jesus my Lord. For his sake I have discarded everything else, counting it all as garbage, so that I could gain Christ ⁹and become one with him. I no longer count on my own righteousness through obeying the law; rather, I become righteous through faith in Christ.* For God's way of making us right with himself depends on faith. ¹⁰I want to know Christ and experience the mighty power that raised him from the dead. I want to suffer with him, sharing in his death, ¹¹so that one way or another I will experience the resurrection from the dead!

Pressing toward the Goal

¹²I don't mean to say that I have already achieved these things or that I have already reached perfection. But I press on to possess that perfection for which Christ Jesus first possessed me. ¹³No, dear brothers and sisters, I have not achieved it,* but I focus on this one thing: Forgetting the past and looking forward to what lies ahead, ¹⁴I press on to reach the end of the race and receive the heavenly prize for which God, through Christ Jesus, is calling us.

¹⁵Let all who are spiritually mature agree on these things. If you disagree on some point, I believe God will make it plain to you. ¹⁶But we must hold on to the progress we have already made.

¹⁷Dear brothers and sisters, pattern your lives after mine, and learn from those who follow our example. ¹⁸For I have told you often before, and I say it again with tears in my eyes, that there are many whose conduct shows they are really enemies of the cross of Christ. ¹⁹They are headed for destruction. Their god is their appetite, they brag about shameful things, and they think only about this life here on earth. ²⁰But we are citizens of heaven, where the Lord Jesus Christ lives. And we are eagerly waiting for him to return as our Savior. ²¹He will take our weak mortal bodies and change them into glorious bodies like his own, using the same power with which he will bring everything under his control.

CHAPTER 4

Therefore, my dear brothers and sisters,* stay true to the Lord. I love you and long to see you, dear friends, for you are my joy and the crown I receive for my work.

Words of Encouragement

²Now I appeal to Euodia and Syntyche. Please, because you belong to the Lord, settle your disagreement. ³And I ask you, my true partner,* to help these two women, for they worked hard with me in telling others the Good News. They worked along with Clement and the rest of my co-workers, whose names are written in the Book of Life.

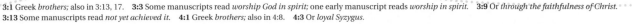

3:1 Greek *brothers;* also in 3:13, 17. **3:3** Some manuscripts read *worship God in spirit;* one early manuscript reads *worship in spirit.* **3:9** Or *through the faithfulness of Christ.* **3:13** Some manuscripts read *not yet achieved it.* **4:1** Greek *brothers;* also in 4:8. **4:3** Or *loyal Syzygus.*

[4]Always be full of joy in the Lord. I say it again—rejoice! [5]Let everyone see that you are considerate in all you do. Remember, the Lord is coming soon.

[6]Don't worry about anything; instead, pray about everything. Tell God what you need, and thank him for all he has done. [7]Then you will experience God's peace, which exceeds anything we can understand. His peace will guard your hearts and minds as you live in Christ Jesus.

[8]And now, dear brothers and sisters, one final thing. Fix your thoughts on what is true, and honorable, and right, and pure, and lovely, and admirable. Think about things that are excellent and worthy of praise. [9]Keep putting into practice all you learned and received from me—everything you heard from me and saw me doing. Then the God of peace will be with you.

Paul's Thanks for Their Gifts

[10]How I praise the Lord that you are concerned about me again. I know you have always been concerned for me, but you didn't have the chance to help me. [11]Not that I was ever in need, for I have learned how to be content with whatever I have. [12]I know how to live on almost nothing or with everything. I have learned the secret of living in every situation, whether it is with a full stomach or empty, with plenty

4:13 Greek *through the one.*

or little. [13]For I can do everything through Christ,* who gives me strength. [14]Even so, you have done well to share with me in my present difficulty.

[15]As you know, you Philippians were the only ones who gave me financial help when I first brought you the Good News and then traveled on from Macedonia. No other church did this. [16]Even when I was in Thessalonica you sent help more than once. [17]I don't say this because I want a gift from you. Rather, I want you to receive a reward for your kindness.

[18]At the moment I have all I need—and more! I am generously supplied with the gifts you sent me with Epaphroditus. They are a sweet-smelling sacrifice that is acceptable and pleasing to God. [19]And this same God who takes care of me will supply all your needs from his glorious riches, which have been given to us in Christ Jesus.

[20]Now all glory to God our Father forever and ever! Amen.

Paul's Final Greetings

[21]Give my greetings to each of God's holy people—all who belong to Christ Jesus. The brothers who are with me send you their greetings. [22]And all the rest of God's people send you greetings, too, especially those in Caesar's household.

[23]May the grace of the Lord Jesus Christ be with your spirit.

SOMETIMES PEOPLE KNOW the truth and still try to find new things to fill the void. The Colossians were kind of like that. They had heard about Jesus, but other people were trying to get them to worship any- and everybody (or thing). It's kind of like when the latest pair of sneakers comes out and you rush to the store to cop 'em—you don't wear your old ones anymore because you have a fresh pair. Paul wanted them to know that Jesus was all that—period.

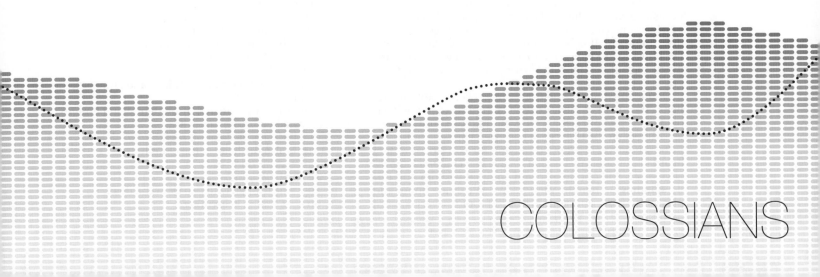

COLOSSIANS

CHAPTER 1

Greetings from Paul

This letter is from Paul, chosen by the will of God to be an apostle of Christ Jesus, and from our brother Timothy.

²We are writing to God's holy people in the city of Colosse, who are faithful brothers and sisters* in Christ.

May God our Father give you grace and peace.

Paul's Thanksgiving and Prayer

³We always pray for you, and we give thanks to God, the Father of our Lord Jesus Christ. ⁴For we have heard of your faith in Christ Jesus and your love for all of God's people, ⁵which come from your confident hope of what God has reserved for you in heaven. You have had this expectation ever since you first heard the truth of the Good News.

⁶This same Good News that came to you is going out all over the world. It is bearing fruit everywhere by changing lives, just as it changed your lives from the day you first heard and understood the truth about God's wonderful grace.

⁷You learned about the Good News from Epaphras, our beloved co-worker. He is Christ's faithful servant, and he is helping us on your behalf.* ⁸He has told us about the love for others that the Holy Spirit has given you.

⁹So we have not stopped praying for you since we first heard about you. We ask God to give you complete knowledge of his will and to give you spiritual wisdom and understanding. ¹⁰Then the way you live will always honor and please the Lord, and your lives will produce every kind of good fruit. All the while, you will grow as you learn to know God better and better.

¹¹We also pray that you will be strengthened with all his glorious power so you will have all the endurance and patience you need. May you be filled with joy,* ¹²always thanking the Father. He has enabled you to share in the inheritance that belongs to his people, who live in the light. ¹³For he has rescued us from the kingdom of darkness and transferred us into the Kingdom of his dear Son, ¹⁴who purchased our freedom* and forgave our sins.

Christ Is Supreme

¹⁵ Christ is the visible image of the invisible God.
He existed before anything was created and is
supreme over all creation,*
¹⁶ for through him God created everything
in the heavenly realms and on earth.
He made the things we can see
and the things we can't see—
such as thrones, kingdoms, rulers, and authorities in the
unseen world.
Everything was created through him and for him.
¹⁷ He existed before anything else,
and he holds all creation together.
¹⁸ Christ is also the head of the church,
which is his body.
He is the beginning,
supreme over all who rise from the dead.*
So he is first in everything.

1:2 Greek faithful brothers.   1:7 Or he is ministering on your behalf; some manuscripts read he is ministering on our behalf.   1:11 Or all the patience and endurance you need with joy.   1:14 Some manuscripts add with his blood.   1:15 Or He is the firstborn of all creation.   1:18 Or the firstborn from the dead.

¹⁹ For God in all his fullness
  was pleased to live in Christ,
²⁰ and through him God reconciled
  everything to himself.
He made peace with everything in heaven and on earth
  by means of Christ's blood on the cross.

²¹This includes you who were once far away from God. You were his enemies, separated from him by your evil thoughts and actions. ²²Yet now he has reconciled you to himself through the death of Christ in his physical body. As a result, he has brought you into his own presence, and you are holy and blameless as you stand before him without a single fault.

²³But you must continue to believe this truth and stand firmly in it. Don't drift away from the assurance you received when you heard the Good News. The Good News has been preached all over the world, and I, Paul, have been appointed as God's servant to proclaim it.

Paul's Work for the Church

²⁴I am glad when I suffer for you in my body, for I am participating in the sufferings of Christ that continue for his body, the church. ²⁵God has given me the responsibility of serving his church by proclaiming his entire message to you. ²⁶This message was kept secret for centuries and generations past, but now it has been revealed to God's people. ²⁷For God wanted them to know that the riches and glory of Christ are for you Gentiles, too. And this is the secret: Christ lives in you. This gives you assurance of sharing his glory.

²⁸So we tell others about Christ, warning everyone and teaching everyone with all the wisdom God has given us. We want to present them to God, perfect* in their relationship to Christ. ²⁹That's why I work and struggle so hard, depending on Christ's mighty power that works within me.

CHAPTER 2

I want you to know how much I have agonized for you and for the church at Laodicea, and for many other believers who have never met me personally. ²I want them to be encouraged and knit together by strong ties of love. I want them to have complete confidence that they understand God's mysterious plan, which is Christ himself. ³In him lie hidden all the treasures of wisdom and knowledge.

⁴I am telling you this so no one will deceive you with well-crafted arguments. ⁵For though I am far away from you, my heart is with you. And I rejoice that you are living as you should and that your faith in Christ is strong.

Freedom from Rules and New Life in Christ

⁶And now, just as you accepted Christ Jesus as your Lord, you must continue to follow him. ⁷Let your roots grow down into him, and let your lives be built on him. Then your faith will grow strong in the truth you were taught, and you will overflow with thankfulness.

⁸Don't let anyone capture you with empty philosophies and high-sounding nonsense that come from human thinking and from the spiritual powers* of this world, rather than from Christ. ⁹For in Christ lives all the fullness of God in a human body.* ¹⁰So you also are complete through your union with Christ, who is the head over every ruler and authority.

¹¹When you came to Christ, you were "circumcised," but not by a physical procedure. Christ performed a spiritual circumcision—the cutting away of your sinful nature.* ¹²For you were buried with Christ when you were baptized. And with him you were raised to new life because you trusted the mighty power of God, who raised Christ from the dead.

¹³You were dead because of your sins and because your sinful nature was not yet cut away. Then God made you alive with Christ, for he forgave all our sins. ¹⁴He canceled the record of the charges against us and took it away by nailing it

"Christ is the visible image of the invisible God. He existed before anything was created and is supreme over all creation, for through him God created everything in the heavenly realms and on earth. . . . He existed before anything else, and he holds all creation together" (Colossians 1:15-17).

say what?

Christ is God in the flesh. He existed before God made anything, so he's in charge of all creation—including you. Nothing existed before Christ.

1:28 Or *mature.* **2:8** Or *the spiritual principles;* also in 2:20. **2:9** Or *in him dwells all the completeness of the Godhead bodily.* **2:11** Greek *the cutting away of the body of the flesh.*

to the cross. ¹⁵In this way, he disarmed* the spiritual rulers and authorities. He shamed them publicly by his victory over them on the cross.

¹⁶So don't let anyone condemn you for what you eat or drink, or for not celebrating certain holy days or new moon ceremonies or Sabbaths. ¹⁷For these rules are only shadows of the reality yet to come. And Christ himself is that reality. ¹⁸Don't let anyone condemn you by insisting on pious self-denial or the worship of angels,* saying they have had visions about these things. Their sinful minds have made them proud, ¹⁹and they are not connected to Christ, the head of the body. For he holds the whole body together with its joints and ligaments, and it grows as God nourishes it.

²⁰You have died with Christ, and he has set you free from the spiritual powers of this world. So why do you keep on following the rules of the world, such as, ²¹"Don't handle! Don't taste! Don't touch!"? ²²Such rules are mere human teachings about things that deteriorate as we use them. ²³These rules may seem wise because they require strong devotion, pious self-denial, and severe bodily discipline. But they provide no help in conquering a person's evil desires.

CHAPTER 3

Living the New Life

Since you have been raised to new life with Christ, set your sights on the realities of heaven, where Christ sits in the place of honor at God's right hand. ²Think about the things of heaven, not the things of earth. ³For you died to this life, and your real life is hidden with Christ in God. ⁴And when Christ, who is your* life, is revealed to the whole world, you will share in all his glory.

⁵So put to death the sinful, earthly things lurking within you. Have nothing to do with sexual immorality, impurity, lust, and evil desires. Don't be greedy, for a greedy person is an idolater, worshiping the things of this world. ⁶Because of these sins, the anger of God is coming.* ⁷You used to do these things when your life was still part of this world. ⁸But now is the time to get rid of anger, rage, malicious behavior, slander, and dirty language. ⁹Don't lie to each other, for you have stripped off your old sinful nature and all its wicked deeds. ¹⁰Put on your new nature, and be renewed as you learn to know your Creator and become like him. ¹¹In this new life, it doesn't matter if you are a Jew or a Gentile,* circumcised or uncircumcised, barbaric, uncivilized,* slave, or free. Christ is all that matters, and he lives in all of us.

¹²Since God chose you to be the holy people he loves, you must clothe yourselves with tenderhearted mercy, kindness, humility, gentleness, and patience. ¹³Make allowance for each other's faults, and forgive anyone who offends you. Remember, the Lord forgave you, so you must forgive others. ¹⁴Above all, clothe yourselves with love, which binds us all together in perfect harmony. ¹⁵And let the peace that comes from Christ rule in your hearts. For as members of one body you are called to live in peace. And always be thankful.

¹⁶Let the message about Christ, in all its richness, fill your lives. Teach and counsel each other with all the wisdom he gives. Sing psalms and hymns and spiritual songs to God with thankful hearts. ¹⁷And whatever you do or say, do it as a representative of the Lord Jesus, giving thanks through him to God the Father.

Instructions for Christian Households

¹⁸Wives, submit to your husbands, as is fitting for those who belong to the Lord.

¹⁹Husbands, love your wives and never treat them harshly.

²⁰Children, always obey your parents, for this pleases the Lord. ²¹Fathers, do not aggravate your children, or they will become discouraged.

²²Slaves, obey your earthly masters in everything you do. Try to please them all the time, not just when they are watching you. Serve them sincerely because of your rever-

---

2:15 Or *he stripped off.* **2:18** Or *or worshiping with angels.* **3:4** Some manuscripts read *our.* **3:6** Some manuscripts read *is coming on all who disobey him.* **3:11a** Greek *a Greek.* **3:11b** Greek *Barbarian, Scythian.*

ent fear of the Lord. ²³Work willingly at whatever you do, as though you were working for the Lord rather than for people. ²⁴Remember that the Lord will give you an inheritance as your reward, and that the Master you are serving is Christ.* ²⁵But if you do what is wrong, you will be paid back for the wrong you have done. For God has no favorites.

CHAPTER 4

Masters, be just and fair to your slaves. Remember that you also have a Master—in heaven.

An Encouragement for Prayer

²Devote yourselves to prayer with an alert mind and a thankful heart. ³Pray for us, too, that God will give us many opportunities to speak about his mysterious plan concerning Christ. That is why I am here in chains. ⁴Pray that I will proclaim this message as clearly as I should.

⁵Live wisely among those who are not believers, and make the most of every opportunity. ⁶Let your conversation be gracious and attractive* so that you will have the right response for everyone.

Paul's Final Instructions and Greetings

⁷Tychicus will give you a full report about how I am getting along. He is a beloved brother and faithful helper who serves with me in the Lord's work. ⁸I have sent him to you for this very purpose—to let you know how we are doing and to encourage you. ⁹I am also sending Onesimus, a faithful and

beloved brother, one of your own people. He and Tychicus will tell you everything that's happening here.

¹⁰Aristarchus, who is in prison with me, sends you his greetings, and so does Mark, Barnabas's cousin. As you were instructed before, make Mark welcome if he comes your way. ¹¹Jesus (the one we call Justus) also sends his greetings. These are the only Jewish believers among my co-workers; they are working with me here for the Kingdom of God. And what a comfort they have been!

¹²Epaphras, a member of your own fellowship and a servant of Christ Jesus, sends you his greetings. He always prays earnestly for you, asking God to make you strong and perfect, fully confident that you are following the whole will of God. ¹³I can assure you that he prays hard for you and also for the believers in Laodicea and Hierapolis.

¹⁴Luke, the beloved doctor, sends his greetings, and so does Demas. ¹⁵Please give my greetings to our brothers and sisters* at Laodicea, and to Nympha and the church that meets in her house.

¹⁶After you have read this letter, pass it on to the church at Laodicea so they can read it, too. And you should read the letter I wrote to them.

¹⁷And say to Archippus, "Be sure to carry out the ministry the Lord gave you."

¹⁸HERE IS MY GREETING IN MY OWN HANDWRITING—PAUL.
Remember my chains.
May God's grace be with you.

3:24 Or *and serve Christ as your Master.*   **4:6** Greek *and seasoned with salt.*   **4:15** Greek *brothers.*

THE POINT

Livin' twice. Maybe you've heard about being dead because of sin. Of course that's not literal. Check the point:

You were dead because of your sins and because your sinful nature was not yet cut away. Then God made you alive with Christ, for he forgave all our sins. He canceled the record of the charges against us and took it away by nailing it to the cross. (Colossians 2:13-14)

There's a reason why some people say they've been "born again." That's exactly what salvation is like. They're not literally being reborn, but Christ gives them a second (or maybe 102nd) chance. Sin can make us feel like we're dead, but when we are down with Christ, the sinful part of us is cut away. Better yet, Christ takes an eraser and wipes out all of the bogus stuff we've done. He did this for us the day he died on the cross.

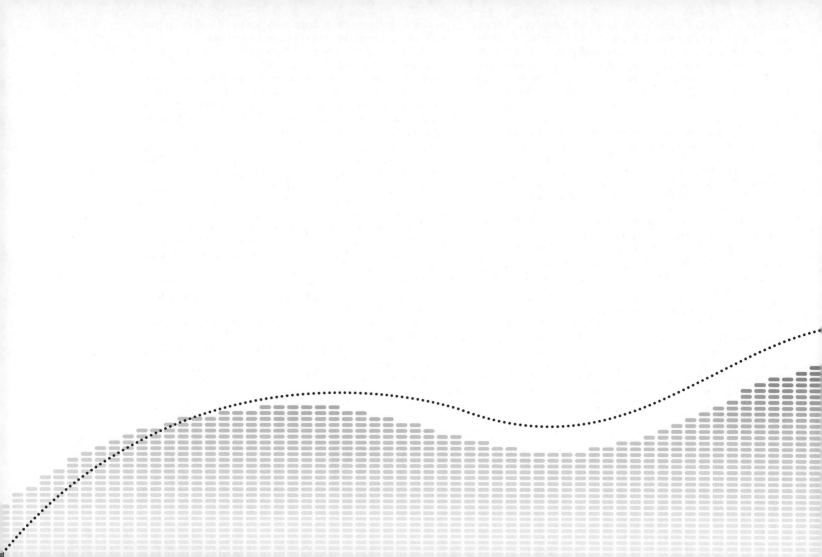

THE BOOK OF 1 THESSALONIANS is similar to the movies where there's a child left home alone with his nose pressed to the window: It's about the Second Coming of Christ. Paul is trying to keep everybody on their toes until Jesus returns. He's reminding them to live in ways that please God and encouraging them to hold things down in his absence.

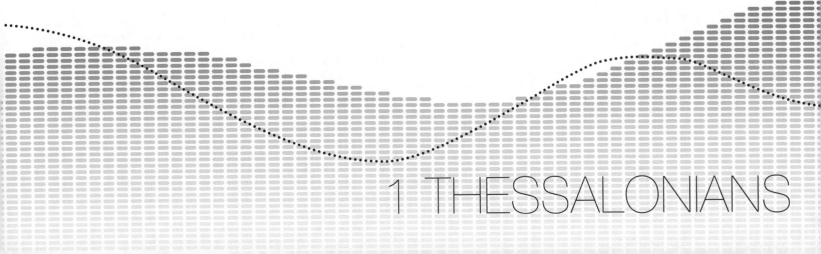

1 THESSALONIANS

CHAPTER 1

Greetings from Paul

This letter is from Paul, Silas,* and Timothy.

We are writing to the church in Thessalonica, to you who belong to God the Father and the Lord Jesus Christ.

May God give you grace and peace.

The Faith of the Thessalonian Believers

²We always thank God for all of you and pray for you constantly. ³As we pray to our God and Father about you, we think of your faithful work, your loving deeds, and the enduring hope you have because of our Lord Jesus Christ.

⁴We know, dear brothers and sisters,* that God loves you and has chosen you to be his own people. ⁵For when we brought you the Good News, it was not only with words but also with power, for the Holy Spirit gave you full assurance* that what we said was true. And you know of our concern for you from the way we lived when we were with you. ⁶So you received the message with joy from the Holy Spirit in spite of the severe suffering it brought you. In this way, you imitated both us and the Lord. ⁷As a result, you have become an example to all the believers in Greece—throughout both Macedonia and Achaia.*

⁸And now the word of the Lord is ringing out from you to people everywhere, even beyond Macedonia and Achaia, for wherever we go we find people telling us about your faith in God. We don't need to tell them about it, ⁹for they keep talking about the wonderful welcome you gave us and how you turned away from idols to serve the living and true

God. ¹⁰And they speak of how you are looking forward to the coming of God's Son from heaven—Jesus, whom God raised from the dead. He is the one who has rescued us from the terrors of the coming judgment.

CHAPTER 2

Paul Remembers His Visit

You yourselves know, dear brothers and sisters,* that our visit to you was not a failure. ²You know how badly we had been treated at Philippi just before we came to you and how much we suffered there. Yet our God gave us the courage to declare his Good News to you boldly, in spite of great opposition. ³So you can see we were not preaching with any deceit or impure motives or trickery.

⁴For we speak as messengers approved by God to be entrusted with the Good News. Our purpose is to please God, not people. He alone examines the motives of our hearts. ⁵Never once did we try to win you with flattery, as you well know. And God is our witness that we were not pretending to be your friends just to get your money! ⁶As for human praise, we have never sought it from you or anyone else.

⁷As apostles of Christ we certainly had a right to make some demands of you, but instead we were like children* among you. Or we were like a mother feeding and caring for her own children. ⁸We loved you so much that we shared with you not only God's Good News but our own lives, too.

⁹Don't you remember, dear brothers and sisters, how hard we worked among you? Night and day we toiled to earn a living so that we would not be a burden to any of you as we

"We know, dear brothers and sisters, that God loves you and has chosen you to be his own people" (1 Thessalonians 1:4).

God has mad love for you. He picked you to be part of his fam. We're all family to him.

PAGE
268

1:1 Greek *Silvanus*, the Greek form of the name.   1:4 Greek *brothers*.   1:5 Or *with the power of the Holy Spirit, so you can have full assurance.*   1:7 *Macedonia* and *Achaia* were the northern and southern regions of Greece.   2:1 Greek *brothers*; also in 2:9, 14, 17.   2:7 Some manuscripts read *we were gentle.*

preached God's Good News to you. [10]You yourselves are our witnesses—and so is God—that we were devout and honest and faultless toward all of you believers. [11]And you know that we treated each of you as a father treats his own children. [12]We pleaded with you, encouraged you, and urged you to live your lives in a way that God would consider worthy. For he called you to share in his Kingdom and glory.

[13]Therefore, we never stop thanking God that when you received his message from us, you didn't think of our words as mere human ideas. You accepted what we said as the very word of God—which, of course, it is. And this word continues to work in you who believe.

[14]And then, dear brothers and sisters, you suffered persecution from your own countrymen. In this way, you imitated the believers in God's churches in Judea who, because of their belief in Christ Jesus, suffered from their own people, the Jews. [15]For some of the Jews killed the prophets, and some even killed the Lord Jesus. Now they have persecuted us, too. They fail to please God and work against all humanity [16]as they try to keep us from preaching the Good News of salvation to the Gentiles. By doing this, they continue to pile up their sins. But the anger of God has caught up with them at last.

Timothy's Good Report about the Church

[17]Dear brothers and sisters, after we were separated from you for a little while (though our hearts never left you), we tried very hard to come back because of our intense longing to see you again. [18]We wanted very much to come to you, and I, Paul, tried again and again, but Satan prevented us. [19]After all, what gives us hope and joy, and what will be our proud reward and crown as we stand before our Lord Jesus when he returns? It is you! [20]Yes, you are our pride and joy.

CHAPTER 3

Finally, when we could stand it no longer, we decided to stay alone in Athens, [2]and we sent Timothy to visit you. He is our brother and God's co-worker* in proclaiming the Good News of Christ. We sent him to strengthen you, to encourage you in your faith, [3]and to keep you from being shaken by the troubles you were going through. But you know that we are destined for such troubles. [4]Even while we were with you, we warned you that troubles would soon come—and they did, as you well know. [5]That is why, when I could bear it no longer, I sent Timothy to find out whether your faith was still strong. I was afraid that the tempter had gotten the best of you and that our work had been useless.

3:2 Other manuscripts read *and God's servant;* still others read *and a co-worker,* or *and a servant and co-worker for God,* or *and God's servant and our co-worker.*

THE POINT

He's comin' back. The Second Coming of Christ is a term thrown around quite a bit. People may not know what it is, and nobody knows when it will happen. The term "Second Coming" means exactly what it says: Jesus has been here once, and he will come a second time. Here are a few verses to help you get the point.

For the Lord himself will come down from heaven with a commanding shout, with the voice of the archangel, and with the trumpet call of God. (1 Thessalonians 4:16)

For you know quite well that the day of the Lord's return will come unexpectedly, like a thief in the night. (1 Thessalonians 5:2)

When will he come again?
People might say they know when Christ will return, but who's so tight with God that they can say they know for sure? Nobody. We can't even know for certain what the traffic will be like on the highway or what the weather will be from one day to the next. Seriously, you could roll outside in a long-sleeve polo and a hoodie, and by noon it's 80 degrees! Don't listen to those cats who claim to know when the Second Coming might happen. No one can know for sure.

⁶But now Timothy has just returned, bringing us good news about your faith and love. He reports that you always remember our visit with joy and that you want to see us as much as we want to see you. ⁷So we have been greatly encouraged in the midst of our troubles and suffering, dear brothers and sisters,* because you have remained strong in your faith. ⁸It gives us new life to know that you are standing firm in the Lord.

⁹How we thank God for you! Because of you we have great joy as we enter God's presence. ¹⁰Night and day we pray earnestly for you, asking God to let us see you again to fill the gaps in your faith.

¹¹May God our Father and our Lord Jesus bring us to you very soon. ¹²And may the Lord make your love for one another and for all people grow and overflow, just as our love for you overflows. ¹³May he, as a result, make your hearts strong, blameless, and holy as you stand before God our Father when our Lord Jesus comes again with all his holy people. Amen.

CHAPTER 4

Live to Please God

Finally, dear brothers and sisters,* we urge you in the name of the Lord Jesus to live in a way that pleases God, as we have taught you. You live this way already, and we encourage you to do so even more. ²For you remember what we taught you by the authority of the Lord Jesus.

³God's will is for you to be holy, so stay away from all sexual sin. ⁴Then each of you will control his own body* and live in holiness and honor—⁵not in lustful passion like the pagans who do not know God and his ways. ⁶Never harm or cheat a Christian brother in this matter by violating his wife,* for the Lord avenges all such sins, as we have solemnly warned you before. ⁷God has called us to live holy lives, not impure lives. ⁸Therefore, anyone who refuses to live by these rules is not disobeying human teaching but is rejecting God, who gives his Holy Spirit to you.

⁹But we don't need to write to you about the importance of loving each other,* for God himself has taught you to love one another. ¹⁰Indeed, you already show your love for all the believers* throughout Macedonia. Even so, dear brothers and sisters, we urge you to love them even more.

¹¹Make it your goal to live a quiet life, minding your own business and working with your hands, just as we instructed you before. ¹²Then people who are not Christians will respect the way you live, and you will not need to depend on others.

The Hope of the Resurrection

¹³And now, dear brothers and sisters, we want you to know what will happen to the believers who have died* so you will not grieve like people who have no hope. ¹⁴For since we believe that Jesus died and was raised to life again, we also believe that when Jesus returns, God will bring back with him the believers who have died.

¹⁵We tell you this directly from the Lord: We who are still living when the Lord returns will not meet him ahead of those who have died.* ¹⁶For the Lord himself will come down from heaven with a commanding shout, with the voice of the archangel, and with the trumpet call of God. First, the Christians who have died* will rise from their graves. ¹⁷Then, together with them, we who are still alive and remain on the earth will be caught up in the clouds to meet the Lord in the air. Then we will be with the Lord forever. ¹⁸So encourage each other with these words.

CHAPTER 5

Now concerning how and when all this will happen, dear brothers and sisters,* we don't really need to write you. ²For you know quite well that the day of the Lord's return will

3:7 Greek *brothers.* **4:1** Greek *brothers;* also in 4:10, 13. **4:4** Or *will know how to take a wife for himself;* or *will learn to live with his own wife;* Greek reads *will know how to possess his own vessel.* **4:6** Greek *Never harm or cheat a brother in this matter.* **4:9** Greek *about brotherly love.* **4:10** Greek *the brothers.* **4:13** Greek *those who have fallen asleep;* also in 4:14. **4:15** Greek *those who have fallen asleep.* **4:16** Greek *the dead in Christ.* **5:1** Greek *brothers;* also in 5:4, 12, 14, 25, 26, 27.

come unexpectedly, like a thief in the night. ³When people are saying, "Everything is peaceful and secure," then disaster will fall on them as suddenly as a pregnant woman's labor pains begin. And there will be no escape.

⁴But you aren't in the dark about these things, dear brothers and sisters, and you won't be surprised when the day of the Lord comes like a thief.* ⁵For you are all children of the light and of the day; we don't belong to darkness and night. ⁶So be on your guard, not asleep like the others. Stay alert and be clearheaded. ⁷Night is the time when people sleep and drinkers get drunk. ⁸But let us who live in the light be clearheaded, protected by the armor of faith and love, and wearing as our helmet the confidence of our salvation.

⁹For God chose to save us through our Lord Jesus Christ, not to pour out his anger on us. ¹⁰Christ died for us so that, whether we are dead or alive when he returns, we can live with him forever. ¹¹So encourage each other and build each other up, just as you are already doing.

Paul's Final Advice

¹²Dear brothers and sisters, honor those who are your leaders in the Lord's work. They work hard among you and give you spiritual guidance. ¹³Show them great respect and wholehearted love because of their work. And live peacefully with each other.

¹⁴Brothers and sisters, we urge you to warn those who are lazy. Encourage those who are timid. Take tender care of those who are weak. Be patient with everyone.

¹⁵See that no one pays back evil for evil, but always try to do good to each other and to all people.

¹⁶Always be joyful. ¹⁷Never stop praying. ¹⁸Be thankful in all circumstances, for this is God's will for you who belong to Christ Jesus.

¹⁹Do not stifle the Holy Spirit. ²⁰Do not scoff at prophecies, ²¹but test everything that is said. Hold on to what is good. ²²Stay away from every kind of evil.

Paul's Final Greetings

²³Now may the God of peace make you holy in every way, and may your whole spirit and soul and body be kept blameless until our Lord Jesus Christ comes again. ²⁴God will make this happen, for he who calls you is faithful.

²⁵Dear brothers and sisters, pray for us.

²⁶Greet all the brothers and sisters with Christian love.*

²⁷I command you in the name of the Lord to read this letter to all the brothers and sisters.

²⁸May the grace of our Lord Jesus Christ be with you.

5:4 Some manuscripts read *comes upon you as if you were thieves.*   **5:26** Greek *with a holy kiss.*

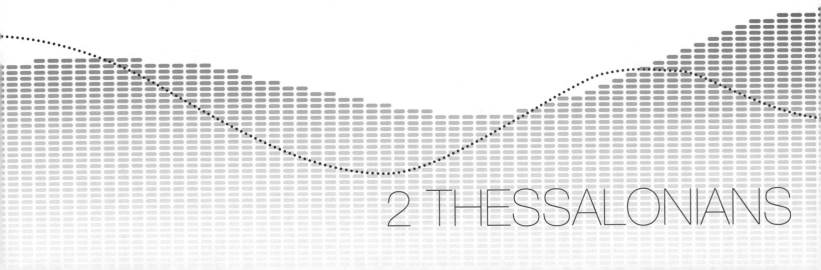

THIS BOOK IS A CONTINUATION of 1 Thessalonians. It's like a double DVD—too much info for just one disc. Paul was still encouraging the Thessalonians to stand firm even though people were comin' down hard on them with false info about Jesus and when he would return. The Thessalonians were facing persecution, and it's hard to stand for Jesus when people are tryin' to force you to fold.

2 THESSALONIANS

CHAPTER 1

Greetings from Paul

This letter is from Paul, Silas,* and Timothy.

We are writing to the church in Thessalonica, to you who belong to God our Father and the Lord Jesus Christ.

²May God our Father* and the Lord Jesus Christ give you grace and peace.

Encouragement during Persecution

³Dear brothers and sisters,* we can't help but thank God for you, because your faith is flourishing and your love for one another is growing. ⁴We proudly tell God's other churches about your endurance and faithfulness in all the persecutions and hardships you are suffering. ⁵And God will use this persecution to show his justice and to make you wor-

thy of his Kingdom, for which you are suffering. ⁶In his justice he will pay back those who persecute you.

⁷And God will provide rest for you who are being persecuted and also for us when the Lord Jesus appears from heaven. He will come with his mighty angels, ⁸in flaming fire, bringing judgment on those who don't know God and on those who refuse to obey the Good News of our Lord Jesus. ⁹They will be punished with eternal destruction, forever separated from the Lord and from his glorious power. ¹⁰When he comes on that day, he will receive glory from his holy people—praise from all who believe. And this includes you, for you believed what we told you about him.

¹¹So we keep on praying for you, asking our God to enable you to live a life worthy of his call. May he give you the power to accomplish all the good things your faith prompts

1:1 Greek *Silvanus,* the Greek form of the name. 1:2 Some manuscripts read *God the Father.* 1:3 Greek *Brothers.*

THE POINT

God's got you. Nowadays—at least where most of us live—not too many are persecuted for believing in Christ. But back in the day, it happened a lot. It still happens in many places around the world. Just in case you run into some persecution, here's a crash course: God will be with you no matter what happens, and he'll use the trouble to help you grow and to bring his justice into a situation. Here's what Paul told the folks in the city of Thessalonica:

We proudly tell God's other churches about your endurance and faithfulness in all the

persecutions and hardships you are suffering. And God will use this persecution to show his justice and to make you worthy of his Kingdom, for which you are suffering. In his justice he will pay back those who persecute you. And God will provide rest for you who are being persecuted and also for us when the Lord Jesus appears from heaven. He will come with his mighty angels, in flaming fire, bringing judgment on those who don't know God and on those who refuse to obey

the Good News of our Lord Jesus.
(2 Thessalonians 1:4-8)

It was tough back in the day when Paul was alive. A lot of people wigged out on the Christians who were brave enough to say they believed in Jesus. But God sees and knows all! When his people are bein' hammered because of their love for him, he knows and he promises to take care of things. Trust me—he ain't takin' it lightly!

you to do. ¹²Then the name of our Lord Jesus will be honored because of the way you live, and you will be honored along with him. This is all made possible because of the grace of our God and Lord, Jesus Christ.*

CHAPTER 2

Events prior to the Lord's Second Coming

Now, dear brothers and sisters,* let us clarify some things about the coming of our Lord Jesus Christ and how we will be gathered to meet him. ²Don't be so easily shaken or alarmed by those who say that the day of the Lord has already begun. Don't believe them, even if they claim to have had a spiritual vision, a revelation, or a letter supposedly from us. ³Don't be fooled by what they say. For that day will not come until there is a great rebellion against God and the man of lawlessness* is revealed—the one who brings destruction.* ⁴He will exalt himself and defy everything that people call god and every object of worship. He will even sit in the temple of God, claiming that he himself is God.

⁵Don't you remember that I told you about all this when I was with you? ⁶And you know what is holding him back, for he can be revealed only when his time comes. ⁷For this lawlessness is already at work secretly, and it will remain secret until the one who is holding it back steps out of the way. ⁸Then the man of lawlessness will be revealed, but the Lord Jesus will kill him with the breath of his mouth and destroy him by the splendor of his coming.

⁹This man will come to do the work of Satan with counterfeit power and signs and miracles. ¹⁰He will use every kind of evil deception to fool those on their way to destruction, because they refuse to love and accept the truth that would save them. ¹¹So God will cause them to be greatly deceived, and they will believe these lies. ¹²Then they will be condemned for enjoying evil rather than believing the truth.

Believers Should Stand Firm

¹³As for us, we can't help but thank God for you, dear brothers and sisters loved by the Lord. We are always thankful that God chose you to be among the first* to experience salvation—a salvation that came through the Spirit who makes you holy and through your belief in the truth. ¹⁴He called you to salvation when we told you the Good News; now you can share in the glory of our Lord Jesus Christ.

¹⁵With all these things in mind, dear brothers and sisters, stand firm and keep a strong grip on the teaching we passed on to you both in person and by letter.

¹⁶Now may our Lord Jesus Christ himself and God our Father, who loved us and by his grace gave us eternal comfort and a wonderful hope, ¹⁷comfort you and strengthen you in every good thing you do and say.

CHAPTER 3

Paul's Request for Prayer

Finally, dear brothers and sisters,* we ask you to pray for us. Pray that the Lord's message will spread rapidly and be honored wherever it goes, just as when it came to you. ²Pray, too, that we will be rescued from wicked and evil people, for not everyone is a believer. ³But the Lord is faithful; he will strengthen you and guard you from the evil one.* ⁴And we are confident in the Lord that you are doing and will continue to do the things we commanded you. ⁵May the Lord lead your hearts into a full understanding and expression of the love of God and the patient endurance that comes from Christ.

An Exhortation to Proper Living

⁶And now, dear brothers and sisters, we give you this command in the name of our Lord Jesus Christ: Stay away from all believers* who live idle lives and don't follow the

"Don't be so easily shaken or alarmed by those who say that the day of the Lord has already begun. Don't believe them, even if they claim to have had a spiritual vision, a revelation, or a letter supposedly from us" (2 Thessalonians 2:2).

say what?

I know they're tryin' to shake you, makin' you think they know when Jesus is comin' back, but trust me—THEY DON'T KNOW. Don't sweat them or the falsehoods they're spittin'. They don't even have a clue.

1:12 Or *of our God and our Lord Jesus Christ.*   **2:1** Greek *brothers;* also in 2:13, 15.   **2:3a** Some manuscripts read *the man of sin.*   **2:3b** Greek *the son of destruction.*   **2:13** Some manuscripts read *chose you from the very beginning.*   **3:1** Greek *brothers;* also in 3:6, 13.   **3:3** Or *from evil.*   **3:6a** Greek *from every brother.*

tradition they received* from us. ⁷For you know that you ought to imitate us. We were not idle when we were with you. ⁸We never accepted food from anyone without paying for it. We worked hard day and night so we would not be a burden to any of you. ⁹We certainly had the right to ask you to feed us, but we wanted to give you an example to follow. ¹⁰Even while we were with you, we gave you this command: "Those unwilling to work will not get to eat."

¹¹Yet we hear that some of you are living idle lives, refusing to work and meddling in other people's business. ¹²We command such people and urge them in the name of the Lord Jesus Christ to settle down and work to earn their own living. ¹³As for the rest of you, dear brothers and sisters, never get tired of doing good.

¹⁴Take note of those who refuse to obey what we say in this letter. Stay away from them so they will be ashamed. ¹⁵Don't think of them as enemies, but warn them as you would a brother or sister.*

Paul's Final Greetings

¹⁶Now may the Lord of peace himself give you his peace at all times and in every situation. The Lord be with you all.

¹⁷HERE IS MY GREETING IN MY OWN HANDWRITING—PAUL. I DO THIS IN ALL MY LETTERS TO PROVE THEY ARE FROM ME.

¹⁸May the grace of our Lord Jesus Christ be with you all.

3:6b Some manuscripts read *you received.*   **3:15** Greek *as a brother.*

DID YOU KNOW THAT LEADERSHIP IS A GIFT? The apostle Paul realized that although Timothy was young, he was a natural-born leader. As a matter of fact, Paul had so much faith in Timothy's leadership abilities that he sent him to pastor the church at Ephesus. Even though Paul was on lockdown, he wanted to make sure that Timothy had all the advice he needed to avoid mistakes that could hurt his people. So Paul wrote Timothy a letter from his jail cell to encourage and instruct him on how to handle difficult situations.

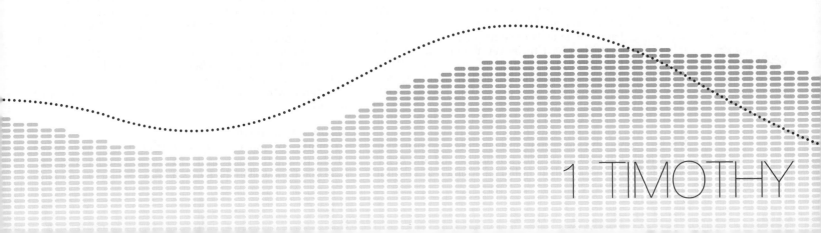

1 TIMOTHY

"Cling to your
faith in Christ, and
always keep your
conscience clear"
(1 Timothy 1:19).

*Keep your faith in
Christ tight and do
what you know is
right.*

CHAPTER **1**

Greetings from Paul

This letter is from Paul, an apostle of Christ Jesus, appointed by the command of God our Savior and Christ Jesus, who gives us hope.

²I am writing to Timothy, my true son in the faith.

May God the Father and Christ Jesus our Lord give you grace, mercy, and peace.

Warnings against False Teachings

³When I left for Macedonia, I urged you to stay there in Ephesus and stop those whose teaching is contrary to the truth. ⁴Don't let them waste their time in endless discussion of myths and spiritual pedigrees. These things only lead to meaningless speculations,* which don't help people live a life of faith in God.*

⁵The purpose of my instruction is that all believers would be filled with love that comes from a pure heart, a clear conscience, and genuine faith. ⁶But some people have missed this whole point. They have turned away from these things and spend their time in meaningless discussions. ⁷They want to be known as teachers of the law of Moses, but they don't know what they are talking about, even though they speak so confidently.

⁸We know that the law is good when used correctly. ⁹For the law was not intended for people who do what is right. It is for people who are lawless and rebellious, who are ungodly and sinful, who consider nothing sacred and defile what is holy, who kill their father or mother or commit other murders. ¹⁰The law is for people who are sexually immoral, or who practice homosexuality, or are slave traders,* liars, promise breakers, or who do anything else that contradicts the wholesome teaching ¹¹that comes from the glorious Good News entrusted to me by our blessed God.

Paul's Gratitude for God's Mercy

¹²I thank Christ Jesus our Lord, who has given me strength to do his work. He considered me trustworthy and appointed me to serve him, ¹³even though I used to blaspheme the name of Christ. In my insolence, I persecuted his people. But God had mercy on me because I did it in ignorance and unbelief. ¹⁴Oh, how generous and gracious our Lord was! He filled me with the faith and love that come from Christ Jesus.

¹⁵This is a trustworthy saying, and everyone should accept it: "Christ Jesus came into the world to save sinners"—and I am the worst of them all. ¹⁶But God had mercy on me so that Christ Jesus could use me as a prime example of his great patience with even the worst sinners. Then others will realize that they, too, can believe in him and receive eternal life. ¹⁷All honor and glory to God forever and ever! He is the eternal King, the unseen one who never dies; he alone is God. Amen.

Timothy's Responsibility

¹⁸Timothy, my son, here are my instructions for you, based on the prophetic words spoken about you earlier. May they help you fight well in the Lord's battles. ¹⁹Cling to your faith

1:4a Greek *in myths and endless genealogies, which cause speculation.* • 1:4b Greek *a stewardship of God in faith.* • 1:10 Or *kidnappers.*

keeping your swagger strong

BIBLICAL PRINCIPLES FOR SUCCESS AND LEADERSHIP

It can be really tempting to compromise what we know to be right for the sake of doing what's popular or what will lead to our outward success. The apostle Paul knew Timothy would have to deal with this, so he warned him not to give in:

Cling to your faith in Christ, and keep your conscience clear. For some people have deliberately violated their consciences; as a result, their faith has been shipwrecked. (1 Timothy 1:19)

Many times Paul had been persecuted and imprisoned for going against popular culture. Now he passed his wisdom on to young Timothy to encourage him to remain strong in the Lord and keep the faith. He wanted to make sure that Timothy's young age or lack of experience didn't keep him from fulfilling God's call on his life.

wants everyone to be saved and to understand the truth. [5]For there is only one God and one Mediator who can reconcile God and humanity—the man Christ Jesus. [6]He gave his life to purchase freedom for everyone. This is the message God gave to the world at just the right time. [7]And I have been chosen as a preacher and apostle to teach the Gentiles this message about faith and truth. I'm not exaggerating—just telling the truth.

[8]In every place of worship, I want men to pray with holy hands lifted up to God, free from anger and controversy.

[9]And I want women to be modest in their appearance.* They should wear decent and appropriate clothing and not draw attention to themselves by the way they fix their hair or by wearing gold or pearls or expensive clothes. [10]For women who claim to be devoted to God should make themselves attractive by the good things they do.

[11]Women should learn quietly and submissively. [12]I do not let women teach men or have authority over them.* Let them listen quietly. [13]For God made Adam first, and afterward he made Eve. [14]And it was not Adam who was deceived by Satan. The woman was deceived, and sin was the result. [15]But women will be saved through childbearing,* assuming they continue to live in faith, love, holiness, and modesty.

in Christ, and keep your conscience clear. For some people have deliberately violated their consciences; as a result, their faith has been shipwrecked. [20]Hymenaeus and Alexander are two examples. I threw them out and handed them over to Satan so they might learn not to blaspheme God.

CHAPTER 2

Instructions about Worship

I urge you, first of all, to pray for all people. Ask God to help them; intercede on their behalf, and give thanks for them. [2]Pray this way for kings and all who are in authority so that we can live peaceful and quiet lives marked by godliness and dignity. [3]This is good and pleases God our Savior, [4]who

CHAPTER 3

Leaders in the Church

This is a trustworthy saying: "If someone aspires to be an elder,* he desires an honorable position." [2]So an elder must be a man whose life is above reproach. He must be faithful to his wife.* He must exercise self-control, live wisely, and have a good reputation. He must enjoy having guests in his home, and he must be able to teach. [3]He must not be a heavy drinker* or be violent. He must be gentle, not quarrelsome,

2:9 Or *to pray in modest apparel.* 2:12 Or *teach men or usurp their authority.* 2:15 Or *will be saved by accepting their role as mothers,* or *will be saved by the birth of the Child.* 3:1 Or *an overseer,* or *a bishop;* also in 3:2, 6. 3:2 Or *must have only one wife,* or *must be married only once;* Greek reads *must be the husband of one wife;* also in 3:12. 3:3 Greek *must not drink too much wine;* similarly in 3:8.

and not love money. ⁴He must manage his own family well, having children who respect and obey him. ⁵For if a man cannot manage his own household, how can he take care of God's church?

⁶An elder must not be a new believer, because he might become proud, and the devil would cause him to fall.* ⁷Also, people outside the church must speak well of him so that he will not be disgraced and fall into the devil's trap.

⁸In the same way, deacons must be well respected and have integrity. They must not be heavy drinkers or dishonest with money. ⁹They must be committed to the mystery of the faith now revealed and must live with a clear conscience. ¹⁰Before they are appointed as deacons, let them be closely examined. If they pass the test, then let them serve as deacons.

¹¹In the same way, their wives* must be respected and must not slander others. They must exercise self-control and be faithful in everything they do.

¹²A deacon must be faithful to his wife, and he must manage his children and household well. ¹³Those who do well as deacons will be rewarded with respect from others and will have increased confidence in their faith in Christ Jesus.

The Truths of Our Faith

¹⁴I am writing these things to you now, even though I hope to be with you soon, ¹⁵so that if I am delayed, you will know how people must conduct themselves in the household of God. This is the church of the living God, which is the pillar and foundation of the truth.

¹⁶Without question, this is the great mystery of our faith*:

Christ* was revealed in a human body
 and vindicated by the Spirit.*
He was seen by angels
 and announced to the nations.

He was believed in throughout the world
 and taken to heaven in glory.

CHAPTER 4

Warnings against False Teachers

Now the Holy Spirit tells us clearly that in the last times some will turn away from the true faith; they will follow deceptive spirits and teachings that come from demons. ²These people are hypocrites and liars, and their consciences are dead.*

³They will say it is wrong to be married and wrong to eat certain foods. But God created those foods to be eaten with thanks by faithful people who know the truth. ⁴Since everything God created is good, we should not reject any of it but receive it with thanks. ⁵For we know it is made acceptable* by the word of God and prayer.

A Good Servant of Christ Jesus

⁶If you explain these things to the brothers and sisters,* Timothy, you will be a worthy servant of Christ Jesus, one who is nourished by the message of faith and the good teaching you have followed. ⁷Do not waste time arguing over godless ideas and old wives' tales. Instead, train yourself to be godly. ⁸"Physical training is good, but training for godliness is much better, promising benefits in this life and in the life to come." ⁹This is a trustworthy saying, and everyone should accept it. ¹⁰This is why we work hard and continue to struggle,* for our hope is in the living God, who is the Savior of all people and particularly of all believers.

¹¹Teach these things and insist that everyone learn them. ¹²Don't let anyone think less of you because you are young. Be an example to all believers in what you say, in the way you live, in your love, your faith, and your purity. ¹³Until I get there, focus on reading the Scriptures to the church, encouraging the believers, and teaching them.

3:6 Or *he might fall into the same judgment as the devil.* **3:11** Or *the women deacons.* The Greek word can be translated *women* or *wives.* **3:16a** Or *of godliness.* **3:16b** Greek *He who;* other manuscripts read *God.* **3:16c** Or *in his spirit.* **4:2** Greek *are seared.* **4:5** Or *made holy.* **4:6** Greek *brothers.* **4:10** Some manuscripts read *continue to suffer.*

¹⁴Do not neglect the spiritual gift you received through the prophecy spoken over you when the elders of the church laid their hands on you. ¹⁵Give your complete attention to these matters. Throw yourself into your tasks so that everyone will see your progress. ¹⁶Keep a close watch on how you live and on your teaching. Stay true to what is right for the sake of your own salvation and the salvation of those who hear you.

CHAPTER 5

Advice about Widows, Elders, and Slaves

Never speak harshly to an older man,* but appeal to him respectfully as you would to your own father. Talk to younger men as you would to your own brothers. ²Treat older women as you would your mother, and treat younger women with all purity as you would your own sisters.

³Take care of* any widow who has no one else to care for her. ⁴But if she has children or grandchildren, their first responsibility is to show godliness at home and repay their parents by taking care of them. This is something that pleases God.

⁵Now a true widow, a woman who is truly alone in this world, has placed her hope in God. She prays night and day, asking God for his help. ⁶But the widow who lives only for pleasure is spiritually dead even while she lives. ⁷Give these instructions to the church so that no one will be open to criticism.

⁸But those who won't care for their relatives, especially those in their own household, have denied the true faith. Such people are worse than unbelievers.

⁹A widow who is put on the list for support must be a woman who is at least sixty years old and was faithful to her husband.* ¹⁰She must be well respected by everyone because of the good she has done. Has she brought up her children well? Has she been kind to strangers and served other believers humbly?* Has she helped those who are in trouble? Has she always been ready to do good?

¹¹The younger widows should not be on the list, because their physical desires will overpower their devotion to Christ and they will want to remarry. ¹²Then they would be guilty of breaking their previous pledge. ¹³And if they are on the list, they will learn to be lazy and will spend their time gossiping from house to house, meddling in other people's business and talking about things they shouldn't. ¹⁴So I advise these younger widows to marry again, have children, and take care of their own homes. Then the enemy will

---

5:1 Or an elder.   5:3 Or Honor.   5:9 Greek was the wife of one husband.   5:10 Greek and washed the feet of God's holy people?

THE POINT

Stand up and lead. Paul knew that because Timothy was so young, he would be up against some serious opposition dealing with church folk. So Paul pointed out a few things:

Don't let anyone think less of you because you are young. Be an example to all believers in what you say, in the way you live, in your love, your faith, and your purity. . . . Do not neglect the spiritual gift you received. (1 Timothy 4:12, 14)

Are you afraid of what people might say or do if you step out in favor of your faith? Paul knew that Timothy would face opposition as he stepped into a leadership role within the church. But Paul also knew that his boy was up for the challenge! Anytime a person steps into a position of leadership, you can rest assured that there will be some haters. The key is to remain faithful to your gift and hang in there no matter what. The Bible tells us that leadership is about serving others, not about who is the most talented, best looking, best dressed, or smartest. Are you an undercover leader?

not be able to say anything against them. ¹⁵For I am afraid that some of them have already gone astray and now follow Satan.

¹⁶If a woman who is a believer has relatives who are widows, she must take care of them and not put the responsibility on the church. Then the church can care for the widows who are truly alone.

¹⁷Elders who do their work well should be respected and paid well,* especially those who work hard at both preaching and teaching. ¹⁸For the Scripture says, "You must not muzzle an ox to keep it from eating as it treads out the grain." And in another place, "Those who work deserve their pay!"*

¹⁹Do not listen to an accusation against an elder unless it is confirmed by two or three witnesses. ²⁰Those who sin should be reprimanded in front of the whole church; this will serve as a strong warning to others.

²¹I solemnly command you in the presence of God and Christ Jesus and the highest angels to obey these instructions without taking sides or showing favoritism to anyone.

²²Never be in a hurry about appointing a church leader.* Do not share in the sins of others. Keep yourself pure.

²³Don't drink only water. You ought to drink a little wine for the sake of your stomach because you are sick so often.

²⁴Remember, the sins of some people are obvious, leading them to certain judgment. But there are others whose sins will not be revealed until later. ²⁵In the same way, the good deeds of some people are obvious. And the good deeds done in secret will someday come to light.

CHAPTER **6**

All slaves should show full respect for their masters so they will not bring shame on the name of God and his teaching. ²If the masters are believers, that is no excuse for being disrespectful. Those slaves should work all the harder

5:17 Greek *should be worthy of double honor.*   5:18 Deut 25:4; Luke 10:7.   5:22 Greek *about the laying on of hands.*

POWERCHOICES

TAKING A POSITION OF LEADERSHIP IS AN AWESOME RESPONSIBILITY. PAUL AND TIMOTHY'S RELATIONSHIP WAS A MODEL FOR WHAT GOOD LEADERSHIP AND MENTORING IS ALL ABOUT. PAUL ENCOURAGED TIMOTHY TO KEEP IT REAL, LIVE RIGHT, NOT BE A FAKE, AND ABOVE ALL TO SHOW LOVE TOWARD OTHERS.

¶ DEANDRE FINALLY GOT HIS FIRST BIG CASE! HE HAD SPENT FOUR YEARS GETTING HIS UNDERGRAD DEGREE, THREE YEARS GETTING HIS MBA, AND ANOTHER THREE YEARS IN LAW SCHOOL. HE WAS ON THE FAST TRACK AT ONE OF THE MOST PRESTIGIOUS LAW FIRMS IN THE CITY. HE HAD WORKED HARD, AND FINALLY THE FIRM HAD OFFERED HIM A HIGH-PROFILE CASE—HE WAS READY! HE FELT HE DESERVED THE CASE, NOT TO MENTION THE LOOT THAT WOULD GO ALONG WITH IT. "SIX FIGURES, HERE I COME!" HE THOUGHT PROUDLY. THIS WAS THE CASE: DEFENDING AN EMBEZZLER, A MAN THEY KNEW HAD STOLEN SEVERAL MILLION DOLLARS OF HIS COMPANY'S PENSION BENEFITS. THE FIRM WAS OFFERING DEANDRE A SIZABLE AMOUNT OF MONEY TO DEFEND THIS GUY, KNOWING HE WAS GUILTY. ¶ IT TAKES SELF-DISCIPLINE AND INTEGRITY TO BECOME AN EFFECTIVE LEADER. A WHOLE LOT OF PEOPLE FALL INTO THE TRAP OF THINKING THEY CAN BUY THEIR WAY OUT OF ANY SITUATION. THEY BELIEVE THAT MONEY CAN BUY ANYTHING, INCLUDING INTEGRITY. BUT NOTHING COULD BE FURTHER FROM THE TRUTH. MONEY ISN'T EVERYTHING; AS A MATTER OF FACT, PAUL TOLD TIMOTHY THAT THE "LOVE OF MONEY IS THE ROOT OF ALL KINDS OF EVIL" (1 TIMOTHY 6:10). YEAH, DEANDRE COULD TAKE THE MONEY AND GET THIS GUY OFF, BUT AT WHAT COST TO HIS PERSONAL INTEGRITY AND BELIEFS? ¶ *WHAT IS REALLY IMPORTANT IN YOUR LIFE? HAVE YOU TAKEN A LOOK AT YOUR MOTIVES? ARE THEY PURE?*

because their efforts are helping other believers* who are well loved.

False Teaching and True Riches

Teach these things, Timothy, and encourage everyone to obey them. ³Some people may contradict our teaching, but these are the wholesome teachings of the Lord Jesus Christ. These teachings promote a godly life. ⁴Anyone who teaches something different is arrogant and lacks understanding. Such a person has an unhealthy desire to quibble over the meaning of words. This stirs up arguments ending in jealousy, division, slander, and evil suspicions. ⁵These people always cause trouble. Their minds are corrupt, and they have turned their backs on the truth. To them, a show of godliness is just a way to become wealthy.

⁶Yet true godliness with contentment is itself great wealth. ⁷After all, we brought nothing with us when we came into the world, and we can't take anything with us when we leave it. ⁸So if we have enough food and clothing, let us be content.

⁹But people who long to be rich fall into temptation and are trapped by many foolish and harmful desires that plunge them into ruin and destruction. ¹⁰For the love of money is the root of all kinds of evil. And some people, craving money, have wandered from the true faith and pierced themselves with many sorrows.

Paul's Final Instructions

¹¹But you, Timothy, are a man of God; so run from all these evil things. Pursue righteousness and a godly life,

6:2 Greek *brothers.*

along with faith, love, perseverance, and gentleness. ¹²Fight the good fight for the true faith. Hold tightly to the eternal life to which God has called you, which you have confessed so well before many witnesses. ¹³And I charge you before God, who gives life to all, and before Christ Jesus, who gave a good testimony before Pontius Pilate, ¹⁴that you obey this command without wavering. Then no one can find fault with you from now until our Lord Jesus Christ comes again. ¹⁵For at just the right time Christ will be revealed from heaven by the blessed and only almighty God, the King of all kings and Lord of all lords. ¹⁶He alone can never die, and he lives in light so brilliant that no human can approach him. No human eye has ever seen him, nor ever will. All honor and power to him forever! Amen.

¹⁷Teach those who are rich in this world not to be proud and not to trust in their money, which is so unreliable. Their trust should be in God, who richly gives us all we need for our enjoyment. ¹⁸Tell them to use their money to do good. They should be rich in good works and generous to those in need, always being ready to share with others. ¹⁹By doing this they will be storing up their treasure as a good foundation for the future so that they may experience true life.

²⁰Timothy, guard what God has entrusted to you. Avoid godless, foolish discussions with those who oppose you with their so-called knowledge. ²¹Some people have wandered from the faith by following such foolishness.

May God's grace be with you all.

"Fight the good fight for the true faith" (1 Timothy 6:12).

Let your faith do what it do—no matter what the cost!

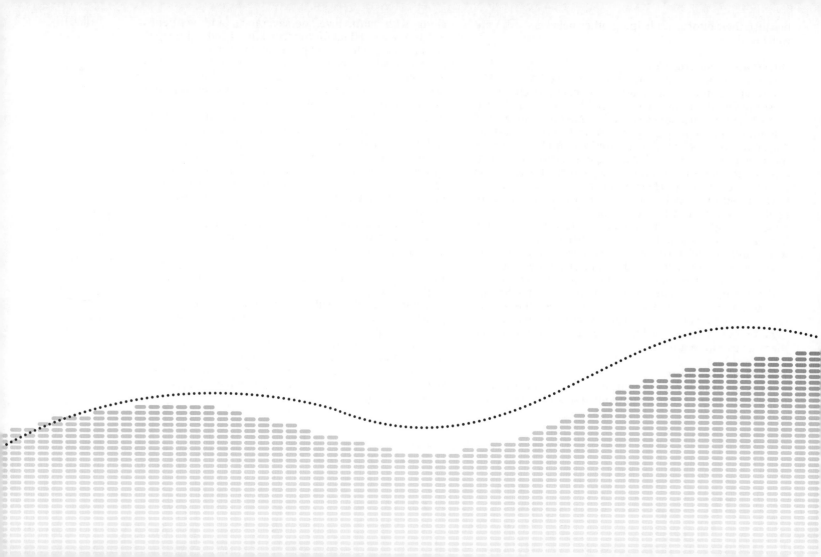

PAUL KNEW HE WAS going to die. But before he died, he wanted to make sure that he gave his young protégé Timothy final instructions about holdin' it down and keepin' the faith even in times when there was drama. Paul challenged Timothy by reminding him that he was handpicked for this job; and as a soldier for Christ, he, like Paul, would be talked about and possibly thrown into jail for his beliefs. Paul reminded Timothy to never be ashamed of his faith or where he came from and to ask God daily to give him strength.

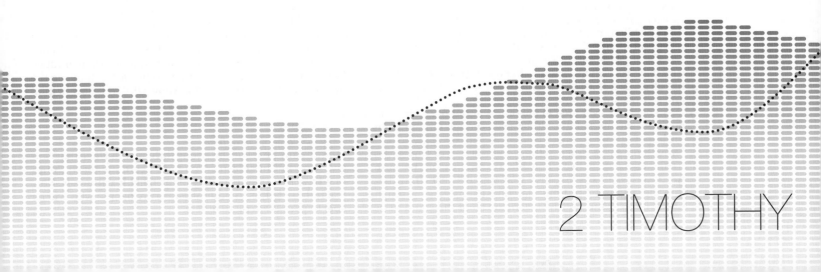

2 TIMOTHY

CHAPTER 1

Greetings from Paul

This letter is from Paul, chosen by the will of God to be an apostle of Christ Jesus. I have been sent out to tell others about the life he has promised through faith in Christ Jesus. ²I am writing to Timothy, my dear son.

May God the Father and Christ Jesus our Lord give you grace, mercy, and peace.

Encouragement to Be Faithful

³Timothy, I thank God for you—the God I serve with a clear conscience, just as my ancestors did. Night and day I constantly remember you in my prayers. ⁴I long to see you again, for I remember your tears as we parted. And I will be filled with joy when we are together again.

⁵I remember your genuine faith, for you share the faith that first filled your grandmother Lois and your mother, Eunice. And I know that same faith continues strong in you. ⁶This is why I remind you to fan into flames the spiritual gift God gave you when I laid my hands on you. ⁷For God has not given us a spirit of fear and timidity, but of power, love, and self-discipline.

⁸So never be ashamed to tell others about our Lord. And don't be ashamed of me, either, even though I'm in prison for him. With the strength God gives you, be ready to suffer with me for the sake of the Good News. ⁹For God saved us and called us to live a holy life. He did this, not because we deserved it, but because that was his plan from before the beginning of time—to show us his grace through Christ Jesus. ¹⁰And now he has made all of this plain to us by the appearing of Christ Jesus, our Savior. He broke the power of death and illuminated the way to life and immortality through the Good News. ¹¹And God chose me to be a preacher, an apostle, and a teacher of this Good News.

¹²That is why I am suffering here in prison. But I am not ashamed of it, for I know the one in whom I trust, and I am sure that he is able to guard what I have entrusted to him* until the day of his return.

¹³Hold on to the pattern of wholesome teaching you learned from me—a pattern shaped by the faith and love that you have in Christ Jesus. ¹⁴Through the power of the Holy Spirit who lives within us, carefully guard the precious truth that has been entrusted to you.

¹⁵As you know, everyone from the province of Asia has deserted me—even Phygelus and Hermogenes.

¹⁶May the Lord show special kindness to Onesiphorus and all his family because he often visited and encouraged me. He was never ashamed of me because I was in chains. ¹⁷When he came to Rome, he searched everywhere until he found me. ¹⁸May the Lord show him special kindness on the day of Christ's return. And you know very well how helpful he was in Ephesus.

CHAPTER 2

A Good Soldier of Christ Jesus

Timothy, my dear son, be strong through the grace that God gives you in Christ Jesus. ²You have heard me teach things that have been confirmed by many reliable witnesses. Now teach these truths to other trustworthy people who will be able to pass them on to others.

1:12 Or *what has been entrusted to me.*

³Endure suffering along with me, as a good soldier of Christ Jesus. ⁴Soldiers don't get tied up in the affairs of civilian life, for then they cannot please the officer who enlisted them. ⁵And athletes cannot win the prize unless they follow the rules. ⁶And hardworking farmers should be the first to enjoy the fruit of their labor. ⁷Think about what I am saying. The Lord will help you understand all these things.

⁸Always remember that Jesus Christ, a descendant of King David, was raised from the dead. This is the Good News I preach. ⁹And because I preach this Good News, I am suffering and have been chained like a criminal. But the word of God cannot be chained. ¹⁰So I am willing to endure anything if it will bring salvation and eternal glory in Christ Jesus to those God has chosen.

¹¹This is a trustworthy saying:

If we die with him,
we will also live with him.
¹² If we endure hardship,
we will reign with him.
If we deny him,
he will deny us.
¹³ If we are unfaithful,
he remains faithful,
for he cannot deny who he is.

2:17 Greek *gangrene*. 2:19a Num 16:5. 2:19b See Isa 52:11.

¹⁴Remind everyone about these things, and command them in God's presence to stop fighting over words. Such arguments are useless, and they can ruin those who hear them.

An Approved Worker

¹⁵Work hard so you can present yourself to God and receive his approval. Be a good worker, one who does not need to be ashamed and who correctly explains the word of truth. ¹⁶Avoid worthless, foolish talk that only leads to more godless behavior. ¹⁷This kind of talk spreads like cancer,* as in the case of Hymenaeus and Philetus. ¹⁸They have left the path of truth, claiming that the resurrection of the dead has already occurred; in this way, they have turned some people away from the faith.

¹⁹But God's truth stands firm like a foundation stone with this inscription: "The LORD knows those who are his,"* and "All who belong to the LORD must turn away from evil."*

²⁰In a wealthy home some utensils are made of gold and silver, and some are made of wood and clay. The expensive utensils are used for special occasions, and the cheap ones are for everyday use. ²¹If you keep yourself pure, you will be a special utensil for honorable use. Your life will be clean, and you will be ready for the Master to use you for every good work.

THE POINT

Last words to live by. Second Timothy is the apostle Paul's way of droppin' jewels on his boy to keep him ahead of the game. Timothy's path wasn't going to be easy, so Paul encouraged him to be ready for whatever might be around the corner.

Endure suffering along with me, as a good soldier of Christ Jesus. . . . Work hard so you can present yourself to God and receive his approval. Be a good worker, one who does not need to be ashamed and who correctly explains the word of truth. (2 Timothy 2:3, 15)

Paul realized Timothy was a little shy and sensitive, but he wanted to make sure that once he was gone, Timothy would be able to handle the pressures of ministry on his own. Paul knew that the people were becoming increasingly self-serving and were living unholy lives. So he encouraged Timothy to remain faithful and live a godly life no matter what might be happening around him.

²²Run from anything that stimulates youthful lusts. Instead, pursue righteous living, faithfulness, love, and peace. Enjoy the companionship of those who call on the Lord with pure hearts.

²³Again I say, don't get involved in foolish, ignorant arguments that only start fights. ²⁴A servant of the Lord must not quarrel but must be kind to everyone, be able to teach, and be patient with difficult people. ²⁵Gently instruct those who oppose the truth. Perhaps God will change those people's hearts, and they will learn the truth. ²⁶Then they will come to their senses and escape from the devil's trap. For they have been held captive by him to do whatever he wants.

CHAPTER 3

The Dangers of the Last Days

You should know this, Timothy, that in the last days there will be very difficult times. ²For people will love only themselves and their money. They will be boastful and proud, scoffing at God, disobedient to their parents, and ungrateful. They will consider nothing sacred. ³They will be unloving and unforgiving; they will slander others and have no self-control. They will be cruel and hate what is good. ⁴They will betray their friends, be reckless, be puffed up with pride, and love pleasure rather than God. ⁵They will act religious, but they will reject the power that could make them godly. Stay away from people like that!

⁶They are the kind who work their way into people's homes and win the confidence of* vulnerable women who are burdened with the guilt of sin and controlled by various desires. ⁷(Such women are forever following new teachings, but they are never able to understand the truth.) ⁸These teachers oppose the truth just as Jannes and Jambres opposed Moses. They have depraved minds and a counterfeit faith. ⁹But they won't get away with this for long. Someday everyone will recognize what fools they are, just as with Jannes and Jambres.

Paul's Charge to Timothy

¹⁰But you, Timothy, certainly know what I teach, and how I live, and what my purpose in life is. You know my faith, my patience, my love, and my endurance. ¹¹You know how much persecution and suffering I have endured. You know all about how I was persecuted in Antioch, Iconium, and Lystra—but the Lord rescued me from all of it. ¹²Yes, and everyone who wants to live a godly life in Christ Jesus will suffer persecution. ¹³But evil people and impostors will flourish. They will deceive others and will themselves be deceived.

¹⁴But you must remain faithful to the things you have been taught. You know they are true, for you know you can trust those who taught you. ¹⁵You have been taught the holy Scriptures from childhood, and they have given you the wisdom to receive the salvation that comes by trusting in Christ Jesus. ¹⁶All Scripture is inspired by God and is useful to teach us what is true and to make us realize what is wrong in our lives. It corrects us when we are wrong and teaches us to do what is right. ¹⁷God uses it to prepare and equip his people to do every good work.

CHAPTER 4

I solemnly urge you in the presence of God and Christ Jesus, who will someday judge the living and the dead when he appears to set up his Kingdom: ²Preach the word of God. Be prepared, whether the time is favorable or not. Patiently correct, rebuke, and encourage your people with good teaching.

³For a time is coming when people will no longer listen to sound and wholesome teaching. They will follow their own desires and will look for teachers who will tell them whatever their itching ears want to hear. ⁴They will reject the truth and chase after myths.

⁵But you should keep a clear mind in every situation. Don't be afraid of suffering for the Lord. Work at telling

3:6 Greek and take captive.

POWERCHOICES

PERILOUS TIMES ARE ALL AROUND US. HARDLY A DAY GOES BY WITH-
OUT SOME SENSELESS ACT OF VIOLENCE TAKING PLACE IN THE
WORLD. A GUNMAN OPENS FIRE IN A BUSY MALL. AFTER KILLING
DOZENS OF INNOCENT PEOPLE, HE TURNS THE GUN ON HIMSELF. A
SEVENTEEN-YEAR-OLD GIRL FATALLY STABS A TWELVE-YEAR-OLD
GIRL OVER A BOY. THE CONFLICT IN DARFUR RESULTS IN HUNDREDS
OF DEATHS EACH DAY. PEOPLE DON'T TRUST LAW ENFORCEMENT DUE
TO THE RISE OF POLICE BRUTALITY ACROSS THE COUNTRY. USING
PAUL'S OWN WORDS, THESE ARE "VERY DIFFICULT TIMES" (2 TIMOTHY
3:1). IN OUR FALLEN WORLD WHERE SIN IS RAMPANT, PAUL'S WORDS
OF WARNING AND ENCOURAGEMENT TO TIMOTHY ARE STILL RELE-
VANT FOR BELIEVERS TODAY. ¶ ON THE REAL, IT MIGHT GET A LOT
WORSE BEFORE IT GETS BETTER, BUT AS CHRISTIANS WE ARE
CHARGED TO REMAIN FAITHFUL TO GOD'S WORD AND TO SHARE OUR
FAITH NO MATTER WHAT. PAUL WROTE, "PREACH THE WORD OF GOD.
BE PREPARED, WHETHER THE TIME IS FAVORABLE OR NOT. PATIENTLY
CORRECT, REBUKE, AND ENCOURAGE YOUR PEOPLE WITH GOOD
TEACHING" (2 TIMOTHY 4:2). ¶ *ARE YOU READY TO OPEN YOUR
MOUTH TO SPEAK TRUTH—NO MATTER WHAT? WE NEED TO BE
READY TO SPEAK DURING THESE DIFFICULT TIMES.*

---

others the Good News, and fully carry out the ministry God
has given you.

⁶As for me, my life has already been poured out as an
offering to God. The time of my death is near. ⁷I have
fought the good fight, I have finished the race, and I have
remained faithful. ⁸And now the prize awaits me—the
crown of righteousness, which the Lord, the righteous
Judge, will give me on the day of his return. And the prize
is not just for me but for all who eagerly look forward to
his appearing.

Paul's Final Words

⁹Timothy, please come as soon as you can. ¹⁰Demas has deserted me because he loves the things of this life and has
gone to Thessalonica. Crescens has gone to Galatia, and
Titus has gone to Dalmatia. ¹¹Only Luke is with me. Bring
Mark with you when you come, for he will be helpful to me
in my ministry. ¹²I sent Tychicus to Ephesus. ¹³When you
come, be sure to bring the coat I left with Carpus at Troas.
Also bring my books, and especially my papers.*

¹⁴Alexander the coppersmith did me much harm, but the
Lord will judge him for what he has done. ¹⁵Be careful of
him, for he fought against everything we said.

¹⁶The first time I was brought before the judge, no one
came with me. Everyone abandoned me. May it not be
counted against them. ¹⁷But the Lord stood with me and
gave me strength so that I might preach the Good News in
its entirety for all the Gentiles to hear. And he rescued me
from certain death.* ¹⁸Yes, and the Lord will deliver me from
every evil attack and will bring me safely into his heavenly
Kingdom. All glory to God forever and ever! Amen.

Paul's Final Greetings

¹⁹Give my greetings to Priscilla and Aquila and those living
in the household of Onesiphorus. ²⁰Erastus stayed at Corinth, and I left Trophimus sick at Miletus.

²¹Do your best to get here before winter. Eubulus sends
you greetings, and so do Pudens, Linus, Claudia, and all the
brothers and sisters.*

²²May the Lord be with your spirit. And may his grace be
with all of you.

4:13 Greek *especially the parchments.*   **4:17** Greek *from the mouth of a lion.*   **4:21** Greek *brothers.*

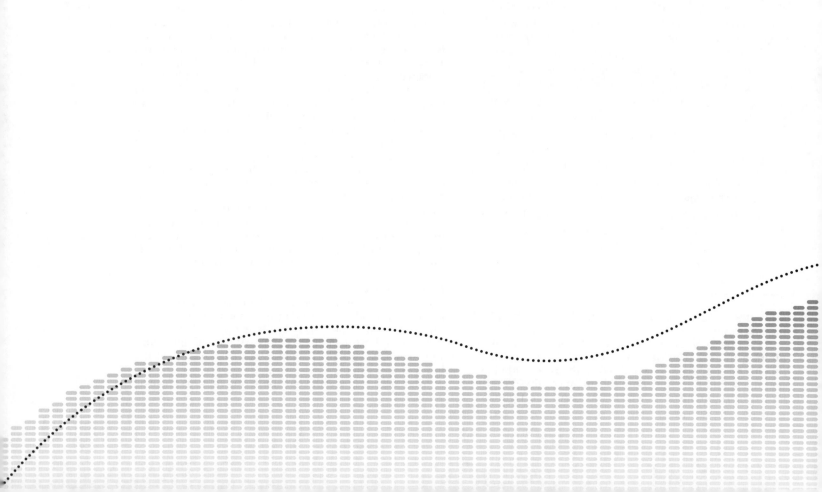

THE BOOK OF TITUS is a small book with a big message: Set things in order! Titus was another one of the apostle Paul's protégés. Like 1 Timothy, Paul's letter to Titus primarily contains guidelines about appointing spiritual leaders and promotes sound teaching within the church. Paul outlines for Titus certain rules for Christian behavior, sound doctrine, and good works with an emphasis on holy living.

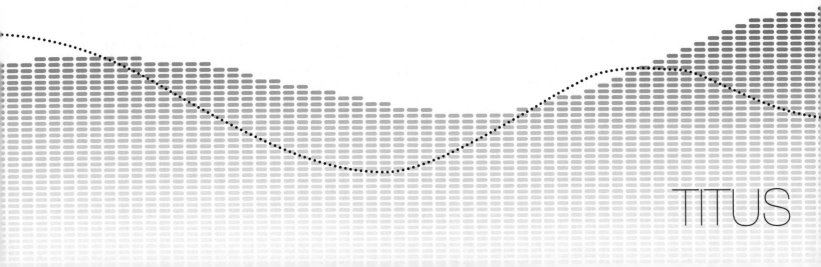

TITUS

CHAPTER 1

Greetings from Paul

This letter is from Paul, a slave of God and an apostle of Jesus Christ. I have been sent to proclaim faith to* those God has chosen and to teach them to know the truth that shows them how to live godly lives. ²This truth gives them confidence that they have eternal life, which God—who does not lie—promised them before the world began. ³And now at just the right time he has revealed this message, which we announce to everyone. It is by the command of God our Savior that I have been entrusted with this work for him.

⁴I am writing to Titus, my true son in the faith that we share.

May God the Father and Christ Jesus our Savior give you grace and peace.

Titus's Work in Crete

⁵I left you on the island of Crete so you could complete our work there and appoint elders in each town as I instructed you. ⁶An elder must live a blameless life. He must be faithful to his wife,* and his children must be believers who don't have a reputation for being wild or rebellious. ⁷An elder* is a manager of God's household, so he must live a blameless life. He must not be arrogant or quick-tempered; he must not be a heavy drinker,* violent, or dishonest with money.

⁸Rather, he must enjoy having guests in his home, and he must love what is good. He must live wisely and be just. He must live a devout and disciplined life. ⁹He must have a strong belief in the trustworthy message he was taught; then he will be able to encourage others with wholesome teaching and show those who oppose it where they are wrong.

¹⁰For there are many rebellious people who engage in useless talk and deceive others. This is especially true of those who insist on circumcision for salvation. ¹¹They must be silenced, because they are turning whole families away from the truth by their false teaching. And they do it only for money. ¹²Even one of their own men, a prophet from Crete, has said about them, "The people of Crete are all liars, cruel animals, and lazy gluttons."* ¹³This is true. So reprimand them sternly to make them strong in the faith. ¹⁴They must stop listening to Jewish myths and the commands of people who have turned away from the truth.

¹⁵Everything is pure to those whose hearts are pure. But nothing is pure to those who are corrupt and unbelieving, because their minds and consciences are corrupted. ¹⁶Such people claim they know God, but they deny him by the way they live. They are detestable and disobedient, worthless for doing anything good.

CHAPTER 2

Promote Right Teaching

As for you, Titus, promote the kind of living that reflects wholesome teaching. ²Teach the older men to exercise self-control, to be worthy of respect, and to live wisely. They must have sound faith and be filled with love and patience.

1:1 Or *to strengthen the faith of.*   1:6 Or *must have only one wife,* or *must be married only once;* Greek reads *must be the husband of one wife.*   1:7a Or *An overseer,* or *A bishop.*
1:7b Greek *must not drink too much wine.*   1:12 This quotation is from Epimenides of Knossos.

³Similarly, teach the older women to live in a way that honors God. They must not slander others or be heavy drinkers.* Instead, they should teach others what is good. ⁴These older women must train the younger women to love their husbands and their children, ⁵to live wisely and be pure, to work in their homes,* to do good, and to be submissive to their husbands. Then they will not bring shame on the word of God.

⁶In the same way, encourage the young men to live wisely. ⁷And you yourself must be an example to them by doing good works of every kind. Let everything you do reflect the integrity and seriousness of your teaching. ⁸Teach the truth so that your teaching can't be criticized. Then those who oppose us will be ashamed and have nothing bad to say about us.

⁹Slaves must always obey their masters and do their best to please them. They must not talk back ¹⁰or steal, but must show themselves to be entirely trustworthy and good. Then they will make the teaching about God our Savior attractive in every way.

¹¹For the grace of God has been revealed, bringing salvation to all people. ¹²And we are instructed to turn from godless living and sinful pleasures. We should live in this evil world with wisdom, righteousness, and devotion to God, ¹³while we look forward with hope to that wonderful day when the glory of our great God and Savior, Jesus Christ, will be revealed. ¹⁴He gave his life to free us from every kind of sin, to cleanse us, and to make us his very own people, totally committed to doing good deeds.

¹⁵You must teach these things and encourage the believers to do them. You have the authority to correct them when necessary, so don't let anyone disregard what you say.

CHAPTER 3

Do What Is Good

Remind the believers to submit to the government and its officers. They should be obedient, always ready to do what is good. ²They must not slander anyone and must avoid quarreling. Instead, they should be gentle and show true humility to everyone.

³Once we, too, were foolish and disobedient. We were misled and became slaves to many lusts and pleasures. Our lives were full of evil and envy, and we hated each other.

⁴But—"When God our Savior revealed his kindness and love, ⁵he saved us, not because of the righteous things we had done, but because of his mercy. He washed away our

2:3 Greek *be enslaved to much wine.*   2:5 Some manuscripts read *to care for their homes.*

THE POINT

Do the right thang! So far, we know that Paul was a great mentor to Timothy and Titus. Paul taught Timothy how to avoid false teachings and urged him to be diligent and faithful in the face of adversity. Paul's letter to Titus instructed him on how to carefully select church leaders, rebuke false teachings, and encourage good works in the church. Paul taught both of these brothas the importance of right living, sound doctrine, faithfulness, and integrity.

Paul chose Titus (whose name means "honorable") because he was a man of integrity and honor. He believed Titus was the perfect person to instruct the people how to grow in their faith and set an example for righteous living. The people of Crete were considered hypocrites because they claimed to be Christians, but their talk didn't match their lifestyle. Even one of their own called them greedy, lazy liars. Titus's job was to point out that their lives should be a witness to the Gospel's power. He was to speak out on the qualities necessary to live a God-filled life, qualities like self-control, spiritual and moral character, and integrity. In short, Titus was called to say, "Do the right thang!"

sins, giving us a new birth and new life through the Holy Spirit.* 6He generously poured out the Spirit upon us through Jesus Christ our Savior. 7Because of his grace he declared us righteous and gave us confidence that we will inherit eternal life." 8This is a trustworthy saying, and I want you to insist on these teachings so that all who trust in God will devote themselves to doing good. These teachings are good and beneficial for everyone.

9Do not get involved in foolish discussions about spiritual pedigrees* or in quarrels and fights about obedience to Jewish laws. These things are useless and a waste of time. 10If people are causing divisions among you, give a first and second warning. After that, have nothing more to do with them. 11For people like that have turned away from the truth, and their own sins condemn them.

Paul's Final Remarks and Greetings

12I am planning to send either Artemas or Tychicus to you. As soon as one of them arrives, do your best to meet me at Nicopolis, for I have decided to stay there for the winter. 13Do everything you can to help Zenas the lawyer and Apollos with their trip. See that they are given everything they need. 14Our people must learn to do good by meeting the urgent needs of others; then they will not be unproductive.

3:5 Greek *He saved us through the washing of regeneration and renewing of the Holy Spirit.*   **3:9** Or *spiritual genealogies.*

keeping your swagger strong

BIBLICAL PRINCIPLES FOR SUCCESS AND LEADERSHIP

What does it take to become an effective leader, to become a leader who shows integrity in all areas of life? Check out what the apostle Paul demanded of Titus:

You yourself must be an example to them by doing good works of every kind. Let everything you do reflect the integrity and seriousness of your teaching. Teach the truth so that your teaching can't be criticized. Then those who oppose us will be ashamed and have nothing bad to say about us. (Titus 2:7-8)

Daily integrity is achieved when you perform those tasks that move you closer to your personal goals and promote godly values. Consider the following quote from Samuel Smiles: "Sow a thought, reap an action; sow an action, reap a habit; sow a habit, reap a character; sow a character, reap a destiny."

15Everybody here sends greetings. Please give my greetings to the believers—all who love us.

May God's grace be with you all.

OUT OF ALL THE LETTERS Paul wrote, this one to Philemon is the shortest. Paul wrote the letter to his friend in defense of a brotha named Onesimus, who had bounced from Philemon and probably stole some money as he left. Back in the day, someone could get executed for either offense, whether running away or stealing. Onesimus met Paul and became one of his closest boys. So Paul sent Onesimus back to Philemon with this letter, asking Philemon to forgive and accept him as a brother in Christ.

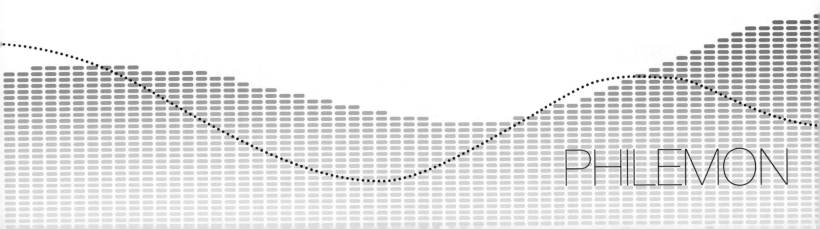

PHILEMON

Greetings from Paul

This letter is from Paul, a prisoner for preaching the Good News about Christ Jesus, and from our brother Timothy.

I am writing to Philemon, our beloved co-worker, ²and to our sister Apphia, and to our fellow soldier Archippus, and to the church that meets in your* house.

³May God our Father and the Lord Jesus Christ give you grace and peace.

Paul's Thanksgiving and Prayer

⁴I always thank my God when I pray for you, Philemon, ⁵because I keep hearing about your faith in the Lord Jesus and your love for all of God's people. ⁶And I am praying that you will put into action the generosity that comes from your faith as you understand and experience all the good things we have in Christ. ⁷Your love has given me much joy and comfort, my brother, for your kindness has often refreshed the hearts of God's people.

Paul's Appeal for Onesimus

⁸That is why I am boldly asking a favor of you. I could demand it in the name of Christ because it is the right thing for you to do. ⁹But because of our love, I prefer simply to ask you. Consider this as a request from me—Paul, an old man and now also a prisoner for the sake of Christ Jesus.*

¹⁰I appeal to you to show kindness to my child, Onesimus. I became his father in the faith while here in prison. ¹¹Onesimus* hasn't been of much use to you in the past, but now he is very useful to both of us. ¹²I am sending him back to you, and with him comes my own heart.

¹³I wanted to keep him here with me while I am in these chains for preaching the Good News, and he would have

2 Throughout this letter, *you* and *your* are singular except in verses 3, 22, and 25.   9 Or *a prisoner of Christ Jesus.*   11 *Onesimus* means "useful."

THE POINT

Forgiveness in the fam. Can you imagine someone asking you not only to forgive the person who stole something from you, but to accept them back into the family like they had never done anything wrong? Well, that's exactly what Paul was asking Philemon to do. He wanted Philemon to forgive Onesimus for his crime, allow him to come back home, and treat him as a brother in Christ. The reference to family here is important. Paul put it this way to Philemon:

It seems you lost Onesimus for a little while so that you could have him back forever. He is no longer like a slave to you. He is more than a slave, for he is a beloved brother, especially to me. Now he will mean much more to you, both as a man and as a brother in the Lord. (Philemon 1:15-16)

You do know that you can't separate yourself from family, don't you? No matter what short-comings your family members have, good or bad, they are still family. Forgiving and accepting those who have done us wrong (especially those closest to us) is an important concept in our Christian walk. Just think where you would be if Christ hadn't forgiven you and accepted you into his family.

helped me on your behalf. ¹⁴But I didn't want to do anything without your consent. I wanted you to help because you were willing, not because you were forced. ¹⁵It seems you lost Onesimus for a little while so that you could have him back forever. ¹⁶He is no longer like a slave to you. He is more than a slave, for he is a beloved brother, especially to me. Now he will mean much more to you, both as a man and as a brother in the Lord.

¹⁷So if you consider me your partner, welcome him as you would welcome me. ¹⁸If he has wronged you in any way or owes you anything, charge it to me. ¹⁹I, PAUL, WRITE THIS WITH MY OWN HAND: I WILL REPAY IT. AND I WON'T MENTION THAT YOU OWE ME YOUR VERY SOUL!

20 Greek *onaimen,* a play on the name Onesimus.

²⁰Yes, my brother, please do me this favor* for the Lord's sake. Give me this encouragement in Christ.

²¹I am confident as I write this letter that you will do what I ask and even more! ²²One more thing—please prepare a guest room for me, for I am hoping that God will answer your prayers and let me return to you soon.

Paul's Final Greetings
²³Epaphras, my fellow prisoner in Christ Jesus, sends you his greetings. ²⁴So do Mark, Aristarchus, Demas, and Luke, my co-workers.

²⁵May the grace of the Lord Jesus Christ be with your spirit.

"I appeal to you to show kindness to my child, Onesimus. I became his father in the faith while here in prison. Onesimus hasn't been of much use to you in the past, but now he is very useful to both of us" (Philemon 1:10-11).

say what?

You gotta show love to Onesimus. I became his adviser in his faith while I was locked up. Onesimus was no good back in the day, but now he's a good look and will be useful to both of us.

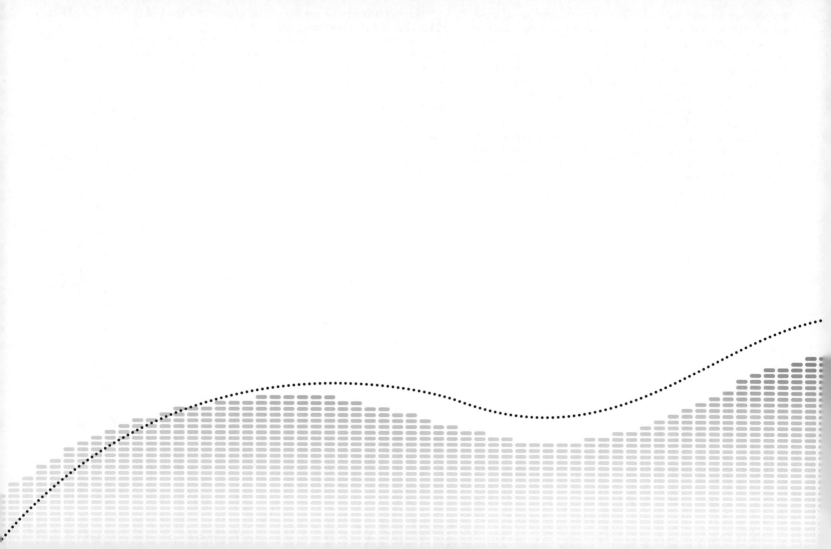

EVEN THE PEOPLE who study the Bible as part of their daily grind aren't sure who wrote the book of Hebrews. Some think it may have been Paul, Apollos, Philip, or even Priscilla. One thing is certain—whoever wrote the book wrote it to encourage the people to hold on. Judaism was old school, and Christianity was new. Many traditional Jews were having a hard time accepting the fact that the Messiah had come and paved the way to a new and better way of life.

Those who accepted Jesus as Lord and Savior were finding that they were being mistreated or ridiculed for their newfound beliefs. The people were tired of all the drama and found themselves slipping back into old habits. The author of Hebrews wanted to reassure those struggling with their new faith that following Jesus and the way of Christianity was far better than the old lifestyle they were used to.

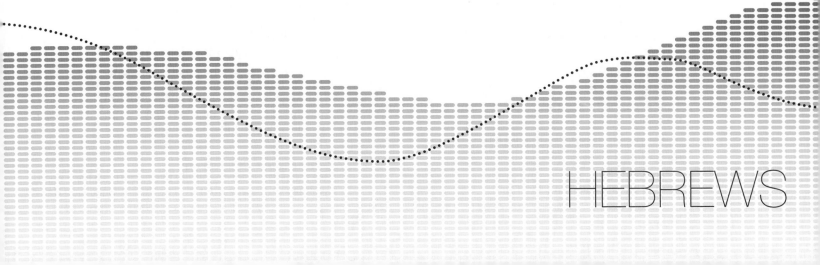

HEBREWS

CHAPTER 1

Jesus Christ Is God's Son

Long ago God spoke many times and in many ways to our ancestors through the prophets. ²And now in these final days, he has spoken to us through his Son. God promised everything to the Son as an inheritance, and through the Son he created the universe. ³The Son radiates God's own glory and expresses the very character of God, and he sustains everything by the mighty power of his command. When he had cleansed us from our sins, he sat down in the place of honor at the right hand of the majestic God in heaven. ⁴This shows that the Son is far greater than the angels, just as the name God gave him is greater than their names.

The Son Is Greater Than the Angels

⁵For God never said to any angel what he said to Jesus:

"You are my Son.
Today I have become your Father.*"

God also said,

"I will be his Father,
and he will be my Son."*

⁶And when he brought his supreme* Son into the world, God said,*

"Let all of God's angels worship him."*

⁷Regarding the angels, he says,

"He sends his angels like the winds,
his servants like flames of fire."*

⁸But to the Son he says,

"Your throne, O God, endures forever and ever.
You rule with a scepter of justice.
⁹ You love justice and hate evil.
Therefore, O God, your God has anointed you,
pouring out the oil of joy on you more than on anyone else."*

¹⁰He also says to the Son,

"In the beginning, Lord, you laid the foundation of the earth
and made the heavens with your hands.
¹¹ They will perish, but you remain forever.
They will wear out like old clothing.
¹² You will fold them up like a cloak
and discard them like old clothing.
But you are always the same;
you will live forever."*

¹³And God never said to any of the angels,

"Sit in the place of honor at my right hand
until I humble your enemies,
making them a footstool under your feet."*

¹⁴Therefore, angels are only servants—spirits sent to care for people who will inherit salvation.

CHAPTER 2

A Warning against Drifting Away

So we must listen very carefully to the truth we have heard, or we may drift away from it. ²For the message God deliv-

1:5a Or *Today I reveal you as my Son.* Ps 2:7.   1:5b 2 Sam 7:14.   1:6a Or *firstborn.*   1:6b Or *when he again brings his supreme Son* [or *firstborn Son*] *into the world, God will say.*
1:6c Deut 32:43.   1:7 Ps 104:4 (Greek version).   1:8-9 Ps 45:6-7.   1:10-12 Ps 102:25-27.   1:13 Ps 110:1.

ered through angels has always stood firm, and every violation of the law and every act of disobedience was punished. ³So what makes us think we can escape if we ignore this great salvation that was first announced by the Lord Jesus himself and then delivered to us by those who heard him speak? ⁴And God confirmed the message by giving signs and wonders and various miracles and gifts of the Holy Spirit whenever he chose.

Jesus, the Man

⁵And furthermore, it is not angels who will control the future world we are talking about. ⁶For in one place the Scriptures say,

> "What are mere mortals that you should think about
>   them,
>   or a son of man* that you should care for him?
> ⁷ Yet you made them only a little lower than the angels
>   and crowned them with glory and honor.*
> ⁸ You gave them authority over all things."*

Now when it says "all things," it means nothing is left out. But we have not yet seen all things put under their authority. ⁹What we do see is Jesus, who was given a position "a little lower than the angels"; and because he suffered death for us, he is now "crowned with glory and honor." Yes, by God's grace, Jesus tasted death for everyone. ¹⁰God, for whom and through whom everything was made, chose to bring many children into glory. And it was only right that he should make Jesus, through his suffering, a perfect leader, fit to bring them into their salvation.

¹¹So now Jesus and the ones he makes holy have the same Father. That is why Jesus is not ashamed to call them his brothers and sisters.* ¹²For he said to God,

> "I will proclaim your name to my brothers and sisters.
>   I will praise you among your assembled people."*

¹³He also said,

> "I will put my trust in him,"
>   that is, "I and the children God has given me."*

¹⁴Because God's children are human beings—made of flesh and blood—the Son also became flesh and blood. For only as a human being could he die, and only by dying could he break the power of the devil, who had* the power of death. ¹⁵Only in this way could he set free all who have lived their lives as slaves to the fear of dying.

¹⁶We also know that the Son did not come to help angels; he came to help the descendants of Abraham. ¹⁷Therefore, it was necessary for him to be made in every respect like us, his brothers and sisters,* so that he could be our merciful and faithful High Priest before God. Then he could offer a sacrifice that would take away the sins of the people. ¹⁸Since he himself has gone through suffering and testing, he is able to help us when we are being tested.

CHAPTER 3

Jesus Is Greater Than Moses

And so, dear brothers and sisters who belong to God and* are partners with those called to heaven, think carefully about this Jesus whom we declare to be God's messenger* and High Priest. ²For he was faithful to God, who appointed him, just as Moses served faithfully when he was entrusted with God's entire* house.

³But Jesus deserves far more glory than Moses, just as a person who builds a house deserves more praise than the house itself. ⁴For every house has a builder, but the one who built everything is God.

⁵Moses was certainly faithful in God's house as a servant. His work was an illustration of the truths God would reveal later. ⁶But Christ, as the Son, is in charge of God's

"What are mere mortals that you should think about them, or a son of man that you should care for him? Yet you made them only a little lower than the angels and crowned them with glory and honor. You gave them authority over all things" (Hebrews 2:6-8).

Who are we that God should think about us? But just think—he made us only a li'l lower than the angels and crowned us with glory. Amazing!

entire house. And we are God's house, if we keep our courage and remain confident in our hope in Christ.*

[7]That is why the Holy Spirit says,

"Today when you hear his voice,
[8] don't harden your hearts
   as Israel did when they rebelled,
      when they tested me in the wilderness.
[9] There your ancestors tested and tried my patience,
      even though they saw my miracles for forty years.
[10] So I was angry with them, and I said,
   'Their hearts always turn away from me.
      They refuse to do what I tell them.'
[11] So in my anger I took an oath:
      'They will never enter my place of rest.'"*

[12]Be careful then, dear brothers and sisters.* Make sure that your own hearts are not evil and unbelieving, turning you away from the living God. [13]You must warn each other every day, while it is still "today," so that none of you will be deceived by sin and hardened against God. [14]For if we are faithful to the end, trusting God just as firmly as when we first believed, we will share in all that belongs to Christ. [15]Remember what it says:

"Today when you hear his voice,
   don't harden your hearts
      as Israel did when they rebelled."*

[16]And who was it who rebelled against God, even though they heard his voice? Wasn't it the people Moses led out of Egypt? [17]And who made God angry for forty years? Wasn't it the people who sinned, whose corpses lay in the wilderness? [18]And to whom was God speaking when he took an oath that they would never enter his rest? Wasn't it the people who disobeyed him? [19]So we see that because of their unbelief they were not able to enter his rest.

CHAPTER 4

Promised Rest for God's People

God's promise of entering his rest still stands, so we ought to tremble with fear that some of you might fail to experience it. [2]For this good news—that God has prepared this rest—has been announced to us just as it was to them. But it did them no good because they didn't share the faith of those who listened to God.* [3]For only we who believe can enter his rest. As for the others, God said,

3:6 Some manuscripts add *faithful to the end.*   3:7-11 Ps 95:7-11.   3:12 Greek *brothers.*   3:15 Ps 95:7-8.   4:2 Some manuscripts read *they didn't combine what they heard with faith.*

THE POINT

Not so lost. Have you ever heard the term "the Lost Generation"? Generally, it refers to a generation of young people growin' up in the United States in the early 1900s shortly after World War I. It included people like Paul Robeson, Langston Hughes, Golda Meir, Ernest Hemingway, and F. Scott Fitzgerald. I'm sure you're wonderin' what a bunch of old heads like this have to do with you, let alone the people in Bible times. Well, a lot more than you think.

The "Lost Generation" was noted for thinkin' the older generation was wack. Ironically, the "Lost Generation" wasn't really lost at all. As a matter of fact, this generation produced some of the most creative writers, musicians, poets, and playwrights of the twentieth century. They were just tired of the same ole thing and were willin' to stand up for what they believed in. They were lookin' to change their culture, just like the Jews mentioned in Hebrews who took a stand for their Christian faith.

The point is, like most people who attempt to change the status quo, they met opposition and were falling back into their old way of doing things. They were tired of church, tired of serving, tired of being persecuted, and tired of the same struggle. They needed encouragement to keep the faith and to keep on keepin' on as they carved a new path. As Christians, we can turn to Christ and give him our troubles. He won't leave us hangin'.

"In my anger I took an oath:
'They will never enter my place of rest,'"*

even though this rest has been ready since he made the world. ⁴We know it is ready because of the place in the Scriptures where it mentions the seventh day: "On the seventh day God rested from all his work."* ⁵But in the other passage God said, "They will never enter my place of rest."*

⁶So God's rest is there for people to enter, but those who first heard this good news failed to enter because they disobeyed God. ⁷So God set another time for entering his rest, and that time is today. God announced this through David much later in the words already quoted:

"Today when you hear his voice,
don't harden your hearts."*

⁸Now if Joshua had succeeded in giving them this rest, God would not have spoken about another day of rest still to come. ⁹So there is a special rest* still waiting for the people of God. ¹⁰For all who have entered into God's rest have rested from their labors, just as God did after creating the world. ¹¹So let us do our best to enter that rest. But if we disobey God, as the people of Israel did, we will fall.

¹²For the word of God is alive and powerful. It is sharper than the sharpest two-edged sword, cutting between soul and spirit, between joint and marrow. It exposes our innermost thoughts and desires. ¹³Nothing in all creation is hidden from God. Everything is naked and exposed before his eyes, and he is the one to whom we are accountable.

Christ Is Our High Priest

¹⁴So then, since we have a great High Priest who has entered heaven, Jesus the Son of God, let us hold firmly to what we believe. ¹⁵This High Priest of ours understands our weaknesses, for he faced all of the same testings we do, yet he did not sin. ¹⁶So let us come boldly to the throne of our gracious God. There we will receive his mercy, and we will find grace to help us when we need it most.

CHAPTER 5

Every high priest is a man chosen to represent other people in their dealings with God. He presents their gifts to God and offers sacrifices for their sins. ²And he is able to deal gently with ignorant and wayward people because he himself is subject to the same weaknesses. ³That is why he must offer sacrifices for his own sins as well as theirs.

⁴And no one can become a high priest simply because he wants such an honor. He must be called by God for this work, just as Aaron was. ⁵That is why Christ did not honor himself by assuming he could become High Priest. No, he was chosen by God, who said to him,

"You are my Son.
Today I have become your Father.*"

⁶And in another passage God said to him,

"You are a priest forever in the order of Melchizedek."*

⁷While Jesus was here on earth, he offered prayers and pleadings, with a loud cry and tears, to the one who could rescue him from death. And God heard his prayers because of his deep reverence for God. ⁸Even though Jesus was God's Son, he learned obedience from the things he suffered. ⁹In this way, God qualified him as a perfect High Priest, and he became the source of eternal salvation for all those who obey him. ¹⁰And God designated him to be a High Priest in the order of Melchizedek.

A Call to Spiritual Growth

¹¹There is much more we would like to say about this, but it is difficult to explain, especially since you are spiritually dull and don't seem to listen. ¹²You have been believers so long now that you ought to be teaching others. Instead,

"For the word of God is alive and powerful. It is sharper than the sharpest two-edged sword, cutting between soul and spirit, between joint and marrow. It exposes our innermost thoughts and desires. Nothing in all creation is hidden from God. Everything is naked and exposed before his eyes" (Hebrews 4:12-13).

The word of God is powerful, sharper than the sharpest knife. It cuts us open and reveals who we really are. We can't hide anything from God.

4:3 Ps 95:11.   4:4 Gen 2:2.   4:5 Ps 95:11.   4:7 Ps 95:7-8.   4:9 Or *a Sabbath rest.*   5:5 Or *Today I reveal you as my Son.* Ps 2:7.   5:6 Ps 110:4.

you need someone to teach you again the basic things about God's word.* You are like babies who need milk and cannot eat solid food. ¹³For someone who lives on milk is still an infant and doesn't know how to do what is right. ¹⁴Solid food is for those who are mature, who through training have the skill to recognize the difference between right and wrong.

CHAPTER 6

So let us stop going over the basic teachings about Christ again and again. Let us go on instead and become mature in our understanding. Surely we don't need to start again with the fundamental importance of repenting from evil deeds* and placing our faith in God. ²You don't need further instruction about baptisms, the laying on of hands, the resurrection of the dead, and eternal judgment. ³And so, God willing, we will move forward to further understanding.

⁴For it is impossible to bring back to repentance those who were once enlightened—those who have experienced the good things of heaven and shared in the Holy Spirit, ⁵who have tasted the goodness of the word of God and the power of the age to come—⁶and who then turn away from God. It is impossible to bring such people back to repentance; by rejecting the Son of God, they themselves are nailing him to the cross once again and holding him up to public shame.

⁷When the ground soaks up the falling rain and bears a good crop for the farmer, it has God's blessing. ⁸But if a field bears thorns and thistles, it is useless. The farmer will soon condemn that field and burn it.

⁹Dear friends, even though we are talking this way, we really don't believe it applies to you. We are confident that you are meant for better things, things that come with salvation. ¹⁰For God is not unjust. He will not forget how hard you have worked for him and how you have shown your love to him by caring for other believers,* as you still do.

POWERCHOICES

IF YOU THINK YOU HAVE IT ROUGH, LOTS OF LEGENDS LIKE LANGSTON HUGHES AND PAUL ROBESON ENDURED COUNTLESS HARDSHIPS TO MAKE IT. AT THE TIME, PAUL ROBESON WAS THE THIRD AFRICAN AMERICAN TO BE ACCEPTED TO RUTGERS UNIVERSITY. HE WAS BEATEN AND HAD HIS FINGERNAILS PULLED OUT, AND YET HE EARNED NUMEROUS VARSITY LETTERS AND WAS VALEDICTORIAN OF HIS GRADUATING CLASS. ¶ LANGSTON HUGHES IS QUOTED AS SAYING, "I WAS A VICTIM OF A STEREOTYPE. THERE WERE ONLY TWO OF US NEGRO KIDS IN THE WHOLE CLASS AND OUR ENGLISH TEACHER WAS ALWAYS STRESSING THE IMPORTANCE OF RHYTHM IN POETRY. WELL, EVERYONE KNOWS—EXCEPT US—THAT ALL NEGROES HAVE RHYTHM, SO THEY ELECTED ME AS CLASS POET." HUGHES WENT ON TO BECOME ONE OF THE GREATEST WRITERS OF THE HARLEM RENAISSANCE. ¶ GET THE PICTURE? WHAT DO YOU HAVE IN COMMON WITH A BUNCH OF OLD HEADS? AS PART OF THE HIP-HOP CULTURE, A LOT MORE THAN YOU THINK. JUST LIKE THE "LOST GENERATION," THE HIP-HOP GENERATION HAS THE ABILITY TO CHANGE MINDS, TO REACH OTHERS, AND TO SHARE CHRIST. THE REDEEMABLE ELEMENTS OF THE CULTURE CAN BE OFFERED UP TO GOD AND MADE HOLY BY THOSE WHO HAVE SET THEMSELVES APART FOR HIS SERVICE. ¶ *EVEN IF THE WAY YOU DRESS AND THE WAY YOU TALK DOESN'T FALL IN LINE WITH TRADITIONAL OLD-SCHOOL WAYS, OR EVEN IF SOME OF YOUR HOMIES THINK YOU'RE A LITTLE WEIRD, DON'T TRIP—KEEP THE FAITH, JUST LIKE THOSE LEGENDS FROM BACK IN THE DAY. GOD'S GOT YOUR BACK.*

¹¹Our great desire is that you will keep on loving others as long as life lasts, in order to make certain that what you hope for will come true. ¹²Then you will not become spiri-

5:12 Or *about the oracles of God.*   6:1 Greek *from dead works.*   6:10 Greek *for God's holy people.*

tually dull and indifferent. Instead, you will follow the example of those who are going to inherit God's promises because of their faith and endurance.

God's Promises Bring Hope

¹³For example, there was God's promise to Abraham. Since there was no one greater to swear by, God took an oath in his own name, saying:

¹⁴ "I will certainly bless you,
and I will multiply your descendants beyond
number."*

¹⁵Then Abraham waited patiently, and he received what God had promised.

¹⁶Now when people take an oath, they call on someone greater than themselves to hold them to it. And without any question that oath is binding. ¹⁷God also bound himself with an oath, so that those who received the promise could be perfectly sure that he would never change his mind. ¹⁸So God has given both his promise and his oath. These two things are unchangeable because it is impossible for God to lie. Therefore, we who have fled to him for refuge can have great confidence as we hold to the hope that lies before us. ¹⁹This hope is a strong and trustworthy anchor for our souls. It leads us through the curtain into God's inner sanctuary. ²⁰Jesus has already gone in there for us. He has become our eternal High Priest in the order of Melchizedek.

CHAPTER 7

Melchizedek Is Greater Than Abraham

This Melchizedek was king of the city of Salem and also a priest of God Most High. When Abraham was returning home after winning a great battle against the kings, Melchizedek met him and blessed him. ²Then Abraham took a tenth of all he had captured in battle and gave it to Melchizedek. The name Melchizedek means "king of justice," and king of Salem means "king of peace." ³There is no record of his father or mother or any of his ancestors—no beginning or end to his life. He remains a priest forever, resembling the Son of God.

⁴Consider then how great this Melchizedek was. Even Abraham, the great patriarch of Israel, recognized this by giving him a tenth of what he had taken in battle. ⁵Now the law of Moses required that the priests, who are descendants of Levi, must collect a tithe from the rest of the people of Israel,* who are also descendants of Abraham. ⁶But Melchizedek, who was not a descendant of Levi, collected a tenth from Abraham. And Melchizedek placed a blessing upon Abraham, the one who had already received the promises of God. ⁷And without question, the person who has the power to give a blessing is greater than the one who is blessed.

⁸The priests who collect tithes are men who die, so Melchizedek is greater than they are, because we are told that he lives on. ⁹In addition, we might even say that these Levites—the ones who collect the tithe—paid a tithe to Melchizedek when their ancestor Abraham paid a tithe to him. ¹⁰For although Levi wasn't born yet, the seed from which he came was in Abraham's body when Melchizedek collected the tithe from him.

¹¹So if the priesthood of Levi, on which the law was based, could have achieved the perfection God intended, why did God need to establish a different priesthood, with a priest in the order of Melchizedek instead of the order of Levi and Aaron?*

¹²And if the priesthood is changed, the law must also be changed to permit it. ¹³For the priest we are talking about belongs to a different tribe, whose members have never served at the altar as priests. ¹⁴What I mean is, our Lord came from the tribe of Judah, and Moses never mentioned priests coming from that tribe.

6:14 Gen 22:17.   7:5 Greek *from their brothers.*   7:11 Greek *the order of Aaron?*

Today I'm makin' a new pact with my people. They'll know what I want them to do, because I will put my laws in their minds and in their hearts. I will be theirs, and they will be mine.

Jesus Is like Melchizedek

¹⁵This change has been made very clear since a different priest, who is like Melchizedek, has appeared. ¹⁶Jesus became a priest, not by meeting the physical requirement of belonging to the tribe of Levi, but by the power of a life that cannot be destroyed. ¹⁷And the psalmist pointed this out when he prophesied,

"You are a priest forever in the order of Melchizedek."*

¹⁸Yes, the old requirement about the priesthood was set aside because it was weak and useless. ¹⁹For the law never made anything perfect. But now we have confidence in a better hope, through which we draw near to God.

²⁰This new system was established with a solemn oath. Aaron's descendants became priests without such an oath, ²¹but there was an oath regarding Jesus. For God said to him,

"The LORD has taken an oath and will not break his vow:
    'You are a priest forever.'"*

²²Because of this oath, Jesus is the one who guarantees this better covenant with God.

²³There were many priests under the old system, for death prevented them from remaining in office. ²⁴But because Jesus lives forever, his priesthood lasts forever. ²⁵Therefore he is able, once and forever, to save* those who come to God through him. He lives forever to intercede with God on their behalf.

²⁶He is the kind of high priest we need because he is holy and blameless, unstained by sin. He has been set apart from sinners and has been given the highest place of honor in heaven.* ²⁷Unlike those other high priests, he does not need to offer sacrifices every day. They did this for their own sins first and then for the sins of the people. But Jesus did this once for all when he offered himself as the sacrifice for the people's sins. ²⁸The law appointed high priests who were limited by human weakness. But after the law was given, God appointed his Son with an oath, and his Son has been made the perfect High Priest forever.

CHAPTER 8

Christ Is Our High Priest

Here is the main point: We have a High Priest who sat down in the place of honor beside the throne of the majestic God in heaven. ²There he ministers in the heavenly Tabernacle,* the true place of worship that was built by the Lord and not by human hands.

³And since every high priest is required to offer gifts and sacrifices, our High Priest must make an offering, too. ⁴If he were here on earth, he would not even be a priest, since there already are priests who offer the gifts required by the law. ⁵They serve in a system of worship that is only a copy, a shadow of the real one in heaven. For when Moses was getting ready to build the Tabernacle, God gave him this warning: "Be sure that you make everything according to the pattern I have shown you here on the mountain."*

⁶But now Jesus, our High Priest, has been given a ministry that is far superior to the old priesthood, for he is the one who mediates for us a far better covenant with God, based on better promises.

⁷If the first covenant had been faultless, there would have been no need for a second covenant to replace it. ⁸But when God found fault with the people, he said:

"The day is coming, says the LORD,
    when I will make a new covenant
    with the people of Israel and Judah.
⁹ This covenant will not be like the one
    I made with their ancestors
    when I took them by the hand
    and led them out of the land of Egypt.
They did not remain faithful to my covenant,
    so I turned my back on them, says the LORD.

7:17 Ps 110:4.   7:21 Ps 110:4.   7:25 Or *is able to save completely.*   7:26 Or *has been exalted higher than the heavens.*   8:2 Or *tent;* also in 8:5.   8:5 Exod 25:40; 26:30.

¹⁰ But this is the new covenant I will make
   with the people of Israel on that day,* says the LORD:
I will put my laws in their minds,
   and I will write them on their hearts.
I will be their God,
   and they will be my people.
¹¹ And they will not need to teach their neighbors,
   nor will they need to teach their relatives,*
   saying, 'You should know the LORD.'
For everyone, from the least to the greatest,
   will know me already.
¹² And I will forgive their wickedness,
   and I will never again remember their sins."*

¹³When God speaks of a "new" covenant, it means he has made the first one obsolete. It is now out of date and will soon disappear.

CHAPTER 9

Old Rules about Worship

That first covenant between God and Israel had regulations for worship and a place of worship here on earth. ²There were two rooms in that Tabernacle.* In the first room were a lampstand, a table, and sacred loaves of bread on the table. This room was called the Holy Place. ³Then there was a curtain, and behind the curtain was the second room* called the Most Holy Place. ⁴In that room were a gold incense altar and a wooden chest called the Ark of the Covenant, which was covered with gold on all sides. Inside the Ark were a gold jar containing manna, Aaron's staff that sprouted leaves, and the stone tablets of the covenant. ⁵Above the Ark were the cherubim of divine glory, whose wings stretched out over the Ark's cover, the place of atonement. But we cannot explain these things in detail now.

⁶When these things were all in place, the priests regularly entered the first room* as they performed their religious duties. ⁷But only the high priest ever entered the Most Holy Place, and only once a year. And he always offered blood for his own sins and for the sins the people had committed in ignorance. ⁸By these regulations the Holy Spirit revealed that the entrance to the Most Holy Place was not freely open as long as the Tabernacle* and the system it represented were still in use.

⁹This is an illustration pointing to the present time. For the gifts and sacrifices that the priests offer are not able to cleanse the consciences of the people who bring them. ¹⁰For that old system deals only with food and drink and various cleansing ceremonies—physical regulations that were in effect only until a better system could be established.

Christ Is the Perfect Sacrifice

¹¹So Christ has now become the High Priest over all the good things that have come.* He has entered that greater, more perfect Tabernacle in heaven, which was not made by human hands and is not part of this created world. ¹²With his own blood—not the blood of goats and calves—he entered the Most Holy Place once for all time and secured our redemption forever.

¹³Under the old system, the blood of goats and bulls and the ashes of a young cow could cleanse people's bodies from ceremonial impurity. ¹⁴Just think how much more the blood of Christ will purify our consciences from sinful deeds* so that we can worship the living God. For by the power of the eternal Spirit, Christ offered himself to God as a perfect sacrifice for our sins. ¹⁵That is why he is the one who mediates a new covenant between God and people, so that all who are called can receive the eternal inheritance God has promised them. For Christ died to set them free from the penalty of the sins they had committed under that first covenant.

8:10 Greek *after those days.* **8:11** Greek *their brother.* **8:8-12** Jer 31:31-34. **9:2** Or *tent;* also in 9:11, 21. **9:3** Greek *second tent.* **9:6** Greek *first tent.* **9:8** Or *the first room;* Greek reads *the first tent.* **9:11** Some manuscripts read *that are about to come.* **9:14** Greek *from dead works.*

¹⁶Now when someone leaves a will,* it is necessary to prove that the person who made it is dead.* ¹⁷The will goes into effect only after the person's death. While the person who made it is still alive, the will cannot be put into effect.

¹⁸That is why even the first covenant was put into effect with the blood of an animal. ¹⁹For after Moses had read each of God's commandments to all the people, he took the blood of calves and goats,* along with water, and sprinkled both the book of God's law and all the people, using hyssop branches and scarlet wool. ²⁰Then he said, "This blood confirms the covenant God has made with you."* ²¹And in the same way, he sprinkled blood on the Tabernacle and on everything used for worship. ²²In fact, according to the law of Moses, nearly everything was purified with blood. For without the shedding of blood, there is no forgiveness.

²³That is why the Tabernacle and everything in it, which were copies of things in heaven, had to be purified by the blood of animals. But the real things in heaven had to be purified with far better sacrifices than the blood of animals.

²⁴For Christ did not enter into a holy place made with human hands, which was only a copy of the true one in heaven. He entered into heaven itself to appear now before God on our behalf. ²⁵And he did not enter heaven to offer himself again and again, like the high priest here on earth who enters the Most Holy Place year after year with the blood of an animal. ²⁶If that had been necessary, Christ would have had to die again and again, ever since the world began. But now, once for all time, he has appeared at the end of the age* to remove sin by his own death as a sacrifice.

²⁷And just as each person is destined to die once and after that comes judgment, ²⁸so also Christ died once for all time as a sacrifice to take away the sins of many people. He will come again, not to deal with our sins, but to bring salvation to all who are eagerly waiting for him.

CHAPTER 10

Christ's Sacrifice Once for All

The old system under the law of Moses was only a shadow, a dim preview of the good things to come, not the good things themselves. The sacrifices under that system were repeated again and again, year after year, but they were never able to provide perfect cleansing for those who came to worship. ²If they could have provided perfect cleansing, the sacrifices would have stopped, for the worshipers would have been purified once for all time, and their feelings of guilt would have disappeared.

³But instead, those sacrifices actually reminded them of their sins year after year. ⁴For it is not possible for the blood of bulls and goats to take away sins. ⁵That is why, when Christ* came into the world, he said to God,

"You did not want animal sacrifices or sin offerings.
　　But you have given me a body to offer.
⁶ You were not pleased with burnt offerings
　　or other offerings for sin.
⁷ Then I said, 'Look, I have come to do your will, O God—
　　as is written about me in the Scriptures.'"*

⁸First, Christ said, "You did not want animal sacrifices or sin offerings or burnt offerings or other offerings for sin, nor were you pleased with them" (though they are required by the law of Moses). ⁹Then he said, "Look, I have come to do your will." He cancels the first covenant in order to put the second into effect. ¹⁰For God's will was for us to be made holy by the sacrifice of the body of Jesus Christ, once for all time.

¹¹Under the old covenant, the priest stands and ministers before the altar day after day, offering the same sacrifices again and again, which can never take away sins. ¹²But our High Priest offered himself to God as a single sacrifice for sins, good for all time. Then he sat down in the place

9:16a Or *covenant;* also in 9:17.　9:16b Or *Now when someone makes a covenant, it is necessary to ratify it with the death of a sacrifice.*　9:19 Some manuscripts do not include *and goats.*　9:20 Exod 24:8.　9:26 Greek *the ages.*　10:5 Greek *he;* also in 10:8.　10:5-7 Ps 40:6-8 (Greek version).

of honor at God's right hand. ¹³There he waits until his enemies are humbled and made a footstool under his feet. ¹⁴For by that one offering he forever made perfect those who are being made holy.

¹⁵And the Holy Spirit also testifies that this is so. For he says,

¹⁶ "This is the new covenant I will make
    with my people on that day,* says the LORD:
I will put my laws in their hearts,
    and I will write them on their minds."*

¹⁷Then he says,

"I will never again remember
    their sins and lawless deeds."*

¹⁸And when sins have been forgiven, there is no need to offer any more sacrifices.

A Call to Persevere

¹⁹And so, dear brothers and sisters,* we can boldly enter heaven's Most Holy Place because of the blood of Jesus. ²⁰By his death,* Jesus opened a new and life-giving way through the curtain into the Most Holy Place. ²¹And since we have a great High Priest who rules over God's house, ²²let us go right into the presence of God with sincere hearts fully trusting him. For our guilty consciences have been sprinkled with Christ's blood to make us clean, and our bodies have been washed with pure water.

²³Let us hold tightly without wavering to the hope we affirm, for God can be trusted to keep his promise. ²⁴Let us think of ways to motivate one another to acts of love and good works. ²⁵And let us not neglect our meeting together, as some people do, but encourage one another, especially now that the day of his return is drawing near.

²⁶Dear friends, if we deliberately continue sinning after we have received knowledge of the truth, there is no longer any sacrifice that will cover these sins. ²⁷There is only the terrible expectation of God's judgment and the raging fire that will consume his enemies. ²⁸For anyone who refused to obey the law of Moses was put to death without mercy on the testimony of two or three witnesses. ²⁹Just think how much worse the punishment will be for those who have trampled on the Son of God, and have treated the blood of the covenant, which made us holy, as if it were common and unholy, and have insulted and disdained the Holy Spirit who brings God's mercy to us. ³⁰For we know the one who said,

"I will take revenge.
    I will pay them back."*

He also said,

"The LORD will judge his own people."*

³¹It is a terrible thing to fall into the hands of the living God.

³²Think back on those early days when you first learned about Christ.* Remember how you remained faithful even though it meant terrible suffering. ³³Sometimes you were exposed to public ridicule and were beaten, and sometimes you helped others who were suffering the same things. ³⁴You suffered along with those who were thrown into jail, and when all you owned was taken from you, you accepted it with joy. You knew there were better things waiting for you that will last forever.

³⁵So do not throw away this confident trust in the Lord. Remember the great reward it brings you! ³⁶Patient endurance is what you need now, so that you will continue to do God's will. Then you will receive all that he has promised.

³⁷ "For in just a little while,
    the Coming One will come and not delay.

10:16a Greek *after those days.*   **10:16b** Jer 31:33a.   **10:17** Jer 31:34b.   **10:19** Greek *brothers.*   **10:20** Greek *Through his flesh.*   **10:30a** Deut 32:35.   **10:30b** Deut 32:36.   **10:32** Greek *when you were first enlightened.*

38 And my righteous ones will live by faith.*
    But I will take no pleasure in anyone who turns
        away."*

39But we are not like those who turn away from God to their own destruction. We are the faithful ones, whose souls will be saved.

CHAPTER 11

Great Examples of Faith

Faith is the confidence that what we hope for will actually happen; it gives us assurance about things we cannot see. 2Through their faith, the people in days of old earned a good reputation.

3By faith we understand that the entire universe was formed at God's command, that what we now see did not come from anything that can be seen.

4It was by faith that Abel brought a more acceptable offering to God than Cain did. Abel's offering gave evidence that he was a righteous man, and God showed his approval of his gifts. Although Abel is long dead, he still speaks to us by his example of faith.

5It was by faith that Enoch was taken up to heaven without dying—"he disappeared, because God took him."* For before he was taken up, he was known as a person who pleased God. 6And it is impossible to please God without faith. Anyone who wants to come to him must believe that God exists and that he rewards those who sincerely seek him.

7It was by faith that Noah built a large boat to save his family from the flood. He obeyed God, who warned him about things that had never happened before. By his faith Noah condemned the rest of the world, and he received the righteousness that comes by faith.

8It was by faith that Abraham obeyed when God called him to leave home and go to another land that God would give him as his inheritance. He went without knowing where he was going. 9And even when he reached the land God promised him, he lived there by faith—for he was like a foreigner, living in tents. And so did Isaac and Jacob, who inherited the same promise. 10Abraham was confidently looking forward to a city with eternal foundations, a city designed and built by God.

11It was by faith that even Sarah was able to have a child, though she was barren and was too old. She believed* that God would keep his promise. 12And so a whole nation came from this one man who was as good as dead—a nation with so many people that, like the stars in the sky and the sand on the seashore, there is no way to count them.

13All these people died still believing what God had promised them. They did not receive what was promised, but they saw it all from a distance and welcomed it. They agreed that they were foreigners and nomads here on earth. 14Obviously people who say such things are looking forward to a country they can call their own. 15If they had longed for the country they came from, they could have gone back. 16But they were looking for a better place, a heavenly homeland. That is why God is not ashamed to be called their God, for he has prepared a city for them.

17It was by faith that Abraham offered Isaac as a sacrifice when God was testing him. Abraham, who had received God's promises, was ready to sacrifice his only son, Isaac, 18even though God had told him, "Isaac is the son through whom your descendants will be counted."* 19Abraham reasoned that if Isaac died, God was able to bring him back to life again. And in a sense, Abraham did receive his son back from the dead.

20It was by faith that Isaac promised blessings for the future to his sons, Jacob and Esau.

21It was by faith that Jacob, when he was old and dying, blessed each of Joseph's sons and bowed in worship as he leaned on his staff.

10:38 Or *my righteous ones will live by their faithfulness;* Greek reads *my righteous one will live by faith.*   **10:37-38** Hab 2:3-4.   **11:5** Gen 5:24.   **11:11** Or *It was by faith that he [Abraham] was able to have a child, even though Sarah was barren and he was too old. He believed.*   **11:18** Gen 21:12.

²²It was by faith that Joseph, when he was about to die, said confidently that the people of Israel would leave Egypt. He even commanded them to take his bones with them when they left.

²³It was by faith that Moses' parents hid him for three months when he was born. They saw that God had given them an unusual child, and they were not afraid to disobey the king's command.

²⁴It was by faith that Moses, when he grew up, refused to be called the son of Pharaoh's daughter. ²⁵He chose to share the oppression of God's people instead of enjoying the fleeting pleasures of sin. ²⁶He thought it was better to suffer for the sake of Christ than to own the treasures of Egypt, for he was looking ahead to his great reward. ²⁷It was by faith that Moses left the land of Egypt, not fearing the king's anger. He kept right on going because he kept his eyes on the one who is invisible. ²⁸It was by faith that Moses commanded the people of Israel to keep the Passover and to sprinkle blood on the doorposts so that the angel of death would not kill their firstborn sons.

²⁹It was by faith that the people of Israel went right through the Red Sea as though they were on dry ground. But when the Egyptians tried to follow, they were all drowned.

³⁰It was by faith that the people of Israel marched around Jericho for seven days, and the walls came crashing down.

³¹It was by faith that Rahab the prostitute was not destroyed with the people in her city who refused to obey God. For she had given a friendly welcome to the spies.

³²How much more do I need to say? It would take too long to recount the stories of the faith of Gideon, Barak, Samson, Jephthah, David, Samuel, and all the prophets. ³³By faith these people overthrew kingdoms, ruled with justice, and received what God had promised them. They shut the mouths of lions, ³⁴quenched the flames of fire, and escaped death by the edge of the sword. Their weakness was turned to strength. They became strong in battle and put whole armies to flight. ³⁵Women received their loved ones back again from death.

But others were tortured, refusing to turn from God in order to be set free. They placed their hope in a better life after the resurrection. ³⁶Some were jeered at, and their backs were cut open with whips. Others were chained in prisons. ³⁷Some died by stoning, some were sawed in half,* and others were killed with the sword. Some went about wearing skins of sheep and goats, destitute and oppressed and mistreated. ³⁸They were too good for this world, wandering over deserts and mountains, hiding in caves and holes in the ground.

³⁹All these people earned a good reputation because of their faith, yet none of them received all that God had promised. ⁴⁰For God had something better in mind for us, so that they would not reach perfection without us.

CHAPTER 12

God's Discipline Proves His Love

Therefore, since we are surrounded by such a huge crowd of witnesses to the life of faith, let us strip off every weight that slows us down, especially the sin that so easily trips us up. And let us run with endurance the race God has set before us. ²We do this by keeping our eyes on Jesus, the champion who initiates and perfects our faith.* Because of the joy* awaiting him, he endured the cross, disregarding its shame. Now he is seated in the place of honor beside God's throne. ³Think of all the hostility he endured from sinful people;* then you won't become weary and give up. ⁴After all, you have not yet given your lives in your struggle against sin.

⁵And have you forgotten the encouraging words God spoke to you as his children?* He said,

"My child,* don't make light of the LORD's discipline, and don't give up when he corrects you.

11:37 Some manuscripts add *some were tested.*   12:2a Or *Jesus, the originator and perfecter of our faith.*   12:2b Or *Instead of the joy.*   12:3 Some manuscripts read *Think of how people hurt themselves by opposing him.*   12:5a Greek *sons;* also in 12:7, 8.   12:5b Greek *son;* also in 12:6, 7.

"Because of the joy awaiting him, he endured the cross, disregarding its shame. Now he is seated in the place of honor beside God's throne. Think of all the hostility he endured from sinful people; then you won't become weary and give up. After all, you have not yet given your lives in your struggle against sin" (Hebrews 12:2-4).

Because he knew good was comin' from it, Jesus took a hit on the cross. Now he's sittin' pretty beside God's throne. Remember all the hatin' he took from sinful people; then you won't get tired and give up.

⁶For the L<small>ORD</small> disciplines those he loves,
 and he punishes each one he accepts as his child."*

⁷As you endure this divine discipline, remember that God is treating you as his own children. Who ever heard of a child who is never disciplined by its father? ⁸If God doesn't discipline you as he does all of his children, it means that you are illegitimate and are not really his children at all. ⁹Since we respected our earthly fathers who disciplined us, shouldn't we submit even more to the discipline of the Father of our spirits, and live forever?*

¹⁰For our earthly fathers disciplined us for a few years, doing the best they knew how. But God's discipline is always good for us, so that we might share in his holiness. ¹¹No discipline is enjoyable while it is happening—it's painful! But afterward there will be a peaceful harvest of right living for those who are trained in this way.

¹²So take a new grip with your tired hands and strengthen your weak knees. ¹³Mark out a straight path for your feet so that those who are weak and lame will not fall but become strong.

A Call to Listen to God

¹⁴Work at living in peace with everyone, and work at living a holy life, for those who are not holy will not see the Lord. ¹⁵Look after each other so that none of you fails to receive the grace of God. Watch out that no poisonous root of bitterness grows up to trouble you, corrupting many. ¹⁶Make sure that no one is immoral or godless like Esau, who traded his birthright as the firstborn son for a single meal. ¹⁷You know that afterward, when he wanted his father's blessing, he was rejected. It was too late for repentance, even though he begged with bitter tears.

¹⁸You have not come to a physical mountain,* to a place of flaming fire, darkness, gloom, and whirlwind, as the Israelites did at Mount Sinai. ¹⁹For they heard an awesome trumpet blast and a voice so terrible that they begged God to stop speaking. ²⁰They staggered back under God's command: "If even an animal touches the mountain, it must be stoned to death."* ²¹Moses himself was so frightened at the sight that he said, "I am terrified and trembling."*

²²No, you have come to Mount Zion, to the city of the living God, the heavenly Jerusalem, and to countless thousands of angels in a joyful gathering. ²³You have come to the assembly of God's firstborn children, whose names are written in heaven. You have come to God himself, who is the judge over all things. You have come to the spirits of the righteous ones in heaven who have now been made perfect. ²⁴You have come to Jesus, the one who mediates the new covenant between God and people, and to the sprinkled blood, which speaks of forgiveness instead of crying out for vengeance like the blood of Abel.

²⁵Be careful that you do not refuse to listen to the One who is speaking. For if the people of Israel did not escape when they refused to listen to Moses, the earthly messenger, we will certainly not escape if we reject the One who speaks to us from heaven! ²⁶When God spoke from Mount Sinai his voice shook the earth, but now he makes another promise: "Once again I will shake not only the earth but the heavens also."* ²⁷This means that all of creation will be shaken and removed, so that only unshakable things will remain.

²⁸Since we are receiving a Kingdom that is unshakable, let us be thankful and please God by worshiping him with holy fear and awe. ²⁹For our God is a devouring fire.

CHAPTER 13

Concluding Words

Keep on loving each other as brothers and sisters.* ²Don't forget to show hospitality to strangers, for some who have done this have entertained angels without realizing it! ³Remember those in prison, as if you were there yourself. Re-

"Don't love money; be satisfied with what you have. For God has said, 'I will never fail you. I will never abandon you'" (Hebrews 13:5).

Don't chase money; be satisfied with what you have. God said, "I will always protect you; I will always be with you."

12:5-6 Prov 3:11-12 (Greek version).   **12:9** Or *and really live?*   **12:18** Greek *to something that can be touched.*   **12:20** Exod 19:13.   **12:21** Deut 9:19.   **12:26** Hag 2:6.   **13:1** Greek *Continue in brotherly love.*

member also those being mistreated, as if you felt their pain in your own bodies.

⁴Give honor to marriage, and remain faithful to one another in marriage. God will surely judge people who are immoral and those who commit adultery.

⁵Don't love money; be satisfied with what you have. For God has said,

"I will never fail you.
    I will never abandon you."*

⁶So we can say with confidence,

"The LORD is my helper,
    so I will have no fear.
What can mere people do to me?"*

⁷Remember your leaders who taught you the word of God. Think of all the good that has come from their lives, and follow the example of their faith.

⁸Jesus Christ is the same yesterday, today, and forever. ⁹So do not be attracted by strange, new ideas. Your strength comes from God's grace, not from rules about food, which don't help those who follow them.

¹⁰We have an altar from which the priests in the Tabernacle* have no right to eat. ¹¹Under the old system, the high priest brought the blood of animals into the Holy Place as a sacrifice for sin, and the bodies of the animals were burned outside the camp. ¹²So also Jesus suffered and died outside the city gates to make his people holy by means of his own blood. ¹³So let us go out to him, outside the camp, and bear the disgrace he bore. ¹⁴For this world is not our permanent home; we are looking forward to a home yet to come.

¹⁵Therefore, let us offer through Jesus a continual sacrifice of praise to God, proclaiming our allegiance to his name. ¹⁶And don't forget to do good and to share with those in need. These are the sacrifices that please God.

¹⁷Obey your spiritual leaders, and do what they say. Their work is to watch over your souls, and they are accountable to God. Give them reason to do this with joy and not with sorrow. That would certainly not be for your benefit.

¹⁸Pray for us, for our conscience is clear and we want to live honorably in everything we do. ¹⁹And especially pray that I will be able to come back to you soon.

²⁰ Now may the God of peace—
    who brought up from the dead our Lord Jesus,
the great Shepherd of the sheep,
    and ratified an eternal covenant with
        his blood—
²¹ may he equip you with all you need
    for doing his will.
May he produce in you,*
    through the power of Jesus Christ,
every good thing that is pleasing to him.
    All glory to him forever and ever! Amen.

²²I urge you, dear brothers and sisters,* to pay attention to what I have written in this brief exhortation.

²³I want you to know that our brother Timothy has been released from jail. If he comes here soon, I will bring him with me to see you.

²⁴Greet all your leaders and all the believers there.* The believers from Italy send you their greetings.

²⁵May God's grace be with you all.

13:5 Deut 31:6, 8.   13:6 Ps 118:6.   13:10 Or *tent*.   13:21 Some manuscripts read *in us*.   13:22 Greek *brothers*.   13:24 Greek *all of God's holy people*.

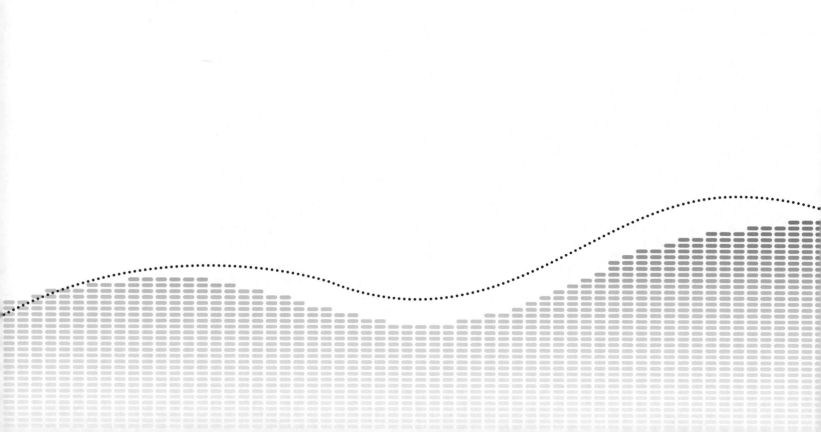

FROM ITS OPENING WORDS to its last, James's letter challenges believers to look at themselves in the mirror and to operate with a sense of integrity in thought, speech, and action. The book of James is believed to be the oldest of the New Testament writings. It was written by James, the half brother of Jesus. While the apostle Paul's writings primarily addressed a Gentile audience and focused on what Christians should believe, James chose to encourage his fellow Jewish brothers and sisters on how they should behave.

James drops little bits of wisdom throughout this small book of five short chapters, but these tidbits—when applied fully to your life—can help you grow into a mature Christian by reinforcing the fact that there is a connection between what you believe and how you should act.

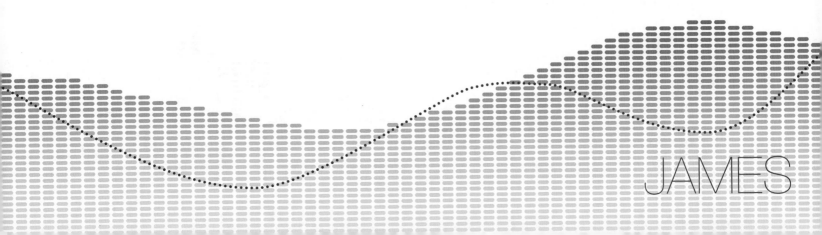

JAMES

CHAPTER 1

Greetings from James

This letter is from James, a slave of God and of the Lord Jesus Christ.

I am writing to the "twelve tribes"—Jewish believers scattered abroad.

Greetings!

Faith and Endurance

²Dear brothers and sisters,* when troubles come your way, consider it an opportunity for great joy. ³For you know that when your faith is tested, your endurance has a chance to grow. ⁴So let it grow, for when your endurance is fully developed, you will be perfect and complete, needing nothing.

⁵If you need wisdom, ask our generous God, and he will give it to you. He will not rebuke you for asking. ⁶But when you ask him, be sure that your faith is in God alone. Do not waver, for a person with divided loyalty is as unsettled as a wave of the sea that is blown and tossed by the wind. ⁷Such people should not expect to receive anything from the Lord. ⁸Their loyalty is divided between God and the world, and they are unstable in everything they do.

⁹Believers who are* poor have something to boast about, for God has honored them. ¹⁰And those who are rich should boast that God has humbled them. They will fade away like a little flower in the field. ¹¹The hot sun rises and the grass withers; the little flower droops and falls, and its beauty fades away. In the same way, the rich will fade away with all of their achievements.

¹²God blesses those who patiently endure testing and temptation. Afterward they will receive the crown of life that God has promised to those who love him. ¹³And remem-

1:2 Greek *brothers;* also in 1:16, 19. 1:9 Greek *The brother who is.*

THE POINT

Do the Word. What influences or motivates you to do the right thing? Is it television, your family, your friends, your man, or your girl? James says that God's Word should be the guiding force in your life, not pop culture. Unfortunately, that's easier said than done. It's a known fact that most people emulate what they see. Unfortunately, what a lot of people see portrayed on television, in their homes, or within their families is wack because

the images are mostly of sex, violence, and wrongdoing.

James tells us, however, that we should emulate Christ by followin' what the Bible tells us to do. According to James, it's not enough to "just listen to God's word. You must do what it says. Otherwise, you are only fooling yourselves" (James 1:22).

The point is, there is a big difference between

knowin' what's right and actin' on it. You've gotta do it—no fakin', no frontin'! Even God did not simply announce his love for humanity; he demonstrated it by sacrificing his only Son, Jesus, to die on the cross to pay for our sins. Likewise, it is simply not enough to say you're a Christian; you have to live the life. If you believe what the Bible teaches, allow the Word to transform your behavior in visible ways.

POWERCHOICES

LIVIN' FAITHFULLY IS NOT AN OCCASIONAL ACTIVITY, BUT A COMMITTED LIFESTYLE. IT'S LIKE BEIN' TRUE TO YOUR GIRL OR YOUR GUY. YOUR CHARACTER SHOULD MATCH YOUR CLAIM. THAT IS NOT TO SAY THAT YOU HAVE TO WALK AROUND BEIN' ALL "HOLIER THAN THOU" OR JUDGMENTAL; STILL, THERE SHOULD BE SOME OUTWARD SIGN OF YOUR FAITH. ¶ *WHAT GOOD IS IT, DEAR BROTHERS AND SISTERS, IF YOU SAY YOU HAVE FAITH BUT DON'T SHOW IT BY YOUR ACTIONS? CAN THAT KIND OF FAITH SAVE ANYONE? . . . SO YOU SEE, FAITH BY ITSELF ISN'T ENOUGH. UNLESS IT PRODUCES GOOD DEEDS, IT IS DEAD AND USELESS.* (JAMES 2:14, 17) ¶ DON'T MAKE THE MISTAKE OF THINKING, LIKE SOME PEOPLE, THAT AS LONG AS YOU HAVE FAITH IN GOD IT DOESN'T MATTER HOW YOU ACT. IT DOES.

---

ber, when you are being tempted, do not say, "God is tempting me." God is never tempted to do wrong,* and he never tempts anyone else. ¹⁴Temptation comes from our own desires, which entice us and drag us away. ¹⁵These desires give birth to sinful actions. And when sin is allowed to grow, it gives birth to death.

¹⁶So don't be misled, my dear brothers and sisters. ¹⁷Whatever is good and perfect comes down to us from God our Father, who created all the lights in the heavens.* He never changes or casts a shifting shadow.* ¹⁸He chose to give birth to us by giving us his true word. And we, out of all creation, became his prized possession.*

Listening and Doing

¹⁹Understand this, my dear brothers and sisters: You must all be quick to listen, slow to speak, and slow to get angry. ²⁰Human anger* does not produce the righteousness* God

desires. ²¹So get rid of all the filth and evil in your lives, and humbly accept the word God has planted in your hearts, for it has the power to save your souls.

²²But don't just listen to God's word. You must do what it says. Otherwise, you are only fooling yourselves. ²³For if you listen to the word and don't obey, it is like glancing at your face in a mirror. ²⁴You see yourself, walk away, and forget what you look like. ²⁵But if you look carefully into the perfect law that sets you free, and if you do what it says and don't forget what you heard, then God will bless you for doing it.

²⁶If you claim to be religious but don't control your tongue, you are fooling yourself, and your religion is worthless. ²⁷Pure and genuine religion in the sight of God the Father means caring for orphans and widows in their distress and refusing to let the world corrupt you.

CHAPTER 2

A Warning against Prejudice

My dear brothers and sisters,* how can you claim to have faith in our glorious Lord Jesus Christ if you favor some people over others?

²For example, suppose someone comes into your meeting* dressed in fancy clothes and expensive jewelry, and another comes in who is poor and dressed in dirty clothes. ³If you give special attention and a good seat to the rich person, but you say to the poor one, "You can stand over there, or else sit on the floor"—well, ⁴doesn't this discrimination show that your judgments are guided by evil motives?

⁵Listen to me, dear brothers and sisters. Hasn't God chosen the poor in this world to be rich in faith? Aren't they the ones who will inherit the Kingdom he promised to those who love him? ⁶But you dishonor the poor! Isn't it the rich who oppress you and drag you into court? ⁷Aren't they the ones who slander Jesus Christ, whose noble name* you bear?

1:13 Or *God should not be put to a test by evil people.*   **1:17a** Greek *from above, from the Father of lights.*   **1:17b** Some manuscripts read *He never changes, as a shifting shadow does.*   **1:18** Greek *we became a kind of firstfruit of his creatures.*   **1:20a** Greek *A man's anger.*   **1:20b** Or *the justice.*   **2:1** Greek *brothers;* also in 2:5, 14.   **2:2** Greek *your synagogue.*   **2:7** Greek *slander the noble name.*

⁸Yes indeed, it is good when you obey the royal law as found in the Scriptures: "Love your neighbor as yourself."* ⁹But if you favor some people over others, you are committing a sin. You are guilty of breaking the law.

¹⁰For the person who keeps all of the laws except one is as guilty as a person who has broken all of God's laws. ¹¹For the same God who said, "You must not commit adultery," also said, "You must not murder."* So if you murder someone but do not commit adultery, you have still broken the law.

¹²So whatever you say or whatever you do, remember that you will be judged by the law that sets you free. ¹³There will be no mercy for those who have not shown mercy to others. But if you have been merciful, God will be merciful when he judges you.

Faith without Good Deeds Is Dead

¹⁴What good is it, dear brothers and sisters, if you say you have faith but don't show it by your actions? Can that kind of faith save anyone? ¹⁵Suppose you see a brother or sister who has no food or clothing, ¹⁶and you say, "Good-bye and have a good day; stay warm and eat well"—but then you don't give that person any food or clothing. What good does that do?

¹⁷So you see, faith by itself isn't enough. Unless it produces good deeds, it is dead and useless.

¹⁸Now someone may argue, "Some people have faith; others have good deeds." But I say, "How can you show me your faith if you don't have good deeds? I will show you my faith by my good deeds."

¹⁹You say you have faith, for you believe that there is one God.* Good for you! Even the demons believe this, and they tremble in terror. ²⁰How foolish! Can't you see that faith without good deeds is useless?

²¹Don't you remember that our ancestor Abraham was shown to be right with God by his actions when he offered his son Isaac on the altar? ²²You see, his faith and his actions worked together. His actions made his faith complete. ²³And

so it happened just as the Scriptures say: "Abraham believed God, and God counted him as righteous because of his faith."* He was even called the friend of God.* ²⁴So you see, we are shown to be right with God by what we do, not by faith alone.

²⁵Rahab the prostitute is another example. She was shown to be right with God by her actions when she hid those messengers and sent them safely away by a different road. ²⁶Just as the body is dead without breath,* so also faith is dead without good works.

CHAPTER 3

Controlling the Tongue

Dear brothers and sisters,* not many of you should become teachers in the church, for we who teach will be judged more strictly. ²Indeed, we all make many mistakes. For if we could control our tongues, we would be perfect and could also control ourselves in every other way.

³We can make a large horse go wherever we want by means of a small bit in its mouth. ⁴And a small rudder makes a huge ship turn wherever the pilot chooses to go, even though the winds are strong. ⁵In the same way, the tongue is a small thing that makes grand speeches.

But a tiny spark can set a great forest on fire. ⁶And the tongue is a flame of fire. It is a whole world of wickedness, corrupting your entire body. It can set your whole life on fire, for it is set on fire by hell itself.*

⁷People can tame all kinds of animals, birds, reptiles, and fish, ⁸but no one can tame the tongue. It is restless and evil, full of deadly poison. ⁹Sometimes it praises our Lord and Father, and sometimes it curses those who have been made in the image of God. ¹⁰And so blessing and cursing come pouring out of the same mouth. Surely, my brothers and sisters, this is not right! ¹¹Does a spring of water bubble out with both fresh water and bitter water? ¹²Does a fig tree produce olives, or a grapevine produce figs? No, and you can't draw fresh water from a salty spring.*

2:8 Lev 19:18.   2:11 Exod 20:13-14; Deut 5:17-18.   2:19 Some manuscripts read *that God is one;* see Deut 6:4.   2:23a Gen 15:6.   2:23b See Isa 41:8.   2:26 Or *without spirit.*   3:1 Greek *brothers;* also in 3:10.   3:6 Or *for it will burn in hell* (Greek *Gehenna*).   3:12 Greek *from salt.*

keeping your swagger strong

BIBLICAL PRINCIPLES FOR SUCCESS AND LEADERSHIP

What distinguishes counterfeit faith from the real thing? Real faith, says James, once put into action, will produce righteous and tangible behavior. On the other hand, counterfeit faith will only lead to self-deception and the false belief that you're all that.

So, how are ya livin'? Does anyone besides you know you're a Christian? Is it apparent in the way you act, the way you talk, the way you treat others, the way you conduct your affairs? Are you a "doer," or are you frontin'?

True Wisdom Comes from God

13If you are wise and understand God's ways, prove it by living an honorable life, doing good works with the humility that comes from wisdom. 14But if you are bitterly jealous and there is selfish ambition in your heart, don't cover up the truth with boasting and lying. 15For jealousy and selfishness are not God's kind of wisdom. Such things are earthly, unspiritual, and demonic. 16For wherever there is jealousy and selfish ambition, there you will find disorder and evil of every kind.

17But the wisdom from above is first of all pure. It is also peace loving, gentle at all times, and willing to yield to others. It is full of mercy and good deeds. It shows no favoritism and is always sincere. 18And those who are peacemakers will plant seeds of peace and reap a harvest of righteousness.*

CHAPTER 4

Drawing Close to God

What is causing the quarrels and fights among you? Don't they come from the evil desires at war within you? 2You want what you don't have, so you scheme and kill to get it. You are jealous of what others have, but you can't get it, so you fight and wage war to take it away from them. Yet you don't have what you want because you don't ask God for it. 3And even when you ask, you don't get it because your motives are all wrong—you want only what will give you pleasure.

4You adulterers!* Don't you realize that friendship with the world makes you an enemy of God? I say it again: If you want to be a friend of the world, you make yourself an enemy of God. 5What do you think the Scriptures mean when they say that the spirit God has placed within us is filled with envy?* 6But he gives us even more grace to stand against such evil desires. As the Scriptures say,

"God opposes the proud
   but favors the humble."*

7So humble yourselves before God. Resist the devil, and he will flee from you. 8Come close to God, and God will come close to you. Wash your hands, you sinners; purify your hearts, for your loyalty is divided between God and the world. 9Let there be tears for what you have done. Let there be sorrow and deep grief. Let there be sadness instead of laughter, and gloom instead of joy. 10Humble yourselves before the Lord, and he will lift you up in honor.

Warning against Judging Others

11Don't speak evil against each other, dear brothers and sisters.* If you criticize and judge each other, then you are criticizing and judging God's law. But your job is to obey the law, not to judge whether it applies to you. 12God alone, who gave the law, is the Judge. He alone has the power to save or to destroy. So what right do you have to judge your neighbor?

Warning about Self-Confidence

13Look here, you who say, "Today or tomorrow we are going to a certain town and will stay there a year. We will do

3:18 Or *of good things*, or *of justice*.   4:4 Greek *You adulteresses!*   4:5 Or *that God longs jealously for the human spirit he has placed within us?* or *that the Holy Spirit, whom God has placed within us, opposes our envy?*   4:6 Prov 3:34 (Greek version).   4:11 Greek *brothers.*

business there and make a profit." ¹⁴How do you know what your life will be like tomorrow? Your life is like the morning fog—it's here a little while, then it's gone. ¹⁵What you ought to say is, "If the Lord wants us to, we will live and do this or that." ¹⁶Otherwise you are boasting about your own plans, and all such boasting is evil.

¹⁷Remember, it is sin to know what you ought to do and then not do it.

CHAPTER 5

Warning to the Rich

Look here, you rich people: Weep and groan with anguish because of all the terrible troubles ahead of you. ²Your wealth is rotting away, and your fine clothes are moth-eaten rags. ³Your gold and silver have become worthless. The very wealth you were counting on will eat away your flesh like fire. This treasure you have accumulated will stand as evidence against you on the day of judgment. ⁴For listen! Hear the cries of the field workers whom you have cheated of their pay. The wages you held back cry out against you. The cries of those who harvest your fields have reached the ears of the LORD of Heaven's Armies.

⁵You have spent your years on earth in luxury, satisfying your every desire. You have fattened yourselves for the day of slaughter. ⁶You have condemned and killed innocent people,* who do not resist you.*

Patience and Endurance

⁷Dear brothers and sisters,* be patient as you wait for the Lord's return. Consider the farmers who patiently wait for the rains in the fall and in the spring. They eagerly look for the valuable harvest to ripen. ⁸You, too, must be patient. Take courage, for the coming of the Lord is near.

⁹Don't grumble about each other, brothers and sisters, or you will be judged. For look—the Judge is standing at the door!

¹⁰For examples of patience in suffering, dear brothers and sisters, look at the prophets who spoke in the name of the Lord. ¹¹We give great honor to those who endure under suffering. For instance, you know about Job, a man of great endurance. You can see how the Lord was kind to him at the end, for the Lord is full of tenderness and mercy.

¹²But most of all, my brothers and sisters, never take an oath, by heaven or earth or anything else. Just say a simple yes or no, so that you will not sin and be condemned.

The Power of Prayer

¹³Are any of you suffering hardships? You should pray. Are any of you happy? You should sing praises. ¹⁴Are any of you sick? You should call for the elders of the church to come and pray over you, anointing you with oil in the name of the Lord. ¹⁵Such a prayer offered in faith will heal the sick, and the Lord will make you well. And if you have committed any sins, you will be forgiven.

¹⁶Confess your sins to each other and pray for each other so that you may be healed. The earnest prayer of a righteous person has great power and produces wonderful results. ¹⁷Elijah was as human as we are, and yet when he prayed earnestly that no rain would fall, none fell for three and a half years! ¹⁸Then, when he prayed again, the sky sent down rain and the earth began to yield its crops.

Restore Wandering Believers

¹⁹My dear brothers and sisters, if someone among you wanders away from the truth and is brought back, ²⁰you can be sure that whoever brings the sinner back will save that person from death and bring about the forgiveness of many sins.

5:6a Or *killed the Righteous One.*   5:6b Or *Don't they resist you?* or *Doesn't God oppose you?* or *Aren't they now accusing you before God?*   5:7 Greek *brothers;* also in 5:9, 10, 12, 19.

PETER WAS A THUG—a straight gangsta—throw down first, talk later. He was quick to defend those he loved. Besides the apostle Paul and Jesus himself, many view Peter as one of the most prominent peeps in the early church. It was Peter who walked on water, Peter who preached to the masses in Jerusalem on the day of Pentecost, Peter who proclaimed that Jesus was the Son of God, and Peter who cut off that cat's ear in Jesus' defense.

Peter knew what it meant to suffer persecution. He was beaten, threatened, and even thrown in jail for his faith, but he stood strong. He wrote his first letter to Jewish believers to comfort and encourage them to endure the persecution they would suffer for following Christ.

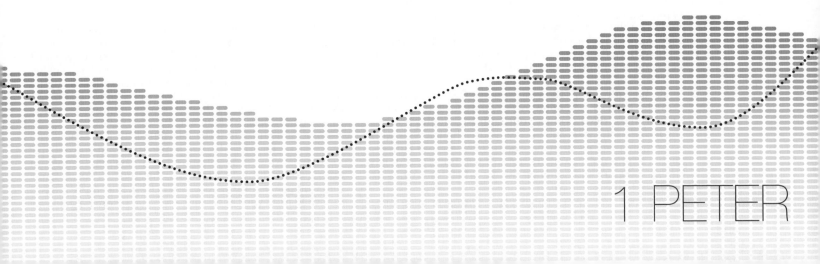

1 PETER

CHAPTER 1

Greetings from Peter

This letter is from Peter, an apostle of Jesus Christ.

I am writing to God's chosen people who are living as foreigners in the provinces of Pontus, Galatia, Cappadocia, Asia, and Bithynia.* ²God the Father knew you and chose you long ago, and his Spirit has made you holy. As a result, you have obeyed him and have been cleansed by the blood of Jesus Christ.

May God give you more and more grace and peace.

The Hope of Eternal Life

³All praise to God, the Father of our Lord Jesus Christ. It is by his great mercy that we have been born again, because God raised Jesus Christ from the dead. Now we live with great expectation, ⁴and we have a priceless inheritance—an inheritance that is kept in heaven for you, pure and undefiled, beyond the reach of change and decay. ⁵And through your faith, God is protecting you by his power until you receive this salvation, which is ready to be revealed on the last day for all to see.

⁶So be truly glad.* There is wonderful joy ahead, even though you have to endure many trials for a little while. ⁷These trials will show that your faith is genuine. It is being tested as fire tests and purifies gold—though your faith is far more precious than mere gold. So when your faith remains strong through many trials, it will bring you much praise and glory and honor on the day when Jesus Christ is revealed to the whole world.

⁸You love him even though you have never seen him.

Though you do not see him now, you trust him; and you rejoice with a glorious, inexpressible joy. ⁹The reward for trusting him will be the salvation of your souls.

¹⁰This salvation was something even the prophets wanted to know more about when they prophesied about this gracious salvation prepared for you. ¹¹They wondered what time or situation the Spirit of Christ within them was talking about when he told them in advance about Christ's suffering and his great glory afterward.

¹²They were told that their messages were not for themselves, but for you. And now this Good News has been announced to you by those who preached in the power of the Holy Spirit sent from heaven. It is all so wonderful that even the angels are eagerly watching these things happen.

A Call to Holy Living

¹³So think clearly and exercise self-control. Look forward to the gracious salvation that will come to you when Jesus Christ is revealed to the world. ¹⁴So you must live as God's obedient children. Don't slip back into your old ways of living to satisfy your own desires. You didn't know any better then. ¹⁵But now you must be holy in everything you do, just as God who chose you is holy. ¹⁶For the Scriptures say, "You must be holy because I am holy."*

¹⁷And remember that the heavenly Father to whom you pray has no favorites. He will judge or reward you according to what you do. So you must live in reverent fear of him during your time as "foreigners in the land." ¹⁸For you know that God paid a ransom to save you from the empty life you inherited from your ancestors. And the ransom he paid was

1:1 *Pontus, Galatia, Cappadocia, Asia,* and *Bithynia* were Roman provinces in what is now Turkey.   1:6 Or *So you are truly glad.*   1:16 Lev 11:44-45; 19:2; 20:7.

not mere gold or silver. ¹⁹It was the precious blood of Christ, the sinless, spotless Lamb of God. ²⁰God chose him as your ransom long before the world began, but he has now revealed him to you in these last days.

²¹Through Christ you have come to trust in God. And you have placed your faith and hope in God because he raised Christ from the dead and gave him great glory.

²²You were cleansed from your sins when you obeyed the truth, so now you must show sincere love to each other as brothers and sisters.* Love each other deeply with all your heart.*

²³For you have been born again, but not to a life that will quickly end. Your new life will last forever because it comes from the eternal, living word of God. ²⁴As the Scriptures say,

"People are like grass;
    their beauty is like a flower in the field.
The grass withers and the flower fades.
25   But the word of the Lord remains forever."*

And that word is the Good News that was preached to you.

CHAPTER 2

So get rid of all evil behavior. Be done with all deceit, hypocrisy, jealousy, and all unkind speech. ²Like newborn babies, you must crave pure spiritual milk so that you will grow into a full experience of salvation. Cry out for this nourishment, ³now that you have had a taste of the Lord's kindness.

Living Stones for God's House

⁴You are coming to Christ, who is the living cornerstone of God's temple. He was rejected by people, but he was chosen by God for great honor.

⁵And you are living stones that God is building into his spiritual temple. What's more, you are his holy priests.* Through the mediation of Jesus Christ, you offer spiritual sacrifices that please God. ⁶As the Scriptures say,

"I am placing a cornerstone in Jerusalem,*
    chosen for great honor,
and anyone who trusts in him
    will never be disgraced."*

1:22a Greek *must have brotherly love.*   **1:22b** Some manuscripts read *with a pure heart.*   **1:24-25** Isa 40:6-8.   **2:5** Greek *holy priesthood.*   **2:6a** Greek *in Zion.*   **2:6b** Isa 28:16 (Greek version).

THE POINT

Followin' is hard. Ever had a really bad day? Week? Month? How about a bad year? Have you ever wondered, why is everyone hatin' on me? What's the point of bein' a Christian if my life is hell? At some point we all have to suffer for what we believe in. You know, your man left you because you weren't ready to have sex. Or you fell out with yo' friends because you didn't want to get high or drink. You're the good guy, the sensitive brotha, the one all the girls trust—and the fellas think you're gay. You're the girl who said no to sex—and now all the other girls think you're a stuck-up diva. Well,

Peter says that reaction is normal—don't sweat it. That type of treatment (persecution) comes along with strivin' to live for Christ.

These trials will show that your faith is genuine. It is being tested as fire tests and purifies gold—though your faith is far more precious than mere gold. So when your faith remains strong through many trials, it will bring you much praise and glory and honor on the day when Jesus Christ is revealed to the whole world. (1 Peter 1:7)

During his walk with Jesus, Peter experienced both success and failure, just like we do. He suffered not because of something he had done, but because he was tryin' to follow Christ. Fact is, it's simply easier to hate on someone than it is to show love, understanding, or compassion. Not everyone is going to roll wit you, and that's okay. The bottom line is you have to answer to God and not other people. So, is it okay to suffer sometimes? Yes. Jesus suffered, Peter suffered, and so will you. But keep it real, keep it right, and know that God is in control.

[7]Yes, you who trust him recognize the honor God has given him. But for those who reject him,

> "The stone that the builders rejected
> has now become the cornerstone."*

[8]And,

> "He is the stone that makes people stumble,
> the rock that makes them fall."*

They stumble because they do not obey God's word, and so they meet the fate that was planned for them.

[9]But you are not like that, for you are a chosen people. You are royal priests,* a holy nation, God's very own possession. As a result, you can show others the goodness of God, for he called you out of the darkness into his wonderful light.

[10] "Once you had no identity as a people;
> now you are God's people.
> Once you received no mercy;
> now you have received God's mercy."*

[11]Dear friends, I warn you as "temporary residents and foreigners" to keep away from worldly desires that wage war against your very souls. [12]Be careful to live properly among your unbelieving neighbors. Then even if they accuse you of doing wrong, they will see your honorable behavior, and they will give honor to God when he judges the world.*

Respecting People in Authority

[13]For the Lord's sake, respect all human authority—whether the king as head of state, [14]or the officials he has appointed. For the king has sent them to punish those who do wrong and to honor those who do right.

[15]It is God's will that your honorable lives should silence those ignorant people who make foolish accusations against you. [16]For you are free, yet you are God's slaves, so don't use your freedom as an excuse to do evil. [17]Respect everyone, and love your Christian brothers and sisters.* Fear God, and respect the king.

Slaves

[18]You who are slaves must accept the authority of your masters with all respect.* Do what they tell you—not only if they are kind and reasonable, but even if they are cruel. [19]For God is pleased with you when you do what you know is right and patiently endure unfair treatment. [20]Of course, you get no credit for being patient if you are beaten for doing wrong. But if you suffer for doing good and endure it patiently, God is pleased with you.

[21]For God called you to do good, even if it means suffering, just as Christ suffered* for you. He is your example, and you must follow in his steps.

[22] He never sinned,
> nor ever deceived anyone.*
[23] He did not retaliate when he was insulted,
> nor threaten revenge when he suffered.
> He left his case in the hands of God,
> who always judges fairly.
[24] He personally carried our sins
> in his body on the cross
> so that we can be dead to sin
> and live for what is right.
> By his wounds
> you are healed.
[25] Once you were like sheep
> who wandered away.
> But now you have turned to your Shepherd,
> the Guardian of your souls.

flo

"For God called you to do good, even if it means suffering, just as Christ suffered for you. He is your example, and you must follow in his steps" (1 Peter 2:21).

say what?

God wants you to do good even if you suffer for it. Christ suffered for you. He is your role model, so you should follow in his steps.

2:7 Ps 118:22.   2:8 Isa 8:14.   2:9 Greek *a royal priesthood.*   2:10 Hos 1:6, 9; 2:23.   2:12 Or *on the day of visitation.*   2:17 Greek *love the brotherhood.*   2:18 Or *because you fear God.*
2:21 Some manuscripts read *died.*   2:22 Isa 53:9.

keeping your swagger strong

BIBLICAL PRINCIPLES FOR SUCCESS AND LEADERSHIP

Between the ages of 9 and 13 is when children begin to develop socially. For many people, that was not a happy time. Think back to when you were that age. Were you the bully or the one everybody bullied? How important was it for you to be the most popular? Now fast-forward to today. Did bein' part of the popular crew make you a better person? Probably not.

When we are young, we believe that success means bein' part of the "in" crowd. However, as we grow older we realize that bein' popular does not always lead to success. In fact, in most cases it's the unpopular people who become the most successful in life. Peter challenges believers to weigh the cost of our unwillingness to lead lives that are visibly different from those of our family, friends, neighbors, and coworkers.

Are you willin' to pay the price to follow Christ? Are you willin' to be different?

CHAPTER 3

Wives

In the same way, you wives must accept the authority of your husbands. Then, even if some refuse to obey the Good News, your godly lives will speak to them without any words. They will be won over ²by observing your pure and reverent lives.

³Don't be concerned about the outward beauty of fancy hairstyles, expensive jewelry, or beautiful clothes. ⁴You should clothe yourselves instead with the beauty that comes from within, the unfading beauty of a gentle and quiet spirit, which is so precious to God. ⁵This is how the holy women of old made themselves beautiful. They trusted God and accepted the authority of their husbands. ⁶For instance, Sarah obeyed her husband, Abraham, and called him her master. You are her daughters when you do what is right without fear of what your husbands might do.

Husbands

⁷In the same way, you husbands must give honor to your wives. Treat your wife with understanding as you live together. She may be weaker than you are, but she is your equal partner in God's gift of new life. Treat her as you should so your prayers will not be hindered.

All Christians

⁸Finally, all of you should be of one mind. Sympathize with each other. Love each other as brothers and sisters.* Be tenderhearted, and keep a humble attitude. ⁹Don't repay evil for evil. Don't retaliate with insults when people insult you. Instead, pay them back with a blessing. That is what God has called you to do, and he will bless you for it. ¹⁰For the Scriptures say,

> "If you want to enjoy life
>   and see many happy days,
> keep your tongue from speaking evil
>   and your lips from telling lies.
> ¹¹ Turn away from evil and do good.
>   Search for peace, and work to maintain it.
> ¹² The eyes of the Lord watch over those who do right,
>   and his ears are open to their prayers.
> But the Lord turns his face
>   against those who do evil."*

Suffering for Doing Good

¹³Now, who will want to harm you if you are eager to do good? ¹⁴But even if you suffer for doing what is right, God will reward you for it. So don't worry or be afraid of their threats. ¹⁵Instead, you must worship Christ as Lord of your

3:8 Greek *Show brotherly love.*   3:10-12 Ps 34:12-16.

life. And if someone asks about your Christian hope, always be ready to explain it. [16]But do this in a gentle and respectful way.* Keep your conscience clear. Then if people speak against you, they will be ashamed when they see what a good life you live because you belong to Christ. [17]Remember, it is better to suffer for doing good, if that is what God wants, than to suffer for doing wrong!

[18]Christ suffered* for our sins once for all time. He never sinned, but he died for sinners to bring you safely home to God. He suffered physical death, but he was raised to life in the Spirit.*

[19]So he went and preached to the spirits in prison—[20]those who disobeyed God long ago when God waited patiently while Noah was building his boat. Only eight people were saved from drowning in that terrible flood.* [21]And that water is a picture of baptism, which now saves you, not by removing dirt from your body, but as a response to God from* a clean conscience. It is effective because of the resurrection of Jesus Christ.

[22]Now Christ has gone to heaven. He is seated in the place of honor next to God, and all the angels and authorities and powers accept his authority.

CHAPTER 4

Living for God

So then, since Christ suffered physical pain, you must arm yourselves with the same attitude he had, and be ready to suffer, too. For if you have suffered physically for Christ, you have finished with sin.* [2]You won't spend the rest of your lives chasing your own desires, but you will be anxious to do the will of God. [3]You have had enough in the past of the evil things that godless people enjoy—their immorality and lust, their feasting and drunkenness and wild parties, and their terrible worship of idols.

[4]Of course, your former friends are surprised when you no longer plunge into the flood of wild and destructive things they do. So they slander you. [5]But remember that they will have to face God, who will judge everyone, both the living and the dead. [6]That is why the Good News was preached to those who are now dead*—so although they were destined to die like all people,* they now live forever with God in the Spirit.*

[7]The end of the world is coming soon. Therefore, be earnest and disciplined in your prayers. [8]Most important of all, continue to show deep love for each other, for love covers a multitude of sins. [9]Cheerfully share your home with those who need a meal or a place to stay.

[10]God has given each of you a gift from his great variety of spiritual gifts. Use them well to serve one another. [11]Do you have the gift of speaking? Then speak as though God himself were speaking through you. Do you have the gift of helping others? Do it with all the strength and energy that God supplies. Then everything you do will bring glory to God through Jesus Christ. All glory and power to him forever and ever! Amen.

Suffering for Being a Christian

[12]Dear friends, don't be surprised at the fiery trials you are going through, as if something strange were happening to you. [13]Instead, be very glad—for these trials make you partners with Christ in his suffering, so that you will have the wonderful joy of seeing his glory when it is revealed to all the world.

[14]So be happy when you are insulted for being a Christian,* for then the glorious Spirit of God* rests upon you.* [15]If you suffer, however, it must not be for murder, stealing, making trouble, or prying into other people's affairs. [16]But it is no shame to suffer for being a Christian. Praise God for

3:16 Some English translations put this sentence in verse 15.   3:18a Some manuscripts read *died*.   3:18b Or *in spirit*.   3:20 Greek *saved through water*.   3:21 Or *as an appeal to God for*.   4:1 Or *For the one* [or *One*] *who has suffered physically has finished with sin*.   4:6a Greek *preached even to the dead*.   4:6b Or *so although people had judged them worthy of death*.   4:6c Or *in spirit*.   4:14a Greek *for the name of Christ*.   4:14b Or *for the glory of God, which is his Spirit*.   4:14c Some manuscripts add *On their part he is blasphemed, but on your part he is glorified*.

the privilege of being called by his name! [17]For the time has come for judgment, and it must begin with God's household. And if judgment begins with us, what terrible fate awaits those who have never obeyed God's Good News? [18]And also,

"If the righteous are barely saved,
what will happen to godless sinners?"*

[19]So if you are suffering in a manner that pleases God, keep on doing what is right, and trust your lives to the God who created you, for he will never fail you.

CHAPTER 5

Advice for Elders and Young Men

And now, a word to you who are elders in the churches. I, too, am an elder and a witness to the sufferings of Christ. And I, too, will share in his glory when he is revealed to the whole world. As a fellow elder, I appeal to you: [2]Care for the flock that God has entrusted to you. Watch over it willingly, not grudgingly—not for what you will get out of it, but because you are eager to serve God. [3]Don't lord it over the people assigned to your care, but lead them by your own good example. [4]And when the Great Shepherd appears, you will receive a crown of never-ending glory and honor.

[5]In the same way, you younger men must accept the authority of the elders. And all of you, serve each other in humility, for

"God opposes the proud
but favors the humble."*

[6]So humble yourselves under the mighty power of God, and at the right time he will lift you up in honor. [7]Give all your worries and cares to God, for he cares about you.

[8]Stay alert! Watch out for your great enemy, the devil. He prowls around like a roaring lion, looking for someone to devour. [9]Stand firm against him, and be strong in your faith. Remember that your Christian brothers and sisters* all over the world are going through the same kind of suffering you are.

[10]In his kindness God called you to share in his eternal glory by means of Christ Jesus. So after you have suffered a little while, he will restore, support, and strengthen you, and he will place you on a firm foundation. [11]All power to him forever! Amen.

Peter's Final Greetings

[12]I have written and sent this short letter to you with the help of Silas,* whom I commend to you as a faithful brother. My purpose in writing is to encourage you and assure you that what you are experiencing is truly part of God's grace for you. Stand firm in this grace.

[13]Your sister church here in Babylon* sends you greetings, and so does my son Mark. [14]Greet each other with Christian love.*

Peace be with all of you who are in Christ.

4:18 Prov 11:31 (Greek version).   **5:5** Prov 3:34 (Greek version).   **5:9** Greek *your brothers*.   **5:12** Greek *Silvanus*.   **5:13** Greek *The elect one in Babylon*. Babylon was probably symbolic for Rome.   **5:14** Greek *with a kiss of love*.

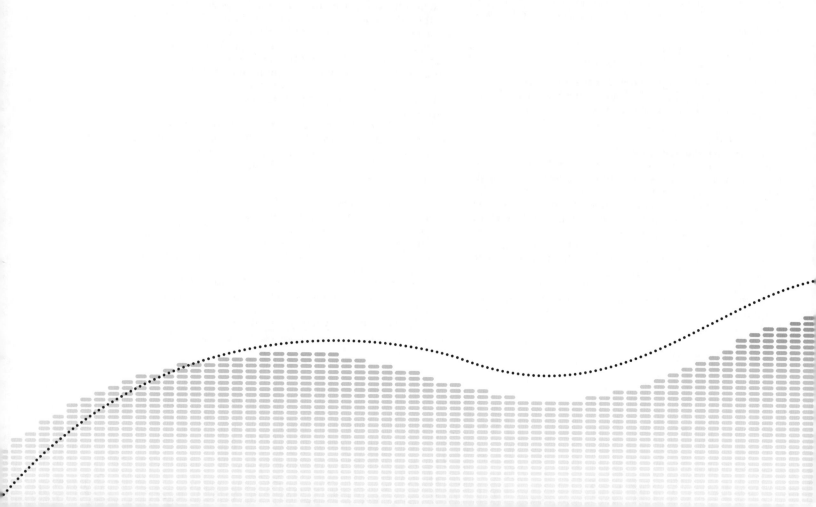

IN HIS SECOND LETTER, Peter continues talkin' about church folk. He warns believers that not everyone in the church is real. It had been three years since Peter wrote his first letter to the believers in Rome, and still false teachers continued to show up. These teachers had no problem makin' up their own ideas about what livin' a godly lifestyle meant, and they wanted everyone to join in on the hatin'. Peter warned believers not to believe everything they heard, but to continue to grow in their faith and get to know God for themselves.

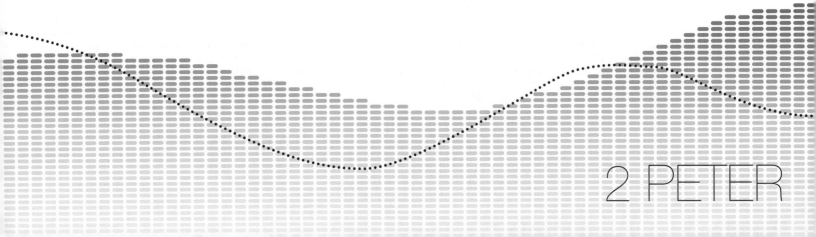

2 PETER

CHAPTER 1

Greetings from Peter

This letter is from Simon* Peter, a slave and apostle of Jesus Christ.

I am writing to you who share the same precious faith we have. This faith was given to you because of the justice and fairness* of Jesus Christ, our God and Savior.

²May God give you more and more grace and peace as you grow in your knowledge of God and Jesus our Lord.

Growing in Faith

³By his divine power, God has given us everything we need for living a godly life. We have received all of this by coming to know him, the one who called us to himself by means of his marvelous glory and excellence. ⁴And because of his glory and excellence, he has given us great and precious promises. These are the promises that enable you to share his divine nature and escape the world's corruption caused by human desires.

⁵In view of all this, make every effort to respond to God's promises. Supplement your faith with a generous provision of moral excellence, and moral excellence with knowledge, ⁶and knowledge with self-control, and self-control with patient endurance, and patient endurance with godliness, ⁷and godliness with brotherly affection, and brotherly affection with love for everyone.

⁸The more you grow like this, the more productive and useful you will be in your knowledge of our Lord Jesus Christ. ⁹But those who fail to develop in this way are shortsighted or blind, forgetting that they have been cleansed from their old sins.

¹⁰So, dear brothers and sisters,* work hard to prove that you really are among those God has called and chosen. Do these things, and you will never fall away. ¹¹Then God will give you a grand entrance into the eternal Kingdom of our Lord and Savior Jesus Christ.

Paying Attention to Scripture

¹²Therefore, I will always remind you about these things— even though you already know them and are standing firm in the truth you have been taught. ¹³And it is only right that I should keep on reminding you as long as I live.* ¹⁴For our Lord Jesus Christ has shown me that I must soon leave this earthly life,* ¹⁵so I will work hard to make sure you always remember these things after I am gone.

¹⁶For we were not making up clever stories when we told you about the powerful coming of our Lord Jesus Christ. We saw his majestic splendor with our own eyes ¹⁷when he received honor and glory from God the Father. The voice from the majestic glory of God said to him, "This is my dearly loved Son, who brings me great joy."* ¹⁸We ourselves heard that voice from heaven when we were with him on the holy mountain.

¹⁹Because of that experience, we have even greater confidence in the message proclaimed by the prophets. You must pay close attention to what they wrote, for their words are like a lamp shining in a dark place—until the Day dawns, and Christ the Morning Star shines* in your hearts. ²⁰Above all, you must realize that no prophecy in Scripture ever came from the prophet's own understanding,* ²¹or from human initiative. No, those prophets were moved by the Holy Spirit, and they spoke from God.

1:1a Greek *Symeon.*   1:1b Or *to you in the righteousness.*   1:10 Greek *brothers.*   1:13 Greek *as long as I am in this tent* [or *tabernacle*].   1:14 Greek *I must soon put off my tent* [or *tabernacle*].   1:17 Matt 17:5; Mark 9:7; Luke 9:35.   1:19 Or *rises.*   1:20 Or *is a matter of one's own interpretation.*

CHAPTER 2

The Danger of False Teachers

But there were also false prophets in Israel, just as there will be false teachers among you. They will cleverly teach destructive heresies and even deny the Master who bought them. In this way, they will bring sudden destruction on themselves. ²Many will follow their evil teaching and shameful immorality. And because of these teachers, the way of truth will be slandered. ³In their greed they will make up clever lies to get hold of your money. But God condemned them long ago, and their destruction will not be delayed.

⁴For God did not spare even the angels who sinned. He threw them into hell,* in gloomy pits of darkness,* where they are being held until the day of judgment. ⁵And God did not spare the ancient world—except for Noah and the seven others in his family. Noah warned the world of God's righteous judgment. So God protected Noah when he destroyed the world of ungodly people with a vast flood. ⁶Later, God condemned the cities of Sodom and Gomorrah and turned them into heaps of ashes. He made them an example of what will happen to ungodly people. ⁷But God also rescued Lot out of Sodom because he was a righteous man who was sick of the shameful immorality of the wicked people around him. ⁸Yes, Lot was a righteous man who was tormented in his soul by the wickedness he saw and heard day after day. ⁹So you see, the Lord knows how to rescue godly people from their trials, even while keeping the wicked under punishment until the day of final judgment. ¹⁰He is especially hard on those who follow their own twisted sexual desire, and who despise authority.

These people are proud and arrogant, daring even to scoff at supernatural beings* without so much as trembling. ¹¹But the angels, who are far greater in power and strength, do not dare to bring from the Lord* a charge of blasphemy against those supernatural beings.

¹²These false teachers are like unthinking animals, creatures of instinct, born to be caught and destroyed. They scoff at things they do not understand, and like animals, they will be destroyed. ¹³Their destruction is their reward for the harm they have done. They love to indulge in evil pleasures in broad daylight. They are a disgrace and a stain among you. They delight in deception* even as they eat with you in your fellowship meals. ¹⁴They commit adultery with their eyes, and their desire for sin is never satisfied. They lure unstable people into sin, and they are well trained in greed. They live under God's curse. ¹⁵They have wandered off the right road and followed the footsteps of Balaam son of Beor,* who loved

---

2:4a Greek *Tartarus.*   **2:4b** Some manuscripts read *in chains of gloom.*   **2:10** Greek *at glorious ones,* which are probably evil angels.   **2:11** Other manuscripts read *to the Lord;* still others do not include this phrase at all.   **2:13** Some manuscripts read *in fellowship meals.*   **2:15** Some manuscripts read *Bosor.*

THE POINT

Read the Word. While Peter's first letter was written to comfort and encourage believers to endure persecution from those outside the church, the point of his second letter was to warn believers against bogus teachers and prophets *inside* the church. He realized that not everyone in the church was sincere. These fake teachers were distorting Bible truths and sayin' things that contradicted Christ's teachings and those of the Old Testament prophets.

Peter urged believers not to fall for the hype—these false teachers were only in it for the Benjamins. He told them the only way they could figure out who was real or who was fake was if they took the time to read God's Word for themselves. "Pay close attention to what they [the Old Testament prophets] wrote, for their words are like a lamp shining in a dark place" (2 Peter 1:19).

In other words, Peter was sayin' if you want to know the real deal, get closer to God by readin' and studyin' his Word for yourself. Don't take what others say at face value and be led down a path of wrongdoing. Check out God's Word for yourself. If you don't, you might find yourself worse off than you were before you got saved.

to earn money by doing wrong. ¹⁶But Balaam was stopped from his mad course when his donkey rebuked him with a human voice.

¹⁷These people are as useless as dried-up springs or as mist blown away by the wind. They are doomed to blackest darkness. ¹⁸They brag about themselves with empty, foolish boasting. With an appeal to twisted sexual desires, they lure back into sin those who have barely escaped from a lifestyle of deception. ¹⁹They promise freedom, but they themselves are slaves of sin and corruption. For you are a slave to whatever controls you. ²⁰And when people escape from the wickedness of the world by knowing our Lord and Savior Jesus Christ and then get tangled up and enslaved by sin again, they are worse off than before. ²¹It would be better if they had never known the way to righteousness than to know it and then reject the command they were given to live a holy life. ²²They prove the truth of this proverb: "A dog returns to its vomit."* And another says, "A washed pig returns to the mud."

CHAPTER 3

The Day of the Lord Is Coming

This is my second letter to you, dear friends, and in both of them I have tried to stimulate your wholesome thinking and refresh your memory. ²I want you to remember what the holy prophets said long ago and what our Lord and Savior commanded through your apostles.

³Most importantly, I want to remind you that in the last days scoffers will come, mocking the truth and following their own desires. ⁴They will say, "What happened to the promise that Jesus is coming again? From before the times of our ancestors, everything has remained the same since the world was first created."

⁵They deliberately forget that God made the heavens by the word of his command, and he brought the earth out from the water and surrounded it with water. ⁶Then he used the water to destroy the ancient world with a mighty flood. ⁷And by the same word, the present heavens and earth have been stored up for fire. They are being kept for the day of judgment, when ungodly people will be destroyed.

⁸But you must not forget this one thing, dear friends: A day is like a thousand years to the Lord, and a thousand years is like a day. ⁹The Lord isn't really being slow about his promise, as some people think. No, he is being patient for your sake. He does not want anyone to be destroyed, but wants everyone to repent. ¹⁰But the day of the Lord will come as unexpectedly as a thief. Then the heavens will pass away with a terrible noise, and the very elements themselves will disappear in fire, and the earth and everything on it will be found to deserve judgment.*

¹¹Since everything around us is going to be destroyed like this, what holy and godly lives you should live, ¹²looking forward to the day of God and hurrying it along. On that day, he will set the heavens on fire, and the elements will melt away in the flames. ¹³But we are looking forward to the new heavens and new earth he has promised, a world filled with God's righteousness.

¹⁴And so, dear friends, while you are waiting for these things to happen, make every effort to be found living peaceful lives that are pure and blameless in his sight.

¹⁵And remember, our Lord's patience gives people time to be saved. This is what our beloved brother Paul also wrote to you with the wisdom God gave him—¹⁶speaking of these things in all of his letters. Some of his comments are hard to understand, and those who are ignorant and unstable have twisted his letters to mean something quite different, just as they do with other parts of Scripture. And this will result in their destruction.

Peter's Final Words

¹⁷I am warning you ahead of time, dear friends. Be on guard so that you will not be carried away by the errors of these wicked people and lose your own secure footing. ¹⁸Rather, you must grow in the grace and knowledge of our Lord and Savior Jesus Christ.

All glory to him, both now and forever! Amen.

2:22 Prov 26:11.   **3:10** Other manuscripts read *will be burned up;* still others read *will be found destroyed.*

IN THE BOOKS OF 1–3 JOHN, the writer shows us God as a guiding force of light, life, love, truth, and faithfulness. In his first letter, John reminded believers that they needed to remain tight with God. He warned of the dangers of talkin' out the side of your neck. In other words, one cannot intentionally walk in spiritual darkness and still claim fellowship with Jesus Christ.

It is simply not enough to say that we know Jesus. We also must have enough faith to roll wit him, no matter what—obeying his commands the best we can and recognizing that none of us is without sin. Also, John's letter reminds believers that God is love, that love is the key to understanding God and the life he wants us to live here on earth.

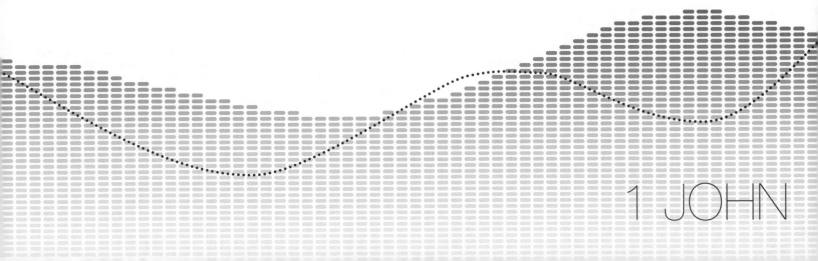

1 JOHN

CHAPTER 1

Introduction

We proclaim to you the one who existed from the beginning,* whom we have heard and seen. We saw him with our own eyes and touched him with our own hands. He is the Word of life. ²This one who is life itself was revealed to us, and we have seen him. And now we testify and proclaim to you that he is the one who is eternal life. He was with the Father, and then he was revealed to us. ³We proclaim to you what we ourselves have actually seen and heard so that you may have fellowship with us. And our fellowship is with the Father and with his Son, Jesus Christ. ⁴We are writing these things so that you may fully share our joy.*

Living in the Light

⁵This is the message we heard from Jesus* and now declare to you: God is light, and there is no darkness in him at all. ⁶So we are lying if we say we have fellowship with God but go on living in spiritual darkness; we are not practicing the truth. ⁷But if we are living in the light, as God is in the light, then we have fellowship with each other, and the blood of Jesus, his Son, cleanses us from all sin.

⁸If we claim we have no sin, we are only fooling ourselves and not living in the truth. ⁹But if we confess our sins to him, he is faithful and just to forgive us our sins and to cleanse us from all wickedness. ¹⁰If we claim we have not sinned, we are calling God a liar and showing that his word has no place in our hearts.

CHAPTER 2

My dear children, I am writing this to you so that you will not sin. But if anyone does sin, we have an advocate who pleads our case before the Father. He is Jesus Christ, the one who is truly righteous. ²He himself is the sacrifice that atones for our sins—and not only our sins but the sins of all the world.

³And we can be sure that we know him if we obey his commandments. ⁴If someone claims, "I know God," but doesn't obey God's commandments, that person is a liar and is not living in the truth. ⁵But those who obey God's word truly show how completely they love him. That is how we know we are living in him. ⁶Those who say they live in God should live their lives as Jesus did.

A New Commandment

⁷Dear friends, I am not writing a new commandment for you; rather it is an old one you have had from the very beginning. This old commandment—to love one another—is the same message you heard before. ⁸Yet it is also new. Jesus lived the truth of this commandment, and you also are living it. For the darkness is disappearing, and the true light is already shining.

⁹If anyone claims, "I am living in the light," but hates a Christian brother or sister,* that person is still living in darkness. ¹⁰Anyone who loves another brother or sister* is living in the light and does not cause others to stumble. ¹¹But anyone who hates another brother or sister is still living and walking in darkness. Such a person does not know the way to go, having been blinded by the darkness.

1:1 Greek *What was from the beginning.* 1:4 Or *so that our joy may be complete;* some manuscripts read *your joy.* 1:5 Greek *from him.* 2:9 Greek *hates his brother;* similarly in 2:11. 2:10 Greek *loves his brother.*

¹² I am writing to you who are God's children
because your sins have been forgiven through Jesus.*
¹³ I am writing to you who are mature in the faith*
because you know Christ, who existed from the beginning.
I am writing to you who are young in the faith
because you have won your battle with the evil one.
¹⁴ I have written to you who are God's children
because you know the Father.
I have written to you who are mature in the faith
because you know Christ, who existed from the beginning.
I have written to you who are young in the faith
because you are strong.
God's word lives in your hearts,
and you have won your battle with the evil one.

Do Not Love This World

¹⁵Do not love this world nor the things it offers you, for when you love the world, you do not have the love of the Father in you. ¹⁶For the world offers only a craving for physical pleasure, a craving for everything we see, and pride in our achievements and possessions. These are not from the Father, but are from this world. ¹⁷And this world is fading away, along with everything that people crave. But anyone who does what pleases God will live forever.

Warning about Antichrists

¹⁸Dear children, the last hour is here. You have heard that the Antichrist is coming, and already many such antichrists have appeared. From this we know that the last hour has come. ¹⁹These people left our churches, but they never really belonged with us; otherwise they would have stayed with us. When they left, it proved that they did not belong with us.

²⁰But you are not like that, for the Holy One has given you his Spirit,* and all of you know the truth. ²¹So I am writing to you not because you don't know the truth but because you know the difference between truth and lies. ²²And who is a liar? Anyone who says that Jesus is not the Christ.* Anyone who denies the Father and the Son is an antichrist.* ²³Anyone who denies the Son doesn't have the Father, either. But anyone who acknowledges the Son has the Father also.

²⁴So you must remain faithful to what you have been taught from the beginning. If you do, you will remain in fellowship with the Son and with the Father. ²⁵And in this fellowship we enjoy the eternal life he promised us.

2:12 Greek *through his name.*   **2:13** Or *to you fathers;* also in 2:14.   **2:20** Greek *But you have an anointing from the Holy One.*   **2:22a** Or *not the Messiah.*   **2:22b** Or *the antichrist.*

THE POINT

Quit makin' excuses! During the time when John was writing, a group called the Gnostics (pronounced nahs-tiks) rolled up in church, spreadin' a lot of propaganda that challenged Christians' faith. Basically, Gnostics believed that it didn't matter what you did with your body and it was okay to sin and live an immoral lifestyle, because the physical body was going to be destroyed anyway. (Gnostics also refused to believe that Jesus was both fully man and fully God, because they viewed the physical body as evil. From their point of view, God could not have possibly been walkin' around in something as evil as sinful flesh!) John flipped the script on these false teachings by making it clear that living in sin is not okay:

If we claim we have no sin, we are only fooling ourselves and not living in the truth. . . . If we claim we have not sinned, we are calling God a liar and showing that his word has no place in our hearts. (1 John 1:8, 10)

John was sayin', "Hold up, wait a minute! God is real; he is love; he is the truth and the light. And it is only through loving and obeying God that fellowship with God is possible. So quit makin' up excuses; just do the right thang!"

[26]I am writing these things to warn you about those who want to lead you astray. [27]But you have received the Holy Spirit,* and he lives within you, so you don't need anyone to teach you what is true. For the Spirit* teaches you everything you need to know, and what he teaches is true—it is not a lie. So just as he has taught you, remain in fellowship with Christ.

Living as Children of God

[28]And now, dear children, remain in fellowship with Christ so that when he returns, you will be full of courage and not shrink back from him in shame.

[29]Since we know that Christ is righteous, we also know that all who do what is right are God's children.

CHAPTER 3

See how very much our Father loves us, for he calls us his children, and that is what we are! But the people who belong to this world don't recognize that we are God's children because they don't know him. [2]Dear friends, we are already God's children, but he has not yet shown us what we will be like when Christ appears. But we do know that we will be like him, for we will see him as he really is. [3]And all who have this eager expectation will keep themselves pure, just as he is pure.

[4]Everyone who sins is breaking God's law, for all sin is contrary to the law of God. [5]And you know that Jesus came to take away our sins, and there is no sin in him. [6]Anyone who continues to live in him will not sin. But anyone who keeps on sinning does not know him or understand who he is.

[7]Dear children, don't let anyone deceive you about this: When people do what is right, it shows that they are righteous, even as Christ is righteous. [8]But when people keep on sinning, it shows that they belong to the devil, who has been sinning since the beginning. But the Son of God came to destroy the works of the devil. [9]Those who have been born into God's family do not make a practice of sinning, because God's life* is in them. So they can't keep on sinning, because they are children of God. [10]So now we can tell who are children of God and who are children of the devil. Anyone who does not live righteously and does not love other believers* does not belong to God.

Love One Another

[11]This is the message you have heard from the beginning: We should love one another. [12]We must not be like Cain, who belonged to the evil one and killed his brother. And why did he kill him? Because Cain had been doing what was evil, and his brother had been doing what was righteous. [13]So don't be surprised, dear brothers and sisters,* if the world hates you.

[14]If we love our Christian brothers and sisters,* it proves that we have passed from death to life. But a person who has no love is still dead. [15]Anyone who hates another brother or sister* is really a murderer at heart. And you know that murderers don't have eternal life within them.

[16]We know what real love is because Jesus gave up his life for us. So we also ought to give up our lives for our brothers and sisters. [17]If someone has enough money to live well and sees a brother or sister* in need but shows no compassion—how can God's love be in that person?

[18]Dear children, let's not merely say that we love each other; let us show the truth by our actions. [19]Our actions will show that we belong to the truth, so we will be confident when we stand before God. [20]Even if we feel guilty, God is greater than our feelings, and he knows everything.

[21]Dear friends, if we don't feel guilty, we can come to God with bold confidence. [22]And we will receive from him whatever we ask because we obey him and do the things that please him.

2:27a Greek *the anointing from him.*   **2:27b** Greek *the anointing.*   **3:9** Greek *because his seed.*   **3:10** Greek *does not love his brother.*   **3:13** Greek *brothers.*   **3:14** Greek *the brothers;* similarly in 3:16.   **3:15** Greek *hates his brother.*   **3:17** Greek *sees his brother.*

POWERCHOICES

DO YOU SHOW MAD LOVE FOR EVERYONE? WHEN ASKED, MOST CHRISTIANS ARE QUICK TO ADMIT THAT THEY LOVE THE LORD. YET MANY ARE HESITANT TO SHOW LOVE TOWARD THEIR BROTHAS AND SISTAS. WHAT'S THE DEAL WIT THAT? ¶ *DEAR FRIENDS, LET US CONTINUE TO LOVE ONE ANOTHER, FOR LOVE COMES FROM GOD. ANYONE WHO LOVES IS A CHILD OF GOD AND KNOWS GOD. BUT ANYONE WHO DOES NOT LOVE DOES NOT KNOW GOD, FOR GOD IS LOVE.* (1 JOHN 4:7-8) ¶ GOD'S COMMANDMENT TO LOVE ONE ANOTHER MUST BECOME REAL IN THE LIVES OF ALL CHRISTIANS. IF WE SAY WE ARE TRUE BELIEVERS OF GOD'S WORD, THERE'S NO OTHER PATH. LIKE JOHN REMINDS US, HOW CAN WE LOVE GOD AND HATE OUR BROTHAS OR SISTAS? TO SHOW BROTHERLY L.O.V.E. MEANS **L**IVING **O**UR **V**ALUES **E**VERY DAY. ¶ *LOVE IS ACTION. IF YOU THINK YOU LOVE GOD, WHAT HAVE YOU DONE TODAY—ON THE REAL—TO PROVE IT?*

23And this is his commandment: We must believe in the name of his Son, Jesus Christ, and love one another, just as he commanded us. 24Those who obey God's commandments remain in fellowship with him, and he with them. And we know he lives in us because the Spirit he gave us lives in us.

CHAPTER 4

Discerning False Prophets

Dear friends, do not believe everyone who claims to speak by the Spirit. You must test them to see if the spirit they have comes from God. For there are many false prophets in the world. 2This is how we know if they have the Spirit of God: If a person claiming to be a prophet* acknowledges that Jesus Christ came in a real body, that person has the

Spirit of God. 3But if someone claims to be a prophet and does not acknowledge the truth about Jesus, that person is not from God. Such a person has the spirit of the Antichrist, which you heard is coming into the world and indeed is already here.

4But you belong to God, my dear children. You have already won a victory over those people, because the Spirit who lives in you is greater than the spirit who lives in the world. 5Those people belong to this world, so they speak from the world's viewpoint, and the world listens to them. 6But we belong to God, and those who know God listen to us. If they do not belong to God, they do not listen to us. That is how we know if someone has the Spirit of truth or the spirit of deception.

Loving One Another

7Dear friends, let us continue to love one another, for love comes from God. Anyone who loves is a child of God and knows God. 8But anyone who does not love does not know God, for God is love.

9God showed how much he loved us by sending his one and only Son into the world so that we might have eternal life through him. 10This is real love—not that we loved God, but that he loved us and sent his Son as a sacrifice to take away our sins.

11Dear friends, since God loved us that much, we surely ought to love each other. 12No one has ever seen God. But if we love each other, God lives in us, and his love is brought to full expression in us.

13And God has given us his Spirit as proof that we live in him and he in us. 14Furthermore, we have seen with our own eyes and now testify that the Father sent his Son to be the Savior of the world. 15All who confess that Jesus is the Son of God have God living in them, and they live in God. 16We know how much God loves us, and we have put our trust in his love.

4:2 Greek *If a spirit;* similarly in 4:3.

God is love, and all who live in love live in God, and God lives in them. ¹⁷And as we live in God, our love grows more perfect. So we will not be afraid on the day of judgment, but we can face him with confidence because we live like Jesus here in this world.

¹⁸Such love has no fear, because perfect love expels all fear. If we are afraid, it is for fear of punishment, and this shows that we have not fully experienced his perfect love. ¹⁹We love each other* because he loved us first.

²⁰If someone says, "I love God," but hates a Christian brother or sister,* that person is a liar; for if we don't love people we can see, how can we love God, whom we cannot see? ²¹And he has given us this command: Those who love God must also love their Christian brothers and sisters.*

CHAPTER 5

Faith in the Son of God

Everyone who believes that Jesus is the Christ* has become a child of God. And everyone who loves the Father loves his children, too. ²We know we love God's children if we love God and obey his commandments. ³Loving God means keeping his commandments, and his commandments are not burdensome. ⁴For every child of God defeats this evil world, and we achieve this victory through our faith. ⁵And who can win this battle against the world? Only those who believe that Jesus is the Son of God.

⁶And Jesus Christ was revealed as God's Son by his baptism in water and by shedding his blood on the cross*—not by water only, but by water and blood. And the Spirit, who is truth, confirms it with his testimony. ⁷So we have these three witnesses*—⁸the Spirit, the water, and the blood—and all three agree. ⁹Since we believe human testimony, surely we can believe the greater testimony that comes from God. And God has testified about his Son. ¹⁰All who believe in the Son of God know in their hearts that this testimony is true. Those who don't believe this are actually calling God a liar because they don't believe what God has testified about his Son.

¹¹And this is what God has testified: He has given us eternal life, and this life is in his Son. ¹²Whoever has the Son has life; whoever does not have God's Son does not have life.

Conclusion

¹³I have written this to you who believe in the name of the Son of God, so that you may know you have eternal life. ¹⁴And we are confident that he hears us whenever we ask for anything that pleases him. ¹⁵And since we know he hears us when we make our requests, we also know that he will give us what we ask for.

¹⁶If you see a Christian brother or sister* sinning in a way that does not lead to death, you should pray, and God will give that person life. But there is a sin that leads to death, and I am not saying you should pray for those who commit it. ¹⁷All wicked actions are sin, but not every sin leads to death.

¹⁸We know that God's children do not make a practice of sinning, for God's Son holds them securely, and the evil one cannot touch them. ¹⁹We know that we are children of God and that the world around us is under the control of the evil one.

²⁰And we know that the Son of God has come, and he has given us understanding so that we can know the true God.* And now we live in fellowship with the true God because we live in fellowship with his Son, Jesus Christ. He is the only true God, and he is eternal life.

²¹Dear children, keep away from anything that might take God's place in your hearts.*

"I have written this to you who believe in the Son of God, so that you may know you have eternal life" (1 John 5:13).

say what?

This is for you who believe in the Son of God, so that you know you're living an eternal life.

4:19 Greek *We love*. Other manuscripts read *We love God;* still others read *We love him.*   4:20 Greek *hates his brother.*   4:21 Greek *The one who loves God must also love his brother.*   5:1 Or *the Messiah.*   5:6 Greek *This is he who came by water and blood.*   5:7 A few very late manuscripts add *in heaven—the Father, the Word, and the Holy Spirit, and these three are one. And we have three witnesses on earth.*   5:16 Greek *a brother.*   5:20 Greek *the one who is true.*   5:21 Greek *keep yourselves from idols.*

Living in Truth and Love
(2 John 1:1-6)

Remaining Loyal to Christ
(2 John 1:7-13)

JUST LIKE 1 JOHN, the second book of John warns Christian believers about the importance of loving one another and the danger of false teachers. At the same time, John warns believers of the dangers of showing hospitality to false teachers. Although the short letter encourages believers to continue to love one another, it warns them not to extend their hospitality by inviting false teachers into their homes.

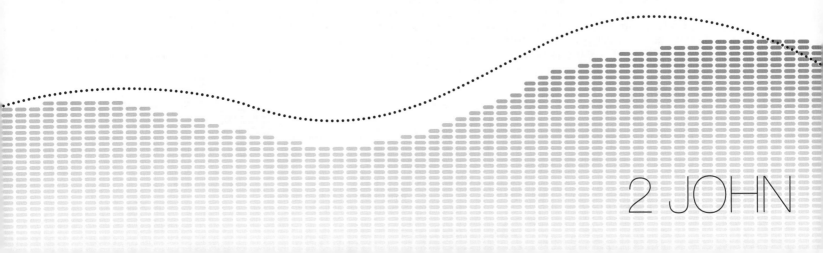

2 JOHN

Greetings

This letter is from John, the elder.*

I am writing to the chosen lady and to her children,* whom I love in the truth—as does everyone else who knows the truth—²because the truth lives in us and will be with us forever.

³Grace, mercy, and peace, which come from God the Father and from Jesus Christ—the Son of the Father—will continue to be with us who live in truth and love.

Live in the Truth

⁴How happy I was to meet some of your children and find them living according to the truth, just as the Father commanded.

⁵I am writing to remind you, dear friends,* that we should love one another. This is not a new commandment, but one we have had from the beginning. ⁶Love means doing what God has commanded us, and he has commanded us to love one another, just as you heard from the beginning.

⁷I say this because many deceivers have gone out into the world. They deny that Jesus Christ came* in a real body. Such a person is a deceiver and an antichrist. ⁸Watch out that you do not lose what we* have worked so hard to achieve. Be diligent so that you receive your full reward. ⁹Anyone who wanders away from this teaching has no relationship with God. But anyone who remains in the teaching of Christ has a relationship with both the Father and the Son.

¹⁰If anyone comes to your meeting and does not teach the truth about Christ, don't invite that person into your home or give any kind of encouragement. ¹¹Anyone who encourages such people becomes a partner in their evil work.

Conclusion

¹²I have much more to say to you, but I don't want to do it with paper and ink. For I hope to visit you soon and talk with you face to face. Then our joy will be complete.

¹³Greetings from the children of your sister,* chosen by God.

1a Greek *From the elder.* 1b Or *the church God has chosen and its members.* 5 Greek *I urge you, lady.* 7 Or *will come.* 8 Some manuscripts read *you.* 13 Or *from the members of your sister church.*

THE POINT

The careful crib. During Bible times, it was common for missionaries to come through and post up at the homes of fellow believers while they were in town preaching. But John warned Christian believers that they should be careful of false prophets seekin' to chill at their spot. He cautioned believers to have discernment about who stayed in their homes, especially for long periods of time.

If anyone comes to your meeting and does not teach the truth about Christ, don't invite that person into your home or give any kind of encouragement. Anyone who encourages such people becomes a partner in their evil work. (2 John 1:10-11)

John was warning the believers to have a spirit of discernment. Even though, as Christians, we're supposed to walk in truth and show genuine love and concern for others, John warns that we are not supposed to get so caught up in other people's drama that it keeps us from God's truth—and that's what discernment is all about.

AS IN HIS OTHER LETTERS, 3 John again emphasizes the importance of walking in the truth of the gospel. In his first letter, John had warned against believing false doctrine. In his second letter, he warned Christians not to invite false teachers into their homes. Here in his third letter, he stresses how important it is to support, encourage, and serve one another in ministry.

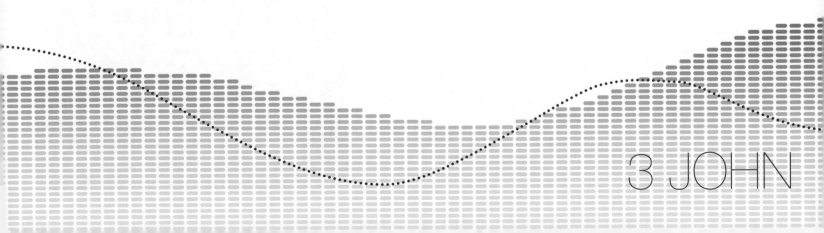

3 JOHN

Greetings

This letter is from John, the elder.*

I am writing to Gaius, my dear friend, whom I love in the truth.

²Dear friend, I hope all is well with you and that you are as healthy in body as you are strong in spirit. ³Some of the traveling teachers* recently returned and made me very happy by telling me about your faithfulness and that you are living according to the truth. ⁴I could have no greater joy than to hear that my children are following the truth.

Caring for the Lord's Workers

⁵Dear friend, you are being faithful to God when you care for the traveling teachers who pass through, even though they are strangers to you. ⁶They have told the church here of your loving friendship. Please continue providing for such teachers in a manner that pleases God. ⁷For they are traveling for the Lord,* and they accept nothing from people who are not believers.* ⁸So we ourselves should support them so that we can be their partners as they teach the truth.

⁹I wrote to the church about this, but Diotrephes, who loves to be the leader, refuses to have anything to do with us. ¹⁰When I come, I will report some of the things he is doing and the evil accusations he is making against us. Not only does he refuse to welcome the traveling teachers, he also tells others not to help them. And when they do help, he puts them out of the church.

flō

"Follow only what is good. Remember that those who do good prove that they are God's children" (3 John 1:11).

say what?

Follow what's good. When you do good, you prove to everyone that you are part of God's fam.

1 Greek *From the elder.*   3 Greek *the brothers;* also in verses 5 and 10.   **7a** Greek *They went out on behalf of the Name.*   **7b** Greek *from Gentiles.*

keeping your swagger strong

BIBLICAL PRINCIPLES FOR SUCCESS AND LEADERSHIP

Real leaders have the ability to serve others. That statement might not be cool wit some people, given the negative view associated with the word "serve." It seems like nobody these days wants to do somethin' and get nothin' in return.

Service is central to Christian belief. Why? Because we follow a God who serves. Jesus humbled himself and washed the feet of his disciples. What makes you any better than him? If you think that serving others is weak, or you're about gettin' paid, check out what some great minds have said about serving:

"I try to make my life about service, and hope that one day we can all 'see' a little better because God is with everyone and everywhere." –Russell Simmons

"Everybody can be great, because anybody can serve. You don't have to have a college degree to serve. You don't have to make your subject and your verb agree to serve. . . . You only need a heart full of grace." –Martin Luther King, Jr.

"To know is to comprehend. Do you know, do you comprehend, in this moment, whom or what you serve? We must all be serving someone or something. Whom or what are you choosing to serve right now?" –Maya Angelou

A servant of Christ chooses to be like Christ and serve others. What are you doing to serve others?

[11]Dear friend, don't let this bad example influence you. Follow only what is good. Remember that those who do good prove that they are God's children, and those who do evil prove that they do not know God.*

[12]Everyone speaks highly of Demetrius, as does the truth itself. We ourselves can say the same for him, and you know we speak the truth.

Conclusion

[13]I have much more to say to you, but I don't want to write it with pen and ink. [14]For I hope to see you soon, and then we will talk face to face.

[15]*Peace be with you.

Your friends here send you their greetings. Please give my personal greetings to each of our friends there.

11 Greek *they have not seen God.*   15 Some English translations combine verses 14 and 15 into verse 14.

prayer

LORD, There are so many people around me, and they're trying to get my full attention. Please help me to be faithful and loyal to you. Give me the good sense to know who is fake and who is real in my life so I won't be led astray by false promises and fake teachings. Amen. (See 3 John 1:11.)

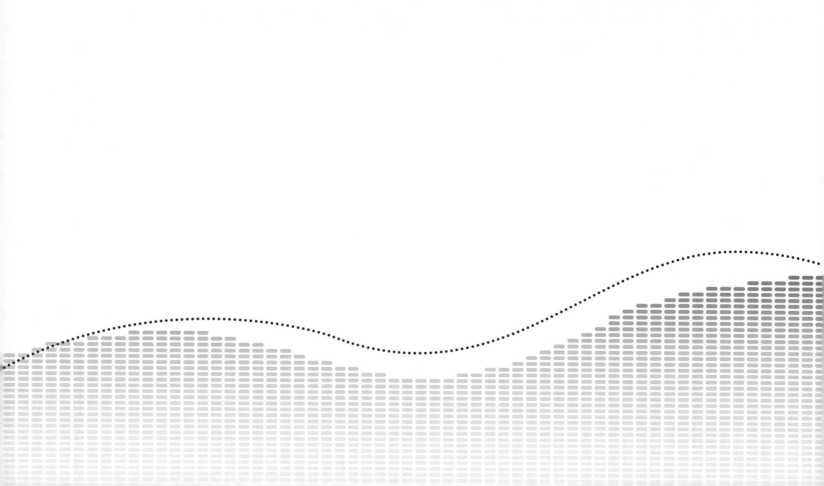

THE BOOK OF JUDE was written to call Christians everywhere to stand up and fight for the gospel of Jesus Christ. Jude begins his letter by sharing that his original intent was to write about salvation. Instead, he thought it was more important to warn the believers to resist false teachers who might cause them to turn from the truth. Even today, Christians should learn to trust what the Bible says and not believe in false doctrine. We must focus on God's love, pray, and do the right thing until Jesus returns.

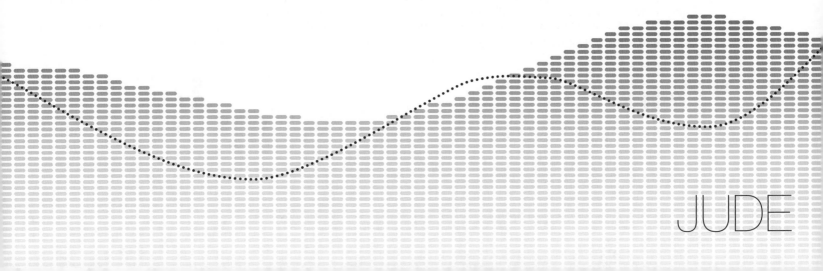

JUDE

Greetings from Jude

This letter is from Jude, a slave of Jesus Christ and a brother of James.

I am writing to all who have been called by God the Father, who loves you and keeps you safe in the care of Jesus Christ.*

²May God give you more and more mercy, peace, and love.

The Danger of False Teachers

³Dear friends, I had been eagerly planning to write to you about the salvation we all share. But now I find that I must write about something else, urging you to defend the faith that God has entrusted once for all time to his holy people. ⁴I say this because some ungodly people have wormed their way into your churches, saying that God's marvelous grace allows us to live immoral lives. The condemnation of such people was recorded long ago, for they have denied our only Master and Lord, Jesus Christ.

⁵So I want to remind you, though you already know these things, that Jesus* first rescued the nation of Israel from Egypt, but later he destroyed those who did not remain faithful. ⁶And I remind you of the angels who did not stay within the limits of authority God gave them but left the place where they belonged. God has kept them securely chained in prisons of darkness, waiting for the great day of judgment. ⁷And don't forget Sodom and Gomorrah and their neighboring towns, which were filled with immorality and every kind of sexual perversion. Those cities were destroyed by fire and serve as a warning of the eternal fire of God's judgment.

⁸In the same way, these people—who claim authority

1 Or *keeps you for Jesus Christ.*   5 As in the best manuscripts; various other manuscripts read *[the] Lord,* or *God,* or *Christ;* one reads *God Christ.*

THE POINT

False teachers are wack. For Jude, fugazi teachers were wack. He knew they were dangerous, godless men to be dismissed at any cost. Jude knew it was his responsibility to make sure people did not get caught up in their lame philosophies and end up stuck on stupid. He held nothing back when it came to exposing their lies.

Some ungodly people have wormed their way into your churches. . . . They are like shame- *less shepherds who care only for themselves. They are like clouds blowing over the land without giving any rain. They are like trees in autumn that are doubly dead. . . . These people are grumblers and complainers, living only to satisfy their desires.* (Jude 1:4, 12, 16)

Don't even hang out with these people, Jude warned—don't even go there. Next, he gives

examples of what happened to people back in the day who rebelled against God's Word and lived to regret it. "What sorrow awaits them! For they follow in the footsteps of Cain . . . Balaam . . . Like Korah, they perish in their rebellion" (Jude 1:11).

keeping your swagger strong

BIBLICAL PRINCIPLES FOR SUCCESS AND LEADERSHIP

"I think we have a profound crisis of black leadership now in our communities. Most of the best leadership is probably at the grassroots level, which is relatively invisible. . . . we just don't have enough fearless truth tellers." This response, by prominent African American scholar Cornell West, was given during an interview in which the question was asked: "What has happened to our people in the last thirty years?" For all you students and twenty- and thirty-somethings out there, the same question needs to be asked today. What's your game plan for takin' it to the next level?

Do you ever wonder why so many folks from the hip-hop generation are seemingly so violent, angry, materialistic, and self-absorbed? You might be thinkin', "That ain't me! I don't have all them issues!" Fo' sho—but undoubtedly you know at least one brotha or sista who fits that description, a person who is wildin' most of the time. Jude challenged the church to look within and become fearless truth-tellers. It's called accountability and responsibility. Jude's fiery letter lets us know that if you speak the truth (in love) and stand up for what's right, God is willing and able to keep you from failing.

---

the footsteps of Cain, who killed his brother. Like Balaam, they deceive people for money. And like Korah, they perish in their rebellion.

¹²When these people eat with you in your fellowship meals commemorating the Lord's love, they are like dangerous reefs that can shipwreck you.* They are like shameless shepherds who care only for themselves. They are like clouds blowing over the land without giving any rain. They are like trees in autumn that are doubly dead, for they bear no fruit and have been pulled up by the roots. ¹³They are like wild waves of the sea, churning up the foam of their shameful deeds. They are like wandering stars, doomed forever to blackest darkness.

¹⁴Enoch, who lived in the seventh generation after Adam, prophesied about these people. He said, "Listen! The Lord is coming with countless thousands of his holy ones ¹⁵to execute judgment on the people of the world. He will convict every person of all the ungodly things they have done and for all the insults that ungodly sinners have spoken against him."*

¹⁶These people are grumblers and complainers, living only to satisfy their desires. They brag loudly about themselves, and they flatter others to get what they want.

A Call to Remain Faithful

¹⁷But you, my dear friends, must remember what the apostles of our Lord Jesus Christ said. ¹⁸They told you that in the last times there would be scoffers whose purpose in life is to satisfy their ungodly desires. ¹⁹These people are the ones who are creating divisions among you. They follow their natural instincts because they do not have God's Spirit in them.

²⁰But you, dear friends, must build each other up in your most holy faith, pray in the power of the Holy Spirit,* ²¹and await the mercy of our Lord Jesus Christ, who will bring

---

from their dreams—live immoral lives, defy authority, and scoff at supernatural beings.* ⁹But even Michael, one of the mightiest of the angels,* did not dare accuse the devil of blasphemy, but simply said, "The Lord rebuke you!" (This took place when Michael was arguing with the devil about Moses' body.) ¹⁰But these people scoff at things they do not understand. Like unthinking animals, they do whatever their instincts tell them, and so they bring about their own destruction. ¹¹What sorrow awaits them! For they follow in

---

8 Greek *at glorious ones,* which are probably evil angels.　**9** Greek *Michael, the archangel.*　**12** Or *they are contaminants among you;* or *they are stains.*　**14-15** The quotation comes from intertestamental literature: Enoch 1:9.　**20** Greek *pray in the Holy Spirit.*

you eternal life. In this way, you will keep yourselves safe in God's love.

²²And you must show mercy to* those whose faith is wavering. ²³Rescue others by snatching them from the flames of judgment. Show mercy to still others,* but do so with great caution, hating the sins that contaminate their lives.*

A Prayer of Praise

²⁴Now all glory to God, who is able to keep you from falling away and will bring you with great joy into his glorious presence without a single fault. ²⁵All glory to him who alone is God, our Savior through Jesus Christ our Lord. All glory, majesty, power, and authority are his before all time, and in the present, and beyond all time! Amen.

22 Some manuscripts read *must reprove.*   **22-23a** Some manuscripts have only two categories of people: (1) those whose faith is wavering and therefore need to be snatched from the flames of judgment, and (2) those who need to be shown mercy.   **23b** Greek *with fear, hating even the clothing stained by the flesh.*

JUST AS GENESIS is the book of beginnings, Revelation is the book of endings. The book of Revelation is the apostle John's inspired vision received while in exile on the island of Patmos. In it John gives the final warning to seven churches that the world will surely end and judgment will come.

The Christian image of Jesus is often very simplistic. Many view him as a long-haired, meek, and mild-mannered man, strollin' down the streets of Jerusalem in a long robe handin' out blessings. The book of Revelation paints a vastly different picture. Here we are given a glimpse of the awesomeness of Jesus as the Lion of Judah—the all-powerful One, the One to whom all creatures bow down and worship.

REVELATION

CHAPTER 1
Prologue

This is a revelation from* Jesus Christ, which God gave him to show his servants the events that must soon* take place. He sent an angel to present this revelation to his servant John, ²who faithfully reported everything he saw. This is his report of the word of God and the testimony of Jesus Christ.

³God blesses the one who reads the words of this prophecy to the church, and he blesses all who listen to its message and obey what it says, for the time is near.

John's Greeting to the Seven Churches

⁴This letter is from John to the seven churches in the province of Asia.*

Grace and peace to you from the one who is, who always was, and who is still to come; from the sevenfold Spirit* before his throne; ⁵and from Jesus Christ. He is the faithful witness to these things, the first to rise from the dead, and the ruler of all the kings of the world.

All glory to him who loves us and has freed us from our sins by shedding his blood for us. ⁶He has made us a Kingdom of priests for God his Father. All glory and power to him forever and ever! Amen.

⁷ Look! He comes with the clouds of heaven.
> And everyone will see him—
> even those who pierced him.
> And all the nations of the world
> will mourn for him.
> Yes! Amen!

⁸"I am the Alpha and the Omega—the beginning and the end,"* says the Lord God. "I am the one who is, who always was, and who is still to come—the Almighty One."

Vision of the Son of Man

⁹I, John, am your brother and your partner in suffering and in God's Kingdom and in the patient endurance to which Jesus calls us. I was exiled to the island of Patmos for preaching the word of God and for my testimony about Jesus. ¹⁰It was the Lord's Day, and I was worshiping in the Spirit.* Suddenly, I heard behind me a loud voice like a trumpet blast. ¹¹It said, "Write in a book* everything you see, and send it to the seven churches in the cities of Ephesus, Smyrna, Pergamum, Thyatira, Sardis, Philadelphia, and Laodicea."

¹²When I turned to see who was speaking to me, I saw seven gold lampstands. ¹³And standing in the middle of the lampstands was someone like the Son of Man.* He was wearing a long robe with a gold sash across his chest. ¹⁴His head and his hair were white like wool, as white as snow. And his eyes were like flames of fire. ¹⁵His feet were like polished bronze refined in a furnace, and his voice thundered like mighty ocean waves. ¹⁶He held seven stars in his right hand, and a sharp two-edged sword came from his mouth. And his face was like the sun in all its brilliance.

1:1a Or *of.* 1:1b Or *suddenly,* or *quickly.* 1:4a *Asia* was a Roman province in what is now western Turkey. 1:4b Greek *the seven spirits.* 1:8 Greek *I am the Alpha and the Omega,* referring to the first and last letters of the Greek alphabet. 1:10 Or *in spirit.* 1:11 Or *on a scroll.* 1:13 Or *like a son of man.* See Dan 7:13. "Son of Man" is a title Jesus used for himself.

17When I saw him, I fell at his feet as if I were dead. But he laid his right hand on me and said, "Don't be afraid! I am the First and the Last. 18I am the living one. I died, but look—I am alive forever and ever! And I hold the keys of death and the grave.*

19"Write down what you have seen—both the things that are now happening and the things that will happen.* 20This is the meaning of the mystery of the seven stars you saw in my right hand and the seven gold lampstands: The seven stars are the angels* of the seven churches, and the seven lampstands are the seven churches.

CHAPTER 2
The Message to the Church in Ephesus

"Write this letter to the angel* of the church in Ephesus. This is the message from the one who holds the seven stars in his right hand, the one who walks among the seven gold lampstands:

2"I know all the things you do. I have seen your hard work and your patient endurance. I know you don't tolerate evil people. You have examined the claims of those who say they are apostles but are not. You have discovered they are liars. 3You have patiently suffered for me without quitting.

4"But I have this complaint against you. You don't love me or each other as you did at first!* 5Look how far you have fallen! Turn back to me and do the works you did at first. If you don't repent, I will come and remove your lampstand from its place among the churches. 6But this is in your favor: You hate the evil deeds of the Nicolaitans, just as I do.

7"Anyone with ears to hear must listen to the Spirit and understand what he is saying to the churches. To everyone who is victorious I will give fruit from the tree of life in the paradise of God.

The Message to the Church in Smyrna

8"Write this letter to the angel of the church in Smyrna. This is the message from the one who is the First and the Last, who was dead but is now alive:

9"I know about your suffering and your poverty—but you are rich! I know the blasphemy of those opposing you. They say they are Jews, but they are not, because their synagogue belongs to Satan. 10Don't be afraid of what you are about to suffer. The devil will throw some of you into prison to test you. You will suffer for ten days. But if you remain faithful even when facing death, I will give you the crown of life.

11"Anyone with ears to hear must listen to the Spirit and understand what he is saying to the churches. Whoever is victorious will not be harmed by the second death.

The Message to the Church in Pergamum

12"Write this letter to the angel of the church in Pergamum. This is the message from the one with the sharp two-edged sword:

13"I know that you live in the city where Satan has his throne, yet you have remained loyal to me. You refused to deny me even when Antipas, my faithful witness, was martyred among you there in Satan's city.

14"But I have a few complaints against you. You tolerate some among you whose teaching is like that of Balaam, who showed Balak how to trip up the people of Israel. He taught them to sin by eating food offered to idols and by committing sexual sin. 15In a similar way, you have some Nicolaitans among you who follow the same teaching. 16Repent of your sin, or I will come to you suddenly and fight against them with the sword of my mouth.

1:18 Greek and Hades. 1:19 Or what you have seen and what they mean—the things that have already begun to happen. 1:20 Or the messengers. 2:1 Or the messenger; also in 2:8, 12, 18. 2:4 Greek You have lost your first love.

17"Anyone with ears to hear must listen to the Spirit and understand what he is saying to the churches. To everyone who is victorious I will give some of the manna that has been hidden away in heaven. And I will give to each one a white stone, and on the stone will be engraved a new name that no one understands except the one who receives it.

The Message to the Church in Thyatira

18"Write this letter to the angel of the church in Thyatira. This is the message from the Son of God, whose eyes are like flames of fire, whose feet are like polished bronze:

19"I know all the things you do. I have seen your love, your faith, your service, and your patient endurance. And I can see your constant improvement in all these things.

20"But I have this complaint against you. You are permitting that woman—that Jezebel who calls herself a prophet—to lead my servants astray. She teaches them to commit sexual sin and to eat food offered to idols. 21I gave her time to repent, but she does not want to turn away from her immorality.

22"Therefore, I will throw her on a bed of suffering,* and those who commit adultery with her will suffer greatly unless they repent and turn away from her evil deeds. 23I will strike her children dead. Then all the churches will know that I am the one who searches out the thoughts and intentions of every person. And I will give to each of you whatever you deserve.

24"But I also have a message for the rest of you in Thyatira who have not followed this false teaching ('deeper truths,' as they call them—depths of Satan, actually). I will ask nothing more of you 25except that you hold tightly to what you have until I come. 26To all who are victorious, who obey me to the very end,

To them I will give authority over all the nations.
27 They will rule the nations with an iron rod
and smash them like clay pots.*

28They will have the same authority I received from my Father, and I will also give them the morning star!

29"Anyone with ears to hear must listen to the Spirit and understand what he is saying to the churches.

CHAPTER 3

The Message to the Church in Sardis

"Write this letter to the angel* of the church in Sardis. This is the message from the one who has the sevenfold Spirit* of God and the seven stars:

"I know all the things you do, and that you have a reputation for being alive—but you are dead. 2Wake up! Strengthen what little remains, for even what is left is almost dead. I find that your actions do not meet the requirements of my God. 3Go back to what you heard and believed at first; hold to it firmly. Repent and turn to me again. If you don't wake up, I will come to you suddenly, as unexpected as a thief.

4"Yet there are some in the church in Sardis who have not soiled their clothes with evil. They will walk with me in white, for they are worthy. 5All who are victorious will be clothed in white. I will never erase their names from the Book of Life, but I will announce before my Father and his angels that they are mine.

6"Anyone with ears to hear must listen to the Spirit and understand what he is saying to the churches.

The Message to the Church in Philadelphia

7"Write this letter to the angel of the church in Philadelphia.

This is the message from the one who is holy and true, the one who has the key of David.

2:22 Greek *a bed.* 2:26-27 Ps 2:8-9 (Greek Version). 3:1a Or *the messenger;* also in 3:7, 14. 3:1b Greek *the seven spirits.*

What he opens, no one can close;
and what he closes, no one can open:*

[8]"I know all the things you do, and I have opened a door for you that no one can close. You have little strength, yet you obeyed my word and did not deny me. [9]Look, I will force those who belong to Satan's synagogue—those liars who say they are Jews but are not—to come and bow down at your feet. They will acknowledge that you are the ones I love.

[10]"Because you have obeyed my command to persevere, I will protect you from the great time of testing that will come upon the whole world to test those who belong to this world. [11]I am coming soon.* Hold on to what you have, so that no one will take away your crown. [12]All who are victorious will become pillars in the Temple of my God, and they will never have to leave it. And I will write on them the name of my God, and they will be citizens in the city of my God—the new Jerusalem that comes down from heaven from my God. And I will also write on them my new name.

[13]"Anyone with ears to hear must listen to the Spirit and understand what he is saying to the churches.

The Message to the Church in Laodicea

[14]"Write this letter to the angel of the church in Laodicea. This is the message from the one who is the Amen—the faithful and true witness, the beginning* of God's new creation:

[15]"I know all the things you do, that you are neither hot nor cold. I wish that you were one or the other! [16]But since you are like lukewarm water, neither hot nor cold, I will spit you out of my mouth! [17]You say, 'I am rich. I have everything I want. I don't need a thing!' And you don't realize that you are wretched and miserable and poor and blind and naked. [18]So I advise you to buy gold from me—gold that has been purified by fire. Then you will be rich. Also buy white garments from me so you will not be shamed by your nakedness, and ointment for your eyes so you will be able to see. [19]I correct and discipline everyone I love. So be diligent and turn from your indifference.

[20]"Look! I stand at the door and knock. If you hear my voice and open the door, I will come in, and we will share a meal together as friends. [21]Those who are victorious will sit with me on my throne, just as I was victorious and sat with my Father on his throne.

[22]"Anyone with ears to hear must listen to the Spirit and understand what he is saying to the churches."

CHAPTER 4

Worship in Heaven

Then as I looked, I saw a door standing open in heaven, and the same voice I had heard before spoke to me like a trumpet blast. The voice said, "Come up here, and I will show you what must happen after this." [2]And instantly I was in the Spirit,* and I saw a throne in heaven and someone sitting on it. [3]The one sitting on the throne was as brilliant as gemstones—like jasper and carnelian. And the glow of an emerald circled his throne like a rainbow. [4]Twenty-four thrones surrounded him, and twenty-four elders sat on them. They were all clothed in white and had gold crowns on their heads. [5]From the throne came flashes of lightning and the rumble of thunder. And in front of the throne were seven torches with burning flames. This is the sevenfold Spirit* of God. [6]In front of the throne was a shiny sea of glass, sparkling like crystal.

In the center and around the throne were four living beings, each covered with eyes, front and back. [7]The first of these living beings was like a lion; the second was like an ox; the third had a human face; and the fourth was like an eagle in flight. [8]Each of these living beings had six wings, and

"I am coming soon. Hold on to what you have, so that no one will take away your crown" (Revelation 3:11).

I'm coming back soon, so hold on to your faith. That way no one can take away your glory.

"Day after day and night after night they keep on saying, 'Holy, holy, holy is the Lord God, the Almighty—the one who always was, who is, and who is still to come'" (Revelation 4:8).

Every day and every night they keep sayin', "Holy, holy, holy is God, the all-powerful One. He has always been, is now, and always will be."

their wings were covered all over with eyes, inside and out. Day after day and night after night they keep on saying,

> "Holy, holy, holy is the Lord God, the Almighty—
> the one who always was, who is, and who is still to come."

⁹Whenever the living beings give glory and honor and thanks to the one sitting on the throne (the one who lives forever and ever), ¹⁰the twenty-four elders fall down and worship the one sitting on the throne (the one who lives forever and ever). And they lay their crowns before the throne and say,

> ¹¹ "You are worthy, O Lord our God,
> to receive glory and honor and power.
> For you created all things,
> and they exist because you created what you pleased."

CHAPTER 5

The Lamb Opens the Scroll

Then I saw a scroll* in the right hand of the one who was sitting on the throne. There was writing on the inside and the outside of the scroll, and it was sealed with seven seals. ²And I saw a strong angel, who shouted with a loud voice: "Who is worthy to break the seals on this scroll and open it?" ³But no one in heaven or on earth or under the earth was able to open the scroll and read it.

⁴Then I began to weep bitterly because no one was found worthy to open the scroll and read it. ⁵But one of the twenty-four elders said to me, "Stop weeping! Look, the Lion of the tribe of Judah, the heir to David's throne,* has won the victory. He is worthy to open the scroll and its seven seals."

⁶Then I saw a Lamb that looked as if it had been slaughtered, but it was now standing between the throne and the four living beings and among the twenty-four elders. He had seven horns and seven eyes, which represent the sevenfold Spirit* of God that is sent out into every part of the earth. ⁷He

stepped forward and took the scroll from the right hand of the one sitting on the throne. ⁸And when he took the scroll, the four living beings and the twenty-four elders fell down before the Lamb. Each one had a harp, and they held gold bowls filled with incense, which are the prayers of God's people. ⁹And they sang a new song with these words:

> "You are worthy to take the scroll
> and break its seals and open it.
> For you were slaughtered, and your blood has ransomed people for God
> from every tribe and language and people and nation.
> ¹⁰ And you have caused them to become
> a Kingdom of priests for our God.
> And they will reign* on the earth."

¹¹Then I looked again, and I heard the voices of thousands and millions of angels around the throne and of the living beings and the elders. ¹²And they sang in a mighty chorus:

> "Worthy is the Lamb who was slaughtered—
> to receive power and riches
> and wisdom and strength
> and honor and glory and blessing."

¹³And then I heard every creature in heaven and on earth and under the earth and in the sea. They sang:

> "Blessing and honor and glory and power
> belong to the one sitting on the throne
> and to the Lamb forever and ever."

¹⁴And the four living beings said, "Amen!" And the twenty-four elders fell down and worshiped the Lamb.

CHAPTER 6

The Lamb Breaks the First Six Seals

As I watched, the Lamb broke the first of the seven seals on the scroll.* Then I heard one of the four living beings say

5:1 Or *book*; also in 5:2, 3, 4, 5, 7, 8, 9.   **5:5** Greek *the root of David.* See Isa 11:10.   **5:6** Greek *which are the seven spirits.*   **5:10** Some manuscripts read *they are reigning.*   **6:1** Or *book.*

with a voice like thunder, "Come!" ²I looked up and saw a white horse standing there. Its rider carried a bow, and a crown was placed on his head. He rode out to win many battles and gain the victory.

³When the Lamb broke the second seal, I heard the second living being say, "Come!" ⁴Then another horse appeared, a red one. Its rider was given a mighty sword and the authority to take peace from the earth. And there was war and slaughter everywhere.

⁵When the Lamb broke the third seal, I heard the third living being say, "Come!" I looked up and saw a black horse, and its rider was holding a pair of scales in his hand. ⁶And I heard a voice from among the four living beings say, "A loaf of wheat bread or three loaves of barley will cost a day's pay.* And don't waste* the olive oil and wine."

⁷When the Lamb broke the fourth seal, I heard the fourth living being say, "Come!" ⁸I looked up and saw a horse whose color was pale green. Its rider was named Death, and his companion was the Grave.* These two were given authority over one-fourth of the earth, to kill with the sword and famine and disease* and wild animals.

⁹When the Lamb broke the fifth seal, I saw under the altar the souls of all who had been martyred for the word of God and for being faithful in their testimony. ¹⁰They shouted to the Lord and said, "O Sovereign Lord, holy and true, how long before you judge the people who belong to this world and avenge our blood for what they have done to us?" ¹¹Then a white robe was given to each of them. And they were told to rest a little longer until the full number of their brothers and sisters*—their fellow servants of Jesus who were to be martyred—had joined them.

¹²I watched as the Lamb broke the sixth seal, and there was a great earthquake. The sun became as dark as black cloth, and the moon became as red as blood. ¹³Then the stars of the sky fell to the earth like green figs falling from a tree shaken by a strong wind. ¹⁴The sky was rolled up like a scroll, and all of the mountains and islands were moved from their places.

¹⁵Then everyone—the kings of the earth, the rulers, the generals, the wealthy, the powerful, and every slave and free person—all hid themselves in the caves and among the rocks of the mountains. ¹⁶And they cried to the mountains and the rocks, "Fall on us and hide us from the face of the one who sits on the throne and from the wrath of the Lamb. ¹⁷For the great day of their wrath has come, and who is able to survive?"

CHAPTER **7**

God's People Will Be Preserved

Then I saw four angels standing at the four corners of the earth, holding back the four winds so they did not blow on the earth or the sea, or even on any tree. ²And I saw another angel coming up from the east, carrying the seal of the living God. And he shouted to those four angels, who had been given power to harm land and sea, ³"Wait! Don't harm the land or the sea or the trees until we have placed the seal of God on the foreheads of his servants."

⁴And I heard how many were marked with the seal of God—144,000 were sealed from all the tribes of Israel:

⁵from Judah 12,000
  from Reuben 12,000
  from Gad. 12,000
⁶from Asher 12,000
  from Naphtali. 12,000
  from Manasseh 12,000
⁷from Simeon 12,000
  from Levi. 12,000
  from Issachar. 12,000
⁸from Zebulun. 12,000
  from Joseph 12,000
  from Benjamin. 12,000

6:6a Greek *A choinix* [1 quart or 1 liter] *of wheat for a denarius, and 3 choinix of barley for a denarius.* A denarius was equivalent to a laborer's full day's wage.   **6:6b** Or *harm.*   **6:8a** Greek *was Hades.*   **6:8b** Greek *death.*   **6:11** Greek *their brothers.*

Praise from the Great Crowd

⁹After this I saw a vast crowd, too great to count, from every nation and tribe and people and language, standing in front of the throne and before the Lamb. They were clothed in white robes and held palm branches in their hands. ¹⁰And they were shouting with a great roar,

"Salvation comes from our God who sits on the throne
and from the Lamb!"

¹¹And all the angels were standing around the throne and around the elders and the four living beings. And they fell before the throne with their faces to the ground and worshiped God. ¹²They sang,

"Amen! Blessing and glory and wisdom
and thanksgiving and honor
and power and strength belong to our God
forever and ever! Amen."

¹³Then one of the twenty-four elders asked me, "Who are these who are clothed in white? Where did they come from?"

¹⁴And I said to him, "Sir, you are the one who knows."

Then he said to me, "These are the ones who died in* the great tribulation.* They have washed their robes in the blood of the Lamb and made them white.

¹⁵ "That is why they stand in front of God's throne
and serve him day and night in his Temple.
And he who sits on the throne
will give them shelter.
¹⁶ They will never again be hungry or thirsty;
they will never be scorched by the heat of the sun.
¹⁷ For the Lamb on the throne*
will be their Shepherd.
He will lead them to springs of life-giving water.
And God will wipe every tear from their eyes."

CHAPTER 8

The Lamb Breaks the Seventh Seal

When the Lamb broke the seventh seal on the scroll,* there was silence throughout heaven for about half an hour. ²I saw the seven angels who stand before God, and they were given seven trumpets.

³Then another angel with a gold incense burner came and stood at the altar. And a great amount of incense was given to him to mix with the prayers of God's people as an offering on the gold altar before the throne. ⁴The smoke of the incense, mixed with the prayers of God's holy people, ascended up to God from the altar where the angel had poured them out. ⁵Then the angel filled the incense burner with fire from the altar and threw it down upon the earth; and thunder crashed, lightning flashed, and there was a terrible earthquake.

The First Four Trumpets

⁶Then the seven angels with the seven trumpets prepared to blow their mighty blasts.

⁷The first angel blew his trumpet, and hail and fire mixed with blood were thrown down on the earth. One-third of the earth was set on fire, one-third of the trees were burned, and all the green grass was burned.

⁸Then the second angel blew his trumpet, and a great mountain of fire was thrown into the sea. One-third of the water in the sea became blood, ⁹one-third of all things living in the sea died, and one-third of all the ships on the sea were destroyed.

¹⁰Then the third angel blew his trumpet, and a great star fell from the sky, burning like a torch. It fell on one-third of the rivers and on the springs of water. ¹¹The name of the star was Bitterness.* It made one-third of the water bitter, and many people died from drinking the bitter water.

¹²Then the fourth angel blew his trumpet, and one-

7:14a Greek *who came out of.*   **7:14b** Or *the great suffering.*   **7:17** Greek *on the center of the throne.*   **8:1** Or *book.*   **8:11** Greek *Wormwood.*

third of the sun was struck, and one-third of the moon, and one-third of the stars, and they became dark. And one-third of the day was dark, and also one-third of the night.

¹³Then I looked, and I heard a single eagle crying loudly as it flew through the air, "Terror, terror, terror to all who belong to this world because of what will happen when the last three angels blow their trumpets."

CHAPTER 9

The Fifth Trumpet Brings the First Terror

Then the fifth angel blew his trumpet, and I saw a star that had fallen to earth from the sky, and he was given the key to the shaft of the bottomless pit.* ²When he opened it, smoke poured out as though from a huge furnace, and the sunlight and air turned dark from the smoke.

³Then locusts came from the smoke and descended on the earth, and they were given power to sting like scorpions. ⁴They were told not to harm the grass or plants or trees, but only the people who did not have the seal of God on their foreheads. ⁵They were told not to kill them but to torture them for five months with pain like the pain of a scorpion sting. ⁶In those days people will seek death but will not find it. They will long to die, but death will flee from them!

⁷The locusts looked like horses prepared for battle. They had what looked like gold crowns on their heads, and their faces looked like human faces. ⁸They had hair like women's hair and teeth like the teeth of a lion. ⁹They wore armor made of iron, and their wings roared like an army of chariots rushing into battle. ¹⁰They had tails that stung like scorpions, and for five months they had the power to torment people. ¹¹Their king is the angel from the bottomless pit; his name in Hebrew is *Abaddon,* and in Greek, *Apollyon*—the Destroyer.

¹²The first terror is past, but look, two more terrors are coming!

The Sixth Trumpet Brings the Second Terror

¹³Then the sixth angel blew his trumpet, and I heard a voice speaking from the four horns of the gold altar that stands in the presence of God. ¹⁴And the voice said to the sixth angel who held the trumpet, "Release the four angels who are bound at the great Euphrates River." ¹⁵Then the four angels who had been prepared for this hour and day and month and year were turned loose to kill one-third of all the people on earth. ¹⁶I heard the size of their army, which was 200 million mounted troops.

¹⁷And in my vision, I saw the horses and the riders sitting on them. The riders wore armor that was fiery red and dark blue and yellow. The horses had heads like lions, and fire and smoke and burning sulfur billowed from their mouths. ¹⁸One-third of all the people on earth were killed by these three plagues—by the fire and smoke and burning sulfur that came from the mouths of the horses. ¹⁹Their power was in their mouths and in their tails. For their tails had heads like snakes, with the power to injure people.

²⁰But the people who did not die in these plagues still refused to repent of their evil deeds and turn to God. They continued to worship demons and idols made of gold, silver, bronze, stone, and wood—idols that can neither see nor hear nor walk! ²¹And they did not repent of their murders or their witchcraft or their sexual immorality or their thefts.

CHAPTER 10

The Angel and the Small Scroll

Then I saw another mighty angel coming down from heaven, surrounded by a cloud, with a rainbow over his head. His face shone like the sun, and his feet were like pillars of fire. ²And in his hand was a small scroll* that had been opened. He stood with his right foot on the sea and his left foot on the land. ³And he gave a great shout like the roar of a lion. And when he shouted, the seven thunders answered.

9:1 Or *the abyss,* or *the underworld;* also in 9:11.   10:2 Or *book;* also in 10:8, 9, 10.

⁴When the seven thunders spoke, I was about to write. But I heard a voice from heaven saying, "Keep secret* what the seven thunders said, and do not write it down."

⁵Then the angel I saw standing on the sea and on the land raised his right hand toward heaven. ⁶He swore an oath in the name of the one who lives forever and ever, who created the heavens and everything in them, the earth and everything in it, and the sea and everything in it. He said, "There will be no more delay. ⁷When the seventh angel blows his trumpet, God's mysterious plan will be fulfilled. It will happen just as he announced it to his servants the prophets."

⁸Then the voice from heaven spoke to me again: "Go and take the open scroll from the hand of the angel who is standing on the sea and on the land."

⁹So I went to the angel and told him to give me the small scroll. "Yes, take it and eat it," he said. "It will be sweet as honey in your mouth, but it will turn sour in your stomach!" ¹⁰So I took the small scroll from the hand of the angel, and I ate it! It was sweet in my mouth, but when I swallowed it, it turned sour in my stomach.

¹¹Then I was told, "You must prophesy again about many peoples, nations, languages, and kings."

CHAPTER 11

The Two Witnesses

Then I was given a measuring stick, and I was told, "Go and measure the Temple of God and the altar, and count the number of worshipers. ²But do not measure the outer courtyard, for it has been turned over to the nations. They will trample the holy city for 42 months. ³And I will give power to my two witnesses, and they will be clothed in burlap and will prophesy during those 1,260 days."

⁴These two prophets are the two olive trees and the two lampstands that stand before the Lord of all the earth. ⁵If anyone tries to harm them, fire flashes from their mouths and consumes their enemies. This is how anyone who tries to harm them must die. ⁶They have power to shut the sky so that no rain will fall for as long as they prophesy. And they have the power to turn the rivers and oceans into blood, and to strike the earth with every kind of plague as often as they wish.

⁷When they complete their testimony, the beast that comes up out of the bottomless pit* will declare war against them, and he will conquer them and kill them. ⁸And their bodies will lie in the main street of Jerusalem,* the city that is figuratively called "Sodom" and "Egypt," the city where their Lord was crucified. ⁹And for three and a half days, all peoples, tribes, languages, and nations will stare at their bodies. No one will be allowed to bury them. ¹⁰All the people who belong to this world will gloat over them and give presents to each other to celebrate the death of the two prophets who had tormented them.

¹¹But after three and a half days, God breathed life into them, and they stood up! Terror struck all who were staring at them. ¹²Then a loud voice from heaven called to the two prophets, "Come up here!" And they rose to heaven in a cloud as their enemies watched.

¹³At the same time there was a terrible earthquake that destroyed a tenth of the city. Seven thousand people died in that earthquake, and everyone else was terrified and gave glory to the God of heaven.

¹⁴The second terror is past, but look, the third terror is coming quickly.

The Seventh Trumpet Brings the Third Terror

¹⁵Then the seventh angel blew his trumpet, and there were loud voices shouting in heaven:

"The world has now become the Kingdom of our Lord
    and of his Christ,*
    and he will reign forever and ever."

🔊

"There were loud voices shouting in heaven: 'The world has now become the Kingdom of our Lord and of his Christ, and he will reign forever and ever'" (Revelation 11:15).

say what?

There was a lot of loud talk in heaven: "Now the world is truly under God's rule, and he will reign for all eternity."

10:4 Greek *Seal up.*   11:7 Or *the abyss,* or *the underworld.*   11:8 Greek *the great city.*   11:15 Or *his Messiah.*

¹⁶The twenty-four elders sitting on their thrones before God fell with their faces to the ground and worshiped him. ¹⁷And they said,

"We give thanks to you, Lord God, the Almighty,
　the one who is and who always was,
for now you have assumed your great power
　and have begun to reign.
¹⁸ The nations were filled with wrath,
　but now the time of your wrath has come.
It is time to judge the dead
　and reward your servants the prophets,
　as well as your holy people,
and all who fear your name,
　from the least to the greatest.
It is time to destroy
　all who have caused destruction on the earth."

¹⁹Then, in heaven, the Temple of God was opened and the Ark of his covenant could be seen inside the Temple. Lightning flashed, thunder crashed and roared, and there was an earthquake and a terrible hailstorm.

CHAPTER 12

The Woman and the Dragon

Then I witnessed in heaven an event of great significance. I saw a woman clothed with the sun, with the moon beneath her feet, and a crown of twelve stars on her head. ²She was pregnant, and she cried out because of her labor pains and the agony of giving birth.

³Then I witnessed in heaven another significant event. I saw a large red dragon with seven heads and ten horns, with seven crowns on his heads. ⁴His tail swept away one-third of the stars in the sky, and he threw them to the earth. He stood in front of the woman as she was about to give birth, ready to devour her baby as soon as it was born.

⁵She gave birth to a son who was to rule all nations with an iron rod. And her child was snatched away from the dragon and was caught up to God and to his throne. ⁶And the woman fled into the wilderness, where God had prepared a place to care for her for 1,260 days.

⁷Then there was war in heaven. Michael and his angels fought against the dragon and his angels. ⁸And the dragon lost the battle, and he and his angels were forced out of heaven. ⁹This great dragon—the ancient serpent called the devil, or Satan, the one deceiving the whole world—was thrown down to the earth with all his angels.

¹⁰Then I heard a loud voice shouting across the heavens,

"It has come at last—
　salvation and power
and the Kingdom of our God,
　and the authority of his Christ.*
For the accuser of our brothers and sisters*
　has been thrown down to earth—
the one who accuses them
　before our God day and night.
¹¹ And they have defeated him by the blood of the Lamb
　and by their testimony.
And they did not love their lives so much
　that they were afraid to die.
¹² Therefore, rejoice, O heavens!
　And you who live in the heavens, rejoice!
But terror will come on the earth and the sea,
　for the devil has come down to you in great anger,
　knowing that he has little time."

¹³When the dragon realized that he had been thrown down to the earth, he pursued the woman who had given birth to the male child. ¹⁴But she was given two wings like those of a great eagle so she could fly to the place prepared for her in the wilderness. There she would be cared for and protected from the dragon* for a time, times, and half a time.

12:10a Or *his Messiah.*　**12:10b** Greek *brothers.*　**12:14** Greek *the serpent;* also in 12:15. See 12:9.

¹⁵Then the dragon tried to drown the woman with a flood of water that flowed from his mouth. ¹⁶But the earth helped her by opening its mouth and swallowing the river that gushed out from the mouth of the dragon. ¹⁷And the dragon was angry at the woman and declared war against the rest of her children—all who keep God's commandments and maintain their testimony for Jesus.

¹⁸Then the dragon took his stand* on the shore beside the sea.

CHAPTER 13

The Beast out of the Sea

Then I saw a beast rising up out of the sea. It had seven heads and ten horns, with ten crowns on its horns. And written on each head were names that blasphemed God. ²This beast looked like a leopard, but it had the feet of a bear and the mouth of a lion! And the dragon gave the beast his own power and throne and great authority.

³I saw that one of the heads of the beast seemed wounded beyond recovery—but the fatal wound was healed! The whole world marveled at this miracle and gave allegiance to the beast. ⁴They worshiped the dragon for giving the beast such power, and they also worshiped the beast. "Who is as great as the beast?" they exclaimed. "Who is able to fight against him?"

⁵Then the beast was allowed to speak great blasphemies against God. And he was given authority to do whatever he wanted for forty-two months. ⁶And he spoke terrible words of blasphemy against God, slandering his name and his dwelling—that is, those who dwell in heaven.* ⁷And the beast was allowed to wage war against God's holy people and to conquer them. And he was given authority to rule over every tribe and people and language and nation. ⁸And all the people who belong to this world worshiped the beast. They are the ones whose names were not written in the Book of Life before the world was made—the Book that belongs to the Lamb who was slaughtered.*

⁹Anyone with ears to hear
    should listen and understand.
¹⁰ Anyone who is destined for prison
    will be taken to prison.
Anyone destined to die by the sword
    will die by the sword.

This means that God's holy people must endure persecution patiently and remain faithful.

The Beast out of the Earth

¹¹Then I saw another beast come up out of the earth. He had two horns like those of a lamb, but he spoke with the voice of a dragon. ¹²He exercised all the authority of the first beast. And he required all the earth and its people to worship the first beast, whose fatal wound had been healed. ¹³He did astounding miracles, even making fire flash down to earth from the sky while everyone was watching. ¹⁴And with all the miracles he was allowed to perform on behalf of the first beast, he deceived all the people who belong to this world. He ordered the people to make a great statue of the first beast, who was fatally wounded and then came back to life. ¹⁵He was then permitted to give life to this statue so that it could speak. Then the statue of the beast commanded that anyone refusing to worship it must die.

¹⁶He required everyone—small and great, rich and poor, free and slave—to be given a mark on the right hand or on the forehead. ¹⁷And no one could buy or sell anything without that mark, which was either the name of the beast or the number representing his name. ¹⁸Wisdom is needed here. Let the one with understanding solve the meaning of the number of the beast, for it is the number of a man.* His number is 666.*

12:18 Greek *Then he took his stand;* some manuscripts read *Then I took my stand.* Some translations put this entire sentence into 13:1.   13:6 Some manuscripts read *and his dwelling and all who dwell in heaven.*   13:8 Or *not written in the Book of Life that belongs to the Lamb who was slaughtered before the world was made.*   13:18a Or *of humanity.*   13:18b Some manuscripts read *616.*

The Lamb and the 144,000

Then I saw the Lamb standing on Mount Zion, and with him were 144,000 who had his name and his Father's name written on their foreheads. [2]And I heard a sound from heaven like the roar of mighty ocean waves or the rolling of loud thunder. It was like the sound of many harpists playing together.

[3]This great choir sang a wonderful new song in front of the throne of God and before the four living beings and the twenty-four elders. No one could learn this song except the 144,000 who had been redeemed from the earth. [4]They have kept themselves as pure as virgins,* following the Lamb wherever he goes. They have been purchased from among the people on the earth as a special offering* to God and to the Lamb. [5]They have told no lies; they are without blame.

The Three Angels

[6]And I saw another angel flying through the sky, carrying the eternal Good News to proclaim to the people who belong to this world—to every nation, tribe, language, and people. [7]"Fear God," he shouted. "Give glory to him. For the time has come when he will sit as judge. Worship him who made the heavens, the earth, the sea, and all the springs of water."

[8]Then another angel followed him through the sky, shouting, "Babylon is fallen—that great city is fallen—because she made all the nations of the world drink the wine of her passionate immorality."

[9]Then a third angel followed them, shouting, "Anyone who worships the beast and his statue or who accepts his mark on the forehead or on the hand [10]must drink the wine of God's anger. It has been poured full strength into God's cup of wrath. And they will be tormented with fire and burning sulfur in the presence of the holy angels and the Lamb. [11]The smoke of their torment will rise forever and ever, and they will have no relief day or night, for they have worshiped the beast and his statue and have accepted the mark of his name."

[12]This means that God's holy people must endure persecution patiently, obeying his commands and maintaining their faith in Jesus.

[13]And I heard a voice from heaven saying, "Write this down: Blessed are those who die in the Lord from now on. Yes, says the Spirit, they are blessed indeed, for they will rest from their hard work; for their good deeds follow them!"

14:4a Greek *They are virgins who have not defiled themselves with women.*   14:4b Greek *as firstfruits.*

THE POINT

Nothin' to fear. Revelation is hard to understand. It is filled with so much imagery and symbolism that many people find themselves asking what it all means. Most scholars hold the view that the book is prophetic concerning what will happen at the end of time and depicts the ultimate battle between good and evil.

The word "Revelation" literally means "to take the cover off." In that sense, the book uncovers the glory of Jesus Christ and the final destruction and judgment during the end times. While some of the images may be shocking and hard to handle, many of them should be a source of hope and encouragement for believers. Rather than frightening us, the book should assure believers that God will triumph, evil will be punished, and the faithful will be rewarded for their faith and endurance with an eternal dwelling place in God's presence.

This means that God's holy people must endure persecution patiently, obeying his commands and maintaining their faith in Jesus . . . Blessed are those who die in the Lord from now on. Yes, says the Spirit, they are blessed indeed, for they will rest from their hard work; for their good deeds follow them!
(Revelation 14:12-13)

The point is, in the end, WE WIN! So be about God's business now.

The Harvest of the Earth

¹⁴Then I saw a white cloud, and seated on the cloud was someone like the Son of Man.* He had a gold crown on his head and a sharp sickle in his hand.

¹⁵Then another angel came from the Temple and shouted to the one sitting on the cloud, "Swing the sickle, for the time of harvest has come; the crop on earth is ripe." ¹⁶So the one sitting on the cloud swung his sickle over the earth, and the whole earth was harvested.

¹⁷After that, another angel came from the Temple in heaven, and he also had a sharp sickle. ¹⁸Then another angel, who had power to destroy with fire, came from the altar. He shouted to the angel with the sharp sickle, "Swing your sickle now to gather the clusters of grapes from the vines of the earth, for they are ripe for judgment." ¹⁹So the angel swung his sickle over the earth and loaded the grapes into the great winepress of God's wrath. ²⁰The grapes were trampled in the winepress outside the city, and blood flowed from the winepress in a stream about 180 miles* long and as high as a horse's bridle.

CHAPTER 15

The Song of Moses and of the Lamb

Then I saw in heaven another marvelous event of great significance. Seven angels were holding the seven last plagues, which would bring God's wrath to completion. ²I saw before me what seemed to be a glass sea mixed with fire. And on it stood all the people who had been victorious over the beast and his statue and the number representing his name. They were all holding harps that God had given them. ³And they were singing the song of Moses, the servant of God, and the song of the Lamb:

"Great and marvelous are your works,
  O Lord God, the Almighty.
Just and true are your ways,
  O King of the nations.*

⁴Who will not fear you, Lord,
  and glorify your name?
For you alone are holy.
All nations will come and worship before you,
  for your righteous deeds have been revealed."

The Seven Bowls of the Seven Plagues

⁵Then I looked and saw that the Temple in heaven, God's Tabernacle, was thrown wide open. ⁶The seven angels who were holding the seven plagues came out of the Temple. They were clothed in spotless white linen* with gold sashes across their chests. ⁷Then one of the four living beings handed each of the seven angels a gold bowl filled with the wrath of God, who lives forever and ever. ⁸The Temple was filled with smoke from God's glory and power. No one could enter the Temple until the seven angels had completed pouring out the seven plagues.

CHAPTER 16

Then I heard a mighty voice from the Temple say to the seven angels, "Go your ways and pour out on the earth the seven bowls containing God's wrath."

²So the first angel left the Temple and poured out his bowl on the earth, and horrible, malignant sores broke out on everyone who had the mark of the beast and who worshiped his statue.

³Then the second angel poured out his bowl on the sea, and it became like the blood of a corpse. And everything in the sea died.

⁴Then the third angel poured out his bowl on the rivers and springs, and they became blood. ⁵And I heard the angel who had authority over all water saying,

"You are just, O Holy One, who is and who always was,
  because you have sent these judgments.

14:14 Or *like a son of man.* See Dan 7:13. "Son of Man" is a title Jesus used for himself.   14:20 Greek *1,600 stadia* [296 kilometers].   15:3 Some manuscripts read *King of the ages.*
15:6 Other manuscripts read *white stone;* still others read *white [garments] made of linen.*

⁶ Since they shed the blood
   of your holy people and your prophets,
 you have given them blood to drink.
   It is their just reward."

⁷And I heard a voice from the altar,* saying,

"Yes, O Lord God, the Almighty,
   your judgments are true and just."

⁸Then the fourth angel poured out his bowl on the sun, causing it to scorch everyone with its fire. ⁹Everyone was burned by this blast of heat, and they cursed the name of God, who had control over all these plagues. They did not repent of their sins and turn to God and give him glory.

¹⁰Then the fifth angel poured out his bowl on the throne of the beast, and his kingdom was plunged into darkness. His subjects ground their teeth in anguish, ¹¹and they cursed the God of heaven for their pains and sores. But they did not repent of their evil deeds and turn to God.

¹²Then the sixth angel poured out his bowl on the great Euphrates River, and it dried up so that the kings from the east could march their armies toward the west without hindrance. ¹³And I saw three evil* spirits that looked like frogs leap from the mouths of the dragon, the beast, and the false prophet. ¹⁴They are demonic spirits who work miracles and go out to all the rulers of the world to gather them for battle against the Lord on that great judgment day of God the Almighty.

¹⁵"Look, I will come as unexpectedly as a thief! Blessed are all who are watching for me, who keep their clothing ready so they will not have to walk around naked and ashamed."

¹⁶And the demonic spirits gathered all the rulers and their armies to a place with the Hebrew name *Armageddon*.*

¹⁷Then the seventh angel poured out his bowl into the air. And a mighty shout came from the throne in the Temple, saying, "It is finished!" ¹⁸Then the thunder crashed and rolled, and lightning flashed. And a great earthquake struck—the worst since people were placed on the earth. ¹⁹The great city of Babylon split into three sections, and the cities of many nations fell into heaps of rubble. So God remembered all of Babylon's sins, and he made her drink the cup that was filled with the wine of his fierce wrath. ²⁰And every island disappeared, and all the mountains were leveled. ²¹There was a terrible hailstorm, and hailstones weighing as much as seventy-five pounds* fell from the sky onto the people below. They cursed God because of the terrible plague of the hailstorm.

CHAPTER 17

The Great Prostitute

One of the seven angels who had poured out the seven bowls came over and spoke to me. "Come with me," he said, "and I will show you the judgment that is going to come on the great prostitute, who rules over many waters. ²The kings of the world have committed adultery with her, and the people who belong to this world have been made drunk by the wine of her immorality."

³So the angel took me in the Spirit* into the wilderness. There I saw a woman sitting on a scarlet beast that had seven heads and ten horns, and blasphemies against God were written all over it. ⁴The woman wore purple and scarlet clothing and beautiful jewelry made of gold and precious gems and pearls. In her hand she held a gold goblet full of obscenities and the impurities of her immorality. ⁵A mysterious name was written on her forehead: "Babylon the Great, Mother of All Prostitutes and Obscenities in the World." ⁶I could see that she was drunk—drunk with the blood of God's holy people who were witnesses for Jesus. I stared at her in complete amazement.

⁷"Why are you so amazed?" the angel asked. "I will tell you the mystery of this woman and of the beast with seven heads and ten horns on which she sits. ⁸The beast you saw was once alive but isn't now. And yet he will soon come up

"Look, I will come as unexpectedly as a thief! Blessed are all who are watching for me, who keep their clothing ready so they will not have to walk around naked and ashamed" (Revelation 16:15).

say what?

I will come without warning, like a thief! Blessed are those waiting for me, who keep their clothes on—ready so they won't have to walk around embarrassed.

out of the bottomless pit* and go to eternal destruction. And the people who belong to this world, whose names were not written in the Book of Life before the world was made, will be amazed at the reappearance of this beast who had died.

⁹"This calls for a mind with understanding: The seven heads of the beast represent the seven hills where the woman rules. They also represent seven kings. ¹⁰Five kings have already fallen, the sixth now reigns, and the seventh is yet to come, but his reign will be brief.

¹¹"The scarlet beast that was, but is no longer, is the eighth king. He is like the other seven, and he, too, is headed for destruction. ¹²The ten horns of the beast are ten kings who have not yet risen to power. They will be appointed to their kingdoms for one brief moment to reign with the beast. ¹³They will all agree to give him their power and authority. ¹⁴Together they will go to war against the Lamb, but the Lamb will defeat them because he is Lord of all lords and King of all kings. And his called and chosen and faithful ones will be with him."

¹⁵Then the angel said to me, "The waters where the prostitute is ruling represent masses of people of every nation and language. ¹⁶The scarlet beast and his ten horns all hate the prostitute. They will strip her naked, eat her flesh, and burn her remains with fire. ¹⁷For God has put a plan into their minds, a plan that will carry out his purposes. They will agree to give their authority to the scarlet beast, and so the words of God will be fulfilled. ¹⁸And this woman you saw in your vision represents the great city that rules over the kings of the world."

CHAPTER 18

The Fall of Babylon

After all this I saw another angel come down from heaven with great authority, and the earth grew bright with his splendor. ²He gave a mighty shout:

"Babylon is fallen—that great city is fallen!
   She has become a home for demons.
She is a hideout for every foul* spirit,
   a hideout for every foul vulture
   and every foul and dreadful animal.*
³ For all the nations have fallen*
   because of the wine of her passionate immorality.
The kings of the world
   have committed adultery with her.
Because of her desires for extravagant luxury,
   the merchants of the world have grown rich."

⁴Then I heard another voice calling from heaven,

"Come away from her, my people.
   Do not take part in her sins,
   or you will be punished with her.
⁵ For her sins are piled as high as heaven,
   and God remembers her evil deeds.
⁶ Do to her as she has done to others.
   Double her penalty* for all her evil deeds.
She brewed a cup of terror for others,
   so brew twice as much* for her.
⁷ She glorified herself and lived in luxury,
   so match it now with torment and sorrow.
She boasted in her heart,
   'I am queen on my throne.
I am no helpless widow,
   and I have no reason to mourn.'
⁸ Therefore, these plagues will overtake her in a single day—
   death and mourning and famine.
She will be completely consumed by fire,
   for the Lord God who judges her is mighty."

⁹And the kings of the world who committed adultery with her and enjoyed her great luxury will mourn for her as they

17:8 Or *the abyss,* or *the underworld.*   18:2a Greek *unclean;* also in each of the two following phrases.   18:2b Some manuscripts condense the last two lines to read *a hideout for every foul [unclean] and dreadful vulture.*   18:3 Some manuscripts read *have drunk.*   18:6a Or *Give her an equal penalty.*   18:6b Or *brew just as much.*

see the smoke rising from her charred remains. ¹⁰They will stand at a distance, terrified by her great torment. They will cry out,

"How terrible, how terrible for you,
O Babylon, you great city!
In a single moment
God's judgment came on you."

¹¹The merchants of the world will weep and mourn for her, for there is no one left to buy their goods. ¹²She bought great quantities of gold, silver, jewels, and pearls; fine linen, purple, silk, and scarlet cloth; things made of fragrant thyine wood, ivory goods, and objects made of expensive wood; and bronze, iron, and marble. ¹³She also bought cinnamon, spice, incense, myrrh, frankincense, wine, olive oil, fine flour, wheat, cattle, sheep, horses, chariots, and bodies—that is, human slaves.

¹⁴ "The fancy things you loved so much
are gone," they cry.
"All your luxuries and splendor
are gone forever,
never to be yours again."

¹⁵The merchants who became wealthy by selling her these things will stand at a distance, terrified by her great torment. They will weep and cry out,

¹⁶ "How terrible, how terrible for that great city!
She was clothed in finest purple and scarlet
linens,
decked out with gold and precious stones and
pearls!
¹⁷ In a single moment
all the wealth of the city is gone!"

And all the captains of the merchant ships and their passengers and sailors and crews will stand at a distance.

¹⁸They will cry out as they watch the smoke ascend, and they will say, "Where is there another city as great as this?" ¹⁹And they will weep and throw dust on their heads to show their grief. And they will cry out,

"How terrible, how terrible for that great city!
The shipowners became wealthy
by transporting her great wealth on the seas.
In a single moment it is all gone."

²⁰ Rejoice over her fate, O heaven
and people of God and apostles and prophets!
For at last God has judged her
for your sakes.

²¹Then a mighty angel picked up a boulder the size of a huge millstone. He threw it into the ocean and shouted,

"Just like this, the great city Babylon
will be thrown down with violence
and will never be found again.
²² The sound of harps, singers, flutes, and trumpets
will never be heard in you again.
No craftsmen and no trades
will ever be found in you again.
The sound of the mill
will never be heard in you again.
²³ The light of a lamp
will never shine in you again.
The happy voices of brides and grooms
will never be heard in you again.
For your merchants were the greatest in the world,
and you deceived the nations with your
sorceries.
²⁴ In your* streets flowed the blood of the prophets
and of God's holy people
and the blood of people slaughtered all over the
world."

18:24 Greek *her.*

CHAPTER 19

Songs of Victory in Heaven

After this, I heard what sounded like a vast crowd in heaven shouting,

"Praise the LORD!*
Salvation and glory and power belong to our God.
² His judgments are true and just.
He has punished the great prostitute
who corrupted the earth with her immorality.
He has avenged the murder of his servants."

³And again their voices rang out:

"Praise the LORD!
The smoke from that city ascends forever and
ever!"

⁴Then the twenty-four elders and the four living beings fell down and worshiped God, who was sitting on the throne. They cried out, "Amen! Praise the LORD!"

⁵And from the throne came a voice that said,

"Praise our God,
all his servants,
all who fear him,
from the least to the greatest."

⁶Then I heard again what sounded like the shout of a vast crowd or the roar of mighty ocean waves or the crash of loud thunder:

"Praise the LORD!
For the Lord our God,* the Almighty, reigns.
⁷ Let us be glad and rejoice,
and let us give honor to him.
For the time has come for the wedding feast of the
Lamb,
and his bride has prepared herself.

⁸ She has been given the finest of pure white linen to
wear."

For the fine linen represents the good deeds of God's
holy people.

⁹And the angel said to me, "Write this: Blessed are those who are invited to the wedding feast of the Lamb." And he added, "These are true words that come from God."

¹⁰Then I fell down at his feet to worship him, but he said, "No, don't worship me. I am a servant of God, just like you and your brothers and sisters* who testify about their faith in Jesus. Worship only God. For the essence of prophecy is to give a clear witness for Jesus.*"

The Rider on the White Horse

¹¹Then I saw heaven opened, and a white horse was standing there. Its rider was named Faithful and True, for he judges fairly and wages a righteous war. ¹²His eyes were like flames of fire, and on his head were many crowns. A name was written on him that no one understood except himself. ¹³He wore a robe dipped in blood, and his title was the Word of God. ¹⁴The armies of heaven, dressed in the finest of pure white linen, followed him on white horses. ¹⁵From his mouth came a sharp sword to strike down the nations. He will rule them with an iron rod. He will release the fierce wrath of God, the Almighty, like juice flowing from a winepress. ¹⁶On his robe at his thigh* was written this title: King of all kings and Lord of all lords.

¹⁷Then I saw an angel standing in the sun, shouting to the vultures flying high in the sky: "Come! Gather together for the great banquet God has prepared. ¹⁸Come and eat the flesh of kings, generals, and strong warriors; of horses and their riders; and of all humanity, both free and slave, small and great."

¹⁹Then I saw the beast and the kings of the world and their armies gathered together to fight against the one sitting on the horse and his army. ²⁰And the beast was captured, and

---

19:1 Greek *Hallelujah;* also in 19:3, 4, 6. *Hallelujah* is the transliteration of a Hebrew term that means "Praise the Lord." **19:6** Some manuscripts read *the Lord God.* **19:10a** Greek *brothers.* **19:10b** Or *is the message confirmed by Jesus.* **19:16** Or *On his robe and thigh.*

with him the false prophet who did mighty miracles on behalf of the beast—miracles that deceived all who had accepted the mark of the beast and who worshiped his statue. Both the beast and his false prophet were thrown alive into the fiery lake of burning sulfur. ²¹Their entire army was killed by the sharp sword that came from the mouth of the one riding the white horse. And the vultures all gorged themselves on the dead bodies.

CHAPTER 20

The Thousand Years

Then I saw an angel coming down from heaven with the key to the bottomless pit* and a heavy chain in his hand. ²He seized the dragon—that old serpent, who is the devil, Satan—and bound him in chains for a thousand years. ³The angel threw him into the bottomless pit, which he then shut and locked so Satan could not deceive the nations anymore until the thousand years were finished. Afterward he must be released for a little while.

⁴Then I saw thrones, and the people sitting on them had been given the authority to judge. And I saw the souls of those who had been beheaded for their testimony about Jesus and for proclaiming the word of God. They had not worshiped the beast or his statue, nor accepted his mark on their forehead or their hands. They all came to life again, and they reigned with Christ for a thousand years.

⁵This is the first resurrection. (The rest of the dead did not come back to life until the thousand years had ended.) ⁶Blessed and holy are those who share in the first resurrection. For them the second death holds no power, but they will be priests of God and of Christ and will reign with him a thousand years.

The Defeat of Satan

⁷When the thousand years come to an end, Satan will be let out of his prison. ⁸He will go out to deceive the nations—called Gog and Magog—in every corner of the earth. He will gather them together for battle—a mighty army, as numberless as sand along the seashore. ⁹And I saw them as they went up on the broad plain of the earth and surrounded God's people and the beloved city. But fire from heaven came down on the attacking armies and consumed them.

¹⁰Then the devil, who had deceived them, was thrown into the fiery lake of burning sulfur, joining the beast and the false prophet. There they will be tormented day and night forever and ever.

The Final Judgment

¹¹And I saw a great white throne and the one sitting on it. The earth and sky fled from his presence, but they found no place to hide. ¹²I saw the dead, both great and small, standing before God's throne. And the books were opened, including the Book of Life. And the dead were judged according to what they had done, as recorded in the books. ¹³The sea gave up its dead, and death and the grave* gave up their dead. And all were judged according to their deeds. ¹⁴Then death and the grave were thrown into the lake of fire. This lake of fire is the second death. ¹⁵And anyone whose name was not found recorded in the Book of Life was thrown into the lake of fire.

CHAPTER 21

The New Jerusalem

Then I saw a new heaven and a new earth, for the old heaven and the old earth had disappeared. And the sea was also gone. ²And I saw the holy city, the new Jerusalem, coming down from God out of heaven like a bride beautifully dressed for her husband.

³I heard a loud shout from the throne, saying, "Look, God's home is now among his people! He will live with them, and they will be his people. God himself will be with them.* ⁴He will wipe every tear from their eyes, and there

20:1 Or *the abyss,* or *the underworld;* also in 20:3. **20:13** Greek *and Hades;* also in 20:14. **21:3** Some manuscripts read *God himself will be with them, their God.*

"And I saw the holy city, the new Jerusalem, coming down from God out of heaven like a bride beautifully dressed for her husband. I heard a loud shout from the throne, saying, 'Look, God's home is now among his people! He will live with them, and they will be his people'" (Revelation 21:2-3).

And I saw Jerusalem, the holy city, coming down from Heaven, like a bride dressed beautifully for her husband. I heard a loud yell comin' from the throne sayin', "Look, God is at home now among his people! He will live with them, and they will be his fam."

will be no more death or sorrow or crying or pain. All these things are gone forever."

⁵And the one sitting on the throne said, "Look, I am making everything new!" And then he said to me, "Write this down, for what I tell you is trustworthy and true." ⁶And he also said, "It is finished! I am the Alpha and the Omega—the Beginning and the End. To all who are thirsty I will give freely from the springs of the water of life. ⁷All who are victorious will inherit all these blessings, and I will be their God, and they will be my children.

⁸"But cowards, unbelievers, the corrupt, murderers, the immoral, those who practice witchcraft, idol worshipers, and all liars—their fate is in the fiery lake of burning sulfur. This is the second death."

⁹Then one of the seven angels who held the seven bowls containing the seven last plagues came and said to me, "Come with me! I will show you the bride, the wife of the Lamb."

¹⁰So he took me in the Spirit* to a great, high mountain, and he showed me the holy city, Jerusalem, descending out of heaven from God. ¹¹It shone with the glory of God and sparkled like a precious stone—like jasper as clear as crystal. ¹²The city wall was broad and high, with twelve gates guarded by twelve angels. And the names of the twelve tribes of Israel were written on the gates. ¹³There were three gates on each side—east, north, south, and west. ¹⁴The wall of the city had twelve foundation stones, and on them were written the names of the twelve apostles of the Lamb.

¹⁵The angel who talked to me held in his hand a gold measuring stick to measure the city, its gates, and its wall. ¹⁶When he measured it, he found it was a square, as wide as it was long. In fact, its length and width and height were each 1,400 miles.* ¹⁷Then he measured the walls and found them to be 216 feet thick* (according to the human standard used by the angel).

¹⁸The wall was made of jasper, and the city was pure gold, as clear as glass. ¹⁹The wall of the city was built on foundation stones inlaid with twelve precious stones:* the first was jasper, the second sapphire, the third agate, the fourth emerald, ²⁰the fifth onyx, the sixth carnelian, the seventh chrysolite, the eighth beryl, the ninth topaz, the tenth chrysoprase, the eleventh jacinth, the twelfth amethyst.

²¹The twelve gates were made of pearls—each gate from a single pearl! And the main street was pure gold, as clear as glass.

²²I saw no temple in the city, for the Lord God Almighty and the Lamb are its temple. ²³And the city has no need of sun or moon, for the glory of God illuminates the city, and the Lamb is its light. ²⁴The nations will walk in its light, and the kings of the world will enter the city in all their glory. ²⁵Its gates will never be closed at the end of day because there is no night there. ²⁶And all the nations will bring their glory and honor into the city. ²⁷Nothing evil* will be allowed to enter, nor anyone who practices shameful idolatry and dishonesty—but only those whose names are written in the Lamb's Book of Life.

CHAPTER 22

Then the angel showed me a river with the water of life, clear as crystal, flowing from the throne of God and of the Lamb. ²It flowed down the center of the main street. On each side of the river grew a tree of life, bearing twelve crops of fruit,* with a fresh crop each month. The leaves were used for medicine to heal the nations.

³No longer will there be a curse upon anything. For the throne of God and of the Lamb will be there, and his servants will worship him. ⁴And they will see his face, and his name will be written on their foreheads. ⁵And there will be no night there—no need for lamps or sun—for the Lord God will shine on them. And they will reign forever and ever.

"Look, I am coming soon! Blessed are those who obey the words of prophecy written in this book" (Revelation 22:7).

I'm comin' soon! Blessed are those who live like they believe what I told 'em.

21:10 Or *in spirit.*   21:16 Greek *12,000 stadia* [2,220 kilometers].   21:17 Greek *144 cubits* [65 meters].   21:19 The identification of some of these gemstones is uncertain.   21:27 Or *ceremonially unclean.*   22:2 Or *twelve kinds of fruit.*

⁶Then the angel said to me, "Everything you have heard and seen is trustworthy and true. The Lord God, who inspires his prophets,* has sent his angel to tell his servants what will happen soon.*"

Jesus Is Coming

⁷"Look, I am coming soon! Blessed are those who obey the words of prophecy written in this book.*"

⁸I, John, am the one who heard and saw all these things. And when I heard and saw them, I fell down to worship at the feet of the angel who showed them to me. ⁹But he said, "No, don't worship me. I am a servant of God, just like you and your brothers the prophets, as well as all who obey what is written in this book. Worship only God!"

¹⁰Then he instructed me, "Do not seal up the prophetic words in this book, for the time is near. ¹¹Let the one who is doing harm continue to do harm; let the one who is vile continue to be vile; let the one who is righteous continue to live righteously; let the one who is holy continue to be holy."

¹²"Look, I am coming soon, bringing my reward with me to repay all people according to their deeds. ¹³I am the Alpha and the Omega, the First and the Last, the Beginning and the End."

¹⁴Blessed are those who wash their robes. They will be permitted to enter through the gates of the city and eat the fruit from the tree of life. ¹⁵Outside the city are the dogs—the sorcerers, the sexually immoral, the murderers, the idol worshipers, and all who love to live a lie.

¹⁶"I, Jesus, have sent my angel to give you this message for the churches. I am both the source of David and the heir to his throne.* I am the bright morning star."

¹⁷The Spirit and the bride say, "Come." Let anyone who hears this say, "Come." Let anyone who is thirsty come. Let anyone who desires drink freely from the water of life. ¹⁸And I solemnly declare to everyone who hears the words of prophecy written in this book: If anyone adds anything to what is written here, God will add to that person the plagues described in this book. ¹⁹And if anyone removes any of the words from this book of prophecy, God will remove that person's share in the tree of life and in the holy city that are described in this book.

²⁰He who is the faithful witness to all these things says, "Yes, I am coming soon!"

Amen! Come, Lord Jesus!

²¹May the grace of the Lord Jesus be with God's holy people.*

22:6a Or The Lord, the God of the spirits of the prophets. 22:6b Or suddenly, or quickly; also in 22:7, 12, 20. 22:7 Or scroll; also in 22:9, 10, 18, 19. 22:16 Greek I am the root and offspring of David. 22:21 Other manuscripts read be with all; still others read be with all of God's holy people. Some manuscripts add Amen.

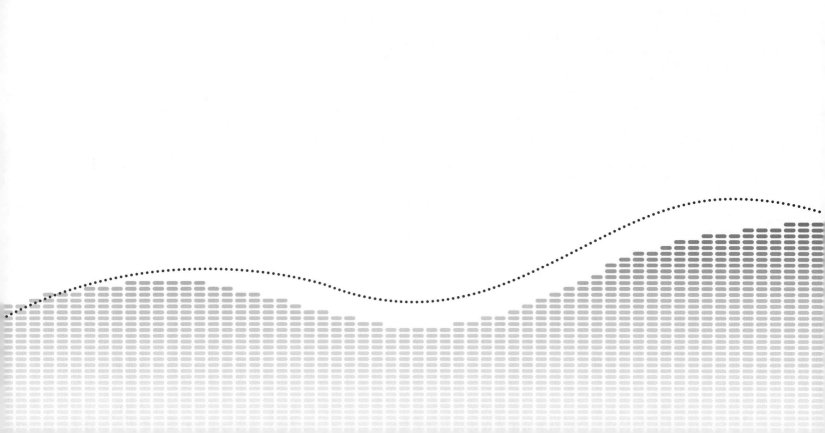

INDEX TO

SOUL INFINITY FEATURES